20/20
THE KERMIT
WASHINGTON
STORY

To Chris Stevens
From
[signature]
24
L. A. Lakers

PATRICIA HA[...]

AND

KERMIT WASH[...]

PAGE PUBLISHING, INC.
New York, NY

First originally published by Page Publishing, Inc. 2017

ISBN 978-1-63568-473-5 (Paperback)
ISBN 978-1-63568-474-2 (Digital)

Printed in the United States of America

WASHINGTON POST: MARC SPLAVER: A CHAMPION

· ·

By Ken Denlinger May 4, 1978

You would have enjoyed Marc Splaver, whose enjoyment came from making life a bit easier for others. His special talents and personality seemed destined to someday force him into the sporting spotlight, until the killer leukemia grabbed him ten months ago and took his life yesterday.

It is impossible to appreciate Splaver without understanding his job, public relations. Splaver's natural inclination was a smile, and not one of those paste-on models other in the business so often affect. His information always was accurate and swift, usually more thorough than anyone else's, and funnier.

Splaver's passion for basketball led him to uncover odd facts, many of which appeared as trivia questions. His mind led a largely unknown AU forward, Kermit Washington, to the player Splaver might have reserved for himself in playground fantasy years earlier.

As AU sports information director after graduation in 1970, Splaver pictured the foreseen prominence of the basketball team, under Tom Young, as "The American Revolution," and Washington as its leader.

Teams, athletes and their publicists must justify and give their attention to Washington who transformed from a skinny sophomore into the 6-foot 8-inch essence of a power forward, the fifth player picked in the NBA draft after his senior season.

But Splaver was the major reason Washington became an All-American. Washington was only the sixth major college player to average 20 points and 20 rebounds, so Splaver developed an eye-chart to illustrate this 20-20 notion.

Other players, among them Julius Erving, were lettered in eye-chart fashion and an influential wire service man later admitted that publicity elevated Washington to first-team All American by the Associated Press.

To Marc Splaver, who formed the clay for the vessel
Pete Newell, who as the potter molded the clay into a vessel
And all the family and friends who saw the
vessel as honorable and valuable

Pete Newell　　　　　　　*Marc Splaver*

AMERICAN UNIVERSITY

. . . .

The Forward

Living in the nation's capital Washington, DC in the late 60's and early 70's was marked by momentous times. The world was exposed to awareness that the accepted norm of segregation was being challenged by whites and blacks across America. Political leaders were voicing a sense of urgency to make changes. Media coverage placed in the spotlight how prejudice, injustice and mistreatment of individuals were on-going and ignored. A failure to knowledge such actions called into question why nothing was addressed to remedy these concerns. Opportunities once forbidden were now viewed as unalienable rights. Tabloids included detailed statements for supporting radical changes with revolutionary ideas be implemented. For the first time, insisting on the acceptance of a paradigm shift in the public's thinking was *the* priority.

The public acknowledgement of Black Panther opposition to the status quo, civil rights demonstrations in which college students readily engaged in and a growing discontent for aggressive efforts in Vietnam, created an anti-war sentiment, drawing advocates from around the country to our nation's capital. Marches on Washington led by acknowledged civil rights leaders, such as Martin Luther King Jr., set in motion a movement many participated in, changing previously accepted disparaging norms.

College campuses demographics no longer reflected an all-White or all Black student population. Athletics no longer provided limited opportunities for a student to attend an institution of higher learning due to rigid and biased requirements set for admission. Interactions between black and whites led to a course of action which focused on peace and the hope for a better future. Demonstrations across college campuses fueled the fires of change that burnt in the hearts of many.

Washington, DC's American University college campus was a perfect locale to spearhead reforms. Its geographic location, in the affluent North West, was ideal for taking note of daily events taking place in the nation's capital. American University's campus, was adjacent to Ward Circle, a pivotal transportation artery where DC, Virginia and Maryland resident's traverse into, around and, out of the city's hub.

In the late 60's and early 70's, media published documentation of America's involvement in foreign affairs. With this increased awareness of actions taken, public sentiment voicing opinions about political responses to current events appeared in print. Impeachment was no longer a term found in the dictionary but was being applied to one of our own. A Vietcong soldier was filmed being shot and killed by a South Vietnamese soldier, and featured on the evening news. This brought to the public's attention the stark reality this man, was not an actor who, later would appear in a different episode of a popular TV program. But, in fact, was the victim of a violent crime, murdered before our very eyes.

College students joined together to protest such actions, collaborate, and make a statement regarding their lack of support for warfare and prejudice. Reported incidents of on-going injustices disclosed the vicious murders of civil rights demonstrators. Such persecution and martyrdom drew attention for the need to acknowledge the depth of commitment civil rights supporters displayed around the country. Changes were beginning to take place and would continue in the future. Daily selfless actions, whether big or small, built a solid foundation to support every effort that moved change forward. Amidst these events were American University's young local athletes, soon to become part of another American University revolution. This

4

revolution included changes in education, athletics, and social aware-ness that would directly impact their future and the lives of many.

Sitting around a table in the Mary Graydon Center on October of 2015, at our college reunion, we took time to remember the rea-sons we chose to attend American University and reflected on the changes made in both ourselves and one another.

American University

CONTENTS

CHAPTER 1

The Importance of Being Optimistic

Grandma Foreman born in 1886, raised in a matriarchal Native America culture without any formal education and limited resources, shaped how she raised Grandma Marion, my father, my brother and me. My brother and I lived with Grandma Foreman until Chris was in the fifth grade and I was in the fourth grade. After learning of Grandma Marion's birth due to an undesirable inter-racial liaison, she traveled to Canada to bring her back to DC and adopt her as her own. Living in DC presented Grandma Marion with many challenges as at the age of thirteen she became pregnant and at the age of fourteen gave birth to my father. Unable to care for a baby being a child herself, Grandma Foreman raised my father. After my parents divorced, she then cared for both my brother and me until my father re-married.

With these humble beginnings, how does one accomplish the following?

Capital One Academic All-America: The program selects an <u>honorary</u> <u>sports</u> team composed of the most outstanding <u>student</u> <u>athletes</u> of a specific <u>season</u> for positions in various sports—who in turn are given the honorific "Academic All-American." American University's Hughes Award: for leadership; First Team All-American: Basketball; First Team All-Academic American: Academic Achievement 1972 and 1973 at American University; NCAA Post Graduate Scholarship:

Basketball Hall of Fame: Springfield, MA. Final game jersey won against Georgetown University, as American University center was taken after the game and hung in the Academic All-American Hall of Fame (1973) I was inducted into the Academic All-American Hall of Fame, along with Raymond Berry- SMU'55, Dave Casper-Notre Dame '74, and Jim Grabowski-Illinois'66, in 1993.

Recognized as the last college player in NCAA history to average 20 points and 20 rebounds for their entire college career; with only six other players have achieved this in the history of college basketball.

1980 NBA-All Star; 1986 Founder Sixth Man Foundation-Project Contact Africa: philanthropic non-profit organization.

When you consider the following accounts of many sad, humorous, intriguing misfortunes, noteworthy adventures and extra ordinary events, will help you better understand the following accounts better understand the decisions and choices made throughout my life. It all began on September 17, 1951, in Washington, DC being the second son of Barbara Robinson Washington and Jimmy Alexander Washington.

The 1950's was the age of segregation in the South, a world quite different from that of today. Outright discrimination was the accepted norm for society. Separate and inferior facilities were made available to those of color and large signs were posted to remind any who might not be familiar with such restrictions if they were not members of the local community. At this time, there were no outright objections to such treatment as history had proven anyone who voiced such an opinion dealt with negative consequences. Therefore, this common practice molded my mind and contributed to a deep understanding and empathy for the plight of others.

As the years brought many positive reforms for equality to the forefront, my daily journey into a world with standards that would continue to undergo metamorphosis and carry me along with this needed transformation. Society was being forced to recognize and acknowledge the current disparity for basic civil rights. Focus was placed on efforts and movements to make changes across America. Education was presented as the answer to solving many inequity issues. People were now looking at prejudice, an accepted norm, as something to be challenged and eradicated. People began to step to the forefront to make civil rights an inalienable right. Legislation was being passed to provide and support equal educational opportunities for everyone.

Education was a strong foundation greatly supported by my parents. Attending school and learning was the expectation expressed by many. In the DC, metropolitan area educational system, the policy to send black students to all black staffed schools was still in place during my early school years. Some felt that such educators were positive role models and would best understand the impressionable minds of black youth. Location was the primary determination of which school's students attended. If you lived in a predominately black neighborhood your schools would also reflect a majority of black students and black teachers. How to attract a more diverse staff was not the immediate priority.

My parents were strong proponents of getting a quality education. My mother attended a local DC college and they were insightful enough to purchase property in the DC metropolitan area that would provide a more well-rounded educational opportunity for their children. My mother was a brilliant woman, recognized summa cum laude graduate from DC's Miners Teacher's College during which time she met my father. Our early years were a mixture of days filled with happiness and stability and days darkened by uncertainty and instability. Were there *really* dolphin people who were my mother's secret friends? Was there *really* a Mr. Ericson who gave her advice and hope for the future?

Somehow, stress or other events contributed to my mother being plagued with a mental disorder. As her increasing instability began to contribute to frequent bouts of questionable behavior it was soon diagnosed she suffered with paranoid schizophrenia. In her final years, she was plagued with a mental disorder. Somehow her gifted mind was accompanied with demons. She began to exhibit signs of a mental instability later diagnosed at paranoid schizophrenia.

My father was born to a fourteen-year-old unwed mother Grandma Marion who left him in the care of her mother, my great grandmother Foreman. Being raised without the support of either father or mother, he longed to have a strong family bond with my mother for his children. For this to be a reality he had to recognize and address many missing pieces needed to complete a successful family puzzle. One major piece was self-esteem.

Not having the nurturing of his mother and raised by a very strict grandmother knowing what it feels like to love and give love was missing in his formative years. Without a male role model and no history of a loving relationship with a female, his relationship with my mother was based on an unsteady foundation. My mother's illness presented a problem he did not know how to address. Unprepared, inexperienced, and lacking a bond of love between his female role models, he simply walked away and left her in the care of her family.

The consequences of his actions had a more negative effect on my brother than me. When my father left my mother with her parents we were placed in the care of our great grandmother Foreman. He simply moved on, leaving his responsibility to the people he felt were more qualified to handle the situation. He frequently made choices that helped him avoid dealing with confrontation. Dealing with conflict was not on his list of strengths. This inability to point out and stand up to negative actions and intents was witnessed by my brother Eric and me. This greatly influenced how we looked at the world and how we felt about ourselves and others.

My older brother, Eric Christopher Washington, was almost two years old at the time of my arrival and entrance into the Washington family. Being a small child about three years old who enjoyed the companionship of an older brother I followed his lead and wanted to be just like him. We were unable to understand the swings of emotion and behavior of our mother. The mental fragmentation of the disease was the cause of several episodes of delusional behaviors, which proved to be problematic for my father.

Such was the case when my mother told my Uncle Buddy that my father had been abusing her. A fireman, Uncle Buddy came over to our house to confront my dad. These accusations resulted in loud harsh words of accusations that had my Uncle Buddy chasing my father around our kitchen. Soon, Uncle Buddy tackled my father to the ground hitting him with his fists. My father's grandmother and caregiver Florence Foreman born in 1886, was there and she picked up a hammer hitting my uncle in the head. Uncle Buddy held his hand up to his head and blood was spurting everywhere. Unable to stop the bleeding he was taken to the hospital. After this incident, I never saw my parents together again.

My mother, my brother, and I moved to live with our Grandmother and Grandfather Robinson, on Maryland Avenue. To this day I remember the smell of frying grease that permeated the air both in and out of their apartment building. It was wonderful living with my grandfather and grandmother; both were very loving and kind. My Grandfather Robinson went the extra mile to make our first Christmas as a split-apart family extra special. I particularly remember him asking me what I wanted for Christmas. At that age, I just knew Santa would be able to deliver my wish so I told him out of all the toys in the world I *really* wanted a robot.

This being the popular item of the year finding one was not an easy task. It required numerous visits to toy stores and ultimately ordering one with the delivery date close to the twenty-fifth. When the robot arrived in the store, my grandfather walked from where we lived on Maryland Avenue to the Sears store on Florida Avenue in the wet and cold to get me this robot. The weather was very damp and he caught pneumonia from his venturing out so late in the evening. He was very sick on that Christmas morning, not able to get out of bed. Thinking Santa Claus had answered my wish by bringing the robot.

It wasn't until years later when I was told the truth about Santa that I realized just how much my grandfather loved me. Walking in the damp and cold, risking his health to make me happy helped me understand and appreciate the importance of being unselfish by putting the needs of others first. His unselfish demonstration to express love and concern is an impression that remains with me to this day. At that time in my life I didn't understand why as I had believed that Santa Claus had brought it.

For a short period of time, my father let my brother and me stay with our mother and her parents, in their apartment on Maryland

Ave. My father stayed at 59 Bryant Street, the house we lived in when my parents were together. When that was sold, he bought a house at 237 Farragut Street where Grandma Foreman moved into and took care of us. My father used this house as his *in and out* residence.

He had a room of his own, and would stay with us periodically. His mother, Grandma Marion lived at 1400 Emerson Street where she took care of blind residents. My father had two Russian wolf hounds, Tasha and Boya, who lived with us at Farragut Street. Perhaps he thought they would be good company and provide us with company to play with. Chris didn't like dogs, so it became my job to care for and clean up after them. Grandma Foreman wasn't very nice to them, but then again she wasn't that nice to most people.

She didn't have any other children as she had some health issues after having my father at the age of fourteen. My father later bought a house on 237 Farragut Street. My brother and I moved in with Grandma Foreman to live with her in this house. I don't know how this all came about. Years later we would walk to Grandma Marion's house on the weekends. She was losing her sight due to diabetes. Her house was located several miles from my father's house at 237 Farragut Street.

While living on Bryant Street my mother began to exhibit signs of instability. There were days when she would sneak us down to the basement and proceed to have a conversation with the wall of imaginary people and animals. She spoke to a Mr. Ericson and his friends, whom she described as dolphin people.

She would explain that these delusions were going to help her take us to a place where we could be happy and no one would harm us. She believed that Mr. Ericson had an airplane and he would be able to do this.

To a small child her behavior just seemed normal until we were old enough to put the puzzle pieces together. At night after we moved in with Grandma and Grandpa Robinson, my mother would sit in a rocking chair all night in watching us closely repeating that she would never let anyone take us from her. My brother and I wondered if that meant she might kill us. After she fixed us a meal I would tell Chris to try it out first just in case she was trying to poison us. We were watching too much TV and our imaginations were all to influenced by such shows as The Twilight Zone, Alfred Hitchcock, and One Step Beyond.

When we moved in with Grandma Foreman on 237 Farragut Street her daily routine was to sit outside on her porch in her rocking chair. Whenever people walked by she would engage them in a conversation. Most families did not own cars, and since our house was close to the side walk, everyone would walk past our front door, whether leaving or returning home. Looking back on those early formative years, there were several positive outcomes from living within such a tight-knit neighborhood. During those formative years, looking back there were some positive outcomes to living within a tight-knit community.

People looked like you, would communicate and interact comfortably daily, and were professionals with successful careers. Neighbors were positive role models who emphasized the value of securing an education in any field. Education was viewed as the key to unlocking a future. Success was possible if you set high expectations. You came to believe it possible to meet and even exceed your expectations as did your neighbors. These interactions with our neighbors created memorable conversations that inspired and motivated me to formulate the desire to contribute positively to society at large. It helped me to dream and look for ways to set and achieve goals, and at the same time fulfill my individual dreams to be successful and experience success in pursuing happiness.

Even with these positive role models, inner city residents were not encouraged to question the norm and made all too aware to never forget their "place." Constant reminders were evident in how blacks boarded and rode on public transportation. Despite being a predominately black community, all black passengers after climbing the short few steps into any bus, passed the front section and sat in the back of the bus due to unquestioned standard expectations.

There were no signs posted to remind anyone of this expected restriction. It was simply understood blacks were to sit in the back of the bus, especially if the bus route meant crossing into geographic locations that were predominately residences for white computers.

As a young child, this practice and the acceptance of this blatant display of prejudice made a lasting impression on my mind and sense of injustice. I simply could not understand how and why this continuous disregard for anyone's civil rights had not be challenged and changes made. It was evident passenger's response to this practice ranged from entitlement, prejudice, complacency, and frustration. These expressions on the faces of passengers indicated that it might be possible to see a change for the better. I was determined to not accept any attitude or action that supported injustice and the lack of concern for the rights of others.

Using location as the determining factor for school enrollment contributed to limited interaction Grandma Foreman walked us to school every morning. Her body language clearly indicated she valued education and believed in how important is was in determining our future. Our neighborhood schools provided limited interaction with white peers and teachers. Most integrated schools were in the suburbs, a term found in the dictionary. At times school presented a few obstacles to overcome. Grandma Foreman had never gone to school and was very limited in helping us with our school work. She could not read or write but when raising our father; she made sure he attended school every day.

My father's absence in our early school years was greatly felt by both Chris and me. Along with Grandma Foreman's inability to help us with our school work, she had a limited budget and we didn't have nice clothes to wear to school. If he was living with us he would have noticed how we were dressed and understood what was happening at school. His support would have meant the world to us. I will always remember wearing a white sweater with brown and gray stripes every day. The kids would make fun of us as especially on dress up day we had nothing different to wear that would eliminate the bullying from our classmates or the looks of distain from our teachers.

There was no acceptance of who we were as individuals or concern about what our home situation was like. At no time was there any display of compassion or attempt to understand why we came to school every other day wearing the same clothes. Ever present was derision and judgmental intolerance. Once you experience this, you never forget what it feels like to be treated unfairly. It reminds you to be more understanding of the many situations one has little or no control over.

We shared this with her one morning while walking to school and she told us what we should say to them to make them stop. The words she shared were curse words Chris and I had never heard before. When we followed her advice, my teacher overheard me and started to slap me. When we got home I told Grandma Foreman what my teacher did after overhearing what I repeated she told me to tell the kids. She got upset with me for not making sure only the kids who were bullying me heard what I had to say to them and not anyone else.

Under her care Grandma Foreman did teach us to always be polite when responding to any adult or authority figure. We were to say, "Yes, ma'am or No, ma'am, Yes, sir or No, sir." Appreciation for any kind gesture was to be acknowledge with "Thank You." Already in her late 70's she relied on a wooden cane with a hook to assist her in getting around. Conveniently enough, she also used it to administer a quick whack if we did something she felt desired correction. Grandma had a great deal of respect for others and had a strong moral sense of right and wrong. Injustice of any kind was always acknowledged and she would share her opinions and feelings openly with both Chris and me. She might not have been book smart but she had a great deal of common sense and taught us how to show concern for the rights of others. It was always her determination to make the world a better place by sharing her high moral standards with others, especially us.

Therefore, we were encouraged to perform acts of kindness without any expectation of reward or compensation. This lesson was always reinforced as she constantly volunteered Chris and my services to neighbors; she always made sure we never accepted any form of compensation. This strict rule of doing well simply because one can, never accepting any compensation and if offered it was to be declined. This rule continues to greatly influence my interactions with people today.

Even though at times her strict rule proved extremely challenging, we valued the joy one experiences when doing something nice for others simply because you can. Whether shoveling snow in the cold winter temperatures or cleaning up yard debris in the sizzling summer heat and oppressive humidity, if that helped a neighbor, it always gave us a sense of fulfillment. This developed in us a work ethic that helped us. This work ethic influenced the choices we made throughout our lives. As it was cold in DC in the winter with an occasional deposit of snow, she made us shovel every senior citizen's walkway on our block. In the summer the heat and humidity was oppressive at times. When we helped a neighbor with a chore in the heat we would get very thirsty. Once a neighbor asked us to help with cleaning up her yard and when we were finished she generously offered us each an ice-cold Coke. Oh, how we wanted to accept but knew if we did, she would find out, and that meant a whack. We grudgingly declined. This refusal to accept the Cokes was related to Grandma, and she was pleased that we followed her direction even though we needed and wanted a refreshing beverage. We, therefore, at times able to make her happy.

Grandma's sense of bringing us up properly rested strongly on her need to control and monitor every hour of our lives while under her roof. After she scheduled our chores for the day, including cleaning up after Tasha and Boya, we were free to play in the neighborhood alleys. We always returned home when we heard her call us and everyone in the neighborhood gave us the nickname the Sundown Kids. If we were outside as the sun was setting and the evening sky grew darker with every passing minute of freedom, her voice could be heard calling our names to come in. The advantage to playing in the alley was the proximity to our house. Once that first call was spoken we had to get home before she called our names a second time.

After moving in with Grandma Foreman and living at 237 Farragut Street, Chris and I were allowed to keep in touch with our mother. She would sometimes call and come over to spend a few hours with us. I remember one day when I was in second grade, she came by unannounced and asked Grandma Foreman if she could walk us to school. Grandma wasn't a trusting sort, but she had never said a negative word about our mother to us or anyone else including our father. It was taken for granted the two of them got along as Grandma never denied our mother any opportunity to spend time with us. She always liked my mother, and felt comfortable in honoring her request. As we were leaving the house and reached the corner, I immediately realized we were walking in the opposite direction of school. Continuing our walk, we arrived at the train station.

We listened as my mother bought train tickets and we soon discovered my mother had decided to take Chris and me on a trip. We boarded a train and started a weeklong adventure. We were excited to sit in our chairs and look out the window as the scenery changed within a matter of seconds. Where we were headed, we had no idea. At one point the conductor announced, "Hold your breath! You just held your breath long enough to cross the Mississippi River." This was significant for the smell that was in the air was truly strong and holding your nose was not as helpful as one might think.

Our first stop was in Chicago, Illinois, where Chris and I had scheduled appointments at the Mayo Clinic. Mother was concerned that we might not be in good health and had arranged for both of us to undergo an extensive physical examination. Having earned a salary from her lucrative job experience funding for this excursion and medical expenses did not present a problem in the first few days of our trip. As the days moved forward funds began to present a set of circumstances she had not taken into consideration. Staying in a hotel was possible for a short amount of time but we were limited in having enough money to buy one meal each day. If we had a ham and cheese sandwich Chris and I would have to share it. We soon learned to eat slowly as if the meal would last longer and help us not feel hungry sooner.

Having to miss a few meals was an inconvenience but well worth the ability to spend time with our mother. She was always loving and kind even if at times her behavior was questionable. Although living with Grandma Foreman gave us a glimpse of what normal interactions with a parent figure looked like, it wasn't difficult to see that our mother was not always lucid and rational in her behavior. She began to spend more hours sharing adventures with imaginary friends. At first we thought this was a way of entertaining us and helping us to understand that we were safe and loved. Realizing my mom needed to get money for us to stay together she would get up early get dressed and look for work. We were left alone in our hotel room and given specific instructions, not to open the door to anyone and assured us we were safe reminding us her friends Mr. Ericson and the dolphin people would be looking after us.

At first we thought it was a game she was entertaining us by trying to make us feel safe. But as this was the order of the day, for several days, we began to wonder if she was playing with a full deck. We were afraid of her behavior as every night she would rock in a rocking chair she put right next to our bed, saying she would never let us go, over and over again. These behaviors presented a series of questions that we couldn't quite formulate answers to and would not be able to fully comprehend her answers if any were given.

We never knew if our father tried to find us during our time with her or if she tried to contact him for financial help. When her funds were depleted we took a cab to the Salvation Army. When we arrived, my mother did not have the money to pay the fare and asked the worker there to pay the driver. When told by the worker that the Salvation Army didn't pay for cab fares somehow the issue was resolved as we were allowed to spend the night in the facility. There was only one room that we shared and before going to sleep the worker told my mother we could expect pancakes for breakfast. Chris and I were so hungry we dreamt all night of the breakfast we could enjoy in the morning. We eagerly got up and sat at the serving table. The requirement of holding hands and saying a prayer seemed to unnerve my mother, and she told us we could not stay there and we were whisked away before eating.

After leaving the Salvation Army facility and having no place to stay, we listened as my mother found a pay phone and place a call to our father. We had no idea what was said between them, but he sent money for two airplane tickets for Chris and me to return to DC. How our mother got back to the DC metropolitan area remains a mystery. Our father met us at the airport and never asked us about our trip or our mother. We didn't see my mother for quite a few years after returning. Her health unfortunately continued to decline, and mentally she seemed to only remember both Chris and me as her small children. We had no idea at that time just how much she was suffering.

Returning to DC presented a dilemma for me concerning whether I would be allowed to finish the second grade or repeat the year. My second-grade teacher, Mrs. Williams, said I had missed too many days of instruction and was going to recommend that I repeat the academic school year. My father had a long discussion with the principal and Mrs. Williams, and fortunately I was moved on the third grade. At this early period of my educational experience, I was genuinely upset and disappointed people had not made a connection between spending time with a mother I loved and missed having in my life with excessive absences. And without taking any of these circumstances into consideration would now present and consider the possibility of my being retained. This dilemma was presented by my second-grade teacher, Mrs. Williams, who felt I had missed too many days of instruction and was going to recommend that I repeat the academic school year.

My brother on the other hand returned to school and quickly returned to his regular school academic schedule. Chris took after our mother in that respect and was extremely talented in many areas. He was a gifted artist and could draw anything. He had beautiful handwriting and passed every test, earning the highest score, although he would not complete any assignment. He was selected to attend special schools due to his ability, with the hope that he would be motivated to actively participate in his education and move forward to reach his potential as a life-long learner. If my mother would have been capable of spending quality time with him, his true potential would have been realized. As our Grandma Foreman, could not read she was unaware of how Chris and I were really doing in school. Chris would read her our grades and teacher comments from our report cards and she simply signed an X and our paperwork was returned to school. If anyone had any questions about our academic performance, these were never voiced.

Family support for me came in the form of my relationship with my brother. I always felt secure knowing Chris would always be there for me. We had each other. The only time I felt abandoned by him was when he started school one year before me. Chris's first year at school created a lot of anxious moments for me. I had tried my best on his first day in kindergarten to remove him from his classroom and bring him back home. This was the first time we would be separated and I wasn't comfortable with the plan. Grandma had prepared Chris for his first day. She talked about how important it was for him to learn how to read and write and basic math skills. As she had not attended school she didn't know a lot about what the average school day looked like, but her only concern was that Chris enjoyed going every day. She told us that Chris was going to tell us all about every day he went to school, as we walked back home at the end of the day.

Chris knew I was not going to stop trying to take him from his classroom. I didn't understand why he got to stay and I had to leave him there without me at his side. Looking inside his classroom, it appeared to me there was plenty of room for me to take a seat beside him. Chris knew I would leave him there without me unless he could convince me. He then told me if he could stay he promised to tell me funny and interesting stories that I would enjoy. It took a while, but he made it seem like this was going to be the opportunity of a life-time. I reluctantly let go of his hand and began to imagine what could possibly happen at school that would replace my companionship. That first day seemed to drag on for hours and when Grandma and I started to walk down the streets to Chris's school, the separation ended and Chris was happy to share the what school was like and the work he had completed his first day.

After sharing how he was learning an alphabet song to identify the letters in the alphabet, he taught it to Grandma and I would sing it to and from school every day. Grandma *really* enjoyed the song and we would sing together at home several times during the day. I remember how she combined letters l, m, n, and o, I thought lmno, was part of the alphabet. Chris would listen to us singing this song and immediately told us the l, m, n, and o were separate letters and not one. He learned this when one of his classmates had recited the song while pointing to the letters his teacher had posted on the wall above the chalk board. He shared that the class laughed at the student for his mistake and made him cry. He felt badly for the student and realized that it was important to learn things correctly.

As the year progressed and Chris was enjoying what he was learning he shared this gift of knowledge with both Grandma and me. Growing in eager anticipation of my turn to enter the educational system, I counted off the days of summer vacation on our wall calendar with Chris. This helped me to learn how to count from 1 to 31. Trying to imitate him as he was completing his homework, I would scribble on a piece of paper and ask "Is this writing? Are these numbers?" I wanted to know how to be just like my older brother. He would laugh and say, "No. Let me show you." He taught me how to write and identify alphabet letters, spell and write my name, memorize my address and my birthday. He would practice with me showing me how to sit in my seat and pay attention. I had trouble at times concentrating as it was still summer and I enjoyed playing outside.

My first day of school soon arrived. Grandma didn't cry but walked with Chris and me to my classroom. Chris took me for a quick tour of where things were in the building, especially the bathroom and the cafeteria. Seeing more than one stall impressed me but it was the size of the cafeteria that immediately caught my attention. The long tables with folding seats were being prepared for the day. In the back of the room was a space where the meals for the day were being prepared. The aroma coming from the ovens made the efforts by the staff peeked my interest in tasting everything put on my plate a welcomed option. I couldn't wait to try for lunch time.

Returning to me to my classroom, Chris explained how students were seated and I noticed each student desk had a colorful name tag on the front across the top of each desk. Individual chairs were placed under each desk and inside were some supplies for us. He told me to walk around the room and find my desk. Remembering what he had taught me I found my seat and tried it out. Not too big, not to small, it was just right. He looked out the classroom door and let me know he had to go to his classroom. I gave him a big hug and promised to do my best to pay attention and make him proud of me and me proud of myself.

I took time to walk around the room noticing each wall and bulletin board was covered with different posters. I recognized the alphabet and number ones but the rest were things I hoped I was going to learn. As the other students began to enter the classroom, my teacher introduced herself and asked we remain standing so she could put our names together with our faces. I met my classmates as the teacher had each of us tell a little something about ourselves. I didn't have a lot to share and when my turn came, I simply stated this was not my first day in kindergarten. Everyone looked at me as I continued to explain last year when my brother came to school I went into his classroom to try and bring him back home. This seemed to amuse my audience and wondered if my comment was well received by my teacher as it was not meant to be funny.

Our first day ended and Grandma didn't come to pick us up. It was arranged that we remain to attend an after-school day care program. We were signed up for this program by her to give us more time to take advantage of extra tutoring to learn the basic skills she was not able to help us with. We didn't mind staying but Chris grew extremely uncomfortable after the director of the program introduced herself. She was an older black woman who reminded us of Grandma. Her voice was deep and her tone harsh. She made it clear she was a no-nonsense person who expected all who attended her program to follow every rule to the letter. Initially this didn't present any concerns as we were used to following the rules laid out by Grandma.

This however was short lived when we were told after using the bathroom and washing our hands we were to sit quietly in assigned seating until our meal was served. After stating "Thank you" we could then eat. That first day set a daily serving of macaroni and cheese. I was happy as it was one of my favorites especially since it was creamy. Chris however, hated macaroni and cheese and turned to me and said, "You know I hate macaroni and cheese, would you help me out by eating mine?" As I was always hungry and one of my favorites, this presented an offer I simply could not refuse. For me my biggest challenge was vegetables. I hated them more than Chris hated macaroni and cheese. With his dislike for macaroni and cheese, there was only one meal choice to avoid eating. Whereas for me there was always some different vegetable being served every day which added to my plan to give whatever vegetable included on the menu to Chris.

Eating next to Chris presented a challenge as he hated when someone touched his arm at any time during his meal. This aversion was on-going both at home and at school. Being seated to his right side made it impossible not to at times have this occur. Each time I received a hard punch not a slight jab or nudge. I soon learned how to eat with my left hand, which made people think I was a lefty.

There were a few times when I used Chris' request to use the bathroom to help me solve my vegetable issue. When he left the table I would scoop my portion of vegetables onto his plate. When he returned to his seat, he would look down at his plate, look at me and ask, "Didn't' I eat my vegetables already?" I put on my best innocent face and would respond, "No." he didn't question me again and he ate this second helping of vegetables as a replacement for the macaroni and cheese. Once our plated empty we were free to join the other students for some tutoring and recess time. Grandma was always waiting for us outside and we then walked home together. Now she had two school day stories to listen to before we returned the house.

This strong bond we had sometimes seemed a bit stretched due to the fact he almost killed me on at least two occasions. On a second occasion when he told me to put the vacuum cleaner hose in my mouth, and it sucked out the air in my lungs, causing me to collapse. He told me to put a lit cherry bomb down a car gasoline tank. This time a stranger was across the street watching us and listening to our conversation, he ran over to where I was just about to put the cherry bomb down the gasoline tank and tackled me to the ground, dislodging it from my hand. It rolled away and exploded before I was dropped it down the tank opening.

On a third occasion, he told me to swallow a hard-boiled egg without chewing. The egg got stuck in my throat, cutting off my breathing and I passed out. Fortunately, Grandpa Robinson was nearby and helped me start breathing again or I would surely be resting in a grave today. On a fourth occasion when playing outside at Fort Totten with our mutual friend Don Morton, we had drawn a thin rope over the cliffs, and Chris told me not to grab it. I didn't listen, and when I grabbed the rope, we all tumbled to the ground after rolling over and over again down the cliffs. Our eyes were filled with dirt and debris and our faces scratched. Amazing enough, after coming home all scuffed up, no one asked any questions about our appearance to show there was any interest or concern about what might have happened to us.

To be fair Chris had his share of mishaps. One summer while we were walking in the neighborhood, we discovered an apple tree full of ripe fruit. As we were always hungry, Chris decided with such an abundant amount of potential harvesting, surely this tree would welcome some relief. He proceeded to climb up the trunk of the apple tree and throw down a few choice morsels for us to enjoy. After reaching a certain height, his arms were not long enough to reach a branch filled with apples. I tried to help by throwing up a large stick. The stick hit a wasp nest and instantaneously angry wasps emerged and began to attack Chris. In a desperate attempt to escape Chris let go of his hold on the tree branch and dropped to the ground. Forgeting about being hungry and the prospect of enjoying the feeling of being satiated from the delicious apples, we ran all the way home to escape attack from the relentless wasps.

Running for your life to escape a wasp attack, being such a memorable experience, would explain Chris' phobia about insects. However, it still leaves me wondering about his phobia about dogs. My father had two Russian Wolf Hounds and grandma Marion had one Russian Wolf Hound named Prince. Prince never interacted with Chris and was kept in the basement. It was my job assignment to care for and clean up after Prince. The truth be told the stench emanating from the basement upon my arrival was both unpleasant and overpowering. Perhaps it was more the chore that Chris avoided and he didn't *really* have a phobia about dogs. He did frequently express his dislike for the stench that always seemed to linger in the basement.

But then again, there were those incidents where he would cross a street to avoid any interaction with a dog and would sometimes turn around and run away if he felt so inclined.

Losing the loving affection and attention of both our parents at an early age made the brotherly bond between Chris and I grow closer and stronger over the years. Fortunately, we had one another to talk to and seek solace when times were uncertain and scary. As we only had each other, we developed a keen insight into the need to be good listeners, being open to presenting support, and at times finding a solution to a problem in a quick but satisfactory manner. We spent most of our evenings after school in our room and sometimes Chris helped me with my homework. This was a bonus as Chris did not do any of his homework but would take the time to work with me on mine. At other times, we played games. Our favorite being Cowboys and Indians. I played the Indian and Chris was always the Cowboy.

We used authentic weapons in our games. Playing in the basement at Grandma Foreman's, I accidently stabbed Chris with a real kitchen knife. He put his hand up in a gesture to respond to one of my requests and I pushed the knife forward, and it made contact with his right hand. The knife went all the way through and he was screaming out in pain. Soon Grandma Foreman called out to us to stop the racked. I pleaded with Chris to not tell on me. To convince Grandma that Chris had sustained his injury from playing outside, we snuck out the back door and came running back into the house. I'm not sure if Grandma could tell from which direction the original screams came, she was so absorbed in Chris' bleeding hand the question was never raised so there was no need to give any additional information. She quickly arranged to take him to the hospital where he received five stitches. He had a scar from that incident to remind both of us of the need to be careful and not to play with or use weapons.

As we had many summer days when no one was concerned about where we went or what we might be up to, any unusual situation that arouse was never discussed. Such was the case on one evening when Chris, and our friends Roland Randall Kenneth Jr,

Brown, and Don Morton, and I met for a campfire picnic. We had a small fire going and were heating up hotdogs. An odd looking white man approached us and exposed his penis, stating that someone needed to rub Peter. He then peed on our fire putting it out and took a very big knife out of his pocket. The four of us ran as fast as we could in all different directions away from him. When we met up again, we thought this encounter was funny not fully understanding the danger we were in until years later.

Perhaps that was why when on one summer evening after calling us in from playing we were surprised at Grandma Foreman's desire to sit us down and talk to us, one day after Chris and I had finished our chore, we learned about her past. We were amazed to find she was born a native American Indian and might not be a blood relative of ours. For reasons never explained, she adopted my father's mother as her own. The result of an interracial relationship, Grandma Marion was abandoned on Grandma Foreman's doorstep, taken in and then adopted by Grandma Foreman. It might seem as if she was a caring person, but let the truth be told, she was not a loving woman. Her staunch rules and rigid lifestyle showed she truly believed in corporeal punishment and exacted it whenever she felt it was needed. There was no such word as "discussion" in her vocabulary, not even "my way of the highway." It was simply my way – end of discussion. She made sure my brother and I did many chores around the house, and we were often left in her care while my father stayed in an apartment on New Hampshire and Georgia Ave when not visiting with us at 237 Farragut Street.

Over the years Grandma Foreman cared for us, we still spent time with our grandma Marion. On weekends, we would walk from 237 Farragut Street to help with chores at her house at 14 Emerson. Our weekend visits to Grandma Marion's prepared us for the times we were left at home on our own. Weekends we watched a limited amount of TV. Chris and I were mesmerized by commercials featuring a mother baking a cake using a box mix and canned frosting. It was a toss-up between having a mom to cook something special for you and the visual image of the cake. Our mouths watered at the very thought of having a piece of cake. Grandma was not a dessert fan and only on a few occasions did she bake. A *from scratch* baker, the idea of buying a boxed mix and a can of frosting was not an option. After delivering groceries for the neighborhood women on Saturday, if we had collected enough money we would pool our resources to buy a $.25 cake mix and $.25 can of frosting. Choosing which kind of cake to try became time for preferences to be considered with lots of discussion and compromise. We decided to try each one and then determine which ones to buy again.

Returning home with our purchase, we would ask Grandma if we could bake a cake. She would agree only if we followed her one stipulation: to clean up after ourselves leaving the kitchen as we found it before preparing our cake. She sat and listened as Chris read the directions. Afterwards she helped us gather the utensils we needed and watched us as we worked. The only time she interrupted our efforts was to demonstrate cooking techniques and give tips we needed to know. As we didn't have a timer and the oven door did have glass we had to use the wall clock to preheat the oven and set a cooking time.

She watched as we mixed the ingredients and checked to see if the batter looked well blended and ready to pour into the baking pan. She greased and floured the pan and didn't let us do it ourselves until we practiced to and gained more experience. Using a spatula, she modeled how to scrap the mixing bowl to make sure we put as much of the batter in the prepared pan as possible. She opened the oven door and let us take turns putting the prepared pan inside. She wanted us to feel how hot the oven was and explained you could put a cold pan inside but to remove the final product you had to use potholders. The heat was a reminder of being safe when in the kitchen.

We watched as the clock counted down the minutes transforming our runny batter into a cake. The aroma of the cake baking filled the kitchen. Grandma informed us this was also a way to determine when the cake had finished baking. To make sure she gave both of us a toothpick to insert into the center of the cake. She would open the oven door, stand back to let the heat out and then using the potholders pull the oven rack a quarter the way out and put the toothpick in the center. If it came out clean the cake had finished cooking. Then she used the potholders to remove the cake and place in on a rack on the countertop to cool.

We watched her closely and after closing the oven door, she turned it off. While the cake was cooling, we practiced taking out a cake pan from the hot oven using the potholders. She did not let us do this by ourselves until we watched her do this several times. We were never allowed to bake in the kitchen unsupervised. Once the cake was cool enough to remove from the pan, she would take a knife and moving it along the sides to the pan loosened it from the pan. She tapped the pan lightly on the countertop and using a potholder, placed the potholder on top of the cake and flipped it onto a plate. Chris and I took turns frosting the cake and let Grandma have the honors of cutting the first piece to taste it. She was kind but honest. To her any boxed cake simply could not measure up to a *from scratch* creation. After sharing her opinion, she let us taste and finish eating her sample piece. She said we did a great job but she didn't want more than one taste. This came as great news to us. Somehow before the light of the following day arrived we had managed to eat the whole cake savoring one piece at a time. We didn't get sick just satiated by the delicious dessert we baked.

Being familiar with the kitchen and how to clean up came in handy in our later years. When our father and his new family went out of town for their vacation trips, Chris and I expanded our culinary arts. We would go to the market and ask the butcher what would be a good kind of meat to purchase with the amount of money we had. After giving his best recommendation, he told us how the fix it. Although we love fried foods, we avoided doing so. In those days, you filled a large pot with cooking oil, placed on the stove top and heated it waiting for the oil to get hot. In the meantime, you put flour and seasoning in a brown paper bag and placed the raw meat inside, constantly shaking the bag to make sure each piece of meat was well coated. Then you had to carefully put the coated meat inside the heated oil and hope it didn't spatter on you. The stove top then required additional cleaning and we soon learned how to broil and bake instead.

To us it was just what we did not realizing the exercise we underwent having to walk fourteen blocks by ourselves. Chris and I simply got up and made the journey, wondering what the funny story that we would remember happening later. We were paid twenty-five cents for our efforts. These included: cleaning the bathrooms, grocery shopping, cleaning the basement and backyard. Grandma Marion had many boarders who were legally blind. You can only image the job of cleaning toilets after blind men one day a week. Despite my instructions to sit down when going to the bathroom, they continued to stand when relieving themselves. This was a source of amusement to the blind men, who would laugh after I reminded them to sit. To this day I never use Lysol as a cleaning agents for whenever I smell Lysol the vivid picture of a urine covered toilet comes to mind.

She would meticulously give us a shopping list with of the items we were to purchase. Being uneducated she would have someone write the list of items for us to purchase, and sometimes they would forget to include things. Not surprising enough, she frequently neglected to give us the correct amount of money. There was always a sense of anxiety when we reached the check-out stand and placed the items on the check stand. If we had enough, it was a good day. However, if not the cashier would set the groceries aside, and we would have to walk back to Grandma's, get the amount deficient, and then walk back to the store. Sometimes, she would add more items to include with her original list, and again we would be short of funds resulting in another return trip to the house and store.

Of the many boarders living at grandma Marion's home, one stands out in my memory, Raymond James. Having a warm friendly and outgoing personality, an older gentleman in his mid-50, Ray was always glad to see Chris and I come visit our grandmother Marion. A truly likeable man he rode the bus to work Monday through Friday, standing outside the Navy Department running a sidewalk candy stand. In the mornings if Chris and I were doing chores for Grandma Marion, I might catch a glimpse of Ray shaving.

It amazed me that all the lights were off in the bathroom as he put the shaving cream on, picked up the razor, and proceeded to move this over and over his face. You would never know he was blind; his hand began the procedure holding the razor in the correct position. He started on his left side and directly under the hair line next to his ear. The razor slowly glided down his face, as he moved the razor up and down with expert handling. He finished moving the razor over his entire face than raised his head to proceed to shave his neck and throat. I was mesmerized by his actions.

When he completed the procedure, he turned on the water, placed the razor under the faucet and counted to ten. Then he placed the washed razor on the counter in the exact positon he took it from, put his hands under the running water and filling his hands washed the remaining shaving cream off his face. Amazingly, his face was smooth and no hair was visible. I imagined when it was time for me to shave I would be able to do as good a job and he did, especially having observed him accomplishing this task in the dark. The careful attention given to such a simple but essential daily task clearly showed what a good, hardworking man he was giving his full attention to complete every task. It needs to be acknowledged he was a good, hardworking man.

Visiting with grandma Marion on the weekends Chris and I would sometimes sit and listen to the latest gossip among the boarders. It was overhearing a conversation that led to us learn about my father's missing father. Apparently, my father knew who his father was. Not having any male role model to follow in caring for the responsibility for a family and children perhaps this information could explain why our interactions with our father were sporadic and brief. Any attention he gave to us was more than he had experienced and might have fostered the understanding any time he shared with us was meaningful and adequate.

Leaving us in the care of Grandma Foreman was how his mother solved her need for assistance in parenting. Raised by Grandma Foreman, as his mother was just fourteen years of age when he was born. Feeling Grandma Foreman had done a good job with him it would be natural for him to assume she would be the best person to be put in charge of our care until other arrangements could be made. When our father would come by and spend the night. We were so happy to see him.

It was a special treat to get into bed with him and know we were together as a family. Wondering where he had been and what he had been doing was answered when he came to Grandma Foreman's one night to announce he was going to get remarried. My brother Chris and I were overjoyed. Would it be possible to be living with our father and regaining the missing component of a loving mother figure? Our trusting minds began to imagine life without a strict and harsh parental figure. We imagined living with someone who would show us love, with hugs and embraces, showing we were both loved and wanted.

With this announcement, we knew why he was often away. We were hopeful he had been looking for someone to make us a family again, someone who would be supportive and understanding of what two young children would need after experiencing the loss of their mother. My brother was about ten and I was eight at the time my father made this decision that would profoundly affect both our lives. My father brought his fiancée, also named Barbara, to the house and introduced her to my Grandma Foreman. There was no mutual admiration for one another and the sparks began to fly when my father added the news she was going to have to move out and live with my grandmother Marion. The scene was truly memorable. Grandma Foreman got up and faced Barbara with an expression I had never witnessed before. She looked directly into Barbara's face and vehemently stated, "Not as long as there is a single breath in my body, am I moving out and letting you take over my grandsons and my home."

My father, demonstrated his inability to face confrontation by his failure to step up to the plate. He stepped back, giving no support or offering any means to settle this heated confrontation. Instead he proceeded to watch and listen to the exchange of words that once uttered could not be taken back, igniting a fire, creating a rift that would never be mended. When it was obvious, Grandma Foreman was not going to bow out gracefully. My father soon realized if he didn't get out of the front door expeditiously a lot of blood was going to be shed.

He took Barbara by the arm and walked to the door. Grandma Foreman was beyond upset and rushing behind them to get to the door first, became to chase my father around the house, she raised her cane and threatened to make sure no changes in her living situation was ever going to happen. Never getting out of breath, she continued to scream and yell a very colorful tirade of profanity to make sure there was no doubt as to her feelings and her intent. The words she spoke were very clear. There was no way another woman was going to force her to change her lifestyle. It was a given this interchange had not gone well and it was imperative for both my father and Barbara to leave as soon as possible to escape with their lives in tack.

Kermit at 3

Kermit's father 1952

Kermit with brother Chris

Aware this discussion didn't go well, both my father and Barbara escaped into his car. Grandma Foreman was not going to give up the chase that easily and hooked her cane on the door handle of my father's car. Under the direction of Barbara, who could be heard saying, "I don't care how old she is we need to get away from this mess now." my father listened to her encouragement to flee. He drove away with such haste down the street. He took no note her cane was hooked to the handle of his car. He did not reduce his speed and continued to drag Grandma Foreman down the street for several feet. She clung to her cane, for as long as she was able. She could still be heard yelling and screaming obscenities, from inside the house, until she could no longer hold on to her cane. Concerned she need assistance to recover from all of this, Chris and I ran into the street to help her to her feet. Her cane was in the street a few yards away and Chris ran ahead to collect it.

I helped Grandma get up and we both held onto her arms as we walked back to the house. We were sure the neighbors had not only watched but also overheard the altercation and would be eagerly waiting to see how things turned out. After settling Grandma inside, we went to our room to give some serious thought to what we had just witnessed. We tried to think things might change for the better, but things did not look promising. We didn't know quite what to expect next.

If this woman could get our father to literally kick our Grandmother to the curb, both literally and figuratively, what else was she capable of doing? Things didn't get much better from that point on in fact they slowly gained momentum and got steadily worse. After this first meeting with my stepmother, she continued to dominate my father and life with her turned out to be the epitome of a true living nightmare, all the Agony but none of the Ecstasy. I didn't think anyone could be any meaner than great Grandma Foreman but my new stepmother *actually* made Grandma look like a saint.

From our first meeting Barbara was openly hostile. She made no pretense about her true feelings about having to care for two children who were dark complexed. Her first impression of how we were raised by Grandma Foreman was not positive and not worthy of her time or attention. Not once did she spend time with us to get to know us as individuals who only wanted to be loved and kindly cared for. To her we were an inconvenience and one she would work diligently to ignore and make our lives miserable. However, Barbara pretended to accept our father as he was, and his meek disposition allowed her to be over bearing and domineering. She took his kind mellow spirit as something she could manipulate and she was very good at it. She was not so kind in her appraisal of us, to her we were crude, ignorant, dirty and uncultured.

Everything Grandma Foreman taught us Barbara found disgusting. To establish her superiority in their relationship, she set her own rules and restricted our use of normally assessable appliances, rooms of the house, TV viewing, and excluded us from being any part of family outings or vacations. She set her own clear rules and restricted our use of normally assessable appliances especially the (e.g. refrigerator). She never addressed any of our daily needs and always made derogatory statements about the mental health status of my mother. Her words were sharp and cutting. She showed no concern for our needs, basic clothing items or food stuffs we could have access to. She never asked if we needed any new items or bought us anything. She made it clear we were burdens she only tolerated because she had to.

Grandma Marion next to great Grandma Foreman and her husband

Grandma Marion

Wanting to please his wife not realizing how much that would negatively affect us, when we asked for anything, he would say, "You won't take care of anything." Really, where does the definition for need and care apply to kids clothing? How many stores would go out of business if a requirement for purchasing items was solely based on the contingency they be cared for by the person it was purchased for? None.

It was my father's support for harsh remarks, tone, and outward dislike for us was hurtful. It made me aware of how sensitive and fragile the human spirit is. Although it made me determined to prove her negative statements false it also reminded me of never trying to please anyone who does not have your best interest at heart. As you identify similar feelings observed in others it helps you to remember not be judgmental. Being over critical of others was something Barbara was an expert at. Instead of trying to show a sincere desire to help Chris and I move past the pain of losing our mother she choose to belittle and humiliate us at any opportunity. Chris and I had to work together and find peace in resolving issues that resulted from her unpardonable actions.

We didn't think our ill-treatment could get any worse, but it did after she had two children with my father. Her negative treatment of my brother and me increased to the point where my brother would get into physical altercations with her. Chris would stand up to her and that wasn't a pleasant scene and was never addressed by my father. He never asked why we were not getting along, never had any family meetings to resolve issues. It as if he was blind to what was happening.

When their two children were of age Barbara started to make plans for family vacation. Family vacations did not include us and we were left behind to take care of ourselves. We had the reputation of helping neighbors with their weekend grocery shopping so we knew how much food items cost. We calculated how much money we would need to purchase the food stuffs we wanted to eat for the week or until my father and his family returned home. We had the physical stamina to work at delivering groceries, and walk back home with our purchased items from money we made that day. No one ever asked how we managed to take care of ourselves. The only concern shown was checking the refrigerator and cupboards to make sure nothing was missing once the family returned. This had its perks as we got to eat what we liked and we learned how to cook. Barbara loved to make macaroni and cheese and it was so stiff and dry we always bought the boxed version that was creamy. Her other favorite was to bake a pound cake. Since we were always subject to some form of punishment and not included to have any we could use our money to buy our favorite cookies and these would last a lot longer than a cake. The only times we enjoyed, while living with my father and his new family, was when they were gone and we had the house to ourselves. We never ventured about or spied through closets, we simply enjoyed the peace and quiet.

Being familiar with the kitchen and how to clean up came in handy in our later years. When our father and his new family went out of town for their vacation trips, Chris and I expanded our culinary arts. We would go to the market and ask the butcher what would be a good kind of meat to purchase with the amount of money we had. After giving his best recommendation, he told us how the fix it. Although we love fried foods, we avoided doing so. In those days, you filled a large pot with cooking oil, placed on the stove top and heated it waiting for the oil to get hot. In the meantime, you put flour and seasoning in a brown paper bag and placed the raw meat inside, constantly shaking the bag to make sure each piece of meat was well coated. Then you had to carefully put the coated meat inside the heated oil and hope it didn't spatter on you. The stove top then required additional cleaning and we soon learned how to broil and bake instead.

Not having to hear Barbara's daily taunts and negative comments was truly like a vacation in paradise for us. As this was not a pleasant household with the unfairness and favoritism not being addressed by my father, his absence was also welcomed. He chose to turn a blind eye to our continuous mistreatment and simply accepted Barbara's harsh tongue towards us and went on with his life. Barbara's constant verbal assaults regarding the color of our skin, or our destiny to become nothing, were the usual comments to be expressed during the day. It wasn't until Barbara and my father retired that he finally acknowledged that he preferred to live alone and Barbara moved out of their home to live with her children.

Chris being the oldest was more aware of the cruelty we were daily shown. He felt it was his responsibility to stand up for us, especially since our father would not or could not. This proved troublesome to Chris who wanted to respect our father but at the same time put Barbara in her place and at bay. This conflict within in made him try very hard to get passed the daily verbal assaults. With every day, he seemed to be coming very close to reaching his limit on patience and forgiveness.

Winning the struggle to forgive and forget was going to take a long time and once his limit was reached it would be comparable to watching a volcano erupt. Daily we spoke about how to not let her actions and malicious intent get under his skin as I shared I was just going to ignore her limiting any conversation to the basic yes or no response. On a good day, we didn't speak to her at all, and this somewhat limited her verbal attacks. When the day did arrive when the volcano erupted it was quite a sight to behold. When given the task to sweep the backyard, Chris took the broom and began to sweep in a back and forth motion. Barbara did not like how he was performing the task and grabbed the broom out of his hand with the stick, hitting him hard in the face. Chris immediately hit her, and an all-out altercation began. I must admit I was secretly cheering him on as she was so mean and cruel someone needed to stand up for us.

After successfully showing her that he was not going to let her continue to get away with her harsh words and physical aggression, Chris ran away for two days. No phone calls or report to police, it was if it was business as usual, my father took Barbara to see a movie. Even upon his return to the house, after doing nothing to find him, there were no questions asked, merely the disappointment felt when a bad penny returns. Barbara continued to display her negative views and her constant remarks that my brother and I would never amount to anything. This did not stop our dream to experience life without Barbara. Plots formulated in our minds as we envisioned a variety of creative yet undetected means for her elimination.

Despite her constant remarks that my brother and I would never amount to anything we continued to dream about a life without Barbara. Her caustic remarks, "Your stupid crazy mother called again. Tell her to stop calling here. The only reason you go to see her is because you have nothing else to do." We rode the bus to visit our mother if for no other reason than that we loved and missed her. I longed to tell Barbara, visiting our mother had a bonus it got us away from you.

The first Saturday morning following Chris' return, we could smell the aroma of a welcoming breakfast being prepared. Could this be a sign that things might be changing? My father was sitting at the table with the family enjoying breakfast. Chris and I quickly threw on some clothes and raced down to the dining room table. We arrived when Barbara had just finished serving the meal. It was clearly our hope and intent to join the family for breakfast. The aroma of freshly cooked eggs and crispy bacon filled the house. It appeared as if we were being invited to join in a true feast of crispy bacon, eggs, toast, pancakes and waffles. When we sat down at the table we were told, in front of my father and her children, "Fix your own breakfast." If fixing our own breakfast included milk that posed a problem as we were not allowed to open the refrigerator. My father sat there and said nothing nor did he get up and open the refrigerator and take out milk so we could have cereal for breakfast. Barbara made it clear, letting us know we were not included in her family. We sat watching everyone else enjoy the meal she had prepared.

Even as we grew older we were limited to the time we could be downstairs and were directed to go to our shared bedroom right after the only meal she did provide for us, dinner. There were no allowances for watching any TV programs and when asked at school if we had seen the latest Star Trek or other current programs, we had to pretend that we had. My half siblings, whom I liked, were of course allowed to get whatever they wanted.

The DC metropolitan area having four seasons, the summers are hot and humid. This did not deter young boys from venturing out in the hope of experiencing an adventure worth remembering. In search of such an adventure my brother and I walked to Fort Totten and looked around for interesting items to play with. A fort held many wonders and sometimes we found fossils or other relics that were interesting to collect and play with. Imagine our excitement when finding a cannon ball (which at the time we thought was a shot-put). This ball was a quite heavy but we managed to toss it back and forth. There were a few times we dropped it on the cement ground and we simply picked it up and continued to walk home at times threw it up and down to try and crack the cement. Arriving home my father noticed our great find and told us it was a cannon ball from the year 1812. We were excited only to discover the reason it was heavy was because it was full of gun powder. In fact, it was LIVE ammunition. We however were convinced it was a shot-put. My father took the cannon ball from us and we never saw it again. He did say that he was taking it away from us because it was dangerous.

My father was not the type who cared for his lawn or automobile. He never washed the car and never mowed the grass. Not mowing the grass was directly related to his not ever watering it. Our front lawn looked like the parched desert. It was filled with dirt a few weeds and lots of rocks. My father began his lifestyle as a hoarder early in life. The outside was merely a sample of what the inside looked like. He used the basement to house a variety of objects simply because he liked them. They were not purchased for any monetary advantage later but simply as a challenge to see if he had room. If he didn't he would make room to store any item that struck his fancy. This meant stock piles of newspapers, along with whatever struck his fancy. Barbara didn't seem to object as the hoarding obsession was gradual and items were out of sight which meant out of mind. Not to best housekeeper, this lack of space meant less to clean.

Our next-door neighbor, Mr. Robinson, could have his lawn on the front cover of Better Homes and Gardens. It was lush and green with colorful plants. We loved looking at it and taking every opportunity to venture over and run and roll in the grass. Mr. Robinson was flattered by our admiration but was also not happy with us taking advantage of any chance to play. We were kind and followed his directive to stay off his grass and only snuck a few play times when we knew he was not at home.

Our neighborhood didn't seem to mind that our father's idea of up-keep was not shared by everyone. They did acknowledge that Chris and I were responsible for most of the yard work and were appreciative for any clean-up and or maintenance we could provide. Realizing that summers were hot and humid everyone sought any means of relief from the uncomfortable humidity and high temperatures. The houses in our neighborhood were small and most didn't have central air conditioning. A simple window air conditioning unit was considered a luxury. Our house on 237 Farragut Street did have one large an air conditioning unit in our family room. Upstairs where the bedrooms were, was like Africa hot. This increased our desire to go to the local recreational center for an opportunity to a swim in the pool. One of my early goals was to learn how to swim. There were several obstacles in achieving this goal. For most of my early years, swimming pools were off limits to blacks. As other recreational facilities were opened in the suburbs, Parks and Recreation in the inner city made the decision to open community pools, on a restricted basis, to the black community. Filled with anticipation and excitement there was also present the element of fear. This fear was multifaceted: fear of drowning by self, fear of drowning by others, fear of not being kept from drowning by life guards who were merely collecting a paycheck.

When finally allowed to take advantage of the pool, the sight was a bit overwhelming. The pool water was quite blue, with a large group of people in the shallow end. There was a long line of prospective participants who were first told to line up outside the pool along the fencing. A white pool lifeguard turned on a large water hose and proceeded to hose perspective swimmers with cold water before we could enter a gate and have access to the pool. The pool was regulation size with most occupants in the shallow end of the pool. The chlorine level must have been doubled as your body was covered with and ashy film and your eyes burned for hours after leaving the water. This noted separation policy, of those who could and those who could not swim, seemed to be in place in the pool as well and in daily interactions. Those early years in DC made clear the need to make rampant changes in society. The injustices observed outside our home could also be mirrored in our home. Having to deal with both was an on-going challenge. As time and practices changed positively for society, it provided hope that in time our situation at home would change also. The changes at home would however, rest more on me and with each day I grew more determined to meet that challenge with success. As there were those who had and those who did not have in the general sense of the word.

This desire to separate from the crowd and venture into new depths aroused my goal to learn how to swim. This open invitation to step outside the norm filled my daily thoughts and nightly dreams. I frequently saw myself swimming in the deep end of the pool with the freedom to enjoy the wide-open space and feel the refreshing cool water. My body glided across the length of the pool and flipped over for another return trip to the wall at the deep end. This constant mental focus on achieving this goal gave me the confidence to put all my mental imagery and envisioning to the test that night I had a dream, I saw myself swimming.

The following day I arrived at to the pool with the sole intention of merely trying not to drown. I closed my eyes saw myself jumping into the water, rising to the top, stretching out my legs, extending my arms, lifting my head to take in a breath, and moving easily through the water. I took the plunge and to my surprise my body followed my vision to a tee and I was indeed swimming. I was amazed and excited by this experience. In my later years, I reflected upon its greater significance in my life. The desire to achieve any goal despite the odds against you, made my future dreams and ultimate success in meeting more formidable goals, seen by others and insurmountable, a reality.

Every day contains 24 hours. We spend approximately 8 sleeping, 3 eating, 6 at work or school, 2 caring for personal needs, leaving about 5or so for other activities. That's not too much to have at your disposal each day. You might think being confined to your bedroom would encourage you to use that time wisely by doing lots of reading and study time but my brother and I simply played slow motion football and basketball. We were bored to tears and dreamt of better times to come. Mental activity was not the preferred way to spend out precious few hours of odds and end's time.

We were eager to participate in any sporting activity that was sponsored by the neighbor recreation center. Any position on a team that was open I would sign up to participate in. Getting out of the house and being considered a valuable part of a group gave me the confidence to accomplish something positive and encouraged me to look to the future. I knew there was a better way of life and if society could change for the better so could my life. If there was a sport that offered an open position, I participated. Anything to get out of the house and feel like I could accomplish something positive. It also encouraged me to look to the future. I knew there was a better way of living and the world as I once knew it was changing. I was determined to benefit from the positive changes and looked to the future with determination and resolve to prove my stepmother wrong and show my father that the life he had given me was worth living and sharing with others.

I tried to keep this frame of mind upon returning to school in the fall, one had to face the daily terrors of being bullied. For me it was Glance Chambers, a student who was repeated retained and was old enough to smoke cigars, have a driver's license and drive a car. He was the legendary elementary school bully. His daily taunts never varied, they were successful even with his limited ability to construct complete sentences. Every day he would say this intimidating line,

"You owe me a dollar, where is my money?" And he and everybody else knew nobody owed him any money. We didn't get an allowance and never had money, so it was either steal from my father's change or get beat up. No one seemed to take any notice of this daily harassment most likely because it wasn't focused at them.

As school was not the best refuge, not being acknowledged as being clean and well-dressed, students repeated the unkind remarks made by our teachers and didn't pay attention to how Glance's daily taunts were hurtful. To add insult to injury, when picture day arrived and we didn't look like we just stepped out of a Gap advertisement, the teacher would put us on blast by calling us out and humiliating us. We tried to act like we had forgotten about picture day but she would send us home to change and we simply stayed there not returning to school until the next day. When we asked our father if we could get new clothes he would say we wouldn't know how to take care of them and that ended that discussion. It appeared that even though we gained another year of life and some wisdom about responsibility, there was never any our father was not aware of to the way our teachers viewed us. He wasn't around enough to ask or listen to how the other student's remarks caused us to be mistreated and overlooked. Both at home and at school no one considered us as being valuable individuals. Being looked at with distain, reminded us of how Barbara looked at us every day we had to live with her. We were constantly reminded to survive, endurance included how one responded to ill-treatment. This was our reality something we either had to ignore or allow to overtake us. The choices forced us to be determined to persevere despite negative comments. A lesson I would have to revisit later in my adult life.

Leaving elementary school and the likes of Glance Chambers was overshadowed by a different group of undesirables in junior high. While attending Bertie Backus Junior High, there were two rival gangs, the Decatur Street Gang and the Riggs Park Gang, who were always fighting on and off campus. Intimidation took on a new meaning. You couldn't go to the bathroom without saying a silent prayer that a gang member might be skipping a class and spending time in a stall smoking a cigarette or merely waiting to assault another frightened student who needed to use the facilities. One occasion I take a chance and went to the restroom just before lunch time. While inside one of the notorious thugs was hiding out in a nearby stall. Before I could escape his attention, he confronted me and told me to give him my lunch money. Now, I wasn't on the lunch line and no one was around do I refused. When he came at me I spun around and hit him as hard as I could. Miraculously I hit him hard enough so that he fell.

It was soon all over the school that I was going to fight him at 3:00 pm in the nearby woods. I thought all afternoon about how I was going to sneak out the building and avoid this much- advertised fight. It held nothing to facing Floyd Mayweather. At 3:00 pm a very large crowd of supports or doubters were waiting for me outside my homeroom door. Mrs. Harrison, my homeroom and typing teacher, asked me why I was so popular today. I was hoping I would see her the following day to give her a satisfying answer. To my surprise my plan to run away was thwarted when my brother Chris was standing outside my homeroom door waiting to walk me to the woods for my 3:00 pm appointment with pending pain.

As we walked towards the awaiting confrontation I did not close my eyes but bawled up my fist that earlier had met with success and again my fist make contact and knocked my challenger to the ground. For a limited amount of time I was held the hero, but still had to deal with the daily intimidation for my lunch money. The average age of junior students is twelve to fifteen, this fact did not apply to gang members who although clearly sixteen, acted like twenty-year-old prison mates.

You could never go to the bathroom as the gang members congregated there. (Monk, Cassius, Al Capone were the names of the top three). The names might have changed but the game was always the same. If you were small or skinny and standing in line for lunch you were easy prey.

Even though we did not dress well and didn't have a reputation for having money we were still the victims of bullying. These guys would see you in the lunch line and getting in your face told you, "Give me your money." In those day's lunch only cost $.30 cents. If you said, "I don't have any money." They would ask, "Why are you in line then?" This was immediately followed with, "All the money I find I can have." And then they would strong arm you to pat down your pockets. While doing so it was clearly stated: "I'm going to knock your teeth out." Once they started the only thing left was to be beat up right then and there. You couldn't tell the principal or these thugs would be expelled and spend their vacation day waiting to beat you up again, when school was over.

These guys would pat your pockets for your lunch money. To get lunch, you had to get in line and pray they would leave you alone. This was never going to happen. Once in line you were a sitting duck, for only those with thirty cents were lined up to pay for their meal. In those days, parents didn't pre-pay, it might have been easier to simply hand over your money and miss lunch, out of choice and not fear of being beaten up. That response could have led to the daily expectation of giving in to this intimidation along with a daily beating just to prove a point or merely for the fun of it. If you got in line and were close enough to the cashier you might just get a meal that day. Odd that these gangsters in training were not hungry, but greedy for cash.

Aware of this daily onslaught of extortion, no adult ever intervened or made any attempt to distract the perpetrators of crime to support a student's desire to eat lunch. Without any stress or presence of having a conscience, these gangsters were never sick or absent and felt free to act as they wanted. So, the bullying continued due to the lack of intervention.

Where were the adults? Quite frankly they stayed clear of these gang members as well. Leaving elementary school and entering junior high was an adventure in survival.

My Junior High was the home of several infamous thugs. Everyone in school and the neighborhood was aware of the infamous thugs, their reputations and sorted criminal actions. Junior High was more of a basic 101 course in criminal behavior and physical assault exercises for these individuals then a place of higher learning. It became a training ground on the art of intimidation. I remember one of my friend's father had just bought him a new pair of tennis shoes. He didn't make it past first period before they were removed from his feet and he was beaten up. When he got home, and told his father, he got a whipping for not telling the principal and trying to fight back.

He tried to explain to his father if he had done either that would guarantee a full group beat down in the front of the school for all the see. This was a way of teaching everyone a lesson. The thugs were in charge as held no fear or respect for anyone. His father infuriated by this decided to go up to the school the next day and get his son's shoes back. What he did get was a full-blown beat down by those thugs.

Graduation meant their criminal activities would continue as they moved on to high school. There new opportunities for perfecting intimidation and physical aggression before committing a punishable crime, that would place them in a new higher educational facility with teachers well versed in a variety of criminal actions, presented itself. It would be comparable to attending college with your choice of electives. Graduation from a penal institution, simply meant time for one on one tutoring to practice your newly learned trade was freely available, before returning to gain additional years of advanced training.

Parents were not immune to fear from these thugs. Social events were advertised in the neighborhood and required an invitation. Ignoring this simple etiquette by attending these events or parties, thugs arrived with ill motives simply because they would explain they didn't need an invitation but decided to stop in for a brief visit. Or they couldn't read the invitation and therefore crashing the event did not apply to their actions or intent. After receiving an invitation to a local party, I walked around Fort Totten down South Dakota Ave. At this time, almost every party would end up with a fight or disturbance. Guns would be pulled and bullets flew or someone who get hit was an open punch that was called "stolen" this meant a victim would be sucker punched for no reason it was simply done to indicate who was the big man to be respected. Despite these well-known acts of violence still parents held parties and kids continued to attend.

I was excited to receive an invitation to a party only one and miles from my house. The family was eager to provide a diversion to the hot summer nights. Music was heard all the way down the block and neighbors were invited to attend. With the presence of more adults it was hoped that the thugs would be less interested in causing any problems by showing up uninvited. The house had two stories with a large space for dancing on the main floor. I walked in and saw Richard Taylor and his group of thugs (I recognized them from elementary school and knew they did not go to Bertie Backus and were not among the invited guests.)

I did say hello and walked downstairs. I went downstairs and walked over to say hello to Darling, a very pretty girl. Then went upstairs to get something to drink. I overheard Richard Taylor tell his thugs about Darling being downstairs and gathered together to come up with a plan to get her alone and rape her. Darling was very pretty and a nice girl and these thugs had singled her out simply because in numbers they could over power her and enjoy the thrill of terrorizing an innocent victim. Quietly slipping down the stairs being careful not to direct any attention to myself, I alerted Darling to what I had overheard and we quickly looked for the basement door and leave before the thugs could carry out their plan to rape her.

We discovered the back door was locked to prevent any would-be party crashers barging in. I asked the person whose party it was to unlock it for us. Leaving as quietly and quickly as possible, I ran with Darling, who lived only a few blocks away from the party and waited for her to go inside her front door. Once she was safely inside her house, I looked around to see if anyone was chasing me and ran as fast as I could one and half miles, uphill home. those one and a half miles in constant fear those blaring headlights were hot my tail… making sure I wasn't being followed, always looking back to make sure no one was following me.

This was a major concern as these thugs drove a yellow Mercury Comet, an <u>automobile</u> produced by <u>Mercury</u> from 1960–1969 and 1971-1977. It featured a split grille with four headlights. Their car's fuel and maintenance was financed by the daily bullying for lunch money and other criminal actions. Unlike the definition of comet:

a celestial object consisting of a nucleus of ice and dust and, when near the sun, a "tail" of gas and dust particles pointing away from the sun. The "tail of gas" from their Comet was something I didn't want to see pointing away from the party, coming after me. I was relieved Darling was safe and even more relieved that Richard and his thugs did not know I was involved in making sure Darling left the party before they could carry out their plan.

There never was a time when something sorted and possibly life threatening was not the order of the day. The student population was tantamount to mixing oil and vinegar, students from two rival gangs, the Decatur Street and Riggs Park, created a constant source of violent behaviors. If you attempted to wear a nice pair of shoes, wanted to keep time with a working watch, tried to stay warm in a new coat, hoped to buy with a few small coins, it was taken from you. There was nothing and no one who could intervene. Any demonstration of rebelling against these acts of tyranny led to a physical beat down. If you managed to run home safely and close your front door, it was pushed in you would be assaulted.

The popular slogan became: If you run in the front door to escape from a beat down you'd better run out the back door. Attending Bertie Backus junior high was destined to prevent challenges daily in one way or another. One day someone called the school to say there was going to be a big gang fight. Rival gangs were always fighting so this was not unusual but this time the school was locked down and sixteen knives were found and confiscated from student lockers. This was but another reason why not going to the bathroom during the school day and not bringing anything of value to school was necessary in to continue living.

As if surviving any of the many incidents faced during the school day was not bad enough, we only ate one meal at home. There was no breakfast or lunch, at school if patted down by the thugs in training. When we came home after 6:00 pm, having participated in some after school athletic program, our dinner was waiting for us, having been placed on the dining room table since 4:00 pm, to get colder. Leaving food on a plate, uncovered for two hours did not improve its taste. Without the benefit of a microwave, or if there had been one having access to use it, we would look at each other and then the food.

We had to make a quick decision, either eat it or chuck it. Believe it or not many nights the choice was chuck it. This was especially true when she fixed macaroni and cheese. It was awful. Not even a starving rat would touch such an offering. Most meals were simply a hodge-podge of items no one wanted to eat over the course of the week. Barbara was not only a bad cook, her attempts to prepare food for a meal looked more like a poor attempt to disguise her plot to commit murder by *food* poisoning. One develops a deep appreciation for a well-cooked meal, served hot, after living in this household.

After years of living in unpleasant conditions, my stepmother's cruelty made us determined to prove her wrong. We were made tougher and stronger to meet a variety of obstacles. She was unaware that I had no desire to try and please her, it was simply a waiting game a countdown to the day I would no longer have to live under her. Chris on the other hand continued to battle with our stepmother and always tried to somehow gain her acceptance and approval. Neither of which was possible as she clearly made it evident how intensely she hated us. He started to take an interest in playing sports. He tried baseball, basketball, and football. He was only successful in football.

In our on-going attempts to enjoy some aspects of life, Chris soon developed an interest in playing football. I'd like to think this interest might have been inspired by me. In my determination to ignore negativity I resolved not to allow Barbara's words, actions, and attitude to dampen my spirits and bother me. I ignored her stinging remarks and focused on becoming an athlete. My lack of responding to her was working and once she found she could not get a rise out of me Barbara seemed to intensify her efforts on annoying Chris. Anything that would thwart her evil intentions was something to take note of and then actively pursue.

Chris and I decided it would be best if he followed my example which meant holding practice sessions to become comfortable with learning these new cognitive behavior skills. To be successful he would need to learn how to play verbal judo, roll with resistance, and reflective listening with me, as his partner in crime. As I was his side-kick it was only natural he clearly expected for me to step up to the plate. Not being found of my psychological solution, Chris opted for some positive physical exertion, football.

This meant getting up at the crack of dawn to walk with him to the football field and catch the many passes he tossed for me to run after. The walk to the playground gave us time to practice how to ignore Barbara's constant negative comments, and throwing the football. This helped Chris lessen his stress. As there was never an option to decline his invitation to join him, I simply went along with his choice on how to handle the situation with Barbara. This meant getting up and joining him on the football field to catch the many passes he tossed for me to run after. Once the invitation was extended, I was woken up and dragged out of bed every morning we were off from school.

Following close behind, Chris didn't wait until I caught up to him before we reached the grassy area on Rudolph's playground field, to begin our practice session. As we walked down the street he started to throw the football for me to catch. The walk to the playground also gave us time to practice ignoring negative comments, and throwing the ball seemed to relieve Chris' stress. As we walked down the street he started to throw the football for me to catch. This was quite a change from the Chris in his early years. The former Chris preferred to sit at home and read books. When it suddenly dawned on him that playing sports might provide some measure of pleasure the fire was lit and soon became a burning passion.

As a junior in High School Chris decided he wanted to play the quarterback position and the need to practice throwing the football became his key focus. His desire to become the best could be seen by our saving up every possible penny to buy a Duke football which cost $21.00. Once purchased absolutely no one could play with it unless they could catch it. If this treasured item ever touched the ground, we would lose out sense of calm and go ballistic. Fortunately, in those days Blacks could still play the quarterback position in high school because our student population was Black. He graduated from McKinley Tech High School being recognized as a very good football player at the quarterback position. When he went to Texas Western University he had to play the defensive back position – also called corner back. Initially, he was not offered a scholarship but with hard work and a talent that was seen he soon earned a position on the team and was offered a three-year full scholarship.

His junior year Chris decided it was time to get his driver's license. He gathered all the necessary material and studied to take and pass the written test. Once this was accomplished he scheduled an appointment for the driving test. His driving appointment scheduled, we rode the bus downtown to the designated Department of Motor Vehicle building. As he got into the car provided by the Department of Motor Vehicles, he appeared confident, but appearances can be deceiving. Within a matter of less than three minutes, Chris stopped the car, exited the driver's side and walked down the street to the bus stop. Shortly after he left the car I noticed he had stopped the car leaving it in the middle of the street. The gentlemen who had been riding in the car with Chris was shaking his head from side to side, walked around to the driver's side of the car, entered and drove back to the designated area for driving tests. I ran to catch up with Chris as he was walking away from the car and towards the bus stop. Racing down the street to find out why this happened Chris told me his driving tester kept yelling at him and he was done for the day.

In DC, you were placed in a high school based on the geographic location of your home address on the school map. I lived in the Roosevelt school area with the Decatur Street gang members at large. Rochester who was the head of the Decatur Street Gang was stabbed several times by the rival gang Riggs Park while walking across the Keene Elementary School campus. Anytime you left your home area to venture elsewhere and had to either cross or enter a gang's territory it was a given your life was in danger. You could never wear anything nice for if seen it was taken and you got beat up. You were told to take off what item they wanted and you still got beat up.

On a Friday afternoon, just before the end of the school day, the counselor was overly tired and asked me in which area I lived so she could place me in my high school assignment. I walked up to the board with the map and quickly responded I lived in the Coolidge High School area. Not getting up to check the map, she simply recorded my reply and I was then placed on the Coolidge High School roster. It was a longer walk from my house but it was safe walk directly down Third Street.

My house was located within in an area of one square block which contained 20 houses on each side. An alley ran between the four blocks running East and West and another alley ran North and South forming a capital letter I in configuration. My friends and I would meet in the alley to play basketball with peach baskets, football, and baseball. One mean neighbor would sit and watch us from his window and cut our ball in half IF we couldn't retrieve it out of his yard before he could get to it first.

Don Morton and other friends from neighborhood joined us by saying they lived in the Coolidge High School area also. Our High School years began with the tenth grade. Junior High started with seventh grade and went on to ninth grade. My sophomore year in High School I tried out for the local 100-pound tackle team. I only weighed 96 pounds but made the team. Our favorite professional football team was the Washington Redskins. We wanted to be football players so badly that after reading an advertisement for gaining weight – Instant Weight Gain, we ordered some. I was so skinny if I ventured outside wearing shorts my neighbors would tell me to go back inside before the wind would blow me away. This added to my need to wear jackets to cover my skinny arms. And so, this advertisement was very appealing.

The only downside of being skinny was the effort we would put forth to remedy this visual affirmation that something had to be done. Therefore, it was when we noticed this advertisement for a ready cure we immediately sought the help of this product Instant Weight Gain. I'm not sure if it was the use of instant or the feature of weight gain or perhaps a combination of both that lured us into buying it. As with any given promise there seems to be some hidden side effect not mentioned at the onset. So was the case with Instant Weight Gain – it only came in one flavor – Butterscotch. This answer to our quest for improvement made my brother Chris so sick he threw up every time he took a pill. Despite this obstacle Chris was determined to bite the bullet and go with the products promised results. Unfortunately, things did not work. We continued to look for the miracle that would allow us to move from following our favorite team and rejoicing when they won or saddened when they lost – to the hope that one day we might play on this team and share in the joy of winning.

After spending mornings working out with Chris my junior year, I made the varsity football team. Phil Gainis was our coach, and we had a very good team. Gainis was a very tough man having two and sometimes three a day practices without water in the hot and humid weather. In those days, we would have sold our souls to the devil for a drink of water. In addition, the coaches thought thinking water would give us cramps. To add to our desperate need for a drink of water, we were given salt tablets. How we managed to survive heaven only knows. As a coach his discipline policy was rigid and unrelenting. In today's world, this form of discipline would have resulted in a long sentence behind bars, wearing the classic orange body-suit with stainless steel accessories. It is noteworthy that not one player was ever late to practice or disrespectful to any of the coaches in word or manner due to a true sense of fear for their lives. In those days one hundred players tried out for the football team, and gaining a spot was very prestigious. Nowadays you can't get fifty players to go out for the football team in the inner city.

I was the back-up quarterback for the varsity in 1968 with very limited playing time. That year I lettered in tennis also (because it got me out of my French II class.) In those days, we were required to follow a strict course to graduate on time and did not have the opportunity to select what we wanted to pursue. My father loved tennis, and every Sunday I would watch him play at the Washington mall with his buddies. There were times he played and practiced with me, so I was a bit better than most players. Mr. Richardson was my driver's education teacher and counselor and the tennis coach. I told him I could play tennis and he invited me to come and try out for the team. I was better than the other kids as I had that practice time with my father, and Mr. Richardson was all too eager to put me on the team. I was undefeated, wining every match I entered, until we played in the playoffs. Warming up for this level of competition was humbling. I knew these suburban kids were good when we were warming up for the matches. Not posing any competition for them they destroyed me. But being on the tennis team still got it out of French class on Friday at 1:00 p.m.

In those days, you had the same homeroom teacher all three years of high school. Mrs. Thomas was my homeroom teacher and the first who took a real interest in motivating me to set and reach higher academic goals. Being still skinny she would ask if I needed lunch money for the day. My financial status rested on whether my buddy Leander Fuller, could be talked into giving me lunch money for the day. If I didn't she would give me thirty cents to buy lunch. Her kindness was expressed in several ways. In the morning before the school day started she would tune us in on WOL or WOOK, both local black radio stations. The favorite song girls wanted to hear was Stevie Wonder's, My Cherie Amour.

Coolidge high school had grade level intramural basketball games. My junior year my homeroom won the Championship. To celebrate our victory Mrs. Thomas provided cake, beverages, and chips. Everyone was happy about winning, and appreciated Mrs. Thomas' efforts to go the extra mile and make this occasion really special.

My junior year I was extremely fortunate to have Mrs. Thomas as my biology teacher. I had no problem earning A's in citizenship but having not applied myself in previous years my grades were C's and D's. As a direct result of consistently telling us she was confident we would all graduate on time and get accepted to colleges and universities, I didn't want to let her down. I began to take seriously the need to become a student and earn better grades. Motivated to please her, my goal was to earn an A in her biology class and earn the highest grade from the students in all her six biology classes. Each quarter I met that goal.

Recognizing my improvement, she asked me to continue working diligently to earn high grades in every class and make the school honor roll my senior year. I put forth a wholehearted effort and made the honor roll. Before my senior year ended, Mrs. Thomas left on maternity leave. She didn't come back before graduation. Mrs. Thomas was the key that unlocked my academic potential. She turned me around helping me to see the value of education. Hard work, setting goals and following through with the determination to succeed, resulted in American University offering me an athletic and academic scholarship.

I would ask Mrs. Thomas if there was any errand or chore I could do to earn lunch money for that day. She would always come up with something so I didn't starve to death. However, when I didn't want to ask her for lunch money I would ask Leander Fuller to lend me money with the promise to pay him back. Now mind you I had no plan on how to do this my immediate concern was to eat lunch. Leander was so nice and he let me pay him back a little at a time. His understanding to this day makes me realize what a good person he was.

Mrs. Thomas helped make studying Biology interesting. I was initially willing to take the time to study about life land living organisms to make her happy. Soon her lessons motivated me to pay closer attention and I enjoyed finding out about cells and genetics and heredity. Chromosomes and how they match up to make us who we are caught my attention. Earning an A in her class made Mrs. Thomas happy and motivated me to start taking academic seriously. I began to think Science might be something I could get into.

Being optimistic, my senior year, I walked into Mr. Chase's Chemistry class with the goal of earning a good grade. Looking around the classroom I was intrigued to understand the Periodic Table, a large chart on the blackboard with capital and small letters with assigned numbers. I sat in my seat and did my best to pay attention, completing my assignments, and actively participant in daily lessons.

The class settled into their assigned seats and proceeded to carry on conversations ignoring Mr. Chase and the information he was trying to deliver. His lesson delivery was different from Mrs. Thomas and if Biology wasn't interesting from the lessons Mrs. Thomas taught us, Chemistry was going to be quite the challenge. Determined to stick to my resolve and focus on academics I listened attentively and would engage in discussions hoping others would follow my lead. At the end of the year I earned an A and that helped my GPA and gain acceptance into American University.

The summer before his senior year to save and prepare for going to the prom Chris worked outdoors taking count of people boarding the public transportation bus to determine when an additional bus might be needed. It was always hot outside and he was only able to endure this uncomfortable job, as he sat in the heat, knowing he would be attending the prom with a date looking his best.

In spite our growing older with more opportunities to find productive use of my few leftover odd's and end's hours, summer continued to be long and boring. As neither Chris or I changed our habits to include spending quality time studying and completing school assignments. If it was summer Chris and I were enrolled in summer school. It was the opportunity to improve our grades in addition to not having to be around Barbara. Often the family planned outings and vacations that excluded us anyway. My stepmother was pleased to have us out of the house and so we sat quietly and improved D's to B's simply by attending. The summer heat and humidity also added to our willingness to attend on a regular basis. We could sit in an air-conditioned room without having to be told what we were not doing right by our stepmother.

The other upside to summer vacation was the opportunity to make some money. We applied for available jobs and planned a budget for upcoming school, social events and basic items our father would not finance for us. Earning some money and putting it aside in a bank to save would help us invite and take a date to the prom, rent a tux, buy flowers and food after the prom, gas money for the driver of the car, order and purchase class rings, senior pictures, rent a gown, and any other paraphernalia that would unexpected need to be addressed. We started this plan by accepting employment from our father to paint the outside of 237 Farragut Street. This included the garage and all needed putty and spackle work. The temperatures were insanely high and the humidity formidable to the point that

Chris was willing to give me his $5.00 salary if I completed the work and went after a different job.

It soon became painfully obvious being employed by our father was not going to end in any successful financial arrangement. We asked around how our friends were getting summer jobs and how we could do the same. We were told about the unemployment office downtown. We arranged to go the very next day. Being only fourteen I wasn't aware of how to obtain a working permit and a social security card. My friend Lawrence's gave me his information as he was already sixteen, and I found a job paying $1.25 an hour as a nurse's aide. My job was to give the patients a bath and feed them lunch.

Chris on the other hand was given a job to count the number of passengers on the K4 bus. He had to sit outside in the blaring sun and when a K4 bus stopped in front of his stationed position he would count the people who boarded and those on board. He was hot at the end of his shift but he knew as did I this job would pay us some money.

As the paychecks came in we gave them to our father to deposit in the bank. When we first requested a sum to pay for any expense, our father told us that he did in fact deposit our paychecks in the bank and whenever we needed anything including a dental or doctor visit he would take our valued savings fund to pay for these services. This came as a complete surprise and we couldn't understand why our father had failed to tell us this.

We had specifically explained why we wanted him to deposit our paychecks in the bank: to buy a suit, a class ring, our school yearbook, take senior pictures, reserve a cap and gown, prom, and pocket change. We were disappointed we were never asked nor informed when funds were taken out to "pay for services" most parents provide for their children. As he informed us these funds were used throughout the year, there were several overlooked opportunities to let us know about these transactions. When we at one time felt it possible to plan, save and use our own money for the extras not the necessities it soon became obvious this plan had not worked out for us. I wanted to take a date but didn't have any money. When I asked my father about the money I had asked him to keep for us, he told me we had already accessed these funds for services requiring payment throughout the year.

Later, as my senior year came close to ending. The painful realization that I wasn't going to my prom was increased as I truly wanted to ask Usher Tate to be my date and now I couldn't. That was no longer an option and my disappointment was greatly felt. My friend Clifford convinced me to go and suggested I take someone else. I had no money and Cliff offered to help me out if I agreed to take Big Debbie. He had a car and wanted me to do all the driving. Now, I did in fact have a limited amount of driving experience. Not on the highways mind you, practice sessions in empty parking lots and up and down the driveway. Wanting to be with his date he asked me to do the driving. We were headed to the beach and Big Debbie thought it would be nice if she sat a bit closer to me while I was driving. Being quite nervous I simply asked her to watch out for me as other drivers on the road were honking at me since I was driving below the speed limit.

I was extremely nervous about driving Cliff's car and driving in general. I don't know how I managed that night to drive to the beach, drive to the restaurant, and drive back home safely. I passed my written drivers test and had my learner's permit but had not gotten my driver's license. I was going to schedule an appointment to take the road test in a few months. As to having the opportunity to practice and refine my limited skills on the road, that would be a NO as I was not allowed to drive the family car.

My lack of experience must have been obvious to Cliff as he often asked me if everything was going okay. I simply stated that the drivers on the road were not the best. Followed with a comment about how rude the drivers were on the roads so early in the morning. Adding, it wasn't surprising people who were out and about must be in a hurry to go nowhere significantly important, fast. This seemed to appease him and I continued to concentrate on the road Big Debbie tried to give me encouragement by moving closer to me in the front seat. Her motives were appreciated but I had to ask her to move over so I could concentrate on the road. After doing my best parking job, we went into the restaurant.

Once seated in a booth, I looked over the menu and knew I did not have enough money to buy two meals. I barely had enough spare change to get a small meal for Big Debbie. I learned a lot about driving that night and it helped when I had to take my driving test. I wasn't nervous as I had already managed to drive a car I wasn't familiar with and to make sure everyone, including myself, got home safely.

Thinking back on the start of my senior year, I was filled with hope and high expectations. I had saved money for the year's expenses and was the starting tight end and back-up quarter-back when needed which required throwing extremely long passes. I loved my senior year. We had huge crowds for games, got out early every Friday, and people acknowledged us as winners. Norman Young made us a very successful team. He was not just good he was a great athlete. He was the star of the football, baseball, basketball and track. He could do it all. His athletic performance earned him many scholarship offers, none of which he could accept due to poor academic status.

Glen Price was a friend of mine who was the star player on the basketball team at Calvin Coolidge High School. His father owned a small neighborhood grocery store. Glen asked if I wanted to try out for the varsity basketball team. He sweetened the offer by stating he would give me a ride to and from school if I made the team. This was an offer I couldn't refuse, so I decided to try out. I hadn't expected to play a lot, sitting on the bench was my second thought after visualizing about the riding in a car to and from school.

Glen was the starting center at six foot nine inches. In the beginning of the year Glen got hurt in practice so the coach put me in the game. When I joined the team my only thought was getting a ride to and from school. As to playing in the game I didn't know if I could meet any of the coach's expectations. Following in Glen's footsteps was a very large role to fill. But I was only asked to stand in for a short amount of time. I did okay the first couple of games and then reality set in.

When I joined the team, I had only played in games until the star player, Glenn Price returned. I was initially embarrassed by my performance. I got lucky and managed to give an adequate performance. My goal was always to improve my skills to be selected to play playground ball. I did not play in our final two games. One was against the 1969 McKinley Tech championship team that was recognized as one of the top high school teams in the nation.

Glen recovered from his injury, and for the remainder of the season when a roster player become ineligible due to failing grades, the coach put me in. I was still focusing on growing a few more inches and my shooting had not made that much improvement. I later read an article about Spencer Hayward, where he revealed one of the secrets to his success was running wearing a twenty-pound weight vest.

I began to think how an absolutely, scathingly brilliant idea of wearing a weight vest while running. I wanted to devise a regular routine that I could do regardless of the time of year, season or temperature changes. The idea of running in the snow or in the intense heat and humidity wasn't going to work for me. I needed to be able to work-out every day, now I had to give this idea of developing and maintaining a regular work-out routine more thought. The next step was figuring out how to save up enough money, without giving it to my father to put in the bank, and use it to buy a weigh vest.

My new plan for saving my money, was to cash one of my paychecks and keep the money from my father. I told him I wanted to have some cash to buy the weight vest and not trouble him to get the money from the bank. I saved up and, right after the basketball season, purchased one. My new focus was on becoming the best basketball player possible. I knew I had to grow, being only 6 foot 4 inches with no great shooting ability. I had a very candid conversation with myself and kept repeating, "You need to grow." Still playing on the tennis team, Coach Harriston kept encouraging me to practice and improve my tennis game. This idea was something I had no desire to pursue. In fact, it wasn't an option to consider in the slightest.

My record of season tennis playoffs was unimpressive to say the least. It came to the point where every player wanted to be matched with me. Some were bidding to play against me as if I was a lottery pick, as I had the reputation of never making it past the first round of play. Any, and all opposing teams were placing bets on how long

I would last on the court and who would the player to accomplish the task of eliminating me from the competition. It was clearly out there, the suburban students held no fear or respect for me on the tennis court.

After an honest conversation with Coach Harriston I made the decision to put all my efforts into basketball. A local talent, James Brown who played for DeMatha High School, the number one basketball power in the DC metropolitan area, most years, was well known for being a great leaper. I started to do some research on trade secrets of those players who were being recognized for their developing talents. In one article, Brown mentioned he attributed his great leaping ability to jumping rope.

My mind began to put a great deal of time into the information I had discovered. I posed the question, "What if I put together wearing a weight vest and jumping rope?" Now this was something I could regularly do any time of day and in any kind of weather. Being regular with this routine, I could determine if my efforts were showing improvement in my leaping and jumping ability. When and if necessary I could make any adjustments when needed. In the beginning, I had to give some thought how to keep focused on jumping rope for over an hour without having to count. I put this question in mind and went to sleep. In the morning, Chris was dancing around the room while listening to one of his favorite tunes playing on our cassette player.

Once this song finished playing he put another tape in. I asked him how many minutes the song had played. He wasn't sure so we timed it. Then I jumped with an imaginary rope to the length of the song as both Chris and I counted the repetitions. Making a sample cassette we then timed and calculated the lengths of songs to calculate how many songs to record. After doing this, we played the songs to match up with the amount of jumping rope repetitions needed to meet my daily goal. As the number of jumping rope repetitions increased we simply added more songs.

In the first month, my routine was to jump rope eight hundred times a night for a week. Doubling each week, it didn't take long until I could to jump ten thousand repetitions a night without having to stop and miss a turn. To help vary my routine I made several cassettes to last for one hour and twenty minutes. Knowing how many repetitions went with each tape it made concentrating on my form and not missing a turn. What also helped was changing how I jumped rope. At first I used two hands as was the standard practice, but when I hit myself in the face a few times I decided to make some adjustments. I started holding the jump rope in one hand and pretending the other rope was in the other hand. It worked out so well I soon could jump rope without stopping.

My daily routine was starting to show signs of improvement. My confidence was growing as was my height. I began researching universities and colleges I might be eligible to apply admittance to. After looking at the thickness of the college handbook, I knew I needed to take my time and look over the information carefully. I had to decide if I wanted to attend a local school or go out of state. I had to think about living on campus or off, transportation to school and back home and then from home, back to school, school fees, meals, laundry.

I soon realized making the choice of schools needed a great deal of thought. My brother Chris went away to school and had shared with me some of the expenses if you weren't a student on scholarship. I took my time and shared by list of potential schools with Chris. He simply said I had some good choices but it might be a good idea to run this by my dad. When I approached him with my list, he clearly stated he would not be able to pay for any college I wanted to apply for. It was time to come up with a plan. I turned all my attention to improving my skills and physical physique to attract the attention of any college scouts in the DC area.

Many college scouts traveled to the DC metropolitan area to view the potential of rising star athletes on the honored and sacred Rudolph playground courts. I was fortunate to live two blocks from Rudolph playground, the choice location for the very best players in the nation to come and play. The best players from DC and Maryland would play on the Rudolph playground Monday through Thursday evenings after finishing summer jobs. The residents supported these games with loyal attendance. People were on-lookers as if watching the championship game in the March Madness college Final Four. Favorite players were cheered on and any and all plays were given loud comments from the neighborhoods best game analysts. Most conversations centered around arguments and profanity about who were the best players on the court on any given night. No shortage of cold beers, blatant comments based on opinion, encouragement and criticism was the established norm

This atmosphere made attending Rudolph playground's evening games an addictive habit. A must, the neighborhood residents need to be present was only satisfied by regular attendance. As for the players, the audience was conducive to playing in front of paying fans, gaining confidence to perform while addressing both positive and negative feedback. This proved very helpful as the regular ten players who walked on the courts nightly with me went on the become NBA starters and stars. The positive results of these evening games, include the influence it had on local football talent. Along the side lines followed the play of gifted basketball players and threw footballs on the side grass area.

My brother Chris was not a basketball player and although enjoying watching the games on the playground courts, he enjoyed taking the time to practice football plays with other interested football players. This interchanged helped to develop his football skills improving his game to the point of being noticed by college scouts and later NFL scouts.

My first home soon became Rudolph playground. You could find me there Monday through Thursday shooting free throws, jumping rope and visualizing playing against the best talented competition available. Sometimes I would stay after playing in games, until the lights were turned off, and jumped rope. Players and local residents would come up and approach me with statements regarding improving in my basketball skills was noticed. I was encouraged to keep doing whatever I was doing. My efforts were paying off and I could even tell I was becoming a better player.

I was asked the secret or key to my improvement and not being willing to share my scathingly brilliant routine, simply stated a lot of practice. That seemed plausible as I was at Rudolph Monday through

Thursday evenings. When I arrived back home my father's once a year come to sell his cabaret tickets friend, Mr. Sickles. He was working his yearly sales pitch knowing my father didn't have the courage to decline and bought the lot with the intent to take Barbara out for a night on the town. He was a nasty man with such a large hammer head he could easily be mistaken for an alien creature in a science fiction movie. He was so mean I tried my best to avoid having any conversation with him.

On this particular visit in mid-April, Mr. Sickles made a cutting remark to me. He shared the word around I had improved in my basketball skills to the point of becoming full of myself. He then continued to confront me with the challenge to try out for the Allen-All-Star team, if I thought I was that good. His sarcasm and taunts infuriated me to the point of needing to put him in his place. It was the idea of being successful and proving him wrong that motivated me to consider his challenge. He was so accommodating he told me when and where the try-outs were being held. My father was listening to our conversation, knew about the event and on the day of try-outs I had to hitch-hike to Saint John's High School to try-out. I had no basketball clothes or fancy shoes. My shorts and old T-shirt and shoes would simply have to do as I did not have anything else to wear.

When I arrived, I was told every senior had to be given a chance to try out. When asked which high school I had played for, I said Coolidge. I was getting a bit nervous while the person checking in players slowly moved her finger down the list of names. I felt a bit sense of relief when mine was found and they had to let me in. Here's where karma comes in. If Glen had not been injured would my name be on the list? I said a silent thank you and was relieved I was allowed entrance. All the players were starters and star athletes who were already signed up with a major college or university. In all honesty, I didn't think I would make the team I had worked hard and gaining more confidence in my improving skills, I was counting on my work effort being my strongest asset. This tryout camp of sorts was five days in duration to select players for the Allen Town Tournament. A lot of coaches were in the bleachers looking for last minute recruits.

The coach from Western New England University in Springfield, Massachusetts came up to me after the first day of try-outs. He offered me a scholarship on the spot if I agreed to not to return for the rest of the try-out camp sessions. I gave that some thought for maybe a second. But I wanted to return to prove to myself I had what it took to play the game at any level and that I was not afraid of the competition but welcomed it. I came back the next day and coaches from Rutgers University, in New Brunswick, New Jersey, High Point University in High Point, North Carolina, and local schools: University of Maryland, Howard University, and George Washington University, approached me offering me the opportunity to play for their schools.

Among those coaches showing some interest in recruiting me was Tom Young and Tom Davis, both were the newly hired coaches from American University. They were in the bleachers and noticed that a section of the arena had a cheering section for me. These were my friends and they were showing me support. Both coaches walked over to this fan club of sorts and asked who I was and if I played well and most importantly if I was a good student. It might sound odd for someone to ask my fan club if I was a good student. In DC, it was a well-known fact if a player remained on the team and made the honor roll he was considered an Einstein.

Directly after the second scrimmage both coaches approached me. They told me they had scholarship available and were specifically looking for five players for American University's freshman team. The fact the university was in DC was a surprise as I had never heard of American University. Having spent the entire life on the other side of 16th Street. My knowledge of the part of town where American University was located was a complete mystery to me. I do remember when my father attempted to take Chris and me to see the movie Fantasia the only theatre it was playing at a movie theatre located in the NW part of town. When we entered, we were told by the attendant this movie theatre was for whites only and told to leave immediately. From that day on we never ventured past 16th Street. At now, this forbidden territory contained the key I needed to find and use to open a hidden treasure that contained a future with a surprising fairy tale ending.

When asked if I wanted to go out to dinner, I accepted as I had never gone out to any full serve restaurant for a meal. We might on occasion drive past a fast food place but not eat in a restaurant with cloth napkins, silverware, and menus with lots of different food items. I ordered a steak expecting to share it with everyone. When everyone else order a separate meal, I started to think the steak might just be for me. When it arrived and the other meals were served separately, I was ready to sign on the dotted line. Following this wonderful meal, I was given a tour of the campus. My fondest imagination could never have prepared me for what I saw. There were beautiful flowers and trees, the buildings were freshly painted, and the sidewalks clean and straight. Colorful banners and welcoming signs were hanging outside along the eves. People were talking and walking at a leisurely pace with no one seeming to be in hurry or worried about who was about to pass them by or who was walking behind them. There was a sense of peace, and the silence was not daunting but pleasant and inviting.

This was a place I could enjoy being a part of. When shown the dorm rooms I was amazed at finding pillows on the beds as I never had a pillow to sleep on before. The windows had blinds something that was on windows downstairs but not in Chris's and my bedroom. People spoke with a sincere greeting, and in my normal daily life, people were too absorbed in the details of their lives that they would rarely acknowledge your presence, let alone extend to you a greeting.

Following this wonderful day, the coaches asked me to set up an appointment with my current basketball coach to discuss my strengths and weakness. As there were extremely limited strengths with more weakness including the fact I had very little playing time, I had to come up with the best possible excuse to prevent any interaction between these two that would make this dream disappear. I eagerly explained my Coach Bernard Dory was out sick and unable to meet with them for a few weeks. Whenever they inquired again, I simply told them that he had not recovered and would be unavailable for quite a while.

A representative from Maryland University came by my house to speak with my father. He was all in favor of my going there because Lefty Driesell had just signed on as the head coach and had proclaimed Maryland University was going to be the UCLA of the east. When we met with Lefty, my SAT scores on my initial testing results were not high enough, and he wanted me to take the SAT again. I did, and my second scores were enough to gain entry and a scholarship. In the meantime, American University sent me two pairs of new Chuck Taylor white Converse shoes. My future began to move forward by making the decision between signing with Maryland University or American University. Someone must have been looking out for me as a meeting never took place between the coaches from American and my high school coach.

CHAPTER 2

Pete's Childhood Memories

Living in Washington, DC, in the '50's was comparable to living in another space and time. Neighborhoods were not integrated and mostly composed of families with working dad's and stay-at-home moms. People were friendly, and everyone was known by their first name. If you needed help, a neighbor was available, but you didn't go next door to borrow a cup of sugar. The neighborhood was relatively established. Many families had lived in their houses for several years. New comers were welcome and it was the expectation that you got to know one another over time.

When Kermit and his older brother Eric, (whom we called Chris), moved in, everyone in the neighborhood was curious or should I say interested in this family. It was noted there was an elderly grandmother whom we later knew to be Mr. Washington's great Grandmother, no wife or mother, and a single "good looking" black man was quite the topic of conversation. Divorce was not a topic to be discussed around young people, and since I was only six it didn't mean anything to me. I remember overhearing my parents one night talking about what Mr. Washington was like. They noticed he was handsome, in good shape, but wasn't around a lot and when he was around he seemed to be very quiet and soft spoken. My mother thought this living arrangement not only odd but questionable, she hoped his absence did not indicate he was the party type. My father seemed less concerned, as being a man, he just knew Mr. Washington had to be a quality person if he was taking care of two small boys with the assistance of his Grandmother.

Most of our neighbors seemed content to give Mr. Washington and the boy's time to get adjusted to the neighborhood. When we first met, both Kermit and Chris were friendly, but not too well-dressed. I didn't want to ask too many questions about their family so we walked to school and back home together sharing our interests in playing sports. We planned to meet in the alley after school and get to know each other better. We managed to spend a few afternoons outside during the school year, but when summer came we got to play together more after Kermit and Chris finished their chores. Our houses were set in a block-type setting with alleys in-between, and this made playing outside a lot of fun. It had other advantages in that you were close enough to other houses where adults could look out for you and then again provide areas to play games and run a lot.

DC also had great parks and playgrounds kids could walk to which had opportunities for exploring what remnants of the past had been left behind buried beneath the surface of the ground. We spent many hours playing around the DC area and forming memories that would last a lifetime. No matter what time of year and what the weather was like, we found the time and the reasons to go outside and play. My parents were always around and provided me with everything and anything I needed and wanted. Unfortunately, Kermit's and Chris's lives were not at all like mine. In those days, you never said anything or made disparaging remarks, but you couldn't help but notice they were often hungry and not well-dressed as they often wore the same clothes.

On one occasion, my mother made my usual lunch sack and gave me money to buy extra treats at school. The aroma from the enclosed pork shop sandwich wasn't that alluring to me I saw a sewer pothole nearby, opened it and tossed the brown paper sack inside. Walking away I notice both Kermit and Chris had stopped, reopened the sewer pothole reached inside to retrieve the brown paper sack. They sat on the curb and opened the sandwich sharing it eagerly. I didn't say anything when both boys said that was the best pork chop sandwich they had ever had. I believed that was the only pork chop sandwich they had. As for me I simply preferred the treats I could buy at school knowing when I got home my mom would fix me whatever I asked for dinner. Kermit once told me he was amazed my mother would ask me what I wanted to eat for dinner and that my clothes were always clean neat and ironed.

In those days, you went to the neighborhood schools from kindergarten through twelfth grade. Families did not move. I remember starting kindergarten with Kermit, and we walked to Rudolph Elementary School, then Bertie Backus Junior high school, and later Calvin Coolidge High School. Over the years the face of the neighborhood changed was one of three neighborhood kids whose parents were married and lived together. Kermit and Chris lived with their sometimes around Dad and their Dad's Grandmother. Being very fortunate, I couldn't help but notice Kermit and Chris lacked the personal care that I simply took for granted.

All the boys and girls in our neighborhood loved playing sports. We cut out a peach basket and put it up on a telephone pole to serve as a hoop for practicing shooting baskets. No matter the time of year we would meet in the alley playing whatever game was being played by the professionals. Kermit's great Grandmother sometimes came outside and played baseball with us. She was funny but scary. She wouldn't use our stick to hit the ball but was quite the hitter using her cane. She would only hit once and the ball would fly over the fence. We didn't like her playing with us because she used her cane, as her bat, and was a good hitter. When asked if we might try using her cane she simply said it was her cane and she only used it to hit baseball and unruly children.

Of the two brothers, Kermit would always come out and play with us. Chris was known to stay inside reading books. It took him a while to join us outside but in later in years he did when we played football. We all loved the Washington Redskins games were shown on TV. At halftime, we would go outside to play catch. We knew every bit of information and statistic about each player and would be greatly disappointed if our beloved team lost a game. Grandma Foreman would use their desire to view every game to make sure we completed their chores or followed all her directions. Basketball games were not televised and only on occasion we watched baseball games and the World Series, but that didn't matter as to us it was all about the Redskins.

When Kermit and Chris could save up enough money we could catch the K-4 or the K-6 bus and get off at Georgia Avenue to watch a professional baseball game at Griffith Stadium, downtown DC. We carried our baseball mitts hoping we would catch a fly ball or a home run ball. We could buy "Knot Hole" tickets for $.25 and had seats located all the way up in the stadium bleachers. This expression came from a knot hole in the fence surrounding a baseball stadium. People who could not afford to buy a ticket would peep through a knot hole in order the view the event. These were usually at the very last rows in the stadium making viewing any game dependent on extremely good eyesight. Still, you were present at the game and could move about if the stadium was not sold out.

My parents always gave me money for anything I wanted to do or needed in addition to an allowance. Kermit and Chris did not get an allowance, and most of the time they would have to walk to the Grand Union grocery store down the street to earn money by helping ladies with their groceries. As not many people owned cars in those days, whenever moms went grocery shopping they had to carry their groceries in their arms or in small rolling shopping baskets. If you were willing, there was always someone who needed a helping hand and Kermit and Chris were the go-to-guys. They would spend all day at the Grand Union grocery store carrying groceries home for the ladies, then returning for their next potential customer.

They would not only carry the bundles of grocery sacks but, once they arrived, after walking up several flights of stairs, they put away the items in the ladies' pantries. As most homes were multi-level, this meant a lot of stairs to climb. (I often wondered if this was the starting point for Kermit's later obsession with running the stairs.) For their efforts, they could earn $0.10 to $0.15 each for every trip. I remember that sometimes they would be so hungry they would stop at Griffith's Hamburger Joint and buy a meal. With $0.35 you could buy a hamburger for $0.10, French fries for $0.15 and a coke for $0.10. With tax, it possibly cost $0.36 for a complete meal.

When they made at least $0.75 each, they would share stories about the ladies and their groceries with me, and it always amazed me how different my life was from theirs. I simply asked for money to go to the baseball stadium, and since my mom always fixed me whatever I wanted to eat, going to Griffith's for a meal was okay but I felt my mom was a much better cook.

Everyone knew Kermit and Chris would be seen walking around the neighborhood with their Griffith's take out bag to show they had some cash. It would make me smile as they seemed to savor every bite of their meal. Personally, my mom's home cooking was still the best and it was free.

Kennedy Movie Theater on Kennedy Street was a frequent stop when they had spare change. Movies cost $0.25 but blacks were not allowed to sit anywhere they chose. We were limited to the balcony section. We often paid to watch Elvis movies until we heard it was said by Elvis that blacks were only good for buying his records and polishing his shoes. I don't know who told us this, but it did make us rethink spending $0.25 on an Elvis film.

When it got very hot in the summer, the idea of going to the local pool for a refreshing dip in the city pool was inviting. We were not allowed access to this opportunity until we were about eleven years old. Kermit was the only one I knew who could swim. I asked him how he learned. He told me a long story of simply seeing himself swimming and when he took the plunge and jumped into the deep end and he was swimming. It sounded too risky for me so Chris and I would venture into the shallow end of the pool, but that turned out to be more dangerous than trying to swim in the deep end.

All the neighborhood thugs couldn't swim, so they made up the Drowning Game. The biggest thugs would grab you and hold you under water until you were so close to death you were released to spit of water and cough until you could gain some composure. This would make them all laugh and wait to eagerly attack their next victims. The water might have been a great way to cool down but in those days, it was truly something to give some serious thought before attempting to live another day by surviving a fearful water experience.

If you managed to survive the "Drowning Game" and lived to tell about it, the experience left you very hungry. We would walk through the neighbor back-yards as Kermit and Chris would grab ripe apples, pears, and peaches from heavily weighed down trees. People seemed to like having this garden in their yards but took little time to work the harvesting aspects of such treasures.

Sometimes the neighbors didn't appreciate their help and would chase us down the street. Trying to catch up with Kermit and Chris, offended homeowners would chase them off their property screaming profanity at them. My job was to divert their attention by asking if they knew where a certain house was on their block. I became the perfect decoy as I got to be good at this. I always asked the homeowners why they were yelling at those boys running away sounding as innocent as a dove. I also knew my parents would back me up if a problem came to pass, knowing I would have no reason to steal food. Kermit and Chris on the other hand didn't have three square meals a day and were often hungry. If they got caught and their great Grandmother Foreman found out she would surely use her cane on them.

Kermit and Chris were mostly cared for by their great Grandmother. She was a strict disciplinarian, and they were always very polite. She would make them help neighbors in the winter by shoveling their driveways and walking paths and in the summer, whatever yard needed some racking or cleanup she would make sure they did it and made them refuse any offer of payment even if it meant a refreshing drink. My parents were consistent but kind in my upbringing. They never yelled at me, and any punishment was reasonable and did not include any whippings. When the end of the day came, and playing outside was over, their great Grandmother would call them inside, and no matter what we were doing, they would stop midstream and book it home. You didn't want to know what would happen if you had to be called by her twice to come home.

Going to school over the years was a lot of fun for me. I had new and stylish clothes, pocket money for treats and enjoy getting whatever I needed or wanted. Sometimes our classmates were not very kind. They noticed that both Kermit and Chris had a limited wardrobe of two outfits. They were not always neatly pressed but clean. The general chant of "I know what you are going to wear tomorrow" was repeated and made them both very uncomfortable. The teachers did not make things any better when they sent Kermit and Chris home on picture day for not wearing their best clothes. To hopefully stop these chants and negative comments from the adults one time Kermit and Chris exchanged outfits, to no avail. Bullies are still bullies no matter what creative thinking you try to make them stop.

Thinking back, Kermit and Chris didn't talk much about their mother. When I asked once about her, Kermit told me she was not in good health and lived on R Street but they would visit when they could. The expression on his face let me know this was not a subject to pursue, and I was grateful I figured that out and never mentioned it again. Being accountable for raising Kermit and Chris was a responsibility their great grandmother Foreman took very seriously, she was a real stickler for both boys to be obedient, listen and follow directions. It was obvious she cared about them and did what she valued as the best way to raise them in the very best way she could. If it were possible for her to provide more suitable clothing I am convinced she would have.

When their father remarried, their new stepmother was not very nice and their lives changed. The first time I overheard her having a conversation with their father it was obvious this she did not want to care for another woman's children. She also mentioned how she disapproved of how the boys were being raised and how dirty they appeared. She had only negative comments to make about them and she did so in front of anyone and everyone. Although she was so open in making such comments, she never said she was going to enjoy having the opportunity to make a positive influence by being the boy's stepmother.

Despite all those years of being ill-treated, by this heartless version of Cruella Deville, both Kermit and Chris were determined to make a success of their lives. Their great Grandmother helped them to develop a strong work ethic and the need to help others without expecting or requesting anything in return. This proved to serve as a protection living with someone who had negative feelings and comments to say to you, and about you. Each focused on the positive aspects for their future, and their great Grandmother made this possible in the formative years of their lives.

Within walking distance from our homes was Rudolph, a great playground close to our elementary school. There were always a lot of activities for the neighborhood kids to take advantage of. There were baseball, football, and basketball leagues based on age. Inside the facility were pool and ping pong tables. The information director was a Mr. Bradford, and he really liked all of us. A lot of fun to be around, he wore these big buckskin shoes that made him seem more important than anyone had the right to be. With so many sports to play with a coach and some supervision Kermit and I signed up for the ten and under teams. When we won a game, Mr. Bradford would show how proud he was of us by treating us to ice cream. That was a treat Kermit and all of us on the team really enjoyed. Kermit blossomed under the kindness extended to him by Mr. Bradford.

Kermit was initially a very good baseball player. Every year he earned the MVP award for our division. Chris was still at this point not interested in playing any sports and had not yet joined us in our daily walks to the Rudolph playground. The friendship between Kermit and myself continued to grow as we were not only classmates all through school but were now building a sports relationship that added another dimension to the word friendship. I thought Kermit would pursue a baseball career as his favorite sport. Even though I was the fastest runner on the teams we played on my expertise was more in the field of track and not in the category of baseball, football, or basketball. I did, however, play to the level of high school football. Soon after Kermit was gaining recognition as a talented athlete, Chris came with us to the playground and found a passion for playing football. He tried his hand at baseball and basketball but was often frustrated by the results, and he centered all his attention on playing football. This was productive as he established himself as a very good football player.

In junior high Kermit was not academically oriented in the slightest. My parents spent many hours going over my homework and making sure I was keeping up with my grades. At the end of the school year I couldn't help but notice that Kermit's books were as pristine as they were on the first day they were issued. To improve his grade point average, Kermit would go to summer school. We both wanted to improve our chances to be accepted to and successfully graduate from a college or university of merit. Chris, on the other hand, was a true genius. Being extremely smart, Chris was always being tested and qualified for the gifted (GATE or TAG) program. He then went to different junior and senior high schools to develop his potential.

Kermit and I then went to Bertie Backus in junior high, and Chris went to McFarland. Before attending high school, the only way, you could play any organized sport, outside the Rudolph playground age leveled play, was to join the CYO, the Catholic Youth Organization. To do so Kermit, Chris, and I went to catechism classes. In high school Kermit and I went to Coolidge, and Chris went to McKinley Tech. Kermit and I played football and basketball but not for Bertie Backus as we barely made the 100- pound tackle team in the CYO league. Sports was the most important way to accomplish their goals. Kermit would often say he was going to get better and make it as a professional athlete. At first he was just an average athlete. In time, with effort and determination he began to improve. Our junior year, he played backup quarterback, then played tennis. I couldn't quite understand the tennis connection and asked him, "Why tennis?" He told me he simply wanted to get out of my French II class, and being on the tennis team, he could leave class early. He did play a few times with his dad, who loved tennis and considered himself a good player. Kermit was better than the regular players, as he did have someone to play against. He won a lot of matches but would always get creamed in the playoffs.

Our senior year, we both knew we were going to have more playing time as athletes. We walked one mile in the summer sun to participate in double football practices. At that time, we were not allowed to drink water during practice and were given salt tablets.

We would be so tired between practices we didn't consider the one-mile walk home and the one-mile walk back to second practice as an option. I always had pocket change, so I would buy us some lunch and, after sharing it with Kermit, rested until the start of our second practice. I started as a defensive end, and Kermit was the starting tight end. At Coolidge, we always had a good football team. During our final season in high school we had a good run, but we were defeated in the playoffs. My career in sports ended, but Kermit went on the join the school basketball team. I figured he might make the team but was truly amazed this would be the beginning of a very exciting and eventful college and professional career.

Following our graduation from Coolidge was a time in America's history when the Vietnam War was unfolding. Without any financial support Kermit and Chris had only two options to attend college or be drafted into the Vietnam War. They had only limited options, the draft or earn athletic scholarships to attend college. Kermit was accepted to American and his options for success became attainable.

CHAPTER 3

John Thompson

Summer nights in the DC metropolitan area provided welcomed relief from the heat and humidity of the day. Monday through Thursday you could always count on a great, on the court, basketball game at Rudolph playground. A variety of local players would arrive armed and ready to compete for the coveted ability to remain on the court. Being selected to continue playing was limited and privilege. By extending playing time for several games required a clear demonstration of talent, receiving the support and attention of onlookers.

Most player's families did not have cars; the general means to move around the city was public transportation. I would pick up the best players driving them to Rudolph to give them the opportunity to learn from the best, improve their game and skills by playing with and against basketball talent from the DC metropolitan area. Sitting on the side lines one evening, a tall, skinny, determined player, Kermit Washington, came to my attention. I watched as he quickly ran up and down the court, held off aggressive moves from recognized players, grabbed rebounds, attempted and made some key shots. His clear focus demonstrated his desire to play hard so he would be chosen to play in follow up games. Having been a former Rudolph player myself there was something about Kermit that made me take notice of him and watch his performance with great interest. At this time, I was the head basketball coach at Saint

Anthony's High School. I attended John Carrol high school, graduated from Providence College and played as a Boston Celtic under Red Auerbach.

The open invitation extended to both players and the community from the hallowed courts on Rudolph's playground, Monday through Thursday, became well known as the place to watch players evolve into future ABA and NBA players. The competition was fierce as every player came prepared to meet the talented opponents present. By participating in a level of competition against such talented athletes was comparable to sword sharpening sword.

Location, location, location, is often referred to by real estate agents as the three most important considerations when clients are looking to purchase property. This held true for Rudolph, it's location played a pivotal role in the later success of players and provide unprecedented entertainment for onlookers. Rudolph had established itself as the playground that attracted the highest levels of talent and competition. This was one reason Kermit came every night to play. The second reason was living only two blocks walking distance from the playground making nightly attendance a bonus. Being able to compete against the best was synonymous with Rudolph playground athletes. Rudolph was the place where you would be tested consistently by some of the roughest, toughest, highly gifted shooters, jumpers, and rebounders one could ever imagine.

Having played on the court for over a year, during that time his on the court performance was in the early stages of development. It was obvious he had a lot of heart and by gaining more time on the court was showing signs of improvement. Kermit might get in a game, but if his team lost, he was not picked up to continue playing in follow up games. In those days, only the best players continued to grace the courts with their stellar performances. Average players were quickly replaced, and it was a known fact this routine was to be respected and honored. It increased the level of competition by motivating every player to give a 100 percent performance knowing what was on the line. To play in a Rudolph playground game, you had to prove your worth on the court every night.

As evenings ended, players ventured home leaving tired, happy or disappointed. Everything depended on how one performed on the court, if given the opportunity to play in a game. Despite these mixed feelings, every player returned nightly to Rudolph with hope of being a chance to compete. It might have meant the end of the evening to many, but not to Kermit. I would hang around the perimeter of the playground and walk over to where my car was parked. This gave me a chance to shoot the breeze with the locals and form relationships that in the future would help me in recruiting local talent.

My curiosity was perked when I watched Kermit put on a twenty-pound weight vest, pick up a jump rope, turn on his tape-recorded music and proceed to jump rope for what seemed like an eternity. As he continued this workout this late hour took its toll on my ability to stay awake. Tired after a long day, I drove home keeping that visual image of Kermit in my head. I wanted to speak with him and learn why he stayed on the court until the lights were turned off. This was a young man with a good work ethnic and a dedication to improving his game and someone I wanted to get better acquainted with.

It took a few nights, but when the opportunity presented itself for me to approach Kermit to find out more about this young man and his routine I took advantage of it. It was shortly after players had gone home and the playground was dimly lit that I walked over to where Kermit was jumping rope. After apologizing for interrupting his concentration, I explained I had noticed him a few nights earlier jumping rope. The need to satisfy my curiosity got the better of me, I had to speak with him. Throughout our conversation I was amazed at his ability to continue jumping rope. It was evident this routine was long standing which made it easier for me to ask him about it. He told me he jumped ten thousand times every night for one and a half hours. I had to say, "Young man, if you keep working as you've been working, one day you're going to be a pretty good player." My prediction could go either way: either he would achieve his goal and become a better player (if his knees held out), drop dead from trying.

A testimony to the value of hard work and dedication, Kermit over the next three years went on to be the starting center for American University. His final, record breaking, game in the Fort Myer gymnasium was against my Georgetown Hoyas team. His performance that evening silenced all doubt as to whether he was ready to play on any NBA team. The level of play demonstrated that evening was one that put a solid period at the end of the sentence: Game over. It also gave incentive to other inner-city players to take a risk and attend schools such as Georgetown and George Washington, both schools were highly esteemed in academia.

This helped support my diligent efforts to mandate academic excellence with the clearly stated expectation, all of my players would graduate with degrees from Georgetown. Kermit established himself not only by accomplishing "20 points and 20 rebounds per game" a record that has never been achieved by any other collegiate player to this day, but in addition recognition for academic excellence. Many local players were now being recruited by DC metropolitan area schools. His accomplishment set one of the greatest statistical game records against my Georgetown Hoyas in the University's entire history.

Due to his physical stature as compared with NBA centers he was considered a better match for the forward position. This change in position required some new training and he was fortunate to have Pete Newell as his mentor. Unfortunately, during this transition one incident involving Rudy Tomjanovich greatly sidetracked that recognition. Not universally understood to be merely a reflex action to seeing someone in his peripheral vision running toward him, he was labeled as a thug and suspended from the league for a while. Newspapers and reporters jumped on the bandwagon of labeling Kermit as someone who was vicious and mean spirited. None of which was accurate and none of which was fair. This kind of public defamation sold papers, and that was the only thing that mattered.

No one took into account the person, the man, the life and spirit of an individual who was the victim of another's actions, and his reaction was the focus of what later resulted in hate mail, death threats, and limited job opportunities. No one cared, no one knew that despite all of this Kermit Washington would rise to meet these unfounded remarks and continue to demonstrate the person he truly was and is. Kermit relied on his persistence and dedication when allowed to return to play in the NBA with the Boston Celtics. He later joined the San Diego Clippers, the Portland Trailblazers, and the Golden State Warriors. Every team he played with after being traded from the Los Angeles Lakers helped him to establish meaningful friendships and provide numerous personal testimonies to the generous nature this man exemplifies.

Few know of his ongoing efforts in Nairobi, Kenya, where he started a health clinic, school, and feeding program in the slums of Kibera. Once you spend time with Kermit, you come to know him not his name and reputation but how he thinks, how he works, and how he sincerely cares about others. He called me once to tell me about his efforts in Africa and when asked if I wanted to help. My response was simply, "How much do you need?" I sent him ten thousand dollars and that moved his project forward for several months. By attending American University, in Washington, DC, he made meaningful changes in his life and in the school and the lives of local DC athletes who saw what he was able to accomplish and set their sights to join him in reaching their goals.

As you continue reading this book, you will come to understand what shaped Kermit Washington's character and appreciate his sincere efforts to make things better for those less fortunate. Despite the pressures he has had to overcome he remains a man of integrity and great compassion.

Georgetown head coach John Thompson

CHAPTER 4

The College Years

Washington, DC metropolitan area. in the late 1960's and early 1970's was a time for many changes in the lives of Blacks. The local Black athlete whose dreams of making it in the professional sports arena was becoming a reality. Many local players were provided the opportunity to play with and against the rising talent on basketball courts around the city. All-Stars in the making were being noticed as they walked onto the legendary Rudolph playground court. Onlookers filled the benches with eager anticipation of what was to become an unedited version of: the college final four, an NBA game, the NBA All-Star game, and the NBA finals.

Although the summer's intense heat and humidity presented multiple challenges for weekend visits to different playgrounds you started to play early in the day and by noon you had mixed emotions. Pleased you were still selected to play, know challengers were waiting for any opportunity to replace you, working through dehydration and physical exhaustion was essential. It was natural to feel tired and yet excited you had to mentally and physically work to face those who aspired to achieve the reputation on the court you had and continued to work hard to maintain and increase. These young guns were armed with talent and tenacity. But then so were you. Meeting each player's challenges and successful maintaining a status of excellence were driving forces that would identify you as being a hard worker who displayed talent.

Players arrived eager and well prepared to present a game to remember by each other and the fans in the stands. It was a time when evenings were not locked into viewing reality TV shows or spending countless hours on YouTube, playing interactive video games, and updating social media sites. People actively engaged in conversations, sometimes a bit heated and off color, sharing their passions or opinions about players and their performance. Every game was a once in a lifetime opportunity to see talent unfold into future NBA stars and legends.

There was no need for referees, the crowd was as familiar with the on-court etiquette. Playground etiquette was different that on-court regulation etiquette. Any player who didn't play well was readily replaced and did not reenter the game and the team lost being finished for the day. Rudolph had two basketball courts. The main court was center stage and the second court ran alongside of it providing some shooting practice for those "waiting for an opportunity to play" hopefuls. The outcome of every game was unknown and presented an exciting mystery to watch being unfolded with a conclusion that was guaranteed to make every player and onlooker eagerly anticipate the next game to be played.

The adventures to unfold right in front of the eyes of those who were giving support for dreams to be realized was felt and appreciated by all. Times were changing for blacks young and old with more positive support being given for individual's goals and dreams to become a reality. This support fostered a sense of unity which began on the court and filtered out into the mindset of individuals to influence daily activities and interactions for the better. Doors once locked and closed were being opened. Now ajar, it was time to move forward and with the encouragement and strength of those who were behind these changes doors were pushed wide open. Doors once open encouraged others to enter and venture to unlock and open more doors along the corridor of life. Local DC metropolitan area talent had a responsibility to themselves and to others who would be following their lead to be bold and discerning to resolve any impending issues or obstacles and make something of themselves.

Urban Coalition: DC Basketball was established to encourage local youth to view basketball as a door to a wider world, athletic or otherwise- and provide a network of former (and current) players to support those opportunities. Summer games were played between our DC Urban Coalition team, the New York Temple League, and the Philadelphia Baker League held at Rutgers University. Highly competitive games were held at Howard University or Georgetown University when in DC. Local attendance was so great, the gymnasium temperature along with high levels of humidity was stifling. When playing, you were drenched with sweat and felt as if someone had thrown a bucket of water over you as you ran up and down the court.

DC players would meet and drive up to New York and Philly. I never made the New York trips but did ride up to Philly on multiple occasions. It was a given if Dr. J was present his team would always win, he simply dominated the court and was literally unstoppable. Despite this we all were eager and excited to play against the legends of our time.

Our DC players included Adrian Dantley, James Brown and Austin Carr. From New York: and from Philly: Dr. J, Nate Archibald, Dean Meminger

Notable Urban Coalition player: College All American -1973- Kermit Washington Coolidge- High School and American University.

By securing scholarships in various sports at schools such as American University, Notre Dame, UCLA, and Maryland University, inspired and motivated local DC metropolitan area talent to reach out, take a risk, and venture into previously uncharted and unexplored geographic locations. Each successful experience encouraged changes which helped player's value academics as well as athletics. This change was paramount for individuals to graduate from colleges and universities by remaining academically eligible to play. The bonus being it placed them in a position to possibly gain NBA status. Learning to be a success now went from simply surviving amidst the mind set of uncertainty to striving to fully embrace and explore what the world could to offer. Living on American University's campus exposed and offered a lifestyle that was previously considered to be unobtainable. Daily interactions, recommended and required reading material, lectures and class discussions, personal reflections and living in an environment that was positive and filled with hope, was a paradigm shift for many. Learning to believe this new lifestyle was not only possible but a reality was embraced and valued forcing one to leave behind the inner-city mentality and break free from the fetters of prejudice and fear.

Unlike my previous inner city school experiences where questioning and posing different perspectives was not encouraged. Attending classes taught by top professors and classmates who were open-minded and well versed due to having a private school education or being taught by teachers in a better public school system was stimulated my desire to learn as much as I could be become a solid academic and athlete student. Conversations were richly centered on world events, local news, and topics of interest. Walking into each classroom meant excepting an invitation to actively participate in an important adventure.

Students played the key role in how the adventure would be conducted daily. Our professors encouraged us to share our ideas and value the understanding of the written word. We were shown how to interpret the meaning behind the words, the intent of the writer and share our impressions with each other. Homework was not simply answering questions found on pages highlighted in yellow. Our assignments were designed to stimulate our thinking and develop skills to process information to make better informed choices for our future and the future of society. We were refined and changed to set an example for those to follow. Every day gave us the opportunity to grow as an individual and not confined or limited to a "group" identity.

Relationships made in those four years helped to make each one of us better people. Support for one another continues to be the focus and having the opportunity to see, experience and embrace the challenges we met prepared us for the many other challenges we would continue to face. When it is said, college was the best time in our lives this statement can only begin to express the gratitude for being offered and accepting the invitation from American University to be the people we are today and will be tomorrow.

The summer before entering college at American University my basketball skills were improving daily and I added longer songs to the length of time I jumped rope with the twenty-pound weight vest, playing at Rudolph long after the lights were turned off, and other playgrounds around the city. Reading did not include assigned college reading text to establish a solid scholarly foundation but Sports Illustrated and a variety of sports magazines. One headline that caught my attention featured a wrestling Olympic hopeful, Dan Gable, from the Iowa State. In the article, Gable shared his thoughts on being prepared to compete and how his focus is always on success.

Gable mentioned that no one would work harder or prepare more than he would for winning the Gold Medal at the Olympic wrestling competition. He admitted it was possible someone might be more talented or even capable of achieving his dream, but he emphasized no one would work like he did to accomplish his goal. This greatly influenced my focus to become to best basketball player I could be. I adopted his thought process and developed a single-minded goal. It had never occurred to me that scoring 20 points and 20 rebounds was an arduous task. I had not really played the game and no one, not even myself set any ceiling or limits to achieving such a goal. I viewed each game, whether for American or on the honored courts at Rudolph, as the opportunity to work harder and prepare more than my competitors.

I knew I was ready to play college basketball. I later met Dan when coach Davis left Stanford University and became the head coach at University of Iowa. Gable was the head wrestling coach and had won the Olympic Gold Medal in 1972. Under his tutelage his wrestling team at the University of Iowa won ten NCAA wrestling championships. I felt privileged to tell Dan how reading his article in Sports Illustrated inspired, motivated, and greatly contributed to my athletic achievements and success. I knew I was ready to play college basketball.

When the competition I would be facing during the season was not as formidable as the tough aggressive players on the playground. There were only four baskets and to play a game you had to be either good enough to start and play the whole game or at least be chosen to play sometime during the game. Without any referees to make calls on any given play you had to be tough to stay in the game. I grew four inches and still did not gain a single pound. I could jump out the gym but my physical appearance was pitiful. I had to play better every day as that was the fuel that ignited my growing confidence.

I didn't know John Thompson personally, our nightly games on Monday through Thursday were well publicized in the neighborhood. Local talent and well-known local legends were acknowledged and when John Thompson frequented the stands, all heads turned to show their appreciation for his support and comments regarding players and plays. Many enjoyed disputing or agreeing with his personal observations and opinions while offering an iced cold beer to further the liveliness of the conversations. He was currently coaching basketball for Saint Anthony's High School. He told me he noticed my improvement and complimented me on making it evident by my play, I was becoming a player to be respected on the court. He wanted to know why I hadn't displayed these skills while playing in high school.

Not willing to tell the truth, the whole truth, and nothing but the truth, I simply gave my standard answer: "I was still practicing." The real answer to his inquiry was already in print. All I did was uncover it, then tweak it a bit and found: never missing a day of working out, staying focused to work harder than anyone else, combined with daily wearing a twenty-pound weight vest while jumping rope with high repetitions was the magic formula that worked for me. I needed to be the hardest worker like Dan Gable stated. Some secrets need to remain such. At this point in my career, I needed an extra edge. And this edge was something I was going to keep a well-guarded secret. I didn't want anyone to start doing my same routine I needed all the extra help I could get to prove to Tom Young and Tom Davis I could make it on their team.

As the hot and humid summer days changed into brisk autumn breezes I started to enjoy thinking about my prospects. Having only one small bag to bring to school, making decisions about what items to leave behind and which ones to take was easy. This might be the first actual identifiable explanation of why and how I came to view downsizing and keeping things simple was based. I had never packed for a trip anywhere before and I didn't want to ask for any assistance from my father.

I did however, take time to take an active interest in what Chris had packed returning to his sophomore year at Texas, El Paso. He wasn't the kind of person who would do a walk through with you, but he did take a great deal of time for me to watch as he packed for school. I knew he'd be the best person to help me choose what to pack, based on knowing what items I would need and those I had at my disposal. When he was all packed and ready to go, he did remind me that being on scholarship was a very important responsibility and told me he knew I would do well both academically and on the court. My confidence in playing basketball on the college level continually grew having played with the best in the country on Rudolph playground courts.

To guarantee I had some money when I went off the school, I opened a checking account over the summer and deposited six hundred dollars. I saved up six hundred dollars and opened a checking account. Being financially solvent, my excitement. I explained to my father it would be a good idea for me to start being more independent and responsible by taking control of all my paychecks. Being financially solvent, my excitement about leaving my father's house increased with each passing day. It wasn't difficult to determine who was the most excited about my heading off to school, my stepmother or me. I truly believe my stepmother Barbara's excitement about both Chris and I being out of the house made her feel comfortable in showing how much our leaving meant to her. It was obvious to any casual observer it was undoubtedly, my stepmother. She no longer attempted to make the effort to hide her dislike for us in front of our father.

Her farewell remarks truly demonstrated the depth of her lack of compassion for me. Her most blatant display occurred on the morning my father dropped me off at the American University's campus which was my first day at college. Barbara had decided to get a ride from my father to work before he dropped me off at school. Just before she got out of the car she told me, "Give me your house key. I don't want you coming back to my house and stealing (not taking but stealing) anything." I turned to my father and asked, "Why did you let her speak to me that way?" He gave no response.

After all those years of being cruelly mistreated I did hope my father would have stood up for me. But he did not. He said nothing. If I wasn't so excited and happy to be starting school and consider what was lying ahead of me, her statement and my father's silence might have upset me. I never spoke to my stepmother after that day. I didn't go home for weekend or vacation visits unless the dorms were closed and it was the only place to rest my head for a few days. In later years, after Barbara and he were no longer living together, he asked me why I never came to visit. I then asked him, "Why would I want to return to an environment where I was insulted and ill-treated?" For the first time in his life, I could see he understood the full meaning of my words.

But on that day, the realization that she was no longer someone I had to deal with was a relief. Her meanness was evident over the years we had to live with her, but on this day, I refused to allow it to take away from the joy my future held out for me. If my father wanted to remain blind as to how we had been mistreated over the years that was his choice as he would have to live with her not me. How he dealt with this was on him. I simply opened the car door, gathered my one bag, and without looking back walk away from the past and into the future. I will always remember this moment where evil intent did not overpower good intent and positive thoughts.

The short walk from the car to the front door at McDowell hall came as a welcome relief from the oppressive atmosphere within my father's car. McDowell Hall was a new building with some finishing touches needing to be done. The hustle and bustle added to my excitement to be a part of college life. I was a bit nervous about the challenges in front of me in the world of academia but for the moment I was more interested in meeting the two people who would be sharing in my first and perhaps more years of my new adventure. Number 207 was my assigned room and my two roommates were Andy Harp and Tom Rowe. My room was in McDowell Hall, a new dorm, and the hustle and bustle energized my excitement to be a part of it all. I was interested in meeting my roommates and experiencing college life. 207 was the magic number. I had two roommates, Andy Harp and Tom Rowe. Andy was waiting in the room. He ran long distance track and was on a scholarship. Tom didn't arrive until two days later and was my teammate on the freshman basketball team.

When I entered the room, Andy's surprise at my appearance was quite noticeable. He quickly welcomed me with the offer to help me with any school work if needed. I wondered what it was about my appearance that gave him the impression I was going to need help. Ones to arrive we selected the best sleeping arrangements. My dorm room was larger than the room at home I shared with my brother. There was a long desk with shelves to put books and two chairs for studying and working on assignments. One wall had two windows that look out over the back of Mary Graydon Center, the amphitheater and tennis courts. When open, the windows let the cool breeze inside. The curtains were dark enough to limit the amount of sunlight coming in when we wanted to sleep in.

We were given clean linens and walking down the to the bathroom I looked inside the other rooms being greeted with friendly smiles and brief introductions to and from the other members on our floor. The bathroom was neat and clean with one side having a row of toilets and on the other side were rows of showers. There was not a bath tub in sight. Walking back to the room in the opposite direction was the lounge. It was supposed to have tables and chairs for eating, but due to some unfinished work, sleeping arrangements needed modification and there were temporary beds to accommodate for this inconvenience.

Being the first occupant to arrive, Andy took sole possession of the single bed, being the second to arrive I choose the lower bunk bed, leaving the upper bunk bed for our third roommate Tom Rowe.

Looking around the room there was a nice desk area. We were given sheets and pillows.

Our third roommate arrived days later. Tom Rowe was a solid player with an intense interest in art. Our freshman year he was focused on playing basketball and was a solid team player in the beginning of the season, and the year's final wins and loses statistics were looking extremely promising for American University's sports record. The team was learning how to play together by complimenting strengths and understanding how to identify weaknesses to be worked on.

My first year at American University, the coaches were concerned I might not be able handle a full five class course load. They suggested I take only four classes and then make up the fifth class later in the year. I was fully aware that although on paper my grades did not reflect my desire to be academic eligible to play on the basketball team, my strong work ethic would be enough to successfully handle five classes. I did not let their concerns sway my decision to meet the challenge to complete the first year of college every freshman was presented. To help new-comers get to know the city, bus tours were provided. I didn't participate in any of these excursions as my brother Chris and I had walked the streets of the DC metropolitan area and visited all the points of interest included in the tours. Taking advantage of some off time I walked down the hill to a local playground looking for a pick-up game. Some varsity players had invited me to join them after briefly running into them in the hallways as we passed one another throughout the days we were settling in.

All the basketball players who lived on campus were housed in McDowell Hall. As we had several brief conversations to get to know one another better, the varsity players told me that the coaches told them about the new recruit who had averaged 14 points a game and 6 rebounds. When we briefly spoke, I was wondering who this person was they were talking about.

Having played on Rudolph's playground with the best competitors in the DC metropolitan area, gave me a better appraisal of the talent on the American University roster and what I needed to do. That first day of practice was a scrimmage between the freshman and varsity roster. I played extremely well against everyone except Gordon Stiles. Physically Gordon was strong and well-built much like an army tank. His legs were spry and he was a leaper to be reckoned with. He could literally jump out of the gym. It was a joke. This was not going to deter me from following the words of Dan Gable I read in a Sports Illustrated article. Gable publicly stated, "*Gold medals aren't really made of gold. They're made of sweat, determination, and a hard-to-find alloy called guts. I'm going to win the gold medal in wrestling, as no one is going to work harder than me.*"

The only sports figure known for his outspokenness about the outcome his athletic performance was Muhammad Ali. Playing against Gordon reminded me about the importance of working harder than anyone else. Whatever that took I was willing to do. All those hours playing on the courts at Rudolph and jumping rope was playing off. He gave me the nickname "Young Buck." Being acknowledged as have a talent he respected I now knew I could play. I began to replay in my mind the many pick-up games I was fortunate to be chosen to participate in. I wanted to focus on one skill that I could truly excel in and that was rebounding. Jumping rope would provide the basis to achieve a high level of success.

Returning to my room, the numerous possibilities set before me continued to provide hours of deep contemplation and self-reflection. Returning to my room I took a long hot shower and enjoyed the comfort of clean linens. At home Barbara did laundry once a week and if she was so inclined washed both Chris and my sheets. If we wanted to have clean linens and towels we would simply have to wait as we were not granted access to the washer or dryer. Having air conditioning was quite a luxury. I had never slept with a pillow before coming to college. My Grandma Foreman worried we would suffocate if we used one and when living with Barbara she simply never considered we might need one.

After my two roommates were in a heated discussion about who could have the one I wasn't using, I decided to give it a try. That was all it took, I was hooked. Another bonus was having a seven-foot bed to sleep in. At home my bed was a typical twin, each new amenity was helping make my transition to college life easier and easier. Clean linens and towels were unbelievable. As I had never had pillows to sleep with my two roommates started to argue about who would get mine. This made me wonder about why this might be something to reconsider so, I told them I was going to try out this pillow issue and get back to them on it. Air-conditioning in our dorm room was truly the most outstanding feature of living in my college dorm.

When classes started, I attended each one with diligence. In the four years attending American University I never missed a class. In my last year in High School I began to understand the need to work hard on academics and athletics. Just as I had a schedule for jumping rope and practicing shooting I made a schedule for preparing my school assignments and studying for tests.

We spent many nights burning the midnight oil. Pat helped me with completing written assignments. Not having done a lot writing in high school it was a challenge for her to keep me focused on making me concentrate on what needed to be done and how to go about it. There were many long hours spent in showing me how to study as we sat at the desk in my dorm room. The hours moved quickly all those nights in McDowell as we worked together. In time, I got the hang of it and she would check my work. After all that was said and done, then she would make me hamburgers and a Nutrament drink to support my efforts to put on quality weight. Having gained 20 lbs. Coach was very happy with my progress. His goal for my game performance was to average 10 points and 10 rebounds a game as a sophomore.

I began to make the connection between working diligently on both academics and athletics. Just as I had a schedule for jumping rope and practicing shooting I made a schedule for preparing my school assignments and studying for tests. Interestingly, enough, the remainder of my freshman basketball scholarship teammates arrived a few days after I did as they lived outside of DC. Bob Rosenfeld was from New Jersey, Frank Witucki was from Pittsburg, Pennsylvania, and Tom Rowe was from Cedar Falls, Pennsylvania. A local walk-on, Jerry Gaston, introduced himself on the basketball court in Leonard Hall.

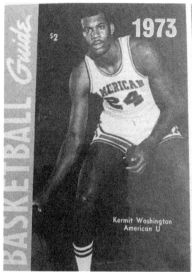

Kermit College Years

Paul Wholey   *Gordon Stiles*

Lenny Lockhart

Bill Demharter

Jim Neurohr

Bill Ulbin

Freshman Gang

Bob Bush

Art Perry

Coach Tom Young

Coach Joe Boylan   *DM Jones*

Frank Witucki

Mike Hill

AMERICAN UNIVERSITY IS PROUD OF KERMIT WASHINGTON

America is a country imbued with the spirit of its athlete-heroes. But the spirit and the reality of Kermit Washington go beyond the usual, for Kermit has displayed qualities of maturity, sensitivity, and intelligence that have established him as an unusual student-athlete. He has previously been named an Academic All American, and now Kermit has been recognized as one of the five greatest collegiate basketball players in America, a rare tribute to his dedication, talents, and self-discipline. But then, Kermit is a rare person, indeed. Whatever honors are bestowed on Kermit Washington are richly deserved.

The American University is proud of Kermit Washington, and knows that you share our pride.

The First Team

Ernie DiGregorio, Providence
Ed Ratleff, Long Beach State
David Thompson, N.C. State
Bill Walton, UCLA
Kermit Washington, American

ON THE COVER: Kermit Washington, American University's potent pivot who topped the nation last year as a rebounder with a 19.8 average after finishing No. 2 the year before with a 20.5 mark. Picked by the 206-member Eastern College Athletic Conference as an All-East choice, he was All-Middle Atlantic as well. With a 21.0 scoring average, and 129 blocked shots to his credit, he was named the Metropolitan Washington, D.C. "Player of the Year", and was the only unanimous All-Metropolitan Washington pick. On the court, Washington's high marks were 30 points and 23 caroms. Off the court he had high marks, too. A psychology major at American, he was named a first team Academic All-American.

ALLY by The N...

105

SPORTS

TUESDAY, MARCH 20, 1973

ermit Washington Makes
Team AP All-America

center of American University's
named yesterday to the first team
merica.

enior almost totally ignored by
he graduated from Coolidge High
of UCLA, Ed Ratleff of Long
orio of Providence and David
State on the first team.

n was named to the third team.
y The Washington Post, Washing-

al times. "I don't believe it. I had
campus, but I thought all those
dn't believe them.

mazing. But why the turnaround
ceived honorable mention in the
ll.

o a 21-5 record and an NIT bid,
l's history, and became only the
to average 20 points and 20 re-
He led the nation in rebounding
s second to 7-foot Artis Gilmore

first-team All-America selection.
I first came here as a freshman,
getting some playing time. Now
ance. No, it's even more than

n't see how I was selected. But
choice. Maybe now people will
merican University. Not many
hool play. Maybe this will help.
ly, you're not kidding me, are

tars from last year's team and

The First Team

Ernie DiGregorio, Providence
Ed Ratleff, Long Beach State
David Thompson, N.C. State
Bill Walton, UCLA
Kermit Washington, American

College Articles

When winter's winds graced our campus the favorite expression universally stated was "the Hawk is out." The Hawk is the Winter NW wind. It's a Chicago term in origin but anywhere you live that can be influenced by a NW wind means the Hawk can come out ... Ever since then if there is a cold wind blowing people say, "the Hawk is out." In DC, metropolitan area everyone knew that the wind was brisk and would literally bite at your face. Because there always seemed the need to provide nicknames to the new rookies, the varsity players chose "Bird" for me. This was penned strictly to point out my skinny legs. However, everything about my body could be called skinny. Andy was given Professor, and to this day when we refer to one another on occasion, those identifications of endearment remain as a reminder of our first few years at American University. It wasn't a bad nickname to accept as one varsity player was always referred to as Cheeseburger.

Greatly influenced by having played with such playground locals as Austin Carr, after these Rudolph playground regulars selected to attend Notre Dame University, whenever their games were televised I was certain to be watching with avid interest. Now being a freshman at American University during the Notre Dame versus University of Indiana I first took note of their star player, George McGinnis. (Played 11 seasons in the <u>American Basketball Association</u> (ABA) and <u>National Basketball Association</u> (NBA). He was drafted into the ABA from <u>Indiana University</u> in 1971. In the 1970–71 season at Indiana, McGinnis became the first sophomore to lead the Big Ten in scoring and rebounding. He averaged 29.9 points per game in his lone season in Bloomington earning All-American and All-Big Ten Honors in 1971.

Just before the game started players were warming up with lay-ups, free throws. Right on the television screen was George taking off his warm-up outfit and as he did so, he revealed to the world one of the most incredibly muscularly defined bodies I had ever seen. My first reaction to this display of muscles convinced me that giving more attention to lifting weights was to be a number one priority. I wanted to look just like George. I knew it would take some hard work and time to achieve this transformation and I was willing to do whatever it took as the results right before my eyes was a true motivating factor. As my improvement in playing my positon and learning about the game was noted by the varsity players, they shared these observations with coach Young and coach Davis who intently listened.

Coaches were not supposed to be present during these scrimmages but when they did they pulled me to the side and expressed their extreme pleasure in the improvement I had made since seeing me at the Allentown try-outs. The two best varsity players were Gordon Stiles and Vince Shaftmeister. Gordon, about six feet three, a very good leaper, was very physical and the only player who as a senior posed any challenge in playing the game. Vince was a tall seven-footer who could rebound if his head was not in the clouds. He was very quiet and introspective due to his frequent close relationship with Mary Jane. Roommates both Gordon and Vince shared many common interests and at times that negatively impacted game performance. As every day drew closer to the start of the season and the beginning of a new life for me, I remembered the words of Dan Gable and stayed focused on continuing to improve in scoring and rebounding. As I continued to do so, the coaches and I were extremely happy.

Determined to stick with my weight vest and jumping strategy, two weeks into the semester I realized if jumping rope was taking away from needed study time a modification was necessary. I cleared my mind one evening, and went to sleep saying to myself I need a solution to this current problem. Upon waking up I walked to the stairwell and remembered a dream I had about running up the steps and taking the elevator down. In my dream this routine was timed and it reduced my training efforts by several minutes. I started running up the seven flights of stairs in McDowell Hall and taking the elevator down ten times every night before going to bed. After my classes ended (I started at 8:00 a.m., business law; 9:25 a.m., history; and 10:50 a.m., biology) at noon, I would eat, start my homework, and then went over to Leonard Hall to play basketball. In substituting running the stairs for jumping rope, the coach suggested I should do some weight training. He straightforwardly stated: "Kermit, you have to put on some weight."

At the time my only knowledge about weight training was watching Jack LaLane, fitness, exercise, nutritional expert and motivational speaker sometimes called "the godfather of fitness" and the "first fitness superhero," wearing his grey polyester jump suit, on TV doing calisthenics. After showing me the school weight facility it was obvious coach had limited experience as well. The school weight room only had one universal machine with some individual weights. After lunch I went to the weight room and then practice. When I began lifting I was six-foot eight inches and 160 pounds. No one was there to show me what kind of training format to follow. I agreed to lift weights for two weeks, and if I didn't see any improvement, I said I would stop. As I walked around campus, fellow athletes would comment that I was gaining some weight and looking stronger. This, although was not noticed by me, was indeed a ploy from the coaches to keep me going. I enjoyed lifting almost as much as how my body responded to this new training coaches. I am assuming – in front of to keep me going.

Being on scholarship was filled with perks. Eating meals at Mary Graydon Center was not limited to weekdays. With having meals on the weekends, I made my six hundred dollars last longer and the best of everything I didn't need to go back to my father's house. For the first time in my life I could eat breakfast and choose whatever I wanted to eat for lunch and dinner. I will always remember those freshly made, warm doughnuts. My first encounter with the cafeteria worker was to ask if I could have anything I wanted to eat. She replied, "As much as you wanted." That meant second helpings, a variety of beverages with refills, and assorted desserts. Life was truly good, and the ability to eat whatever I choose was absolutely, incredible. In time, I did begin to gain weight. To me the food at school was hot and delicious. Just a bit of salt and pepper and my plate was soon empty.

All I had to compare the meals served at school with was the reality, starvation was more appealing then eating one of Barbara's home cooked meals. I now hoped my new diet would help me gain weight, quality weight, and lean muscle and not fat. To me it was a tremendous feast. In time, I did begin to gain eighty pounds, over the four years at American University. Averaging twenty pounds each year. My daily routine included turning off the alarm at 7:00 am, shower, get dressed, gather books, eat breakfast, attend classes, eat lunch, lift weights, shower, start and complete as much as possible assignments, study for tests, go to practice, shower, go to dinner, change to run the eleven flights of stairs taking the elevator back down and then run back up, shower, and then bed. Jumping rope had taken one hour and thirty minutes, so I substituted running the stairs every night and would jump rope a few nights when I had a few extra minutes to spare.

Coach Young and Davis recruited me but our freshman coach was Billy Jones. As freshman players, did not play on or against varsity teams, our games were restricted to local high school team and junior college players. Our freshman coaches were Joe Boylan and Billy Jones. Our competition was against local high school teams or college freshman teams. My first freshman game was against Georgetown I scored 16 points and grabbed 14 rebounds. We scrimmaged against the varsity team daily and would have to endure the physical aggressiveness of Gordon Stiles. My first year at American University, our freshman team played well together. We became true friends both on and off the court. We spent hours getting better acquainted with college life and each other. This comradery resulted in setting the best winning record the freshman team. My freshman year I averaged 19 points and 23 rebounds and was named one of the Top 10 freshman in the country. Quite an improvement from 6 points and 6 rebounds a game in high school.

Earning good grades, I held B+ grade point average which helped the coaches to relax and show more confidence in my ability to select courses that best suited my interest in psychology. At the end of my second semester I met Pat and her roommate Vickie Valsecchi, during the half time of a varsity game at Fort Myer, Virginia military base. Both lived on campus in Anderson Hall which was a long walk from McDowell Hall past the amphitheater. From that point forward I was never asked about my academic status again. The end of the second semester I met Pat. Now this meeting took place during the half time of a varsity basketball game at Fort Myers. Pat and her roommate Vickie Valsecchi lived on campus in Anderson Hall. Vickie was from Baltimore, Maryland and Pat from Long Island, New York.

Vickie had attended a freshman orientation activity before school started. While on campus she noticed a rather tall, slim, lighted young man named Lionel. She tried to get acquainted with him at that time but was so occupied with the weekend activities she never got the opportunity. Pat was provided a big sister who was a Delta Gamma sorority sister to help make the transition to college life easier.

During the first weeks of school while buying textbooks in the school book store, Gordon Stiles took notice of her. Gordon, known as the Big Man on Campus asked around to find out more about her. Her soon learned she lived in Anderson Hall and had a big sister in the Gamma Delta sorority. He asked one of the Gamma Delta sorority sisters he knew if she would talk to Pat to see if she could arrange a date with him. The sorority sister readily agreed and was quite insistent that meeting Gordon would be an enjoyable outing and set up the date.

Vickie helped Pat dress for her date and gave her those sage words of advice a seasoned dater would give to a novice. When the room buzzer rang, Pat answered the phone, thanked Vickie for her help and walked up the short flight of stairs to the lounge. Walking to the front desk, there stood Lionel whom Pat recognized and made to assumption the person with him must be Gordon. Pat had never met Gordon before and but was shown a photo by her Delta Gamma big sister. Gordon introduced himself and Lionel. He then asked if she could possibly arrange for a friend to accompany them and be Lionel's date for the evening.

Without a moment's hesitation, Pat literally raced down stairs and looked for Vickie. Finding her in the lounge curled up with a good book, Pat told her that in a few minutes her life was about to change. Vickie moved faster than a speeding bullet and looked absolutely, knock-out gorgeous. She walked up the stairs with Pat as if gliding on a cloud. Her composure and self-confidence seemed to fill the room. For Vickie, the evening was a big success. She finally met and spent time with the man of her dreams and it was not disappointing in the least. As for Gordon, Pat was told he had a long-time girlfriend who visited regularly. As Gordon failed to share this information with her, Pat let him know she was aware he had a girlfriend and a casual friendship would be the only kind of relationship they could have. This later resulted in many physically aggressive practices with Gordon once he found out Pat and I were dating.

Pat's other roommate was Marty Levy. Marty was born and raised in White Plains, New York in a prestigious neighborhood. Her parents were very wealthy and extremely hospitable. I was once invited to visit and was amazed by how much different the suburbs in New York were from the streets in the heart of New York City. Shortly after Pat and I started dating, Marty became sick with mononucleosis. The school infirmary diagnosed her condition and informed her parents she would need to be temporarily removed from the dorms as she was highly contagious.

Her parent's long-time friends were a local family and they immediately came to the school to collect her. Pat and Marty kept in touch and a few days after settling at the home of her parent's friends, she called to ask Pat to bring over a few items she needed. Pat asked me to drive her there as she wasn't familiar with the DC metropolitan area. I agreed and we drove to an area off New Mexico Avenue. The location of the house immediately sent up red flags.

We rang the doorbell and were greeted by a friendly face. The homeowner invited us in and two very large drooling boxers jumped up to share their slobber with us. It was a real mess. After several tries to apologize for the dog's wet welcome we were asked to step in the kitchen to wash up and enjoy freshly baked brownies. The house was filled with an aroma that simply insisted you taste the baked goods. The brownies were still warm and Pat was in seventh heaven, stating, they were the best brownies she had ever tasted. She asked for the recipe and that meant we were going to be there longer than I intended. The brownies were delicious and having one meant you had to have another. I think the compliment given to the baker was clearly revealed by the plate slowly dwindling down to only two brownies. The ladies were gabbing away, and I was getting anxious about leaving, as upon my immediate entrance into the house my eyes noticed a lot of Boston Celtics memorabilia on the walls. I instinctively knew this family were Boston Celtics fans to the extreme.

Noticing my attention had gone from the brownies to a large collection of Boston Celtic memorabilia, the homeowner's youngest daughter, Randy and I started to have a conversation and I asked her why there were so many items from the Boston Celtics. She told me that her father was Red Auerbach. My reaction was to leave as soon as possible. It took a few minutes for my mind to make the connection as being associated with the Boston Celtics I merely assumed Red Auerbach lived in Boston, Massachusetts. Shortly after making this statement, the door opened and in walked the legendary Red Auerbach. He took one look at me and said "Sit down, young man." He then immediately asked, "Who is your favorite basketball player?" I replied, "Bill Russell." He smiled and said, "Good Answer."

My inner fears were soon realized. If I had had any inkling that this was the home of Red Auerbach I would never have gone with Pat to the front door. I would have stayed in the car and let Pat drop of Marty's bag. This was the man who won nine NBA championships; and was currently running the Boston Celtics franchise. George Washington University games or followed players on George Washington University's team. He asked me if I thought I was a good player. Then he told me now we had met, he was going to keep a watchful eye on me. He ended our brief conversation by inviting me to keep in touch with him, and over the summer I could work in his basketball camps in Marshfield, Massachusetts, as a counselor. This would give me the added opportunity to play with other college players from around the country who would also work as counselors play and against some of the Boston Celtic players.

Surprised by Red's open and easy going personality I was looking forward to keeping in touch. With Marty staying at his house and my taking Pat over to visit on other occasions our relationship developed over time. Driving back to school it was time to get to work. Every night we burnt the mid-night oil studying and completing assignments. Pat helped me with writing papers as I didn't type and my grammar was badly in need of help. She once asked me if I had taken typing in High School. I explained, in junior high, which at that time was seventh to ninth grade I sat quietly in a typing class but never got the hang of it. That might be because I daydreamed the entire time in class.

I had asked my teacher, Mrs. Harrison, if I could change my seat. I was sitting next to a girl who constantly coughed and her breathe was so foul it made me feel sick to my stomach. Knowing I ran groceries home for neighbors on Saturday's, she suggested if I brought her a nice calendar and helped her with school chores like cleaning blackboards and erasers, she would let me move and give me a C in class. Every week Grandma Marion gave Chris and me a quarter for doing chores around her house. I took my quarters to school where I bought government saving stamps. Each stamp was worth a quarter. I saved my weekly money by purchasing stamps. You were given a small booklet where you kept your stamps. When the booklet was full, you had saved ten dollars.

Known for being quiet and well-mannered she knew my request was something I wouldn't have brought to her attention unless it was important. After giving Mrs. Harrison the calendar, she moved me to a corner in the classroom near the window. Sitting away from the girl whose cough was annoying I was now at leisure to daydream. She was focused on helping me use a highlighter properly and how to take marginal notations. We spent more hours sitting at the student desk in Room 207 to earn high grades that resulted from the fruits of our labor to graduate on time. The hours moved quickly all those nights in McDowell as we were working together. We worked well together, and she would make me hamburgers and a Nutrament drink in my efforts to put on quality weight.

For the summer the Coaches arranged for me to work at American University with Lloyd Mayes and I was a counselor at Mt. St. Mary's college, Gettysburg college, and Rider University. I didn't stay in the dorm but went back home, which allowed me to return to my routine of jumping rope 10,000 times a night and walking down to Rudolph playground to play basketball, when college players such as Collis Jones, Austin Carr and other college notables returned home. It was quite rewarding to hear from them when they saw me how much I had grown.

I remembered to get in touch with Red in early July worked his basketball camp in Marshfield, Massachusetts as a counselor. The price of my round-trip plane ticket was forty-five dollars. As a counselor, I responsible for a cabin of fifteen campers. The day started at 7:00 a.m. and ended at 11:00 p.m. In the evening when all the camp activities were over, Red brought the Boston Celtics stars to play games with the counselors. I played well and at the end of the week he gave me an extra twenty-five dollars. Having to go back home for a part of my summer vacation I was subject to inferior home cooked meals which made me miss the cuisine served at Mary Graydon Center. Being at Red's camp was truly life-saving as the food was good. When I shared with Red that I was thankful for my twenty-five dollars but it I had to pay forty-five for my plane ticket, he simply said, "That teaches you something about business." I responded, "That teaches me I'm losing money." Red simply laughed and assured me, "This was a good investment for you." and it was.

I enjoyed my life and routine at American University during the school year. Some students looked forward to intercession break and other opportunities to return home. As for me, the only pleasure in having to live at home in the summer was the thrill and anticipation of playing playground ball. Returning from basketball camps I reunited with the local stars on Rudolph playground. The competition was still stiff and I was more readily picked to play. Sid Catlett (Notre Dame), Collis Jones (Notre Dame), Austin Carr (Notre Dame) Ed Epps (Utah State), and Bill Gaston (Oregon) were some to name a few. The Notre Dame trio were on the team that upset the winning record held by UCLA. The word on the playground was out. Players spoke about what a very good year as a freshman I had. Adding to the quality level of playground basketball, John Thompson would bring the best high school players to Rudolph playground even though he was coaching at Saint Anthony's High School. Every Monday to Thursday night a basketball game of extreme excellence would always be played at Rudolph. The courts were deserted one day a week. No one played basketball in the DC metropolitan area or the area on a Friday night.

After work I would come home and attempt to grab a bite to eat. I missed the food served at American University during the school year. I walked two blocks to Rudolph playground with the excitement of having an opportunity to play with and against the best. If I was not successful, it simply added more determination to work harder, jump rope longer, and continue to work on improving my game. They kept the lights on at the playground until eleven. as the city wanted to encourage kids to be involved in something positive, hoping to reduce any opportunity to get into trouble.

Going home for the summer meant retuning to jumping rope as my training routine to improve my leaping. The noise of the jump rope hitting the pavement and the music I played to keep me focused would disturb the neighbors. To prevent any negative comments from Barbara I stayed on Rudolph's playground long after the games ended. Chris was home for the summer and had managed to earn a scholarship his sophomore year in football. The difference between football and basketball was the inability to practice football by yourself. With basketball, you could always go and shoot hoops alone if a game was not available. The summer before my sophomore year I got back to school early to earn money helping knew students get settled into the dorms, carrying luggage, giving directions, and answering any questions that couldn't be found in any printed flyer.

Most important was providing those assuring worried parents that their child made the best decision in choosing American University as their college for the next four years. As many parents noticed my height, I shared, the basketball team was guaranteed to help provide a sense of community. The team might not be able to initially cure homesickness but it was a given by second semester when the season began their child would feel quite at home and adjust well to college life. It was always exciting and exhilarating to return to campus before students moved in. The meals at Mary Graydon, a pillow to rest my head on at night, air conditioning, clean linen, and the absence of my stepmother were all welcome advantages I had missed.

Soon the campus would be filled with new and returning students who attended concerts in the amphitheater and other planned activities designed to help them face and successfully meet the challenge of learning how to properly manage new found independence. Little Richard, Chicago, The Chamber Brothers, Richard Pryor, and other groups entertained us for hours. These few additional days before classes began gave me time to look over class options for the year and I decided to add an extra night course from six to nine once a week. As professors rarely held students to the three-hour limit, I filled out my class list form and added the extra class. I added an extra night course from six to nine once a week. Since the professors rarely held us to the three hours, I added an extra course.

Jerry Gaston was my roommate sophomore year. A local, Jerry attended John Carrol high school and was raised by a very possessive single mother. Freshman year he was not allowed to live on campus, but his sophomore year after finding the love of his life, his mother agreed to let him stay in the dorms only if he came home every week-end. She always sent him back to school with a small care package providing an excuse for these mandatory weekend visits. Therefore, he was locked into going home to spend at least one day and evening with her. His only legitimate excuse for staying on campus was being involved with basketball team practices and games.

I went from sharing a room with two roommates to having pseudo single arrangement. During the week, Jerry was always at his girlfriend's dorm room and being away on weekends made being able to concentrate on academic and athletic pursuits ideal. We first met on the court when he tried out for the freshman basketball team. He was a marginal walk-on player who was more concerned with how he looked in a uniform than being a player on a team. He seemed to desire the ability to play the game, but lacked the talent necessary to pull it all together. This "want to be" attitude was noticed by every-one and provided a source of humorous comments by the coaches and the team. He traded in his team uniform for that of the assistant manager his sophomore year.

His focus shifted from "watch me try being a player" to "notice how much you need me to help you play, and get through the game." He frequently wore a smile on his face and often chuckled over sit-uations no one else found amusing. He traveled with the team and helped when needed. While working with the team it was discovered that his gym shoes were beyond the stinky stage. Airing them outside the dorm window was not working and it was all too tempting to pretend a strong wind had blown them off the ledge and onto the pavement below.

The first person I met at American University who had a financial work ethnic equivalent to my athletic work ethic was Alan Meltzer. Alan was a motivated and talented wrestler who was injured off and on through his college career. As a freshman, his porcelain god, was the toilet. The location of his god, John, was where he spent many hours in close physical contact and the men's restroom became known as Alan's second home. His daily routine always included regular sessions with the dorm porcelain God – *John*. Making his weigh was constantly his focus. The need to balance meeting nutritional requirements and not gaining unwanted pounds, was his focus every day. To achieve this delicate balance, sounds of his daily communication with *John*, let everyone know where and what Alan was doing any time of the day. This however, did not overshadow Alan's true love, making money. He was always engaging into a business venture and was an entrepreneur before that word became a household expression.

Alan enjoyed visiting Mary Graydon Center to partake of spirits as well as the cuisine. With Jerry's frequent absences, Alan became my stand in roommate. Alan and Jerry did not see eye to eye on most if not all subjects. But both did enjoy spending time at the Tavern in the Mary Graydon Center drinking a brew or eating a quick snack. Some weekends they would give me a list of food stuffs to bring back from the Mary Graydon Center as my meal plan included weekends. If I brought something in my dorm room I wanted to eat later, if Jerry was on campus, it would be gone.

Jerry joined a fraternity and sought to find his perfect love match by attending every party given on campus at the fraternity house. He found success one night when he met Marylou. Once they made that special connection, he was a lost man. His emotional stability whether he was happy or sad rested solely on the status of their relationship. Being his technical roommate and having him come in and out of our dorm room, depended on the status of his relationship with Marylou.

At any moment, the status of their relationship provided ample entertainment for hours and surpassed the standards for engaging soap opera viewers. This was comparable to viewing a reality show with added drama and uncertainty. Living with him was like being the eyewitness to major drama at its finest. Current soap opera plots could learn a lot from Jerry and his real-life drama and provide ample entertainment for hours. On one occasion, there was a misunderstanding that led to an argument that led to a break up. Jerry's reaction was great material for a Hallmark Romance movie. He was so devastated he blackened out the date on the calendar hanging on the wall. It took several days to resolve the issue, but once it was settled, the calendar was replaced so as not to remind him of the darkest day of his life. To guarantee that life would continue to bring him more happiness than sorrow, the couple secretly married our junior year.

With the graduating of the senior varsity players I was acknowledged as the upcoming star on the varsity team. Coach Davis would be with us one more year before accepting a head coaching job at Lafayette University in Easton, Pennsylvania, and Coach Joe Boylan was named as his replacement. Coach Boylan was very nice and worked well with Coach Young and the team. Our first game of the season was at home, Fort Myer's gym in Virginia, against Salisbury State. I scored 19 points and grabbed 23 rebounds. The newspaper reported I had an auspicious start. I had to look the word up in the dictionary and found it meant "showing signs of promise and success." My sophomore year I thought the newspaper reporters were saying I played poorly.

Our second game was against Saint John's University, known for being, a powerhouse in the East. The game was held at Georgetown. I scored 27 points and 25 rebounds. We lost a very close game but being able to play against such talent helped me to stay focused on achieving my goal by continuing my work-out routine which was proving successful. Two of the players on St. John's roster were later first round NBA draft picks the year I was drafted by the Lakers. My sophomore year I was second in the nation behind Artis Gilmore in the category of rebounds, Dr. J. close behind me in the number three position.

Academically, the average SAT score for American University students was 1300 and a perfect SAT score was 1600. My SAT score was 800 and indicated I had a lot of catching up to do. After practice ended at 5:30 p.m., I went to Mary Graydon Center for dinner until 6:30 p.m. and then relaxed from 6:30 pm to 7:00 pm. From 7:00 pm until 11:00 pm I studied Monday through Thursday. On Sunday, I looked over my class syllabus and using a daily planner calendar, marked when assignments were due and tests scheduled. My academic schedule mirrored the time I spent on Rudolph's playground during the summer. As this routine was proving helpful on the court, I had full confidence I would also make academic improvement. I took some time off on Friday and Saturday, unless I needed more time to read and complete assignments. Sundays, I resumed my study time, checking the upcoming week's calendar notes, from noon to 10:00 pm.

It was interesting how college classes and assignments differed from attending high school. Now, instead of going to every class every day, we had altering days such as: Monday – Wednesday, Tuesday – Thursday, this gave you time to catch up on course work and forced you to be organized and consistent in following your outlined calendar. In addition, the rigor of reading material was more than double. In high school, we might be required to read two novels a year, whereas in college we read an average of two novels a semester for each course, and included studying textbook materials.

Pat showed me how to locate key points to make comments during class discussions by using a yellow highlighter. It took a few times to master the art of limiting highlighting entire sentences and paragraphs, which contained too much information, and learned how to identify and highlight only main points and ideas. We would then talk about the information I had just read and discuss its relevance to the assignment. These conversations focused my attention on how to gain a clearer understanding and comprehension of the material.

The next academic area I required assistance with was writing. Run-on sentences and failure to use commas was frequently brought to my attention after Pat read over my responses to open-ended questions. We would talk over my answers and after taking short notes I then wrote down more information for elaboration and clarification. Then I read it aloud to see what needed to be revised. From there I worked on my handwriting as I did know how to type. When an assignment required the final copy to be typed, Pat would type these assignments for me. This was also helpful in that I do a better job of revising to catch any corrections missed before turning in the final product. My grades started to improve along with my ability to present my thoughts on paper. During the weekends when the campus was quiet, anyone staying around soon learned that I would be in my room studying and venturing out for my free weekend meals. I was often asked to bring back some items for others' consumption and this added to my already increasing popularity.

My interest in lifting weights was greatly influenced by my changing physical appearance. I gained twenty-pounds and this weight was well distributed with the one exception of my calves, as my legs were still skinny. Upon leaving the weight room and walking back to my dorm, I was approached by a tall, muscular, gentlemen who introduced himself to me. A football player from the University of Nebraska, Trey Coleman was working on his master degree at American University. He centered our brief conversation by extending a few words of encouragement to stay focused on academics and consider basketball as the means to acquire a very lucrative future.

He noticed I was leaving the weight room and asked me how often I lifted and if I would be interested in having him as a work-out partner. The offer was too good to refuse. We exchanged information and met the following day. During our initial work-out session he shared his intent to earn his master's degree, had tried out for the Washington Redskins but broke his jaw in practice and missed out on making the team. It was soon evident how his serious and intense personality dominated every aspect of his life. His knowledge about work-outs was just what I needed. This combined with his willingness to share his words of wisdom helped me to appreciate how someone with life experience and sincere concern for your welfare could prepare and direct you to the right path that leads to happiness and success.

His biggest gift was to instill in me the importance of viewing all opportunities from both perspectives and how all pieces of the puzzle come together. He emphasized how the choices we make influence our decisions. Taking time to meditate on the known and perceived consequences require time to understand how any one choice can be life altering.

My sophomore year when winter arrived and the "hawk was out" students were eager to return home and spend some time with family and friends. I was in no hurry to go home for intersession break and put off making any arrangements for as long as possible. Over winter break, as in my freshman year, I remained on campus playing in holiday tournaments. The ability to have a selection of food choices at Mary Graydon Center during the week and on weekends made my goal to gain weight a lot easier. I had not heard from my father after returning to the American's campus. It came as a surprise when Chris knocked on the door to my dorm room a few days before winter break was to begin. I was very happy to see him but even more surprised as to why he was there and what he told me.

Flying home to DC from El Paso, Texas, Chris got a ride to our 237 Farragut Street, in DC. He told me it was an odd feeling when he quickly noticed the house was vacant. He asked me if I knew what was going on as he had not been told by our father there were any plans to relocate. Knowing he would need a ticket to fly home and then return to school after winter break one of the first things Chris arranged was to secure a part-time job. After earning the funds needed and making flight reservations Chris called my Dad to tell him his travel arrangements. Having been made aware of Chris' memory to return to DC for winter break it would be logical to expect he would go to the 237 Farragut Street house expecting to find the family there. As no communication regarding this vital information was given to either to Chris, or me several questions hung in the air. If plans were already in place for moving why did Barbara insist on giving her the keys to the 237 Farragut Street my first day at American? When was, this house bought? School started early September and it was now late December and the family had already moved and settled in the new house? When Chris called to give my father the date and time of his return why he was not told they were moving and given the new address?

Thinking I might know something he didn't Chris got a ride to American University hoping to find out what was going on and where Dad had moved. After exchanging the usual good to see you, scenario when he told me that the house at 237 Farragut Street was vacant I was as surprised as he was. It was too late that night to do any investigating so I extended the invitation for Chris to spend the night with me. If we couldn't find out where they moved to Chris could always stay in the dorms with me as during winter break our basketball team participated in Christmas tournaments and arranged for the team to have meals and housing. We got up early the following morning and began or search for Red October.

We sat down and had breakfast at Mary Graydon and put together a plan of action. Our first step was to take the bus to the 237 Farragut Street house. If we could gain access there might be some clues as to when and where the move took place. Then if no clues were found the next step was to contact neighbors who might tell us when the move took place and possibly where the family had moved to. Having lived in the neighborhood for so many years, people would feel comfortable telling us what they saw and heard as they were always watching and talking about the latest news on the street. Arriving at our old stomping grounds we walked down the block to the front door. Looking around, the house was vacant and we noticed the back door was unlocked. We carefully entered the house and looked around. There were some items left behind and it hadn't been cleaned up. There were some items left behind, no mail but some old newspapers scattered about. The fact that there was no mail gave us our first lead.

We walked over and knocked on Don Morton's front door to see if he had any idea where my Dad had moved to. As it was Saturday we had a pretty good idea he was still at home lounging around the house. We were warmly greeted and invited in. He was genuinely glad to see us and somewhat surprised when Chris asked if he knew when and where the family had moved to. He shared it had crossed his mind that we might be stopping by but wasn't certain. Chris explained how he arrived in town late the night before to a vacant house with no idea of where Dad moved to? He then asked Don could fill us in on any details.

He told us everything he knew. The day before the moving van pulled up to the house Dad came over to speak with my Mom. He told her he had found a brand-new house in Silver Spring, Maryland. It was a three-story split level house with a large back yard and basement. The movers came just after Thanksgiving and they left the house vacant. My Dad gave his mother the new address and asked if she would check on and forward any mail that might get misdirected before he had a chance to fill out the forms for a change of address form. He did say, considering it was the time of year when most families and friends arrange to spend time together, being excluded was more likely to be expected than not.

After gathering the mail his mother had collected for my Dad, he drove us to American and collected Chris' luggage. This was an opportunity for Don to see my dorm room. He liked all the sports photos I decorated my walls with and met my roommates. Once we put Chris' luggage in the trunk off we went. As we drove down the highway to 6 Countryside Court, in Silver Spring, Maryland we spent time catching up on what we had been doing over the past few months.

As we were entering the neighborhood, Don reviewed the plan: We were to stay in the car while he went to the door, rang the doorbell and handed my Dad's his mail. Then turning towards his car, he signaled for Chris to open the car door and walk up the driveway to the front door.

Ringing the doorbell, we patiently waited a few minutes before anyone answered. When the door did open there stood my father who extended a warm greeting. Don returned the gesture, handed my Dad his mail. Seeing both Chris and me open the car doors and walk to the front door, my Dad was surprised. We were all invited in. Once made aware of our arrival the household stirred and we were given a brief tour of the new house. Chris walked us back to Don's car, retrieved his luggage from Don's trunk, and then dropped me off at school. On the drive, back we laughed so hard, Don had to pull over a few times to regain his composure.

Sophomore year at American University continued to provide opportunities to master more academic and athletic skills. My brother and I communicated more regularly and he kept me informed about how he was doing at the University of Texas at El Paso. This being his junior year he had earned an academic and athletic scholarship to play football. He told me lots of stories about his college basketball team and one player he knew quite well. This was his roommate "Tiny" Nate Archibald., a playground legend who grow up in a rough-and-tumble neighborhood in the South Bronx, New York City.

Nate had a car and was driving back to New York at the end of the year. Chris extended an invitation for Nate to spend a night or two at the house and told him about the legendary Rudolph playground. When we first met, I was amazed at his small stature. One might quickly access this as a weakness and consider this player of no great consequence.

Walking onto the court Nate was immediately selected to join the game. A willing passer and a very good shooter from midrange, it was his quickness, speed and shiftiness that made him difficult to guard in the open court. He would drive past defenders on his way to the basket. He soon silenced his critics to show his great skills on the court and we all had to eat crow followed by a large slice of humble pie. He is the last player in NBA history to lead the league in scoring and assists in the same season.

As my sophomore year and basketball season ended, our final record was 13 and 12. This was a winning record and our improvement along with my recognition for 20 points and 20 rebounds resulted in my making All-American honorable mention. This was noteworthy as it was not simply first, second, or third recognition but outright All-American honorable mention status. This recognition resulted in a phone call from the Miami Floridians from the American Basketball Association. They wanted me to accept and early-out proposal leaving American University to explore the bright lights offered in professional basketball. I declined because I was having too much fun, and the ABA was not a stable entity.

A recruit joining our team sophomore year was Lloyd Mayes. The first time we met he was riding in the front seat of coach Young's car while being driven around campus. Lloyd was an older player about three or four years our senior. After being introduced, coach Young informed me that Lloyd would be working with me over in the summer with Steve Hines, the assistant equipment manager, and Curly White, the equipment manager, in the Cage. The Cage located in the lower floor of Leonard Hall, was where all sporting equipment was housed.

Our job responsibilities included signing in and out of sports equipment by student athletes. As most students went back home for the summer, there wasn't a big demand for anyone visiting the Cage to inquire about or check out sports equipment. A cushy job, most days you would find both managers with their legs propped on the table top viewing soap operas. Having a job indoors was truly ideal. The oppressive heat and humidity felt whenever going outside was not missed as it did not take its usual toll on our bodies. The welcomed air conditioning helped to extend our stamina as we could shoot around, practice free throws and play multiple one on one games.

Having the free time to play basketball made getting to know Lloyd both easy and enjoyable. He lived off campus and sometimes had a car. On weekends when available he would come by, pick me up and take me to play ball at Luzon playground or Rose Park. At either location, there were hundreds of guys eager to play quality ball. On the downside, he never wanted to stop playing which presented a problem in how I was going to get home. Art Perry was also signed to join our team having been in the Air Force. Both added a great deal of personality to the team. Lloyd seemed to have a comment about every aspect of the game. Art was quiet and a solid player who lived on Hamilton Street two blocks from my home on Farragut Street.

The countless opportunities to visit local playgrounds in and around the DC metropolitan area increased the ability to play against outstanding talent demonstrating exceptional competitive and athletic ability. Playground names might be different from the familiar Rudolph, but the rules and standards remained the same. There were no referees and once you were eliminated from play your day was over.

Each game provided a learning opportunity. Observing how players handled the ball, set up shots, worked the court and one another taught me how to read footing moves and anticipate player shot preferences. No one was your teammate, each man was out for himself, to achieve the goal of remaining in the game and on the court. The ultimate benefit was making an honest appraisal of your strengths and weaknesses. Each game forced you to take time and reflect about your performance to determine where you were amongst the large array of talent.

Each game forced you to take time and reflect about your performance in order to determine where you were amongst the large array of talent. Insert: The Urban Coalition: DC Basketball was established to encourage local youth to view basketball as a door to a wider world, athletic or otherwise- and provide a network of former (and current) players to support those opportunities. Summer games were played between our DC Urban Coalition team, the New York Rutgers League, and the Philadelphia Baker League held at Temple University. Highly competitive games were held at Howard University or Georgetown University when in DC. Local attendance was so large, making the gymnasium temperature along with high levels of humidity stifling. When playing, you were drenched with sweat and felt as if someone had thrown a bucket of water over you as you ran up and down the court.

DC players would meet and drive up to New York and Philly. I never made the New York trips but did ride up to Philly on multiple occasions. It was a given if Dr. J was present his team would always win, he simply dominated the court and was literally unstoppable. Despite this we all were eager and excited to play against the legends of our time.

Our DC players included Adrian Dantley, James Brown and Austin Carr. From New York: and from Philly: Dr. J, Nate Archibald, Dean Meminger

Notable Urban Coalition player: College All American -1973-Kermit Washington Coolidge- High School and American University.

It was my sophomore year, Marc Splaver, the newly hired sports information director joined American University. Basketball played a dominant role in Splaver's life while growing up in Bridgeport, Connecticut. His freshman year at American University brought the reality that the moves and shots from his slender frame would not lead him to basketball stardom. He was an avid sports fan who knew lots of trivia about the game and players. His focus was bringing attention to American University to the next level.

He had been following the school's statistics and was eager to motivate continued improvement. He spent many hours sharing his ideas on how to advertise our success which centered around my being recognized as both and Academic All American and winning the coveted first place title in the on-going competition for averaging 20 points and 20 rebounds. Spalver's passion for basketball led him to research and uncover odd facts which encouraged his out of box thinking. His strategies to draw attention to my achievements both on and off the court, gave me the key I needed to unlock my treasure chest.

His accurate and imaginative public relations releases were noteworthy and helped me to live a fairy tale come true. One strategy included a front-page photo, in the Washington Post, of the Washington monument in the background with me in my American University uniform in the foreground under the heading: Washington and the American Revolution. He then created an eye chart with individual letters in my name arranged in an eye chart with the heading: The 20-20 club. He sent copies of his creative exploits out to the media for distribution and awareness of what level of basketball was unfolding at American University. Before Marc's extensive media blitz and campaign, the sports world knew about Artis Gilmore, Dr. J, Sidney Wicks, and Spencer Haywood, and soon they were made aware of me. Marc was determined to have my accomplishments and name join these athletes for my ability to score points and grab rebounds.

With the freshman players moving up to join us on the varsity roster our confidence in becoming a more solid team was well founded. Upcoming sophomores, Peter DeHaven and Johnny Lloyd led their freshman team to a winning record that surpassed my freshman's team record. Pete lived across the hall and we started to spend more time together after practice. It felt natural and comfortable to simply hang out together and soon it became a part of our daily campus life. If I wasn't in the weight room, the gym, or in my dorm room studying, you would find me hanging out with Pete. He by mid-year joined me in the weight room and as neither one of us was proficient in this area, we learned from each other and enjoyed to results of our work-outs. He was willing to try running the stairs but after a few flights decided that part of training was better left for me.

Pete's quiet and easy going personality made him well disciplined with no desire to stay up late and party. Being quiet, getting him to open and share his feelings and interests was well worth taking the time and effort. Once you got him relaxed and comfortable he surprised me with his sense of humor and humorous observations of the interactions between two of our more colorful teammates, Lloyd Mayes and Johnny Lloyd. Both inner-city recruits would go after each other about anything that would result in a rise.

The physical aggression with the onslaught of insults that resulted provided lots of interesting displays of what playground etiquette with additional knit-picking looks like. I'm sure it was envy that motivated this rivalry but either way it made practices the topic of many dinner conversations. Pete could figure this rivalry out and over dinner conversations took note of who had the heads up for the day. If anyone was a betting man a fortune could be made on tallying points for who was on-top on any day.

By the end of my junior year my physical appearance continued to improve along with my game. I tipped the scales at 210 pounds of muscle and despite my constant efforts to see some noticeable improvement in my calves, my legs were not so willing to cooperate and remained slim. The media coverage of American University games increased interest in my on-going quest to achieve the title of the college player to average 20 points and grab 20 rebounds for the season. My name spread as Marc Splaver continued to remind the media about American University's stats, which were well published around the DC metropolitan area.

The community showed their support whenever and where ever I played on the summer playgrounds in the DC metropolitan area. Now, I was considered one of the players to always be picked for a game. This preferential treatment meant even if my current team lost the game, before the start of the next game I was chosen to play again. This was especially significant for to earn a spot on any playground team, you had to be considered a good solid player who consistently demonstrated athletic prowess for the game. Players always picked to be on a team were either the current best college players who lived in the area, or soon to be ABA or NBA players.

With this invaluable experience, I was confident American University was going to have a better team than the year before. Our scheduled games included top teams with a formidable line up of players. This would help media exposure and further refine my individual talents. My junior year was marked with a decided amount of improvement in my game both as an individual player and as a teammate. Going against the well-known and recognized talent displayed by Dr. J., I won the coveted rebounding title leaving Dr. J.'s stats in the number two position. Close behind Dr. J. in third place, was Marvin Barnes, another adversary competing for the title. Averaging 20 points and 20 rebounds our teams winning record was 16-8, making coaches and players very happy.

As my junior year, the NCAA started to question the validity of my rebounding stats. They alleged my rebounds recorded by our statisticians were padded. To investigate this allegation a representative from the NCAA was sent to personally tally and record my rebounds in a game against LaSalle. This would determine if my rebounds were being recorded with accuracy and integrity. Our school statisticians were not intimidated and when the game ended, Marc Splaver had recorded 23 rebounds with the NCAA representative recording 27. At this point in my college career this was at least one of two games in which my individual rebounds outnumbered those recorded for the entire opposing team players.

A change in our team roster included more inner-city recruits then in previous years. The team's dynamics underwent many changes. The playground aggressive behavior combined with the inner-city street communication patterns were brought into practice and game sessions. Players raised the level of competition to vie for starting positions, which previously were assigned and not challenged. Competition encouraged players to bring into daily interactions any opportunity to "put on blast" the weakness of others. Sometimes it appeared as mere jesting but it was comparable to new renditions of "dueling banjoes." This onslaught of verbal and sometimes physical aggression to win those coveted positions at times went too far.

As the team captain, my role was to develop relationships with every player. Time was spent sharing with the new recruits how college life at American University was different from what was perceived as acceptable in the inner-city. It isn't easy to accept change unless willing to see the need and then take the steps to follow through. Change takes time and with this group we needed all the time we had available and a little more. Getting to know each player as individuals it was possible to lessen these awkward interactions and smooth things over with the coaches as well as the players. My focus continued to be working harder than anyone else in both academics and athletics. Comparing team photos over my four years at American University document changes taking place.

With a more multi-racial team with diverse experiences and personalities we shared common interests which formed friendships that went beyond the court, beyond American University, and remain solid to this day. With teammates, being local talent, demonstrating the playground mentality it motivated me. There were games where I did not miss a single shot including free throws and grabbed over 30 rebounds. It is said: iron sharpens iron. This proved to be true with the team my senior year at American University.

The unfamiliar college campus environment presented a challenge to one player Johnny Lloyd. One's first impression of this young man was here stands "a true rebel without a cause." He projected an air of defiance and confidence on his athletic ability. Academically, he was developing skills which later resulted in his graduating on time and earning post graduate degrees. Half way through my junior year coach kicked Johnny off the team. He was an important member of the team and without him our season ending with 16 wins and 8 losses. So, instrumental was he, our season record would have been 18 and 6, had he been present. Somehow, coach had to put Johnny back on the team, not just for the team but for Johnny.

I prepared my entreaty and made an appointment to meet with coach Young. Lou Carnesecca from the New York Nets and ABA team called Coach Young to discuss my interest in coming out early stating they wanted to draft me as their number one choice. Coach Young called me and asked me to come to his office to discuss leaving American University. I didn't hesitate with my reply. I was having too much fun and the idea of leaving school early never crossed my mind. I could say I wanted to get my degree, but the truth be told I just wanted to keep enjoying my college career. If Coach Young had allowed me to take classes in the summer and provide housing, I could have graduated early and possibly pursued getting a master's degree. My academic status was getting much better and this idea of leaving early was not on the agenda.

Coach Young showed his relief and happiness at my decision to stay in school. This was an Olympic year, and he encouraged me to try out for the Olympic basketball team. That summer I was working at Giant Food Store in the warehouse. It was like Africa hot outside with the oppressive heat and humidity. The air conditioning sometimes worked and sometimes did not, giving the inside of the warehouse little if any welcome relief. Having to wear a shirt and tie made working in the oppressive warehouse conditions there more uncomfortable. As coach Young made the contacts for me to work there, I simply sweated profusely in silence. Joining me in this job was a fellow teammate, Steve Garrett, who was usually the silent type. However, working under these conditions showed me a different side of his personality. Looking at his physical appearance he was built like Adonis, his legs were strong and I envied his large calves.

A star athlete at DeMatha in all three sports: basketball, baseball and football – quarterback, he transferred from North Carolina leaving his spot as their quarterback to play basketball at American

University in the guard position. Making such a change was helpful to rounding out our team. Knowing more about his physical stamina I figured there wasn't anything that would unnerve his quiet demeanor. This was not the case, his reaction to the inferior temperature conditions, surprised me. He tried to make jokes about the lack of air conditioning to make it through the day. He once wondered if the temperature inside the Giant food store warehouse was higher than the temperature outside. Or stated, "who needs a pool when you can swim in your clothes?"

Being acknowledged as an NCAA second-team all-American player I was invited to try-out for the Olympic basketball team. Coach Young took one-on-one time to work with me to get me into better shape. When I arrived, there were sixty-seven players from all different schools and sections of the military in the dorms. There was one TV for all sixty-seven hopefuls. The Air Force Academy site was stunning. The rules were very rigid. There was a rule that limited the number of players to be present in all dorm room to three. The idea was to prevent congregating or hanging out with the brothers.

My coach was Joe B. Hall, the coach from the University of Kentucky, who followed his job description to the letter. This stressed the importance of training athletes as if they were in boot camp. He followed his job description to the letter. Signs must have been printed in bold letters to read, "SCREAM!", to encourage the coaches to scream on demand, at all times for any reason. The first week of practice I did tremendously well. When the games started, I got on the wrong side of the coaches. A player named Jim Forbes from Texas El Paso got injured on the court with a big gash in his face. The coaches wanted him to get stitched up on the court. I told Jim there was a good medical facility on site and to go there instead of letting the trainer's stitch you and you winding up looking like a bad version of Frankenstein. The coaches told me to shut up and sit down, as their motivation was to make Forbes appear to be tough. From that point on, it was downhill with a consequence in the end. My playing time was cut in half but I still ended the trials as the second-leading rebounder. I was doomed to be excluded simply because I showed concern for a fellow athlete and didn't keep mouth shut.

After the games, what would normally be a casual walk uphill back to the dorms, seemed like the last mile climb to reach the summit of the Himalaya's, due to the high altitude. This daily excursion was quite a challenge to get accustomed to. It was uphill and being tired I took a minute to rest. Sitting on the steps I was joined by a reporter, Steve Hershey, who did not disclose his job description with or his reason for befriending me. He asked me about how things were going and I was open and honest. I told him the coaches were crazy, always yelling and screaming at players and grabbing them without showing any respect. Although these words were accurate and truthful they didn't need to be put on blast in the newspaper the next day.

The following morning, I was called in by Coach Frank Iba for a "special meeting." He said, "Boy, I hear you're not happy with how things are going here." I didn't see the paper until Coach Iba put the front page of the local newspaper on his desk for me to read the headline. It was a given I would not make the team.

The overall experience did have several outcomes. I met and played with and against the best college players, some whom I would meet again in some competitive arena with the opportunity to form life-long friendships. During the practice sessions and games at the trials one player stood out above the rest. He was Marvin Barnes. He was outstanding in all facets of the game, a real superstar in every sense of the word. Marvin was not a favorite due to his on court and off court activities at the camp. The newspapers clearly painted a poor picture of my Olympic try-outs and that made coming home difficult. I learned people will be judgmental freely making negative and cruel comments simply because they feel they have the right to their freedom of speech. As this lesson came early in my life it proved to be an insulation when I later faced an even greater attack on my reputation.

A popular sports magazine seeking to sell more copies printed the following statement: Washington's performance in Colorado, and was not good and he might have an off senior year. This provided more incentive to work harder than anyone, keep to my routine of running the stairs and jumping rope, and lifting weights and playing against at the best competition available on local playgrounds. Mere words were not going to deter my efforts and my ability to achieve what I knew was possible.

Returning from the Olympic trials despite the negative comments reported in various magazines, the opportunity to play with and against the very best in the nation added to my personal belief that my senior year at American University was going to be my best yet. Wilbur Thomas, another inner-city athlete, was the star of his freshman team. Now joining varsity, I knew we were on the road to success. To start the year, I had now added sixty pounds to my physique since freshman year. Lifting weights, running the stairs with my twenty-pound weight vest and jumping rope ten thousand times whenever I went back home simply reinforced my confidence.

My junior year, following his senior year at Texas El Paso, Chris was drafted by the Saint Louis Cardinals, NFL team. Returning home before reporting to training camp, he bought a Heavy Chevy with a big engine and drove it to DC. My father was at that time driving a car in much need of repair. Every morning he would start the engine and let it run for five to ten minutes to warm up. Putting the car into reverse he would back down drive way and continue to drive the car in reverse until he reached the main street. If all went per plan, the five to ten-minute warm up would be enough to get the car to the main street and into the flow of traffic.

His strategy was slowly resulting in success and you would see him driving the car back to the house in reverse. Chris was amazed at this solution to the obvious need to buy a new car. Not ready to drive his new car to St. Louis, he gave me his car keys and told me to be the only one to drive it as my father's car was in such at state of disrepair due to his lack of maintenance. The Heavy Chevy had a standard stick shift which was new to my driving experience. Pat had a red 1971 General Motors (Chevrolet) Chevy Vega (named from Vega, the brightest star in the constellation Lyra) Hatchback coupe with a four-speed transmission, two doors, and accommodated four passengers.

One night needing to drive home she lent me her car and after a quick four speed shift lesson to teach me the basics I ventured down the road. The hills and steep inclines were the most terrifying. Trying to find that exact balance between the clutch and the transmission gears created several instances where my blood pressure increased to stroke level. Add to that anxiety, the car directly behind you is so close the driver could very well be a back-seat passenger in your car.

Keeping Chris's car posed several problems. Despite adjusting to driving a manual transmission with clutch and shift issues, there was the constant time consuming task of trying to find an available and legal parking space in the limited campus parking lots. Combine that with not being able to afford the gas. It was a risk as Dad, never took care of the anything and could be clearly labeled as the first and foremost pack rat. Chris reluctantly agreed and soon made plans to have his car sent on to him in St. Louis. As feared, even with his brief use of Chris's car, Dad did not take good care of this generous offer. If Chris had not requested his car to be sent to him when he did, I hate to think what might happen next.

Confident I would have a successful senior year and our team would have the best winning record for a season, I looked over our game schedule and circled the games we would win and which ones we would lose. I placed the schedule into a plain white envelope inside my desk. My prediction was twenty-one wins and four losses. After the final game of the season our record was twenty-one and four. The bonus came when my academic performance awarded my efforts by being named an academic all-American, graduating on time with a solid GPA.

Adding pounds, my physical strength improved and in some ways made my ability to move around the court a little slower. What helped me adjust to this change was the great support from team-mates, Wilbur, Rosie, Peter D., Johnnie, Steve, and Art. Realizing that my ability to run up and down the court had changed with the addition of a few pounds, my teammates provided support on the court in a variety of ways. Wilbur was our leading scorer on the team and Johnny was right behind him scoring quickly at will from my fast break passes. He didn't slow down the game but was ever aware of player positioning on the court and passed the ball to an open man or take a good shot.

Rosie, by being the physical force we needed for the inside play. Rosie would come in with his aggressive play and keep opposing players from beating on me as much as they would have if he wasn't out there. Art remained on the perimeter looking for opportunities to shoot the ball. These team efforts were valued and recognized. Players who came in off the bench did not deviate from this form of play and could contribute points that made us a team to be reckoned with. This inner-city group of tough players successfully brought the talent from local playgrounds onto American University's basketball court. I played well, not having a single bad game due to poor performance.

My ability to achieve this was dependent on being in the best physical shape and more mentally prepared than my opponents. My record of being a consistent player put the spotlight on me. Attempts to hinder my goal to join the 20-20 club, like Marvin Barnes added a new dimension to games. Being the target for players on opposing teams my teammates were aware of and readily stepped up to provide support and protection against obstacles I had to face. With every winning game, the atmosphere on campus became more and more exhilarating. The winds of change carried its positive impact on American University's campus.

Coach Young advised us on game nights not to venture out after curfew to visit any establishment serving alcoholic beverages. We were finally told to wear a wrist watch that kept accurate time with a working battery. We won the game at Madison Square Garden and some players felt the need to celebrate with family and friends. Rosie and a few teammates went out into the Big City breaking curfew. No one would have been the wiser, if coach had not been in the lobby just as Rosie and the others were entering the hotel. Being caught breaking the stated curfew a few players were suspended from the team by Coach Young. It was vital that our team stay together. After hearing about the incident, I personally went to Coach Young to speak on their behalf. It wasn't as if I was playing the role of the devil versus Daniel Webster, but the pressure to make sure things were reconciled was definitely on the table.

The conversation between Coach Young and myself was to convince him of the importance of how close the team was and working so well together. We were a close unit and if any piece of the unit was removed we would soon fall apart. Players who were willing to support one another both on and off the court was something to be considered. Knowing the players involved in this display of disobedient behavior was the direct result of peer pressure. Family and friends could draw on the glitz and glamour of city life and offer a seemingly once in a life-time opportunity when gone was gone forever. Being young the lure of the invitation overshadowed the possible consequences of any indiscretion.

The plan to sneak out of the hotel and return seemed foul proof. Who knew coach would go down to the lobby to see how the New York Times sport section had reported the game? Believing coach should be still in bed, bumping into him in the lobby, came as both a surprise and shock. These players knew they had disappointed coach and the team, and that hurt to the bone. I hoped coach could see that although showing understanding for their behavior did require some form of disciplinary measures the squad hoped these would not require a long-term suspension or removal from the team. The coach had to admit the players involved were not problem children and, with time to reflect on the situation, made the best decision that helped make our team a more cohesive unit.

My senior year was a fairy tale come true. The months and games passed quickly, Wilbur was the leading scorer, I led the nation in rebounds for the second year, and every player was having career years. As a team our goal was to win twenty games. When we beat LaSalle for our twentieth win, this was the only game I fouled out my entire college career but pulled down 30 rebounds. Wilbur and Johnny played well to lead our team to a win. The crowd at Fort Meyers went was going crazy. The crowd at Fort Meyers went crazy. We had only one game left against John Thompson's Georgetown Hoyas.

Having played against these guys on the playground, I knew all players, and it was a given we were better than them. Before the game, our last game of the regular season, all the students kept sharing with me word of encouragement. The night before this game, a group gathered around McDowell and stood beneath my dorm room window. Verbal chants of encouragement were echoed, and soon others joined in. The support was infectious. I knew I needed to give my best effort to be up to live up to the expectation of my successful career ending performance. Instead of trying to relax, I proceeded to run the stairs in preparation for the game that was important.

Going to bed and trying to relax slumber soon overcame my nervousness and I slept. To my ultimate surprise and utter humiliation, the front page of The Washington Post was truly a nightmare come true. There for all the world to see was a photo of me my freshman year. (Now one might think, "Okay, so you were skinny and having a really bad hair day. But now you are more physically strong and in great shape.") This might have been the case if the haircut wasn't so obviously the result of a slip of the clippers. The day I went to the barber shop I specifically asked for a trim. I was working on letting my hair fill out and grow into a neat Afro. Somehow the barber didn't remember to adjust the blade on the clippers, and instead of starting in the back of my neck, as he moved the trimmer across the front part of my head he had shaved that portion right down to my scalp. Once this happened there wasn't much he could do. He simply continued to move the clipper across the front part of my head and then trimmed the rest. I looked like a good idea that went south.

The barber still charged me after making me look ridiculous. I knew my hair would grow back but had no idea team photos would be one of the first item on our team agenda. Mortified, I only prayed this photo would somehow disappear and never be used. Later, I did a retake but somehow, someone with a warped sense of humor selected the bad hair photo to give to the Washington Post for a front cover story. My final game before me, that front page image of the before and after Kermit Washington was out there for all to see. Put on blast, I had to concentrate on giving the performance of a life time.

As I left my dorm room and walked over to Mary Graydon to eat breakfast the support of my peers was clearly shown. No one made a joke about the article. I was built up by words of encouragement for this last game of my college career. I was ready to meet the challenge set before me. I was nervous before the game. Riding to the games with Rosie was nerve wracking enough. His fuel tank was always on empty and many times we arrived on fumes only. With the game being so important I needed to be more self-assured we would arrive on time and not tired from pushing a car down the road.

As a freshman, I met Marc Splaver who was a senior and an avid sports fan. He worked as an apprentice with the current sports information director and was always around practices and games. My sophomore Marc as an American University graduate became the assistant sports information director. Keenly interested in the school being recognized for having some local talent, he was very active in finding out tidbits of information that would otherwise go unnoticed. In point the 20-20 club. After reviewing my stats Marc set out on a publicity campaign that would feature me. He held a photo session with me shooting a basketball with the Washington monument in the background. He specifically mentioned the need for me to maintain if not exceed a B grade point average to be considered as an academic all-American.

My junior year Marc came up with the original and brilliant idea of an eye chart featuring 20-20 using the letters in my name. It was posted around campus and made everyone aware of my goal to make this elite club. Marc was diligent in keeping me up to date on other college players who were close to catching up with my stats and to focus on my game. The night before my final game Marc came by my dorm room to visit. He told me that although I was very close to making history by averaging 20 points and 20 rebounds for my college career, there was something I needed to do.

Marc Splaver sat down and very calmly but firmly told me to make the 20-20 club I needed to score 40 points. I had never scored over 30 points in my entire career. I made first-team academic all-American first team my junior and senior years, and he constantly reminded me of what I needed to do to achieve my goal to join the 20-20club, like Marvin Barnes from Providence, Rhode Island, was close behind me, riding my tail. And on this last game day he was on me to make this 20-20 club. Driving to the game my nerves were a mess, everyone was there, my friends from the neighborhood and my father. As the team was warming up for the game, I was too nervous to warm up and sat down on the bench. There were banners hanging all around the Fort Meyer gym, each one saying, "Thank You Kermit." It was like living the final scene of a fairy tale.

As I walked out of the locker room, cheers ran out from the crowd. The game began and during the first couple of minutes I had to call a time to sit and gather my thoughts and composure. Somehow I felt like someone had put a warm blanket around me and I was a different person. I don't think I missed a shot after that. The crowd went crazy. By the end of the game I was exhausted. The usual game plan was to pass the ball and other players would score. But this day the players only passed the ball to me. My final shot to score 40 points was a left-handed hook which I had never done before not in practice and not even in my fondest dream. The crowd erupted in support. Red Auerbach who was sitting in the audience, got up and mouthed, "I don't need to see anymore." He then walked out.

After the Georgetown game, the entire experience felt surreal. People came up to shake my hand and congratulate me on a great game. I can still remember taking the ball out of bounds and passing it to Wilbur. I told him to go on and run it down the court; as I was experiencing the feeling of growing tired. He said," You can do this, let's go." The look on his face showed both support and belief. I rallied and made it down court to score that phenomenal fortieth point. John Thompson came over to shake my hand after the game. In those days, only the conference winners could go into the NCAA tournament. We were then headed to the NIT tournament. Splaver told me that I could not have a bad game in this post conference play or I wouldn't be a 20-20 player anymore.

Playing Louisville in the first round of the NIT at Madison Square Garden in New York there were fifteen thousand people in the stands. As the game was underway our team was in bad shape. Nothing seemed to be going right. We missed easy shots, free throws, and had to call a time out to regroup. We were literally being blown out of the game. We held a group timeout redirected our focus and put our best effort to come within five points towards the end of the game. Despite losing, we could hold our heads up high for having made it to the NIT and giving it our best effort against a level of play higher than what we could demonstrate.

I scored 29 points. Grabbing 20 rebounds was an easy feat to accomplish, scoring 20 or more points was my main concern. With my team, aware of this they were unselfish in their play and made sure I could accomplish this. My college career ended with my earning the 20-20 club distinguished title, and named first-team all-American, first team academic all-American, making Marc Splaver ecstatic. His confidence in my ability was much appreciated and by making me aware of what needed be done throughout the season and school year proved invaluable. He played an instrumental role in by both my past and future.

Boarding the train from New York to DC, I wondered if sometime later in my life I would be on an NBA team playing in Madison Square Garden and this time the final score would show my team won the game. My college career closed one door and another one opened. The media was advertising the list of possible NBA draft picks. Although I had made a name for myself the other players in the running were formidable. With the recognition from the awards I did receive a few all-star game invitations that were nationally televised.

I accepted invitations and quickly learned players did not pass the ball. Guards would shoot as soon as they gained possession of the ball. Their focus was to be identified as the star of the game and forgot how to work as a team. This was perplexing to me as over the four years at American University I was used to playing team ball. Not even my years playing on Rudolph, with and against inner-city talent, prepared me for these game experiences. I began to wonder if my being drafted would be negatively impacted by my performance in the two tournaments I participated in. Neither allowed me ample opportunity to demonstrate the level of my playing ability.

I remember playing in one game held in Philadelphia, Pennsylvania, under Al McGuire head coach from Marquette University. My team won the game but no one passed me the ball and I was only able to grab rebounds. Returning home to the DC metropolitan area and American University gave me time to re-think going to anymore tournaments where my performance could leave much to be desired. Getting picked up from the airport the, twenty-five minute, drive back to campus gave me a chance to share my frustrations.

To my surprise I was encouraged by Pat not to give up and attend the next tournament. I was reminded all tournaments might not be run the same and it was a chance to go to Hawaii. Who could or should refuse such an invitation? Driving back to the airport the next morning I boarded the plane and hoped this trip would work out a lot better. The schedule and agenda for this tournament was a welcome change. We stayed five days and played three games, versus playing one game in the previous two tournaments. We were divided into four teams, and practiced as a team. This instantly placed me back into my comfort zone as plays were called and expected to be executed. At the end of the tournament my east team had the best record with the bonus of being named one of the all-stars of the tournament.

It was at this tournament I met Pete Newell, who was currently working for the Los Angeles, Lakers. After one of our games he approached me to ask if I could run up and down the court. As my usual role was to grab the rebound, throw it down the court to an open man, and then take my time getting back down the court, he wanted me to run up and down the court. He asked me to demonstrate the extent of my stamina and show what kind of basketball playing shape I was in. After doing what he requested, Pete mentioned how impressed he was by my play throughout the tournament. Not actually comprehending the full meaning of his words, I was willing to accept the fact my name and reputation as the 20-20 title holder had been restored.

The plane ride back to the metropolitan area of DC and American University it was time to relax and feel confident that my name and athletic ability was restored if not enhanced. As the days wound down to the draft I continued to attend classes and focused on graduation. Coach Young made me aware of agents calling about meeting with me to sign and represent me. After meeting, a few, I didn't know very much about them, and I didn't trust them. Donald Dell was different. I liked him and felt comfortable with him. I selected him to represent me and he was extremely happy.

Leaving my room a few days later I was walking across campus to go to class. Josh Rosenfeld, one of the team managers, saw me and told me I had been drafted as the number five pick by the Los Angeles, Lakers. My first response was, "Josh that's nice." Afterward I headed off to class.

Graduation meant packing up my dorm room knowing I was not coming back again. It was a time to think back on the four years that led to earning the Hughes Award for leadership and a NCAA post graduate scholarship. Looking around the room, I remembered that first day. Handing my keys over to Barbara, walking into McDowell Hall, opening the door to room 207, seeing Professor sitting on the single bed with and anxious expression, meeting Pat, running the stairs, jumping rope, lifting weights, gaining eighty pounds, attending classes and making lifetime friendships.

I must state of the many people I have lived with, played with, and grow up Marc Splaver will always stand out as memorable. He influenced my life and the lives of others, encouraging them to venture outside of their comfort zone, reach for and set high goals by creating solid plans to achieve them. He left American University that fall after my graduation and rookie year in the NBA to pursue the position of Sports Information Director for the Washington Bullets NBA team. Both embarking on careers in the NBA, we kept in touch and spent quality time in the summer and NBA off-season until he lost his battle with leukemia.

Splaver had been in remission but his condition worsened while traveling on the road with the Bullets in San Antonio, Texas. He had planned to come visit me after the playoffs, between the Washington Bullets and the San Antonio Spurs. There he suddenly fell ill and upon his return to the DC metropolitan area entered the hospital. On May 3, 1978, he left behind a legacy I continue to draw from to overcome the many hardships I've dealt with throughout my lifetime. We kept in touch, and he visited me every summer until he died. Marc was on the road in San Antonio with the Washington Wizards when he became ill and soon entered the hospital after being diagnosed with cancer where he passed away. He played a major part in what was to happen next in my life.

CHAPTER 5

College Friends

Tom Young

Prior to accepting the job at American University, I had been the head coach at Catholic University for nine years and an assistant at University of Maryland four two years. My senior year at University of Maryland, I was the co-captain of the basketball team that won the Atlantic Coast conference chairmanship, and that was a factor in me getting the coaching job at Catholic University when I graduated. I've been fortunate enough to be inducted into the Hall of Fame at the University of Maryland, Rutgers University, and Catholic University when the head coach at University of Maryland was fired, and of all the assistants, I had the opportunity to return to Catholic University as the athletic director and basketball coach, as well as the head basketball coach at American University. The coaching job at American University was a step up from Catholic University even though the returning team had been a disaster and needed plenty of help in the area of talent and discipline. I chose American University, which also gave me the opportunity to hire Tom Davis, who had been the freshman coach at University of Maryland. The American University basketball team had a record of 4 and 19 the year before I accepted the job.

The first-time Tom Davis and I saw Kermit was when he was trying out for a local all-star team. The team was coached by Morgan Wooten and Joe Gallagher, two of the better-known coaches in the DC metropolitan area. Kermit was very quick, aggressive, and never complained about any problems in the practice. We thought he had a chance to become a good player, even though it was obvious he needed work to become a good college player.

After the last practice of this local all-star team, we spoke with Kermit. Even though he did not make the team, to see if he was interested in exploring the possibility of playing college basketball at American University. We in turn were hopeful that American University would be able to provide financial assistance along with an athletic scholarship. We wanted to make sure Kermit was able to meet all requirements for admission, and given the proper support and direct supervision, he would have a successful college career while at the same time helping the basketball program.

We approached the athletic director and the director of admissions to see if it was possible to get Kermit admitted and offer him a scholarship with financial aid. Both offers were agreed upon and worked out, and it turned out to be in the best interest for Kermit, the basketball team, and especially American University. Believe me when I say that we would've been happy to get just a good player, a good person, and a good student, but never expected to get a great player, a great person, and a great student. It was beyond our wildest dreams that Kermit could accomplish what he did in his four years at American University. I had never known Kermit to use profanity, drink alcohol, do drugs, or present any kind of discipline problem. His conduct was exceptional, and to this day I view him as not only one of the best players but also the hardest worker and one of the best persons I have been pleased to coach and call my friend. I believe this says a lot about Kermit because I've been fortunate enough to coach four first-round picks as centers by the NBA.

Kermit was determined to improve his game. He went to the weight room every day without fail. We advised him to only work out every other day as most players did. Kermit's response was that he needed to catch up with the level of play exhibited by other great players, and if he only did what they were doing, he would fall short of his goals. His daily routine was strictly followed and included never missing a class, studying, lifting weights, and running the dorm stairs. He later achieved first string all-American honors on the AP. Kermit is also the last player to score 20 points and 20 rebounds for their college basketball career.

Kermit made a great deal of improvement during his four years at American University academically, as an athlete, and as an individual. He worked well with others and focused on how to make every situation have a positive up-building outcome. Truly an all-American guy, he was later falsely portrayed negatively due to an unfortunate incident in his NBA career. Out of all the NBA players who are currently or formerly in the league, this should have never happened to Kermit Washington.

Our American University coaching staff spent a great deal of time and effort in recruiting in the DC metropolitan area since it was obvious the city had an abundance of outstanding basketball players. I mentioned earlier that before I accepted the head coaching position at American University, the team record was 4–19, and unfortunately all the players were returning. A team that is 4–19 has major problems, and this team was no different. Attitude and discipline along with other problems had to be solved. Recruiting Kermit and other players with his positive attitude and athletic potential helped get turn our program around and move forward.

Major schools in conferences such at the ACC being well-known for having winning records had their pick of the best players in the city. That forced our staff to recruit good players with good attitudes that we felt had the potential to develop into outstanding players. Our freshmen team with Kermit leading the way his freshman team had a good year. This helped us in our recruiting efforts. Being a local inner-city kid who played on Rudolph's playground, his improvement in playing basketball was followed and opened the way for us to offer the opportunity for others to come to American University. With each new recruit, those our program at American University improved as did the caliber of players we could sign.

One such local talent was Johnny Lloyd. His sophomore year he joined the varsity team and soon was involved in divisive conflicts. Despite several one-on-one conversations and restating what rules must be followed, Johnny could not make the adjustments. His on the playground basketball etiquette flowed over onto American University's on the court etiquette and it did result in an equitable arrangement. Johnny needed time and distance from the team, his current behavior, and attitude to evaluate his actions. It was essential he understand and accept changes had to be made by him to be successful athletically and academically. A coach never wants to suspend a player, but if you're going to maintain discipline, sometimes you have no choice. Without a doubt, it was the right decision for that year. Kermit talked to me over the summer about letting Johnny come back. The staff talked with Johnny and felt that it was willing to and had made changes in his behavior and attitude, about himself, and the role we expected and he needed to fulfill. There was no doubt that everyone understood the consequences if you didn't adhere to the rules set up by the coaching staff. Without a doubt the outcome of my decisions about Johnny made us a better team.

Marc Splaver, the sports information director, was a key in helping promote American University and Kermit's accomplishments. He had the brilliant idea of an eye chart with 20/20. This was to promote Kermit's 20 points and 20 rebounds per game. By the way, I believe Kermit is also the last college player to achieve 20 and 20. Marc's efforts to support all the hard work done by Kermit was a major factor in making the all-American team.

A big win for American University was the game against Saint John's. St. John's well-acknowledged player of merit was Mel Davis. Davis was known for being one of the better rebounders in the country. That night Kermit got 20 rebounds and without question was the better player. Having some national attention, the ABA started to contact Kermit regarding signing early. After another request to sign early was made by a friend of mine from the ABA, I called Kermit into my office and discussed the possibilities with him. I believe he made the right decision when he clearly declined and told me his goal was to stay at American University and after four years earn his college degree and graduate with his teammates and friends.

With many agents wanting to sign him to a contract, we coaches sat down and selected three we thought were good agents, and Kermit couldn't go wrong with any one of the three. Kermit chose Donald Dell, and it turned out to be a good decision. None of the coaches questioned his decision because we knew from experience that he was capable at this time to make a good choice.

After making the NIT and losing to Louisville in the first round, Tom Davis and I were at the final four in Saint Louis. Tom had become the head coach at Lafayette College, in Easton, Pennsylvania, after serving two years as our assistant at American. He suggested that I call Rutgers University in New Brunswick, New Jersey to inquire about the basketball position that was open. I called and was invited to visit the campus for an interview by the athletic director. I was happy at American University, but after the interview at Rutgers, I felt that was a better situation for my future. This was Kermit's final season to play for American, and although we had great talent in Wilber Thomas, Johnny Lloyd, Pete DeHaven, and others, the decision to leave came after much soul searching. The fact that the athletic director Bob Frailey and I had been longtime friends didn't make the decision any easier.

I was very fortunate upon graduating from University of Maryland that I got the head coaching job at Catholic. I played for an outstanding coach at University of Maryland and took everything that he taught me to my first coaching position. He was a no-nonsense coach and tough to play for, but you knew that he was doing everything to make you and the team better. I followed that approach throughout my college career. Most players respond to that type of coaching, which involves a loud voice in certain situations and on occasion getting in a player's face. Kermit was not one of those, and he suggested to me that he would respond better when corrected with a calm voice. I agreed to give it a try and see if it worked; it did, and he was right. Having said that, I also told him that in his career he would have to respond to many different types coaching.

Unfortunately, that proved to be the problem when he tried out for the Olympic team. He called me one night to tell me the coaches would yell at the players and grab players physically to get their point across. I called Bobby Knight, who was a friend of mine and also on the coaching staff to discuss Kermit's situation. He told me that was the philosophy of Hank Iba, who was the head coach. The coaches were instructed to be tough on the players, so when they made the team, they could handle any type of situation. Looking back, I believe Kermit might have been better prepared for that situation if I had been a little tougher on him in practice. I am really not sure what would've been best.

Either way, Kermit soon learned it was one thing to confide in me, but it was not wise to share sentiments with the press. Granted he didn't know when approached by local sports writer Steve Hershey that his honest appraisal of what was happening would be put out there on the front page of the local paper and wording the article to be more of a sensational piece than a factual one. Steve taking Kermit's sentiments and doing whatever he wanted with them was a good learning experience as he could have made that team. This situation really bugged me, and my words of advice to be careful were the best I could share to console myself and him. What rings true here is there will be some time in one's life when you meet someone who can make your life difficult.

In his final game, I have never seen a player more physically exhausted. Marc Splaver had been very diligent in telling Kermit the importance of getting good grades and scoring 20 points and 20 rebounds a game. The team was determined to give Kermit all the support he needed to achieve this without neglecting what was in the best interest of the team, which was to secure a win. This helped me to appreciate how our efforts to coach this group of individuals was not only a success but also extremely rewarding.

Joe Boylan

In 1969 I was the American University freshman coach. At that time the basketball program and the current varsity team was a disaster, and this is an understatement. This was my first time coaching a college team, and I found it was a different set from coaching in a public high school. Head coach Tom Young had been my brother's college coach, and we had a history. This was an incredible time in American history and the history of Washington, DC. The changes in the world at large had a major impact on all Americans had spilled over to American University campus.

I was told by Coach Young about the freshman players recently recruited. Tom Rowe, who was the first freshman to get a scholarship from Pennsylvania; Frank Witucki, from Tom's hometown outside of Pittsburg; Bob Rosenfeld, a big man from New Jersey; and a kid named Kermit Washington, really skinny, six feet and five a half inches, 160 pounds, and who had played football and tennis in high school.

The first time I saw Kermit was when he was trying out for a DC all-star team. He was the last player to be cut. There were several good local talents, so this was truly a compliment and acknowledgment of his level of play. All the other ballplayers wore nicely coordinated outfits, and Kermit stood out by wearing all-white gym shorts and a white T-shirt.

It is interesting to note that every player on our freshman team got along well with one another. The genuine comradery was felt by everyone, and it helped to solidify relationships both on and off the court. There was no jealousy or backbiting; it was an "all of one and one for all" group motto. Freshmen at that time could not play on the varsity team. Unfortunately, students were often influenced to use marijuana. Drugs were a campus share date, and some players on the varsity roster were all too eager and willing to accept any on multiple occasion's invitation to explore and experience this drug.

Kermit had an innate ability to rebound. This knack was unusual in that I have never seen it demonstrated by any other player. At six feet six inches, he would jump up and grab ball and with quickness and agility get back down and run with the ball. Although freshmen could not play on the varsity team, Coach Young held several practices between the freshmen and varsity players. The two best varsity players, Gordon Stiles and Vince Shaftmeister, were bullies on the court. They took great delight in beating up Kermit. I often had the coach stop practice to remind him that Kermit was not a punching bag and to tell his big guys to leave him alone. Kermit never complained and stood up to their overly physical play and soon earned their respect.

On one occasion our freshmen played a game against Lefty Driesell's University of Maryland team. Kermit played so well that one of the University of Maryland assistant coaches told me, "That kids is going to be good." How right he was. A lot of people with good work ethics helped to influence Kermit in positive ways. Dan Gable, world-famous wrestler from the University of Iowa, told Kermit that working hard had to be as important as breathing air. His motto was "My opponent might be better than me, but they didn't work harder than me." Kermit lifted weights before practice and then ran the seven- to eight-story-dorm stairs wearing a weight vest every night. I often think if it were possible to package this routine, he would be a millionaire today.

Kermit didn't put anything in his body that would hurt him. He never smoked, did drugs, nor took a sip of alcohol. Pulitzer Prize–winner David Halberstam was a personal friend of Portland Trailblazer coach Jack Ramsey. He was taking a break from his usual nonfiction pieces about world events and venturing out to investigate the lifestyle of NBA players. He told us that he had spoken with and interviewed a great deal of people in his professional writing career. Kermit was one of the most interesting people he had ever known. Kermit was interested in what was happening in the world around him and was always curious.

Kermit helped transform American University from a subpar basketball program to play in the NIT. Just thinking of this, you must admit this feat was an extraordinary accomplishment. Only forty-two college teams make it to the post-conference tournament. Kermit energized the freshman team; he started as a sophomore, junior, and senior and outrebounded an entire team in many games. In his final game for American University our win against Georgetown University was truly incredible. Kermit scored 40 points and grabbed 26 rebounds. He is the last college player to score 20 points and 20 rebounds in his college career. A great deal of credit must be given to Marc Splaver, the sports information director. On February 4, 1973, Splaver had printed on the front page of the sports section in the Washington Post newspaper a piece entitled, "Washington Leads an American Revolution" and created and distributed the 20/20 eye chart using all the letters in Kermit's name. Marc was relentless in his efforts to make sure all of America knew about the integrity Kermit had displayed during his four years at American University.

It was without a doubt that Kermit was the most known and recognizable person on the American University campus. He made me a better coach, and I saw what a person with focus, purpose, and pride could do. Kermit was always someone who knew how to get things done and stood out as the person who knew where they came from and knew where they were going to end up.

The players on freshman and varsity teams from 1969 to 1973 were an interesting group of individuals. Players ranged from Kermit to the likes of Lloyd Mayes and Johnny Lloyd. It was a transformation from different personalities to a cohesive group of lifelong friends. I began my American University career as the freshman coach, and when Tom Davis accepted the head coaching position at Lafayette, I moved up to the assistant coach spot. Billy Jones, the first African American to attend an ACC school, joined us.

Of all the honors and recognitions Kermit received, the most impressive was to be selected first-team all-American with the likes of David Thompson, Bill Walton, Ernie DiGregorio, and Doug Collins. Also, the way in which Kermit was able to come back after an incident which resulted in hate mail and threats is remarkable. It amazes me how mean and nasty people can be and echoes the desire of the youth in the late '60s and early '70s to revolutionize the world. Those years were tumultuous, and the intense desire to make much-needed changes spilled over to the American University campus and student body, leaving a lasting impression on all those who were living in the world during that time.

Bob Rosenfeld–Rosie

I only played one year of basketball in high school and had knee surgery my senior year. We had a great high school team and had seven division-recognized players being highly recruited. When coaches Young and Davis came to my school (which was actually in the spring as they were just newly hired coaches for American University), I had already signed a letter of intent with New York University. A good friend of mine, Charlie Blank, was attending University of Maryland, and he told them about me. I liked their proposal and asked Coach Davis if there might be a way of my getting out of this commitment. The coach from New York University, Lou Racini, was upset but did release me. New York University two years later discontinued their Division 1 program, so my decision proved to be a fortuitous one for me.

When I arrived at American University, I didn't know many of the players except that one Frank Witucki was from Coach Young's hometown, as was a later recruit, Bill Demharter. My first year at American University, there were four scholarship players, and I arrived on the Wednesday before classes started on the following Monday. On that Monday, I went home with mononucleosis. Four days I had been sleeping fifteen to sixteen hours a day. My roommate Frank Witucki also slept fifteen to sixteen hours a day because he was homesick. I was able to return to school by the end of October. By that time, I had missed a lot of school, and the team players didn't have a chance to get to know me yet. I had to reintroduce myself and try to catch up both in schoolwork and on the court.

Our freshman year marked the ending of the Vietnam War, and our campus being in the nation's capital was a focal point for college demonstrations against the war. Our campus was filled with students from around the country leading and organizing protest marches and demonstrations. I had only six credits for the first semester and had to load up on classes for the second semester, taking twenty-two credits. Our professors were staunch supporters of all efforts to end the war and establish peace. In acknowledgment of our determination to be heard, they were supportive in that they allowed us to provide a limited amount of schoolwork and in some classes eliminated the need to take a final exam. This was like a gift from above and helped me to catch up on my courses, setting me in line to graduate on time.

One particular morning, standing at Ward Circle, over ten thousand protesters faced the local police department armed with tear gas grenades. Some not-too-bright protester started to throw rocks at the police, and then in retaliation they began to throw tear gas grenades onto the campus. In my attempt to escape with a friend, Mark Lowenstein (now Mark Grabow), while running back into the campus, we tripped over each other, landing but a few feet from a tear gas grenade. The sting we felt in our eyes was painful and memorable.

In those days' freshmen were not eligible to play on the varsity team. We had four scholarship players and two or three walk-ons, Marty Yam, Dave Kusher, and David Carter. When my first year ended, I didn't want to go home. I wanted to stay in DC as I had fallen in love with the American University and the DC area. That first summer I worked for two weeks at Mount Saint Mary's basketball camp with Kermit. When the day's activities were over, Kermit and I would pass the football back and forth on campus. Now I really felt I had a good arm and could throw the football seventy-five yards, but Kermit was really good and threw the football eighty yards, and he still weighed about 175 pounds at that time. I never saw anyone that skinny with an arm so strong; of course, he did eventually weigh 220 pounds two years later. The nuns yelled at us to get off the hill where we had been tossing the football to one another, and that put an end to our football-passing days.

One Friday of the two-week camp, we played a pickup game against Gettysburg campers. This school had a good reputation, but Kermit and I kicked butt. This was when I really knew that Kermit was a great player as he dominated every aspect of the game. Returning to campus, a few of us were playing pranks on each other. Kermit would throw water on us. In return my roommate Witucki rubbed two clothing hangers together, and when Kermit opened the door to our room, Witucki pressed the warmed hangers on his arm. He got a nasty burn and still has a scar on his arm to this day. The pranks abruptly ended.

At the end of the season, Kermit invited a few of us to come and play ball on his famous Rudolph playground. I was amazed to find the court was surrounded by three hundred people. I had never seen so many people watching a pickup game in all the years I had played on my home turf. These were not just fans but die-hard followers who booed us as we entered the court. Not only was the talent on the court acknowledged but loyally supported and appreciated by the onlookers.

Beginning our sophomore year, we kept hearing about all the big-time freshmen Lefty Driesell had coming to the University of Maryland (Lenny Elmore and Tom McMillen being two). Kermit and a few other teammates got tired of hearing all the hoopla, so we decided to drive over University of Maryland and challenge these players to a pickup game. The actual time frame was in September, just prior to the start of the regular college season or any official practice. We walked into Cole Field like the Magnificent Seven, minus one. Mentally and physically armed and ready for the challenge, we were warming up shooting baskets waiting for the enemy to appear. Within twenty minutes the assistant coach George Raveling entered the field house, yelling at the top of his lungs, "Get the f—— out of this gym." To establish our "right" to be there, we replied, "We are varsity players from American University and want to play a pickup game against your guys." These words were not like a soothing melody. In fact, it seemed to escalate his anger and aggressive actions. Our agenda had been quickly changed from playing a pickup game to running for our lives. If we were all literally armed with guns, Raveling would have emptied his with such accuracy we would never have left the court alive.

Our sophomore year started, and we ended the season with a 13–12 record. During the Christmas tournament, we played in Erie, Pennsylvania, against Brown University from Providence, Rhode Island. We lost, but I had a great game, scoring 14 points with 1 rebound. After the game Coach Young told me if I didn't get more rebounds, I would lose my starting position. I asked how I could grab more rebounds when Kermit always pulled down 20 every game. I had to remind him there were only so many rebounds to get, and Kermit was there getting most, if not all, of them.

Wanting to keep my position, I was learning I had a much better game with my back to the basket. After having a really good game against Brown, sports reporters expressed an interest in asking me to give an interview, but I wasn't willing to give them the time of day. It soon became a tradition with those of us who were only asked for an interview if our performance stood out. Kermit thought this was really funny, especially since one reporter was Maury Povich's father and the other reporter was a well-known sports TV reporter, Werner Wolf. It didn't matter who they were related to or what notoriety they had; I was just not going there.

After games played at Fort Myer, a favorite watering hole on campus was the Tavern. Campus life was indeed a wonderland as I had attended a male-only high school, and it definitely did not have an establishment like this. I will admit, I loved to drink beer, so I was truly happy with this additional feature of college life. There were times when Coach Young would join us, and for three hours we would pull down beers. The very next day in practice (as we practiced every day including Sunday), the coach made me run his twenty-eight-second drill after saying it looked like I had been out late last night drinking. (He was buying the beers.) On one occasion, we persuaded Kermit to come and watched as he poured his glass of beer on the floor under the table. Kermit never drank. But he would always join us at the Tavern after games for a few hours as we would laugh and break one another's chops—a great group of diverse but terrific teammates.

I remember another occasion junior year. We were in a Christmas tournament in Erie, Pennsylvania. Not a vacation spot to be envied. A couple of us paid one of our managers, Paul Schwartz, to go out and buy us a couple of six-packs of beer. We left them outside our motel room door to stay cold, and the next thing we heard was someone laughing and running away with our beer. It was Coach Young, who like beer as much or if not more than we did.

Practice was like watching a TV reality show. Johnny Lloyd would tease Lloyd Mayes about his very close veins instead of varicose veins. Kermit would block every one of our shots if he was upset with you. Billy Ulbin was pushed around by Steve Garrett. Coach Young would sometimes have to bring his two children to practice, and they would throw whiffle balls at us while we were doing drills. Coach was a stickler for using every minute wisely and ended weekend practice at six fifteen. Now you must consider that the à la carte dining room closed at six thirty, and we had to literally run to get there before the doors closed.

That Sophomore year we played some really quality teams: St. John, Syracuse, Duquesne, Old Dominion had Dave Twardzick, and Virginia Tech had Allen Bristow. We ended the year 13–12. Our last game was against George Washington at Fort Meyer. Odd enough, we both played our home games there, so it was a "home team versus home team" game.

Every year Coach Young brought in more talented local DC players. Our team had bonded, and despite Johnny Lloyd's daily verbal comments junior year, we all stuck up for one another. It could easily be noticed that we had different interests, but at times Johnny crossed the line and landed in Coach Young's doghouse. This resulted in his being kicked off the team for the remainder of my junior year.

Funny story, when Johnny came back as a junior (my senior year), he came up to me after practice one day and thanked me and another teammate, Lenny Lockhart. When I asked him why, he said that since

Lenny and I were always getting into trouble with Coach Young, it took the pressure off him to constantly be on his best behavior.

At the start of my senior year I went in and had a heart-to-heart talk with Coach about my request to have more playing time. Now I understand that as coaching was his livelihood, he had to play the players who would provide the best effort to help him sustain his job and possibly move on. For when faced the choice to play one player who would be leaving and another who would be returning and both players were comparable in ability, it now makes sense his choice to use me when needed but not give me a starting position. I had to face the fact that Johnny Lloyd, Wilbur Thomas, and Peter DeHaven were the future for American University basketball.

Every one of us graduated on time, and during the year we lost Frank Witucki and Tom Rowe. Frank was still homesick after all these years, and Tom found a true love for art and a girl who had that similar passion for art and for him. Earlier in the year we played Fairleigh Dickinson University from Teaneck, New Jersey in Madison Square Garden. The night after the game, my sister's boyfriend had a connection with the Playboy club. Even though Coach Young gave us a curfew of eleven, my sister's boyfriend had arranged for six of us to have dinner and snack. There were two of my teammates and me, and we each had dates.

We waited until ten, and when ten thirty came around, we snuck out the hotel and went to the Playboy club. We had a great evening, and after feeling we were going to return unnoticed, we walked into the hotel at 1:00 a.m. And when we entered the lobby, we ran into Coach Young, literally bumping into him in the lobby. Coach didn't say one word, but his look was very intense. As it was, if looks could kill, I would have been dead and buried for five hundred years.

I will always remember finding out that ABA teams were trying to recruit Kermit and offered him money to leave American University for the glamour of professional ball at the end of this junior year. In those days Julius Irving led the way and influenced many college athletes to follow his lead to leave college early and enter the professional basketball ranks. Everyone was both happy and impressed that Kermit was loyal to the school and, most important, to his teammates. I particularly remember the very night he refused to sign a contract, I had to lend him fifty cents so he could do his laundry. His decision made college life much more enjoyable for everyone.

Of all the games, I played for American University, our final game against Georgetown University was the most fun and memorable. At that point Kermit and I were the only two seniors left on the team. It was like all the stars were aligned that night; everything came together in the universe that night, and the magic was felt by everyone who had the privilege to experience it.

I tell everyone to this day Kermit and I combined for 42 points and 32 rebounds as we crushed Georgetown. Oh, and by the way, I had 2 points and 4 rebounds.

Lloyd Mayes

From the life and times of Lloyd Mayes, who is known for attending University of Minnesota on a hockey scholarship.

I grew up a skinny kid in NW, Washington, DC. My "hood" was considered the worst area of NW – The infamous 14th & U Street corridor. Despite its negative notoriety of the 60's, U Street of the 1940's and 50's was considered a pretty progressive and thriving moderate income, middle class Black neighborhood.

It was called Black Broadway due to its variety of theaters, clubs, movie houses, hotels, upscale eateries, speak-easy's and the like. It was a vibrant enclave for Black life in the Nation's Capital. On any given day or night, you might see the famous and near-famous strolling up and down U Street. Duke Ellington, James Brown, James Baldwin, Count Basie, Ella Fitzgerald, Pearl Bailey were regulars on U Street, as well as Sam Cook, Jackie Wilson and Harry Belafonte and more...the Who's Who of Black America paraded the boulevards of my neighborhood.

I spent countless hours playing the usual sports like baseball and football, but not basketball. I played any sport which involved throwing a ball. Despite being a skinny kid, I had a great throwing arm but I never played basketball, primarily because there were no nearby courts, nor hoops in the alleys where I spent most of my childhood playing and fighting.

It was in tenth grade, at Cardozo High School, that I attended my first high school basketball game. When I saw it, I knew I was hooked, I still am! I was immediately impressed by the game and the athletes. They resembled gifted ballet dancers, demonstrating grace, yet strength and style, as they zoomed up and down the court, dribbling, passing and shooting the round ball with so much speed and skill. I knew I had to learn to play this game!

After this eye, opening event, I began to work at basketball. But, to me, this wasn't work....it was a joy! I had found my passion and I slowly began to develop my skills! For the next year and a half, I played nonstop on the playgrounds and in a few Saturday morning youth leagues. However, I was dumb as hell on the court and a victim of constant 3 second calls, but I kept trying. Finally, someone told me what the three-second lane was and to, "stay the hell out of it." It took a year for me to comprehend what "camping out" in the lane meant. By then, I was so scared I would hear a whistle that I would run through the lane like my drawers were on fire. Like I said, Dumb as hell! Since most kids start playing ball at 8 or 9 years old, my starting to play at 16, meant my skills were dubious, at best.

Coming home to D.C., for the summer meant that I could play summer basketball against other college and pro players in leagues or on the playgrounds of the city. To me, there was no better basketball in the country than D.C. There wasn't a quadrant of the city that you could not find Division 1 caliber basketball on the playgrounds. The competition was fierce throughout the city! Everybody could hoop, you could "ball" in Northwest, Southwest, Northeast or Southeast, on ANY playground and be served up an ass-kicking for breakfast, lunch, dinner and dessert, anytime, anywhere in Washington.

D.C. playgrounds had already produced many legendary collegiate and pro players and the pipeline was replete with players "waiting in the wings" for their turn in the national limelight. Some notable players were Elgin Baylor, Dave Bing, John Tresvant, George Leftwich, James Fox, Ollie Johnson, John Austin, Willie Jones, John Thompson, Tony Upson, William Brockenberry and Genie Littles, all talents from the mid 50's to early 60's. They were soon followed, in the mid 60's by Jerry Chambers, Tom Little, Phillip 'Bo' Scott,

Bernard Williams, Dickie Hood, Austin Carr, Leapin' Louie West, Collis Jones, Joe 'Radar' Carr, Wendell Hart, Sid Catlett, Andrew White, Bob Whitmore, Billy Gaskins, Andrew Agnew, Ed Epps, 'Biggie' Cunningham, Reggie Green, Harvey Sebreeze, Louie Grillo and Jim McBride. Late 60's and early 70's saw the likes of 'Young Turks' like 'Easy' Steve Higgins, Garland 'Big Garloo' Williams, James Brown, 'Apple' Milam, Tim Basset, Ronnie Hogue, Michael Bossard, Curtis Perry, The Campbell Brothers, Kevin Tatum, Howard 'Satch' Matthews, The Dunmore Brothers, Glen Price, Floyd Lewis, Donnell Bullock, Donald Washington and Kermit. This is just a sampling of the talented players throughout the City that were waiting to test and punish anyone coming home from college or the pros, every summer. You made your reputation as a player off of some and some made their reputation off of YOU! Every day was like the Final Four and it was 'sink or swim' in the deep waters of D.C. summer basketball.

Not having grown up in a rural area, I needed to attend a college located in a city. I didn't want to return to DC and attend a school there as it felt awkward to do so. I waited to receive a letter of intent from the University of Denver, in Denver, Colorado. I was either going to return to the University of Minnesota or attend the University of Denver. Coach Tom Davis was visiting family and read about my interest in signing with the University of Denver in the local papers. He contacted me and mentioned the article, and even though he had never heard about me, he decided to come visit with me at the University of Minnesota. Afterward, American University began to actively recruit me.

Returning home for the summer in mid-June, my mother told me American University coaches were calling due to an interest in recruiting me. Despite my intention to never return to DC for schooling, when Coach Davis requested the opportunity to meet with me and extended an invitation to visit American University, I accepted. This was how I met Kermit. Kermit was a passenger in the coach's car parked outside my mother's house and would *not* get out. He had the windows closed and the doors locked and no air-conditioning on in over-ninety-degree temperature in the hot and humid summer in

DC. Aware of the reputation of the neighborhood, he later told me my block looked like a war zone with dead dolls that could have been real people. I will agree it was a rough inner-city neighborhood, but he was a lot bigger than me, and I had survived. And it was truly in the heart of the ghetto, but it was still home.

I walked out of the house and approached the car to introduce myself. He seemed pleasant enough, but it wasn't until I met him on my campus visit that we got a chance to get to know one another. Every recruiting rule was violated—I did not visit while school was in session, as it was summer when students were out of school. The campus was empty, except for a few students attending summer school. Coach planned for a meal at Mary Graydon Center where I was asked for the transcript of my grades. My GPA was now 3.9 from the University of Minnesota. Twenty minutes later I was told American University was interested in signing me.

After high school, I had no real aspiration for a career. I was fortunate at nineteen that even though drafted, I did not meet the medical requirements. I was declared ineligible due to gout and arthritis. Now I really did not have gout. I was simply still growing. I left high school five feet ten inches, and in college I was six feet three inches and continued to reach six feet six inches. I believe it was growing pains but appreciate the label as it greatly improved my situation in life.

From nowhere I went somewhere. I had just come home for the summer anticipating playing ball all over the city, but I also needed a summer job. Since I was visiting the American University campus, I thought I would I would ask about employment. A few days later, I was offered a summer job on campus, working in the gym's athletic cage or equipment room with Kermit. It was great getting to know him, to learn about the team and school and to play ball together every day, during that summer. The hours we spent together helped us develop a bond and a true personal relationship that we still enjoy to this day. American University's coaches, Tom Young and Tom Davis, were always cordial and didn't bug me about changing my mind about Denver University. They never used the summer job as an inducement for me to attend American University. They let me make up my own mind. I finally decided to attend American two weeks before school opened, having not heard from Denver.

I accepted the scholarship to American University. On a Friday, then, over the weekend, I got a letter from Denver offering the scholarship I'd been waiting for. The following Monday, I took the letter to Coach Young, who told me that I was free to sign with Denver if I wanted to go. He said that since I'd always told him where I wanted to go to school, he would respect my decision. However, playing ball with Kermit and meeting some of the other local players over the summer was instrumental in making my decision to attend American University easier. Nevertheless, the biggest factor in my change of heart was the opportunity for my family to finally see me play Division 1 college basketball. That said, without a doubt, I would *NEVER* have gone to American University if I had not met Kermit.

My usual playground haunts varied during the week, but weekends it was Luzon (Ft. Stevens) and Rose Park. On Saturday or Sunday morning, players descended on certain courts to slice and dice their way to playground immortality and R-E-S-P-E-C-T!! Legends and reputations were built on these pitched battles so, there was no shortage of competitors or spectators. Luzon, Kelly Miller, Rose Park, all had similar reputations as mythical sites for this trench warfare. During my first week working in American University's "cage" with Kermit, we talked a lot, shot around a lot and played some 1-on-1 in the gym. When the weekend arrived, we agreed to meet at Luzon on Saturday morning.

Kermit introduced me to the rigors of the legendary Rudolph playground. I was extremely impressed by the crowds and quality of athletic ability but more so about Kermit's talent. When I arrived with my cousin, Kermit was already playing. There were several notable college players in the game with him. Having never seen Kermit play, as I walked toward the court, my eyes were following Kermit's actions. I wanted to see if he could swim with the 'sharks' in the deep end of the pool. I saw Kermit block a shot, get a tip in and finish with a two-hand slam before I could sit down on the sidelines. "*DAMN....* *young-un can PLAY*!!" Watching him play, I noticed his ability to grab rebounds and never put the ball on the floor. I was taken back that with his first few attempts making shots was a challenge. He put the ball in the air but it missed the net, and seemed to struggle making a simple lay-up. I had to take a moment and analyze this. I then noted he was more focused on being a team player and not a star. When he was free and open, he did make shots. However, if he forced a shot and missed he grabbed the rebound and passed the ball. He got the ball working inside, and I soon realized I would have a partner on the court that would I count on, which was not the case at the University of Minnesota. I like having a strong post up around. Kermit was not a selfish player, and it should be noted he couldn't dribble a lick. Thankfully, he never put the ball on the floor.

Being there was an established hierarchy on Rudolph's playground rules, when told by future superstars what to do, you simply did and it worked. With great players like Billy Gaskin, Adrian Dantley, Austin Carr, Collis Jones, Sid Cattlit, and Aubrey Nash, to name a few, taking direction was the natural course of events to follow. Kermit could run the floor. He was fierce on the boards and not intimidated by these current college stars and future NBA greats. He was unaware they were more impressed with his skills and talent than he was of theirs. I regarded Kermit as a diamond in the rough who exploded on the playground scene. This Rudolph playground was hallowed ground with the most difficult competition in the inner city. If you were looking to play against Division 1 basketball players, you could find it on any city playground. DC was overflowing with talent.

As we visited playgrounds, talent was wherever we went. These talented basketball players were being recognized across the country and representing the DC area. Being fierce, able to handle the ball, shoot, quick and tough were all hallmarks to identify the quality of talent in the DC area. Respect was the nature of the game, and everyone came out to play hard and give their best effort. Mutual respect was displayed by all at a level of competition not found in your normal pickup playground games. Once participating in this level of play, I knew at American University we could achieve a level of respect after making a name on these local playgrounds.

After work Kermit expressed an interest in playing ball after work, and on weekends I stepped up to the plate and borrowed a blue Volkswagen and collected other teammates, Mike Lynch and Mike Hill. We drove to Rockville, Maryland; Fredrick, Virginia; and wherever the competition was available. At one location, the court ended in a yard with clothes hanging on a line. At one playground, we played against Kenny Boyd, who attended Boston University in Boston, Massachusetts.

Kermit never wanted to play ball all day. Two hours on the court was more than enough given the humidity and intense heat during summers in DC. His excuse was that unlike me, he could not bear the heat as I was like those Africans who could run and play all day long. Luzon, Watts, Hillcrest, Ridge Road, and Kelly Villa offered no shade. We were like young gunslingers that arrived to play ball and make a statement to leave a lasting impression. Monday through Thursday we could visit Rudolph; Friday was off limits. No one played ball on a Friday night. Saturday and Sunday, it was open season anyplace from Luzon to any open court. You woke up to play ball knowing the best competition in the city was going to be somewhere eager and waiting to play with and against you.

D.C. playgrounds had already produced many legendary collegiate and pro players and the pipeline was replete with players "waiting in the wings" for their turn in the national limelight. Some notable players were:

Players such as Johnny Lloyd came from Anacostia, and attending American University changed his life for the better. American University could do the same for so many local players. In fact, that is how Georgetown established their reputation. John Thompson prided himself on acquiring local talent. With this approach Georgetown was recognized as a powerhouse with such players as Patrick Ewing. The best basketball every played at American University was in the late '70s and early '80s, serving the black athletes well. All who attended benefitted in every sense of the word. This could have been the start of a legacy. Athletes who met entrance requirement would handle the academics.

I have to say that I enjoyed being around Kermit, but I did not like his roommate Jerry Gaston. Jerry was a local athlete who was a casualty of the "wimp factor." Jerry wanted to be tougher than he was. He had no game and no name. He tried out for the team and later became the manager for the team. As a manager, he never did this job. When you were called to the bench, he didn't move to let you have a seat near the coaches; he didn't have water and a towel for you. He simply sat enjoying having front-row seating. Once, we were in Syracuse, New York, playing Saint John's. It was cold and windy out. Jerry drove us to practice and the game. He never warmed up the car and was solely concerned on whether he had managed to make his Afro hair style as full as possible. For Jerry, did not have a lot of hair on his head, in fact he was losing more and more every day. You couldn't tell him that as his self-esteem was defined by how large he could make his thinning hair appear to be. He primped in the car's rear view mirror even though the ants could hear our teeth chattering. He was like a jock sniffer; he wanted to be around athletes but wasn't one himself.

Coach Davis had become aware of my stats, but Coach Young had not seen me play and invited me to campus and play one-on-one against Mike Lynch. Coach considered Mike to be the best player he had in my position, and I destroyed him on the court. He never was able to outshine my ability. I was determined for that to never happen as I was fighting for a chance that I knew was offered, and I needed to take full advantage or lose out and be denied. Having averaged 16 rebounds a game before coming to American University, I was not afraid to mix it up.

Mike Lynch came from Kensington, Maryland, a suburb. We both made the team, and I regret that Johnny Lloyd, Mike Lynch, Mike Hill, and I were never on the court to run together during my four years at American University. Although we were quick and fast, Coach Young was more of a half court coach. He already knew we could run like racehorses; he feared this would lead to more turn-overs. This approach took something away from players and did not add anything to the game.

My senior year was rocky to say the least. This was not among my happiest and fondest memories. I must also say I was not really happy. But I have no regrets about any of my four years at American University. I will always remember a friend whom I lost in a tragic accident. Mary Sorenson. Mary was very helpful in making me feel welcomed in a predominately white school. Keep in mind, I was forbidden to date white girls. At American University, *everyone* was color blind. Friendship were lost or found based on common interest, and conversations among the students were normal, natural, and enjoyable. Mary loved sports and athletes. She enjoyed cheering on everyone as they went about playing whatever sport or activity they were engaged in. The end of my junior year, we were standing outside the dorms, and she told me she was sad to realize that the year was coming to an end and our final year at American University was to follow. For after our senior year ended, all the people she really enjoyed being with would be leaving. She grew tearful, knowing we might never see one another again.

I left American University and played ball in Europe but made a special visit to see Mary before going. Upon my return after that year away, I learned that Mary had died when she returned to her burning apartment to rescue her puppy. I had gone to the gym to play a game and asked if she was still in town living off campus. This news greatly saddened me.

Kermit was the major reason for my attending American University. If not for him, I would *not* have stayed in DC but pursued my need to venture out away from home. There are so many stories I could tell that have nothing to do with Kermit and basketball but do tell about Kermit and life.

All in all, I am very grateful for the fundamentals I learned from being coached by Tom Young. It made me a more solid player, and when playing in Europe, I coached and applied these fundamentals. I found myself doing things I didn't want to do, which made me more disciplined and a better coach. I knew where players needed to be on the court, where the action was, and if not there, to keep driving to find it.

Mike Hill

Growing up in Frederick, Maryland at six foot one inch, playing the guard position, I was recruited by coaches Tom Davis and Billy Jones from Prince George's Community College and played two years. On the court, they felt my style of play would complement the formation of a revised team as seniors, Gordon Stiles and Vince Shaftmeister would be graduating the following year. They flew me down to DC from Hagerstown, Maryland, nicknamed, the Hub City and given a tour of the campus. My first time flying I felt like I was sitting on top of the world. Checking into the Fredrick Airport filled me with both awe and excitement. The ticket agent was very helpful and directed me to the gate area and noticing my lack of travel knowledge, took the time to explain to me some basic travel tips to make my trip both enjoyable and hassle free.

Finding my seat on the plane was made easier as the ticket agent explained the numbering system and where to look on the overhead bin for the letters which let you know if you had a window, middle or aisle seat assignment. Most passengers ignored the stewardess explanation of seat belts and evacuation procedures. Not me, I listened intently and followed along using the pamphlet in the pocket of the seat in front of me. When asked if I wanted a beverage I was please to get a full can of a soft drink and two packets of peanuts. I ate one packet and put the other in my pocket for later.

When the plane landed and we exited the plane the one stewardess asked me how I enjoyed my flight. I told her it was great and then asked how to find out where someone would meet you once entering the terminal. She was about to explain when a fellow passenger invited me to walk with him as he was being met by his family in the seating area directly outside the doors leading into the airport. I was relieved to find Coach Davis and Jones who were waiting for me. The drive from the airport to American University seemed short as both coaches shared what my visit would be like and mentioned we would be eating at Mary Graydon Center on the campus.

Having heard so much about the legendary Gordon Stiles, the star center on the varsity team, I inquired if he was on campus. It was extremely appealing to think I would be able to play every varsity game and scrimmage with him during practice or better yet play with him on the court. This initiation into the college level of basketball of playing with returning sophomores Kermit and Bob (Rosie) Rosenfeld.

Meeting Kermit, before the start of Kermit's sophomore year, I was an incoming junior at American University was during the summer of 1970. We worked together as counselors at Mt Saint Mary's College basketball camp. Fred Carter, a current Baltimore Bullet NBA player, was an alumnus and was invited to speak to the group. He asked if anyone in attendance was willing to play against him. The students volunteered Kermit and the game was on. Kermit killed him and being mortified, Carter got angry and wanted to fight. Rosie and I helped settle things down and managed to salvage Carter's broken ego. That summer we also worked together with Bob (Rosie) Rosenfeld at a basketball camp in Gettysburg, Pennsylvania.

As a counselor, Wally Walker was a small kid under my supervision. He later became a big star for the University of Virginia and played in the NBA. After our daily supervision of students, we spent our free time getting to know one another and playing basketball. I had officiated in local high school basketball teams and this helped in making calls on the court as we played. I later held the positon of a junior college coach, and my years of playing playground ball, college ball, and seeing the game from the perspective of an official proved invaluable.

Senior year during the 1971-1972 season my role was varsity captain. Grand Funk Railroad was one of my favorite group at the time and since it was constantly being played, it became my signature piece. I did however listen to the Stylistics, and the Fifth Dimension to broaden my music repertoire.

Being a college student in DC during the Vietnam War and the height of anti-war protests, one day while walking to class on campus, students had gathered at Ward Circle to participate in a peaceful demonstration. Somehow things got out of hand, and a potentially dangerous situation developed into an explosion of mixed emotions. Students were running away from the outlining grassy knoll to escape tear gas canisters and agitated policemen following closely on their footsteps. The frenzy included a policeman running over a student with his motorcycle. He stopped only because he fallen off his bike, not to check on the status of the injured student. My mind was filled with questions, the most memorable being, "What did I get myself into?"

As the days settled down to a more routine style of college life, I was amazed to find Kermit diligently running the stairs using a twenty-pound weight vest. He never missed a night and was a weight lifting junky. Although his efforts were paying off and I admired his tenacity, personally this was just not something for me to join him in doing.

As a junior year, I started along with Mike Lynch and Lloyd Mayes. Both were interesting characters with Mike being the quiet stay to himself type and Lloyd, affectionately known at string bean, wore his crotched hat with a tassel, carrying a bag – we dubbed his purse, always having something to say about anybody and everybody. It was good hanging out with Josh Rosenfeld and constantly arguing with Jerry Gaston our team assistant manager. Lloyd would invite Kermit, Rosie and other teammates to join in playground games and we played against Kenny Boyd from Boston University.

I got my nickname "Black Moses" from Kermit after seeing the 1971 Issac Hayes album cover from with that title released in November 1971. I drove an older model convertible car with a top that was stuck in the down position, leaving any contents exposed and providing lots of fresh air especially in the winter. DC is known for its cold winters, and the expression the Hawk is Out will always remind me of my college years driving a convertible car without a working top. I had to put a warm blanket over my head to keep from catching pneumonia.

My roommates were Chris Heslin, a long-distance runner, and John Shakerman. Chris was quiet but outgoing and Shakerman a stay at home type with a girlfriend, Merrie who was a constant guest. My freshman year was enjoyable as I got to start and play a lot. Moving up to varsity my sophomore year I became disillusioned and started to lose interest in the game. Watching a game from the stands was not the same as watching from the bench. So as not to lose my enthusiasm for the game I decided to broaden my options and get more involved with campus life. Junior year brought the opportunity to contribute my ball handling skills, help with a few rebounds as I was not afraid to play in traffic being assigned to guard the opposing team's best offensive guard.

Graduating from American University held mixed emotions. Successfully earning a college degree helped to open doors for employment but it meant the end of my true love for the game. I didn't touch a basketball after graduating.

Playing on a team with Kermit was an incredible opportunity. Watching a young talent emerge into a star athlete who was a true team player was unforgettable. Setting his goal to be a 20-20 scorer and rebounder never took president over a team victory and individual game accomplishments for his teammates. Watching from the stands to provide moral support in his final game against Georgetown, my only regret was not being on the court to play with him to as he reached his goal.

Josh Rosenfeld

In 1970, I was an entering freshman at American University and Kermit was a sophomore. The move to DC from New Jersey leaving my family and friends was made easier by meeting with head coach Tom Young and head manager Paul Schultz. I had been the manager of my high school team and wanted to be the manager for American University's varsity team. After this meeting with the coach and head manager while returning to my dorm room I distinctly remember watching a rather tall student walking down the woods between Hughes and McDowell Hall. My first impression was that this student reminded me of a high school classmate, John Shumate.

In those years' freshmen, couldn't play on varsity, and when I watched this tall guy later to be known to me as Kermit Washington, I would constantly compare him in my mind to John. In a pregame scrimmage between returning varsity stars against the current varsity team, I watched Gordon Stiles, Willie Jones, and other former students match up with the current team. Kermit was bigger than these guys and played so well it was obvious to me I was about to become a part of something special.

There was a lot going on in the world at that time with antiwar protests, and many college campuses embraced this "peace and love" mantra with fierce conviction and determination to make their voices heard. The campus was united in politics and in sports. Protestors came from colleges universities around the country and were welcomed on campus. There was one incident when a student threw something at a policeman which sent the police rushing on campus and exploding tear gas canisters. Kermit and a lot of us were sitting on the wall near Ward Circle and fell backward, crawling to get away from the tear gas. Running into the center of campus, everyone was anxious to avoid the noxious effects of the tear gas. Needless to say, with so many guests on the campus, it resulted in invitations to join parties where free love and free drugs were ever present. This open-door policy, both literally and figuratively, are still legendary today.

As a sophomore, Kermit was the dominant force on the court. Every game, he was focused on going after every rebound he could get. My job was to keep stats, and Marc Splaver, the current sports information director, was adamant that we collect accurate numbers and not to do any padding as Kermit did not need any help. By the third or fourth game of the season, the *Washington Post*, a local paper, sent a reporter to cover American University's game and Kermit's rebound stats in particular.

Dunking was not allowed in those years, and this required taking three to four shots with one or two rebounds to pin a field goal low for an inside player. At halftime, the *Washington Post* had Kermit for 12 rebounds. As Marc was concerned with Kermit's field goal percentage, some rebounds were not counted, and with Kermit's jumping ability to make more than one attempt to grab a rebound by the end of the game, our stats were validated. The NCAA also sent a representative to attend the Drexel game to count rebounds. Splaver had reported 23, but the NCAA representative counted 27. After playing in the game against Saint John's, we had to send a tape of the game to the NCAA, who gave Kermit more rebounds than our stats had reported. There were games, such as Loyola Marymount, when Kermit grabbed more rebounds than the entire opposing team, with a total of 33.

In all my years working with athletes, including my seven years with the Lakers, I have never seen any player do this: Kermit would let a guy take a jump shot, and as the ball went past him, he would block the ball on the backboards. When free throws were missed, he would leap from off the basketball rim, get the rebound, and dunk it. The crowd went crazy. This was in college American University versus Kings College in Philadelphia. On the road, we taped games, and we had to send this tape into the NCAA, and the points scored were not disputed. When shots were missed, inside players went back up for the rebound. If dunking had been allowed in those days, Kermit would have scored more points being more of a leaper than the power forward he became his sophomore year.

Back then there was no ESPN, and American University never played a game on television. There were no region telecasts, for perhaps the exception of the Duquesne game. With little to no exposure, getting Kermit's name and accomplishments out there was masterfully engineered through the hard work and professionalism displayed by Marc Splaver. One of the many key publicity ideas Marc designed was the 20/20 eye chart. It was symmetrical and simple with a clear message behind it. This one item played a pivotal role in Kermit's career. This eye chart was displayed on the desk of the college basketball editor; whose role was to calculate votes for the top five athletes to be recognized as first-team all-Americans. He had watched Kermit play in Madison Square Garden against Fairleigh Dickinson from Teaneck, New Jersey and knew him to be a legitimate candidate. However, his vote total was not high enough to be considered for one of the five spots. Considering the names of previous 20/20 players, the editor was so impressed with Kermit's achievements, especially coming from American University. Realizing the significance of leaving Kermit out, he made the executive decision to include him. Both Spalver's incredible genius and Kermit's talent were truly a match made in heaven.

Marc Splaver enjoyed his job as the sports information director for American University and set a standard that would mold and influence the lives of many, but me in particular. Both Kermit and Marc had a lot in common. They set the standard and combined talent, focus, and determination to reach any goal possible. I remember on weekends when the dorm would feature parties on the fifth and sixth floor, and I walked up the stairwell to enjoy this merriment, I would bump into Kermit, who wearing his weight vest would be running up the stairs, sticking to his usual conditioning routine.

There were just some teams American University could not beat. Pennsylvania was the state with teams that were a challenge. Mike Bantom from Saint Joseph's University in Philadelphia, Pennsylvania to this day shared that after playing against Kermit, he returned to his dorm and was harassed by his classmates who raged on him when Kermit blocked five or six of his shots. This motivated Mike to the point that he was more determined than ever to play his best against Kermit.

Kermit's senior year, all five American University varsity starters grew up inside the Beltway. American University had captivated the town. We played home games on the army base gym on Fort Myer.

We would cross over to the state of Virginia carrying kegs of beer. The school's antiwar stand was a direct contrast to the army base philosophy, and it was dreary, run-down, and in dire need of improvements. We played some great games, making major statements to the college basketball scene. Saint John's and Syracuse entered this dismal place undefeated and left with a loss on their record books. At that time players, such as Mel Davis, Bill Shaffer, and Greg Close we notable stars. These were by far among the best teams with acknowledged success in our conference.

Kermit's final game against Georgetown will always be the one game that was truly a fairy tale come true. Kermit needed 40 points to earn the 20/20 title for his college career. Marc Splaver had put all his efforts in featuring the importance of this game and frequently brought it to Kermit's attention. Everyone on campus knew what was at stake. There was standing room only. The fort was packed. Signs, chants, anything and everything imaginable were done to show Kermit how much this game meant to both him and everyone.

Being selected for the NIT was quite an honor. Fans were supportive and were rooting for the underdog. University of Notre Dame in Notre Dame Indiana, and the University of Southern California (USC) in Los Angeles, California, preferred playing American University than the University of Louisville, in Louisville, Kentucky. The first half was not good as American University was down by 23 points. We rallied in the second half and were coming back within five. The crowd grew louder and louder, hoping the odds would fall in our favor. A bad shot was taken and we lost. Kermit still had to score a certain number of points and rebounds and did so. But the defeat was felt by all.

I truly enjoyed my college years at American University and can sincerely say my closest friends to this day were my college classmates.

Johnny Lloyd

Many might call me the "bad boy of the team." In reality, I always focused on academics. The "bad boy" turned out to be a good student, who later became a successful business owner. I did not graduate in the spring with my class. So many people questioned if I ever made that quantum leap. For the record, I graduated from American University that summer with a bachelor of science degree in physical education. I later returned to American University to earn a master's degree in public administration (MPA), two degrees now proudly in my hands.

My life in DC started in an Anacostia apartment building. My parents then moved into a small house in Barry Farms. Although this was by no means the Beverly Hills of DC, our house placed me closer to the basketball courts on the playground. At thirteen years of age I was in love with basketball. My favorite player was Delanore Dunmore. He was a local legend, and my dream was to play just like Delanore. Everybody wanted to be like Delanore. I was fortunate that we established a close relationship. He took me under his wing and became my first mentor.

Spending many hours on the courts shooting free throws and jump shots, I felt I had perfected the craft of playing basketball. Because I was a superstar basketball player, folks in my community looked out for me. No one bothered me; they left me alone. Everyone thought I had a shot at becoming a professional basketball player. That would have been good for the community. With dedication and determination to the game, my basketball skills grew as the direct result of hard work and discipline. While my friends were out partying on weekend nights, I was on the basketball court, alone, perfecting that beautiful jump shot.

Saturday and Sunday mornings, I often visited local playgrounds to play ball with some of the best players in the country: Austin Car, Johnny Jones, Collis Jones, Garland Williams, Warren Armstrong, Sid Catlett, James Brown, Billy Gaston, and Delanore Dunmore.

Attending Anacostia High School, I was fortunate enough to be mentored by the legendary coach Dave Brown, who coached Elgin

Baylor and Dave Bing. Coach Brown taught me all the moves: turn-around jump shot over your right shoulder, turnaround jump shot over your left shoulder, head fakes, the whole ball of wax.

Coach Brown was quite the philosopher. When he talked, I listened. He always told the story about a dog playing on the railroad tracks. A train came by and cut off its tail. When the dog went back to get his tail, another train came along and cut off his head. The moral of the story is don't lose your head over a little tail. Coach Brown's motto was "Everything should be done in moderation."

Thanks, in part to Coach Brown, I played on the 1970 DC all-star team, playing under Coach Armstrong and Coach Billy Coward. What an opportunity!

My senior year in high school, we played Ballou in the first round of the city's high school Christmas tournament. We lost the game. But I outscored every player, and after this game American University scout Billy Jones approached me and asked if I would be interested in signing with American University. At this time, I was being recruited by High Point University, located in High Point, North Carolina, Winston Salem State in Winston-Salem, North Carolina (where Earl Monroe attended), and another school in Texas. I had not really thought about staying in DC. But I told Jones I would think about it. My visit to American University was like visiting a totally different part of the country. Located in uptown DC, when I rode the bus to Glen Echo Park, I would pass the school and once asked what that place was. Traveling down Fox Hall Road, I was amazed to see such beautiful, obviously expensive homes. I wanted to knock on every single door simply to ask if I could see inside. It almost seemed like the backdrop of a movie lot with only the front as a facade. I couldn't believe people actually lived like this.

I signed with American, and my freshman year was a blast. I once asked Art Perry, another freshman who was four to five years older than me and had been in the military, "Where did all these white people come from?" My environment, until this point, had been predominantly African American. I had a few white teachers in high school.

The freshman basketball team had very good players whose winning record and personal accolades showed tremendous potential. We played well together, the student body fully supported us, and we were fun to watch. I was the leading scorer. I averaged 25 points a game. Academically, this first year was difficult as class syllabuses contained so many books that I had not read before and required a lot of effort to catch up and keep up. It felt like my normal homework assignments had quadrupled. My nemesis was grammar. I knew I could master this, but it would take a lot of time and extra effort.

I was excited to move up to the big leagues and play with Kermit Washington. When I first heard, players call him Bird, I thought they nicknamed him that because he could fly. But it was because he was considered skinny. Kermit was a rebounding and shot-blocking machine.

My sophomore year did not turn out as expected. I thought since Kermit was the prolific rebounder and shot blocker and I was a pure shooter and big-time scorer, along with the rest of the guys, it would be a winning combination and we would have a good season. That was not to be. This turned out to present a confusing situation. At this time, I was the all-time leading freshman scorer in American University history. I was six feet one, which was considered to be a big guard at the time, solid as a rock. I could play point guard, shooting guard, I even blocked shots. I could score on anyone, even Kermit sometimes. Relegated to the bench, I was never a starter, just a second stringer. Go figure!

It was all downhill for me after that. Not long after the season started, the coach permanently suspended me from the team. To this day, I do not truly know why. Coach Young was quoted in the *Washington Post* as saying it was a "lot of little things. He just couldn't get along with his teammates. We got to a point where 11 guys were doing what I wanted and Johnny was doing what he wanted."

The coach later called my parents and spoke with my mom. I don't think he knew I was at home that day and heard my mother's response to his conversation. He offered to help me find a place at another school. My mother firmly told him, "My son will not be transferring from American University. This is the best place for him to get a good education." My mama had spoken, and I knew what I had to do. I went to the registrar's office and had a wake-up call. I was behind in credits. I went to Bob Frailey, the athletic director, and asked if I could attend summer school to catch up. He said yes. I hit the books.

I would like to thank Coach Tom Young for forcing me to shift my focus from athletics to academics. When he kicked me off the team, I got a chance to work on what was really important for my future success, my education. (After all, my mom had given me no choice.) Knowledge is valuable. It allows you to be comfortable with yourself and with others.

During my sophomore year, I did not get a chance to really play with Kermit that year. As disappointed as I was, it turned out to be a very, very good learning experience for me.

My junior year, unbeknownst to me, there was a move led by Kermit Washington to have me reinstated on the team. This was a very good year. I was back on the team. It would be a very good team. I also met the young lady who would become my wife. Kermit pulled it off; I'm thankful for that. Not only could Kermit fly, he was Superman.

The decision to reinstate me to the team turned out to be in everyone's best interest, mine, Kermit's, the team, the coach, and the schools. Thank you, Kermit. All these years, I never knew how it happened.

I don't remember when I first met Kermit Washington. I just remember seeing him running up the stairs in the dorm with a weight vest on. I would see him going to class with books in his hand. He always had a pleasant look on his face, like he was happy about something. To this day I wonder what in the world he was so happy about. He epitomized the perfect college student. Kermit looked like a scholar. On road trips, he was always studying. He later became acknowledged as a scholar athlete. Kermit looked like he could be on the student council or the student body president. I respected Kermit as a person and as a player.

Junior year, we were a formidable basketball team. We played like a well-oiled machine: Kermit in the middle, Pete DeHaven and

Wilbur Thomas as forwards, and Steve Garrett and me, Johnny Lloyd, as guards. To me the most memorable game of the season was the Duquesne game. The outcome of which determined if the history of the school would be forever changed. The outcome of this game would determine whether American University would be invited to the National Invitational Tournament. The teams selected would play at Madison Square Garden, and that was a big deal!

On game day, Fort Myer gym was packed full to the rafters with hopeful, supportive fans. Everybody who was somebody was at the game: Lefty Driesell, University of Maryland head coach; Larry Brown, the star running back of the Washington Redskins; Glen Harris; Adrian Dantley; and many others. The fans were going crazy. They were yelling, "NIT! NIT!" Kermit was his usual stellar self, grabbing 26 rebounds and scoring 19 points. I was the beneficiary of most of his rebounds, scoring 29 points, mostly on fast breaks. Wilbur was consistent, scoring 22 points and 13 rebounds, DeHaven had 10 points, and Billy Mann scored 12 points.

It was a great team effort fueled by Kermit's control of the backboards. We won the game 109–94. We were invited to the NIT at Madison Square Garden in New York City. Kermit led us to the big time.

The Georgetown University game was the last game of the season. This game was monumental due to its singular importance. Kermit had to score 40 points to become one of the elites in college basketball. I had no thoughts about how Kermit would score 40 points. I just knew that he would. Coach John Thompson and his Georgetown Hoyas had a big dilemma, how to win the game and prevent Kermit from getting 40 points. Our schools were bitter rivals. Georgetown wanted to win and prevent Kermit from scoring 40 points.

The game was surreal, like a dream. Kermit got the first few rebounds and kicked the ball out to me. I went down court and shot two or three jump shots in a row, making them all. I believe that loosened up the Georgetown University defense. After that, everything went inside to Kermit. He played as if possessed. He scored every way imaginable. Jump shots, layups, tip-ins, you name it, he did it.

Kermit scored his 40 points, we won the game, and the rest is history. He made first-team all-American and was the first player since Dr. J and the last player since Dr. J to make the 20-20 club. He is to date the last college basketball player to accomplish this feat. He was the first-round draft choice of the Los Angeles Lakers. It was the perfect end of the season and Kermit's college athletic career.

Although I only played one year with Kermit, it was a good experience. I got to play with one of the best teams in the history of American University. I also got to play with the best player in American University history. Kermit was not only a great player; he was a good person and still is.

Peter DeHaven

I first met Kermit when being recruited by American University along with Stanley Washington, who went to Spingarn High School. That year in 1970, the final four was played at Cole Field House at University of Maryland, and the coaches at American University got tickets. As I am frequently thought of as being quiet and reserved, I prefer to take time and listen to conversations before adding any comments. This allows me time to consider how words are spoken and try to figure out the intent behind them. In college, and especially during practices this proved to be both helpful and useful. My first introduction to Kermit is one in which I don't remember engaging in much conversation. I had heard a lot about Kermit and this was a chance to get to know a little more. That year most of the players on the team were from inner-city DC, and I was from Fairfax, Virginia. A couple other players were from Coach Young's hometown.

My first year at American University, I played on the freshman team. As a sophomore and junior, I played with Kermit on the varsity team. As Kermit and I lived on the same floor, we lifted weights, ran the dorm stairs, and jumped rope together. At that time workout rooms were not fully equipped with the best machines and free weights that are an established essential in all facilities today. We had one universal machine and no free weights. We made up our own workout routine of five to six exercises and had no one to help or supervise what we were doing. We worked out every day and put forth a great deal of energy. I guess you could say we were ahead of the times.

On road games, we were roommates, Kermit was a great motivator who brought people together. New recruits on my freshman team included Johnny Lloyd, Billy Ulbin, and Bill Demharter. Our coach was Joe Boylan. As a team, we enjoyed the pushing and shoving that occurred on a regular basis during practices. Johnny Lloyd would always find ways to single out and make fun of Lloyd Mayes. Lloyd was four to five years older than us and Johnny took great pleasure in finding nicknames that daily brought this to our attention. One of his favorite remarks was, Lloyd had very close veins instead of varicose veins. Lloyd was extremely thin and his veins did at times seem to pop up from out of his skin. Taunts would flow between them both, but Johnny was clearly more adept in this tactic than Lloyd.

Then you had Steve Garrett, in the guard position, with his Adonis physique pushing around Bill Ulbin, a freshman guard, both jockeying for a starting position. Garrett and Ulbin might have been physical but there was the level of etiquette that demonstrated respect superseded desire. With this obvious contrast in how players interacted, many days we would find Johnny Lloyd in the dog house as he would do or say something that coach Young did not appreciate. Coach Young often pulled Johnny aside to see what he might be able to say to him that would help him respect his new on the court etiquette and rules of play. We soon began to wonder how much more the coach was going to be able to deal with before something drastic was going to be done.

There were times when coach Young would raise his voice and yell at the team regarding plays and moves. He was a really good coach and balanced soft spoken words with those he yelled out which helped us to pay closer attention to his directions given in practice. Coach Davis our other coach was constant in his approach and always yelled at us. When he left American University to take the head coaching position at Lafayette, we were excited for him and continued to move ahead without him.

I particularly remember Kermit's final game at Fort Myer against Georgetown University. We had a small practice facility at American University and had to drive to Fort Myer, a US army post next to Arlington National Cemetery in Arlington, Virginia, across the Potomac River for our home games. This night Marc Splaver was really advertising the 20/20 eye chart and reminded Kermit he had to score enough points and rebounds to secure this title of the 20/20 club. Being a real team player, Kermit did not expect or ask any of us to pass up open shots just to feed to him. He reminded us that we were a team and he wanted to remember, no matter how the game ended, that in his final game he played with his teammates as a team. Knowing how important it was for him to score a record amount of 40 points we resolved to help grab rebounds and set up every opportunity for him to meet this challenge. There were many opportunities in that final game when he could have continued to make shots to meet his challenge but unselfishly as usual he would pass the ball and encourage us to take the open shot when available. This resulted in all of us scoring well and feeling proud we had helped him make the 40 points he need to score in his fairy tale ending college regular season career.

Our team consisted of several talented players: Johnny Lloyd, Steve Garrett, and Wilbur Thomas, along with Kermit and me as the starting five. Although he had a lot of pressure on him to perform his best, he met that challenge and exceeded it. Part of his success was due to a strong work ethic, determination to be the hardest worker, commitment to achieving goals, natural ability combined with his understanding and appreciation for the team concept. Always a team player he looked out for the interest of others. The highlight of my playing on the American University basketball team, was the NIT game against the University of Louisville. Even though we lost and did not advance to the next level of play, it was one of the most rewarding games we played as a team. We got off to a rocky start due more to nerves than talent. Mentally, we were overwhelmed with the large arena, full stands, players who appeared more physically in shape and worst of all we doubted ourselves. It took a while and several reassuring compliments from Kermit as our captain to get us back on track. After every play, he would encourage us to keep giving such a good effort. We were gaining our confidence and control of the ball with being down only 5 points near the end of the game. Despite taking one bad shot, no one yelled or screamed at this catastrophic mistake. Kermit simply encouraged us to be mindful of the clock and play harder than our opponents.

After graduating from American University, I still had the desire to play basketball and pursued a career abroad in Germany and then with the Eastern league in the States. I later taught public school for thirty years and am now retired. As I think back on my college years, I must say that was the greatest time in my life. Everyone on the team got along, and Kermit has remained a close friend over all these years. We keep in touch and often think fondly of our days playing college basketball on the Fort Myer court.

Wilbur Thomas

How do I explain to a Martian the difference between basketball played in the inner city and everywhere else?

Local talents that include: Alonzo Patterson, Duck Williams, Donald Washington, Ed Epps, Billy Gaskins, James Brown, Floyd Lewis, Adrian Dantley, Dr. Carr (e.g. free one) Kenny Carr, Glen Price, Bud Stallworth, Austin Carr, Lloyd Mayes and many others help define and mold each other to excel well beyond the playgrounds and gyms throughout the Washington Metropolitan Area.

It was on the hallowed playground named Rudolph were games and players met to compete for the converted chance to make a name in the local basketball history books. It was a principle written in stone that every Monday through Thursday evening whenever the weather permitted, with temperatures ranging from 70 degrees to over 100 degrees, it did not matter as, 30 to 40 players lined up waiting to play the game against winners advancing to another level of excellent athletic performance.

Not leaving out any day of the week, it was Fort Stevens early Saturday and Sunday mornings before the sun producing uncomfortably hot weather really started to set in. There was the Armory on the University of Maryland campus that had several indoor basketball courts. To accommodate the desire and need to always find a game in town, the best players from D.C., MD, and VA could be found competing on weekends when the weather outside was too cold.

Also, located on the University of Maryland was Cole Field House. Legendary head basketball coach Lefty Driesell's held a summer basketball camp where after our day's assignment as counselors were concluded, college division 1 players from all over the country arrive ready for face to face games between a variety of local talent and visiting players from around the country. These games took on a different perspective as the familiarity of style of play was non-existent presenting an unknown variable to provide a more valuable game performance from all who participated.

The solitude singular opportunities to practice and refine one's basketball skills performance and ability work together to develop and improve.

On my journey to master basketball skills to a level of excellence people who played pivotal roles in my success include: Mr. Mathews, Mr. Billups, Harriet Seay, Dickie Wells, Willie Jones, Chuck Taylor, and Charles Smith. Every basketball player who has or will reach a certain level of athletic accomplishment has their own list of people who helped them along their journey.

Which brings me back to my initial question; how does a person explain to a Martian the difference between basketball played in the inner city and everywhere else? Playing on the concrete jungle without referees only the strong survive. When you have played against some of the most talented and competitive basketball players in 90 to 100 degree temperatures. Participated in and won or lost arguments. Started and ended fights. Engaged in more arguments. Threw more jabs in fights. Were followed by one player not letting you, the guy he is checking, score a bucket. With the added pressure of talking trash while running beside you moving up and down the court to throw off your concentration. Now put into the mix having to wait, sometimes for hours, to have a chance to play. Even this might not be enough to help you grasp the magnitude of the playground atmosphere at all times. But I loved every minute of it.

Then include the experience of a high school senior playing against Austin Carr one of the leading scores in college basketball at that time, telling me "You're are going to be OK.", or John Thompson hugging me and at the same time playfully calling me a SOB after I scored the winning basket against Georgetown my senior year at American University.

A list that could include everything associated with an answer to this question simply does not exist. There are something's or defining moments which words can never suffice that could help the Martian understand the scope of the details, unless he actually EXPERIENCED IT.

My first year playing with Kermit was as a sophomore. There was a freshman rule that prohibited freshman from being on the varsity roster. This was the last year this policy was in place. I had previously attended Theodore Roosevelt High School in Washington, DC. One of thirteen children, playing basketball provided the opportunity to have some time and space away from my family and ultimately led to the best years of my life and a wonderful, loving marriage mate. I simply could not have asked for a better time in my life than when I was a student at American University. The comradery exhibited by my classmates and teammates. We to this day are called the Dirty Dozen, and we meet once a month alternating living spaces to stay in touch, enjoy good memories, and create new memories. I met my wife at American University. We were married at the Kay Spiritual Center on campus. My son attended and graduated from there. American University provided me with the opportunity to become a professional and do well financially.

Living in a rough area in DC, my academic skills were solid, and my love of sports was enhanced by playing basketball on the legendary courts in the inner city. American University was not an easy school to compete academically as many students had attended private schools and many of the required readings on our syllabus were ones they had read and discussed at length in high school. Who would know that *The Grapes of Wrath* and *All the King's Men* were top sellers in local bookstores? In the inner city, you learn to be tough, welcome challenges, and develop the will to survive. Reading to develop intellectual capacity was not introduced or encouraged.

Kermit set the best example for us. Without him, there would be no me as I am today. He was the foundation of the positive changes for all of us. We saw how he set high goals and how he met each one. His attitude and desire to be the very best was only matched by his drive to achieve all things possible and impossible. As a player, he was well respected both on and off the court. Many players were given the task to check him in a game, leaving me open to score. I then led the team in scoring, and I have to thank Kermit for the accolades I achieved because of this.

My freshman year, academically I performed well. I was a solid student in high school, and studying was something I knew went hand in hand with keeping my athletic scholarship. Leaving home,

I didn't want to go back. I declined many an invitation to just hang out and party to keep up and, in some instances, make up for missed learning experiences in the inner-city school system. Each year my confidence increased, and being at American University was a dream come true. Our record was 14–2, the best yet for the school. Bob Bush, Billy Mann, Lenny Lockhart, Kenny Ripple, and John London were some of my teammates. We lost only to George Washington University and Navy University, in Annapolis, Maryland.

I loved going to our daily practices. Playing basketball was the time to develop a sense of comradery and honing in on plays and skills. I always thought of it like a chance to get into better game shape. I distinctly remember how preparing for games in practice was always enjoyable, but actually going out on the court made me extremely nervous. I might have looked calm and ready, but inside my stomach was doing cartwheels and flips. Before games I would literally run to a trash can and throw up.

The following morning, I could barely crawl out of bed. Getting up and walking down the dorm corridor to reach the bathroom was like being a dead man walking. I understood what it felt like on the last mile on death row and having to walk down the longest hallway to face your execution. The hallway seemed to stretch out in front of me. I wondered if I would be able to make my legs meet the challenge of reaching the bathroom door. My legs felt like a ragdoll's. I had never been so sore and felt as physically drained as I did that morning. This feeling of lethargy and pain remained with me for the rest of the day but gradually went away throughout the day.

There were times when Coach Young would let the freshman team scrimmage against the varsity team. We did win a couple of times, but the varsity always managed to let us know they had a better collection of players. Such games like these helped me to take stock of myself and to realize you either had what it takes to make basketball a career or you didn't. To identify areas, you needed to improve on and to know if you had what it takes or not to do so. It kept me reaching to become better and to know where I was as an athlete. Despite making as one of five selected All-Metropolitan Players of the Year, an honor I shared with Adrian Dantley, I knew scoring those points were directly related to having Kermit on our team when I was on varsity.

My first year as a varsity player at American University we beat LaSalle University, from Philadelphia, Pennsylvania on our home court at Fort Myer, and I was matched against Jimmy Crawford, who played high school basketball with Rosie. This game was extremely physical. That was our twentieth win of the season and we were invited to the NIT directly after the game.

I enjoyed my college career at American University for the mere fact that I got to know Kermit. I would not have selected this school if it were not for Kermit. He made it easy to be a team and team player. He set a model for us to follow. It was the expected and established norm that we all care about one another, be supportive and up-building whenever circumstances dictated. The one player I was disappointed not to have stuck to his commitment to sign with American University was Glen Price. He was a local favorite, and we played many hours together on Rudolph playground. We were all disappointed to learn Glen had signed a letter of intent the night before with Saint Bonaventure. If he had been a part of our team, there would have been no holds barred for us to win many a championship. I probably wouldn't have scored as many points, so who is to say what might have been and what was.

Of all the games, I played for American University, the NIT stands out as the most memorable. I have to admit that doesn't match the moment I met my future wife, but it sure comes close. I was matched up against Junior Bridgeman from University of Louisville, who later played in the NBA and was on the same all-star team as Kermit. Louisville had a good run, but we were able to cut their lead to only 5 points. There were many times I was accused of yelling and screaming at players while on the court. I merely helped direct actions that needed to be done to win, even though Billy Ulbin complained to the coach that I was yelling at him. I was merely emphasizing and reminding my teammates about what needed to be done.

Playing in the first round of the NIT was an instance when I should have continued my regular routine to emphasize something that needed immediate attention. And to this day I regret that I remained silent. As a team, we were tired, really tired, and a time-out was definitely the call to make. Coach did not see it that way, and I constantly question why I did not insist on us taking that time-out. Therefore, to this day I consider that a mistake that caused us to lose that game. Because of being exhausted as a team, we took a bad shot that kept Louisville's momentum going, and a time-out would have cooled them down, allowing us to refuel and come back with a vengeance.

The most important night of Kermit's career was his final game at Fort Myer against Georgetown University. He was under a lot of pressure, and that took a toll on his energy. Later in the final quarter, after pulling down a rebound, he passed me the ball and voiced he was tired. It took him awhile to get back on his feet, and I yelled, "Let's go." He again said, "I'm tired, really tired." I looked at him with intensity and yelled at the top of my lungs, "Let's go." He got up, ran down the court as if having had a shot of adrenaline, and played out his final minutes as if he were just starting the game. A memorable moment to remember, he scored a record 40 points, pulled down 28 rebounds, and had 10 blocked shots.

Lloyd Mayes, who grew up in a similar neighbor as I did, gave me some good advice on what I needed to do to make it. His list of dos and don'ts read like *Robert's Rules of Order.* Steve Garrett, Johnny Lloyd, Mike Lynch, and Mike Hill had a lot of worldly knowledge to share and took me under their wings. Johnny Lloyd was the most consistent of all the guards, but we could have used a third man like Glen, who would have made us a team to be reckoned with. When Kermit graduated, I became the leading rebounder at six feet five inches. A better position for me would have been as a shooting guard. In those early years, you concentrated more on wins and losses than on which position you were best suited for. We were a fast-breaking team with Kermit as the number one guy, me as the number two; we needed that strong number three to be complete and carry us over into the next year.

My senior year I played against Joe Bryant (Kobe's dad), and we beat University of LaSalle on the road. I was named the MVP of the league and beat out Joe Bryant for this award. I also played well against Temple with their star player Channey. When the year ended,

I was contacted by Gary Greenburg to play in Europe. Greenburg had coached a losing team in Israel and transformed them to a championship his first year as their coach. Greenburg was my college dorm mate, and he later worked for the Portland Trailblazers. He got me an opportunity to play on an all-star team with Jim McGregor. McGregor would assemble a group of American basketball players and travel from city to city in several countries. This was more like a showcase of talent, and if a team was impressed with your performance, you were offered a contract to stay and play for that team. I was offered a contract, but my heart was not in playing in Europe. Today the money and advertising is a very lucrative opportunity for players who didn't make the NBA but are talented enough to play on a professional level.

Knowing what I know now, if I had worked more on perfecting my outside shot, I would have made the Milwaukee Bucks team, who had traded Kareem for Elmore Smith. Bridgeman and other good players at my position which made it difficult for me to make the team.

I must consistently state and reemphasize that the quality of education at American University was exceptional. As scholarship athletes, we were expected to graduate in four years. This means attending a four-year school and graduating on time. Life is a wonderful opportunity to become all you can be. American University opened my eyes to a future filled with hope and success. These years will always be treasured and share with the Dirty Dozen for an eternity.

Art Perry

In 1970 I left the air force. While doing my military stint, I played basketball on the AAU team. Good players could make the Olympic team from playing for the military. The last year of my service my coach asked if I would be interested in attending American University and playing on the freshman team. At that time freshman, could not play on the varsity roster. He explained that Tom Young was a long-time friend and if I was thinking about going to a four-year school, he could arrange for me to have an interview with the coach from American University.

This sounded good to me, and I agreed. After meeting with Coach Young and visiting the campus, I was really excited about the possibility of being an American University Eagle. I was accepted and joined the freshman team. My sophomore and junior year at American University I was able to take advantage of a basketball scholarship. Freshman year, my team consisted of Johnny Lloyd, guard and the leading scorer; Pete DeHaven, forward and the second-leading scorer and leading rebounder; Bill Demharter, center, a tall, solid shooter; and Billy Ulbin, a fast and quick guard. I was the third guard on the team. Our final record was 16 and 4.

Having been in the military for four years, making the adjustment to college life was not really difficult. I did have to buckle down and learn how to make a schedule; sticking with it wasn't the issue. In the military, following schedules was part of my daily routine. Managing time to include practice, classes, study, and a social life was the challenge to meet. My teammates were very helpful, and we were all aware of how Kermit had been successful in doing this, and his model was easy to follow. It wasn't an easy routine, but it was doable with some modifications. Especially the running of the stairs at night.

Returning to DC was also a bit of an adjustment. Living in the Northwest area of DC was different from where I had grown up. Johnny Lloyd was from Anacostia, and I was from Eastern, which was very close to his neighborhood. Johnny was a close companion as we both loved sports, and coming to American University was like living a dream. Lloyd Mayes was an older player like me, and we became friends almost immediately. Lloyd was quite the big man on campus with the ladies and always presented something amusing for all of us to constantly laugh about. He loved to wear his large-brimmed hat with tassels and carry an over-the-shoulder body bag we jokingly called his "purse."

1972-73 American University Basketball Team

1973 NIT Team

I wanted to do well in school, and I loved playing basketball. All the players were great to be around and individuals who focused on the team effort. Comradery was the order of the day. Hard work was our motto. And to this day we remain close friends. I must admit I was amazed at how much work Kermit did. He worked out all the time, making it clear that to be successful, hard work was a key part of that equation. When I moved up to varsity, it was Kermit's final season, and what a season that was.

Kermit would walk down the streets of DC to find a game of basketball. Rudolph was a close jaunt, and he played Monday through Thursday nights on the most prestigious court in DC. During the summer, I would drive and pick him up in my green VW station wagon. It came in handy for me to get around the city as I lived off campus and not in the dorms. Lloyd Mayes was also living off campus as we were more mature than our identified classmates. I lived about two blocks from where Kermit stayed at home in the summer months. I could literally cross the street and enter Rudolph's courts. Kermit and I would pick up Johnny, Lloyd, and Wilbur, squeezing into the green fighting machine.

After a long day of classes, jumping rope, lifting weights, and running the dorm stairs, you could find Kermit in the small gym shooting free throws. To this day Lloyd Mayes will remark that he didn't practice enough as his average on the court wasn't that good. This from the legendary Lloyd Mayes, who, once we hit the courts on a weekend, would not want the day to end. Despite the hot and humid summers, Lloyd had only one agenda on the weekends, and that was to play ball on every available playground basketball court, be it Rudolph, Luzon, or Rose Park. He pretended to have a deaf ear whenever Kermit wanted to end the day and replenish his strength with a good meal and some much-needed water.

The final game of Kermit's college career against Georgetown University was played in the Fort Myer gym. Kermit needed to score 40 points and grab 26 rebounds to be noted as the seventh player to score 20 points and 20 rebounds in their college career. To this date no other player has become number eight. As a team, everyone worked to get Kermit the ball and still play their game. It was like watching a fairy tale. There was the feeling of such support and respect that it remains to this day as a memorable moment never to be matched.

Some can say it was misfortune we lost to University of Louisville in the first round of the NIT, but others might say it was fortune that we even made it to the NIT. It did help American University move up in status and recruit some talented local DC players. Either way, Kermit demonstrated how hard work and integrity can and will result in reaching individual goals. This is a lesson that each one of us learned, and as a direct result our post-college years have been filled with a lot of happiness and satisfaction.

My senior year I suffered a knee injury, and I had surgery. Coach Joe Boylan always asked me basketball questions. The game, the players, the plays, my interest to pursue coaching, these topics were open for discussion. After Kermit left American University, Coach Tom Young was offered the head coaching job at Rutgers University located in New Brunswick, New Jersey. Both Coach Young and Boylan agreed to take the offer and told me they were looking for a graduate assistant. I was offered this position with the ability to receive my college degree from Rutgers University. That offer was too good to pass up, and I left American University my senior year and graduated from Rutgers University.

CHAPTER 6

Summer Following Senior Year

After graduation, it was time to pack up my room and say farewell to friends with the promise to keep in touch. Changes meant waiting for a formal signing with the Los Angeles Lakers and the addition of some tendinitis in my knee. Seeking relief, I saw a doctor who recommended and administered cortisone shots. It wasn't until years later it was discovered this was the worst treatment that could have been prescribed. This condition was the direct result of a change in my training routine.

No longer living in the dorms, there were no stairs to run and returning home I couldn't jump rope after coming home from work without disturbing the neighbors. If I had could continue my routine without this hiatus my knee would have been fine. I learned that when I worked out with consistency, gaining weight gradually, my body could make the adjustment without any injury.

My first job upon securing a four-year college degree was to lifeguard at American University's swimming pool. It was always hot in the summer, and the pool was seldom used. Some local college professors' families would spend a few hours, but in all, it was a quiet job. I liked the water and, knowing how to swim, enjoyed the opportunity to access the facilities. Campus seemed different. My former safe haven over the past four years transformed the moment I was handed my undergraduate degree. The original version of my fairy tale had started a sequel. With this came some sadness and some excitement. I enjoyed being a student at American University, where I gain weight, height, and confidence.

Between making sure no one drowned, I worked at University of Maryland for Lefty Driesell as a counselor. The usual salary was $100, but Lefty gave me $350. I lifted weights and waited to hear from Donald Dell, who was working on a contract with the Los Angeles Lakers organization. The Lakers had just come from a championship season of play, and with such heavy players as Wilt Chamberlin, Jerry West, and Gail Goodrich, signing me was not a too-high priority.

I was attending Red Auerbach's summer camp, and he honored me by letting me stay with the big boys. I got a chance to interact with NBA legends firsthand. Sometime within the first few days of the camp, Red came to me to let me know I needed to fly out to LA and sign a contract. My plane ticket and hotel accommodations were arranged through the Lakers organization. About a week later I boarded a plane in Washington, D.C. and flew to Los Angeles, California to begin my NBA career. My brother shared a great deal with me about steps to take to be successful in my goals towards making it in the NBA. He was drafted by the St. Louis Cardinals and every day during a scrimmage he would line up and go against the best receiver on the team. His goal was to literally destroy the best players on the roster. He hit hard, tackled furiously, ran hard and fast. He knew if he did his best and performed well he would make the team. He did just that. In fact, he started as a rookie and I could drive down to Baltimore and watch him play.

Chris and I had always been close. We would do anything to support one another. This included taking a cruel spanking so as not to rat on one another and providing support to complete any task we needed to accomplish. As we moved forward in our lives this mutual support proved invaluable. When landing in LA, John Barnhill, the Lakers Assistant Coach, picked me up at the airport and literally deposited me at the hotel. That was the last time he spoke to me prior to practice.

Being drafted number five by the Los Angeles Lakers was the beginning of the sequel to my fairy tale dream come true final game performance against Georgetown University at Fort Myer army base gymnasium. Post season tournament play had not left me hopeful that playing with a new team was going to be a walk in the park. Playing with the professionals who were earning an income most people envy, added to this realization. Being in LA was quite an eye-opening experience. Across the street from the hotel was a car rental agency. You had to be twenty-five to rent a car, but I was fortunate the workers were Lakers fans and cut me a break. After renting a car, the next problem was how to pronounce street names: La Cienega Blvd, Sepulveda Blvd, Centinella Ave were a few choice ones. I did recognize Manchester Ave though. One night I was watching Johnny Carson and made a remark about how newbies to the city often mispronounce these streets, and after saying them correctly, I felt much more confident to venture out on the road.

The very next morning I drove down Sepulveda Blvd, going away from the hotel as far as it went. The next day I drove in the opposite direction. Then I drove down La Cienega Blvd. When I drove down Manchester, I knew why that was a familiar street; in one direction was a part of town I didn't want to get lost in. Still uncomfortable about exploring, I limited my drives to only include leaving and returning to the hotel. I did not make any turns and remained on one street. One day I discovered Loyola Marymount University in the Westchester Community of the Westside of Los Angeles in California and pulled into the parking lot, parked the car and walked around the campus looking for the gym. After a short perusal of the campus I walked through the open doors of the gym and knew I had found a place where I could play some basketball. The ocean was in the opposite direction and so beautiful and very different from the beaches on the East Coast.

No longer under the financial support of my American University athletic scholarship I was now going to be playing for a living, earning a livelihood, practicing a profession that would last for several years, only if my efforts proved successful. As a rookie moving across country held several firsts. This was the first time I was unfamiliar with my surroundings, as I had lived in the DC metropolitan area. The first time living on my own, previously surrounded with supportive friends. The first time I would live on my own, no more daily meals at Mary Graydon, although I did at times prepare and fix a simple meal, now grocery shopping and buying cooking utensils and other household items that would last longer than a few weeks required some research and comparison shopping. The first time I would need to handle a budget that would include rent for an apartment, car payments, basic utility bills, and recreation or entertainment.

With all that to consider my priority continued to be growing stronger, and not losing the eighty pounds I had gained over the past four years. Signing with the Los Angeles Lakers gave me more incentive than ever to gain a spot as a starter on the team.

Staying in a hotel was starting to get old, and I got a newspaper and looked for someplace to call home. I needed to stay on streets I had recently traveled and made an appointment for the following day. I arrived early and looked around. The area was really nice, and the sign still read Vacancy. As I knocked on the apartment manager's door, I introduced myself, and he responded I must have made a mistake as there were *no* vacancies. It amazed me after seeing the Vacancy sign still posted that prejudice was still alive and continuing in the West.

My spirits were not dampened, having grown up in DC with prejudice an integral part of my upbringing. I simply returned to my hotel room, changed into some basketball shorts, and headed off the Loyola Marymount. I met Elmore Smith, Travis Grant, Jimmy Price, and Nate Hawthorne, who were also new additions to the Lakers roster. Of all the players, I met in those first weeks in LA, one stands out in mind. Walking into the gymnasium and playing against Raymond Lewis left me awe struck. I'm not going to say he was a good player, for he was an exceptional shooter and playmaker. In my mind, he was in the same class as Austin Carr, the D.C. playground legend. He was a local who was drafted in the second round by the Philadelphia 76ers. The 76ers first round pick was Doug Collins a player Lewis felt was not as talented as himself. He thought Collins was aptly gifted to prove this on the court, but Lewis was less apt to show how he made his feelings about Collins known. Labeled a "problem," his inner-city view of what was right did not match the establishments, and the world was deprived of enjoying a talent bound to entertain for years in the NBA.

When I asked about housing, they told me they all lived in a complex on Manchester close to the Forum. I checked it out, and it was nice, but the noise from the weekly garbage pickup was quite annoying. Not knowing about furnishing an apartment, I rented some furniture and bought a few odds and ends until I sent for Pat to join me. After we got married, she could do all the household stuff. It seemed to come easier for her as she left her home in New York to attend American University in DC. Having been on her own for those four college years provided some experiences that I had not yet known about.

Elmore soon looked for a house and moved out, which encouraged me to do the same. I found a condo located behind the Forum in a place called Briarwood. It had a security guard, swimming pool, clubhouse, and nicely manicured grounds. You walk around the complex enjoying the peace and quiet. Being so close to the Forum, it guaranteed never being late to practice or games due to traffic.

Arriving at training camp was very different than the first day of college ball practices. I met Stan Love, who was recently traded from the Baltimore Bullets. He was true California beach boy whose brother Eric was a member of the Beach Boys singing group. Most players were in their mid-thirties and very seasoned. The only veteran who instantly decided to provide me with a less-than-warm welcome was Bill Bridges. His contract had one more year with less pay than my new contract, and he was not happy. In his attempt to make me feel like part of the fold, he decided if he wasn't happy, I wasn't going to be happy either. My first fight in the NBA was in this first day of training camp going head to toe with Bill Bridges.

When Wilt Chamberlin did not show up for camp, it soon was made clear that he had decided to pack up the basketball shoes and bask in the warm California sun. This was particularly disappointing. When invited to LA and watch a championship game, I was given the opportunity to have a conversation with Wilt. No doubt you would consider an in-depth conversation filled with words of sound advice about the game and all that went along with my entering the world of the NBA to be the topic. Wrong! Wilt gladly shared his ability to do anything better than anybody. I mentioned that might appear to be the case on the basketball court, but suppose he had to encounter Mohamad Ali in the boxing ring. He laughed and then with all seriousness plainly stated he could beat him without working up a sweat. His exaggerations were pervasive throughout the evening. I was disappointed to lose out on many great stories I could now remember and relate.

College practice was hard, and wind sprints required 100-plus percent effort to be expended. In Lakers practices, if players were at 25 percent, that was an accomplishment. I felt like I was running in slow motion, but the veterans set the pace, and I didn't want to draw any additional attention after my altercation with Bill Bridges. In these years NBA players were tough and ready to fight at the drop of a hat. The going fine was fifty dollars. Against a game in Seattle between the Los Angeles Lakes and the Supersonics, Bill Bridges, our 6'6" power forward from Hobbs, New Mexico, played collegiately for the University of Kansas, literally beat up the entire SuperSonics team. He single-handedly knocked-out five SuperSonic players. I had never witnessed so may bodies hit the floor. He was ejected from the game and at half-time he was really upset. He asked why no one had stepped in to help him out. My response was," You looked like you had everything under control."

Later in this year, Boston Celtic great, Dave Cowens, retired professional basketball player and NBA head coach. At 6'9", he played the center and occasionally the power forward position. He was inducted into the Naismith Memorial Basketball Hall of Fame in 1991. During a game against the Los Angeles Lakers was elbowed. Being close to him in proximity he thought it was me and immediately started swinging. Kevin Stacom a 6'3" (1.90 m) guard from Holy Cross High School, Flushing, New York; and Providence College, Stacom played six seasons (1974–1979; 1981–1982) in the National Basketball Association as a member of the Boston Celtics,

Indiana Pacers, and Milwaukee Bucks, got in the way and knocked down by Dave Cowen's swinging at me.

Later in my career I was privileged play with Dave Cowens after being traded from the Los Angeles Lakers to the Boston Celtics. Dave was the kind of individual who was quiet with many talents. I remember traveling on the team bus from practice. As we drove along the highway, Dave noticed a family stranded by the side of the road. Dave taking note of the situation walked up the aisle of the bus and told, not asked, the driver to stop. It didn't take Dave long to convince the driver to open the door to let him off the bus. The team was aware of Dave having done this before were not concerned and would have joined him if they could have been of any assistance.

We watched as Dave approached the driver and the problematic car and then looked under the hood. The driver waited for a few minutes and when Dave began to work on a solution to the problem, he slowly drove off. All eyes were turned to watch Dave until he was no longer in sight and we continued our drive back to the hotel. Along with Dave Cowens, Dave Bing, John Havlicek, and Jo White, future Hall of Famer's, having the opportunity to be around such high-quality individuals made my playing days as a Boston Celtic memorable and enjoyable.

The word was now out that trades would be made to new players joining the ranks. The first one I was aware of was trading Jim McMillan for Elmore Smith, but we had met previously. Connie Hawkins joined us, and he was filled with amorous nicknames daily. He was always making fun of someone or something. You just learned Some days I was Germ, then Worm, Bacteria, and on those *really* fun days, Comet Kahoutek. to live with the man, but most important, *never*, and I mean *never*, mess with his Stickum a sticky substance when after making skin contact with the surface of the basketball acts like glue to make this connection between skin and the leather of the ball stay fixed for a longer period to enable more control by the ball handler. It was more important than water. He used it like most people us Chap Stick.

Jerry West, Gail Goodrich, Pat Riley, Happy Hairston, and Bill Bridges were returning players. Bill Sharman was the head coach, with a pleasant demeanor and solid, good, strong coaching talent. When the team traveled from LA to play any East Coast team, you were sure to find the veteran/starters sitting in first-class sitting on the airplane floor, playing poker and consuming unlimited airline alcoholic beverages. There was limited seating in those days for team players. If you were on "F troop," you were sentenced to fly coach. F troop was the label nonstarters were given, and in every practice, they were made to wear the purple jerseys. Being on F troop roster meant you only got into a game if the team was winning by 20 points or losing by 20 points. I specifically informed Pat Riley that I was going AWOL from this F troop. Even in first class, there is a limit to how many "free" drinks you were allowed. Readily reaching these limits, they engaged me to collect a variety of alcoholic blends they had been cut off from. Connie Hawkins requested whisky sours, Zelmo ordered Jack Daniels, and as I proceeded to fill orders, the stewardesses were amazed that my behavior did not match that of my very intoxicated teammates.

There were times when we did not hold practice as the players were too hung over from the flight. It gave jet lag a whole new meaning. Then there were those games when a player requested to sit down on the bench due to a hangover. Meeting Stu Lantz was the beginning of a great friendship. As he sat on the bench looking over the playbook, he simply did not believe me when I informed him that we only ran two plays, the 11 and the 22, one for Gail and the other for Jerry. After a few more games, he turned to me and said, "We only run two plays." Cazzie Russell also played with us that year. He was outgoing and always had something to say. Quiet times were never possible as he and Stu would constantly argue over any topic. Cazzie was a great shooter, and he and Stu became close friends. The three of us became good friends and we always ate our meals together.

It was soon obvious I was going to need some work if I would be able to make it in the league. I had played the center position in college and now was expected to know and play as a forward. Following the advice of Michael Cordoza, an attorney in Donald Dell's law firm, I approached Pete Newell to request his help. Mike told me Pete was the best coach and teacher he knew, and it would be most beneficial to get him to work with me as soon as possible. I kept asking for two years, and then one day Pete let me into his office. He explained his intentions to retire, and previously a general manager, he could not work with me as it would appear to slight and insult the coaching staff. He told me if I worked hard and worked with him diligently, he assured me I could make it in the NBA. He then retired and told me to pick him up at seven the next morning. Pete was an excellent teacher, and I learned many lessons that would influence my future both on and off the basketball court. He taught me the importance of positioning and angles on the basketball court. His approach was straightforward and deliberate. His unrelenting "get it done" attitude was inspiring to do my best as to not disappoint him and prove that with hard work many things can be accomplished.

My third year, Kareem joined our team, and things were beginning to look up. Working with Pete and playing with Kareem were dreams coming true. This first year, I worked with Pete one-on-one. Later I invited Kiki Vandeweghe to join me. He was a high school player whose father was my daughter's pediatrician. His dad frequently visited with me, and it seemed like a good idea to include Kiki in these practice sessions. In later years Purvis Short, Jerome Whitehead, Kenny Carr, and Sven Nater joined me.

CHAPTER 7

Danny Padilla – The Giant Killer

Danny Padilla

From my many years of weight training and body building it is always a challenge to support and meet the unique goals individuals set for themselves. Reading and researching nutrition and how the human body functions has provided me with information to share and put into practice. Each sport has specific requirements as to body type and function. A basketball player and a football player are primarily athletes and that's where the similarities end.

I first met Kermit while living in Los Angeles, California, working out in World's/Gold's gym. I noticed he would occasionally work out with Robbie Robinson and at other times workout on his own. He complimented me on my physique and we began to engage in a conversation about what my workout routine was like. He confided in me that he always wanted to have large calves and hoped I would be able to provide him with the secret to achieve this dream.

This conversation lead to his questioning how he could gain weight and build strength. He joined me in my workout routine and I was impressed he was able to survive the short, ten second rests between sets. He told me about how he jumped rope and ran stairs using a twenty-pound weight vest. This provided his body with a solid foundation of endurance that would serve him well.

We trained together and established a routine to include squats to build strength in his legs, bench press, curls, and military press. I constantly reminded him he was an athlete first, not a body builder, and to be successful as a basketball player he needed to focus on speed, endurance, capability of functioning muscle. This was during the time when sports management was against athletes lifting weights. It was later understood that to build muscle tissue and compete in all sports weight lifting had to be included. We worked out as if under the cover of night.

Nutrition was the next key to include. Food is essential in gaining weight. But the achieve a twenty-pound weight is simply not scientifically possible. For every pound of muscle gained, twenty-five percent is fat and for every pound of fat lost, twenty-five percent muscle is also lost. In gaining weight through lifting weights one must consider what they are trying to accomplish. Basketball players and football players have different weight lifting needs but nutrition remains the same. It is important to eat five to six small meals each day. Not to include a lot of protein. Balance is the key. Athletes must always remember endurance requires fuel to participate in training and playing their individual sport. If weight is gained too quickly the effect will slow down one's performance.

In training with Kermit, he had to embrace the ten to fifteen second rest between sets. This tests one's ability to have a quick recovery time from one exercise to the other. It builds endurance, raises the heart rate like jogging. If one gets physically sick following this routine, it is clear they are not in shape. Once this is stabilized then little by little we increase the amount of weight used, then push for the quick recovery time to make such gains as lifting 135 lbs. to 300 lbs. We then add multiple sets with the short rest period.

When Kermit was traded to Portland, he sent for me and I took note of his current training routine. I was not correct and the first week of correcting several concerns we worked out with a great deal of intensity. It was important to re-teach good habits and replace the ones that were not designed to lead to any success. His body had to rediscover the fundamentals once established through jumping rope and running the stairs. Once his body remembered this he could apply the correct workout routine of weight training. In addition to learning the correct way to lift weights he also realized the best way to train an athlete was to join them in the training. A lesson he still incorporates when working with athletes today. He continues to include squats but is careful to not over burden knees as basketball players must run full court with short rest periods in-between.

A solid generic workout will stabilize muscle, give the athlete control by increasing strength in their legs, back, chest and abdomen. Legs must be the first to consider as they hold up the fort, without strong legs your nothing. The proverbial statement: he lost his legs; after losing a boxing event. If not eating a balanced meal the athlete will gain weight that will be more fat and not muscle. There can be no off season when it comes to weight training, it is now a part of who you are and it is a constant reminder of where you are and where you want to be. Nutrition, lifting, rest and recovery become your main objective each day. When increasing in amount of weights used in your routine, only do one to two sets with the new weight. Give your body an opportunity to learn to adapt to these new weights.

Mentally ask yourself: Do I like lifting weights? This question will undoubtedly reoccur as your body will be sore with a lot of work yet to be done before achieving your goal. You must continue to work out and get into condition despite of any weight resistance.

One's mindset is essential to working through those days when you wonder why weights were ever identified as beneficial for anything.

When people ask me why I love weight training I must simply say it is who I am and who I want to be. I grew up in a family of ten children, seven sisters, and two brothers. At the age of seven I didn't know a lot about life never mind body building, but I watched my older brother who was a wrestler and a cousin who was jockey develop incredibly strong bodies while enjoying the process of getting there. I started to read magazines at eighteen and researched the sport of body building.

After entering the Amateur Athletic Union (AAU) World Championships in the lightweight division, I won titles in the World Champion competitions. Always told it was too small to compete I was never deterred in my goal to Be a viable competitor. My only regret is that genetics plays the key role in what anyone can achieve. My father was strong and my mother had great body proportions but in the long run they were both short.

I continue to work with Kermit when training athletes. He like myself can't imagine going a day without working out. Nutrition continues to be part of our on-going conversations and has allowed me to continue in my success at being tall in head knowledge if not physical stature.

CHAPTER 8

Gold's Gym

Golds Gym

As a rookie coming to Los Angeles, California, I was determined to continue in my efforts to get stronger and not lose the eighty pounds I gained over the past four years. Signing with the Lakers gave me more incentive than ever to gain a spot as a starter on the team. I had established a routine of lifting weights and asked around where people went to do weight training. The consensus was the local YMCA. I managed to find a gym at Rogers Park located at 400 West Beach Ave, in Inglewood, California. The gym was adjacent to a playground, but the equipment was limited, and you had to wait behind ten other people before you could use a machine.

World's Gym founded in 1976 by Joe Gold in the glory days of "Muscle Beach" in Venice, California. The small 2200 square foot gym was loaded with the best body builders such as: Lou Ferrigno, Arnold Schwarzenegger, Zabo Koszewski, Franco Columbu, Danny Padilla, Dave Drapper, Rick Drasin, Eddie Giuliani, Casey Viator, Lee Haney, Chris Dickerson, Sergio Oliva, and Frank Zane and I set out to find it. I set out to find it. The building was stark white with a parking lot in the back. You had to walk down a flight of stairs and gain entry through a gated area manned by Ed Giuliani. The rules of the gym, music, no dropping weights, and no poor hygiene (stinking up the gym), or you were gone.

I walked in and paid the daily fee. At that time in 1974 no women were going to these gyms, only men. Finding a leg-press machine, I noticed a bodybuilder pressing seven hundred pounds. The seven one-hundred-pound plates were stacked without any small weights in between to make lifting the plates easier to handle. As the bodybuilder finished his last set, he simply got up and walked away without making any effort to remove the weights. I said, "Excuse me, how am I going to lift off the weights?" He smiled and told me, "If you can't lift off the weights, Pencil Neck, you don't need to use it."

That was one machine I didn't use that day. In college, I had no instruction on how to lift weights. Peter DeHaven and I would go to the weight room and lift for the same body parts every day. I continued to follow the same routine in the gym. I warmed up with 225 pounds for bench press, hoping to impress someone and gain a bit of respect even though my limit was 240 pounds. By becoming a frequent flyer, I was privileged to see at least ten out of the top-twenty bodybuilders working out in the gym each week.

After a week of coming in and working the same body part every day, Robbie Robinson, Mr. America and Mr. Universe, said to me, "I watch you work out the same body part every day."

"Yes, aren't you supposed to?" I asked.

He said, "No, you're supposed to work each body part twice a week, and if you are a power lifter, it could be one time a week. If you want me to show you, I can." Knowing the NBA had a lot of tough guys, although I had gained eighty pounds, I still needed to increase my strength.

I began lifting with Robbie, and he was killing me. I knew I had to get stronger to play the NBA game of intimidation. I was falling in love with Gold's Gym but was still called Pencil Neck. Robbie only lifted Monday through Friday, and I was coming seven days a week. On the weekends, I noticed Bertril Fox, another Mr. Universe, came in every Saturday and Sunday. Bertril would rest three to four minutes between sets whereas Robbie only rested ten seconds between sets. Bertril wanted you to lift the weights to him when doing dumbbell flat bench or dumbbell incline. He wanted me to get two two-hundred-pound dumbbells and give them to him on the incline at the same time. This was something I could not do by myself, and I had to get someone else to help me.

Bertril was very patient and pushed me. I worked out with Robbie Monday through Friday, and Bertril Saturday and Sunday. Even when I was traded to Boston, I would always come back to lift at Gold's. I gained weight and could lift heavier weights. The following year Samir Bannout came to the gym, and Robbie was out of town. Samir was the upcoming bodybuilder, and I asked him to train me. He told me he was going to win the Mr. Olympia contest that year, and he did. I learned that setting a goal and visualizing it lead to success. Setting a goal is just as important as achieving it.

As the summer progressed, I would walk into the gym to see a rather small bodybuilder standing about five feet one inch, with the most incredible body I have ever seen, yelling at Lou Ferrigno, who was six feet six inches, weighing 260 pounds, "Shut up! You're making too much noise while you're lifting." Lou, the incredible hulk, was hearing impaired and probably had no idea he was doing this. I said to myself, "Who is this guy yelling at the big man? Doesn't he realize he could be swashed like a bug?" That was my first introduction to Danny Padilla. I didn't say anything to him that day. As I continued to come to the gym and see Danny on a regular basis, we started a casual conversation that led to a friendship that still exists today. Danny was tough and didn't take anything from anybody. His height had nothing to do with how big his heart was.

Sometimes Arnold Schwarzenegger would walk into the gym, and the energy level would skyrocket. He received respect from every bodybuilder in the gym. He was Mr. Olympia and so charismatic he made everyone feel special. These tough men were honored and in turn returned the compliment. The list includes Robbie Robinson, the greatest bodybuilder simply because of longevity, a disappointment in that he never could meet the presentation standards required of a champion; Franc Zane; Franco Columbu; Tom Platz, known for his great legs; Greg DeFerro; Dave Johns; Samir Bannout; Lou Ferrigno; Casey Viator; and Bertil Fox who could bench press five hundred pounds for several reps.

Zane is a three-time Mr. Olympia (1977 to 1979). His reign represented a shift in emphasis from mass to aesthetics. Zane's proportionate physique featured the second thinnest waistline of all the Mr. Olympias (after Sergio Oliva), with his wide shoulders making for a distinctive V-taper. His abdominals were considered by some bodybuilders to be the best in bodybuilding history. He stood at 5'9" and had a self-declared competition weight of 198 pounds when he won Mr. Olympia (He weighed over 200 lbs. when he competed in the 1960s). Zane is one of only three people who have beaten Arnold Schwarzenegger in a bodybuilding contest (1968 Mr. Universe in Miami, FL) and one of the very few Mr. Olympia winners under 200 pounds. Overall, he competed for over 20 years (retiring after the 1983 Mr. Olympia contest) and won Mr. America, Mr. Universe, Mr. World and Mr. Olympia during his illustrious career.

Franco Columbu won the title of Mr. Olympia in 1976 and 1981. At 5 feet 5 in. in height, Columbu was shorter than most of his bodybuilding competitors. In 1977, Columbu competed in the first *World's Strongest Man* competition and was in fifth place in total points during the competition; a remarkable outing, considering that Franco weighed much less than all his competitors. Then came the refrigerator race, which called for a downhill race in which a heavy, bulky, unwieldy refrigerator is strapped to the racer's back. While ahead, Franco stumbled, and was shown on national television collapsing with a grotesquely dislocated leg. This ended his participation in the World's Strongest Man contest, in the end, he finished in fifth place. After <u>Arnold Schwarzenegger</u>'s comeback victory in the 1980 Mr. Olympia, Franco followed suit and won the 1981 Mr. Olympia.

Tom Platz became famous for his remarkable leg development. He developed a high intensity, high volume method of leg training, which led to his unparalleled size and definition for his time. Platz began his competitive bodybuilding career in the 1973 Mr. Adonis competition. He competed as an amateur until he won the 1978 World Amateur Championships middleweight division. In 1978 and after completing his degree at Wayne State University, he moved to California. He arrived there with $50 and a dream to win <u>Mr. Olympia</u>. For the following nine years Platz competed as a professional, aiming for <u>Mr. Olympia</u>. Though Platz never took first at the Olympia competition, he had a string of top ten finishes, with a third position in 1981 being his best.

Platz became famous for his remarkable leg development. He developed a high intensity, high volume method of leg training, which led to his unparalleled size and definition for his time. Regardless of what was found lacking elsewhere, it is still widely claimed in bodybuilding circles that Platz holds the mark for the best legs in bodybuilding of his time and some of the best legs in bodybuilding ever. <u>Flex</u> readers agree: In a "best body parts of the 20th century" poll, Platz was deemed to have the best <u>quads</u> and <u>hamstrings</u> of all time.

Tom Platz retired from professional bodybuilding competition in 1987 and did a 'Comeback' in 1995 when he was awarded Honorary Mr. America. He still promotes the sport wholeheartedly. Tom says, "I just want to give back to the sport I love which has been really great to me. He played the part of "Body Builder" in the 1990 film <u>Book of Love</u>. His character portrayed the <u>Charles Atlas</u>-like character from those "tired of bullies kicking sand in your face and stealing your girlfriend"-type of advertisements that were in a lot of comic books for decades.

Platz was and is one of the most sought-after guest speakers in the world of bodybuilding, nutrition and general fitness. He was a Professor and the Director of Bodybuilding Sciences at ISSA for 14 years. Tom has a Masters in Fitness Science, Bachelors in Science Physiology and Nutrition from Wayne State University and Michigan State University, and a Master's in Business Administration from the University of California.

Greg DeFerro, in 1979, IFBB Mr. International, five top 4 placing in IFBB shows from 1981-1984. He participated in the following shows: 1984 IFBB World Pro 2nd, 1983 IFBB Grand Prix Las Vegas (Caesars) 4th, 1983 IFBB Night Of The Champions 2nd, 1983 IFBB World Pro 2nd, 1982 IFBB Night Of The Champions 9th, IFBB 1981 IFBB Grand Prix California 6th, 1981 IFBB Grand Prix New England 4th, 1981 IFBB Pro World NP, 1980 IFBB World Pro 6th, 1979 IFBB Mr. International 1st, and 1977 IFBB Mr. USA 3rd.

Samir Known as "the Lion of Lebanon", Samir Bannout won the Mr. Olympia title in 1983. At that time, only six men had held this most prestigious title since the contest began in 1965. The extreme muscular definition that Bannout achieved in his lower back region helped to shape "Lebanon Cedar" when referring the shape made visible during a back pose on the competition stage. Bannout took 4th place at the 1982 Mr. Olympia contest and returned the following year to take home the title in 1983.

After placing 6th at the 1984 Olympia, the IFBB suspended him for three years as punishment for his participation at the World Championship competition of a rival federation, the WABBA. (The real reason was because Samir had an argument with one of the officials over mistreatment.) Bannout did not again get a top six placing again at a Mr. Olympia contest despite competing at the event many more times. In 1990 he won his second IFBB pro show, the IFBB Pittsburgh Pro Invitational. His professional career lasted 17 years.

Lou Ferrigno, in 1969, won his first major titles, IFBB Mr. America and IFBB Mr. Universe, four years later. Early in his career he lived in Columbus and trained with Arnold Schwarzenegger. In

1974, he came in second on his first attempt at the <u>Mr. Olympia</u> competition. He then came third the following year, and his attempt to beat Arnold Schwarzenegger was the subject of the 1975 <u>documentary</u> *Pumping Iron*. The documentary made Ferrigno famous.

Casey Viator was the youngest ever AAMERICAN UNIVERSITY Mr. America–gaining the title at the age of 19 in 1971. The following year, he came in sixth in the 1969 Teen Mr. America, but won in the categories Best arms, Best Abs, Best Chest, Best Legs and Most Muscular. In 1970, Casey Viator's upper arm measured at 19 5/16 inches, and his forearm at 15 7/16 inches. All in the same year, Viator won three separate <u>bodybuilding</u> championships; Teen Age Mr. America, Jr. Mister America, and lastly, the title of Mr. America. In 1982 he capped off his bodybuilding career by placing third in the <u>Mr. Olympia</u> competition.

Bertil Fox won the 1969 Junior Mr. Britain at 18. He went on to win nearly every major bodybuilding contest outside of the IFBB, including the 1976 AAU Mr. World, the amateur 1977 <u>NABBA</u> <u>Mr.</u> <u>Universe</u> and the professional NABBA Mr. Universe in 1978 and 1979.

Lee Haney is the joint record holder along with Ronnie Coleman for winning the most Mr. Olympia titles, with eight wins. His bodybuilding titles include: 1979 Teen Mr. America Tall, 1st, 1982 Junior Nationals Heavyweight & Overall, 1st, 1982 Nationals Heavyweight & Overall, 1st, 1982 World Amateur Championships Heavyweight, 1st, 1983 Grand Prix England, 2nd, 1983 Grand Prix Las Vegas, 1st, 1983 Grand Prix Sweden, 2nd, 1983 Grand Prix Switzerland, 3rd, 1983 Night of Champions, 1st, 1983 Mr. Olympia, 3rd, 1983 World Pro Championships, 3rd, 1984 Mr. Olympia, 1st, 1985 Mr. Olympia, 1st, 1986 Mr. Olympia, 1st, 1987 Mr. Olympia, 1st, 1987 Grand Prix Germany (II), 1st, 1989 Mr. Olympia, 1st, 1990 Mr. Olympia, 1st and 1991 Mr. Olympia, 1st.

Chris Dickerson One of the world's most titled bodybuilders, Dickerson's competitive career spanned thirty years; he was known for both his heavily muscled, symmetrical physique and for his skills on the posing dais. Dickerson first entered <u>bodybuilding</u> competition in 1965 by taking third- place at that year's Mr. Long Beach competition.

He was the first African-American, Mr. America, the oldest and first openly gay winner of the IFBB Mr. Olympia contest at age 43, and one of only two bodybuilders (along with Dexter Jackson) to win titles in both the Mr. Olympia and Masters Olympia competitions. Dickerson won the Mr. Olympia once (1982), a distinction he shares with Samir Bannout (1983) and Dexter Jackson (2008).

Sergio Oliva, in 1966, won the AAU Jr. Mr. America and again he claimed the trophy for "Most Muscular". He then joined the International Federation of Body Builders IFBB in which he won both the professional Mr. World and Mr. Universe Contests. In 1967, he won the prestigious Mr. Olympia contest, making him the undisputed world champion of bodybuilding.

Oliva then went on to win the Mr. Olympia title three years in a row, at 5 feet 11 inches and at a contest weight that went from 225 lbs. up to his most massive at 255 lbs.

In addition to seeing these world-renowned professionals on a regular basis, Mr. Gold the owner of the gym was welcoming and later refused to make me pay, for working out, because he said I was so polite. By working out there I knew I would always be prepared to meet almost every player on the court except for Darrell Dawkins. I gained confidence to compete because of working so hard in the gym and with Pete Newell. As I learned from Samir I was going to be a good NBA player.

When Jerry West became head coach of the Los Angeles Lakers, he would specifically tell me not the lift weights. To show me the seriousness of his directive, he promised to fine me $2,000 if I did. This increased my need to lift at World's Gym in California. No one from the organization ventured there, and I was safe in pursuing what I knew was what my body required to perform at the best level I could. In those days, it was thought that weight training would be harmful to your shooting arm. As I wasn't a shooter, this did not concern me, as my legs and back needed to be strengthened, and weight lifting was a tremendous help in making that happen.

There were many interesting bodybuilders who joined the regulars at the world-famous Gold's Gym. George Sampas, an attorney in Santa Barbara, California, and I struck up a conversation one day about this well-built young man who was very self-conscious about a thick keloid scare running across his throat and up the left-side of his face. As I always strike up a conversation with anyone who has a body that looks like they know the key to building such a physique. He became relaxed and comfortable with our conversations and shared how while in prison a group of fellow in-mates attacked him and using a razor cut his throat and the side of his face. Lacking the best medical care, he was stitched up and the result was a large, thick, disfiguring scar.

George entered the conversation and we learned a great deal about prison life. This young man was placed in solitary confinement following this attack and to keep himself from going insane pushed his body to the limit by doing countless push-ups, sit-ups and squats until he was exhausted only to fall asleep and wake up to the same daily routine. The result was an extraordinary physique. George and I held several days trying to figure out if there was some way we might be able to help him.

George's knew a plastic surgeon, and arranged for us to meet with him. He helped us understand how keloids form. He explained when skin is injured, fibrous tissue, called scar tissue, forms over the wound to repair and protect the injury. In some cases, scar tissue grows excessively, forming smooth, hard growths called keloids. Keloids can be much larger than the original wound. The decision to treat a keloid can be a tricky one. Keloid scarring is the result of the body's attempt to repair itself. After removing the keloid, the scar tissue may grow back again, and sometimes it grows back larger than before.

He shared there are several treatments for keloid scarring. Examples of keloid treatments include corticosteroid injections to reduce inflammation, moisturizing oils to keep the tissue soft using pressure or silicone gel pads after injury, freezing the tissue to kill skin cells, laser treatments to reduce scar tissue or radiation to shrink keloids. In any event, the decision about the treatment should be carefully weighed.

We scheduled an appointment for the surgeon to meet with the young man to decide if treatment was a feasible solution for his situation. We explained we were going to tell the young man that a research study was being conducted by this surgeon and he was looking for patients to consult with. Both George and I shared the $5,000.00 expenses and a date for his surgery was set.

To help with his recovery, he had to wear a very tight face mask and not exert himself or workout for three months. As the recovery time was long and the young man could not do any intensive training, by the time he had recovered both George and I had moved from LA. We did learn that the surgery was a success and the young man when able to return to the gym he asked if anyone knew if both George and I were still coming to work-out there. He was happy with the results and never knew how George and I had helped.

By working out at Gold's Gym, I knew I would always be prepared to meet almost every NBA basketball player on the court except for Darrell Dawkins and play to the best of my ability. I gained confidence to compete against the best by working with the best. Those grueling workouts, daily challenging myself to meet and set higher goals those hours in the gym along with my workouts with Pete Newell I believed when Samir told me, "One day you are going to be a NBA player to contend with."

One morning I noticed this rather well-built Hawaiian athlete who was feared around the city. Everyone knew he was not to be messed with. I was often asked why I worked out with him and my response was because he was tough and would make me work hard. For instance, one day I watched as he was bench pressing 420 pounds and then benched 225 lbs. with 35 repetitions. Now this was more like the body-building efforts I was used to seeing at Gold's. I started to engage him in a conversation and was quickly warned of his notorious reputation. This only further intrigued my curiosity and I felt compelled to follow my instinct to speak with him.

Mel DeLaura was all muscle and was currently working as a personal trainer for professional athletes in the Portland, Oregon area. He played college football as a wide receiver and was given a free agent contract with the Atlanta Falcons and the Washington Redskins. He injured his quad muscle during training camp which prevented him from further pursuing his desire to play in the NFL.

This turn of events did mold his resolve to provide well balanced conditioning and strength training workouts. He was so intense that he worked out with his clients to show if he could do it, so could they. With this Modus Operandi. I was often asked why I wanted to work out with him. It was quite the learning experience and to this day when training with athletes I follow his example.

Every NBA player or professional athlete should train with bodybuilders of this caliber. To be better, you have to be around the best. You should endeavor to find someone who is a good match to show you and work with you to make you successful.

CHAPTER 9

The NBA Years

Being a rookie in the NBA is a daunting experience. Add this to being privileged to play with the Los Angeles Laker greats was memorable in many ways.

Billy Ray Bates

Cedric Maxwell

With the Lakers

With the Blazers

With the Celtics' Coach Satch Sanders

Mychal Thompson

Blazers

1980 NBA All-Star Game

Pete Newell

My rookie year was the first time in playing basketball that resulted in an injury. Prior to this I had managed to escape and stumbling blocks to playing the game. After healing from this, when playing against Tom Burleson (a 7'2" center, who played for North Carolina State University's 1974 NCAA national championship team.

Burleson was known throughout his amateur and pro career as a good shot blocker. He played eight seasons in the NBA with three different teams (Seattle, the Kansas City Kings and the Atlanta Hawks). Burleson fouled me during our pre-season game as I went up for a dunk. With the ball being held in both of my hands I fell on my back to keep the ball in the Laker's possession. I did not let go of it, falling to the floor, resulting in the full impact of the fall on my back. My back hurt as soon as I got up, but continued to play in the pain. As the pain increased I was placed in traction at Centinella Hospital for several days. This back pain was a constant Achilles Heel throughout my nine-year career. In those days, the adage was grin and bear it, and you simply listened and followed the advice given. In a conversation years, later with a doctor, I was informed if I had taken off one week to rest my back I would have never had back pain throughout my career.

The second game in the NBA with the Los Angeles Lakers we played in Seattle against the Super Sonics. We flew into Seattle the day before the game and stayed at the Washington Plaza Hotel. I went down to the hotel restaurant for dinner by myself and as soon as I walked into the restaurant there right before my eyes was Spencer Haywood having dinner with his wife Iman. It didn't seem like he knew who I was. Being star-struck, I was surprised when he looked over at me and motioned me over to their table inviting me to join them for dinner.

Somehow I regained my composure, as my stomach was filled with butterflies and nervousness. Here right in front of me, was someone I idolized for years. I told him I watched him play in the Olympics and remember seeing him block a shot using two-hands. I followed his career closely and after reading an article while still in high school about his secret to success was wearing a twenty-pound weight vest. I went on to share how I saved for weeks to purchase one and was still using it to this very day. He paid for my meal and I thanked him for both the invitation to join him and his wife for dinner and for the secret he shared in print. As I didn't get into the game the next night, during warm-ups I made a point to thank him again.

We still keep in touch and recently while dinning out at P.F. Chang's in Las Vegas, our waitress, Tara Gordon, gave me a message from him to give him a call. Tara told Spencer whenever I am in town I come in to have dinner. A few days later, when I came in for my usual meal favorites, before taking our order, Tara reached into her billfold and handed me the note, saying Spencer made her promise to give it to me.

In in my second year I broke my ankle and could not walk. I was literally crawling around the house as I could not put any pressure on it. I explained this to the doctors who told I would be fine. I again emphasized it didn't feel right. I went in the next day to get and X-ray only to discover I had indeed broken it in half. The doctor's apologized for not having put more stock in my initial concern. In the 1976-1977 year at half time in the game before the All-Star game my knee was hurting and when I told Dr. Kerlan he advised to play through the pain, after telling me to ice it and play with the pain. My knee was hurting at the start of the second half, I jumped up for a rebound and my knee popped I had ruptured my patella tendon and required knee surgery.

When packing my luggage for away games, I was always thinking about how to stay sharp and in shape just in case my opportunity to get in the game would come. In those days, hotels did not have work-out rooms with weights and cardio-machines. To stick to my routine, I packed my twenty-pound weight vest and two 30-lb. dumb-bells.

After checking in and grabbing a bite to eat, before going to bed I put on my weight vest and ran the hotel stairs. Connie whose room was next to mine was not an early to go to bed person, and he saw me walking back to my room wearing my weight vest. He stopped me in the hallway and wondered if I were feeling okay. He noticed my chest looked a bit extended and putting his hand on my chest felt the weight vest.

He immediately asked me if I needed some mental help. I laughed and explained how I was doing what I needed to do to be ready when, not if I was put in a game. In the airport, I was putting my luggage on the check in scale and Connie was waiting to check in his luggage. He noticed how many pounds the scale registered. Just before the ticket agent hauled my bag onto the conveyer belt Connie asked what was inside my luggage.

After we walked away from the ticket counter I whispered, "My twenty-pound weight vest and two 30-lb. dumb-bells." He looked at me in sheer disbelief stating: "Are you really in need of an intervention? That poor agent could have sued you for causing a serious health problem. I doubt if missing one or two days of working out is going to be instrumental in getting off the bench. Personally, I would highly suggest you get some help in learning how to play the center position in the NBA. Think about it, you already have the desire and the know-how for getting and staying in shape. Consider what is missing. Just a thought from one veteran who might just have some good advice to share."

Pete Newell was unavailable to work with me my first two years with the Lakers. Upon his retirement, my career started. I had been like a man consistently rowing a boat toward the ocean with a course set to land. I wanted someone who knew how to help me learn the fundamentals of the forward position. My Lakers coaches were very good but had played the point guard position and could not help me make the transition from playing center in college to playing forward in the NBA. As a center, your back faced the basket, but playing forward, you had to turn around to face the basket, positioned at a distance away, with footwork, angles, spacing, and other positions I had not experienced or understood how to put all together to make sense. This change in perspective posed a problem for me.

Pete lived a few minutes from me in Palos Verdes, California, and I drove to his house that first of several mornings at seven not knowing what to expect. It didn't matter; only learning, mastering, and coming to understand this new position was my ultimate goal. The first day, Pete took the time while we were heading down to Loyola Marymount University to tell me what we were going to do, not just today but over the next few weeks. He made it clear that the process was going to be methodical and sequential. We would start at A and move to Z. We would not move from A to C without thoroughly understanding A and B. There was going be an order to learning everything.

Workouts were unbelievably strenuous. Pete knew what was needed to produce a successful player, having won a National Championship while coaching at Cal Berkley and winning the NIT while coaching at the University of San Francisco 1948–49. Being trained in the military, he was mentally focused, showing little to no compassion for any excuse offered, and goal oriented with the view that no obstacle presented would prevent success. The Pete Newell Big Man's Camp was like Navy SEALs training. All of workouts could be comparable to military training.

The infamous Pete Newell defensive "sliding drill" started off for five minutes without stopping and extended to twenty minutes without stopping by the end of the summer's workouts. Everyone knew about this drill. If you were not positioned properly, Pete would yell at you. In a normal practice during the regular session, a drill like this would last no longer than three minutes. However, nothing was normal about Pete's workouts. After doing the first set for five minutes, I told Pete that there was no way anyone could do this drill for twenty minutes. He simply looked me and said nothing, which told us we would get it done.

While doing this sliding drill, we could see the large clock directly in front of us in the gym. Pete could not see this clock and used the watch on his wrist for timekeeping. The five-minute drills turned into seven-minute drills. No one said anything to Pete, but we all knew we had gone overtime. Wanting the much-needed relief to come sooner than later we were never sure if Pete's watch was unable to keep accurate time. In those minutes and seconds as we agonized to push our bodies to complete each drill, did Pete know how to tell time? Was his timepiece accurate? Was it synchronized with the wall clock? Did he calculate time based on if players were about to threw up or run outside? We were thoroughly spent at the end of every day's session. And people asked me, Why I would I be going to bed at 5:00 in the afternoon? Did that require an answer?

Pete Newell's sense of humor was sometimes difficult to access. Therefore, how could one approach this subject using a little levity? Being a drill sergeant, your words if not delivered in a manner that is not offensive might not be a good idea. On the ride, home one day, in an attempt to make this time issue a joke, I asked if he had any difficulty telling time. I went on to explain his five minutes were seven, his ten minutes were actually thirteen, and finally his twenty turned into twenty-three minutes. He simply laughed. Timing was never mentioned again.

I'm going to describe what we had to go through when doing the infamous Pete Newell defensive sliding drill. You have to get down in a bent-knee defensive stance and armed raised in a defensive position, and positioning your feet to match his directions, you would either slide forward, backward, to the right, or to the left.

The biggest advantage working with Pete was not only gaining knowledge but gaining respect from other people because of Pete's reputation. Now coaches took notice of me because Pete was working with me. The respect they held for him was extended to me. The first summer it was one-on-one training until the last few weeks when Pete invited rookies Don Ford and Tom Abernathy to join us.

He was keenly aware that two to three hours straight without assistance from other players could be modified. He did tell me that he expected me to enter training camp at 225 pounds.

My fourth season began with a new coaching staff. Jerry West made the transition from player to head coach. Jerry was smart enough to get top coaching assistants Stan Auerbach and Jack McCloskey to work with him. Jerry never had been a coach before selected seasoned assistant, with experience and knowledge to work with him and the team. Jerry recognized Kareem as the star and leader of the team but didn't see me as adding a great deal to the mix and, therefore, didn't plan on giving me a lot of playing time. My only saving grace was his being aware of my having spent the off season working with Pete Newell. He gave me a shot and opportunity to demonstrate what I had learned.

In the pre-season, I played a few minutes but twisted my ankle badly. The next pre-season game I was left behind and wasn't included in the team's travel plans. When the team returned, my ankle was still injured, but I had the trainers tape it tightly as if it were in a cast. Directly afterward I spent hours icing it to get the swelling down and numb the pain. If I didn't know anything else, I knew if I didn't get better, this year would prove to be my last chance to play in the NBA. My teammates Cazzie Russell, Earl Tatum, Kareem, Lucius Allen, Don Chaney, and Don Ford were a good collection of players, but the word was that no one expected this team to win a championship. It was known we had Kareem, but as to how the rest of us fit into the mix was still to be seen.

As pre-season games continued to unfold, so did I. Continuing to hustle and push myself as players got hurt, I was put in the game. Having the opportunity to play more allowed me to show the coaches what I had come to understand about playing as a forward and put into practice what I have learned from Pete Newell's "A to Z" court course work.

By the start of the regular season I was playing twenty to twenty-five minutes as a backup power forward and backup center. That year we had the best winning record in the NBA. Before the All-Star Game, about the sixtieth game of the season, we were battling the

Denver Nuggets for the best record, and my knee was hurting badly. I asked Dr. Kerlan about this during halftime and he explained I had tendinitis. In those days, only the pain was addressed, and no one knew that cortisone was the worst possible solution as it weakened the tendons, only adding to the problem.

Sometime in the third quarter while playing against Paul Silas, I went up to block a shot, and my knee popped. I thought someone had thrown something at me from the stands. At that point in the season I was averaging 10 points and 10 rebounds per game. After my injury, Lucius Allen, our starting point guard, broke his toe. During the regular season, we had beaten the Portland Trailblazers 3 out of 3 before these injuries. Thus, we were beaten in the Western Conference Finals by the Portland Trailblazers, who went on to win the Championship series. I was taken to Centinella Hospital with a ruptured patellar tendon. The operation was the next day. Pat brought our daughter Dana to see me in the hospital, and she spent all of ten minutes jumping all over and the bed. The pain it produced was intense, and I had to ask Pat to take Dana home.

Barely recovering from the warm enthusiasm of my daughter, I was visited by my eccentric teammate Earl Tatum. He strolled into my hospital room singing an Al Green tune. He wanted to spend some time just shooting the breeze. It wasn't often that he chose people to sit and have a conversation with. He was a frequent visitor at my house simply because he knew I understood his highly sensitive nature. A word uttered in a harsh tone would send him into a state of silence that lasted for a long time. This flaw in his personality ultimately shortened his NBA career, one which showed great promise, as in one quarter he scored 24 points as a Laker setting a record at that time.

My next challenge proved to be rehabilitation. Dr. Lombardo his expertise includes arthritis of the hip and knee, tendon and ligament injuries of the hip and knee, general orthopedic surgery and trauma with a specialty in hip and knee replacements and MAKOplasty surgery. Pete Newell came up with an inventive plan for our off-season workouts. We met only when he was available, so we didn't meet every day. I still picked him up at 7:00 a.m. on these days, and we worked out at Loyola Marymount University or El Camino College. Pete would tell me, "Kermit, we've got to get your leg stronger." I was beginning to understand what he was trying to teach me.

I was now gaining knowledge about the game but, more important, needed to overcome my injuries. As the season began, I knew my knee wasn't ready for me to come back. A full year of recovery time would have been optimal but was not an option. As I really wanted to play and Pete had worked with me to an intensive extent, I was prepared to play. If I had been able to miss a few practices my performance would have improved at a better rate.

This season introduced me to new players who joined our team, Ernie DiGregorio, Kenny Carr, Norm Nixon, Brad Davis, Jamal Wilkes, and James Edwards. If my memory serves me correctly, the first game that season we were preparing to play the Milwaukee Bucks. Their rookie Kent Benson was interviewed and reported he was going to play Kareem very aggressively and try to push him around. A rookie talking about one of the greatest players in basketball history—this was totally out of line. When the game began, Benson deliberately elbowed Kareem in his stomach, and he doubled Kareem over in pain. When Kareem was able to gather himself together, Kareem punched Benson in the face, breaking his own hand. Kareem was immediately thrown out of the game, later suspended, *but* nothing happened to Benson, who instigated the entire incident.

To fill in the empty hole, James Edwards, our rookie from the University of Washington, started as center, rounding out our team. He averaged 18 points a game and played well. He was among the top-five scoring centers in the league. However, a year earlier playing against the Buffalo Braves (later the San Diego Clippers and currently the Los Angeles Clippers), I got into a brawl with John Shumate. I was fined $50. Fred Foster hit me in the back of my head, Don Adams then attacked me, and soon the Buffalo bench emptied out onto the court, throwing punches at me. I had knots on my head and had several stitches on both of my hands of which I still have scars today. Before Buffalo came to LA to play us again, a few players on the Buffalo Braves team personally called me to apologize for their actions.

Perhaps they were remembering reading the *Sports Illustrated* issue that came out earlier in the year and featured me along with six other NBA players as "the Enforcers," and began to wonder if the title of enforcer would actually apply to how I would play against them. They had no reason to give that a moment's thought, but they did not know that until they called and spoke with me. I didn't want to do that article in the first place, as throughout the year it proved to be detrimental. Maurice Lucas was on the front cover. In those days to be considered an enforcer came to be defined as the team member who protects the star or to intimate or police the opposing team players. Jack Kent Cooke, the LA Lakers owner, insisted I do it, and despite my objections I complied. Photo shots and all, there I was joined by Bob Lanier, Maurice Lucas, Calvin Murphy, and Dennis Archery, put out as one of the NBA's more aggressive players.

Jack Kent Cooke, in addition to owning the Lakers, also owned the Kings and Redskins. He lived in Las Vegas but followed all our games on television. The game against the Celtics, was very physical, and we were both getting creamed on the scoreboard and being pushed around on the court. Watching us play against the Boston Celtics, Jack made a phone call to our then coach Bill Sharman during halftime. Bill took me aside to the training room and told me Jack wanted me to play physically aggressive and start a physical altercation and would pay for any imposed fine. I told Bill that I wasn't going to do that. I could understand the frustration our owner was feeling as he watched us being bullied night after night. He felt I was the only one would be up to and capable of holding my own after the Buffalo incident.

Earl Tatum was one of the most interesting individuals I had the privilege to know. He was truly unprepared for living on his own. Playing for Marquette University, Earl was very comfortable living in the heart of the inner city. He came to LA not knowing how to find an apartment, purchase furniture, open a bank account, and write checks, where to buy quality clothing, and how to buy a car. He asked me to take him around and show him how to get things done.

It took me a few outings to convince him not living in the inner city was the better plan with his new financial status.

Earl loved playing ball. He was a great athlete who literally could run all day long. He loved Jerry West's opening three-man weave drill. This was a painful drill and regarded with dread by everyone except Earl. We were expected to run sprints up and down the court twice, then four, six, eight, and then ten times without missing a layup shot. If you missed, you had to start back at two times and continue up to ten times. Personally, I didn't want to be paired with anyone who might miss. Earl thought this was funny and would at times deliberately miss so he could run it again. Each day somehow I figured out a way of not being his partner. At the end of a three-man weave drill, your butt was already as hard as a rock.

Kareem joined our team in 1975-1976. He was just as good as one expected and was quiet and soft-spoken. He was an avid reader of philosophy texts and when he learned that was something I was interested exploring shared some of favorite book titles with me. When on the road he would see, me reading one and then briefly ask my impression was of the texts. Any conversation with Kareem was short. But he would ask an interesting question, pose a thought provoking answer, or give me another book title to consider. He wasn't pushy but stimulated and encouraged an out of box thinking mindset. My assignment was to check Moses Malone; this was to keep Kareem from getting into foul trouble. I was expendable, but Kareem needed to remain in the game. It was a normal start to the game, and at the beginning of the second quarter, there were three players under the basket for a rebound, Kareem, Kevin Kunnert, and myself. We all went up to rebound the ball. Kevin got the rebound and pushed it forward to the guard for a fast break. I turned to run down the court and placed my hand in front of Kevin to propel myself past him so I could catch up with the other players in front of me. As I did so, Kevin proceeds to elbow me in my face.

At first I thought Kevin's actions were simply accidental. But I stopped to look at him, and he deliberately punched me in my face. That started the fight. Kareem hurried over to break it up. Kevin was hunched over, and out of the corner of my eye I saw a figure running toward me. Remembering the incident in Buffalo, I simply reacted to this by throwing a punch. I did not know who was coming toward me or their intent. I simply wanted to defend myself. I didn't want to be involved in another brawl where someone joined in to hit me. It was a reaction to an anticipated aggressive act.

I didn't know who this was until I saw Rudy hit the floor. Everything stopped. It took him a while to recover but could walk off the court with assistance. I got thrown out of the game, and Dr. Kerlan came over to me to check on the condition of my hand. He asked if I was okay. Rudy, walking next to me, yelled, "Why did you do that?" I answered, "Why don't you ask Kevin why he punched me in the face?" The unanswered question regarding the incident that has labeled me as a notorious criminal remains unanswered to this day. What was Rudy's intent? Why did Rudy run down the court towards a situation that had already ended? Standing with Kevin and my other teammates I saw out the corner of my eye a figure running towards me. In any situation where an event has occurred and someone not involved comes to see or intervenes, the reactions of any individual involved will be directly connected to prior experiences or simply a reaction to the unknown or perceived danger imposed. With the recent Buffalo Braves bench emptying incident my experience led me to base my response on the physical aggressive actions of others as a problem. Being made aware of someone running towards the situation all that came to mind was the incident in Buffalo.

Did I misinterpret Rudy's actions? An answer to this question can help to present the incident clearer, but after all these years does anyone really want to hear the answer? It doesn't make the incident any less injurious but it does present a framework that accurately labels a person's reputation.

Now that Rudy and I have been better acquainted; I truly believe he was not coming to hit me. But at the time I did not know him, only that he was running toward me. I slowly walked to my car, and the attendants who were black assured me that all would be well. Instinctively I knew differently. It was 1977, and Kareem was a black star and attacked by a marginal white player. Kareem was suspended, and *nothing* happened to Benson. I think Benson should have also been suspended. In this instance, Rudy was white and I was black. I punched him, resulting in severe injuries. I knew I was in deep trouble. When I got home, Pat greeted me at the door. She had stayed home that night and was talking on the phone with Jessica Smith, Elmore's wife, when Jackie Chaney made an emergency interrupt call to let her know what had happened and to be prepared for an ill wind.

Pat had been referred to an OB/GYN doctor in Torrance, California. On her next regularly scheduled visit, her doctor sent into the examination room his partner. This doctor gently explained that her original doctor could not stand the sight of her and would no longer offer his medical assistance. He went on to say he did not agree with his feelings and offered to become her doctor as it would be a pleasure to do so. She agreed and although visibly upset managed to drive home. Immediately after she shared this communication with me, it became all too evident that my new status as the most notorious criminal was affecting the members of my family. Similar snide remarks were exchanged when she went shopping and after a while it became evident who our true friends were and who were the haters.

I played in the next game, and during the following day the NBA office called my house. When Pat answered, she was asked if she was the maid and where I was. When she responded, "At practice," the NBA representative rudely ended the phone call with and abrupt tone. She related this to me when I got home, and I wondered how the game would go that night and when I would be contacted by the NBA. We were slated to play against the Buffalo Braves. The crowd was really cheering for me. The fans that night were very supportive. Stu Naham, a sports caster in LA, was on my side (he was a former hockey player). On his TV show, he expressed I had the right to defend myself, but he was quickly quieted and advised to say no more.

I played well and the next morning boarded a plane with my team members heading to New Orleans. After checking into the hotel Ted Green, a writer for the LA newspaper knocked on my door. He asked me, "What do you think about the NBA league's decision?"

As I had not heard anything, I asked him, "What was the decision?" I had been suspended indefinitely and fined $10,000. In reality the fine was $20,000, and I had only received one paycheck so far for the season.

The severity of Rudy's injuries was announced, and it was reported he was still in the hospital. The NBA didn't care if my actions were justified, if I was right or wrong for a reaction to a possible dangerous situation. Their sole concern was how the response would be viewed by the public. Taking into consideration it being 1977, if we were completely honest and reversed the races of everybody involved, I would never have been suspended. I would have been hailed a hero. My reaction would have been accepted as defensive. No one would doubt the intention was aggressive in nature to cause bodily harm. The words in the press would headline as "You Got Him—you know he was going to hit you!" My being right or wrong was never the issue. As the Enforcer, I was going to pay for the label I was given.

I came home and was under a lot of stress. Newspaper articles were front-page cover of the evil villain I was painted to be. I was depicted as 260 pounds instead of my real weight of 220 pounds, as Pete had suggested this to alleviate the pressure on my healing knee. Hate mail was delivered in bundles to my house daily. One envelope that was sent to me in Boston was opened by the ball boy. It was enclosed with open razor blades to ensure whoever opened it would be cut. The ball boy was. From that point on there was no opening of mail. Boxes of letters from the Forum were also forwarded, all racist, all malicious in nature. Each one was read and kept.

I was deeply hurt only three of my teammates called and came by to see me, Earl Tatum, Ernie DiGregorio, and Don Chaney. No one from the front office called or contacted me. Years later Jerry West told me it was a directive that no one was to have any contact with me. I was no longer allowed to interact with the players. There was one positive to all of this, my knee still needed time to heal. The three months of my suspension helped this to happen. It was a wet winter, and that did not allow me to run or do any outdoor activities that would interfere with my knee's required rest.

I would go to bed early and always felt tired and drained. Our second child, Trey, was born, and it helped to make the adjustment from one child to two. Dana was two, and she enjoyed entertaining me by dancing to Stevie Wonder's song "Isn't She lovely." A few days later, Chick Hearn, the radio announcer for the Lakers, called me to say I had been traded to Boston along with Don Chaney for Charlie Scott. No one else from the Lakers organization contacted me. Donald Dell called to tell me although I was traded, I was still suspended and not allowed to practice with or join my new team assignment. I was not in basketball shape, mentally depressed and tired. Death threats, bad press, ill treatment from strangers and alleged friends were the stay of my daily existence.

Larry O'Brien, the commissioner of the NBA, requested a meeting with me and wanted me to fly to New York. Donald Dell shared with me this meeting would result in whether the NBA would reconsider the length of my suspension and if I would return to the league. I told Donald I wasn't interested in spending money on a plane ticket or hotel for what might be. It was more important for me to limit my spending and hold on to my resources. He phoned several times and finally convinced me to go. At that time David Stern was the deputy commissioner of the NBA under commissioner Larry O'Brien. My hotel accommodations were not comfortable. The room was small and very expensive. It was literally the size of a clothes closet. I did bring a dress shirt but forgot to bring a tie. Donald offered to let me use one of his, but somehow wearing a bolo tie was just not the right look. I went without.

O'Brien began the interview with an insulting statement, "We don't need your *kind* in the NBA." My immediate response was to ask, "What is my *kind*?" Donald tried to hold me back, but I kept on. "I've never had a drink of alcohol, never did drugs, or smoked. I have never had a technical foul and was never disrespectful to referees. The only technical received was fighting technical. I graduated from college with honors, and you say the NBA doesn't need *my* kind? You wouldn't have any players in the league *if* I'm *not* your *kind*!"

He then wanted me to write and apology and have it printed in every newspaper. I asked, "Apologize for what? Being punched in the face and fighting back?" I flatly refused by saying, "I will *not* apologize, and I won't write any letter of apology. If I'm not going to be permitted to play in the NBA anymore, so be it. I'll do something else."

The interview ended, and Donald and I left his office. I later learned the announcement that my suspension was to be lifted would be reported on Friday following this meeting in New York. Waiting to hear word of the resolution of this situation, hate mail continued to be delivered. I still could not join the Boston Celtics team until I was given an official reinstatement date. Once this happened, I gave the boxes of letters to Fred Slaughter, a law professor at UCLA who requested to use them in one of his law classes as part of his syllabus.

A Saturday-night TV skit aired that made a parody of the fight. Unfortunately, the stigma of my actions was now memorialized for the world to see. The call to report to Boston finally came, and I left my family in LA. This was the winter of the terrible snowstorm and blizzard that closed the city. Red Auerbach, who was the head of Boston Celtics organization, was a strong advocate for restoring my reputation. He made positive statements to be recorded in the newspapers and continually stated how pleased he was that I was joining the team. He did this even though there were strong racial tensions in the city over bussing concerns. His support was both powerful and exceedingly kind. Because of Red's support, a front-page article with a photo of me and my daughter Dana was printed in the *Boston Globe* written by Bob Ryan.

Red offered me the use of his townhouse, but I declined and asked him to book a room in a hotel. Because our relationship began when I was eighteen years old, he knew me for the person I really was and not the villain depicted in the media. It was sobering to realize that arriving in Boston meant moving from one of the most powerful franchises in the NBA to another powerful one. Red's choice of the Sheraton Prudential Hotel at Copley Square proved to be one of the best experiences during those tumultuous months. The staff was so open and excited to have me staying there. After games, they would eagerly wait for me to share all the "no disclosed" details of the game. They would sit and eagerly hang on to my every word. Most nights they would save food for me. While they were closing the kitchen, they wanted me to tell them about the games. They always wanted to know if I had run the stairs. I had to remind them that I ran the stairs just before going to bed. I had no one to give game tickets to, so I would give them away. I made sure that everyone had the chance to go to a game. The night of Havlicek's final game, I gave my tickets to the people who worked in the kitchen. The joy they expressed could be heard all the way up the last stairwell. They were jumping up and down, not being able to contain their excitement.

My room was located right next to the elevator; the walls were red. It was not a pleasant decor, but it served its purpose. With the weather being so bad, I couldn't move around the city to get better acquainted with where things were located. My friendship with the staff made coming home at night at bit less lonesome, and I was determined to prove that I was well worth the trade.

That first day I practiced with my new teammates, Cedrick Maxwell came up to me and said, "I thought you were going to be a crazy man." This sentiment seemed to be that, shared by my other teammates, everyone was leery of me at first. Cedrick Maxwell even said, "Kermit, I thought you were a mean, nasty guy, but you're one of the nicest people I've met." On this team, I was fortunate enough to play with four future Hall of Famers (John Havlicek, Joe White, Dave Cowens, and Dave Bing).

As this team of players had great character, they were getting long in the tooth. If the players had not been allowed to smoke during halftime and knew what we know today, perhaps some might have played in the league longer. The veteran players always provided instruction to me on the plays and pointed out areas I needed to improve on. This was very similar with the Lakers when I was playing with Jerry West. During the time-outs in the games, we would frequently look to Jerry for direction. Now in Boston I looked to Dave Bing, Joe White, and John Havlicek for the same guidance.

As an older team, the Boston Celtics didn't practice as hard as the Lakers did. I knew I had to get in the best shape I could as soon as possible. It was obvious the masses wanted to see me fail. I was more determined than ever to prove everyone who sent hate mail, anyone who falsely accused me of malicious intent, and everyone who were judgmental wrong.

I brought my weight vest and decided running the stairs twice a day was my best strategy. Twenty-five or twenty-nine flights of stairs were my sole focus to achieve this goal. I rode the elevator to the basement and ran up the stairs and then rode the elevator down again. This arduous regiment was five times in succession in both the morning and evening. I did not relish waking to this every morning or going to bed every evening, so I had to play a mental game to challenge myself. For each flight of steps, I pictured a player I would have to play against during the season. That helped me get up every flight of steps to guarantee that player would not be able to destroy me when we met on the court. Another secret was to never look up to see what floor I was running up to. If I looked up, being tired already, I knew if I was on the fifteenth floor and I had eleven or fourteen more to go, I might not make it. I might have to lie there and not get up to complete the task at hand. I simply envisioned I was closer to reaching the top. Then I would pray the elevator was in use, and I had a few extra minutes to rest before starting up again.

Even if I tripped and fell having to rest for a few minutes, I stayed focused. I knew getting in the best shape would be my only chance to succeed. Knowing in every city every fan would be hoping for me to play poorly, be embarrassed, and fail. The first ten flights of stairs focused on the following: the first set, Adrian Dantley; the second, Maurice Lucas; the third, Jamaal Wilkes; the fourth, Bernard King; the fifth, Truck Robinson; the sixth, Lonnie Shelton; the seventh, Elvin Hayes; the eighth, Marcus Johnson; the ninth, Julius Irving; the tenth, Moses Malone; and so on. I had to be ready to play every game against the very best players in the NBA.

Our first few games were cancelled due to snow, but the first one was on the road against the Golden State Warriors. My coaches Satch Sanders and K. C. Jones were two of the finest people you could ever meet. There were nights Satch would call me just to talk. He would say, "Hoss, what's up?" When I would ask why he called, he would say, "Just to talk." The day of the first practice before the game, I asked Satch how much playing time I would get. He paused and then answered, "Kermit, you might get from ten to fifteen minutes." Now that was something I knew I could do.

A policeman was seated behind our bench being on guard. I was advised not to shake hands with anyone, not to make eye contact, and not to engage in any conversation, if possible, with people I did not know. I was also told not to order room service as one would never know what someone might put in my food. When the Boston Celtics team was introduced, after saying my name, the loudest "boos" I have ever heard in my life were shouted out by the Golden State Warriors fans. To this day I have *never* heard such a loud response to anything before or since then.

Satch put me in the game, and now the crowd yelled even more "boos." Walking down the short line toward the announcer table, I stopped, sat down at the scorer's table, and waited for the play to end. I was so nervous I could hardly see straight. Then suddenly, just like in my final game of my college career against Georgetown University, I felt a warm blanket cover me, and I could relax. Relying on the fact that all the time and effort of running the hotel flights of stairs would get me through the next ten to fifteen minutes of playing time. Although I was mentally prepared for my estimated playing time of ten to fifteen minutes, I ended up playing for twenty-five minutes. I played well, scoring 11 points with 14 rebounds, but couldn't stop sweating for five to six hours following the game due to my still being out of shape.

The next day we flew to Los Angeles. I came home to play against the Lakers. I had to face the first of my flights of stairs opponent, Adrian Dantley, and I could stay at home with my family instead of staying at the hotel. I was again the center of media attention. Everyone wanted to interview me; I was tired from all the stress with the reminder of how it all began one night at the Forum and that initial game against the Golden State Warriors. Memories of how I was thrown under the bus by the Lakers organization, I did my best to stay focused, scoring 12 points with 12 rebounds. In the end, Adrian killed me. I just wasn't in good enough shape to present a challenge to this great player. But next time I would hope things would be different.

We traveled to Denver to play the Nuggets, and one fan remained standing at the beginning of the game screaming obscenities at me. My only consolation was that surely by the end of the evening he must have lost his voice. When the Boston Celtics players were introduced, I received a resounding boo. However, when the Denver Nuggets team was announced, first Calvin Mack and then Dan Issel ran over to me to shake my hand and extend a welcome. This settled the crowd a little and showed what they thought about me as a person. Especially after witnessing the reaction from the crowd, their efforts were much more noteworthy and admirable in addition to being appreciated. One particularly irate fan was throwing ice chips at my back. As I went down the line to enter the game, I mentioned this to a police officer who happened to look up and see who this fan was. I pointed to him and said, "Gotcha!"

When we traveled to Cleveland to play the Cavaliers, the boos were still being voiced, but I was beginning to focus more on the positive support than the negative. I transformed that energy to fuel my fire to succeed in my goal to play every game to the best of my ability whatever it took. Soon it was time for Boston to play the Houston Rockets in Houston. I was prepared to join the team, but Red came to me and said the league would not permit this to happen, and I was left behind. I told him I was willing to go as it was going to happen sooner or later. But he again stated the league did not want that kind of scene.

As a Boston Celtics player, wearing green game shoes was a requirement. When the team returned, Red asked me if the green game shoes ordered by him for me had come in yet. Now I must admit I hated any shoe color other than white. White shoes were my preferred color choice for my game shoes. Wearing green shoes was something I just could not do. I didn't have the heart to tell him this. He would repeatedly order me a pair, and when they arrived, I made a deal with one of the ball boys. His job was to take them home and never mention that they had been received by me. It worked until one day Red let me know that the gig was up. He simply smiled at me and flicked the ashes from his always lit cigar after asking why his shoe orders were never being worn.

Our first home game at the Boston garden was against the Phoenix Suns. I was called to go into the game and scored around 14 points with 14 rebounds. I put forth my best effort. From that point on I was one of the fans favorites. They loved my sincere hustling effort. Red would always come into the locker room during halftime smoking his cigar. He would always say, "I do not want to see any fake hustle out there. I can live with a loss, but I can't live with a loss without players giving 100 percent effort."

While staying at the Boston Sheraton Prudential Hotel during my return to the NBA. One morning I went down to the hotel restaurant and ordered breakfast. I had three scrambled eggs, three pieces of bacon, two slices of toast and one glass of orange juice. The usual NBA game schedule included the Celtics playing the Philadelphia 76ers on weekends. The Celtics would play Philly on Friday night and then Philly would come to the Boston Garden to play us in a nationally televised game on Sunday. To get settled in the Philly team would arrive in Boston on Saturday. With such a talented roster with Dr. J., World Be Free, Doug Collins, George McGinnis, Bobby Jones, Caldwell Jones, and Chocolate Thunder – Darryl Dawkins, the hotel was filled with fans seeking autographs and photos. This one Sunday morning of the game, I made a point to go down to the restaurant earlier than usual to avoid the clamoring fans.

Looking out into the lobby I see Darryl walking into the restaurant. As I always had to play against him my goal was to be nice and give him lots of compliments. Known as the most powerful dunker in the league this morning I invited him to join me and proceeded to comment on how good his jump shots looked in Friday night's game. My primary objective was to direct his attention from dunking (on me) and shooting away from the basket. His strength and powerful presence was formidable. Hoping my efforts would pay off later, I listened to Darryl place his breakfast order with the waitress.

He quickly listed the following food items from the menu: one dozen eggs, a large plate of bacon, seven slices of toast, and a large pitcher of orange juice. My mind quickly formed a deep appreciation for is thoughtfulness. I would have never imagined his being so close with his teammates that he would order breakfast for them.

Wanting to acknowledge how impressed I was by his consideration, I asked Darryl how he knew what his teammates ordered for breakfast, when the rest of the team was expected to come down and join him. He looked at me, perplexed by my inquiry. With a straight face, he stated, "This is for me!"

I couldn't help but smile and try my very best to refrain from bursting out laughing. Four of our team's games were cancelled due to the blizzard had to be made up before the regular season ended. Already the preplanned schedule was packed tightly with games. This did not leave much room between makeup games for rest and recovery from playing. After most home games, Red, would ask me to join him for dinner at his favorite Chinese restaurant. I would always say no. I knew my hotel staff friends were waiting for me to come back and tell them about the game. Red would extend the friendly middle finger salute and walk away. He didn't know about my routine of visiting with the hotel staff and then engaging in a conversation with my constant companions the twenty-nine flights of stairs. In the final games of the season I had played with four great players, Dave Bing, John Havlicek, Dave Cowens, and Jo White. Two of these greats played in the final games of their careers. In the final two weeks of the season, my weight dropped from 235 pounds to 216 pounds. Catching up on the missed games with travel and play, I was willing to forgo eating to get a few more minutes of sleep.

Of all the games, I played in my NBA career one stands out as the most memorable. John Havlicek's final game (number 17, John "Hondo" Havlicek). John came dressed in a tuxedo, and the stadium was standing room only. Fans showered their hero with gifts and words of praise before the game began. I went to John before the game and asked him, "Are you sure you want to check Randy in your final game?" I recognized two things: first, Randy Smith was young, and second but most important, he was probably the fastest player in the league. Red came into the locker room just before the game began and clearly stated, "I will kill each and every one of you if you lose this game."

The first half against the Buffalo Braves proved to be a difficult start. John was matched up against Randy Smith, who had just won the MVP award in the recent All-Star Game in Atlanta, Georgia. John would not trade off and was determined to meet this challenge. Even though John started off slowly, the supporting crowd continued to yell out his name and would not allow him to have a bad game. John proceeded to score 29 points, 8 assists, and 4 rebounds, and after each basket was scored, the crowd went crazy. This showed all of us the depth of talent and courage. At one point, he scored seven buckets in a row, and the roof on the building literally seemed to be blown away.

Coming home to LA from Boston after Havlicek's final game, I didn't realize I was a free agent. Pat went to Boston with Don Chaney's wife, Jackie, to look for a house. It was interesting to learn that in Boston a new house was one hundred years old or younger. At the LA airport, Pat and Jackie met Dee Crawford, a friend of Charlie Scott. Dee shared that Charlie was looking to sell his house and suggested the two go by and see it. Dee was in real estate and gave them all the information they needed to speak with Charlie. After seeing the house and the price, Charlie agreed to make the deal. When selected by Red to make my return to the NBA as a Boston Celtic, his support and confidence in me as a player and individual was greatly appreciated. Shortly, thereafter I became a free agent with the option to play with the Celtics for another contract or choose to take advantage of other offers. The Denver Nuggets offered me an additional $50,000.00 a year for an extended contract of five years. Red approached me to tell me he would understand if I decided to take the Denver deal as he was not able to increase my salary to make me earn more than the established stars. I reassured him that I had no intention of leaving the Celtics. Interestingly at the end of the season the Celtics changed ownership and I went to play for the San Diego Clippers.

Before the paperwork can be processed, it was learned that the Buffalo Braves were going to switch ownerships, along with Sidney Wicks and myself as players included in the deal. Boston Celtics owners Mr. Levin and Mr. Lipton were living on the West Coast, in Beverly Hills, California. They wanted to move their franchise to the West Coast to eliminate cross-country trips and increase their active participation in their business interest. The switch meant moving to San Diego instead of Boston, which was closer to our roots in Palos Verdes, California. Donald Dell called me to tell me that the Denver Nuggets had offered me a contract for the same amount of years but $50,000 more in salary per year. I explained that Boston's offer might pay less, but there was no price tag on the loyalty and support Red had demonstrated when I needed it the most. Even though I didn't get to remain a Boston Celtics, my friendship and connection with Red Auerbach remained strong throughout his lifetime.

That summer Pat's brother came out to spend the summer and started friendships with local Palos Verdes High School juniors Marc Mills, Reggie and Leo Childs, and John Prassis. This was the summer I built a gym in my garage and worked on rehabilitating my knee. The five of us did five sets of twenty-five reps of squats to get stronger without killing ourselves. On the weekends Marc Mills, would ride with me down to Venice, California, to be around the very best bodybuilding competitors in the world.

Upon graduating from Palos Verdes High School, Marc choose to attend Harvard University and while there I was playing for the Boston Celtics. He supported my return to the NBA as a faithful attendee of my NBA games. Marc graduated from Harvard University. He later secured a degree in Finance from the London School of Economics.

Returning to Palos Verdes after graduation, he made me aware of his becoming gainfully employed. I asked Pete Newell who was at that time working for the Golden State Warriors if any of his players might be looking for a Harvard grad with a tremendous work ethic. As it happened, he did. One player was the President of Beverly Hills Savings. He was given an interview and hired right on the spot. Seeking a place to live, not that returning home was a problem, but after being on your own for four years, returning home is just not going to cut it. We had a home in San Diego that was fully furnished but vacant.

Marc moved in but after a few months realized the drive from San Diego to his new location was too much wear and tear on both the car and the body. Taking some time to look around for a more suitable living arrangement, I agreed to give the down payment if he could find what he wanted at a reasonable price. Once that was arranged, we let him have any of the furnishings and household items he would need to set up his own place. He then found a townhouse in San Clemente.

We have remained friends over the years as later when returning to live in Portland, Oregon, Steve Johnson contacted me and asked if I knew of someone who would be interested in taking a job paying $100,000.00 a year. I thought of Marc and put the offer to him. He was doing quite well and told me he appreciated the thought but his current salary was very comfortable and more than the current offer. He also stated he liked living in California and wasn't interested in moving to the Northwest. Later, when I tried my hand at a Sports Bar in Vancouver, Washington, he helped me out.

We keep in touch and when in Los Angeles we get together to lift weights and keep out friendship active.

I enjoyed working out with the group, and although I knew they needed to move on, I missed their companionship. Marc Mills attended and graduated from Harvard, John Prassis attended and graduated from Brown, Reggie Childs attended and graduated from American University, and Leo Childs attended and graduated from San Luis Obispo.

I continued to work with Pete Newell. Because of the success of players who had been working with Pete, more coaches requested their players work with Pete as well. His camp now included a lot more players but was still as regimented and intense as it was in the beginning. Two of the returning players, Kiki Vandeweghe and Purvis Short, were the best at performing Pete's techniques than any other attendees. Larry Smith and Joe Barry Carroll from the Golden State Warriors returned with the interesting addition of Bernard King. An interesting addition was Bernard King. Pete called me one evening and asked if I thought it a good idea to allow Bernard to join us. Now Bernard was a very talented and gifted athlete who had some issues with previous teams. His behavior was frequently misunderstood. I truly believed if Bernard was willing to attend Pete's camp and perform well, he was prepared to give his best effort into shape. No one could survive the rigors of Pete's camp if they were not serious about getting into shape.

Bernard joined us and experienced exactly what we knew from day one. Pete could not tell time and did not know how to blow a whistle. You played ball until the ball went out of bounds or was in the bucket. None of this fazed Bernard; he came to play every day with an aggressive, fearless, and competitive drive. A free agent that summer, he played so well in camp he signed a contract with the Golden State Warriors. Now Pete was working for the Warriors as a scout. He had an impressive season making the All-Star team. The New York Knicks knew a diamond in the rough when they saw one and immediately offered Bernard a very lucrative contract. He signed with them and went on to establish himself and a superstar and legend.

After camp and with two solid performance years under my belt, the time spent with Pete in the off season had begun to pay off. More coaches were interested in how I had improved, and this added to the desire to send their players to work with Pete during the off season. A bonus for me in many ways. This provided opportunities to play with and against NBA players I would otherwise have never met.

My former Lakers teammate Stu Lantz lived in San Diego and helped me find a home. It was in a new community, Hidden Mesa Estates. The lots were large and the houses individual and custom built. The neighbors were very reserved and not very welcoming. It was later disclosed that many were concerned about blacks moving into the area and had joined forces to buy the house we had put an offer on to prevent an unwanted resident. Our offer went through, and we moved in. After meeting us, the neighbors were not exactly friendly but less hostile than at first. As the season progressed and my profession a point of conversation, the warmth from the neighbors was an improvement.

The new franchise needed a name, and the San Diego Clippers was chosen. Our head coach was Gene Shue, and the roster included a hodgepodge of interesting talent, Sidney Wicks, Randy Smith, Swen Nater, Nick Weatherspoon, Kevin Kunnert, and myself. Kevin

Kunnert's addition came as a bit of a surprise considering the Rudy T. incident. It was an ongoing concern that a lawsuit might be initiated regarding that, and Kevin was my constant teammate from this point forward. Later, World B. Free, formerly of the Philadelphia 76ers, Brian Taylor, and Freeman Williams joined the mix.

The arena in San Diego was small, seating twelve thousand. Fans masquerading as arena seats were prominent for most of our first games. As the season progressed and we were winning, real fans started to attend. The first part of the season, we were off to a slow start. As the season went on, we started to become a team and not a group of individual players. By the end of the season, we were one game away from making the playoffs. It is important to note the following about our four guards.

We had World B. Free. World was averaging 30 points a game. When David Thompson from the Denver Nuggets came to play us in San Diego. World announced in the locker room just before the game started he was going to score 50 points against David Thompson to prove although he wasn't making the big bucks like Thompson, he was definitely worth more in salary, and David Thompson had just signed a new contract for 900K and World B. Free was making 125K. That night World ended up with 49 points. This was because his final bucket worth 2 points was taken from him for committing an offensive foul. World left the game with his sixth foul just falling short of his prediction. World could score on anybody and anytime from anywhere on the court. Truly unbelievable. At the end of the season, if he wasn't the leading scorer in the league, he was up there.

Our other starting guard, Randy Smith, was the fastest and quickest player in the league. He averaged 20 points a game as a San Diego Clipper. Randy was infamous for his outspoken nature. He would talk about anybody and anything that might embarrass someone, not to be mean, but to make people laugh. He was the team jokester. He had a nickname for the coach, and he used it in front of him daily. It was Donny Osmond. This was because Gene Shue had a full head of hair that he dyed to perfection. Whenever the coach would yell at us and say, "None of you will be coming back next year. I don't want any of you guys." Randy would say, "Donny Osmond is going off again." The coach had no idea Randy was talking about him. Later when the coach would say, "I love all of you guys, dinner is on me." Randy would repeat, "Donny Osmond is happy today."

Randy lived in Mount Helix and always drove expensive, fancy automobiles. He liked to race down Highway 8 and wave farewell as he passed me on the way to practice or a game. One day as we were driving to practice, me in my conservative car and he in his expensive ride, he passed me by and waved his usual gesture. A few miles down the highway, there was Randy standing on the side of the highway outside his expensive, fancy automobile. He tried to flag me down, but I simply waved and drove on. He gave me the friendly gesture as I passed him by. Of course, I turned around at the next exit and returned to give him a ride. But I had to admit there was a wide smile across my face. Randy Smith and Sidney Wicks enjoyed playing practical jokes on anyone and everyone whenever a golden opportunity presented itself. Especially since I had made fun of Randy he was all too eager to pay me back. Such was the case on a road trip when playing on the Clippers while staying in a hotel in Cleveland, Ohio. Unaware that Ali was staying with his entourage in the same hotel as us I got up and went down to the hotel dining room to have breakfast.

Randy and Sidney after seeing him having breakfast approached him. Normally a fan would ask for an autograph or request having a photo taken but not these two. Capitalizing on my infamous name and the Rudy T incident both proceeded to inform the heavy weight champion of the world that a player on their NBA team boasted how he could kick his butt. They specifically identified this player as Kermit Washington.

Ali was in Cleveland preparing for his upcoming bout against Chuck Wepner. As soon as I entered the dining area, Ali walked up to me all the time boxing with swings that sting like a bee extremely close to my face. He voiced, "You think you can kick my butt!" while never missing a swing. He had a devilish look on his face while moving around me. I was scared to death and gaining my composure managed to repeat, "Please don't hurt me!"

Even after hearing Randy and Sidney laughing to the point of being overcome with another successful prank. Ali was truly gracious and I somehow was able to order and eat breakfast. The news of their successful prank was the talk of the road trip.

Later we met again, while he was in LA staying at the Marriott in the Marina, preparing for his bout against Ken Norton. I didn't ask if he remembered our Cleveland meeting, and simply joined the throngs of fans who listened to his never-ending tales. Ali was a great story teller and enjoyed working a crowd whether in a ring or outside of one.

Brian Taylor, my teammate on the San Diego Clippers, was a Princeton graduate and an opponent during my college years. We were the only professional basketball players who could say they had a brother who was playing professional football at the same time we were playing professional basketball. His brother played for the San Francisco 49ers, and my brother played for the Saint Louis Cardinals. One of the most intelligent players in the league and the best defensive player on the San Diego Clipper roster, he could run a basketball clinic designed to teach how to move your feet defensively without committing a foul. He was that good.

Freeman Williams was a Portland State star recognized as the leading scorer in the nation while in college. A Division 1 scoring champion became the first San Diego Clipper to win the Player of the Month award. A quick jumper in one college game, he scored 76 points in one game. A rookie, he could score against anybody, anywhere, but not in the same manner as World B. Free. Freeman was a quick, smart dribbler whereas World would literally jump over people.

Swen Nater, our starting center, was built like a Greek god. A good rebounder and defensive and offensive player, he made a very positive contribution to our newly formed team. Every day Randy would make a comment about Swen more than any other player on the team. Swen always wore those double-knit stretch pants when on the road. To make matters worse, they were always the same pants. Randy picked up on this right away as he noticed the knee area was showing signs of wear and tear. Swen tried to dye his pants to stop the constant comments from Randy. He was not successful and the dye job was a mess, resulting in even more comments from Randy. Swen took many things seriously; fortunately, Randy's tirades were not one of them. I remember Swen making the Olympic team only to quit because he felt he wasn't being fed enough. As an NBA player Swen was the only player in professional basketball history to lead the NBA and ABA in rebounds.

By the end of our first season, Swen and I were in the top ten for field goal percentage in the league. I was 8-11 and Swen was 3-12 in the final game. When I looked at the stats, I noticed that our stats had been recorded incorrectly. In fact, they had been switched. Swen, after looking over the same information I was looking at, stated, "I didn't think I played that well tonight." I then said, "You didn't." But the stats remained, and he beat me in field goal percentage. That's all you need to know about Swen.

My senior year at American University, I spent hours decorating my room with a collage dedicated to those players I admired. It was truly a wall of fame. Prominent magazine photos of Sidney Wicks and Kareem and others provided inspiration daily. When I made the NBA and these greats became my teammates, it was like a dream come true.

After having a very successful first season as a San Diego Clipper and feeling more at ease, reality set in. I began to sense fans were now seeing me as an individual separate from the fight. That summer I learned I would have to go to Houston to testify in the lawsuit Rudy filed against the Los Angeles Lakers. Although the original venue was Los Angeles, the change was made without any protest from the Lakers organization. This demonstrated there was no concern or effort going to be made to clear my name of any wrongdoing regarding this incident.

The Los Angeles Lakers had the deep pockets and seemed prepared to pay Rudy for damages. It was perceived that as my owner, it was their responsibility to keep me under control. I was portrayed as the wild dog that got out of the front yard and attacked an innocent bystander. Going down to Houston for the trial, I knew the Lakers and I had no chance of coming out of this smelling like a rose. The message sent by the Lakers organization was to simply pay up and permanently remove me from their database. I was dismissed, erased, and forgotten.

Before walking into the courtroom, one attorney shared with me there seemed to be a good chance of winning this lawsuit. I looked at him and simply said, "We didn't have a snowball's chance in you know where." Entering the courtroom, the twelve-man jury looked at me, and if they could, I would have been strung up before the door could close behind me. The looks of contempt could be felt as if a hot fire were consuming a piece of paper. Just as I predicted, the Lakers lost the lawsuit, and Rudy was awarded about two million dollars.

Coming back home to San Diego, I was excited about next year's team. About this time rumors were being circulated that Bill Walton wanted to play in his hometown city of San Diego. He grew up in the Mount Helix area. This news did not immediately become a concern until my name was added as compensation for this trade of signing of Bill Walton, depending on his current contractual status.

The season started, and I attended practice with Bill Walton as the newest member of the team. Gene Shue called me over and shared, "We tried to hold on to you, but you are part of the compensation for acquiring Bill Walton." Here I am in the past year and a half on my fourth team (Los Angeles Laker, Boston Celtics, San Diego Clippers, and Portland Trailblazers). The rumors were soon confirmed, and along with Kevin Kunnert, the trade was made, and we were both headed to the Portland Trailblazers. This affirms my contention of the NBA's fear of a lawsuit as since Los Angeles lost in Rudy T.'s lawsuit, the next logical recourse for me would be to file a lawsuit against Kevin and the Houston Rockets. To ensure this would not happen, the NBA made sure Kevin and I remained teammates until our careers were ended.

Coming home I had to tell Pat I was traded to the Portland Trailblazers. I gave this matter a great deal of thought. Donald Dell called me, and I simply told him I wasn't going. I was tired of having to constantly start again in proving to people the real person I was. I remained in San Diego for a few weeks to do some serious reflection about my future in the NBA. My having to go through another stressful situation so soon after the Houston trial was more than I wanted to deal with.

Donald Dell convinced me to go, after giving me two weeks to decompress. I packed my bags and headed up to the Northwest. Arriving in Portland, pre-season had gotten under way, but to my advantage, starters Mychal Thompson and Maurice Lucas were injured along with a couple of other players. This moved me directly into the starting lineup. The first day of practice, I met my new teammates. Jim Brewer and Abdul Jeelani stayed in the same hotel as me. I wasn't in the greatest shape, having missed a couple of weeks of practice.

My first pre-season game was against the Phoenix Suns in Portland at the Memorial Coliseum. I got into the game and played extremely well for me, 14 points 10 rebounds with a lot of hustle. From that point on the fans loved me, and I was a starter for the Portland Trailblazers. At this point I had played 100-plus games straight. While playing in Maurice Lucas's position and Mychal Thompson's position, playing a great deal resulted in my making the All-Star Game held in Washington, DC. The 1980 Portland Trailblazer team was composed of good group of guys: Maurice Lucas, Mychal Thompson, Jim Brewer, Billy Ray Bates, Ron Brewer, T. R. Dunn, Bob Gross, Lionel Hollins, Abdul Jeelani, Kevin Kunnert, Calvin Natt, Tom Owens, Jim Paxton, and Dave Twardzik. Our head coach was Jack Ramsey.

We won our first nine games in a row without Mychal Thompson, Maurice Lucas, and Lionel Hollins. We thought we were on a roll. The city was overjoyed and all caught up in the magic of success. This was particularly amazing as this team was not composed of any notable superstars. Our head coach was instrumental in handling a team that was undermanned. Our tenth game was against the Phoenix Suns. If we won this game, the Portland Trailblazer record book would show this team achieved the best start of the season in the history of the Portland Trailblazers franchise. In the last second of the game, Walter Davis took a shot from the corner, winning the game for Phoenix and shattering our ability to put our names in the record book.

From that point on we were just an average NBA team. Maurice and Lionel returned, but Mychal was out for the season with a broken leg. With their return, the two stars who were on the championship team expected to get their spots back. Coach Ramsey had other ideas and did not immediately agree. Lionel won his back quickly, but I had Maurice's spot and that was not given back to him as quickly as he had expected. Maurice's growing animosity made practices dangerous because he was extremely aggressive. His outward display of such aggressive behavior was evident and continued to elevate to an all-time level of physical play. His mental and physical frustration on the court let everyone know it was best practice to stay out of his way. But you should realize that before he was injured he was the best player on the team in his starting position.

He had the mentality of a heavyweight champion; he wanted his spot back and was determined to hurt anybody that got in his way.

Before playing the Chicago Bulls in Chicago, I talked with Coach Ramsey. "Coach, you can let Maurice start in front of me, and I will come off the bench. This is not going to bother me. If we don't make this happen, you won't have a team to coach. He will kill all of us." And so, Maurice was a starter from that point on, but Tom Owens, the current starting center, got hurt, and Coach moved Maurice to the starting center position and returned me to the starting power forward.

When playing the Milwaukee Bucks in Milwaukee, we lost the game. Jack came into the locker room to go over what went wrong. He asked the team, "Does anybody have anything to say about why we lost tonight?" Now everybody in their right mind knew better than to open their mouth. Maurice opened and started telling Coach Ramsey what was wrong with everything he was doing. That was the kiss of death. Maurice was traded one week later to the New Jersey Nets for Calvin Natt, a very aggressive player. Maurice still had a lot to add to our team, but frankly, Jack had had enough of him.

Calvin Natt was a six-foot-five-inch forward and could play the 3 or the 4 position. He was not tall enough to play the 4 but was strong enough to. He earned the nickname Pitt Bull. Ron Brewer, out of Arkansas, was dubbed Boothead, because his head was shaped like a boot. He was a solid shooter and defensive player. T. O. Tom Owens, from South Carolina, was a seven-foot center. If you took one look at him, your first impression was he didn't look like an athlete. But TO could play the game. I shared with him that since leaving the Lakers team, no matter what team I was on, we never beat the Lakers in LA. TO simply said, "We beat the Lakers when we play them down there." True to his statement, the Portland Trailblazers *did* beat the Lakers in LA. T. R. Dunn from Alabama was a strong defensive player. He was very quiet and could best be described as a man of few words and currently coaching in Houston, Texas. Jimmy Paxton from Ohio, University of Dayton, had a sensitive nature who later became an NBA All-Star. At first he did not have a lot of playing time due to having good guards on the team, but when he got into the game, he made a positive contribution.

After getting Calvin Natt, Larry Steele was injured, and we needed a replacement in the guard position. Larry Steele was a left-over from the championship year and a very good utility player. He could play a lot of different positions. A great teammate, he came out of Kentucky. Jim Brewer was my roommate for a while and came from Minnesota. We met during the Olympic trials and was a good rebounder. Dave Twardzik was the other leftover from the championship year. He hailed from Old Dominion.

It is times like this that you remember this adage, "Be careful of what you wish for as it just might come true." So, entered Bill Ray Bates from the Maine Lumberjacks, a CBA team. While practicing in New York before the New York Knicks game, we saw Jack Ramsey working out this strong looking country brother on the other end of the court. Testing to see if he had what it took to join the team, Jack was running the hell out of him with drills. Billy Ray did everything they asked and more. His appearance was an unkempt version of Hercules. His hair was disheveled, but the brother could run.

Billy joined the team while we are in New York. He fit in like an old glove. From Kentucky State, Billy's congenial personality was engaging and a welcomed addition to the team. He didn't play in the New York Knicks game, but we were all interested in getting to know him better. From Mississippi, we boarded a plane headed to Detroit to play the Detroit Pistons. Checking into our hotel, T. R. Dunn and I we sitting downstairs in the Hyatt Regency Hotel having a bite to eat in the coffee shop. The elevator doors were made of glass, allowing you to see who was in the elevator and what, if anything, they were doing.

T. R. Dunn, Ron Brewer, and I looked over at the elevator, and we both noticed Billy riding up and down in the elevator. As we continued to eat, we couldn't help but notice Billy was still riding up and down in the elevator and was not getting off. TR told me to go and get that boy since I was the elected captain of the team. I walked over and got Billy out of elevator. Billy said to us, "I've never been in an elevator I can look out of the doors before. This was great, just like a ride in an amusement park. I just like riding up and down." He sat down with us and looked down at our shoes. Billy asked where we got our shoes. He wanted to know what size I wore and was happy to learn we both wore the same size. He then asked if he could have some of old shoes. I told him he would be getting his own new shoes. He then said, "Do you mean for free?" When I said yes, he got up, walked back over to the elevators, got in, and continued to ride up and down.

T. R. Dunn and Ron Brewer burst out laughing. The next day in the locker room, changing before the game, we looked over Billy's body, and he was six feet two or six feet three and about 225 pounds. He was a taller version of Bo Jackson. His legs had scars all over them. He told us he had to run through many thicket bushes in his youth. Billy was notorious for exaggerating the simplest story or explanation about anything. He had a six-pack but never touched a weight in his life. During warm-ups before the game, we were amazed that he would dunk like a mini Darryl Dawkins. He was exerting such power we wondered if the rims would withstand his strength.

Of all the athletes, I had ever played with, he was by far the greatest athlete, not the best basketball player, but by far the greatest athlete, hands down. Playing against the Chicago Bulls with Artis Gilmore in the center position, Billy had his first opportunity to play in the NBA. When Billy Ray got in the game, it was obvious he had not learned the plays. Not knowing any of the plays and operating on basic instinct, he knew to go to the hole and score. When he did this, he was dunking on every player. Despite our optimism, we soon realized he would never learn and remember the plays. His style of play demonstrated the abilities Bill Ray did have. He could palm a ball like a grapefruit. He was considered one of the best leapers in the league. A very good shooter, not just scorer. One of the few players in the league who could go to the right or the left off the dribble with him being closely guarded and shoot a jump shot over them.

In one game against the Los Angeles Lakers, he must have had seven dunks. This was the beginning of the legend of Billy Ray *DUNK* Bates. From this point on he was *the* fan favorite. Billy Ray joining the team added more than talent on the court. Off the court Billy provided hours of amusing entertainment. After his first year with the Portland Trailblazers, the organization signed him into a rehabilitation center for alcohol and drug abuse intervention treatment. Billy knew he had a problem but would always say, "Yeah, man, I got it." But he didn't. Billy was truly a crowd favorite. He was brutally honest, and his only goal once he had the ball was to score. His baskets were incredible feats that bedazzled the eyes of all onlookers. After a game Billy, would sit for hours signing autographs and simply talking with all fans waiting around to share time with him. During the holiday season Billy, would get hundreds of gifts which he could not fit into his locker. It was acknowledged and openly appreciated his attitude of coming to give his best effort on the court every night.

The All-Star game on February 3, 1980, was held in Washington, DC. The names of all twenty-two players selected were announced in January. Scott Wedman from the Kansas City Kings was one. The 1979-1980 NBA season was my first year on the Portland Trailblazer team. Knowing the date of the upcoming NBA- All Star game I was looking forward to having a few days off allowing me to settle into the Northwest lifestyle. After driving back home from taking my daughter Dana to gymnastic lessons, the phone rang and one of the staff from the Portland Trailblazers organization's voice sounded a bit odd. At first I thought the message I was given was a joke. Could it really be? I was told I had been selected by the NBA coaches to replace Wedman, who having sustained an injury would not be able to play in the game.

I was excited to be chosen but the prospects were even more rewarding. When nominations were being made for the NBA All-Star team local Blazer fans turned in copious copies of nomination forms. However, despite their concerted efforts I was not initially included. The rooster for the Western Conference included: Marques Johnson, Adrian Dantley, Kareem Abdul-Jabbar, Jack Sikma, Paul Westphal, Magic Johnson, Walter Davis, Lloyd Be Free, Dennis Johnson, Kermit Washington, Otis Birdsong and for the Eastern Conference: George Gervin, Eddie Johnson, Moses Malone, Dan Roundfield, Larry Bird, Nate Archibald, Julius Erving, Bill Cartwright, and Micheal Ray Richardson.

What is most appreciated about having this opportunity to play with such NBA All-Stars was being selected to replace an injured Scott Wedman by the NBA coaches. I was at home thinking about having a few days off and watching the All-Star Game as usual on TV. The phone rang and the secretary in the front office told me I was selected to replace Wedman in the upcoming All-Star Game. I had to ask if this was a joke, as the reality of such a possibility seemed unimaginable. Not only was the opportunity of a lifetime, with playing in front of my Washington, DC family and friends an added bonus. Although I was in a state of shock I packed my bags and was ready to board the plane leaving Portland.

The pre-game activities were filled with players making a few classic remarks about one another, showing how each appreciated being there and the level of competitive spirit was still alive and well. The gifts and memorabilia given still holds sentimental value.

Being held at the Capital Center in Landover, Maryland with an attendance of 19,035 on February 3, 1980, I played fourteen minutes, had 1- FGM – field goal made, 6 FGA – field goal attempts, 1 PFS- personal foul shot, and 4 PTS – points. It was exciting and nerve wracking at the same time to be playing with such greats. Although it was cold outside I was warmed by the exhilaration of simply being a part of the game. Not expecting to be a starter and content to be included in the game, the final score of East – 144 and West – 136.

We went into overtime and Larry Bird, with 1:40 left in the game, made the first 3-pointer in All-Star Game history. The crowd went crazy. My coach was Lenny Wilkens, and I was on the same West team with: Marques Johnson -Milwaukee Bucks, Adrian Dantley – Utah Jazz, Kareem Abdul-Jabbar – Los Angeles, Lakers, Jack Sikma – Seattle Super Sonics, Paul Westphal – Phoenix Suns, Magic Johnson – Los Angeles Lakers, World Be Free – San Diego Clippers, Dennis Johnson – Seattle Super Sonics, Walter Davis – Phoenix Suns and Otis Birdsong – Kansas City Kings. The coach for the East team was Billy Cunningham with his players being: George Garvin – San Antonio Spurs, Eddie Johnson – Atlanta Hawks, Moses Malone – Houston Rockets, Elvin Hayes- Washington Bullets, Dan Roundfield – Atlanta Hawks, Larry Bird – Boston Celtics, Nate Archibald – Boston Celtics, Julius Erving – Philadelphia 76ers, John Drew – Atlanta Hawks, Bill Cartwright – New York Knicks, and Michael Ray Richardson – New York Knicks. I could return to my home town, play in the NBA All-Star game, and spend time with friends and family. It was quite cold in DC, but I felt warm and content to be present for this event.

The pre-game activities were incredibly wonderful. I had the opportunity to renew old friendships with Adrian Dantley one of my Rudolph playground partners, Kareem a former teammate on the Lakers, World Be Free my most recent former teammate from San Diego, Moses Malone who met when he was first drafted into the NBA in our agent's Donald Dell's Washington, DC office, and Nate Archibald my brother Chris' college roommate. Sharing stories and experiences with the players was quite interesting. My altercation with Rudy T always led to many conversations filled with questions and words of support from the players who could relate to how the incident went down. I was both honored and excited to be heard, understood, and accepted by worthy of being in the company of such legendary greats.

The day of the game the players boarded a chartered bus and drove from downtown DC to Landover, Maryland where the game was being held in the Capital Centre. In front of a crowd of 19,035 I played fourteen minutes, scored one basket, two free throws for 4 points and grabbed 8 rebounds. I didn't feel too badly with these stats it was an experience I was happy to be a part of. George Gervin was named the MVP the final score: The East 144 and the West 136. Both the game and the day ended all too quickly, but the memories and friendships initiated remain.

My second year with the Blazers, Jack opened camp with a two-mile run. The goal was for the big men to complete the course under thirteen minutes; for the rest of the team the goal was to beat twelve minutes. The night before Billy stayed out late drinking. He came to camp hung over. As he ran past everyone, you could smell the liquor on his breath. He finished to course in less than ten minutes. He was legendary. Billy did not understand pressure; he just went out every night to play ball. He had the capability to become a Hall of Famer; that's what a great athlete he was.

Mychal Thompson returned, making us a better team. He was the number one pick in the draft of 1978--79 from the Bahamas. Along with Billy, Calvin Natt, Kelvin Ramsey, and Jimmy Paxton, we were a good team, not the greatest team, but solid. Coach Ramsey wanted Mychal to throw in the pass to Billy Ray for a final shot to win the game against the Philadelphia 76ers. Philly team was well noted to have on its roster the most talented current NBA players in the league. With this fact, ever present in all our minds, this was a big game for us to win. An example being the game against the Philadelphia 76ers at the Portland Memorial Coliseum. The talent displayed on Philly's team kept us on our toes all night.

We were trailing by one point with three seconds left in the game. We had to inbound the ball full court. Coach Ramsey called a time out. He says to Mychal Thompson, "I want you to throw the full court pass." Billy had expressed his ability to make the final bucket and win the game. Sitting on the bench I had already visualized I had thrown the ball to Billy and we won the game. I said to Coach, "Let me throw in the pass." I was good at throwing long inbound passes. Coach then agreed, stating, "Alright Kermit you throw in the pass." Returning to the court, I throw in the out of bounds pass. Billy performs an aerobatic move, catches the ball and immediately makes the basket. This was one of his better moves as he scooped the ball before taking the shot. The crowd went *crazy, the bench emptied as players spilled out onto the court to congratulate Billy by physically jumping on top of him.*

Billy was amazing, continuing to provide spectacular performance night after night. Jimmy Paxson was our steady, hardworking teammate who added in scoring points. Kelvin Ramsey was the ball handler who created opportunities for everyone else to score points and make baskets.

On road trips Jack was always worried about Billy's use of alcohol. His strategy was to assign different players with the responsibility of making sure Billy did *not* drink. This accomplished two things: Billy knew everybody was aware of his problem with alcohol, and he also knew his teammates were concerned about his welfare. Although this helped him to understand and accept our efforts to look after him, he still needed his fix.

Mychal Thompson was Player of the Year when he graduated from University of Minnesota and was awarded an all-you-can-eat gift certificate from the Victoria Station restaurant chain. To say that Mychal single-handedly contributed to the chain's future financial problems would be an understatement. It was his normal practice to invite the team to dine with him in any city where a Victoria Station restaurant was offering services.

On a Dallas trip, Mychal extended this offer to me, Billy, and Calvin. While seated at our table, Billy looked over the menu and said, "I want some of those *swimpy* things." I looked over at him and asked, "What do you mean those 'swimpy things'?" He said, "You know, those white and pink things with tails." I then realized he meant *shrimp*. The first-time Billy tasted shrimp was when he had a meal with me and I offered him some.

After ordering our meal and a few drinks, Billy turned to me and said, "I need something to drink. Let me have a drink." This statement wasn't uttered once but repeatedly. Calvin finally said, "Let him have one drink." And Mychal agreed. Billy then ordered one drink of sixteen ounces of assorted rums. When it arrived at the table, I looked at it and said, "Billy that is more than you can have." He said, "You said I could have one drink, and this is just that." As he proceeded to consume this "more than one drink" drink, his demeanor started to change. His eyes got glassy, and the whites of his eyes slowly turned red. He then shared his observations of the clientele entering the restaurant.

Although his comments were genuinely amusing, he then turned his comments to each one of us at the table, specifically focusing on our on-the-court performances. The comments were also equally amusing, and we continued to finish our meal and returned to the hotel. I was literally praying incessantly Billy would have a peaceful night's rest and wake up refreshed, ready for our scheduled shoot around practice on time or even miraculously arrive early. That did *not* come to pass. He was stone-cold drunk. I knew we were in trouble. When shoot-around actually began and Billy was not there, Coach Ramsey asked me where he was.

I was then directed to go and get him. Walking back over to the hotel, I found Billy in a deep sleep in his room. Waking him up, he quickly got dressed, and we raced over to shoot-around practice. Coach Ramsey was *beyond* upset and let us know this by giving us his "I'm mad at you" Ramsey stare. He pulled me aside and yelled at me and then allowed Billy to start practice. Billy was held afterward and made to do some extra running exercises, which to him was a cake walk. I wasn't sure if Jack actually knew Billy had been drinking, but he could probably tell.

That night nobody knew if Jack was going to let Billy into the game. He was adamant about his rule: No practice, you don't play. Late to practice, you might *not* play. We simply had to wait and see. As Billy wasn't a starter, we were prepared to adopt the wait-and-see attitude. We weren't doing very well, and we needed Billy out on the court. Coach put him in, and before the last minutes of the third quarter, Billy had scored around 40 points in three quarters. He was so hot if left in, he might have scored 60 points before the final buzzer sounded. We all knew if Billy wasn't late that morning, Jack would have left him in the game, and we also knew if Billy remained in the game, it would give him an added edge of truly being identified at the star.

Jack was smart enough to realize this would make Billy recognized at deserving a starting spot. As it was, Jack was a poster boy for being a control freak. We had to run plays exactly as dictated, and everything we were told was to be done without question or comment. He couldn't and wouldn't let Billy gain the upper hand. He would never give up any of his control no matter how small. With Kelvin Ramsey, the starting point guard and Jimmy Paxton the starting shooting guard, having Bill come off the bench was working, and it would remain so. Billy, although a superior athlete, did not run plays, but when he got the ball, he simply went to the basket to score.

As the year progressed, all road trip included my looking for a place to wash my clothes and finding a place to work out to lift weight. Mychal Thompson was also interested in lifting, and we would go to the gyms together. Mychal has a very outgoing personality and would engage in a conversation with people working out in the gym. I focused on my workouts whereas Mychal took on the role of a professional trainer, pointing out what people were doing wrong and demonstrating the best way to train. "You're not lifting right," was the phrase he would use to initiate a conversation. This is because Mychal always thought he knew more than the average guy about anything and everything. That is the main reason nobody wanted to sit next to him on the airplane rides we would take. This resulted in two empty seats on either a plane or bus. One empty seat was next to the coach and the other next to Mychal.

After completing a workout session, Mychal would remove his T-shirt and walk around the hotel showing off his six-pack. I would be embarrassed and would tell him, "Get away from me, and don't walk near me." The team would simply laugh, and this group was not the kind who complained about salaries, playing time, or positions. Each one was concerned with playing together and winning games.

We made it to the playoffs, and we faced Kansas City in the first round. Our opening game was in Portland, and we were beat at home. In those days, the team who won the best two out of three moved on. Otis Birdsong, Phil Ford, Sam Lacey, and Scott Wedman were players whom we faced. We traveled to Kansas City and beat them on their home court. Returning to Portland to play game 3, we packed our bags and were ready to board a flight directly after winning this game. Unfortunately, we lost as Otis Birdsong had an exceptional game. It was a close win for Kansas City, and the final bucket in the last few seconds moved them forward, and we stayed home, and the season ended.

The summer of 1982, David Falk organized an All-star game and trip to Japan. Among the NBA players to accept his invitation were primarily his clients. John Lucas, Moses Malone, Adrian Dantley, Elvin Hayes and the greatly revered Kareem Abdul-Jabbar where among the list of players. When we arrived at LAX we took note of a Japanese woman who had a large hotel luggage cart filled to the brim with See's candy boxes. I wondered about this and made a joke about Japan not having any quality chocolates to eat.

The plan ride was long but with the many interesting personalities on board the time passed rather quickly. Landing in Japan at Narita International we boarded a charter bus to the Hotel ibis Tokyo Shinjuku. A modern building in the cosmopolitan Shinjuku district it was three to five minutes from the Tokyo Shinjuku train station. The city was pristine and I saw new models of cars that would come to the States year later.

There were set rules to be strictly observed. When someone in our group tried to walk down the up staircase, before making up down five steps was carried down the stairs encouraged to walk in the correct direction. Then shown where to stand inside a drawn white slash mark to wait for the soon to arrive train. Eager to practice their English you could ask anyone a question and be sure to get a response. That helped us to move around the city.

With time, off to sightsee we walked down major streets and encountered shrines in various sizes of Buddha. Shrines were literally everywhere. Bakeries were scarce and Nate seeing a tempting apple pastry in the window walked in to buy one. He quickly exited the store and shared the one pastry cost five American dollars. With the yen worth more than the American dollar on this day he passed on the pastry and later purchased an apple for the bargain price of five American dollars. Curious as to sweets in general we chocolate candies were the size of current day miniatures and cost three American dollars each. The understanding of the large hotel luggage cart filled with See's Candy boxes was now made very clear.

One evening we were invited to an authentic Japanese restaurant. Locals were seated on the floor with legs crossed and the restroom facilities featured a large hole in the floor without a toilet to sit on, there were no toilet covers and toilet tissue was merely a memory. We soon learned to carry tissues or pieces of toilet paper in our pockets. The meal they arranged for us was more than interesting. On a long wooden tray, each of us were given a small fish, reminding one a dead goldfish, a moldy piece of cheese and a variety of "things" that looked like someone cleaned the kitchen and found insects that might serve and appetizers. The locals seemed to enjoy the cuisine and eagerly encouraged us to try it you might like it motto. At one point, a player picked up his fish and asked who was brave enough to give it a go. No one bought into the invitation. When we returned to the hotel we went to the restaurant to order some familiar cuisine. It became the standing joke to count the number of French fries or peas to see which plate had the most.

Breakfast was lots of bacon, toast and soft-boiled eggs. If we were going on an all-day excursion, not being able to return for a mid-day meal, we made bacon sandwiches and left the eggs behind. The tours arranged were informative and showed us the vast differences between the city and the rural farming life-style. Rolling cultivate field grew a large variety of fruits and vegetables. Workers wore the typical Japanese outfit one would associate with a scene from a Hollywood movie.

We ventured to a local strip mall with lots of European clothing shops. Many stores were busy and lots of new designs were displayed in store windows. It was interesting to note the mannequins all had blonde wigs. It wasn't unusual to see many Japanese teenagers with dyed blonde hair. Prices for many items was high and locals in the city limits wore expensive and tailored attire. Apartment building seem to reach for the heavens as land space was limited. It was pointed out the any structure with bamboo finishes let you know the occupants were well off.

The day of the game came quickly and we just had one day to explore the city. We were told that on the weekends Japanese teenagers would dance in the city streets to American 50' rock and roll music wearing the sock hop pink poodle skirt complete with bobby socks and black and white saddle shoes. Leaving homes wearing normal clothing then change into the 50's, Grease, outfit and let it all hang out. Males combed their hair like Elvis and females sported ponytails. Everyone was enjoying the activity and invited us to join in.

On a short shopping trip when Moses wanted to buy a camera, our bus driver took the group to downtown Tokyo to an electronic warehouse type establishment. The space was small but the inventory impressive. Having done his research, Moses knew what he wanted found the prices much lower than in the States even with the yen being worth more than the dollar. He made his purchase and before we arrived back at the hotel, managed to break the camera on the bus ride back to the hotel. Springs were flying everywhere. John Lucas added to his frustration and Moses continued to complain. Not being able to read the directions he tried the *fly by the seat of my pants approach* to finding out how to work it. He repeated, in his usual fashion – as he would tend to mumble and not speak as clearly as he would when calm, that the camera was the problem. He insisted the bus driver take him back. After spending five thousand dollars he wanted true customer satisfaction and it didn't matter he made a purchase in a foreign country. Bottom line he wanted to complain and either get a replacement or his money back.

Kareem spent most of his on his own as he brought his current girlfriend and their baby alone on the trip. He was always polite and friendly just private and unassuming.

As a family, we headed to San Diego, California, and over the summer bought a ten-acre farm in Boring, Oregon. Being well known in Portland had its advantages, but when one wanted to have privacy and downtime, living in the city limits posed a problem. We looked for a place that was quiet and had enough space for two dogs who loved being outside and running free. We had six neighbors each with large lots, and they were friendly from a distance unless needed. Closet neighbor asked if he could have the use of our barn and the large field for his livestock. In exchange, he would cut the hay, bail it, and store it in our barn for future use by his livestock. I agreed, and the property was well-kept.

One morning I decided to take a walk to the far end of the property. I knew the perimeter was lined with an electric fence but had never ventured to see how far this fence was from the house. Walking across the field, I noticed the land sloped down, and there was a small creek running across. Once you crossed over the small creek, the land sloped upward. I then noticed something moving on my right in my peripheral vision. A large, very large bull was advancing toward me. I quickly looked back to the house and tried to determine if I could get back down to the front of the property before the bull charged me. My two dogs immediately sensed the danger I was about to face and distracted the bull's attention long enough for me to run back safely to the house. I waited for them to run back as well, and I closed the gate before the advancing bull could hurt me or my dogs.

Driving down to San Diego, it was time to spend the off season working out with Pete. Jerome Whitehead joined Swen Nater and me as we drove to Los Angeles three times a week to meet Pete at Loyola Marymount College. Pete would train us, and if he tried to give us a break, we pointed out that this was not acceptable and to train us as if we were Spartan warriors. Driving back home after Pete's workouts proved to make for long days.

In the same way Pete, had helped Bernard King, he did the same for Jerome Whitehead. Jerome had not been playing, and the San Diego Clippers had offered to extend his contract for $50,000 for three years as he was a free agent. By attending Pete Newell's Big Man Camp, Pete could work with him and determine what kind of player he was. When I returned to Portland, Jack Ramsey and Stu Inman, the general manager, asked me if I could recommend someone to fill in the backup center positon. I immediately thought about Jerome. I suggested they call Pete Newell. Jerome had worked out with him over the summer. Following this phone call, the Portland Trailblazers offered Jerome a three-year no-cut contract for $125,000 a year. The San Diego Clippers countered with $150,000 a year for a three-year no-cut and Jerome stayed in San Diego and went on to play for the

Golden State Warriors, where Pete was working as a scout. He later established himself as a good, solid center in the league.

This was the summer my brother Chris and his family moved to San Diego, California. We headed up to Portland, Oregon. In pre-season, I injured my Achilles tendon. I wasn't healing as rapidly as I had anticipated. I managed to practice in pre-season and expected I was getting well to play in games, but it just wasn't happening. As this had been the case with my previous injuries when it wasn't healing as expected, I knew it would be difficult to keep my starting position. Jack's staunch rule "If you don't practice, you don't play" resounded heavily in my mind. My back was also hurting as I had injured it during my rookie year. It came to the point in the thirtieth game that I could hardly walk and required constant icing and heavy doses of aspirin.

Even knowing what Jack's response would be, I went to him and made a request to not have to practice as hard or as often for me to give my best performance on the court. He firmly stated, "If can't fully practice. I can't play you." I then held a meeting with Jack and Stu Inman about the seriousness of my situation. I explained about my back and my knees and stated my body just couldn't take it anymore. They offered me the option of sitting the remainder of the year on the bench and giving my body some time to rest and then come back the following season.

I was afraid I was never going to be healthy again, because I could always taste pain in my mouth. Bending over was so excruciatingly painful. I had to do something to end the pain. That was the end of my NBA career.

San Diego Clippers full team

First year with the Lakers

Billy Ray Bates

Billy Ray Bates the best athlete I ever played with

Jerome Kersey, My die-hard workout partners

Kevin Duckworth, My die-hard workout partners

Ran the stairs in this hotel in Boston, 29 stories, 10 times a day, 25 lb weight vest

CHAPTER 10

Pete Newell – My Dad
"The Master Teacher"

My father, Pete Newell, and mother, Florence Newell, raised my brothers Peter Junior, Tommy, Roger, and me with a love of sports and people. My mother was before her time in that she led by example. She had a very positive and strong female personality that she eagerly shared with the women she interacted with. This was especially true of rookie wives who entered the lifestyle of glitz and glamour. She was helpful in showing them what was important and what was superficial. Florence was a voracious reader. It was not uncommon for her to frequent the local library and check out five or six books. After reading each one, she on occasion would check them out again to reread them. Her reading choices varied and her interests insatiable. Authors such as Saul Bellow, John Steinbeck, Langston Hughes, Eldridge Cleaver, James Baldwin, Ernest Hemingway, Carl Sagan, David Halberstam, and James Michener provided literature that was enjoyed and shared with others. Being well versed on a variety of subjects, she could interject interest points for others to consider, and at times conversations would be limited as to her audience.

With my dad being away a lot, the responsibility of parenting fell largely on her shoulders. She confidently filled these roles with style and grace. Florence was family oriented and with such strong beliefs that she and my father were a perfect match for one another. It has often been said that my dad, Pete Newell, changed the lives of many people. I must admit that is not only a true statement but also an understatement. In fact, my dad changed the way professional basketball, its players, and management interacted and, ultimately, improved the game.

My dad was the head coach at the University of San Francisco with its main campus located on a 55-acre setting between the Golden Gate Bridge and Golden Gate Park, in San Francisco. Not long before the season started, World War II broke out, and he was enlisted and served in the armed forces. He returned home to San Francisco after meeting Red Auerbach. who was on the same ship with him in the service. Odd enough, Red wanted to be sent back East, and my dad wanted to be sent out West. At the time of his return from the war, my parents had started a family. My dad had a longtime colleague, Jimmy Needles, who heard my dad was coaching and offered him the head coaching job for basketball, golf, tennis, and baseball. When my dad decided to move on, he chose to accept the head coaching job at Michigan State. He was there for four years, and although the team's initial record of 4-19 improved, the school never achieved any recognition for being a basketball powerhouse.

My dad did lead the team to the NIT, which in those days would be comparable to the final four NCAA tournament level of play. Although improvement was established, my parents missed the warmth of the California sun and accepted the head coaching job at University of California the center of health sciences research, patient care, and education; located in San Francisco, California. While coaching for University of California, he won the leagues Pac 8 championship honors three to four years in a row. At forty-four to forty-five years of age, my dad retired from his position as head coach and became the athletic director due to the political tensions that existed in the '60s. In 1969 there was a lot of antiwar sentiment. The Black Panthers and other similar protests brought unwarranted attention to the basketball program at California Negative racial slurs about black athletes being controlled and manipulated by slave mongers led to unfair and false allegations personally directed to my dad.

Who at this time in America's history wanted to send their kid to go to a school like California, which was being negatively viewed in the public's eyes?

My mother was particularly upset and concerned about their children having to be negatively affected by my dad being called a "white pig" and was eager for my dad to leave the Bay Area and find different employment. She was always thinking about family. My mother understood the establishment but viewed it as undergoing a paradigm shift. The shift was happening at Berkley, the campus, the city, and the nation. In later years, she knew it was going to be especially difficult for Kermit's family to withstand so much negativism and hatred. In 1968 we moved to San Diego, and my dad worked for the Rockets as their general manager. At this time, Pat Riley was dating his wife, Kris, who spent time visiting with my mom. Kris always felt a close kinship with my mom and once stated Florence was the epitome of what a wife, mother, friend, and human being was. Kris labeled her "the woman who led the women's movement before anyone knew what the women's movement was all about."

As the youngest son, I overheard many a conversation held between my parents about events at California and the importance of raising a family in an environment that was positive and supportive. My parents loved people of all ethnic backgrounds for the people they were and not the people others tried to portray them to be. Both had the instinctive ability to look beyond the physical and see the inner person for what it truthfully was. In fact, Bobby Knight, who is known for his straightforward personality, showed my mother the ultimate respect and paid her the highest compliment in that he attentively listened to her words of wisdom with appreciation.

When my mom first met Kermit, there was a mutual admiration as if love at first sight. When the incident happened between Kermit and Rudy, my mother was particularly hurt in that it brought back those unpleasant memories of my dad's coaching days at California. She really knew Kermit, his qualities, thoughts, and actions; she did not simply know him by his name or face. Understanding how statements can blow the truth out of perspective, she was greatly concerned about the impact it was going to have on Kermit's family. It would be mandatory for the family to remain strong despite what Kermit was personally going through. Such media coverage was being intensified with the undertone of racial undercurrents. Hatred, no matter how felt, is an ugly animal that rises to the occasion when called into action.

I remember my dad immediately reached out to contact Kermit when learning about the incident. My dad reached out to Kermit and my mother, Florence, was a frequent visitor at the Washington household. When Kermit was waiting to hear if he would be returning to play in the NBA, my dad provided the support and positive feedback that helped Kermit upon his return. After playing in games, Kermit would call Pete to discuss how things went. When my dad could watch Kermit's return performance, he would share positive comments about what Kermit did well and areas he should focus on. Kermit took note, and when the Big Man's Camp took place after the season, my dad was impressed that Kermit had been applying his advice, and noticeable progress to improving his game was evident. One of Kermit's accomplishments following the incident was his selection for the All-Star team held in DC.

My dad had a very superstitious nature. He was always nervous about whether his team would win or lose a game. To settle his nerves, he would walk outside the Forum and follow a routine he felt would make a difference in the outcome of a game. If the team was winning, he would walk around the parking lot in one direction; if the team was losing, he would walk around the lot in another direction, and if the team needed support to keep the momentum flowing, he had another course to pursue. The security guards were aware of my dad's superstitious actions, and mindful that the Forum was not located in the safest part of LA, they would leave the arena and look out for him to make sure he wasn't rolled.

My dad's camp was really all about hard work. I was eighteen years old when my dad arranged with Kermit to work with him during the off season. The first year it was just my dad and Kermit, and the second-year Don Ford and Tom Aberthany joined in. The third-year Kermit's daughter's pediatrician was Kiki's dad. When meeting during one of her visits, they started talking basketball and, being a close friend with my dad, he asked if his son Kiki could join the sessions. Pete agreed, and Kiki became the solid participant along with Kermit. It was often said that my dad's camp was comparable to navy SEALs training. The camp was two hours, and with only two or three players in the early years, the sessions were intense. There were no days off, and my dad volunteered his time simply because he loved to see progress.

As Kermit progressed, you must remember that it was my dad who drafted him in the first round of the NBA draft. He had watched Kermit play in Hawaii and saw past the physical appearance and saw what great character he possessed. The heart and soul my dad could see went beyond the talent that showed potential to become a successful NBA player. This is truly a statement that lets people know what kind of man my dad was. I distinctly remember one occasion when he drafted Rudy T. and not Pete Malevich when general manager for the Houston Rockets. Now, Pistol Pete was my all-time favorite player, and I gave my dad the silent treatment for two weeks. I might have prolonged this deliberate failure to communicate with him if I had not exhausted my allowance and needed cash.

We were able to resolve my disappointment when we did talk, and he explained that talent was important, but integrity was more important. My dad always had a plan. He knew talent. When asked why he drafted Kermit from a little-known school as American University with so many other noteworthy college players, he explained to Bill Sharman, the head coach for the Lakers, that it was more about character and Kermit's display of a heartfelt work ethic that would make a difference on the team. At that time Sharman had eight or nine veterans and not making any sign of moving forward. Bill was a good coach but not a teacher, and when my dad retired, Jerry West became the head coach. With such a warm relationship with the Lakers organization, my dad would not overstep his role to work with Kermit until he left the organization as the general manager. Respect and wanting to make sure no one would felt intimidated; my dad was insightful enough to provide Kermit with the help he needed and to show that progressive improvement was happening and would continue to benefit the team.

My dad working with Kermit gave Kermit credibility. But his biggest public relations man was Chick Hearn. Chick regularly spoke of Kermit's progressive improvement from working with my dad. Broadcasting heard around the league, Chick was instrumental in sharing Kermit's improvement. This widely reported information helped to open the door for invitations to NBA players from Pete as the years progressed. It helped Kermit to also understand why Chick was the one who personally called him when he was traded to the Boston Celtics. Chick was a true fan of Kermit, and he felt he would be the best person to have to relay this news.

In those early years Kiki, being a college player, had to really put up the fine fight against Kermit daily. He struggled with Kermit's ability to block his shots and needed to figure out a way to step back and then release the ball to make his shot. It took time, and when Pete observed how Kiki was concentrating on this move, he spoke to him about it, and the step-back move was then renamed the Kiki move. In all the years in basketball, both college and professional, he had never seen this move perfected as it had been by Kiki. Kiki's motivation was to score against Kermit and not embarrass himself. He gained self-confidence and admits to this day that having a move named after him truly was the key to helping him become the player he became. My dad absolutely *loved* this move. This move literally blew his mind; it was innovative and was simply designed to get a shot off against Kermit Washington.

Players in the early years came to my dad's camp knowing it was going to be hard work. Pete had a reputation that was felt around the league. Kermit approached my dad for help, and this made Kermit near and dear to his heart. In the beginning when he was about to retire, he spoke with my mother, Florence. I remember one conversation where he told her that he wanted this for Kermit. He knew there was a lot of moving parts in the Lakers organization, and to provide this help, he would need to be have a plan. Knowing Kermit had an incredible work ethic, he knew it was doable.

Players like Kenny Carr my dad thought had a great deal of natural talent. Coming to his camp this was the first time he had seen him play as he had not scouted him for the Lakers. My dad was impressed with all the possibilities set in front of him and knew he was destined to become an All-Star in the NBA.

My dad called Kermit and asked what he thought about including Bernard in the camp. Kermit was blatantly honest and told my dad if a player with a reported problem with management could make it through the camp, the player was no longer had that problem but was determined to be a successful NBA player. He wholeheartedly felt Bernard deserved this opportunity to show himself, Pete, the other camp attendees, and the NBA what he was made of. Bernard performed extremely well, but Utah waived him.

Bernard went on to show everyone what his true nature was. My dad was grateful for the encouragement from Kermit to allow Bernard to attend his camp. Bernard arrived the first day to demonstrate a phenomenal talent and work ethic. He would sometimes struggle to perfect a move that my dad wanted his players to learn and execute. Bernard wouldn't wait for my dad to point out that he didn't get it right. Bernard would approach my dad and ask if he could do again and again until he was able to master it. My dad never got frustrated with Bernard but watched and gave positive feedback until Bernard felt confident that he had pleased my dad and mastered the skill.

During this first session of my dad's camp with Bernard, he formed a close personal relationship with Kiki. Kiki would drive all the way out to Westwood to get him to and from camp. They had a lot of good conversations during those daily drives. To this day Bernard always shares how much his friendship with Kiki means to him. Bernard also had a close relationship with my dad. After an NBA game as a Boston Celtics, he played against Cedric Maxwell. He was averaging 42 points a game in the first of five games in the series playoff. Cedric circled him in moves Bernard had never seen before. Cedric limited his scoring to 15 points. He immediately called my dad and told him about the game and asked what he could do so that this would never happen to him again. My dad spent time sharing some advice with Bernard, which he immediately put into practice. Bernard went off and blew the remaining games with exceptional skill and regained his high scoring totals.

One player, Akeem, attended camp and demonstrated extraordinary footwork. Learning other court skills was a challenge, but my dad was most impressed by Akeem's footwork. He moved up and down the court faster than any other player with equal grace and ease. My dad asked how Akeem was able to do this. He shared that in his country every small child played soccer. At that time, I had a small son, and my dad called me and told me to sign his grandson up for soccer.

The 1978 summer session Kermit as usual came to the house to pick up my dad. You had to be on time to get him as Dad would be waiting outside the front door by 7:30 a.m. Kermit had to drive from San Diego up to Los Angeles. Kermit was never late, and every morning my dad wanted to explore a different way to get down the Loyola Marymount College. Sometimes the drive seemed similar, but my dad had somehow managed to create a new route to explore. Kermit had just bought a new car, a Datsun 240 Z 2 + 2. Part of his desire to explore different road options was that he would come home and say how much he enjoyed riding in Kermit's new car. On the last day of this camp, Kermit handed my dad the keys to the car and told him he was giving the car to him so he could explore many other interesting ways to drive around the city. My dad was speechless. Kermit simply wanted to let him know how much he appreciated their friendship by giving him something he knew my dad would not only appreciate but enjoy.

Then there was Shaq, by far the most dominate player ever to attend my dad's camp. He was known to be a big jokester, and he came to camp when it was held in Hawaii. The morning before Shaq told Kermit that he wanted to rent a moped and ride the streets of Waikiki. Kermit hoped he was just kidding, but just in case he wasn't, he explained that it often rained in the evening and the streets would be too slick to even think about doing this. When Kermit's phone rang in the early ungodly hours of the morning of the third day, he answered with a silent prayer that this call would have nothing to do with the conversation he had with Shaq earlier in the day. Not. Shaq was calling from a local hospital to report he had fallen off the moped and donated a large contribution of flesh to the streets of Waikiki.

David Stern called a doctor to check Shaq out, but all went well as Shaq. He was able to attend three of my dad's camps.

My dad was always anxious to leave the Staples Center arena before the game ended to miss the traffic and mayhem that attending a Lakers camp caused. One night he forgot where he had parked his car and became extremely agitated. At the age of eighty-five he returned to the arena and walking through the tunnel ran into Shaq, who was leaving through the VIP exit. Shaq sensed there was a problem and immediately motioned to two Los Angeles policemen to help my dad find his car and escort him from the arena. My dad always remembered the kindness Shaq showed him and shared this account whenever he could.

To this date it remains a common quote: "There will never be another camp like Pete Newell's Big Man Camp." My dad was a tremendous person, coach, teacher, and overall basketball expert. His career is well underplayed as his success as the founder and teacher of NBA professionals is memorialized by his Big Man's Camp. He focused on angles, positioning, footwork, and the value of repetition. Intensity was the basis for everything connected with the camp. My mother often noted that when my dad was sick during the NBA season, he would rally and focus on the summer Big Man's Camp sessions. He came alive with his love and passion for helping players improve. He later in life had cancer surgery and refused to make use of chemo. He lived for my son Peter's high school games played in San Diego. A family friend, Dr. Earl Shultz, remarked that my dad, after seeing his grandson Peter play, had two things to live for. Number one, to watch my grandson play and, number two, his Big Man's Camp.

On his deathbed nearing the end of his life, my dad would work at getting into shape to walk up and down the court. He would walk around his complex of his San Diego townhouse in order to build up his strength. At the beginning of his training, he could barely walk past eight townhouses. He would struggle and often be out of breath. He was utterly exhausted. Over a three- to four-month regiment, he got his gait back and was no longer hanging on to me. He would daily say he had to be in shape for "my camp."

My dad died only three months following his final Big Man's Camp, the first camp his grandson Peter could participate as a player and not as a ball boy or ball passer. This last camp he could not stand and had to be seated to run the players and plays. When he grew tired, Mike Dunlap became his mouthpiece.

When I reflect, and consider the positive impact my father had on the lives of so many people, it reminds me of the movie *What a Wonderful Life*. It could easily be said the main character George Bailey's life was based on Pete Newell's real life story.

Kiki Vandeweghe

My sophomore year at UCLA, my father took advantage of his long-time relationship with the legendary Pete Newell. In a conversation between my father and Pete, Pete shared his plan to work with the Los Angeles Lakers forward Kermit Washington. Pete knew I was playing basketball and asked if I might be interested working out one-on-one with Kermit on basketball basics. His initial focus was on defensive skill improvement. My dad, realizing this was an opportunity of a lifetime, wanted me to learn fundamentals of the game that I would be exposed to as a college player and possibly an NBA player.

Confirming these arrangements, I met with Pete and Kermit for no less than two hours a day, three days a week. We met at Loyola Marymount University and started working on offensive drills. These sessions were full practices with only Pete, Kermit, and me. In later years, other players joined us, but initially we worked out every other day three days a week, and it was the greatest experience I have ever had in my life.

Sessions focused on footwork, reading defense, basketball, and life in general. As I was skinnier than Kermit, it took a lot of effort to keep up and withstand the rigors of being pushed and shoved around. This helped me when I later had to work with Kenny Carr,

Larry Smith, and Jerome Whitehead, who were also formidable participants. All of these interactions with professional, seasoned NBA veterans gave me the confidence to play against college competition. These big men and powerhouses of the NBA were stronger, quicker, and knew more about the game than I did and provided a well-rounded, solid educational experience that greatly benefited me personally and professionally.

The comradery displayed by every participant over the years should be noted. We worked to help each other reach a single goal: to get better as players. It was a special time that can never be duplicated. It is impossible to recreate Pete's vision. Pete worked with us every year for free with the sole purpose of helping players reach their potential at least and become the better at most. He stated this purpose before every session to water the seed of success he planted and nurtured in our minds.

These early small intimate sessions later evolved in the Pete Newell's Big Man Camp. From humble beginnings at Loyola Marymount University, the camp later moved to Hawaii. The early-session participants gained more from the three-day sessions over the summer than a one-week session. Most notable was the effort extended and the friendships developed over a longer period of time. *Repetition* was the word of the day. Drills were to be perfected, and Pete had the patience and insight to provide as much repetition to master a skill as needed by each individual player.

Pete became known for the final twenty minutes of every practice. The dreaded sliding drill. After the better part of a two-hour intense workout, we were soaking wet, dripping with sweat. Pete standing on the sidelines would issue directions. He called it the hands-up drill, but we were in effect sliding up and down, moving forward and back on the court for a minimum of twenty minutes. Looking back, I truly don't know how we made it. Perhaps it was Pete Newel's will that made it possible.

The step-back drill was one Pete named after me. I was constantly trying to figure out how to get off my shot as quickly as possible without being pushed and shoved by the other big men. Not matter how hard I tried, I always seemed to be forced to step back before getting my shot off. Pete asked me one day, "What are you doing?" I told him, "I keep getting hit so hard I am forced to step back before I can get my shot off." That recognition by Pete became a hallmark in my professional career as it was included in all future years of the camp and named the Kiki move.

I tried to perfect this Pete Newell move against the likes of Kermit and Kenny Carr. I would step back and get my shot off as fast as I could. This naming a skill after me was an inspiration to me. I was going to meet this challenge in a way that worked for me and was seen by Pete as valuable.

Bernard King and I became very good friends as a direct result of Pete's camp. I picked him up every morning of practice for two years. Driving to and from Loyola Marymount University gave us time to engage in many dialogues that I hold very special to this day. Bernard was a very talented athlete who had never been acknowledged for his greatness. I consider him to be the most underrated, explosive, quick player with the ability to release a jump shot that was almost impossible to block. He was serious and brought this measure of professionalism to every practice. I was fortunate enough to go against him, and this helped my game in addition to providing fond memories.

Bernard was so quick that at times learning a Pete Newell move proved to be quite a challenge. His first few practices proved to be a challenge, and he would ask if he could try it again and again and again. Pete gave him the practice time he needed and gave him only positive feedback even when Bernard struggled to master a move. Being insightful, Pete knew being as quick as Bernard was, it could be compared to those gifted students who could give an accurate answer but couldn't explain *how* they arrived at the answer as it was simply the answer which required no explanation. Bernard was that talented athlete who could not slow down to perfect a skill as he simply performed at a higher level.

Later holding camp at California State University, Dominguez Hills a public university located in the city of Carson, California in the South Bay region of Los Angeles County, J. B. Carrol and Purvis Short accepted an invitation from Pete to attend. Most people didn't realize you could not show up to his camp; you had to receive a personal invitation from Pete. Pete also considered how other participants viewed additions to the camp experience. There were the superstars: Shaq, known for his explosive quickness, and Shawn Kemp, whose attendance moved the camp to another level.

I attended Pete's camp for twenty-five years. During that time, there was only one year when I was injured and could not be a participant, but Pete allowed me to be a passer. This was an opportunity I would never have believed would allow me to view the camp through another perspective. This later helped in my post-NBA jobs. When I was able to participate in the camp, Pete asked me to play against Shaq two on two and show him how to pick and roll to separate quickly, spacing and post up. He was physically better than anyone else.

Shawn Kemp was a legend walking among humans. He would come to practice and dunk five to six times before even warming up. His jumping ability was unmatchable. We all watched in amazement. Shawn was the nicest person with such *raw* talent you were anxious to follow his career to see what kind of player he would become.

Comradery was the word of the day. Pete began each practice with a talk to help us understand what our roles were to be. He emphasized we all had one common goal—to get better. He stated the harder we played one another, it would result in all of us getting better. These efforts would make our NBA careers easier. We were to expect getting hit hard and shoved around, and we were to do the same. If you had to dive to the ground, you were to simply get off the floor and hit somebody else. Competition was to be made and met as a group for the group to get better. You were never to compete against one another. Pete kept emphasis on the need to *not* foul but to get as physical as was necessary.

Pete taught you where you should be on the court for all positions played. He made sure we understood the *why* of what you did. If you understood the why, that would lead to the most improvement in your game. It was important to take your time and *read* the defense no matter where you are on the court. Whatever your position was on the court, spacing and knowing how defense was being played was invaluable.

Pete focused on offense while at the same learning about defense. When you understand the why and read the defense, you would know how to react when playing the game. Being able to read defense and use appropriate counter, you would be able to react and execute the counter better. Understanding spacing and timing better allows you to slow down and take your time and gain control over your actions. Pete clearly stated there was *no* perfect defense. Every defense gives you something to learn. Never panic on the floor, always be under control, and "practice what I preach."

Kermit didn't have to agree to let a skinny college sophomore to come and work out with Pete. I will always be appreciative for this. Other than college myself, Hank Gathers was the only college player invited by Pete Newell to participate in his Big Man's Camp. Using the Loyola Marymount University gymnasium, the coach, Paul Westhead, knowing Pete asked if join his camp. Westphal having been well acquainted with Gathers potential and talent was please when Pete agreed. NBA participants Shawn Kemp, Jerome Kersey, Scottie Pippin, and James Worthy noted Gathers play and leadership.

Pete remarked Gathers played with the NBA veterans as if he was a five-year NBA veteran who was selected as the MVP of each NBA All-Star those five-years. Gathers play was exceptional with and unbelievable motor. Gathers became the second player in NCAA Division I history to lead the nation in scoring and rebounding in the same season, averaging 32.7 points and 13.7 rebounds per game.

Bernard King

Kermit Washington and Kiki Vandeweghe, two great forwards, were the foundations of Pete Newell's Big Man's Camp. Pete was pivotal in assisting me in improving my game. He was helpful, and I was delighted to experience the opportunity of a lifetime. Daily sessions of his camp could be compared to All-Star games. The camp provided instruction and practice on how to become a more well-rounded basketball player. This is key as every team varies in plays and roles, but the basics taught by Pete were consistent and invaluable. I needed to develop a perimeter game. I was well versed in the high post game that we played in college at the University of Tennessee and carried over with my play on the New Jersey Nets team, now based in Brooklynn as the Brooklynn Nets.

Camp was very competitive, and everyone worked up to Pete's level of excellence. Nobody got upset with one another for being pushed and shoved around. We knew this was the reality in the NBA, and to be prepared for this, practice that included this essential part of the NBA court life was instrumental for us all. I was able to join the Golden State Warriors under head coach Al Attles after leaving Utah. Pete shared my performance in his camp and helped to give me a chance to play for the Warriors. This was a very important opportunity that made the major change in my career and resulted in my becoming an MVP of the playoffs, making the NBA Hall of Fame, making first-team all-pro, and making the All-Star team.

Every day after camp I would come back to my apartment, eat something, and then ride over The University of California, Los Angeles located in the Westwood district of Los Angeles, California, on my bike. I ran the stadium stairs then went to the track to run sprints and then headed off to the UCLA gym for two hours to play ball. I loved practice and considered practice the same way I thought about games. I was always mentally up for games and, therefore, always mentally up for practices.

My NBA career began when I left the University of Tennessee in Knoxville, Tennessee early in my junior year. My teammate Ernie Grunfeld also left. He went to play with the Milwaukee Bucks, and I signed with the New Jersey Nets. We often played against one another in NBA games as we both played the same position. In college, together we scored 50 points a game between us, and I won't really say who scored the most points.

My years with the Golden State Warriors provided the opportunity for me to truly blossom as both a person and player. When I ended my years there, I became a free agent and was extremely pleased to be offered a contract to play with the New York Knicks. I was able to come home and play games in front of my family and the New York fan base. My head coach was Hubie Brown.

The one instance that will always mark how much Pete Newell influenced my career happened after we played the Detroit Pistons in the first game of a five-game series featuring the great Isaiah Thompson. The first half of the season we played well, but the second half of the season we were known as a winning team. Now you must realize I averaged 42 points in five games of this series. With the game on the line and a few seconds left, we called a time-out. Coach wanted the final play to go to the center, Billy Cartwright. I didn't want to question his choice, but I knew I should be the one to take the ball for the last shot.

Earl Cureton on the Detroit Pistons was guarding me for the final shot. He turned to me and said, "Come on and take it!" A few seconds later the game was over and my team moved on to play Boston, not his. With my 42 points against Detroit, I now became the focus of the Boston Celtics, who wanted to prevent me from accomplishing my usual performance. Cedric Maxwell performed a move on me that I had never seen before, and being a very physical player he would circle me and would not let me make contact with his body. He started at the back of me, then came top side to circle around me, and came back to the bottom side. He again circled me, and I wasn't able to adjust to this new form of defense against me. In all my games, it was my goal to always make contact with my opponent. I needed help to figure out what to do.

I immediately called Pete and asked him what I could to do to counteract the defense played against me. Pete's advice was to talk with the guards and tell them exactly when to pass the ball to me. This is when Maxwell was going around me. When he was directly behind me, the ball needed to be passed to me then and not when he was coming around the side again.

I did this and was able to get 46 points in the next game. We won the next two games at home. I never shared this secret as I did not want anyone in the NBA to know how I was able to learn this strategy against this kind of defense. I didn't want them to discover that Pete had the answer and solution to any basketball question or scenario and then go to him for help. This ability to provide such valuable and timely assistance is a testimony to the great coach Pete Newell was.

As a Golden State Warrior, I did not see Pete a lot. He was getting up in age and was not fond of doing a lot of traveling at this time in his life. When he was in town and we had the opportunity to spend time to talk Pete, it was very insightful and up-building. The many drills and focus on footwork and skills I learned from Pete's camps allowed me to move my game to another level. I used my aggressive nature and combined it with determination, and you could tell by the look on my face "I'm going to go." I loved the jump shot and the push stop. Taking jump shots, I never broke my wrist. I was shooting against bigger players, and if you spin a ball in the palm of your hand, you will find if you do not break your wrist going up in the post, you will see how much quicker you will be able to play on the open court.

Playing with the Golden State Warriors was enjoyable, and I was very open to resigning an extended contract with them. Having been an All-Star player, my attorney was actively involved with securing me a contract with the team who provided the best financial offer. Larry Bird was a rookie this year, and Dr. J was scoring 30 points a game. The Denver Nuggets were paying Alex English with a large salary, and the Golden State Warriors were not willing to offer me a comparable contract. The contract they offered me I turned down as they low-balled me.

When the New York Knicks offered me a contract, the owner of the Golden State Warriors flew to New York and held a press conference to show how upset he was that New York was interested in signing me. My contract negotiations went to arbitration. The Golden State Warriors were as required to match New York's offer; they declined, and I ended up in New York.

In 1985 I injured my knee when playing for the Knicks. The injury was an ACL, and no player had ever returned with success at the same level of play as an NBA player following such an injury. We were playing the Kansas City Kings. I was guarding Reggie Theus; he was going to the basket, and I was defending him. Checking him very aggressively as I planted my foot to stop his progress, that is when I tore my ACL cartilage and broke a bone. I knew it was over at the age of twenty-eight.

I had surgery with forty-one staples down my knee, which was reconstructed with the iliotibial band. At this time in NBA history, *no* player had ever been able to return to play after experiencing these injuries. Mitch Kupchak also came back after his surgery, and despite being the talented player he was, he still limped the rest of his career and was never as effective.

After surgery, I asked for medical journals, a tape recorder, and pad and pencil. I spent hours researching my injury and wrote down specific questions regarding the procedure performed and the best way to establish a rehabilitation regiment. I then shared my outline regiment with the Knicks and requested their help in carrying it through. I wanted to have all equipment put in my home and the assistance of a qualified physical therapist. I interviewed their recommended therapist, and after making sure that she understood this was going to be consistent workouts with the expected results of my returning to play at an All-Star level, we made arrangements and began. She came every day over a period of two years.

Not being mobile sitting in a wheelchair for a while made me cognizant of the things Pete had us at practice in his camp. The angles, positioning, and mental concentration of being aware of the full court continually played over and over in my mind. I had always been an analytical player, and working with Pete helped me to become more of a mental player. I became a thinking player for the remainder of my basketball career. I mentally practiced every day from a distance, and this made me a more complete player. I watched videotapes of my games, and after one year of working with my therapist, I hit the court and worked on making changes in my game. I practiced faithfully and did not focus on what if I reinjured myself. I practiced falling. The one thing players feared was being off balance and falling, which might result in reinjuring themselves. The game is very physical, with bumps, pushing, and shoving about. I had to remember all those Big Man's Camp sessions where this was the order of the day. I focused on how it felt to be off balance on the floor and how to fall without fear of getting hurt.

I came to understand how an ACL injury affected the flexibility of movement. If this tendon was severed, there would be no blood flow to the area, and leaving scars would deaden the patella tissue and make moving around as one did prior to such an injury impossible. Despite all the negative comments such as being sorry I was injured and would never play again, I dismissed all negativity and only focused on knowing I was going to come back and play as well as I had in the past. I was working with a therapist and every day saw improvement. I learned that you have to distance yourself from people who lack faith in your conviction to succeed. If someone tells you for one and a half years you can't do something, you will believe it. Therefore, I kept reinforcing the statement that I would be returning and be successful.

The previous year I made first-team all-pro. I thank Dr. J to this day for entering the league. He was the standard I wanted to model my basketball career after. In time, I was voted an MVP. Imagine how devastating it was to go down at the age of twenty-eight after scoring 32.9 points a game.

After two years of following this regiment, I was able to return and play the final six games of the season. I needed to come back as I had been out of sight, out of mind for two years, and it was time to negotiate my contract. It was similar to not having any history in the NBA, and I wanted to make it clear Bernard King was back in the house. I averaged 22 points a game for these final six games and went on to play for six more years. I retired at thirty-six and achieved the offensive production that I did before my injury. At thirty-four years of age I was the oldest player (at that time) to start on the NBA All-Star team.

Remembering those early years and attending Pete's camp, we had at most eight players. It started with Kermit asking Pete for help, and they worked one-on-one that first year. Later Kermit was joined by other Lakers rookies who did not return, and when Kiki joined, he lasted twenty-five years as a Big Man's Camp participant. The very first year I joined the camp, Kiki gave me a ride to and from the camp. I will always hold fond memories of the time we spent together on the court. To this day I continue to cherish the close relationship I have with Kiki, and that is something I can also thank Pete for.

Jerry West

It's about time somebody wrote about Kermit Washington. First and foremost, I was sort of thrust into the coaching position for the Los Angeles Lakers, and I didn't know the complexities of coaching. As a player, you pretty much manage your own affairs in terms of preparing yourself for a game. You try to mentally prepare yourself for every game you play. In addition, there is the emotional part of playing, and that is what separates good athletes from the best athletes. More important, each player has their own particular skills which allows them to maintain a place in the league. Skills are what makes any player invaluable, but only if they utilize these skills consistently to win games.

I was trusted into the head coaching position to replace Bill Sharman, who was a Hall of Fame coach. At this time the Los Angeles Lakers didn't have any flexibility as it was pretty much the same team as we had the year before. I looked at the team and knew I needed to hire two assistant coaches. I selected Stan Auerbach and Jack McCloskey, two people who were invaluable to me. To organize a practice was one of the most difficult things that I ever had to do and even think about, to be honest with you. Their experience really helped me in that area. Looking at the team, I considered the strengths of each player and the fact that we did not make the playoffs for a couple of years, knowing that the Lakers would have to become a defensive team to be successful. This was a new identity I was pushing onto the team. Realizing Kermit was a very good rebounder and shot blocker in college, we were going to try to capitalize on those skills on a professional level..

Kermit brought us size and quickness and, more important, an enormous effort on the court. Kareem Abdul Jabbar always attracted the most attention on every play. We were hoping that Kermit could do all the dirty work and without getting into foul trouble as a result. However, it was more important that Kareem didn't get into foul trouble. As the star of the team, Kareem needed to be free to play the entire game from start to finish if necessary; this was the main objective if we were going to win games.

The one thing you never had to worry about with Kermit was his work ethic. I mean he put in 100 percent effort every night, and that's one of his biggest contributing attributes. Some players have the ability but won't put out the effort to reach their potential. But Kermit was an average basketball player who put out the extra effort needed to become a better-than-average player.

Kermit initially didn't understand how to play the forward position. I think what happens with players like Kermit is they have the willingness to learn the position but he needed a teacher to help guide him. Kermit took it on himself to reach out to Pete Newell for help as he recognized this was the man who could work with him. After working with Pete over the summer and seeing Kermit's improvement in the first few pre-season games, I knew Kermit would fit perfectly into my plan for the team.

The one identifying incident that changed his life and professional career was undoubtedly the punch. My recollection is such—it hasn't been talked about enough! And I think from a personal perspective, it was one of the worst things that I have ever seen in my life; it was just horrid to see. I went home that night knowing that this was a very serious matter. I said to myself, "Honestly did I have anything to do with this, because we were an aggressive defensive team." I looked in the mirror long and hard, and finally I said, "You know, this is something that happened, and the way it happened, it was the result of perfect timing, everything had to be fall into place in order for an injury like to occur." But it didn't take me very long after reading the newspaper articles and hearing people's comments that I felt the way he was treated was disgraceful.

We couldn't say anything. I couldn't say anything, and I had to keep my mouth shut because we didn't know what the heck was going to happen next. It must be noted and clearly stated that Kermit was not the cause of that punch—bottom line—period! Kevin Kunnert was the cause of that fight. And to this day if anyone has escaped any consequences as a result of his aggressiveness, it's been him. Now, Rudy suffered a terrible injury, and Rudy is a great guy. And as I say if you just look at how it happened, it was like a flash, and I said to myself, "Oh my gosh, what the heck just happened here." Like most of us at the time, we did not realize the seriousness of Rudy's injuries. And it was one of a million punches that have been thrown in this league forever, and no one ever sustained anything like that.

At the end of the day, in my recollection, I remember Kermit got traded to the Boston Celtics, and the things that were written about him, uncontrollable, you name it, okay, they were written about him. But in fact, Kermit was and is a fantastic guy, a great person. I have watched him over the years. I think he's definitely been affected by this. He's a gentle soul. The competitive part of him is what made him stand out as a player at that position, and to be remembered by something that had happened to numerous players in the league who have hit guys, this was just the perfect scenario to have damage like that.

Now, I was actually happy when the Boston Celtics picked him up! Oh, my gosh, I was thrilled for him that somebody decided that not only was he a good basketball player, but he was a good person. In watching him play, I don't think I ever saw the same person again, I really don't. I think this thing that made him was his aggressiveness, and suddenly I'm sure in the background people were watching him like a hawk, and this was going to be something that was going to follow him around for the rest of his life.

And Kermit Washington should be known more than just for having thrown a punch. Kermit should be known more as a really good guy, a guy who has given his time to make other people's lives better, and he has served out his term under public scrutiny with incredible dignity. And in terms of public opinion, he has weathered a storm better than most individuals would have been able to do as far as I'm concerned.

I wouldn't say any of this about Kermit if it weren't true. I have followed his career and personal life over the years. Despite the things that have happened to him, he has been able to refine himself and be identified with who he is as a person and not with one incident that was an accident that came about in an instant of time without any malice. An incident he did not start but that he is solely linked with the consequences that followed the incident's conclusion. It makes me sad to see that people so quickly judged him and were very quick to classify him as ... Oh, I don't know what. Most everything that has been said about him, especially in print, just go and read articles and letters to the editor; it's just horrid what people said about him, and they didn't know him.

And honestly, I'll be honest with you, that's why I never wanted to coach again, never. Even though it was tough for me to be a coach because of a lot of other things that were going on in my life that were personal. I didn't want to coach anymore because it's not who Kermit was in reality that was shared with the public. Those negative remarks and hurtful, untrue comments are statements that should never have been printed, those vicious words I would never stand behind simply because I believe in fair play. I also believe in aggressive play. And every time I see Kermit, I see him working with kids and trying to be a mentor to a lot of kids who are coming into the NBA, and he's given his time to a lot of causes. I think his giving back to basketball doesn't surprise me, but the other thing is that he's gone out of his way to show people he is something other than the false perception painted by individuals who were more concerned in selling newspaper without any regard for the lasting impact their words would have on the life of a fellow human being. That stigma that people have given him is one that should never have been allowed to be created.

Stu Lantz

In 1974 I was extremely happy to be traded to the Lakers. I had played my final game the night before joining the Lakers team. Arriving early for the shot-around practice as we had a game that night, I was eager to learn the plays. As a guard, this position requires that you know where you need to be and where other players are on the court. I felt the need to put forth extra effort to learn plays and be ready to show I was capable of making a positive contribution to the team.

Seeing me with my head buried in the playbook, Kermit approached me and asked why I was taking time to look over the team playbook, as it was to explain the team only ran three plays. Not thinking this could possibly be true that first game, I closely watched and was amazed to discover only three plays were called during the game.

The group was a much more talented group of players, even though the Lakers did not make the playoffs that year, which was a surprise. It was especially noticed the comradery displayed among the players. There are usually a few players who gravitate to one another, but in this instance, everyone got along and was supportive of one another's efforts to be champions.

Cazzie Russell and Kermit were helpful in finding housing that was in a safe location within a short period of time. This was of particular interest to me as my wife and three small children would be soon joining me. As a family, we did have a solid base in San Diego, but we always were together in whatever city when the season started.

In 1974–75 Pete Newell was the general manager of the Lakers organization. Peter and I had a history going back to him drafting me into the NBA following my college graduation. Later he played a role in having me traded to the Lakers. Having Pete as the general manager was an added bonus. Pete would often state that Kermit was his first project, but in reality, I was. I might not have been a big man, playing as a guard, but working the Big Man's Camp with Pete was instrumental in my positive experiences throughout my career.

Kermit continued to work with Pete over the years, and as the Big Man's Camp grew, both of us worked with Pete as nonparticipants. Everyone who had the privilege to work with Pete owe their success both on and off the court to working with Pete Newell. Where would Kermit be without Pete? That's a question that would end in a negative answer. Pete's support during the most trying time in his professional career can never be understated. Kermit is one of the nicest individuals you will ever know.

Pete showed Kermit how to improve his defensive and rebounding machine, and he learned offensive rules. He knew how to shoot; he just wasn't a shooter. He did know what to do in his role on the court, and he accepted the role he was delegated to perform for the benefit of the team. He was the rebounder and defensive backbone of the team.

There were so many talented players that attended Pete Newell's Big Man's Camp; to not name one of them would be a failure to acknowledge each player's growth as an NBA player and the value of working with Pete Newell. We can mention a few such as Shaq, who was a three-hundred-pound monster. At one camp held in Hawaii, Shaq was determined to ride a motorcycle. It is well known that it might rain in the night resulting in slick streets. Did this dissuade Shag from attempting to ride like the wind? Not at all. Needless to say, when skin met the pavement, no one was surprised. Then we had the talent of Kevin Duckworth, Dale Ellis, X-Man, Scottie Pippin, Antoine Carr, Steve Johnson, and Shawn Kemp.

The first-time Shawn Kemp attended camp, it was held at Loyola Marymount University in Los Angeles. Now Shawn was not late, but according the Pete Newell time, he was. Shawn walked into the gym wearing low-cut tennis shoes, and it looked like he didn't have any socks on. I went up to him and asked, "Do you need time to go the locker room and dress?" He responded, "I'm ready to go." Shawn was the ultimate definition of raw talent. He was able to cultivate an appreciation and application of Pete's fundamentals and soar to greater professional excellence. Then there was Kurt Rambus, who complained when Shawn jumped from the free throw line and dunked on him. He repeatedly shouted, "Nobody should be able to do that!" Kiki Vandeweghe also joins this list. He started working with Kermit and Pete while still in high school. The news rapidly spread that working with Pete Newell was like winning the lottery. This made more players want to attend and benefit from Pete's extensive knowledge.

Purvis Short and Kenny Carr can also be added to that list of memorable attendees. Pete's ability to teach the fundamentals was impressive. Pete emphasized the fact that no matter how much talent any player possesses, if they didn't have the fundamentals under their belts, it didn't matter how talented they were. He helped all players understand you could never downplay learning, mastering, and applying fundamentals as contributing to a player's success.

Every practice session under Pete Newell's tutelage was like an All-Star team showing up to learn from the guru of basketball. As the word spread about the camp, Pete was very selective in including players to participate in this opportunity. It changed from a "first come, first serve" sign-up to players Pete felt would work well together and to those he extended an invitation.

After my NBA career came to an end, I returned to my permanent residence in San Diego and got a job with the San Diego Clippers organization as a color man in broadcasting game information. I started in broadcasting for CBS and with a limited number of games to call (less than ten for the season). I later got a phone call from Jerry West and Chick Hearn to join Chick of the Los Angeles Lakers on their broadcasts. This was indeed the opportunity of a lifetime. Chick Hearn was legendary, well respected, and so gifted in his craft this experience was memorable and career influential. It's sometimes hard to believe I've been able to perfect this craft for almost twenty-nine years as the direct result of working with Chick.

Ernie DiGregorio

Kermit and I played on two NBA teams together, the Boston Celtics and the Los Angeles Lakers. We were also first-team all-Americans in 1973. Living in Providence, Rhode Island, my father was a hard worker who scraped hardwood floors for a living. He wanted me to follow in his footsteps. My mother was determined I did not need to spend time playing basketball but would gain better benefits if I went to work with my father. I tried to convince her to let me practice basketball, I could make a great living so one day I could buy her a nice house. Being the loving son, I went to work from 6:00 a.m. to 4:00 p.m. When my father noticed, I was getting better in basketball, he reduced my work schedule hours to a half a day. With even more improvement, he graciously released me, and I could put all my energy into practicing basketball.

I began to concentrate on basketball at the age of twelve. I played Little League baseball and soon discovered that improving baseball skills required help from eleven other players. With basketball, you could work on improving in the game and working on your own. I would get up at 6:00 a.m. and leave the house by 6:30 a.m., dribbling the basketball one mile to the playground. The basketball never left my hands. I imagined that there was a player in front of me all the time and practiced dribbling crossing over from one side to the other, imagining that with only ten seconds left in a game, I

305

had to make the winning shot. My imagination created a variety of scenarios to which I dribbled and shot the ball to meet the challenge. I looked around the court and worked very hard to make difficult moves and shots over and over. I would make a pass behind my back or dribble the ball between my legs, then take the shot.

My eyes looked at the court and not at the ball. The ball was simply a part of me, and it was an extension of my arm—dribble left, dribble right, then score. Using both hands improved my ability to drive to the hoop quick and hard; there was no favoring one-hand play from another. The ball was a part of the whole me and was therefore used by both hands to meet the challenge. Attending North Providence High School, our basketball coach was really our baseball coach and was not capable of providing any assistance in my goal to improve my skills. Not knowing a lot about basketball, he felt everyone should have the opportunity to play even after seeing me score 10 points in one quarter of play.

This effort might have been overlooked by him, but it gave me more confidence to stay focused and step up my efforts to improve. My senior year we had a new coach, Dave Turbidy, who had more knowledge of the sport and would have us run five miles before each practice. We did sit-ups and push-up, and my senior year I averaged 37 points per game. Our school played in a championship tournament, and I was named MVP of the tournament. Our team traveled to various schools along the East Coast, which include a stop in DC.

I was offered a four-year scholarship at Providence University and enjoyed playing with a colorful collection of players including Marvin "Bad News" Barnes and Kevin Stacom. The three of us all wanted to play professionally. Our bond was strong, and our motto could rightly be stated to be "All for one and one for all." Playing together both on and off the court, it became instinctive to know where Marvin and Kevin were on the court and pass the ball to any if suitable to respond with a scoring basket.

College basketball was the most fun, the game pure and simple. Money was not a factor; it was exciting and filled with memorable moments. I was selected as one of top-ten freshmen in the country. At that time freshmen, could not play on the varsity roster. Fans would come to the small 3,300-capacity Alumni Hall gym to watch us play and leave before the varsity team hit the floor. Sophomore year I started on the varsity team, averaging 18 points a game, and we made the NIT. We lost to The University of North Carolina at Chapel Hill, also known as UNC, or simply Carolina, is a public research university located in Chapel Hill, North Carolina, after giving it a good shot.

Junior year, we were tied with The University of Rhode Island, commonly referred to as URI, located in Kingston, Rhode Island, with an undefeated record of 12–0. Before the game, I went outside to shoot some hoops and badly twisted my ankle. It swelled up like an inflated balloon. I called my coach, who instructed me to go the doctor. I was given a shot of Novocain, and never really played the same afterward. I averaged 17 points that season, but that injury really set me back. We won twenty games in a row in my senior year and finished 24-2, ranking fourth in the final polls that year. We played in a tournament in Utah and was beaten by Santa Clara University located in Santa Clara, California. I was named MVP of the tournament, and when we returned to campus, Coach Gavitt invited me to his office. He told me to sit down and proceeded to play a recording of the Santa Clara game we had just lost.

He never said a word about the game. When the film was over, I stood up and said, "Okay, I get it." He then told me that he was giving me the keys to the engine, and it was my game and to go as far as I could to carry us to success. His message was clear by showing me how I had played and what needed to be changed in order for a loss like this to never happen again. Like Red Auerbach, he knew how to handle players. Lenny Wilkins had a similar approach. He never yelled at his players. He knew how to speak to people and handle issues. Mistakes were just that and not made on purpose. Lessons are learned from mistakes, and it is not necessary to belittle someone for being human.

Our senior year Marvin and Kevin helped us get to the final four. Marvin was a junior, and Kevin, like me, was a senior. We spent countless hours working on our game. Freshman year, when Coach Gavitt introduced me to Marvin, he encouraged me to get better acquainted with this kid from south Providence. Gavitt told me Marvin loved to play the game just like me and to pick him up to get to know him better and play ball with him. Marvin was a great rebounder and shot blocker and was the backbone of our defense. He would tell me to let opposing drive by me as he would simply block their shots. A true team player, he was never jealous even when I was recognized for being the leading scorer on the team.

We exuded confidence and seemed to feed off each other to support this display of assurance that we would succeed and met with every challenge with a positive outcome. Kevin was another good match. As Marvin, would get the rebounds, he was there to pitch the ball out to me so I could cut across at an angle. Kevin reminds me of John Havlicek. He transferred from Holy Cross, and his day on campus we dropped off his gear and headed directly to the basketball court. I picked him up every day, and we would run the 440s at the track every morning at six o'clock. Marvin would always say at practice that we were running and getting into condition so we could get the BR. That stood for "bank roll." Back then college games were not widely televised. If you wanted to get any recognition, you have to win to really make a statement and stand head and shoulders above the crowd. We played against The University of Memphis, also called the U of M, located in the Normal Station neighborhood of Memphis, Tennessee and was ahead by 16 points before Marvin hurt his knee, but we lost when Marvin blew out his knee. If that had not happened and we won, we would have played UCLA. Marvin was really disappointed as his main goal in this series was to meet the famous Bill Walton again and show him that the first-time UCLA beat us at Pauley Pavilion, it wasn't going to happen again, but we never got that chance.

My biggest asset I feel as a player was passing the ball. As a point guard, I could see the whole court. Ball control was part of my game as the ball was actually connected to my hands. On the fast break, I never looked down at the ball; my mind concentrated on imagining the best way to either score the bucket myself or pass the ball to the open man in the best position to score. I looked to pass to the open man in many creative ways to confuse my opponent who was checking me. My aim was to put them off guard and wondering not only what I was doing but also how I was able to do it, giving me an advantage and feeding my imagination to continue to inspire my play.

While playing in Los Angeles against a Russian team, I was told at a practice I had been the third-player pick in the 1973 NBA draft by the Buffalo Braves. This was nothing like today where there is a big press conference, TV team hats, and media attention is at its finest. Buffalo had Randy Smith, a quick player, faster than a speeding bullet; Bob McAdoo, a scoring machine; and traded Elmore Smith for Jim McMillian. Randy Smith was quite the talented athlete even though he smoked during halftime. He came to play and led the team in running a mile in under six minutes. Now I ran as fast as I could, but Randy seemed to put his motor into another gear as he passed all of us to cross the finish line first. He turned to watch as we moved as fast as we could, he wasn't out of breath and simply encouraged us to keep going.

The pro game was different from college ball, and I changed my style of play to meet the needs of the team. I hit open shots and was named Rookie of the Year. My free throw record of .902 was a record that still stands today. I also led the league in assists, 8.2, perfecting my passing skills to meet the needs of my teammates. If they could catch a hard pass, that was how the ball was delivered, and if they needed the soft pass, that was the manner of delivery. My goal was to pass as the situation dictated.

Moses Malone was on this team for a very short period of time. His game was much like a strong Bill Walton when he was healthy in college. Moses only played for a total of six minutes in a game as he learned he was soon to be traded, and neither team wanted him to get injured. Those brief six minutes clearly gave evidence that Moses was a star in the making and would make a major statement in the league. He was quite young and joined the NBA straight out of high school. He was very quiet and was a gentle giant off the court but an aggressive warrior on the court.

In the game against the Golden State Warriors, I felt a pinch in my knee and tore my cartilage. I had surgery and wore a cast for what seemed like an eternity. In those days, there was no microscopic surgery; they went to fix something which could mean removing something that might have needed to be left where it was. This injury shortened my NBA career. I played four years for Buffalo, a half year with Los Angeles, and a half year for Boston. I had been cut by LA and was a ten-day-contract player for the Boston Celtics.

I was Kermit's teammate in LA and had been sitting on the bench when the infamous "fight" happened. I still remember vividly what I saw that night. There had been a lot of pushing and shoving between Kermit and Kevin Kunnert. I saw Kermit was partially turned away from the far court, and when the pushing stopped I saw Rudy running full speed up the court, and Kermit caught Rudy running, and I felt he assumed Rudy was going to hit him. Kermit instinctively punched Rudy.

The consequences were severe, and I wanted to show my support and went to his home to visit Kermit. I felt he was very distraught and down on life. I wanted him to know I cared about him. I brought his daughter a teddy bear and a riding toy and spent time simply talking about a variety of topics and to assure him that he was still the great person and friend I admired. Kermit was always the type of person who put other people's needs and concerns ahead of his own. There aren't a lot of people in the world like that, and he needed to know this quality was both recognized and appreciated. To this day he is still that kind of person, and we have remained friends.

Kermit arrived in Boston a few days after me. Kermit was exactly the kind of player Boston needed. He was a strong rebounder and shot blocker and knew his role and stuck to completely performing that role to the highest level possible. He was the kind of player every team was looking for to win games, and I was privileged to play with him.

This year was John Havlicek's final season as a Boston Celtics, and I was able to make a major impact in that final game. Havlicek was really struggling the first half. John was a guy that loved to fast break, and that was exactly complementary to my game, hit the open man going to the basket. When I spoke with Bob Ryan, a Boston reporter before that game, I said I had eyes for Hondo, but only said

I was going to throw every pass to him. When I was put in the game, I remained true to my words. I made sure John hit the fast break, and he ended up scoring 29 points. I still have a signed basketball from him that personally says, "One more pass, Ernie." He was extremely appreciative for my help, and I know I helped to make his final game a memorable one for all his fans and particularly for me.

I have received many compliments about my ball handling ability, but the most memorable one was given by Bob Cousy. When asked, "Which of the many NBA players to ever play the game would you say was the most like you?" he answered, "Ernie DiGregorio is the one player most like me." He told me in all the years of playing basketball, I reminded him of how he played the game and admired how I handled the ball.

If I was asked the same question today, I would have to name three players who I consider to be on top of their game. I would say Stephen Curry, Golden State Warriors; Derrick Rose, Chicago Bulls; and Kyrie Irving, Cleveland Cavaliers.

Cedric Maxwell

During my rookie year as a Boston Celtics, when I found out we had traded for Kermit Washington, I was scared. Kermit was in the news and having known him prior to the recent incident between Houston Rocket star Rudy Tomjanovich, as a formidable player, everyone was shocked by the reports and the incident itself. My first reaction was, "This fool is unbelievable." I knew Kermit to be a nice guy who was suspended for a while, and the next thing I know he was going to join our team and be my teammate.

Initially my main concern was my personal being. I was skeptical that this man was going to kill me. I was only six feet seven inches, and Kermit outweighed me by forty to fifty pounds. He was known as a big bruiser, and I had to go against him in practice. The first day he joined us in practice, he was surrounded by media. I wondered how I should approach him or if I should approach him. Either way the situation itself was crazy.

During practice, instead of being extremely aggressive, Kermit didn't push me around but simply ran past with a casual brushing aside. Instead of the expected aggressive play I had previously observed and experienced, this situation took a little of his aggressive nature out of him. As I became better acquainted with Kermit, I came to understand who he was as a person. If it possible to use the expression "man crush," that is how I would describe my feelings toward him. Kermit is truly a very nice person. I did go up and speak with him that first day and was a bit relieved that Don Chaney helped with the interchange. I knew Don, who had previously played for the Celtics, and he had joined us in the trade that brought Kermit to our team.

The team locker room conversation was full of lighthearted humor. The running joke that you had to watch your back now that Kermit was on the team gradually faded as Kermit's presence was acknowledge and respected by all of us. I watched Kermit come into a situation that was a challenge and see the class he showed despite all the media attention. He shared with me the hate mail he was regularly receiving and noted the cursing and the inclusion of the *N* word. People wanted to make Kermit into the person they wanted him to be, but Kermit rose to the challenge and made himself. He was humble, classy, and aggressive but not to the point that people were going to hate him.

Odd enough, Don Chaney's babysitter later became my wife, and in later years I personally experienced the "hater" syndrome, and it was because I had seen how Kermit responded to such behavior that I was able to get past a situation with the dignity and class Kermit had displayed. It isn't until you personally experience things that you gain a deeper appreciation of the example left for you to follow and meet with a successful outcome.

That year Kermit joined our team, we had seven greatly respected and well-known All-Stars who were older and established in their careers. Along with the usual circus that accompanied their reputations came Kermit with another circus. As the other power forward, I witnessed how Kermit's reputation was perceived by others on the court. His newly portrayed persona was that of an invisible enforcer, someone who you couldn't push around. He was "the guy" to go to both on the court and in life. He had gone through a lot and was fully aware of the challenge to reinvent himself. It was important to establish the fact he was not the monster everyone thought. As the punch changed the history of basketball, it is interesting to note that some years later during the playoffs in Philadelphia, I ran into the stands and punched a fan with no consequences. I went on to receive the MVP in those playoffs. I was never suspended for my actions.

That same year Kermit joined the Boston Celtics was marked by the end of John Havlicek's career. John was all class. He started the game with his usual routine of pulling on the bench and stretching. I remember saying to myself, "I do things like John, and I could last in the NBA for twenty years." Being class personified, when John was introduced, the crowd went crazy. He stood midcourt and turning to the crowd bowed to every section of fans in the Boston Garden. He started on the right and turned full circle to acknowledge everyone in attendance.

Life as a Boston Celtics was always filled with some sort of chaos. Regular circus performances were given due to the addition of

Kermit, and the usual Jo White, Dave Bing, and the other All-Stars unique and talented performances night after night and game after game. Even though we knew this year we weren't going to make the playoffs, it was still drama as expected.

One of the most positive things that happened that year was to see John play in his final game. He played well and left the fans and his teammates with a memory to last a lifetime. After the season San Diego wanted to make a trade with the Celtics. I was the original player under consideration, but they took Kermit instead. Years later a similar situation arose when Detroit wanted me in the Bob McAdoo trade for M. L. Carr in compensation. The ability to stay in Boston helped keep me on solid ground.

John Havlicek

Although it was going to be my final year playing basketball for the Boston Celtics, I was excited to hear that Red Auerbach was bringing Kermit Washington to join our team. He was known for being a solid rebounder and would set good picks. As a shooter, this was important to me as this meant more opportunities to take shots and make winning baskets. Kermit was an intense player in that he never took a day off and always put forth and gave 100 percent effort.

That year Kermit came to Boston, we had an intense winter blast that immobilized the Boston area. We had to cancel several games, and in order to make these up before the regular season ended, at times we played three games back-to-back quite a lot. When I think back on my final game, many memories flood my mind, and it was so intense that most of these escape my mind. I do remember how my mind was filled with many things, and it was racing all over the place, moving from one thought to another. At times, it seemed like I was randomly moving about as my entire focus was on winning my final performance as a Boston Celtic.

My eight-year-old son, my wife, my mother, my mother-in-law, all my relatives, and my former Ohio teammates were in the Boston Garden to support me. It was an extraordinary day, and at halftime the Celtics gave me a camper as a token of their appreciation, which I used for many years. We took two trips out West and all over the country; it was a gift I truly enjoyed receiving from the Celtic fans. Regardless of what else was happening in the world that day, my mind was focused on winning that final game. When I was introduced, I followed the Japanese tradition of bowing to all four sections in the Boston Garden. Dave Bing and I were the starting guards, and at that time we were probably the oldest back court players as our combined ages was seventy-four years. I always liked playing the small forward position; it was in fact my favorite position to play. That night started as a guard, but in the later part of the game they let me play the small forward position, and I shot the ball every time it was fed to me. I scored 29 points.

I checked Randy Smith, who at that time was by far the fastest guard in the league. I had played a pretty good position and played defensive game with my head and legs, which allowed me to successfully guard an opponent in the later end of my career. I just figured if he's a guard and I'm a guard, why not match up? Every year I would take of a little bit of weight before the training camp. I liked to come in underweight as it was easier to get in shape when you are underweight. I had a tendency to gain weight with work. So, with the work of all the practices as the season progressed, I would start out eating three meals a day and then eating three to five meals; it was good weight that I was putting on. I just reversed the process of a lot of things. I felt I knew my body really well, and I knew I could gain weight with work. My training camp weight was 192 to 193 pounds, and when the season started I would gain 15 to 17 pounds to get to 210 pounds at the beginning of the season and then gradually stream down to 205 pounds throughout the remainder of the season.

Looking back, I was the only first-round draft pick of the Boston Celtics who initially declined their offer. I knew this greatly disappointed Red as I was the only player who did not sign with the Celtics even though I signed with a football team, the Cleveland Browns. As it was not customary for any player not to sign with the Celtics, I knew I had to do a lot to gain Red's respect. When I was cut by the Browns, the first time Red saw me play was when I attended his Marshfield camp. I wanted to show him I could play a little bit. Red never saw me play as a collegiate, and I had to work my butt off in order to gain his respect and interest in my signing with the Celtics.

Red had a very interesting way of signing players. He had a very close relationship with Kurt Jo sports caster well-known as the longtime voice of the Boston Red Sox's, who was a basketball player The University of Wyoming, located in Laramie, Wyoming, situated on Wyoming's high Laramie Plains, at an elevation of 7,220 feet, between the Laramie and Snowy Range mountains. He knew the game well and was broadcasting the NCAA final four. Red, during a luncheon during the final four, asked Kurt if he was enjoying the games. Kurt said he was. Red then mentioned to take a look and see if there were any players who might fit in to play with the Celtics. When Kurt came back to Boston and Red asked if Kurt saw anyone he might be interested in, he said, "There's a kid named Havlicek, he runs around like a motor is up his ass, and he might be a good fit for your team." This was one of the ways Red recruited players over the years. I was able to gain Red's respect and had a very good relationship with him over the years.

Red was my coach for four years from 1963 to 1966. Red let people know when it was going to be his last year coaching, and it was well known everyone wanted to play for Red; he let it be known this was going to be their last chance. Practices only lasted forty-five minutes; he let us cut loose, and Red put more time with the seventh, eighth, and ninth men on the team. This was because starters often get injured and needed to be replaced. Red knew if he spent quality time with these players, working them out and keeping their weight in check and working on executing plays, he knew they would learn where he wanted them to be, and when called in the play, they would be ready and eager to fill in the gap.

Red was not the X-and-O chalk coach. At the end of a season if you gave him a piece of chalk, he probably would have had nine-tenths of it remaining because he just felt if you executed the plays the way he designed them, then you'd be in that good position to score, make a good pass, or take it to the hoop. If you weren't on the spot to start the play as he wished, he said, "I will find someone who could get to that spot and make this play work." He wanted players to be at designed spots in order to execute plays. There were no gray areas with Red; everything was either black or white. There was no discussion as to "don't do this" or "don't do that." He was a great guy for motivating people. When we won, he was always honest, and when we lost, he never said a lot. He used reverse psychology by making us reflect on how we performed.

To prepare for later years and build a solid financial foundation on my own, I worked with Frank Ramsey former professional basketball player and coach. A 6-3 guard, he played his entire nine-year (1954–1964) NBA career with the Boston Celtics and played a major role in the early part of their dynasty, winning seven championships. Ramsey was also a head coach for the Kentucky Colonels of the ABA during the 1970–1971 season. I would take $200 or $300 and put it in stock like AT&T or General Telephone and blue chip stocks and finally had a portfolio going, and after a while I said, "I don't care what it does right now but when I'm sixty or seventy years old, I want it to be something substantial." I feel it's a great lesson to come away from the game by giving something to it, but you will also take away something monetarily if you invest properly.

Looking back on all the successful years as a Boston Celtics and playing with such talented and really terrific guys, it's hard to say I had a favorite. Red never traded anyone, which added to our success. I think I was on the Boston Celtics team for eight or nine years before the first trade Red made was Mel Counts for Bailey Howe. Red felt that even if a player wasn't that good, he was going to stay around. He stayed with the team. I remember Frank Ramsey, who was the original sixth man when I came to the Celtics. He said he was glad I was there because he was getting too old. "And you're going to be able to take over for me. It will be a couple of years, but I'm glad you are here." Everyone was sort of on the same page most of the time in the way we approached the game, playing and that sort of thing. Former Boston players always stay in touch with the Boston Celtics organization. I see a lot of my old teammates, and it's always good to stay in touch with your friends.

I am currently seventy-five years old and feel pretty good. I keep my weight down and am careful to take care of myself.

Satch Sanders

The first thing I remember about Kermit Washington was that everyone thought of him as a very nice man, and he was well respected for his hard work. Red Auerbach often spoke to me about Kermit before he was drafted into the NBA by the Los Angeles Lakers. Red shared with me while I was coaching at Harvard University in Cambridge, Massachusetts, established 1636, whose history, influence and wealth have made it one of the world's most prestigious universities.

Prior to the Celtics bringing Kermit on board, I watched the video of the "infamous punch." I saw Kevin Kunnert holding his own in an altercation with Kermit. I observed Kermit turn his head as if someone had called his name or someone was trying to warn him about something that was about to happen. Then Rudy came running toward Kermit and made the connection with Kermit's extended fist.

It was portrayed as Kermit doing something awful when in actuality Kevin Kunnert was holding his own in an altercation with Kermit. Rudy, on the other hand, had no reason to come into the equation. If Rudy had not sustained such serious injuries, there might not have been presented such a negative consequence for Kermit. In any situation where someone makes the decision to get involved, there is the risk of a misconception of intent. This is what happened in this situation.

With the concern of reinstatement as Kermit's suspension was coming to an end, Red came to me and discussed how much he wanted Kermit to join us on the Boston Celtics team. For me it was simply a done deal as Kermit was a tough player with the ability to become even a better player. He had tremendous potential prior to the incident, and the only question was if his time off from basketball would become an issue. It's never a good thing to have time off from playing ball, and coming back with the adversity he had to face simply added to the intense pressure Kermit had to overcome.

When he put on the Boston Celtics uniform, he continued to show his quickness and ability to rebound and block shots. I was impressed that he could get up in the air after two and even three tries to grab a rebound. He demonstrated quick recovery, and at first I thought we might only use him for ten to twelve minutes a game.

After the first game's performance on the court, he was looking as good as if he had never been away from the game, and it was obvious that he was going to get a lot better. We played him longer in games than at first intended, and Kermit became instrumental in helping us out to win more games.

K. C. Jones and I were aware that with our older players, our practices were not strenuous. We had the blizzard that year, and that meant catching up with many nights of back-to-back games. Kermit was working hard to get back in shape, and Red had booked him in the Sheraton Prudential Center for housing. This hotel provided Kermit with several flights of stairs he would run up wearing a twenty-pound weight vest. He once told me that after his first game as a Boston Celtics, he couldn't stop sweating for several hours, and I had to smile as he had played so well. I was afraid to tell him he would be playing more minutes in the games to follow even though he felt he needed to get into shape.

Kermit was always easygoing, and living in the hotel helped provide a comfort level he needed to settle into the Boston Celtics routine. On the road, we had certain requirements, one of which was wearing a suit. No one brought this to his attention until after he was fined for not having one. I simply reminded him that he could go out and buy one, but it should be noted that his per diem envelope often came up with a note: You Owe Us.

John Havlicek played his final game that year in the Boston Garden. John was checking the MVP of the All-Star game held in Atlanta, Randy Smith. As everyone knew, this was John's final game. The Buffalo Braves team put out a very physical game to prevent him for going out with style, leaving his mark, and wanted to make sure Boston lost their last game of the season. John was really being pushed around in the first half and once was knocked to the floor. I put Kermit in the game so he could set some better picks for John to continue to make baskets. John was then able to get open, which lessened the physical nature of the game for him and allowed him to score more points.

In the end John came out like a loaded gun and scored 29 points. He left his mark, and to this day his career performance as a Boston Celtics is long remembered by many.

Adrian Dantley

Growing up in the Cordoza area in Washington, DC, at the age of eight and nine you could find me playing basketball for Monroe Elementary School. I was always being made fun of for being "chubby." This motivated me to become the best basketball player in the DC area. I loved the game, and it became my passion in life. Over the years I was able to accomplish this due to working myself into the best mental and physical shape possible to achieve.

I knew I was going to be good, for at the early age of eight I could go against the bigger players and destroy them. I could consistently outplay bigger opponents, and this had its negative and positive consequences. Being acknowledge for my skills was the plus; being threatened to be beat up or actually being beaten up was a true minus in this equation.

When playing for Monroe Elementary School, in the community where I grew up, every four to five blocks there was a playground with ten-and-under, twelve-and-under, and fourteen-and-under basketball teams you could play on. Mr. White was the recreational director and coach for my playground and was the first person to recognize my talent. I played on the twelve-and-under team with him as my coach.

It was the established practice to go out and play basketball around the city. When my team entered a local Christmas tournament, Coach White promised if we won our games we would go out to celebrate. When we did win, I was leaving the locker room and had not taken the time to put on a shirt. Coming down the steps without a shirt on, I was soon made aware of a sinister plot to jump me. As I had no intention of accepting this possibility becoming a reality, there was no need to try and reason on this or ask any questions. I simply responded with the fight-or-flight reaction and ran all the way home. In those days, it was a well-known fact that if you won the game, you were going to lose the fight. To avoid this from applying to my case, I took off until I reached the safety of my home. Another advantage to working hard and being in better condition than anyone else.

When I attended Bertie Backus Junior High, this local motto continued to follow me. I was given notice that I was going to be beat up. A contract had been put out on me, and it was open season. Somehow providence intervened, and the contract was not fulfilled, and I managed to continue living. My family moved to Sergeant Road, and I played on Saint Anne's playground with the legendary player James Brown. This helped me to improve my skills on the court.

I walked or rode the bus to visit Langley Park, Mount Rainer in Hyattsville, Maryland, Taft High School, and Bunker Hill playgrounds. At twelve and thirteen I was like the determined gunslinger with only one intent. I wanted to play with and against the very best talent on any court on any given day. During my ninth-grade year I would frequent Luzon playground while a student at Bertie Backus Junior High School. When playing a game against DeMatha High School, Eugene was the guy local high schools were seeking to recruit. DeMatha showed an interest in me when Chuck Taylor asked if I might be interested in attending DeMatha High School in the upcoming school year. Chuck made a wonderful pitch about playing under the auspicious tutelage of Morgan Wooten.

During that summer, I had to attend summer school and pass math and English classes to apply and be considered entrance. When the session began, there were twenty players enrolled in the summer school mandatory classes. By the end of the third and fourth day, fourteen players back out. I completed summer school and after passing all classes was accepted for admittance to DeMatha High School. I tried out for the junior varsity basketball team and, having made it, blossomed as a player.

My freshman year I averaged 10 points and 10 rebounds per game. During that summer, I started going to a lot more playgrounds and ventured to Cole Field House at University of Maryland, where I met Kermit. In those days, you played ball based on word of mouth. Once you learned which local talents were playing, you went there to meet the challenges of playing with and against the very best. Kermit was well-known around the city and recognized as a player of merit. This summer I also played in the Bethesda Chevy Chase league, scoring 50 points against Jim O'Brien from Saint John's High School, four years my senior, who later attended Boston College.

Monday through Thursday the place to be was on the courts of Rudolph playground. John Thompson, Merlyn Wilson, and Austin Carr were the players to look for. They might be at Fort Stevens, Turkey Thicket, or anywhere in the city. Rudolph was the established site for play, but on the weekends, it was open season in DC to locate local talent. I mainly went to Aubrey or Cole Field House. You never knew who would be in the stands. Red Auerbach lived in DC during the off season and was known as a regular attendee. Everyone in the city knew where to be to watch quality basketball competition. It was unbelievable the support that was shown. In those days with limited access to quality entertainment, local playground basketball games could be compared to ESPN sports specials.

Local high school coaches such as John Thompson brought his players from Saint Anthony's to Rudolph to play against the playground greats. The perimeter of the playground was filled with fans who sat in the sun drinking beers and shouting words of encouragement to their local favorites. Not having comfortable seating or any stands to speak of was no obstacle to fans that loyally came to watch DC talent play.

My sophomore year I played against Austin Carr, five years my senior, and made first-team All-Met. On my team was Ricky Hunt and Michael Hunt, with players you might not recognize as they did not go on to play in the NBA. Carrol Holmes, Kenny Roy, and Kenny Carr played on that team, Kenny being the only acknowledged star. The level of talent was exceptional. The talent was so good; if you lost in the first game, you we out for the rest of the morning. It got extremely hot in the afternoons on any given summer day in DC.

Playground game rules were different from organized basketball. On the playground, the goal was to reach 30 points before the opposing team. When you got to 28 up, you would have to foul for the opposing team not to score, or you needed to have a great outside shooter. Because you couldn't foul as easily with an outside shot, you wanted to have an Austin Carr on your team. As a guard, somebody better not let the other team score. You had to call fouls. If you lost, the prospect of playing in other games that day was slim and none. Once removed from the court due to a loss, you would not get back on the court unless you were recognized as super good.

Reputation was more important than anything else. With having obtained a good reputation, I was respected for my hard work. It helped me to appreciate that my efforts were not in vain as no one else was going to put in as much time and energy as I was willing and determined to do. I jumped rope, shot three throws, and practiced every skill known to basketball. The rumor going around reported that even on Christmas Day I spent six hours working on my game. You could find me running the stadium stairs of DeMatha to improve my conditioning routine.

When my senior year was coming to an end, I was not really interested in going to The University of Notre Dame. I was a shoo-in to go to North Carolina State University, considered the possibility of Indiana, and was not keen on University of Maryland as I didn't want to stay in the DC area. I was aware of three key players from DC: Sid Catlett, Austin Carr, and Collis Jones. When extended an invitation to visit, I accepted as it was a car ride out of the city. When I drove up to the campus and saw the golden dome, I was smitten. The personnel and a spot for me to play right away was enticing, but the clincher to seal the day was the fact that games were televised locally. I knew it was the best choice I could make.

Attending the University of Notre Dame, located adjacent to South Bend, Indiana, was both enjoyed and helped to widen my knowledge of traveling beyond the confines of the DC area. People were basically the same, and both blacks and whites were a positive aspect of my educational career. It didn't take notice the diversity of my fellow students was markedly different from my previous educational experience and that people of color were in the minority on campus. I was focused on my academics and, most important, my training to improve my basketball skills and overcome the stigma of being that "chubby" kid. Playing on the local playground courts was the foundation for my enjoyment of any and every challenge. I attended school with a positive self-image and the goal to complete my college years with a degree and a future I would embrace on with the confidence needed to be successful.

My freshman year, John Shumate was a senior with Gary Brokow, both first-round NBA draft picks. Of the memorable games, I played, The University of Notre Dame, versus UCLA game stands out as the most significant in my college years. At that time UCLA, had won eighty-eight straight games. Bill Walton was the player of note. Before the game started, Bill walked by our bench whistling the UCLA fight song. We were encouraged to keep our composure and give it all we had. During the game Tommy Curtis continually shouted out disparaging remarks about us. Our team put forth a spurt in the last three minutes of the game. That matched with unexpected turnovers made by UCLA. Norte Dame went down in history as defeating the formidable nemesis of every college team, the UCLA Bruins.

After the game, Bill Walton cried holding his head in defeat to hide his tears. We still could see the tears running down his face, which showed his disappointed over the outcome. As the team went on to celebrate, I had to keep an appointment with my tutor. Somehow I could focus on the academic requirements to be met, but later I dreamt about the game and had one of the best nights of sleep of my life.

I played in the NBA, being drafted by the Buffalo Braves, playing with the talent of Bob McAdoo, Ernie DiGregorio, and Randy Smith. Traded to the Indiana Pacers, my teammates included Ricky Sobers and John Williams, with coach Slick Leonard. When traded to the Los Angeles Lakers, I had the privilege to play with Kareem, Jamaal Wilkes, and Norm Nixon. I was traded to the Utah Jazz as the consensus was that even though I stared with Jamaal, the team could not win with two small guards. While on the Utah team, I had my best scoring season. I personally enjoyed being a part of each of these teams.

Guys in the NBA played me tough, but by the second half they would lose their steam, getting tired. Being in better shape due to my intense conditioning regiment. Knowing this made me a second-half player to be reckoned with. Later becoming an assistant coach for the Denver Nuggets, I noticed current players did not demonstrate the same level of working out as players in the past had done. Current players had a coach to accompany them in these efforts and were available to run after missed balls. In my time players worked out on their own and they had to run after the ball before they tried any move again. More effort was needed to do this and added to increased stamina. I always made it a point to work out even if I was tired. If I didn't want to do any footwork, I would shoot five hundred free throws. Not a day was skipped, and each workout was at the highest level I could achieve on any given day.

Brian Taylor

Living in New Jersey, I attended Perth High in Amboy, New Jersey, located a half-hour drive from New York, was close to Rutgers, about ten minutes away, and a half-hour drive from Princeton University, in Princeton, New Jersey. Sports played a big part of my early life. My dad was a semi-pro football player. My first love was baseball. I was a bat boy, then Joined the Little League and then the Babe Ruth league. Baseball was my favorite sport until I started playing basketball at the local recreation center, but I also loved football.

I found out I had a lot of athletic ability as I loved all three sports: baseball, basketball, and football. I played varsity football, basketball, and baseball with my older brother, who was a senior when I was a freshman, Bruce. Our school was number one in basketball but was knocked out of the state finals. We were known as being the best basketball team in the state of New Jersey.

I played quarterback and defensive back in football and came into my own as an all-American quarterback. I played baseball and was watched by pro scouts. My older brother Bruce later played professional football the same time I played professional basketball, something Kermit and I share as a one-time event in professional sports.

My senior year I injured my foot and concentrated on playing basketball with the goal of attending Princeton University. My high school was basketball state champion my junior year, and I averaged

40 points a game. I had two outstanding games that year. In one game, I scored 85 points, but a foul was committed and 1 point was taken away, so the record of 84 points to be scored in thirty minutes of one game. I also scored 71 points in a high school game. This record remained in place until a kid named Wagner broke it by scoring 90 points in one game. I was known as a gunner in high school. Coaches came to watch me play, and the head coach from Princeton offered me a spot if I wanted to accept it.

Being a good student with leadership skills as I was the school vice president my junior year, I accepted the offer and took the opportunity to attend Princeton. After doing a lot of reading about black athletes who failed to prosper from such opportunities, I decided not to fall into the stigma of being dumb. I had grown up in the projects, and being given the opportunity to attend such a highly recognized school was unbelievable. I was excited and ended up having a great career at Princeton.

Playing for Princeton was different than high school ball. Princeton had a slow-down game. I was used to the run-and-gun plays with the freedom to shoot. I felt like I was in the embryo stage as Princeton ran a score from transition game. Points were obtained from defense with the concentration on full court pressure. It was a man-to-man full court defense, and I felt like a gambler on defensive end and encouraged to go after the ball. Coach gave me the confidence to go after the ball, be defensive, and rely on my alacrity and agility. Princeton scored 100 points in a couple of games due to this approach.

In 1969–1970 freshmen were not allowed to play varsity basketball. As a freshman, my team was undefeated with a 17–0 record. The varsity team featured future NBA players Jeff Petrie and John Hummer. We played against this varsity and gave them a run for their money but were not able to beat them. My sophomore year I had a lot of injuries, but our team had a winning record. In my junior year, American University came to Princeton to play us. I remember meeting Kermit Washington in 1971–1972. He was American University's leading rebounder and shot blocker. I had heard about him, and this was an opportunity to play against a future NBA standout.

Princeton beat North Carolina State University when Bob McAdoo with Bobby Jones, George Carl, and Bill Chamberlin were starters. North Carolina was number two in the conference, and we back-doored them to death. The arena went wild.

After having played a great season my junior year, I was approached by Lou Carnesecca from the ABA New York Nets team. He invited me to meet with him at the Waldorf Astoria and asked me this question, "How much are you worth?" All I could think of was $5 the cost of catching the train back to school. He responded, "I can change that overnight." My interest was aroused. Leaving Princeton was not a difficult decision to make. If I remained to complete my degree, I would have to prepare a one-hundred-page thesis. The choices were to prepare a thesis or play professional basketball with the legendary Dr. J. Seriously, there was only one choice to make. I made the choice to take him up on his offer.

My childhood dream to play professional basketball was actually going to come true. Icing on the cake was to play with the legendary Dr. Julius Irving. My first year as a New York Net I was named Rookie of the Year. I had three great years playing with the doctor. He was a superstar in the very essence of the word. A classy gentleman, I looked up to him both on and off the court. We had some great times together, and those years remain special to me. This first year we had Billy Paultz, who was an all-around player, good rebounder, scorer, passer, and shot blocker. The team was filled with loopers. Dr. J was the leader on the court. He was inspirational by example. He was not a playmaker but focused on making his teammates better. John Williams was also on the team who was the quick athlete who sent balls into the rafters. You could always pick him out on the team as he always had a toothpick in his mouth. Then there was Larry Kenyon. People liked to call him Dr. K, but he preferred to be called Mr. K as there was only one doctor on the team. Add Billy Melchionni and John Rhodes, a team of terrific people and talented players.

My second year on the ABA Nets, the team began to fall apart. It's a known fact that being able to know, accept, and carry out your role on the basketball court leads to success. When this is not done, the glue that holds together the unique puzzle pieces loses its ability to hold things together. Everyone wanted the ball. J knew this, and as prolific at the fast court game required, he passed the ball to whoever was open, and if he was double-teamed, he would look for the closest open man. He never raised his voice but worked to redirect those puzzle piece that were losing their staying power on the court. He was never the coach on the court; he preferred playing the wing.

The Spirit of Saint Louis team featured Maurice Lucas and Marvin Barnes. We beat this team all eleven times we played them. Remember, we only had seven teams in the ABA, and we played each other over and repeatedly. In the first round of the ABA playoffs, they knocked us off, and we were out of the playoffs.

In 1976 the ABA was about to merge with the NBA. With a limited number of teams, the ABA featured only seven, and we played each other anywhere from ten to twelve each season. We were on the road in Utah and freezing our butts off. We were excited to be leaving the cold weather on the East Coast and travel out west to play the San Diego Conquistadors. The night before we were to leave Utah, my bags were all packed and I was ready to go. We got a message that we would have to remain in Utah a couple of days as the San Diego team had folded. We were so disappointed we had to hold up in the cold, especially since we had packed our lovely light gear to enjoy the warm California sun.

We beat the Denver Nuggets in the last ABA finals, a team that featured David Thompson, Bobbie Jones, and Dan Issel. As the teams merged, it became our new focus to prove an ABA player could meet the challenge of playing in the NBA and excel. In the first year after the merger took place, it was heartwarming to see that half of the players in the All-Star game were former ABA players.

I had a fantastic final year in the NBA and played with Tiny Nate Archibald. Tiny was the leading scorer for the Kansas City Kings with Phil Johnson. I had scored 17 points a game and was soon acknowledged as a good player. Many people were not aware of ABA player skills as our games were not televised. When the trade was made for Tiny, everyone thought Phil Johnson was crazy, but after having such a great year Tiny was recognized as a true gem. My contract was up for negotiation, and I was signed, sealed, and delivered, or so I thought. Upon deeper inspection, the team discovered I had not been guaranteed an unconditional guaranteed deal and the contract had more holes than Swiss cheese.

Larry Brown put into play and asked for me in a trade to join him in Denver. I signed a new deal for $750,000, which at that time was a phenomenal deal. It in fact changed the economic landscape of the game. When David Thompson learned of this, he complained that he was more than twice the player I was and demanded to have his contract renegotiated. Denver was not willing to pay both of us the upscale salaries, and I soon exercised my free- agent status and signed with San Diego.

This was a good move as the coach was Gene Shue with whom I had a previous connection. Many people questioned this decision, but Gene had a plan under his belt. He wanted to get Bill Walton from Portland and knew he would have to give up players, and he actually cried when they chose Kermit, Kevin Kunnert, and Randy Smith. Now he knew Bill wanted Kermit to be his backup rebounder and protector under the bucket to play the power forward role. He also had to choose between giving up World B. Free or Randy Smith in compensation. Gene made the choice and lived with the consequences. Bill was never healthy enough to play well, and I had to sit out the remainder of the year to not be included in the trade as additional compensation. In fact, he would arrive at practice a minimum of fifteen minutes after we started, and nothing was ever said.

Although I was going to miss lifting weights in Kermit's El Cajon garage and spending hours of being entertained by Randy Smith, I was looking forward to the beginning of the season. Bill only played fifteen games, but I was able to make a statement and establish myself as a credible player. Freeman Williams rose to the occasion and scored 20 points a game. With the loss of Kermit, Gene instituted a new game strategy. It focused on the three-point shot. I made my living off the boards. Swen Nater grabbed rebounds along with Sidney Wicks. Swen had attended Pete Newell's Big Man's Camp and learned how to develop the basic hesitation game from the baseline.

Swen got better with Pete's hesitation and spin move. He played seven down low and double-teamed Swen, which left me open. Swen would look for me in the corner, pass me the ball, and let me shoot the three-point shot. Our team set a record for making three-point shots for years to come as Gene designed this play off the big man inside and outside. I had another good year when I snapped my Achilles. Gus Williams is the person I like to blame for this career-ending injury. Jack Sickma was an eyewitness to his play. Swen set the swing for me to take the shot, and I stepped away quickly. My shot was blocked. I got back up and tried to go up in the air when I snapped my Achilles. After playing in the ABA and NBA for a total of ten years, my career ended due to having surgery and wearing a cast beyond a reasonable amount of time. I could never build up my calf strong enough to come back and play.

I returned to Princeton as I had promised my classmates and earned my degree in African American studies and political science. This was the smartest decision I ever made. Without a degree, working the professional arena is not a possibility. A former classmate heard of an administrative position in a private school, Harvard Wesley, and my twenty-five-year career as an educator began.

Mychal Thompson

In 1972 it would be safe to say you could find me living the life under the warm Bahamian sun. Have you ever been mistaken for someone else? I answered an unexpected knock on my parents' front door and was greeted by a stranger who would ultimately change my life forever. A high school coach from Miami Jackson Senior High was looking for a Charles Thompson, and when he realized his mistake, he was thought quickly on his feet and immediately made mention of my height. After he explained the purpose of his visit to the Bahamas, he was honest when speaking that since I was tall, why not give some thought to coming to Miami and attend his high school with the explicit objective of playing basketball.

I took some time to research the school and was impressed with its successful history in winning tournaments and receiving accolades for championship performances. I spent many hours sharing this information with my father and convinced him it was worth taking a risk and see if this move would be a positive one for me. After all, I could come back home if it didn't work out. I Joined the school as a junior and never looked back.

My senior year in 1974, I was a part of the starting lineup, and we were nicknamed the Jackson 5. My teammates were three other Bahamians and a Cuban. Known as the Generals, we beat opponents by an average of 30 points per game to have a winning record of 33–0. We won the Class 4A state championship over Winter Park High School.

As my basketball ability was being acknowledged by colleges across the country, college scouts started to recruit me, leaving me with some choices to consider. Personally, I wanted to play in the Big Ten Conference and compete in the NCAA division or the Pack 8. The University of Minnesota Twin Cities located in Minneapolis and St. Paul, Minnesota fit my requirements and was a basketball powerhouse. They offered me a scholarship, and I readily accepted. As a Golden Gopher, our men's basketball team was ineligible to participate in the NCAA tournaments due to being on probation. In 1977 I was named second-team all-American and had my best season ever. We were slated to play against Marquette in the NCAA. In 1978 I was named first-team all-American. We were good enough to play in an NCAA tournament, but being on probation, we were not eligible to participate.

My junior year I was selected Player of the Year and offered an NBA contract but decided to remain in college and earn my degree. I was having such a good time at the University of Minnesota; the glamour and excitement of an NBA career could wait until later.

The Portland Trailblazers made me their number one pick in the 1978 NBA draft, being the first foreign-born player to be selected first. I played for Portland eight years and missed part of one season when I broke my leg. In 1979 I made the All-Rookie Team, and my best season statistically was in 1981–82 averaging over 20 points and 11 rebounds per game. Jack Ramsey was my coach, who was creative, and his system involved all of his five starters or combinations of five players on the court. He was smart, innovative, was easy to play for and knew how to help players play to their strengths. Maurice Lucas was a key player on the team. He was known as one of the better power forwards in the league. Lionel Hollins was another class act and quick point guard. As a rookie, my transition to the NBA was made a lot easier with the help my teammates gave me.

Early in my career with Portland, Kermit Joined the team when the San Diego Clippers traded for Bill Walton. Bill was not healthy, and Portland received Kermit and Kevin Kunnert in compensation. In the long run Portland did the best from this trade. Kermit was always ready, willing, and able to go to the gym and work out. I often met him in Lake Oswego at River's Edge Athletic Facility. On the road, we would visit any gym located close to our hotel. People were really friendly, and I was able to share my conditioning secrets with many people who would have otherwise missed out on the opportunity to learn from my successful efforts.

I enjoyed going on road trips and sharing my growing knowledge on a wide variety of topics with the people we'd meet on our travels. Most people were quite surprised to learn about the many interesting bits of information I was willing to share. Far too often people want to limit your conversations to professional basketball and the star players they want juicy gossip about. Being a highly intelligent individual, I enjoyed providing other topics to discuss and learn more about other people. I think this impressed many of them as when we arrived at our destination, many were speechless after our conversation. I'm saying this with tongue in cheek.

Now do you wonder why I often had an empty seat next to me on an airplane? But that's okay. I enjoyed watching my soap operas and had a chance to escape the usual tirade of insults simply because I had an avid interest in fictitious drama. Schedules are important, and people who follow them are very organized in their thinking. For me I was a strict believer in being back to our hotel rooms in time to watch my favorite soap. Why this was a subject of contention, I have no idea. Didn't most of the players want to be seated in front of their TV screens to watch a game? I simply wanted to relax and escape into the imaginary world of those characters that provided amusement and the very hint of suspense.

Of all the colorful players to join the team, there was Billy Ray Bates. A crowd favorite, Billy was down to earth, a raw talent, and provided many hours of entertainment for all of us. He could score numerous ways in on court traffic. Like Russell Westbrook, Billy could dunk on you from anywhere. He was a six-foot-four version of LeBron James. He was so naturally strong, he never lifted a weight, and had the body of a bodybuilder. He had a very limited basketball IQ and played straight from the hip. His game was like watching an episode of *Entertainment Tonight*. Off court he had the ability to drink four men under the table, and this later proved to be responsible for his shortened professional career.

In 1986 I was traded to the San Antonio Spurs for Steve Johnson, and to this day I was never given any clear reason for this trade. I was playing well, making a positive contribution to the team, and was continuing to enjoy playing with my teammates.

My stay in San Antonio was brief, lasting only half the year. I was then traded to my dream team, the Los Angeles Lakers. I was privileged to play with Kareem, Magic, and James Worthy and won consecutive championship titles in 1987 and 1988.

World B. Free

Raised in Brooklynn, New York, after attending Canarsie High, I played basketball for Guilford College, a small school in North Carolina located in Greensboro, North Carolina. I helped to lead Guilford College to the NAIA national championship, as well as named MVP of the tournament. I consider myself to be a great jump shooter that could score on any player on a given court on a given day.

In 1975 I was the twenty-third pick in the NBA draft, along with Darrell Dawkins by the Philadelphia 76ers. I played with such NBA legendary, great All-Stars as Dr. J, George McGinnis, Doug Collins, Darrell Dawkins, and Henry Bibby as a Philadelphia 76er for three years. I was traded to the San Diego Clippers and played there for two years. I played with Kermit the first year the team was moved and renamed, and later played with the Golden State Warriors for two years.

At six feet two inches, 185 pounds, I was privileged to enjoy the daily comradery of such great athletics and super-special people. Fans came early to watch warm-ups as if viewing a slam dunk contest between All-Star teammates. My first two years on the 76ers team I didn't get to play very much with Doug Collins and Henry Bibby as the starting guards. I enjoyed being a part of the traveling circus with faithful fans; however, I deeply wanted to have a chance to play with these greats on a regular basis.

When traded to the San Diego Clippers, I had mixed feelings. I missed the euphoria of being a 76er. Having known Gene Shue when he was my head coach of the 76ers, my only real concern was whether this sense of well-being would be achieved with such a new team. I feared my new teammates knowing I was a shooting guard, that I would not pass the ball. I needed time to reflect on the facts: The Clippers had Freeman Williams, Brian Taylor, and Randy Smith, all guards who could and did match up with any NBA guard.

It didn't take long to become relaxed and enjoy my new teammates and playing time. Our season started off slowly but that was to be expected. As the season progressed, we jelled, and I was able to score 28 points a game. Randy Smith scored 20 points per game. Freeman Williams scored 13 points per game. Brian Taylor scored 9 points per game but was the best defensive player on the team who ran the offensive well. That first year every player knew what their delegated role was to perform and did so with diligence. We missed making the playoffs by losing one game to Portland. That first year, only four games were missed by the starters. We ran well as a team, and the prospects of success were on the horizon.

At that time my salary was $125,000 per year. David Thompson had just signed a $900,000-a-year contract with the Denver Nuggets. The night we played against the Nuggets, I let everyone in the locker room know that David Thompson was not nine times better than me. I clearly stated that I was going to personally make it my objective to score 50 points on him that night to show him and everybody else who was worth the money.

I scored 51 points that night, and we won the game. The stats will not show this figure as I was called on an offensive charging foul, and they took my last basket from me. I had to leave the game having fouled out and feel technically one point short of my goal.

Living in San Diego was both enjoyed, and I was saddened to find that we lost Kermit in a trade for Bill Walton. If we had been kept together as the team we had been forming during this first year, we would have been more successful. When numerous injuries Bill didn't play a lot and we missed Kermit's presence. The following year both Kermit and I made the All-Star team held in Washington, DC. For Kermit, being traded to Portland made that possible for him, so maybe in the long run it wasn't such a bad move after all.

Kiki Vanderweghe

Teammate and
coach Jerry West

Hall of Famer Bernard King at Pete Newell's Camp

CHAPTER 11

Stanford University—The Cardinal (a tree not a bird)

John Arrillaga Stanford Alumnus and benefactor

If you were to ask the average person to define retirement, most would include: ultimate bliss, no worries, sleeping in, spending the twenty-four hours previously scheduled by others now as you see fit, security, comfort, and unlimited options. Reality tells you it boils down to boredom which for me meant a lack of mental stimulation. When leaving Portland, Oregon, the one daily regiment I truly have not missed was running up the hill on Southeast Wally Road, in Boring, Oregon. The climb up that hill was comparable to running the stairs in Boston. However, not having anything to motivate me to start my day, left me constant wondering how I was going to make the adjustment without a new routine and then asking what will that new routine look like? I was left feeling a sense of urgency in filling this void.

Boredom is said to be a state of mind. Therefore, I wasn't really bored or confined in a state of boredom but, merely in need of consider options which were viable. Any new options worth consideration had to include: physical activity; reading; it truly is amazing how much information I could access and enjoy, socializing: I had to be around people who shared similar interests at best or were open to thinking outside the box at least: and of course, had some connection to athletics be it a sport, or an athlete. Life without having to ice an injury or being in constant pain had become a part of my new retirement status and I was pleased with having a peaceful night's rest. My comfort level regarding my current life had plateaued and the linger embers from being physically and mentally active began to flicker sparks and soon ignited into a burning desire to get on with my life. This fire was soon a blazing fire I could not ignore.

Having kept in touch with both Coach Young and Coach Davis, I picked up the phone and spoke with Coach Davis, who was currently coaching at Stanford University in Stanford, California. Coach Young was on the East Coast coaching at Rutgers University in New Jersey. I considered the possibility of remaining on the West Coast and not buying any more real estate, or venturing back East to old roots. My years of being traded to different cities, usually meant purchasing real estate. It soon became evident that was not the best way to do things. I should have listened to Stu Lantz who bought one home in San Diego and only rented housing when he was traded. The idea of remaining in California was a possibility. Having friends in the area would be a bonus versus moving back to the east coast and having to adjust to the seasons and humidity. But the familiarity with the DC metropolitan area, American University and life-long friendships might have been the better choice. I mulled these options over and over and thought more about the comfort and convenience remaining in California offered.

My brother Chris, his wife, and son had moved into our San Diego home while we were in Portland. Coming back and sharing living space proved to create unexpected problems. I then decided to sell a piece of property in Palos Verdes, California, buying a larger home and moved there. Chris and his family remained in San Diego, where he was attending San Diego State University to obtain his degree in electrical engineering.

Having a close tie to family has its pluses and minuses. Chris's wife, although she enjoyed the comfort of a beautiful home in San Diego, her family and friends and decided to move back to Missouri. She had support and a Job connection there which was more appealing than living in a large house she couldn't enjoy without family and friends to share it with. Being miles away from those she missed intensified her loneliness and desire to go back home. Leaving Chris on his own in San Diego and returning home was a choice made that left Chris hurt but he tried to consider what was in the best interest of the family. Little Eric would have the benefit of spending time with his grandparents and this would motivate Chris to finish up his course work with the objective of joining his family sooner.

Shortly after his wife and son returned to Missouri, Chris drove up to Palos Verdes from San Diego to share his concerns about being separated from his family. Initially, after he married he was still playing professional football. This provided a stable and lucrative financial arrangement for his family. After Little Eric was born, he was playing well as a defensive back when at the end of a play and opposing player slammed into his knee. This cheap shot resulted in an ACL injury that ended his career. Today, surgery would have been able to repair the damage so he could recover and return to playing football. But back then this was a game breaker.

Not knowing how to provide the kind of support that would have been long-lasting, I should have encouraged him to immediately enroll in school and get a degree in Engineering. Instead I sent money for buying a house, car, and supporting his living expenses. Realizing this arrangement should not go on indefinitely, he called me from Missouri one evening to thank me for my help but indicated he wanted to be independent and find a solution that would be long-lasting and restore his pride. That was when I extended the offer to move his family to San Diego and while he attend a local college and completed credits to earn his degree. This conversation took on a different tone. He was alone in the large house in San Diego, missing his family and unable to concentrate on his studies. He expressed a keen desire to move back to Missouri and hoped I would understand. I gave him the pink slip to the new Camaro and wished him well. A few days later he had packed up the car and drove back to Missouri.

With Chris gone I decided to move back to San Diego. Putting the recently purchased house in Palos Verdes on sale. I now put more serious thought in a new routine and possible forms of employment. Coach Davis had move from the east coast and was the head basketball coach for Stanford University, in the San Francisco Bay area. Having visited there on many occasions and thinking about the requirements I outlined for a new routine, I gave coach a call. I inquired if he knew of any open assistant coaching positions. And was more specific by adding I was interested in working with him if there was a position available at Stanford. I based this request on the fact that Coach Davis had known me for years, and we had always kept in touch. I didn't give any thought to the realization that Stanford University was a very conservative institution of higher learning and probably identified Kermit Washington with "the fight." I later thought I had actually placed coach Davis in an awkward position. I knew he had full confidence in his coaching abilities and if I joined him that would indicate his confidence in me. If this worked out I know what coach Davis had done for me. In would show me the extent to which he believed in me. This added to the extent of my appreciation for who he was as a person as he gained more respect in my eyes.

Coach Davis returned my call and asked me to fly up and talk about joining him as an assistant coach. At this time one of his assistants was pursuing a head coaching job and was waiting to hear about it. The day I flew in, we met, and he told me he would get back to me. While sitting in the airport waiting for my return flight home, I happened to pick up a newspaper. In the sports section I read an Eric

Washington formerly in the NFL had died. I had to take hold of my emotions and forced myself to continue reading the article. I knew at the time my brother was playing professional football there were two Eric Washington's on NFL rosters. Without the current technology of cell phones or other devices I continued reading. Sadly, the Eric Washington mentioned in this article was indeed my brother. I was in a state of shock to read further and discover it was my brother who had died.

Depression rapidly set in, and one week later Coach Davis called to offer me an assistant coaching job. I enjoyed working with and being around athletes. To step into the role of coach I had a lot of work to do. I still thought as a player and not as a coach. I didn't have any experience under my belt yet and watched coach Davis closely. Not comfortable with that in the beginning, I later found myself easily slipping into that role when needed, once I could separate the player from the coach. The first year I rented a small home in Palo Alto. With two children and two dogs, it was soon obvious we needed to find more suitable housing. After getting better acquainted with the area, we found a house in Redwood City, California, that had a large front and side yard. This space was perfect for the dogs and the Stanford students who spent many hours with me and my family for barbecues and hard-boiled egg challenges. After making hard-boiled eggs with Miracle Whip and ketchup students wondered why the eggs looked orange, they were used to using mustard and mayonnaise. This led to a challenge to determine which recipe was the best. The outcome was hours of humorous memories and a combine recipe that included all four ingredients.

Arriving in Palo Alto, the campus located on El Camino Real was absolutely amazing. It was a city within a city. Buildings and streets were part of an artist's rendition of Shangri-La. It would take a minimum of one hour to walk around the perimeter of the campus and then walk throughout the campus to see all the features this facility offered to the students. Bicycles were primary means of moving around the campus. Row upon row of bicycle racks housed locked and chained well-oiled machines that lined the outside and inner courtyards of the campus. Parking lots and open streets provided additional bicycle racks to safely store a student required and much needed means of transportation. Cars were also parked in lots for other activities off campus and the eager pursuit of recreation on the bay area could provide. Classrooms were much the same as I remembered with clamoring students eager to be present in any and every class offered. Making the transition from professional basketball to college coaching required adopting a new mind-set. I was now provided an office with a desk and work space, and a secretary. The women's basketball offices were located on the same floor and directly opposite the men's basketball offices. After entering the door from the main hallway if you turned to the right you would enter the women's basketball offices and if you walked to the left you would enter the men's basketball offices. My desk was the third one on the left directly in front of the head coach office. Coach Davis had a room with a view I had the view of the other assistant coaches and staff working directly under him.

Part of my Job assignment was to recruit players. This included, after identifying potential players, making phone calls, visiting practices, watching games, and meeting with families. It was all about establishing a relationship and impress upon the players how the value of a Stanford degree far outweighed the fleeting glitz and glamour of college basketball as portrayed on TV.

Meeting the two assistant coaches, Bruce Pearl, currently the head coach at Auburn University located in Auburn, Alabama, and Gary Close, current assistant coach at The University of Wisconsin–Madison located in Madison, Wisconsin, they were helpful in showing me the ropes and explaining what my Job description actually entailed. Coach Davis spent a great deal of time going over the rules of college ball recruiting. What you could do and could not do were clearly outlined and reviewed to make sure I knew all the ins and outs of being a college coach.

I was relieved I could train players in the weight room. I would occasionally play a pickup game on neighborhood courts. In one incident, a local player reported that playing in such a game I had tried to recruit him to come to Stanford. I then learned playing on any court was not going to be an option. After being called in about this, the player was questioned, and when it was revealed he had lied, I learned a valuable lesson. Palo Alto basketball courts were not like the metropolitan DC area playgrounds. A pick-up game could be easily misconstrued by a player as an outright recruiting tactic. For me it was simply a chance to play a game without any pain and an enjoyed avenue to stay in shape. As this was potentially an opportunity to cause trouble in the future I only played ball with Stanford students on Stanford courts.

Being around such talented individuals both on and off the athletic arena was inspiring. It was enjoyed being around the football and basketball players. Working out in the weight room, I met James Lofton, a Stanford graduate and Hall of Fame inductee, and Dave Wyman, a current football player who was working diligently to rehabilitate a very bad knee injury. James was quite the well-rounded athlete. He lifted for all body parts and incorporated running the legendary hills of Palo Alto. Like all the Stanford athletes, James was motivated and dedicated to achieving success. This provided the opportunity to be constantly supported and surrounded by the very best competitive athletes in the world.

My first year of coaching in college meant a lot of work off the court. Mentally I was still thinking as an athlete in the capacity as a player. I didn't like yelling at the players. I was prepared to share in one's workout and help my partners know I understood the pain needed to meet a goal joining to join. I was joining them in their efforts while at the same time setting goals for myself. It soon became evident that making the transition from player to being a coach was going to take time. I was a work in progress. If I were asked to evaluate my performance that first year, sadly I would say a D+. It didn't help that Coach Davis was such a good coach; he didn't need any assistance. Coach Davis's strengths as a coach was evident when he was the assistant at American University, head coach at Lafayette, head coach at Boston College, head coach at Stanford, and later head coach at the University of Iowa.

My first real assignment was to recruit Howard Wright. Howard was from San Diego, California and in my efforts to sign him to Stanford shared with him this, "I'm much older now, but a Stanford degree will be the most significant accomplishment of your life. At Stanford, you don't gain admission on athletic ability. There are *no* exceptions to entrance requirements." The strict adherence to maintain high entrance standards later led to Coach Davis's decision to leave Stanford University and coach at The University of Iowa in Iowa City, Iowa.

Howard's SAT scores were formidable and on an equal footing as others aspiring to attend such a prestigious institution. His father a former NFL playing for the San Diego Chargers, realized the value of a Stanford degree and was instrumental in helping Howard not select a school based on their national recognition for basketball on the court.

This second year, Todd Litchi entered as a freshman, along with Howard Wright. These new recruits were more talented than last year's roster. Although were many talented players who would have made Stanford a powerhouse to be reckoned with, too many could not meet the academic entrance requirements. The efforts of recruiting and the freedom to weight train with the ballplayers this first summer made me start to enjoy being an assistant coach. I could now play in a few pickup games without experiencing pain as I now had time to rest my body, giving me time to recover my stamina on the court. The other athletes soon noticed how much fun the football and basketball players had working out with me and asked if they could join us.

Pam Dukes, who was in her sophomore year, approached me about working out with her. A well-renowned shot putter, she later went on to win a bronze medal in the Olympics. Pam had a physique like Serena Williams. She was stronger than most of the basketball players I worked with, and I had to make sure we worked out at a time when they would not be in the gym for fear she would intimidate them. She reminded me of something Bruce Lee once said. "If you want to be a better basketball player, play basketball. If you want to be a better swimmer, swim. If you want to be a better runner, run. So, whatever you want to be good at, do that. For this is more important than all the peripheral things. First be good at the skill you are seeking to improve."

Those years of working out with a variety of students resulted in my gaining strength. I had achieved my personal best and was stronger. My highest bench press was 385 pounds, cleaning 340 pounds, and squatting 400 pounds for ten reps (as if it were nothing). The weight room was overseen by the head strength coach. To better meet the varying schedules of athletes who wanted to work out in the gym, I asked the strength coach for a key to the weight room. I was denied this, but after speaking with Coach Davis, I was given one. This perceived invasion of "personal space" was met with animosity, which festered during my duration as a coach.

Once I had a key, I could open the weight room on the weekends, late evenings, and early mornings. I ran the hills and sometimes had a training partner join me. Jerry Rice might have made these hills famous, but running them with so many athletes who went on to achieve remarkable feats made these hills legendary.

Pam Dukes knew I had a key to the weight room and would call to see if I could meet her on Sunday evenings. She was always focused and set high goals for her workout sessions. James Lofton, after seeing me working out, approached me and asked me a series of questions before asking if he could lift with me. He wanted to know if I could lift 225 pounds for ten reps on the bench press. I told him, "That is nothing." He said, "Let me see." I readily demonstrated so. He then remarked, "Your kind of strong." I told him again, "That is nothing."

We became lifting partners as he was serious about fitness and working out. Even though I had been going to Gold's Gym for years, this time spent at Stanford got me in the best shape of my life. Dave Wyman soon Joined our regime while recovering from such a bad knee injury; it was doubted by the experts that he would ever be able to play again. This view was unfounded. If you knew anything about Dave Wyman, you knew what a fierce competitor he was. He was more determined than death and taxes. He would participate in performing five sets of twenty-five squats, which could result in a near-death experience, with the will and fortitude of a Spartan. This one exercise was a favorite of the bodybuilder Robbie Robinson and greatly strengthened ligaments and tendons, exactly the focus Dave needed.

We did have three other athletes work out with us in our squatting ordeal, but they didn't last; the only regulars were James, Dave, and me. Dave was drafted by the NFL and played for the Denver Broncos and Seattle Seahawks. His toughness served him well. Mentally he was like a seasoned rodeo rider determined to hold on to that horse and, when the time allotted is over, walk the horse leisurely back to the stables. Nothing could ever stand in the way of him playing football.

Being still young at thirty-four years of age, I was up for the challenge of squats, but the night before doing them in the gym was always fretful. I knew the pain I was going to experience, and anxiety set in. My only comfort came from knowing I wasn't going through this alone.

The second year at Stanford, we had a strong basketball team. I would evaluate my performance as an assistant this year with a solid C. Todd Litchi and Howard Wright were Joined by Greg Butler; each one went on to play in the NBA. Bruce Pearl and Gary Close were much better assistant coaches than I was. Their concentration was on mastery of techniques. Not having played ball, they weren't thinking like an athlete. As a coach, you need to step away from the player mode. Bruce and Gary were always in coaching mode. Something as a former NBA player I had to learn.

Coaching with Coach Davis was a great experience. After my third year, Davis left Stanford to become the head coach at Iowa University. A lot of top recruits were unable to qualify for entrance to such a formidable institution such as Stanford University. Of all the individuals, I met or came to know, the one person who stands out far above anyone else is John Arrillaga. I met John after my first game as assistant coach. He walked up to me and asked, "Do you still play basketball?" I said, "No." John asked me this question multiple times, and my response was always, "No." Coach Davis pulled me aside and simply stated, "I think you should play with John."

Once a week for several weeks the league John was playing in was filled with a variety of former NBA players. It was quite impressive, and I did enjoy playing. I later found out John was the most generous of all the Stanford benefactors, having donated over 150 million dollars, and he responsible for the construction of eighty buildings. John was a former Stanford player who made all-American status. Off the court he was a talented magician and displayed great skill with card tricks. He once shared with me his humble beginnings. Living in California, his home did not have bathroom facilities as we know them today, and he had to use an outhouse. His first Job was to persuade a potential boss to allow him to prove his work ethic by allowing him to work for free. He did so, and his boss became his mentor.

John knew the value of money and would frequently tell me that it was important to buy things outright. He owned several properties, which were all paid for. He explained if there was a recession and he couldn't get all his rent, he could at least get something and it would be all his income as he didn't owe on any loans. His constant question, "Is that car paid for?" This was said to remind me of his words of wisdom regarding finances. At twelve to thirteen years my senior, he had sponsored the league we were playing in by paying for the referees and gym. Although he was older, physically he was in good basketball shape and could shoot. He needed help getting the ball, and that's where I came in. I set picks and got rebounds for him and thus we won games.

This wasn't an easy, guaranteed-win kind of arrangement. John enjoyed the competition but enjoyed winning and the trophy at the end of the season. The first round included seven weeks of games that ended with playoffs for a championship trophy. John averaged about 15 points a game, and we easily won the trophy. He played really well this round, and that made him extremely happy. I'm thinking it's all over, but a week later John called to let me know the next round of games would start in two weeks. I told him I had enjoyed the first round but had to politely decline his invitation. I took a very deep breath and told him I felt the need to be honest. I let him know I enjoyed the first round of games and was pleased we had placed first and won a trophy but at this stage of my basketball playing days I had to take time off. After explaining about my need for down time to take a rest.

John, however, had a serious hearing problem in that he selectively refused to ever hear the word *no*. Although *no* is universally understood in any language, that fact was permanently removed from his level of comprehension. When John wanted something, or wanted you to do something, it was simply to be acquired and the task carried out. Even though the leagues schedule was on Monday nights, John did not hear my explanation regarding the sacredness of Monday night football. So, on the first Monday of games when the scheduled game was comparable to a Bo Jackson–Barry Sanders matchup, John drove up to the house. Trying to pretend I don't see him wasn't an option as he proceeded to honk his horn until I came out. There was no choice. I got in the car, and off we went. As one of the richest and influential men in the country, it was rewarding to learn that the one thing his money and power could not buy was the joy of playing basketball with me.

Coach Davis took Bruce and Gary along with him to the University of Iowa as assistant coaches. Although he extended me an invitation, I declined his offer. I didn't want to relocate to the Midwest. He really didn't need my assistance, and I really wasn't head coach material. I was more of the "working one-on-one with individual" kind of coach and not a true team coach. I knew where my strengths lie, and it wasn't as a college coach—assistant or head. Coach Davis invited me to come, work-out and play a few games with his team. As he was just beginning to get to know his players, to substantiate his accomplishments as a coach, I could share how his working with me to improve my basketball skills resulted in an NBA career. I spent time discussing and emphasizing the importance of having a good work ethic and setting a clear goal. I expressed my deep enjoyment of lifting weights, jumping rope and running stairs as each helped me to gain strength and confidence. Playing on neighborhood playgrounds to uncover talent, both in yourself and that of opponents was also pointed out. All in all, the visit went well. Of the twelve players on coach Davis roster his first year as head basketball coach at The University of Iowa, five players were drafted by and played in the NBA.

The interim between Coach Davis left and the hiring of Mike Montgomery formerly head basketball coach at the University of Montana.

I was asked by Andy Geiger, Stanford's athletic director to hold things together until a new coach was selected. I had always been very good when in charge of an assignment but did not give my best effort when asked to carry out menial tasks. After giving it my best effort, I was not asked to interview for the head coaching Job, and John Arrillaga approached me with an offer I could not refuse. He asked me to work with his son John on weight training and to be the head coach at Menlo Park High School for his son's final year. Having been pleased with my efforts, John offered me an assistant strength coach position at Stanford. I would be accountable to John, and my Job description gave me leeway to schedule and work with all athletes. It was a great Job match, and I readily accepted.

To show respect and not to overstep my bounds regarding the basketball team, I limited my interactions with weight training and occasional playground pickup ball. I could use the knowledge I had gained from years of working out and training with the very best bodybuilders who worked out at Gold's Gym. Bodybuilders have a different mind-set altogether when it comes to workouts. They focus on working specific body parts to strengthen or rehabilitate an injury. That helped me to design specific workout sessions to meet the individual needs of the student athletes. Most of the athletes who were previously limited to working out with me could now take advantage of my open status and schedule training times with me.

My day began at 5:30 a.m. working with swimmers and divers. It was admirable that despite the long hours required to meet academic obligations, athletes were always punctual. The early hours supported my need for to keep my key, and as the head strength coach was not about to get to the weight room that early, things went along as smoothly as could be expected for a while. Later in the morning the tennis players trained, followed by the football players. The addition of the football player's added fuel to the flame as the head strength coach felt the football team was his sole responsibility to work with.

Joining me on a regular schedule was Patrick McEnroe, current commentator for the US Open. Patrick was very quiet and reserved, much like most of the students. He came across as guarded and, with a famous brother like John McEnroe, was keenly aware of the onslaught of questions that would follow if he left the door open. With him knowing my personal history, we would talk about nothing significant, and I always stayed focused on the workout to provide praise or further instruction to Pam Dukes and other track athletes. I had established a growing relationship with all the students, and this made my Job extremely enjoyable but also posed a threat to other members of the athletic staff.

At the same time, I was working with students, a few of the Golden State Warriors came up to Stanford to play ball in the gym. Now that I wasn't coaching, I could play with the Stanford players and go against the Golden State Warriors players. Every three days I would play and perform well, as my body had healed from my NBA days, and I played a day or two, then took off a day or two.

I knew I could still play in the NBA, but my body could not take the everyday rigors of games, practice, and traveling. When the general manager of the Golden State Warriors, Don Nelson, came to watch our pickup games, he was impressed with my performance. Toward the end of the season, Coach Nelson invited me to try out for the Golden State Warriors team.

Toward the end of the school year and John Arrillaga's son was preparing to start attending Stanford University, Andy Geiger called me into his office to tell me my contract was not going to be renewed. The athletes I had worked with met with Andy to petition for my return in my capacity as assistant strength coach. Andy agreed and called me in to let me know that by popular demand I would be offered and extension on my contract. Reflecting on the fact that the athletes would be soon graduating from Stanford, I decided not to accept his offer. But was very thankful for their support.

The years I spent at Stanford was a tremendous experience. The students regularly came over for BBQs, informal chats, and the normal family-type gatherings. Our Redwood City house was always filled with laughter and the exchange of good company. In fact, it was the *best* company. Before leaving Stanford, Don Nelson asked, "If I was to offer you a certain salary, would you be willing to come back?" My body was like a worn tire. If you chose to drive with it, you would go a distance, but in time it would wear out. Don was persistent in increasing his offer, and after one very appealing salary amount, I replied, "What time do you want me there?"

My Stanford days had come to an end, and I was now getting ready for the Golden State Warriors.

Coach Tom Davis, Kermit's assistance coach at American U and head coach at Stanford

John Arrillaga - Stanford's biggest donor and Alumni

CHAPTER 12

Catching Up with former teammates: Jerome Kersey and Kevin Duckworth

Once my years working with talented athletes who played a variety of sports at Stanford University, which was a both enjoyed and not soon forgotten, I began to think about moving back to Portland. Having lived there and worked out in at the River's Edge, I knew there would be someone I would be able to partner up with to work out on a regular basis. I held on to the highly motivated athlete concept as a standard set to find an ideal partner.

While driving to pick up my daughter from school I saw Jerome Kersey driving down the road in the lane right next to me. He honked his car horn, we looked at each other and pulled over to chat. It was a nice friendly catch up kind of conversation and he told me that Kevin Duckworth was also living in the neighborhood and suggested we all get together to catch up on what was new.

We met at my house the next day. It was interesting to find out that Jerome had bought some weight equipment and was still working out. Kevin on the other hand was interested in getting into better shape to improve his game. Jerome could maintain his playing weight and physique and all too eager to begin a workout program with the two of us. His natural athletic ability helped him develop into a very valuable basketball player for the Portland Trailblazers.

His only rival in receiving the award for athlete of the year would be Clyde Drexler.

We agreed to start running five days a week during the off season. We met at 7:00 am at my house and ran the course with an upward slope like climbing Mt. Everest. It was a five-mile run uphill with no breaks in the rise of the slope formula. Both arrived on time and for Kevin at 300 pounds this was going to be an interesting first day. As we began our upward trek it was amazing how competitive we became. This keep us focused on reaching the top of the hill and not stopping at any time. When we reached the top, Jerome was game for another go, but Kevin was clearly ready to call it a day.

We met every morning and followed this routine for several months. On one morning, early in July, Jerome phoned me around 6:30 am to say he had been out all night and was going to pass on running with Kevin and me that morning. His closing words were, "I'll see you tomorrow." Kevin and I laughed about it and started our run. The first part was flat and as we rounded the corner barely reaching the one-mile mark, who was waiting at the bottom of the hill for us, but Jerome. He arrived looking a bit disheveled and tired but remarked, "You guys didn't think I was going to let you run without me, did you?"

Usually, Jerome takes the lead when we run the hill, that day Kevin and I were leaving Jerome in the dust. Gaining confidence that this would be the first time we would beat Jerome to the top of the hill, we smiled at each other and push ahead. We did not lessen our pace but kept moving forward. Before Kevin and I could reach 100 yards from the top, we heard approaching footsteps. If we didn't know any better, we might have imagined Secretariat closing in on us from behind us. Before we had the chance to look to see who was behind us, we see Jerome run past us as if he was about to cross the finish line and win the Kentucky Derby.

Not out of breath or even sweating hard, Jerome sailed past us leaving us in his dust. Reaching the top, we had to smile and once we recovered our breath broke out laughing. Jerome had to laugh too. He calmly told us, "I could be dying of a heart attack and I would still beat you. Now, I'm going to go home and go to bed dreaming of how I beat two guys who can only dream of beating me."

Jerome told this story to all his teammates about what happened the day Kevin and Kermit thought they could beat me running up the hill. Terry Porter heard about it and would join the three of us from that day on. Terry was a good runner but none of us could beat Jerome. When Clyde heard about this tall tale he would make it known that even though Jerome was a good athlete he was still second to him in athletic ability.

After running the hill, we extended our workouts to include weight lifting. Now, I was feeling more comfortable about my decision to return to Portland. Spending time with Jerome and Kevin created a friendship that lasted until their sad passing. I will always think of both fondly, but that morning run with and against the likes of Jerome Kersey will be one memory I often think about.

CHAPTER 13

Golden State Warriors

Chris Mullin

Arriving to training camp, I knew with the time I had taken off along with lifting weights that I could successfully play in the NBA *only* if I was on a good team and could come off the bench. In practicing and working out with this team with Chris Mullings, Sleepy Floyd, Chris Washburn, and Joe Barry Carroll, I played well. In pre-season Coach George Carl and Don Nelson let me practice with less intensity than demanded in between games. When camp broke, I knew I had made the twelve-man roster.

Waiting to rent a place in Foster City, California, Chris Mullins extended to me an invitation to stay with him. He had a very nice condominium, and I accepted. I would go to practice, then from there head to a gym to work out. Chris was always focused on working out and had an exercise bike and treadmill in his condo. You could always find him on a machine working on cardio. After cardio, he would make it over to the courts and work on his basketball skills. His routine included working on all facets of his game and hours of shooting.

Money did not mean anything to him. It was all about the game; it was about hoops. He wasn't a true homemaker as he never cooked or prepared a meal at home. Not even a bowl of cold cereal. Chris would eat out every meal and gave it no thought as to how eating at home would be a better financial move. I asked him, "Chris, eating out is really expensive. I can cook. If I cooked a meal, would you join me?" But if he didn't, I assured him I felt comfortable with his returning to his routine of eating out.

When he got checks for endorsements for very large amounts, he would put them on the refrigerator under a magnet. I would say, "Chris, put these checks in the bank." His reply was, "I'll get to it. I'll get to it." I would ask every day and would soon find that they were gone. But he had merely started to put them under a magnet on top of the refrigerator, thinking I would not notice. He still laughs about this today. You will never find a better-quality person. He was truly color blind, and if you were blind, you would assume he was black. He went out of his way to help anybody. He is currently head coach for Saint John 's.

Chris Washburn was the number one pick this year, 1986. I knew him well, having played with and against him during my last year at Stanford University. Chris came from North Carolina State as a freshman. Six feet eleven inches, about 245 pounds of natural raw talent like Billy Ray Bates, he could run, jump, and shoot with the best. The similarities between him and Billy don't stop with athletic ability. Chris was a victim of innocence mixed with ignorance and addiction. His number one problem: he was still a kid.

Realizing the need for guidance from a trusted family member, the Golden State Warriors sent for his uncle to mentor and live with him. The unexpected turn of events happened: his uncle started to do all the crazy stuff Chris was doing. I'm talking women, drugs, and alcohol. Chris started to date older women (twenty-four to twenty-five), and he was only eighteen or nineteen. He had to undergo unscheduled drug testing and had his uncle provide the urine sample for testing. Now seriously, as both were abusing and using drugs, what would you think the results would reveal?

In my limited three months on the Golden State Warrior team, I started the first few games and then my body started to show signs of losing momentum. I was like a car tire with worn down treads driving in the Indianapolis Five Hundred. It was a choice of parking the car on the side and enjoy the race from the sidelines or continue to race until the disaster of a flat or blow out occurred. I had to be content with knowing after being away from the game for four years I was still in the starter category and if healthy would have had a successful season.

CHAPTER 14

China

Leaving Portland, Oregon, I moved back east and I received a phone call from a coach I knew in Eugene, Oregon. He asked if I might be interested in coaching a basketball team in China. Having a passport and never having been to China, I decided to venture outside the box and give it a try. It had been several years since my days at Stanford University in Palo Alto, California. The team was called the Chen Zen Dragons, and all but one player was native Chinese, speaking only Mandarin and another dialect. The assistant coach served as the translator. The season had already begun, and the coach was demoted due to a losing record.

Although a contract was agreed upon and signed, to be receive a salary of $8,000.00 American dollars a month as the head coach of the Shenzhen Dragons team. Actually, I received a $4,000.00 in American dollars a month. Unfortunately, in foreign contracts, there was no guarantee you would be paid what was on paper. You simply had to rely on the grace of God to see to it you get any financial compensation. Thinking back, I'm not quite sure it was the discrepancy in pay that influenced my decision to return to the states after six months. Perhaps, it might have been the way things were managed. Everyone was housed together in a hotel. Meals were served and eaten together, and all travel, wherever the destination, was together.

One of these scathingly brilliant ideas was to go on a shopping excursion to Shang-hi. Not realizing the need to always carry passports with you when leaving the hotel, my other American companion and I left our passports in our hotel room. Boarding the bus, no thought was given as to whether that was a bad idea. We took no notice of the fact that we had left one province and entered another. Suddenly from out of nowhere, a military entourage appeared and ordered our bus driver to pull over. Two soldiers board the bus, ordering everyone to show their passport.

Not having ours, my companion and I were ordered off the bus. The bus traveled north, and the military entourage traveled south, leaving the two of us on the open highway on our own. We tried to hitchhike back to the hotel, and a passing vehicle was driven by a British businessman on vacation. He dropped us off at a bus terminal, and we tried to get back to the hotel. But we only knew the name of the hotel in English, not Chinese. We had a key with the name of the hotel, but we could not pronounce it correctly. We say China, but they say it differently. We then asked how to get back to Shenzhen. A small city is about twenty to thirty million people. We did know what the hotel looked like and knew how to get back safely. If the British tourist had not stopped to help us, I would still be there stranded in the middle of nowhere.

The hotel did not have heat. During the day, the sun heated the room, but at night you had to wear layers of clothing to stay warm. Mealtime, we all ate together. One custom that was rather disgusting was the spitting out of bones to the middle of the table while we were eating. If you ordered spaghetti with meatballs, the meat would always be dog. Dogs were hauled like we haul pigs and cattle. Dogs were not considered pets, only food. I stuck with rice and fish.

It was not unusual to see playgrounds filled with basketball players in much the same style as we played growing up in DC. This dedication to the sports will result in future quality athletes. My team had good shooters, but players did not work hard. A strong work ethic was definitely lacking. One American player from Kansas got injured and wanted to return home. He was insisting that his no-cut contract be honored. The Chinese paid for and gave him a plane ticket but did not give him any money. He was determined to remain in China until he was paid in full. When the team left the hotel to go on a short road trip, the owners stopped paying for this player's housing. I have no idea what happened to him as he was gone when we returned.

Today Chinese basketball players are playing the game at a higher level of excellence, such as Yao Ming, making the world take notice of them. Despite this increasing recognition of athlete improvement China places a higher value on resources and commodities that promote the country's economic status and furthers production of what the world will continue to shop for. Bootlegging of movies is a very lucrative business. Movies are available on DVD months before they are released in American movie theatres. DVD's selling for less than $1.00 are of high quality and much sought after versions of older but popular movie titles.

Blacks are rarely seen in China, and whenever I ventured out on the city streets, I would attract a crowd. People would follow me down the street, and local business would wave me inside, knowing the entourage would enter the store and might possibly make a purchase. Walking along the perimeter of a school fence, the children ran to get a closer look at me. It was an awkward feeling being the center of attention due to people not being used to seeing a person of any ethnic background different from themselves.

The Chinese society began to have a very off-balanced appearance. The schoolchildren were predominately male. Families had only one child, and the preference was a male child who would be responsible for taking care of parents in their old age. As the males grew up and it became evident that females were needed to provide companionship, wives and mothers, some males were reported to raid outlining provinces to secure a partner.

As the season in China came to an end, I returned to the States. David Stern called me to ask if would be interested in an assistant coaching position in the D league. I agreed, and after working with the Ashville team later that season, we won the championship. Ashville, North Carolina, was not a hustling, bustling metropolitan city. As a team, we traveled by bus. On one occasion our bus driver was falling asleep while driving us to our next game. The rest of the bus was also asleep, and I was the only one awake, and that was including the driver who was swerving all over the road. I had to tell him to either pull over or let me drive or wake up.

I must admit this was a good group of players, and the main reason they were not in the NBA was due to their being deficient in acquiring certain key basketball skills.

CHAPTER 15

The Adventure Begins

Have you ever had one startling visual image have such a profound impact on you, that your perspective and its meaning influences every aspect of your life? One evening in 1969, the graphic image on the nightly news report captured the execution of a Vietnamese man by a Vietcong soldier. Standing with his hands tied behind his back the fear and desperation on the man's face made a lasting impression on my mind. As the soldier pointed his gun at the man's left temple and pulled the trigger the man's body fell limp to the ground. As the reality of this event shook my heart and awakened my mind it is an image I have never could forget. It is an image that remains with me to this day. This image was not a trailer for an upcoming movie, this man was not an actor who would be cast for a different role in an upcoming Hollywood feature. This man was someone like you or me realizing his life was about to end.

Journey to Zaire and Rwanda in 1994

During my life, I have faced situations presenting me with challenges to make difficult decisions. Whether choices made were right or wrong is irrelevant. It is the perception of who I am as a person, has led many to create their own definition of me as a person. One individual who desired to taking time to meet and get to know me and not blindly believe the image depicted by the media was David Halberstam. Many enjoyed hours were spent sharing personal thoughts, opinions, good and bad memories, as well as life changing experiences. Every conversation influenced how our relationship grew into a life-long friendship. A long-time friend of Phil Knight, the chairman of NIKE, Inc. David was earnestly interested in understanding how character and personality affected interactions between teammates and the impact these had on how the game was played. Having recently returned to the league, my recent trade from the San Diego Clippers to the Portland Trailblazers afforded him the opportunity to gather information on these two points while getting better acquainted with the notoriously infamous Kermit Washington. Questioning if my publicized image was accurate and fair, and arrived in town with the explicit purpose of determining for himself through first-hand interviews and informal conversations.

It was in the pursuit of discovering the truth about both me and the ins and outs of the NBA that I first met the1964 Pulitzer Prize winning author, David Halberstam. When he was introduced to the team, we were told he was writing a book, The Breaks of the Game, about the Portland Trailblazers. Traveling with us on the road, David became recognized as our Sixth Man during the season. Being such great author, David gathering facts and details to complete his work, he eagerly shared many of his personal experiences during conversations that drew people into his confidence. His open and welcoming ability put me at ease and throughout the 1979-1980 season, I contributed words, impressions and feelings to be included along with numerous details for the book he was writing about the Portland Trailblazers.

During that 1979-1980 NBA basketball season, David and I became friends spending numerous hours in Portland, Oregon while doing research. My friendship with Phil Knight began one night when David, thinking Phil and I would have a lot in common, invited me to join them for dinner. I accepted the invitation. Phil was very open to our keeping in touch and thus I got to know Phil Knight quite well.

David's book was a top-seller and helped to clear up false, inaccurate, and derogatory statements concerning my character. After retiring from the NBA due to injuries, I worked closely with Pete Newell organizing and working with NBA teams and their player's in his Big Man's camp. Watching me demonstrate moves and work with current highly talented players on the basketball court, Pete encouraged me to try and make a comeback in 1984. I spoke with Larry Weinberg, the owner of the Portland Trailblazers, about the possibility of doing so.

Remembering how the people of Portland, Oregon, were always supportive of my efforts both on and off the court. I made it perfectly clear to Larry Weinberg, the idea of coming back as a player was something I would consider only if my entire salary was to be used to further the efforts being extended to the community through the

Sixth Man Foundation. The ability to give back the support shown to me from such a warm and welcoming community. I gave Pete's suggestion to return to the NBA serious thought. However, my one contingency was stated upfront, IF I made the team my entire salary was to be given to the Sixth Man Foundation. This charity was initially founded to help any individuals who was identified by a third party who was aware of what assistance would best benefit the individual in need and their positive contributions to others was covered under a very large umbrella. Just as there are times extending a helping hand to one person has a positive domino effect on others, we based our criterion for the foundation from the concept of a sixth man.

The value of having a sixth man ready and willing to leave the bench, enter the game, set up shots, and make baskets to score points for a victory was essential to guarantee a successful outcome. Using my salary to initiate funding, would raise public awareness of the sixth man's positive contributions to the community, to the next level. Funding efforts with my salary would take this idea, of the sixth man's positive contribution to the community, to the next level. It would ensure meeting the needs of many. It was clearly stated one-hundred percent of all contributions, monetary support and donations were used to meet individual requests for assistance, everyone could benefit. Larry Weinberg pledged his support by making a sizeable donation, in addition to the contribution of my salary to promote the start of the foundation. Unfortunately, I was unable to make that comeback and join the team. It was time to explore other alternatives.

The foundation's criteria required potential recipients of assistance be named in a letter written by an individual or group. Specific details and documentation were to be provided in order that each request could be investigated for accuracy and authenticity. All given facts regarding a potential recipient's current circumstances and how assistance would positively benefit both themselves and others was to be included. For example: We helped a blind man purchase a braille machine needed to gain employment and meet his financial responsibilities. A truck was purchased for a man whose current mode of transportation use to provide services to the community broke down beyond repair leaving the community at a loss on how to provide services. Recipients of a variety of requests encouraged us to continue in our efforts to keep the foundation in operation. Living in Lake Oswego, Oregon, we frequented Albertsons as our supermarket of choice. The manager, Monty Atkinson was an avid Blazer fan and enjoyed working out and lifting weights. As more publicity was being given to the Sixth Man's Foundations on-going community assistance, as the Thanksgiving holiday approached, Monty asked if there was something he and Albertsons could help with. Contacting the local homeless shelters, it was arranged that 50 -100 turkeys and all the items that go with the traditional Thanksgiving meal be provided by Albertsons. The turkeys were prepared in the Albertson's store and after a long night before Thanksgiving, the store and all the helpers were noticeably covered with the aroma of an enticing fare. Transportation was arranged, the food was boxed up and delivered to each designated sight. All volunteers spread out over the city and shared with the serving of meals. This arrangement began a regularly scheduled event for over four years. As the awareness of the Sixth Man's Foundations successful efforts in helping and supporting the community continued to increase, Phil Knight reached out to me. Conversations focused on the direction being taken by the Sixth Man Foundation and formulating ideas on how to secure financial support to keep the foundation moving forward. I asked for suggestions on how to access contacts, leads, and ideas to secure funding.

To draw the most public attention to the meaning of the concept behind the Sixth's Man Foundation, I planned and organized an All-Star game held in Portland, Oregon, at the Portland Memorial Coliseum. To ensure that this venture was a success I personally contacted, spoke with and received the support of twenty NBA players who willingly agreed to participate in the event. The event was well advertised and tickets were sold raising $56,000. Red Auerbach donated me signed jerseys for EVERY Boston Celtic and we held a silent auction and these in the mezzanine that was frequented throughout the game. The highest bidder went home with a valuable item as well as having experienced an All-Star game featuring: Carl Malone, John Stockton, Larry Nance, Kiki Vandeweghe, Dominque

Wilkins, Purvis Short, Clyde Drexler, Kevin Duckworth, Steve Johnson, Jerome Kersey, Terry Porter; all current Portland Blazers, Cliff Robinson and more. Harry Glickman, president of the Portland Trailblazers, and Stu Inman were instrumental in coordinating activities to organize this event. Despite their concern we could not get players to participate during the off-season, they diligently worked to help this event to be a success.

With the help of local radio and TV media exposure to the upcoming All-Star game to promote the Sixth Man Foundation, Phil's interest in being more involved in the project became evident. His asking more detailed questions and sharing ideas on what to do next let me know his willingness to help in a greater capacity in the project. He began his involvement by providing Nike athletic shoes as incentives for an inner-city honor roll awards program. We planned and held an assembly at Harriet Tubman Middle School and kept several pairs of Nike's latest athletic shoes on display in the school in a glass case students passed daily. The program was a success, and student grades began to improve, showing an increase in academic performance. We extended the program to five other inner-city schools. Nike donated over a thousand pairs of shoes every year to support this incentive program objective.

As with any venture, it's probable unexpected glitches to resolve will present themselves. Such was the case when holding our first incentive assemblies at Harriet Tubman Middle School, King Elementary School, and three other inner city schools in the Portland, Oregon, area neighborhoods. Students failing to appreciate the motive behind being selected to receive a pair of Nike athletic shoes questioned why the Nike athletic shoe models presented were not the latest or soon to be released models. Although our goal was to provide an incentive to show the value of hard work, the concept was becoming lost in the minds of students who were raised in the entitled mentality of the inner city.

In 1994 viewing the nightly news with my family in Portland, Oregon, the image viewed back in 1969 of the murder of that Vietcong man, flashed across my mind. Each news report depicted horrendous accounts of murder and terror in war torn Rwanda.

Daily, thousands of people became casualties of the current war in Rwanda as it ravaged the country. The impact was on-going with little hope of ending the conflicts against people whose only crime was to have been born of a different tribal affiliation. Graphic footage documented the massive genocide with piles of dead and mutilated bodies. The devastation resulting was a stark reminder of the seriousness of this situation currently happening. With each day, my anxiety regarding the reported conditions of unrest and death in Rwanda constantly intruded on my mind. As the organizer of Pete Newell's Big Man's Camp my energy and focus for the next two weeks needed to be directed towards scheduling, arranging, and preparing, for this upcoming event.

I didn't get a lot of sleep at night. My mind was constantly searching for the answer to the question my daughter raised. Once I had decided to become actively involved in helping in any way possible, it was clear, a plan of action was required. To ensure success no detail could be overlooked. The first step was to locate, connect, and work with an organization of trained professionals, who knew what needed to be done. I organized my thoughts, then compiled a list of things to do. The next step was find contacts, and phone numbers to gather information about current efforts in place regarding the situation in Rwanda.

Questions requiring immediate answers were: Who could I contact to decide to go to Africa? What would I need to do to prepare? How long will it take to get a passport updated? Where was my passport? How soon can I schedule a doctor's appointment to get vaccinations? What supplies and personal items would I need to pack? Where would I stay? What arrangements for travel, transportation, and meals needed to be made? What would I do when I got there? Is this venture the answer to that constant nagging question: What are you going to do?

My daughter's words continued to echo in my head reminding me how the Sixth Man foundation came into existence. As reported in the news there was a situation where a family needed assistance. My daughter turned to me and asked, "Dad what can you do?" That question created a seed and once planted, roots to the foundation took hold and began to grow.

Just as the family requesting help, the situation in Rwanda continued to disturb both me and my daughter. Every day she asked me if I had an idea of how to help and make a difference. I then saw a TV broadcast that reminded me of the problems in Somalia where Somalis were suffering and dying from the drought. As I had not done anything about that situation the idea of not doing anything about this current carnage would not be dismissed from my mind and greatly concerned me. My mind began to consider some options to explore. I looked through the telephone book for agencies and organizations that might provide me some answers to questions about what efforts were in place and what was needed to be done to support these.

Having limited experience in traveling outside of the United States the mere idea of going abroad to a country embroiled in warfare and strife present challenges. In addition, going into a war-torn city without any connections posed with additional interesting questions. Having no experience in how to plan such a venture, to pursue this line of thinking and be successful I needed to develop a plan and find out what to do. I looked through the telephone book for agencies and organizations that could provide me with information about any efforts currently in place that I could help with, or even participate in. From gathering this information, I could make a better decision on how to complete working on Pete Newell's Big Man's Camp and answer my daughter's question.

Looking through the phone book there was a listing for Doctors Without Borders. This was an organization I associated with a documentary where doctors performed surgery on children born with cleft palates. Along with this listing I recognized the American Red Cross. I made phone calls to both, not reaching anyone I left voice messages on their answering machines. Undeterred, I continued to pursue the telephone pages where I saw a listing for the Northwest Medical Team. A live person answered the phone and we conducted a brief and informative conversation. I offered to donate money to support their efforts. I also mentioned I would be interested in going on a future trip to check out the situation, but at this time had a previous commitment that I needed to attend to within the next two weeks.

The idea of actually going to Africa, in the immediate future, really didn't occur to me as I was focused on the upcoming Pete Newell's Big Man's Camp. When the person on the other end of the phone recognized who, I was, as a representative for the Northwest Medical Team, she was very excited to learn I had expressed a willingness to join a team of medical professionals on a future scheduled trip. The representative shared that the team was planning to make a trip in the next few days. The offer to accompany the team was then put out there. "You can go with us next week we are taking a group over. Let me put you through to Ron Post." Ron, the head of Northwest Medical Teams, told me more about the upcoming trip to Africa. He took a few minutes to share the trip's agenda and explain how I could accompany the group. As his goal was to convince me to make this trip, despite the short notice, he extended the invitation for me to join the team.

Once the invitation was extended I expressed my gratitude and assured him I would give it some serious thought after talking it over with my family. I wasn't sure how they would feel about my going off the Africa without any concrete plans of my own. When I got home we all sat down and after sharing the invitation from Ron Post and the Northwest Medical Teams, everyone encouraged me to accept the invitation. I called Ron the next day. To help me prepare for the trip he gave me advice on what needed to be done, included a list of medical requirements, vaccination shots, confirmation of valid passport status, acquisition of a visa, and packing specific supplies cover personal needs. My mind now had to shift from Pete's camp to a trip to Africa.

The vaccinations for this trip were very painful. You were injected in your thigh and the serum made you feel sick for a few days once the serum entered your blood stream. Then there were the personal needs to be addressed? What clothing to bring wear? Did anyone mention netting? Shoes-what kind of footwear does one need for the African terrain? The climate being different from the

Northwest how would I deal with the intense heat? On this first trip to Africa I later found out despite gathering all the items on the necessities list I did neglect to bring a few basics. These were items returning members of the team simply took for granted and failed to bring to my attention.

Determined to complete all the requirements within this short time frame I made a: To Do List for both Pete's camp and the trip. There were several important tasks to complete and being organized was the best way to accomplish both objectives. Having been accustomed to traveling on pre-arranged itineraries, this impromptu plan; made me wonder how to get everything accomplished to meet the Africa deadline and keep on track with the planning and coordinating Pete's camp.

Although an invitation extended for an unexpected opportunity may make you feel uncomfortable and even doubt your ability to successfully meet what is proposed to you, somehow you gather the strength to step outside your comfort level and accept. Facing your fears and insecurities you become determined to move forward and put forth your best effort. With each step forward you feel more self-confident and gain more determination to continue until you have completed what you started to achieve. And before you know it, the opportunity is realized and you are now motivated to do even more. For me, agreeing to travel with the Northwest Medical Team to Africa, was to be one such unexpected opportunity that helped me to find a meaningful answer to my daughter's nagging question. It is the start many travels and connections with Africa.

CHAPTER 16

Goma, Zaire–Refugee Camp

Refugee Camp in Gomo Zaire

The flight from London, England, to Nairobi, Kenya was ten hours. The flight provided me the opportunity to get better acquainted with the North West Medical team doctors and nurses. They were very open and friendly and shared with me some of their other relief efforts around the world. Confident that everything would work itself out no one seemed to know where we were going. How we were to get there? But they did know what to do once we had reached our destination. I didn't know whether to be concerned or if their demeanor of travelling to a vacation spot should allay any of my fears. I opted to go with the second viewpoint as I couldn't believe anyone who left their families and the safety of home to help others would be that cavalier if danger was truly eminent.

My first impression of the team of North West Medical Team doctors and nurses was extremely positive. My anxieties lessened allowing me to relax. With every minute getting to know and learn about each one as individuals allayed any reservations I previously had. I was comfortable and more confident about the success of this trip. The team's personalities were warm and open. In fact, if you didn't know where they were headed and why you would have sworn they were preparing for an all-expense paid vacation to paradise. It was obvious these doctors and nurses were sincerely good people without any personal agendas to cloud their goals. Each was willing to leave the safety of family and home, put their lives on the line, and pay their own expenses incurred to plunge head-first into a dangerous situation simply to help others.

After we had traveled for ten hours, we landed in Nairobi, Kenya, after departing from London, England. Our first order of business was unloading and then loading all our supplies, medicines, tents, and personal items. It was a laborious effort and when completed there was no place to sit comfortably to recharge our energy and relax while we waited for our connecting transportation to arrive. The temperature was nice and we were told "Hurry up and wait." Here transportation was truly make-shift as you go, the state of affairs was such no scheduled transportation could be confirmed and one simply had to wait and see who was available to get you to your destination then help reload supplies. We never knew by means of what kind of transportation to expect but were assured, and informed where we were traveling to would be handled.

The directions given were to head directly to Entebbe, Uganda. We landed in seemingly deserted airport, which at one time was the center of international travel but due to international conflicts was now an airstrip housing United military personnel awaiting further orders. Walking around this isolated location a soldier was walking around showing forty-pound python snake he had recently killed. I had never seen anything like this before. The soldiers unimpressed by his actions were diligently working out in a make-shift gym to physically prepared to fulfill any commission given them to carry out.

In Entebbe, Uganda, were not advised of any set schedule, or particular arrangements as to how we were going to travel to Goma, Zaire. Due to the unrest in the region arrangements could not be set in stone strictly depending on ever-changing variables. This was the direct result of the strife in the region. Planes and transportation were being handled as best they could. The phrase "Hurry up and wait" were the words of the day. It appeared the military was used to these conditions. For me I felt like I was watching a movie I had been cast in as a supporting character but was not given a script to follow. Everyone else simply sat around for instructions. The time slowly passed by with us waiting.

Standing around with so many American military soldiers in the region, I looked around and noticed the large supply of K-rations and food surplus items that were provided to the army soldiers. Since my first encounter with how things were run or not run in Africa, my immediate reaction to seeing the number of rations available, I started to consider the value of obtaining some K-rations for my journey. I began to contemplate the wisdom to be prepared for any unexpected food issues by obtaining food stuffs I was more familiar with. Therefore, as not leave the question of where my food would be coming from to chance. I began to eavesdrop and listen to the conversations between the soldiers to get an idea of how items were obtained. Apparently, the barter system was the rule of the day. My mind raced as to what I had brought with me that might be considered worth using in the form of trade. When I packed clothing for the trip, it never occurred to me that the many NBA logo T-shirts I brought would be perfect to barter for military food. When I asked if K-rations were available for trade, the soldiers laughed at me and inquired, "Why would You want K-rations." I simply said, "You just never know." The T-shirts represented home for the United States soldiers and they enjoyed the possibility of having them. I was happy to part with them for a limited number of K-rations.

My mind was still actively taking in my unknown surrounding yet my sense of time was slowly being scrambled in my mind. I don't remember how long we stayed in Entebbe, only being extremely confused as to when we were going to leave. The one thing that is vivid in my mind even today, is how American soldiers were extremely professional staying in their assigned positions while waiting for their orders. It was clear they represented the United States and were well disciplined and mannered that is to be recognized and appreciated. By the second night, Ron Post found an efficient means of transportation for us to travel from Uganda to Goma, Zaire, which today is the Republic of Congo. Ron was instrumental in arranging our transportation, along with the Canadian Red Cross. We flew inside of a large and heavy duty cargo carrier which held and secured us with cargo nets and no seats. The other cargoes were placed in large desert Hummer trucks, with tents and miscellaneous supplies.

Being inside the cargo carrier plane was scary, and it crossed my mind if the plane were to crash, the trucks could come unhinged and subsequently crush us all like bugs. The plane was so large and heavy I was relieved it took off like a flight like transporting one across the country; in fact; the overall experience was as smooth as silk. The plane engine was quite loud but as, I could not feel it leaving the ground I began to relax and use this time to reflect on the reality soon I would be able to see first-hand the news had been portraying and learn about global issues and about myself.

Our crew was able to make the necessary adjustments to this form of travel as they were not the sort of people who would complain about having to sit in the cargo netting without seat belts. We were happy to be on a plane taking us closer to our destination. Traveling was exhausting, and there was no food or fresh water readily available, a flight attendant, and bathroom accommodations. I was growing more anxious as to where we would be landing but as soon as the team seemed to be unconcerned and relaxed I followed their lead. We landed at military base at about four o'clock in the early morning.

The soldiers assisted us in getting all our supplies and medicines unloaded and then put on a military transport vehicle. The truck was huge with an enclosed cab and open sides. The military personnel directed us to climb into the back with all the equipment and "stay down." We obeyed the order and stayed down. As time, would have it, my instincts were correct as we were informed if stopped and it was discovered we were in the rear of the truck without having proper travel documents that would present a serious problem.

When arranging to join this trip, I was unaware of these facts as shared with me by the medical team. Just as I was unable to identify a Tutsi from a Hutu, I would not be able to identify victims of the many aspects of the conflict. The goal was to provide aid to any of the tribe members whether responsible for starting the conflict or not. My focus concentrated on what needs were to be addressed and how many people required assistance. It didn't matter how or when the war shifted, people were trying to escape, along with the defeated members of the military. Everyone arriving at the camp was a victim.

When I initially agreed to take the trip to Africa it was my understanding I would be working out of an established facility assisting the medical team, trained in setting up and dispensing supplies and medical care in a war-torn country. My knowledge of the current situation, we were about to encounter, was limited to news reports and discussions held with the medical team. I was clearly unaware of the extent of the actual circumstances the African people were up against. It soon became evident everyday people regardless of social class, from doctors, teachers, to families who were one-day living normally and the next minute; struggling for life as refugees. A sad, tragic, and seemingly insurmountable situation was before us.

The genocide committed against the Tutsi's in the 1990's, was similar to the start of WWI by the assassination of Franz Ferdinand, the archduke of Austria-Hungary. On April 6, 1994, the Minister of Defense, Habyarimana's died as the result of an airplane crash. The following day the direct response to this event sparked the beginning of massive killings. Conflict between Hutu's and Tutsi's having a long history fueled the animosity and the devastation which resulted is still felt today. Traveling for about an hour, in the dark, we could barely make out what the accommodations for us were like. In the dark the long winding road lead to a small house located about forty yards from the road. It was one story building with five bedrooms and lots of windows, giving a clear view of any activity moving about. Safely arriving at the house, we were greeted by an organization leader from the Adventist Relief Agency; (ADRA). We all helped to unloaded the military vehicle and went inside to our rooms. The trip inside the tail end of a military vehicle was long and taxing but worth it.

Settling in at about 4 am, I fell fast asleep. Waking up later in the morning, to find we were in Goma, Zaire, about a mile outside of the Mugunga Refugee Camp. I walked out onto the porch and witnessed a stream of refugees traveling on the narrow stretch of road towards the refugee camp. You were close enough to see the desperation on the faces of each person as they walked past the house. The distance between the porch and the road was approximately forty yards.

The landscape was lacking massive foliage, with lots of abandoned houses nearby. Other houses had broken windows and were in general disrepair. All the trees had been chopped down and the ground was bare. The ground was covered with a powder-like dirt. As we began the day, one of the sights that continue to be with me is the hundreds of refugees that were tired and listlessly standing in lines and walking by. As we began the day, one of the sights that continued to be with me is the hundreds of refugees that were tired and listlessly standing in lines and walking by.

About every hour refugees fled Rwanda with nothing but the clothes they were wearing when forced to leave their homes. The only thing they had in common was the desire to preserve were lives and nothing more. It was very sobering, and I was beginning to understand what true despair and heartbreak feels like. As the growing number of refugees walked into the camp I was watching a death march. We quickly found out the people we were watching were ordered and forced to leave their homes with only a very few minutes' notice or they would be killed. This clear evidence of man's inhumanity to man was humbling. It would not matter whom this was happening to, but these people from all economic status from low, middle, to and upper class were visually devastated and broken in spirit.

The earth was incapable of facilitating the growth of crops, or sustaining any kind of life. As the entire top layer of earth was volcanic rock it was impossible for the refugees to dig the necessary holes for disposing of their human waste at a safe distance from their living accommodations. Their access to bathroom facilities was a major concern as was the need to provide adequate provision for graves. This site created an environment where dead bodies were left on the side of the road, wrapped in blankets. I looked at one of the nurses and stated, "This is awful, to have family members leaving their loved ones on the road for someone to pick them up for mass burials."

The refugee camp was filled with row upon rows of make-shift tents and shelters. The living quarters were close and tight together. People were scrambling for any supplies available and looking to find anyone who knew them, their family members, or any news from Rwanda. The long trek into the camp was both exhausting and difficult. Mentally, people were in a state of shock and disbelief. That mental exhaustion played heavily on the realities to be faced leaving little hope for the present or the future. Those with family stayed together and those who were uncertain as to where or what had happened to family members attached themselves to one another for support.

Even though we were not housed in a five-star hotel, we comfortably bunked five people to a room with no working bathroom inside. We used an outside latrine that was small, hot, and smelly! One of the necessities not included on my list of supplies to bring with me was a mosquito net. I quickly discovered everyone else had brought one. Since I distinctly remember the doctor reminding me that my vaccinations would not be effective; or offer any protection from disease for many days beyond the date I arrived in Africa, I insisted that no one open a window while we were living in the house.

After all the travel and stress of being in Africa for the first time, it might appear that exhaustion would set in and place one into a deep sleep, but that was not the case. I found it difficult to sleep. It was hot and stuffy with so many of us in the room. With the unrest and strife of warfare, my first trip to Africa held additional concern over the recent outbreak of the Ebola virus. This was a concern as not much information was known, or being disseminated in the United States at that time. The clearest dissemination of information was that it was cureless if exposed. Without either the protection from vaccinations or a mosquito net, I knew I needed to take any and all necessary precautions from an encounter with mosquitoes. Windows had to remain closed.

In the morning before leaving for the camp, some of the medical professionals brought their breakfast bowls to eat a meal on the porch. The road on which the refugees walked to reach the camp site, it was apparent to me that having a clear of them meant they had a clear view of us. The idea of showing food was readily available from our location was not safe or considerate of the situation at hand. After sharing this thought with others, it was decided that eating inside would be the procedure to follow at all times. Others worked at unpacking and organizing the supplies we would be using the day. Once the supplies were organized, there was no set schedule for where to set up for the day. Drove around and looked for location to our operation.

After driving through the area designated for the refugees for we stopped several times to see if the ground was soft enough to dig holes needed to set up and secure tents. After many repeated attempts using a variety of tools at our disposal I was soon event this plan of action would not work. We were not able to dig holes in the ground and this meant the clinic would otherwise be exposed in the open and vulnerable to theft. The supplies were mostly of a medical nature and proving security for them was of paramount concern. Ron Post made the decision to go to the Mugunga camp where the Red Cross and World Vision were already setup. We would be able to set up our facility next to theirs giving us security and protection. In addition, the time we would expend to daily set up and tear down a portable facility would require more time and energy we could use in working with the refugees.

On the first day, half of the group had begun to assemble the equipment and medicine so that we could be ready once we searched and found a place appropriate to set up our clinic. The other half of our group got into a car and conducted a location search by driving up and down the road for a site most accessible for refugees to be able to readily be seen by the medical team. Noticing some of the medical team were capturing the current conditions in to relay an honest appraisal to others, I felt very uncomfortable silently observing the use of cameras. It might be assumed that we were more interested in recording the plight of the refugees and showed a lack of compassion and understanding for the need of these people to have a sense of dignity despite current circumstances. I tactfully suggested to those who were taking such photographs for whatever reason, that this may be misinterpreted by any one and negatively impact the relationships we were hoping to establish to provide the medical care needed.

The way in which we carried ourselves and the way we interacted with the refugees was of paramount importance to me. All our intentions were with the upmost respect for the devastation being experienced. Our primary reason for leaving our homes and loved ones was to help facilitate the up building of the many lives and families currently in a state of extreme distress. Our presence should only reflect our desire to provide comfort and meet the physical needs that must be addressed to support the efforts to reestablish normalcy in the lives of the refugees. They needed hope and support not to be the objects of any exploitation.

Realized we needed to join another group after several attempts to dig holes in the ground to erect a tent and set up our care center. We were originally hoping to find a place on the side of the road being traveled to help any who were having difficulty reaching the camp and then having to walk further to seek medical assistance. When we were unable to make this work, we had to switch to Plan B. We soon join the efforts with the Red Cross and other agencies that were to erect and secure a safe place to work out of.

With the presence of various reporters from around the United States, once I was recognized, I was approached and asked if I would mind being photographed carrying an ailing refugee. It was not my intent to receive any media attention and I quickly declined informing the reporter my Job was to assist when necessary and I would only provide services required to carry out any Job requiring my immediate attention.

As one day turned into two; and waking up in the morning with curiosity, I looked out the front door, and my eyes were met with a growing number of people experiencing great distress. I began to contemplate our safety as the severity of their situation suggested to me the reality of being an American meant to these people we had things they desperately needed. Again, some of the very people I was watching were or might have been responsible for great atrocities involving the massacre of thousands. Point of fact: although we had good intentions we were certainly not exempt from the potential of violence. Most all Americans feel a sense of safety in the United States because of the law enforcement we pay for. We even use terms such as "response time," when we call for police. As there were no police or military to speak of, the most creative, industrious, and strongest were among the survivors.

I advised my companions to stay mindful and refrain from standing out on the front porch and watching desperate, hurting, and hungry people while they freely enjoyed a meal. Little things such as having food to eat and the leisurely way we Americans view any opportunity to enjoy a meal might would be more than what a starving person could bare. I did not want anyone to assume we were insensitive to the seriousness of the current situation. I personally felt we were a part of this present situation in we came to provide help and give hope placing us in the middle of it. Circumstances withstanding, the daily routine faced by the refugees applied to us as well.

Refugees were lined up by the hundreds, women giving birth, and babies of all ages in need of medical attention. Half of the doctors were working with other agencies to treat those who were too weak to stand in a line or come to shelters. The other half worked in makeshift shelters treating many who were subject to dying from heat exposure and dehydration. This was unfortunately a common occurrence and dead bodies were strewn along the side of the road, until buried in mass graves.

As there was no place to bury the dead, the French would come by to pick up and bury the bodies in a nearby sand lake. Unfortunately, the wild dogs were digging up the bodies and eating them. On one morning, a group of men came and asked if I could help them re-bury the bodies and I said, "No, you have the wrong man." I simply didn't have the intestinal fortitude for that kind of mission. Because I was already having nightmares it was out of the question. I wanted no part of that particular job assignment.

Getting a good night's rest or not the next day arrive and it was time to get to work. We set up our station, put up our tent, and organized all the medicines. African people lined up by the hundreds, there were women giving birth, babies of all ages in need of medical attention and everyone needing water. Water was the one commodity everyone needed. Without which making through a day presented many challenges. As I only brought one bottle of water with me to the camp site, once the children saw me take a small sip, a growing number of thirsty children began to ask me for something to drink. I soon found myself without water. I had to work in the extreme heat until I returned to the house. Although I realized water was a necessity the one item needed to make it through the day's taxing demands. I resolved to exercise caution to both provide minimal requests for me and share when it was possible.

The French delivered water from a huge truck that was equipped with an enormous water pouch that looked sort of like a huge hot-water bag but contained thousands of gallons. As there was not enough water to supply everyone, the truck would leave when empty. Knowing another truck was coming the next day, people lined up for hours so that when the truck returned, they would have a place in line being closer to the possibility of getting water during the next shipment. If anyone was to get out of line, their position was immediately lost, resulting in not getting water. Water was the most important commodity. No one shared water as people didn't have enough for their own families. It was understandable. I knew; and we all knew without water people simply died.

Looking out the windows after returning from the camp I particularly remember observing the local Adventists did not have ready access to meat and most of their meals featured a limited supply of vegetables. I watched the women cook a meal standing over a large kettle filled with potatoes and assorted vegetables. As vegetables are not my first choice at any time for any meal the absence of meat was a concern I needed to address. Although in my later years I have come to appreciate a small but growing interest in eating vegetables; at that time, I was not so inclined. It didn't help that the vegetables being cooked were unfamiliar to me and made the prospect of consuming them even more unpalatable. People may wonder how an athlete, or retired athlete can refuse to eat vegetables simply consider the wonderful addition of supplements to make up for this deficiency. It was times like this, I was glad to be alone in my room to sit and eat my military K-rations. I found them to be quite eatable under the circumstances.

One the third day Moses, a three-year old orphan and survivor of a bridge bombing, was brought to the house where I was staying. His family members were killed during an attack that bombed a bridge in an attempt to prevent people from crossing into the next region. Moses soon became my best buddy in the house.

Later in the evening, we saw two young boys whom we later knew to be brothers. These boys were carrying a young girl, and I requested they bring her into our tent. The little girl was clearly sick and about six years of age. The doctors immediately observed how ill she was and after examining her, they determined she was suffering from pneumonia and set her up with an IV drip and a shot containing antibiotics. The doctors had a difficult time inserting the needle because she was so small, dehydrated, and frail. They finally got the IV set-up, and her brothers never left her side. They looked after her. I wanted us to take her back to the camp so that we could continue to monitor her.

Being extremely concerned about her welfare I wanted to take her with us back to our house. She could have my bed. I was new, and because it was my first time being one this type of mission, I was not insistent we take her. I let my inexperience get the better of my willingness to push and insist we care for her, longer. To this day I am haunted by not insisting on it! This is a very difficult memory for me to share because I still see her laying there. I still see myself putting Chap Stick on my lips when she pointed at my chap stick. She watched me using it on my lips and I can tell she had never seen it before. She motioned with her empty hand, a Chap-Stick moving across her own lips. I put Chap Stick on her parched lips and then gave it to her so that it could help make her a little more comfortable.

The following day we returned only to learn the little girl had died during the night. After learning she died I felt very guilty that I did not insist we take her. I couldn't get her out of my mind, nor did I want to, and I thought how terrible it was going to be for her brothers to return to their family without her. I was not sponsoring this trip but I made a very deep and personal decision at that very moment. I realized that for me to avoid circumstances where I'd feel like I did less than I could do, I needed to exercise my voice and to have it taken very seriously. I knew that when I return in the future, a more assertive role was necessary.

For me, it was heart wrenching to see a little African girl, who because she was born in Africa, had minimal chances to survive and in America she might have been ill for only about a week. I also learned that even if the doctors had stayed an entire year and used an unlimited supply of medicines, long lines would not have gotten any shorter. This was the magnitude of the endless suffering we were observing. The eyes of those people in long lines were window views into their unmistakable depression. I felt it. I felt guilty to the core of my bones and my inner most reach of humanity was being breached. I knew that I could get on a plane and leave at any moment and it seemed almost cruel to those people. In fact, I knew that in just a few days I'd be arriving at my Lake Oswego home in Portland, Oregon, and then traveling straight to Hawaii to stay in a luxury suite for Pete Newell's Big Man's Camp.

These felt like conflicts to me at that time. I was conflicted because no matter how much we did it would fall very short in the big picture. These people were dying and in few days after returning to the states I would be in Hawaii, playing inside on the beach or in a swimming pool with my son and daughter; but still thinking about the suffering people in Africa. I put these thoughts aside during the day while working the camp and then revisited then at the end of the day. My mind refused to let these images and reality of the situation fade or be forgotten. I actually had a haunting memory of the time in Goma, Zaire, when blowing my nose, cleaning my ears, and looking at the black fecal dust on my tissues afterwards. Also, I was eating K-rations which had little M&M's candies inside for energy that I shared with the kids in Africa. These experiences were giving me night-terrors, nightmares of the starvation and helplessness. I always told the people that I would be back to help. I didn't lie to them. I needed more knowledge and information prior to returning to be more effective. I did all I could to ensure the people that I would certainly return to help and would never forget about them.

After the fifth day, Ron Post asked if I wanted to stay any longer. I told him no, as I had complete arrangements for Pete's upcoming Big Man's Camp. My concern about the plight of the people I had come to know and those who were strangers to me but held similar needs would stay weigh heavily on my mind. I needed to get back home. Because I learned what was needed and saw how the organized efforts by a group of people with the same focus could make a difference in people's lives, I continued to reflect on how an operation was conducted and prepared a list of options to explore further. This experience in Goma, Zaire was not only an extremely valuable lesson, but the catalyst to coordinate efforts for setting up a means to provide health care on a long-term basis

Those five days of limited bathroom facilities, water and clean fresh air, messed up my system. Nothing about this trip was enjoyed or comfortable. It was however, extremely enlightening, informative, to the point of thinking outside of the box. When you watched the TV reports you could observe the horror and terror. Being there took the visual stimulus to another level. All your senses began to work on overdrive. The air was constantly filled with the stench of death and exposed excrement. Your sense of touch and sight felt the blazing heat of the sun on your face and exposed skin and the heat that penetrated your clothing. Your sense of taste longed for clean cool water after experiencing what true thirst was, not the mere need for staying hydrated, but thirsty to the point of having difficulty being satiated. Along with that was the constant fear for your safety. You knew if any kind of chaos were to erupt you were left unprotected.

Throughout the trip, my mind working on a long-lasting solution to several issues that required attention. I kept thinking to myself if living in those deplorable, I would get away from the area due to the large and increasing concentration of desperate people. I thought; I'd sleep during the day and stay up during the night because without shelter, it was the most terrifying time. My thoughts raced throughout the night; preventing me from being able to take advantage of a much-needed restful night's sleep. The people were destitute and living in the open in temperatures reaching extreme heat, the stench from rotting corpses', unwashed bodies and clothing and waste penetrated the air. everywhere. The human waste would dry and become dust and part of the soil.

There was no escape from air filled with pollutants. As people moved about their activity stirred the air and carried this dust with human waste. The effect was felt by everyone as bacteria was rampant and directly impacted the state of refugee's health. We daily took in with every breath this dust of circulated, as people moved around, so bacteria were rampant. Again, my shots would not take effect for several more days. I went from living a retired NBA player's life in the United States to facing the stark reality of life in Africa. Leaving my home life seventeen my goals were to earn a college degree and pursue a career in the NBA. Life does present circumstances you either control or except. The choices made regarding each circumstance will result in consequences with ups and downs. However, knowing about certain aspects of needing support from my personal experiences, nothing I was witnessing could have ever prepared me to feel a desperation to make things better.

You gain a deep understanding for being a lone reed, an island by yourself. When Ron asked if I wanted to stay I had to decline the offer. I had an obligation to fulfill to prepare for Pete's Big Man's Camp. He did ask if he needed to get extended VISA's for the remaining medical team as Ron was going to be returning to the states with me. I mentioned the advice given by the soldiers regarding this and so he arranged for this to be done before he left.

We met a Canadian relief plane bringing in a large load of supplies. Ron and I asked if we could get a ride back to the air strip and catch a plane back to Nairobi, Kenya, the pilot was eager to help. Having my travel arrangements made by the Northwest Medical team upon arriving in Nairobi, Kenya, entered the airport ready for my departure. After walking up to the ticket counter, I showed my ticket to the agent who then informed me my ticket had been cancelled due a failure to provide confirmation twenty-four hours before the flight.

This experience remained ever present on my mind and I slowly began to put together a plan that help people over time through a different venture. I learned a great deal from this experience and appreciate the ability to work with individuals that demonstrated a passion for their profession and for doing anything and everything to help people in need to achieve a sense of peaceful conditions. Little did I know this adventure would be the first of over forty to fifty additional visits to Africa.

This current situation was too dangerous and overwhelming for the Sixth Man's Foundation. Project Contact Africa was about to be established.

There was a constant need to understand and then determine how to address all concerns I could control. Yet, the harsh, reality daily demonstrated no matter how much support was extended, the gravity, severity, and magnitude of this situation presented colossal obstacles to overcome. I asked myself, "Are we merely providing a band-aide solution that would fall short of the big picture?" People were struggling to survive, many dying and, yet in few days, I would leave this place, return home, but the situation faced by these refugees would still exist. Working Pete's camp in Hawaii, I would still think about the refugees and the situation I was leaving behind. My mind would constantly remind me of the people suffering in Africa. I focused my mind on the day's tasks to be completed, helping the refugees.

While working Pete's camp it was imperative I put all my energies in doing the best I could. There would be many opportunities to share my recent trip with both players and contacts associated with the camp. Support for making any effective change in the circumstances faced by the refugees, needed to come from many sources. Information shared from someone who was present and keenly aware of the situation needed to be put out there.

I was anxious to get home and begin assembling my ideas into action for future trips. At the time, I made the decision to leave I was physically and emotionally drained. I saved only one pair of shoes and one change of clothes. All my other clothing articles were dirty and I decided to leave them behind at the advice of the other doctors. I was told that all the bacteria present in the clothing could possibly spread disease. I was now wondering how I was to get back to Nairobi without a visa or transportation.

If we had remained for a minimum of two years we could never address the needs of so many people who continuously walked down that narrow road to the refugee camp. I got lucky and hitched a ride with the Canadian Red Cross who took us to Nairobi. The Canadian Red Cross was very happy to assist us and all that needed to be said was that we were relief workers. They, without question, gave us rides and any other assistance we needed. We were again flying in a large transport plane, but this time it was empty due to returning to collect another cargo load. I pulled out my ticket and got ready to fly out of Nairobi as I headed towards the gate.

I soon learned African traveling requirements were not like the stated norms as expected when using any American airline companies, in terms of flight check-in procedures. There are no people at the gates waiting to assist you into the airport. Entrance doors for flights remain locked until approximately three hours or so prior to plane departure times. Finally, I walked in and approached the woman at the counter who checked my ticket and advised me the flight I booked was full because I hadn't called in a twenty-four-hour confirmation. I'd never heard of this. In America, when you pay for a seat on a plane, that confirms you are flying on that plane.

As the result of this failed confirmation my seat was given away. I advised the woman that I was in an area with no phones. She responded by stating they were sorry and the best they could do would be to get me on a flight the following day.

In Africa, there is no such thing as sleeping inside the airport overnight. This meant I had to leave the airport and go somewhere. Because I didn't know where to go I asked to speak with a supervisor, who I assumed would give me an opportunity to plead my case for getting on the fight I paid for. Well, in a desperate situation my imagination took the better of me and I proceeded to exclaim that there was a terrible accident with a family member and I needed to return quickly or else I'd miss the funeral services. I told her that it was imperative for me to get on that plane! I guess the emotion on my face looked convincing because the woman began to cry and immediately booked me first class to London.

After boarding the plane, I was greeted by a flight attendant who brought me a Coke a Cola with ice. I can still remember how wonderful ice was at that moment, and how refreshing the cola was inside my mouth. I don't drink sodas but at that moment I couldn't imagine anything else tasting better. I was so exhausted that I had no recollection of the plane taking off and it was nine hours later when I was awakened by the flight attendant to inform me we'd arrived in London. I was also informed, that I had missed my connecting flight. The only set of clean clothing was what I was wearing on my back as I stood looking at the Departure wall with total exhaustion. The help counter agent took mercy on me and provided me with a complementary pass to the Heathrow Hilton. It was very nice for the woman to assist me in this way. As a traveler in distress, I couldn't show enough humility and appreciation to her. I checked into the hotel, went to the room, and slept for the next twenty hours straight.

I missed my next connecting flight because I slept right on through the alarm due to extreme exhaustion. I remember that it was also the first time I felt safe and clean in almost a week. I left a house in Zaire that was surrounded by death and danger, and there were no locks on the doors. I couldn't help but think the United Nations should have stepped in and done something to keep the peace. I always heard the phrase "Never again" when referring to Nazi camps from World War II and the violence that came with it. I just wanted the UN to intervene. Once I awakened, I headed downstairs to a Chinese restaurant, where I ordered seven courses from the menu. The waiter asked whom all the food was for, and I said, "Me!" I told him that it had been days since I had could eat a meal I could truly enjoy. Without hesitation, I proceeded to eat every single item ordered served to me. I'd lost about twenty pounds in Africa. When I returned to Portland, Oregon, the Oregonian newspaper wrote a front-page article about my trip. Tens of thousands of dollars were donated to the Northwest Medical Team because of this article. It also raised awareness.

The dead to be buried in mass graves

CHAPTER 17

Vienne- Searching

Searching for Vienna brothers in Kibera

During those first few days of working in the refugee camp in Goma, Zaire, my curiosity as to what these masses of survivors had once called home continued to intrude in my thoughts. Throughout the days of assessing health concerns the stark reality of the current situation could not turn aside my interest to find out more. Down times provided the opportunity to learn more about the other members of the health care team. All health care workers stayed at the Adventist

Relief Agency house. Some groups had separate plans and agendas and my team was from Beaverton, Oregon, the Northwest Medical Teams. In particular, was the group from either Norway or Sweden. Two women in their early twenties and one man in his early forties. They had been working with the refugees for a few weeks before we had arrived.

After being introduced they shared how their day's agenda had been pre-arranged and was followed to every last detail. They were up and out the door just as we were getting loaded up and organized to start our day. Their sincerity and work ethic was obvious and greatly impressed me. On the third evening of my five-day stay, the older gentleman and I was talking about the genocide that was being reported in the media. He shared he was a frequent visitor to Rwanda and mentioned he was going to make a trip there the following day. He asked if I would like to accompany him as I was filled with questions that such a venture would help me answer.

Having worked in Kigali, Rwanda prior to the genocide he had some follow up work to do. As he had not been back to assess the degree of devastation caused by the massacre of his former patients, he offered to drive me over the border. The distance was 60 miles, and within an hour and a half we were driving into Kigali, Rwanda. The ride in the open jeep afforded us the opportunity to get an up-close view of the refugees walking past us. As we drove along the same road traveled by the continuous flow of refugees it was soon obvious something truly horrific had transformed this tranquil landscape into a burial ground. I needed to see for myself how much this tribal rivalry left its mark and changed a positive outlook of a future into the bleak and dismal struggle to get through another day.

Looking around the country limits, the corpses which lined the side of the road were rolled up in blankets. With naked feet sticking out from the partial covering it was easy to determine which bodies were female and which were male. The jeep we rode in traveled easily past the remains of individuals who no longer existed. Death was everywhere, in the air, on the ground and most significant in one's mind and memory. The land was void of any sign of life. My guide, the health care worker, pointed out the homes he had previously visited and were now empty vestiges of a life-style that once made a house a home and people a family. We stopped leaving the jeep to walk around a house that was partially furnished. Inside the house had been ransacked, closet turned upside down and inside out. It was clearly the intent to collect any valuables left behind or pillage through any item that might be of use to its finder.

Livestock pens were bare as any farm animals were gathered and confiscated by the perpetrators of this pillage. Blood stained walls and floors made the truth regarding what happened all to heart wrenching. Imagining what evil would encourage such murderous intent made the plight of the refugees more personal. Looking at the fear and sadness on the faces of those we assessed in the camp now made the need to help make their current situation better more of a priority.

The stark silence was disturbing. There were no birds signing, people talking, children playing, or farmers working with livestock. The air once filled with the natural smells of farm life were replaced with the stench of rotting flesh. Man's inhumanity to man was clear and it was difficult to remain a casual observer. What once was the normal routines of daily life being now a distant memory? No families carried extraneous supplies on the flight from what was and now no more. The spoils of war were collected and with no reason to stay any longer a sense of urgency ignited our resolve to focus on a promising future and not dwelling in a past that should never have happened.

The return trip to Goma seemed a lot shorter than to trip from Goma to Rwanda. Our jeep continued to pass an ever-growing throng of refugees traveling along the same road we traveled. This time after seeing where they were journeying from, we were motivated by their determination to complete their journey and look ahead with hope. The trust required to continue searching for lost loved ones and challenging hunger and thirst to step aside was evident and respected. It isn't easy to understand the trauma these people had to endure, but it was easy to appreciate their resolve to move forward and conquer evil with good.

Returning to the triage tent I took more notice of a young man who spoke several languages and was helping to gather information from patients being seen by the medical care givers. I learned his name was Vienne and he was currently living in Houston, Texas. He had been working with the health care team for several weeks. While working with the Northwest Medical Team we worked closely with Vienne who served as a translator. He was a native born African from Rwanda, twenty-five years old, and a current United States citizen. Having been born and raised in Rwanda, his explicit purpose was to locate his two younger brothers who were still living in Rwanda at the time of the genocidal atrocity. I took more note of how he interacted with each patient. His conversation was through but included a bit of personal attention to determine if any of these patients knew his brothers and had any word as to where they might be, if indeed they were still alive. He was extremely compassionate in conducting each interview and his demeanor was extremely helpful. It impressed me how no matter what information he could compile his immediate attention was to provide relief for any infirmity identified. In fact, he would arrange to have those patients with immediate health concerns and see they were transported to the triage tent. His efforts were noticed and appreciated by everyone who acknowledged what an asset he was.

Taking a five-minute government break one morning, I walked over to where Vienne was sitting. He was organizing patient information forms and setting up appointments for the next round of refugees. I wondered why he was being so diligent with paperwork and decided to ask him. I was impressed that his notes were taken to put together some time line of when his brothers might have left Rwanda and arrived in Goma, Zaire. From this information, he would be able to get some perspective on how to fine tune his search and ultimately locate his two younger siblings among the multitude of vulnerable refugees.

Those five days passed quicker than expected and soon I was saying my farewells to the health care workers and everyone who had worked with me. I wanted to show my support in Vienne's search for is misplaced family members. I did not know when he would be leaving Goma, Zaire to return to Houston, Texas, and we exchanged contact information. I told Vienne I would contact him and expressed my willingness to return to Africa and work exclusively with him to do whatever was necessary to help him to find his lost brothers.

In the months that followed Vienne returned to Houston, Texas and contacted me. He had not yet been successful in locating his lost brothers and I told him after making arrangements for both his and my airfare and hotel accommodations I would meet him to follow through on my promise. The Adventist Relief Agency had been so helpful during my initial visit to Africa and were closely connected to the refuges who were fleeing from Rwanda seeking assistance in relocation and health care. The Agency recommended a local hotel in Nairobi, Kenya. Accommodations were said to be nice, and the cost was reasonable, about $10.00 a night.

The expression, the price is right didn't quite match the other well-known phrase, you get what you pay for. I did inquire why Nairobi, Kenya and was told most refuges were directed to a community named Mathare. After contacting Vienne, he seemed familiar with the area in Nairobi and felt confident that this would be a good starting place. His parents and two other siblings, had moved to Houston, Texas a few years prior to the war in Rwanda. They were hopeful with the added resources I was going to provide, the possibility of finding their two missing sons would result in success.

The first six trips to Africa, Goma, Zaire and Nairobi, Kenya, were financed by me as we had no donors. Later trips were financed using my NBA worker's compensation funds, and NBPA salary. Funding for air fare/travel, meals, lodging, and transportation around Nairobi, Kenya, and medical supplies, medicines, equipment, and other incidentals were all covered by Project Contact donations and my personal funds. There was limited use of credit cards and checks as most establishments accepted cash only for transactions.

I made my second trip to Africa with Vienne in September of 1994. We needed a strategy as we would be in a foreign country and I was not familiar with Nairobi, Kenya at all. Vienne had been there a few times and had some connections for us to contact once we arrived. Having this initial lead provided some direction in how to pursue our efforts the next day. Heading to our hotel I was looking forward to a restful night with a positive attitude about our first day of searching for Vienne's brothers. Trusting the information given was accurate, I was hopeful but not overly confident. Financed by me, except for when Howard Hedinger paid for the two doctors who went with me on my third trip. I was expecting a Marriott but knew a Motel 6 might be the real thing, after all it was said to be safe, reasonable and provided moderate accommodations and facilities. I assumed or more than that hoped, the appraisal of the hotel was both trustworthy and accurate. Following this advice along with the assurance the hotel was nice, the cost reasonable and at $10.00 a room for each night I booked two rooms for a minimum of five days.

The flight to Nairobi, Kenya was long and comfortable seating a definite challenge for my long legs. I left Portland, Oregon, stopped in Minneapolis, Minnesota, re-boarded a plane for London, England, and then from London, England arrived in Nairobi, Kenya. After nineteen hours in the air, we landed in the ever busy Jomo Kenyatta International airport. I stood in an ever-growing long line of other travelers to clear customs. This process sometimes takes a while. You can't help but casually observe the unfolding nightmare description of the well-known term *break time*. In the United States, we have the five-minute government break. In Africa, our five-minute government break turns into twenty minutes of off time at best. It gives a whole new meaning to "being late to your own funeral." This practice of making you wait is designed to increase your desire to do anything and pay any fee simply to get on with your trip. Signs are posted to make you aware to enter the country a fee is required and required payment is to be paid with cash only. You must have exact change as no credit cards are accepted. You are to provide two ten dollar bills not one twenty. If you have currency higher than ten dollars you are asked to leave the line and informed you may get back in line once you can provide the exact fee requested.

Whenever traveling I am always grateful when I land. The ability to stand and regain the feeling in my limbs can only be compared to what a butterfly emerging from its chrysalis stage feels once it is free to take flight after being enclosed during its transformation. The long line to leading to acquiring a visa and customs did give me some additional time to stretch my legs which alleviated any anxiety or frustration for the long wait. Walking the short distance from the airport baggage claim and required documents for entry, Vienne and

I stood on the sidewalk, and were faced with a barrage of taxi cab vying for chance to collect our cash. This resulted in a mad rush by a minimum of a dozen taxi drivers racing to approach us. They were all offering their services as if I were an auction item up for bidding. The taxi cab ride to the hotel was at the least interesting. Vienne was able to work with one driver on a price, but his driving ability left much to be desired. Adding to my anxiety was the lack of street lighting. How could the taxi driver see where he was going? That could account for some of the less than perfect driving but I would still have to wager his ability to simply drive was also a factor to be considered.

I put my trust in the driver to make sure we arrived safely to the hotel. When the taxi stopped in front of the hotel, I felt a small sense of relief. The area of the city where the hotel was located appeared somewhat safe. So far, so good. The street was set back and in the late evening darkness I looked around. The view of the city was beautiful. This of course was before the reality of stepping inside the hotel became apparent. This was the first time to understand how much front exteriors were exactly like Universal Studios sets with nothing to support the sides and back. Although the building looked well maintained. It was not what the outward impression presented. This fact became quickly obvious as I carried my small backpack through the front doors. My first impression was the city had at one time been very beautiful but the years of wear and tear had not been kind.

I knew I was in trouble when I noticed what was missing in the lobby. This was a different take on reality. For the most part we look at what is present in front of your eyes. This was just the opposite; you were keenly aware of what should have been there but was obviously not. This reminded me of the famous line in Paul Newman's Cool Hand Luke, "What we have here is a failure to communicate." What was related regarding the accommodations and what was actually available was definitely a failure to communicate accurate information. Could it have been a translation glitch? Could it be a total difference in perceptive? Either way, in Nairobi, Kenya, you get exactly what you pay for, if you are fortunate to be in the right place at the right time.

The word reasonable has many definitions, at this current place in time it simply meant housing that will provide the basic and I mean the bare necessities of life minus what is available at the time you check into the hotel. The rooms were small, with one bed, a mattress that had seen better days (years might be a better explanation), one set of sometime in the past was white, soap the size of most after-dinner mints placed on your pillow in a swanky hotel in New York City, and the bathroom did not provide shampoo, conditioner, or lotion samples.

When speaking with the older residents in the city, they told me their memories of how beautiful the city was in those earlier days. The test of thirty years of turmoil and strife proved to pay a large toll on what once was quite exquisite with well-maintained and a thriving center of economic stability. It appeared the city Kenya won its independence from the United Kingdom and in its attempt to provide stability, simply replaced their former governmental structure with tribal affiliations that presented more problems than solutions to existing conditions. Broken windows were left as is, not replaced or boarded up. Over time, this sort of prolonged failure to address needed repairs dramatically impacted the city's overall aesthetic. The city's state of neglect was simply disappointing that reflected a lack of concern. This, although upsetting, helped me better understand the desperation felt by the inhabitants, as well as their lack of feeling any sense of urgency regarding identifying a problem and reaching a viable solution.

Traveling anywhere in or outside the city of Nairobi approved to present various challenges. The roadways and road signs were ignored, people pushing hand carts would join cars and people on bikes to get from one place to another. One morning a man was pushing a large hand cart, in a round-a-bout, and almost hit by a driver who insisted he had the right of way. Careless driving was not limited to round-a-bouts and streets. My first morning, I was attempting to cross the street when I was very nearly rundown by a car. The drivers were extremely aggressive in Nairobi, Kenya. Being used to looking in both directions prior to crossing the street, I stepped off the curb. I was almost hit by an oncoming car traveling from the opposite direction of my on-going traffic. In the United States, you can step off a curb or attempt to cross a street after taking a quick glance to the left then the right to see if cars oncoming cars in the closest lane to the curb. Not here!

After my brief but impressionable stay in Goma, Zaire, I was somewhat prepared for such conditions as no running water, toilets or electricity. I reasoned that conditions on my prior trip were because of the war. I was surprised to discover, in the "slum" area of Kibera, the conditions were almost identical. The Kibera "slum" is the largest on the continent of Africa and inhabited by one million people. The ground was muddy and the air filled with the stench of rotting garbage and pollution. The community did not have access to running water or any connection to modern conveniences. Housing was poorly constructed, mostly shacks made of tin. This community clearly made me aware of what poverty was like.

The entrance to a one room space featured a make shift covering. There were no windows, and a small cooking grate was placed in the center of the room. The air was filled with the smoke lingering due to a lack of ventilation in the small room from preparing a meal. The only light source was small candles place around the room. Living in such conditions contributed to poverty and distress. The lack of food and medical support were daily challenges to be faced with little hope of relief that influenced how residents dealt with life.

Being told a family from his neighborhood in Rwanda were living in Nairobi, Kenya. using this tip, he decided to ask local merchants about his brothers. We took a taxi to the market area in downtown Nairobi. Vienne stopped to talk with local merchants. Initially my accompanying Vienne proved to be a deterrent, until Vienne introduced me and the word quickly spread among the vendors. One vendor approached us and advised Vienne to ride the local Matatus and speak with the passengers.

There were several Matatus available and we chose the first one that looked less crowded than the one before. The passengers were friendly and Vienne easily engaged in conversations with several of them. He explained why we were traveling together and his interest in locating his two brothers. Interested in helping, the passengers were so friendly, and told us on this Matatu the passengers were regulars. As such many shared how they came to be living in Nairobi and there was one passenger who related how she had fled from Rwanda. Hopeful she would know something. To help Vienne recognize this woman, the passenger agreed to point her out. He was told today this passenger got off the Matatu a few stops before we boarded. Usually she continued to travel further on the route and suggested if we were to get on at the same stop the next day we would be sure to meet up with her. Following her advice, we returned to our hotel with a growing anticipation, "this could be the day we find Vienne's lost brothers." He was told they had managed to leave and relocated to Nairobi, Kenya. Asking assistance to get this families phone number, Adventist Relief Agency, was a big help. The contact number was up-to-date and after making one call, Vienne and I were invited to dinner. I sat listening to the story about this family's escape and wondered how terrifying those times must have been for many. These people were survivors but many families were not so fortunate. I began to wonder if this might be the case for Vienne's two brothers.

Vienne spent most of the evening asking about any people they had both known who left Rwanda, and are now living in Nairobi, Kenya. This family shared a list of possible people to contact. These were friends who lived nearby in the Nairobi, and might have information to share about his brothers. We left that night hopeful and eager to get started the next day. Having gotten a good night's sleep, we got up early the next morning. While eating looked over the list and then asked the local waiter to help us organize the list according to addresses.

The addresses given were close to the hotel and the suggested approach to visit each and then return to the hotel proved very useful, both in saving time and energy. Most were within walking distance of each other with few requiring we brave the streets and hail a taxi or board a Matatu. After settling in, Vienne started to visit with the passengers. The passengers being so friendly, we were told that each day new and returning regulars board this very Matatu and one of the names Vienne inquired about was expected to be on it the following day. We returned to our hotel with the growing anticipation "this could be the day we find Vienne's lost brothers."

The next morning Vienne was up early and the hope on his face was clearly evident. We walked back to the place we had boarded the day before after grabbing a quick bite to eat for breakfast. The hotel cuisine was not the best but it managed to lessen my hunger and desire for some real food. The long waited for Matatu arrived jammed packed to passengers. The people boarding and departing were open and friendly, once they understood why Vienne was asking so many questions. As time and unforeseen occurrences would have it, one of the persons included on the list provided the night before boarded the Matatu.

Vienne approached the passenger and started a conversation. Although Vienne's brothers were not known to the passenger she told Vienne one of her friends had mentioned two brothers in a recent conversation. She might have some information for him and when asked, she gave Vienne another lead to pursue. Vienne took down the information and decided to get off the Matatu and wait for the next one that would return us to the hotel. The weather was pleasant and trying to consider this need lead, Vienne wanted to walked a few yards to gather his thoughts.

The next morning Vienne was up early. I had to remind him that to contact the woman on the list we had to board the Matatu at the same time. We sat down to breakfast and Vienne although excited about the possibilities ahead managed to consume a large breakfast. The waiter we had the previous morning asked how our search was going and that conversation left Vienne more hopeful than ever. The hope on his face was clear. We left the hotel and walked down the street to catch the Matatu.

The passengers on the Matatu entered and exited and the passenger who was so helpful the day before was already seated and motioned for us to move closer. Vienne continued to engage in conversations with the passengers. With more questions answered by interested and helpful passengers, everyone seemed to be focused on looking out for the woman who had related her experience in Rwanda and could possibly be the name on his list. The helpful woman passenger again stated she usually boarded a few stops before we boarded, but on this morning boarded just as we were settling in. Giving her a few minutes to sit down, Vienne introduced himself. He shared his reason for approaching her and they held a brief conversation about his reason for seeking her help. Although Vienne's brothers were not known to her, one of her friends had recently mentioned meeting two men who might be his brothers. They were living somewhere in the area and looking for Jobs. She agreed to ask her friend for more information. She knew of a family who had also fled from Rwanda and had their address. Giving Vienne this lead to pursue, he wrote down all the details and we decided to exit the Matatu and catch another to return to the hotel.

Upon returning to the hotel we asked our waiter, how to locate the address of the family were given. He suggested we contact the Adventist Relief Agency to verify this information and knew they had helped other families both relocate and find other family members. He was able to provide the agency's phone number and we immediately made a phone call. The family contact information was up-to-date, and we were surprised to find it was not too far from our hotel. Eager to follow up on this lead we took a taxi and walked up to the front door. Unexpected, we took a chance and rang the doorbell. We found the family's home and a maid answered the door. To our surprise the building was quite large and in situated in a very nice neighborhood. The maid was very pleasant and we were warmly greeted. After Vienne introduced us, the maid went to tell her employer why we were there and invited us in. The employer was the wife of the homeowner; she was well dressed and the house was decorated with quality and expensive items. Her three children were at school and the maid servant prepared tea and cakes. She could speak English fluently and were held a conversation about why we were given her family's name and address in connection with locating Vienne's two brothers. I explained how I met Vienne and why I had agreed to join him in Nairobi, to assist in his efforts.

The wife related the need to escape from Rwanda. Her family left secretively in the late hours of the night constantly fearing for their safety. There was no time to communicate their plans to anyone and this level of secrecy proved to be beneficial as her husband was a very influential member of the community and his life was in danger. She did not know Vienne's brothers but knew several refugees who had fled Rwanda and managed to find housing and Jobs in the area, although having limited resources. She suggested we search in the slums of Kibera. We were told this was not a pleasant place to visit but with so many people living in such close quarters someone was sure to be able to help. Very grateful for both the information and the tea, we were invited to return with Vienne's brothers. This added to our confidence that we were on the right track.

Locating Kibera was easy. Leaving the dusty and unpaved roadway we entered the Kibera slum. After my brief but impressionable stay in Goma, Zaire, I was somewhat prepared for the conditions in Kibera or so I thought. There was no running water, toilets, or electricity. I reasoned that conditions on my initial trip was directly related to the war, and was surprised to discover, in the "slum" area of Kibera, these conditions were almost identical. The Kibera slum is the largest on the continent of Africa and inhabited by one million people. The ground was dusty and the air filled with the stench of rotting garbage, human waste and pollution. The community did not have access to running water or any connection with modern conveniences. Housing was poorly constructed, mostly shacks made of tin. This community clearly made me aware of what the poverty level was.

People moved about caring for their daily needs. Women carried large plastic containers to be filled with water located at the top of an incline. Trash and garbage was strewn along the roadside and the air was filled with dust and the stench of rotting garbage and human waste. Stopping to ask people about his brothers I looked inside one of the structures. The small space had one entrance and exit. A piece of cloth covered the opening. There were no windows, and a small cooking grate was placed in the center of the room. The air was filled with smoke lingering in the stuffy area due to the lack of ventilation in the room from preparing a meal. The only source of light were small candles placed around the room. This one room served as the kitchen, bathroom, and bedroom for a family of six. Living in such conditions contributed to both the level of poverty and distress. The lack of food and medical support were daily challenges to be faced with little hope of relief that would positively influence how residents dealt with life.

Each structure we visited looked the same and residents were eager to see why we had come in hope of gaining some material gain. One resident thought he might know where Vienne's brothers might be. He knew of two men who had fled from Rwanda and were asking about housing and employment. He directed us to an area just outside Kibera where small huts and stables were located. He suggested we asked a resident in that area for information. Following this lead, we walked through the slums and found the area described by the resident.

The road was dusty and filled with rocks and other debris. We continued along the path and found a small hutch on the side of the road. We walked across the heavily dirt-covered landscape and saw a mud shack with a tin roof. It looked much like a small stable. The outside had evidence that someone was living inside. Looking at this structure we did question if it was fit for human habitation. Hoping the resident or residents were there, we walked up to the front of the structure and looked inside through the open upper portion of the Dutch doors.

We gained strength and momentum with every step we took heading down that dusty road. We continued to walk and soon found a small hutch on to the side of the main road. We walked across the heavily dirt-covered road and found a mud shack with a tin roof. It looked like a small stable. Perhaps someone might have more information for Vienne. I questioned if we were at the right location as this structure couldn't possibly be fit for human habitation. Vienne walked up to the front of the building and looked inside through the open upper portion of the Dutch doors.

The inside could only be described as a stable. The presence of the Dutch doors might have been an attempt to appear as a possible place for a humble abode, but failed miserably to pull it off. The whole environment looked like a place to keep sheep. Walking up to the Dutch doors we looked inside, there were two men sitting on the dirt floor without any furnishings, light source, and or heat.

Vienne called out the names of his brothers and to my surprise these two men walked out this stable and ran up to him. So many words and emotions passed between the brothers. I might have been able to give a word for word translation, but instinctively knew everything was going to be alright. We soon discovered after leaving the women who had helped them escape his two brothers could not impose on her kindness and move into these current lodgings until they could find more suitable accommodations they could afford. It amazed me how these two men had been living in conditions only suitable for animals. Vienne was both relieved and happy to be reunited with his brothers. He didn't seem concerned about any lack of amenities but would now be able to focus on what to do next.

It was a miracle we found Vienne's brothers healthy and alive. He was anxious to take his brothers back to the hotel to get cleaned up and phone their parents. I thought that a wonderful idea and once this was done we went out to eat a proper meal. Now that the brothers had been reunited I was curious as to how they managed to get from Rwanda to Nairobi. They shared their drive from Rwanda to Kenya was approximately twenty hours and forty-eight minutes. As flying was not the safest or affordable means to travel and the most expensive, the one hour and thirty-three minutes' flight was not an option. The idea of walking briefly crossed their minds until viewing a map. The walking distance of 525 miles would take a month and the terrain held several missing sidewalks and unsafe pedestrian paths. So, how did they manage to leave Rwanda and arrive safely in Nairobi?

After hearing several reports about the killings and outright persecution from neighbors and locals, Vienne's brothers learned about the approaching Hutus' planned siege upon their local village. Not being able to sleep, both ventured out of their small lodgings in the late evening to develop a plan of escape. While walking, they encountered a fellow neighbor who was loading his truck with one cow, one heifer, one calf and Bachiara (livestock feed farmers grow in their fields.). He was alone and in need of help.

Stopping to ask if they could be on some assistance the farmer welcomed their help. After one hour of packing the feed, the livestock, and a few personal items the farmer extended his appreciation by sharing his plan to leave the area that night and drive to Nairobi, Kenya. The brothers knowing the danger that was coming asked if they could accompany the farmer if they got in the truck without returning to their home and left with him directly.

Realizing this opportunity would not be available again, it didn't require a great deal of thought to decide to take advantage of this solution to their very serious dilemma. Returning home to collect anything would mean alerting others about their plan to escape and this was not an option. The farmer agreed if both traveled with the livestock and feed, just in case there was an issue, the farmer would be able to inform anyone that the brothers were workers on his farm and helping to deliver of his cargo.

The journey began that night as the loaded truck headed North to Goma, Zaire. They stopped in Goma to refuel, take a brief restroom break and then continued to Uganda, stopping at another gas station north of Entebbe at Kampala. The drive seemed like it would last forever, but each mile brought the brothers closer to Nairobi without any interference. It was a welcomed relief to reach Kampala where they stopped in Bungoma, then Nakuru. From there they arrived safely in Nairobi, after traveling for close to nineteen hours, over 725 miles, in the bed of a small truck with smelly livestock and feed. In Nairobi, the brothers were able to clean up after helping the driver unload his truck.

The driver asked the brothers where they intended to stay and provided what information he knew about an area known as Kibera. He explained it was not the best of accommodations but was some- place to stay until other arrangements could be made. Kibera houses approximately 2.5 million slum dwellers in about 200 settlements. It is the biggest slum in Africa and one of the biggest in the world. The average size of a shack is 12 ft. by 12 ft. built with mud walls, a cor- rugated tin roof with a dirt or concrete floor. The cost is KES 700 per month = $6.93. Shacks often house up to eight or more with many sleeping on the floor. Only twenty percent of Kibera has electricity. This includes street lighting, security lightning and connection to shacks (this costs KES 900 per shack = $8.91. Water had to be collected from the Nairobi dam. The dam water is not clean and causes many cases of typhoid and cholera. Water is collect at KES 3 per 20 liters = $0.01. In most of Kibera there are not toilets. One latrine, a hole in the ground, is shared by up to 50 shacks. Once full, young boys are hired to empty the latrine and take the contents to the river. As safety at this point was their main concern and they had escaped death, any arrangements would be welcomed.

The farmer's friends and connections were limited but names were exchanged and later proved instrumental. As news of the 100-day siege that claimed more than 800,000 innocent Rwandans through the slaughter in one grisly massacre reached the brothers a great sense of sorrow and relief filled their hearts and mind. The Tutsi's and moderate Hutus and children, fled to refugee camps in bordering countries. Women were raped and livestock considered the "spoils of war." Already a country landlocked with few natural resources, Rwanda became a location for landless peasants. Had they not left the night they did the soldiers would have stopped them along the way, confiscated the livestock and grain and murdered all three of them.

Vienne had made some inquiries as to where refugees from Kigali, Rwanda might have gone and following that lead traveled to Goma, Zaire. His goal was to find his brothers among the throng of refugees. Most of the refugees were women and children which presented major challenges in locating men. Determined to interact with as many people as possible, Vienne Joined a group of health care providers and worked as a translator. One refugee remembered a neighbor who was a farmer whose truck had been parked in front of his lodgings one night and was gone the following morning. It had been thought he had taken his livestock to Nairobi for his family to care for as the rumors about the on-going reprisals from the Hutus was emanate. It was also noted that two young men had also suddenly left the neighborhood and might have gone with this farmer to Nairobi, Kenya.

Now safely in Nairobi, Vienne's brothers used their ability to translate to help secure employment. Locals knew the difference between Hutus and Tutsi's and were very prejudice. After several attempts to gain employment, both were hired for a minimal wage to work in a local market a few hours a day. They checked invoices and merchandise deliveries. Realizing their status as Tutsi's and their need for work, their employer was accommodating in allowing them to work together but was not so amiable as to provide a higher wage to help them obtain suitable housing. They therefore, rented a small space that simply provided shelter.

Vienne had been so helpful to all of us when in Goma, Zaire, in the refugee camp improving dialogue through conducting meaningful and accurate translations. Fluent in English, French, and several native dialects. Before leaving the refugee camp I asked Vienne if there was anything I could do to show my appreciation for is assistance in making people's lives better.

Reflected on Vienne's only request that I return to Africa and help find his two brothers and being successful in doing so, traveling back home, and my mind began to take into consideration many possibilities. Thinking back on my own early beginnings the objective of the Sixth Man Foundation-Project Contact Africa, to help anyone in need of assistance whether in America or Africa, began in my early childhood years.

CHAPTER 18

Trips to Africa

Our kids on annual picnic

NBA sponsored these Somalian refugees to help them start businesses

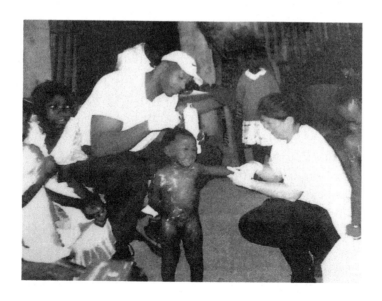

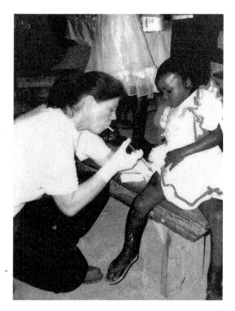

First trips with medical tram from the US

Experiencing success in helping Vienne locate his two lost brothers and be reunited in Nairobi, Kenya, I returned to Portland, Oregon, with conflicting emotions. By walking the thoroughfares of Mathare, the oldest slum in Nairobi amidst 180,000 residents, my mind was filled with a realistic awareness for the need to find answers to considerable questions relating to current living conditions there. What needed to be put into place to improve the health and welfare of the local residents? How could consistent medical assistance have provided through an established, qualified, affordable, and supportive on-going health care system present viable solutions to existing problems? Mychal, during KFXX air time, asked me to compare my first trip to Goma, Zaire, to my recent second trip to Nairobi, Kenya. While sharing this second trip was to fulfill a promise made to Vienne to return to Africa and help him find his two brothers. Knowing they escaped the carnage and warfare in Rwanda, it was relief not returning to Goma to continue his search.

This second trip with Vienne introduced me to Mathare, its residents, and sparked my interest in exploring this community further. Housing for residents are 6 ft. x 8 ft. shanties made of old tin and mud. These inadequate living spaces lack beds, electricity, and running water. People sleep on pieces of cardboard on the dirt floors of the shanties. There are public toilets shared by up to 100 people and residents have to pay to use them. Those who cannot afford to pay must use the alleys and ditches between the shanties. "Flying toilets" are plastic bags used by the residents to dispose of their human waste at night. This accepted disposal method encourages throwing these flying toilets into the Nairobi River, the source of the residents' water supply.

In the slums of Mathare, approximately 600,000 people share an area of three square miles. Their shanties although not connected their proximity adds to a sense of claustrophobia. As there is no front door entry is easily obtained by simply walking inside. The residents are open and friendly at quite at home with your visit. A small candle was lit and placed in the center of the room providing the only light source. There are no beds with limited furnishings, no electrical outlets, bathroom facilities, running water or kitchen space. Most residents live on an income of less than a dollar per day. Crime is prevalent and the occurrence of HIV/AIDs widespread. Many parents die of AIDS and leave their children to fend for themselves.

It is estimated that one of every three adults in Mathare is HIV positive. The average life expectancy for a person who is HIV positive in Mathare is five years or less. Common health problems for children in Mathare include dysentery, malnutrition, malaria, typhoid, cholera, infections, tetanus, and polio. There were several juvenile heads of households, 8 or 9 years old, left to care for younger siblings, since both parents have died of AIDS.

There are an estimated 70,000 children in the Mathare Valley, with too few schools for so many children to educate. Many children do not attend school, due to required school fees, uniforms, school supplies and meal fees for admission. Without an education, many children in Mathare Valley's future choices are limited to criminal activity, prostitution, drug abuse and disease. The long-term effect on the quality of any resident's life is devastating.

Before returning home, I spoke with several local residents about the children. They were quite vocal about how limited their resources were and asked if I might be offering financial assistance. I mentioned my interest in arranging to provide health care services to the local residents and everyone I spoke with was eager to know more.

My attention was directed to the closest school within walking distance of Mathare's community. Kicking up red dust into the air, I soon noticed a school surrounded by a tall fence with a guard posted in front of locked gates. Approaching the fence, it took a few minutes to get his attention. It wasn't that he failed to see me; it was more that he didn't see the importance of why I was standing there.

Continuing to motion him over to where I was standing I called out and asked if he spoke English. To my relief he did and I asked if I could speak with speak the administrator. The guard told me to wait and he went to see if anyone was available to speak with me. Several minutes later I watched a woman walking over to the fence. It was school principal who introduced herself and speaking fluent English invited me into her office.

Exchanging introductions, I shared my interest in using her school as a base for a two-week health clinic to provide free health services for the residents of Mathare. Before making a commitment, we exchanged contact information and I agreed to send her an action plan with an itinerary within seven to ten business days. I took advantage to the sixteen hours of air travel time home to create a T-chart. One side listing the problems to consider and the other side listed solutions.

Initially, my idea was to encourage interest in supporting these efforts and then utilize personal funds for all incurred expenses. My third trip came together after sharing my concerns with two doctors who I lifted weights with at Gold's gym. Both offered to volunteer their medical assistance if that would be something I would be interested in. I then started to explore how this school site might serve as a possible location to host this visit from a group of medical care providers. The idea that this could be the opportunity to determine how to make this plan work was invigorating. It was evident to pursue this plan and achieve any beneficial results my first priority would be obtaining funding that would be on-going.

A plan was needed to incorporate a system to most efficiently assess patient needs, distribute medical supplies, dispense medicines, and treat diseases most prevalent in the area. Research into this information was necessary and gathering an adequate supply of medicines a top priority. Being able to provide care to local residents would relief and comfort to those who needed much more. Health care is expensive and there are no free clinics available.

Deeply reflecting on how medical caregivers set up, and worked with patients in the refugee camp, I took time to think about how things were organized, what supplies were needed, and how to address needs, and put it all together. I had to clearly identified one key need and then what could be done to meet that need not just once but continuously. Funding was that need and after people saw how much was being accomplished perhaps that might stimulate interest and financial support. The basic idea to help one person at a time under whatever circumstance exist is the mission of the Sixth Man Foundation- Project Contact Africa.

At Gold's gym two doctors arranged to meet with me after working out to develop a proposal for the school administrator in Mathare and formulated an action plan on how to move forward. We listed what steps must be taken to achieve our specific goal, to reach local Mathare residents to assess, treat and dispense medication. The purpose of our action plan was to clarify what resources were required to reach our goal, formulate a timeline for when specific tasks needed to be completed and determine what resources were required.

I was invited to speak at Wilson High School where the daughter of Howard Hedinger, an executive officer and director of American Steel, a West Coast steel service center chain based in Portland, Oregon. American Steel is a subsidiary of American Industries, which has interests in real estate and other investments, was a student. Telling her father about my presentation, she arranged for the two of us to meet at his office to discuss my action plan. After doing some research I discovered Howard was noted as a philanthropist and during our meeting elicited his advice. His interest peaked he generously paid for the airfare for two doctors. I paid for the airfare for two nurses and covered housing, food, and other incidental fees.

In seeking out resources, I was directed to a website where pharmaceutical companies, such as Pfizer, donated medicines to charitable organizations. The lead representative for Pfizer was Jay Donkers. After meeting him he shared his interest in not only providing pharmaceutical supplies and medicine but would like to accompany me on my next trip. Jay later organized and monitored the distribution of all medications in our African clinics. He accompanied me on several trips after his initial introduction to Project Contact Africa and the clinic in Kenya. A valued asset his knowledge and meticulous management of medications helped our supplies reach more individuals and positively impacted their health status. Donations of powerful antibiotics were generously made. As our action plan was well on the way, it was time to contact the principal of the local school in Mathare.

I paid for the airfare for one nurse, Elsa Marie and myself and covered housing, food, and other incidental fees. The two doctors Joined my circle of friends from working out at Gold's Gym. Both having just been assigned to residencies at different hospitals across the country knew one nurse and met Elsa Marie, an employee at Key Bank of Oregon. Elsa Marie after listening to my conversations about my trip to Africa on KFXX- the FAN sports radio show, came to listen to me give a presentation at a local school in Gresham, Oregon. She approached me and gave me her contact information stating she was very interested in going on my next visit to Africa and was willing and able to pay for her expenses. She supported our health care services by following medical directions given by the doctors and the nurse. Her primary role was to assist in the pharmacy. In addition, I promised the doctors and nurse a two to three day paid for lay-over in Amsterdam for their volunteer efforts.

As agreed I contacted the principal at the school within 8 business days to share my action plan and we worked out a timeline that worked for both of us. Once steps were in place to make the trip, I forwarded our itinerary information to the school principal in Mathare. After reviewing the details, it was approved for us to use the school facilities. The only stipulation made by the principal was the students and staff be seen before extending services to Mathare residents. We readily agreed, scheduled the date for our arrival and finalized travel plans.

We flew to Amsterdam and stayed overnight catching a flight to Nairobi the following day. After a good night's rest, we arrived at our lodgings and settled in. Unpacking the medicines and medical supplies was a long and tedious Job. Sorting and labeling all dosages was time consuming and labor intense but the most important component in our action plan meeting its goal. When dispensing antibiotics, we had to carefully count out 21 pills – 3 pills a day for 7 days.

Traveling anywhere in the city of Nairobi was a challenge. The roadways and road signs were ignored, people pushing hand carts would join cars and people on bikes to get from one place to another. One morning a man was pushing a large hand cart and was almost hit by a driver who insisted he had the right of way. Careless driving was not limited to circles and streets. The first morning waking up and attempting to get better acquainted with my surroundings, attempting to cross the street, looking both ways, I was nearly run-down by a car. The drivers in Nairobi were very aggressive, with only one agenda, theirs. An oncoming car coming from the opposite direction appeared out of nowhere, ignored my presence and continued to drive down the road.

Now a passenger in a rented van with a local driver, we left the Methodist Guest House and headed to the local school in Mathare. On our first day, the principal welcomed us and greeted us as we entered through the school gates. The guard was told we would be holding a special health care clinic for the next few days and to expect our arrival in the morning and our departure in the late afternoon. Having been given permission to use the school as the site for the dispensing of medications and medical care, it took a while to set up our working space. The principal was quite open to our request provided we strictly followed her one stipulation; we were to provide care to the students and staff before anyone from the community. We readily agreed and began to unload the supplies.

The room we were assigned to was dusty and small. Located in the center of the school the room next door was available for the pharmacy and supplies. As you entered the make-shift clinic an area was set aside for receiving patients. The rest of the space was set aside for doctor examinations, treating scabies and ringworm, and a space for the urgent care services. The local children standing along the fence watched as we unloaded the van with our medical supplies.

Our first patients were the students and staff of the school as we had pre-arranged. By the time we were ready to begin seeing local patients, we noticed the children who were standing along the school perimeter were nowhere to be seen. We soon realized they had gone back to their homes to tell everyone what was happening at the local school. Soon local residents lined the perimeter of the school with inquisitive minds wanting to know what was going on and how and if they could be included. We soon learned many of the patients desiring medical attention had never been seen by any medical professionals.

This experience presented a two-fold opportunity, as both the medical team from the United States and many patients had limited if any interactions with languages spoken by people of different cultures. It soon began evident both had a lot to learn about the other and in the end people are the same and should be viewed as individuals who at any given time will need support and a helping hand. The realization a change in a person's circumstance could easily result in living in similar conditions as the patients was thought-provoking.

Our number one priority was to establish communication. The next obstacle to overcome was how to best use the space in the location assigned. It was evident providing a permanent location that was easily accessible, with an established structure in place to provide health care on an on-going basis under the management of local doctors and health care workers was needed. We had to select procedures that worked well and those requiring modification to better meet patient needs. Most noteworthy was the decision to distribute numbered cards to patients without clearly explaining how they were to be used.

Not understanding each numbered card was to be used by one person being seen by the doctor caused a great deal of confusion. The health care provider failed to collect each numbered card after seeing each patient. This resulted in cards being passed along to family members or friends allowing them to see the doctors without having to wait a turn in the long and growing patient line. This increased the number of patients seen and medicines were running out in proportion to the larger number of patients seen. The task of meeting the needs of such large number of people was overwhelming due to this oversight.

It being the very first trip orchestrated by myself, I brought $5,000 cash because credit cards were of limited use at that time in the region. The cash was to be used for the purchase of medicines, guest house lodging and food while we were there. At my hotel, I went to the lobby area and attempted to pay for the guest room but was told that I had to pay in shillings. I didn't have shillings and needed to obtain the conversation later. I immediately returned to my room, showered and headed to get a car so that I could have the money exchanged to shillings. While I was showering, my bags were left in the open area of the room and not hidden in any way. After showering I hailed a taxi and while on the way to exchange my US currency to shillings, I had the taxi driver stop along the road. His driving was making me carsick so I briefly stepped out of the car for a few minutes.

When I got back into the taxi, I picked up my bag and opened it. I was looking for something to help settle my nausea. It immediately came to my attention, money from my bag was missing $4,600.00 was gone! Unfortunately, I was not sure if the money was stolen from my hotel room while I was in the shower, or after the taxi driver stopped and I left the taxi to get some air. Feeling confused and angry, my mind began to take stock of what options were available to pursue. The money was gone and I was devastated. With only four one-hundred dollar bills left in my bag, I kept my composure and asked the taxi driver to take me back to the Methodist guest house. Paying the driver, I maintained my composure and asked to speak with the manager I told the manager I needed to speak with the police to request a theft be investigated.

The manager didn't seem concerned that one of his employees might be thief. To add insult to injury he casually informed me to speak with a police officer I would have to pay for a taxi to find an available police officer and have him brought back to the guest house. It then became apparent an investigation of any kind was not going to take place and no effort would be made to recover the money. If I tried to pursue any investigation was going to be both timely and costly. I needed to consider what to do next. My first inclination was to contact the US Embassy but decided against that option. As a government agency, this would probably be just as time consuming with little assistance and at present I needed to recover some capital.

Conveniently, I was able to find an American Express office where personal checks with the presence of a gold card would be accepted. I immediately charged $5,000.00 to cover for the remainder of the trip. This experience forced me to exercise patience to understand the thinking, and actions people take to survive. Without gaining this perspective it would be difficult to proceed in assisting the people of Africa. I was learning there were many ways of being victimized when trying to provide assistance to people living in despair. I was not alone in this position as there are people like me who want to assist the people in Africa; but have no idea how demanding it can be. You need a support structure to successfully carry out your mission as the small details often overlooked are the ones that impede the successes of a mission. Finding the right people to assist in setting up the clinic, distributing medications and health care services to make things run smoothly was the structurally support we began to establish.

The second day we used a local translator to explain one person per numbered card would to be treated, the need to turn in cards before receiving treatments or pharmaceuticals. We also had the help of Kenyan doctors and paid those a salary of fifty dollars twenty-five US dollars a day for assisting us. I incorporated the local medical students and doctors because they were more familiar with local and chronic diseases. The impact of patients receiving treatments was both significant and rewarding. News of our visit spread quickly and patients arrived at the clinic with the hope to gain relief from their pain and suffering. After being given strong antibiotics, many returned within three days, able to walk on their own two feet with hugs to show their appreciation for our efforts.

Following the corrections made with our card system, we treated one hundred people before and then an additional hundred people after lunch. These adjustments helped us to accomplish our priority to increase efficiency in dispensing medicines. We needed to dispense services and all medicines and supplies judiciously. Every night we had to pack up the medications to avoid theft. I decided that to save time and energy we were going to leave the medicine in place and trust that it would be kept safe. We clearly made the stipulation, if any supply or medication was stolen, we would pack up and leave the location immediately. We never had a problem, and the locals would spend a night just to ensure the security of our operation and the supplies.

We treated one hundred people before and then an additional hundred people after lunch, following the corrections in our system. The adjustments in the system were made with efficiency in handling medicines as the priority. We needed to portion the services wisely.

Overall, the doctors after assessing patient wellness found many to be in good health. Children generally suffered from scabies and ringworm. Many were impacted by water borne diseases, respiratory pneumonia, malaria as well as airborne diseases due to the poor sewerage system. The red soil was dry and the dust in the air from walking along the unpaved streets accounted for many respiratory conditions. While staying in Nairobi, and several weeks after returning home from being exposed to this environmental hazard, particles of red dust, was expelled from your lungs when sneezing, coughing or blowing your nose.

It became the expectation, on days off from working in the clinic, time to explore the city be set aside. On trip three we had two weekends open to explore Nairobi. For our second outing places considered were: Kenya's first National Park, the Karen Blixen Museum, and the Giraffe Centre, on the edge of Nairobi National Park, The National Museum in Nairobi, The Ngong Hills, Tsavo National Park, and Lake Nakuru National Park.

Nairobi National Park is a haven for wildlife and only 7 km from the skyscrapers of Nairobi's city center. The park is also a rhino sanctuary, which protects more than 50 of these critically endangered creatures. In addition to the rhinos, visitors may spot lions, gazelles, buffaloes, warthogs, cheetahs, zebras, giraffes, and ostriches, and more than 400 species of birds have been recorded in the wetlands Lion, cheetah, zebra, wildebeest, giraffe, rhinoceros, and buffalo roam the sun-soaked savanna here, and animal lovers can cuddle baby elephants and connect with giraffes at the excellent animal sanctuaries nearby.

At the main gates of Nairobi National Park, the orphan-elephant rescue and rehabilitation program is a must-see for animal lovers. The center cares for young abandoned elephants and rhinos and works to release the animals back into the wild. Visitors can commune with these lovable creatures as they frolic in the mud and drink from giant baby bottles.

The Karen Blixen Museum at the foot of the Ngong Hills is the former home of the famous namesake Out of Africa author. Karen Blixen, also known by her pen name Isak Dinesen, lived in the house from 1917 to 1931 where she ran a coffee plantation. Visitors can tour the well-preserved colonial farmhouse, a kitchen in a separate building, a coffee-drying plant in the woodland, and an agricultural college on the grounds. Furniture that belonged to Karen Blixen and her husband is on display, as well as photographs, and books owned by Karen and her lover, Denys Finch Hatton. Enthusiastic guides bring the story of Karen Blixen and colonial Kenya to life.

The Giraffe Centre, on the edge of Nairobi National Park, visitors can come face to face with endangered Rothschild's giraffes. The visitor center displays information about these graceful creatures, and a raised platform allows visitors to feed them at eye level with specially prepared pellets. Visitors can enjoy a 1.5 km self-guided forest walk in the adjacent nature reserve.

The National Museum in Nairobi is an educational way to spend a few hours on a city stopover. The museum displays diverse cultural and natural history exhibits including more than 900 stuffed birds and mammals, fossils from Lake Turkana, ethnic displays from various Kenyan tribal groups, and exhibits of local art. In the Geology Gallery, visitors can explore an impressive collection of rocks and minerals and learn about tectonic plates and the life cycle of a volcano. The Hominid Vault contains a collection of prehistoric bones and fossils, including the preserved fossil of an elephant. At the museum, visitors can purchase combination tickets, which include entrance to the adjacent Snake Park with live specimens of Kenya's most common reptiles.

The Ngong Hills: "Ngong" means "knuckles" in Masaai since these beautiful pointed green hills resemble the back of a fist facing the sky. The hills are the peaks of a ridge overlooking the Great Rift Valley, and many white settlers established their farms here in the early colonial days. Half- timbered houses and flowering gardens remain, but seem more suited to southern England than Africa. Several walking trails traverse the hills offering beautiful views of the valleys below. Wildlife is also visible in the area. Buffalo, gazelles, giraffes, bushbuck, the occasional klipspringer, and troupes of baboons are often glimpsed grazing along the roadside. For Out of Africa fans, the grave of Denys Finch Hatton, the lover of famous Danish author, Karen Blixen, lies on the eastern slopes, graced by an obelisk and garden.

Kenya's largest park, Tsavo National Park, is divided in half; Tsavo West and Tsavo East. Together these parks comprise four percent of the country's total area and encompass rivers, waterfalls, savannah, volcanic hills, a massive lava-rock plateau, and an impressive diversity of wildlife. Midway between Nairobi and Mombasa, Tsavo East is famous for photo-worthy sightings of large elephant herds rolling and bathing in red dust. The palm-fringed Galana River twists through the park providing excellent game viewing and a lush counterpoint to the arid plains. Other highlights here include the Yatta Plateau, the world's longest lava flow, Mudanda Rock, and the Lugard Falls, which spill into rapids and crocodile-filled pools.

Lake Nakuru National Park, in Central Kenya, is famous for its huge flocks of pink flamingoes. The birds throng on Lake Nakuru itself, one of the Rift Valley soda lakes that comprises almost a third of the park's area. The park is the home of 450 species of birds has been recorded here as well as a rich diversity of other wildlife. Lions, leopards, warthogs, waterbucks, pythons, and white rhinos are just some of the animal's visitors might see, and the landscapes range from sweeping grasslands bordering the lake to rocky cliffs and woodland.

This group of doctors was extremely adventurous and headstrong. They decided to spend a day at Tsavo National Park. Before we left I was very clear to remind them that no matter where we went, the cardinal rule was "don't get out of the car, or vehicle." Or "NO, we are not going to venture off the driven path." However, on this first excursion we had a driver who simply was not a good listener. I specially shared with him the group's idea of what was safe and the inclination to take uncalculated risks. But to no avail. Shortly after entering a Tasvo National Park, one of the doctors asked the driver if he would drive down a short stretch of land, leaving the park's chosen path, for him to take photos of the park's panoramic view from a different perspective.

It didn't matter as the driver, despite my on-going protest, left the main road and slowly drove down a small hill which immediately landed the vehicle in a gulley. The gulley was not within sight of the road and the driver asked us to get out and push. There was NO way I was leaving the vehicle to push a vehicle out of gulley no that was just not happening. Now that we were in this precarious situation, no one felt the need to exit the vehicle and attempt to push it back on the main road. Perhaps the reality of understanding the driver seemed a bit uneasy might have been a signal. Either way, the driver looked around and knowing what possible dangers were nearby, decided to take matters in his own hands.

The driver knowing the terrain quickly walked up the embankment and flagged down two rangers. Both spoke a little English, but carried out their conversation in Swahili. They kept looking around and shaking their heads as they worked to push the vehicle out of the gulley. Once the vehicle was removed from the gulley, one ranger asked how this happened. All eyes were blank as everyone looked to me to explain. Great, just great, no one listens to advice and then you are the one placed in the catbird seat. I wanted to say the driver, no one followed my directions and this group simply has a mind of its own. Although that was the truth, sometimes it's best to just let it go.

I simply explained we got off track from the main road and the rest was history.

Did the group learn to stay in the vehicle? No, as after leaving the park we stopped for lunch and they exited the vehicle before the driver could alert them to any impending danger. I wonder if he simply knew his words would not be heard. We had plenty of room in the vehicle for a quick bite before returning to our rooming accommodations, but not this group. As soon as the driver parked they had cameras in hand, and off they went to take more pictures. After a few minutes, they returned to the vehicle and climbed a small rise in the ground to enjoy a picnic lunch. We arrived safely back to our living quarters and of course the highlight of the days evening conversation was the adventure with the vehicle and the gulley.

Still inquisitive as to Kenyan life style and daily routines, this group was interested in visiting Biashar's Business Street in downtown Nairobi's shopping district. The Yaya center was a well-known shopping mall most patrons are local residents. You had to press an entry button for some shops. One was a jewelry store owned by an Indian woman who was extremely prejudiced. She was kirk and not anxious or even open to showing me any items. She would have been different if my companions were not in attendance with me, as her clear distain for anyone of color was clearly displayed by manner and demeanor. This seemed odd as most patrons would be people of color. Walking around the center it was obvious that most shop owners were either Asian or Indian. You had to look hard to find any business that had an African owner. Most vendors in the downtown area were African run and operated as rent for store space must have been quite high.

We then went over to the Uchumi supermarket and experienced a paradigm shift in Brand items back home. A package of potato chips looked nothing like a Lay's potato chip bag. The contents were made from potatoes but the chips were cut like Red Robin French fries left to dry after being flattened by a rolling pen. These unrecognizable imitations of the real deal were prevalent throughout the store. The most unusual occurrence was when the electricity went out and people continued to shop. When we asked the cashier about this he remarked that it happened often and not to worry as the electricity would come back on for a while and possibly go out again.

On the second weekend excursion, the two doctors made arrangements to visit the Nairobi National Park–"The World's Wildlife Capital"." It is a short drive out of Nairobi's central business district is the Nairobi National Park. Wide open grass plains and backdrop of the city scrapers, scattered acacia bush play host to a wide variety of wildlife including the endangered black rhino, lions, leopards, cheetahs, hyenas, buffaloes, giraffes and diverse birdlife with over 400 species recorded. Visitors can enjoy the park's picnic sites, three campsites and the walking trails for hikers. We were warned to remain in our transportation vehicle and no matter how safe and inviting it appeared the threat of real danger was everywhere.

But did anyone listen? That would be a NO. Now this might seem like a simple request but it came directly after reminding the doctors about the recent dangerous predicament we were placed in, just last week. Directly due to not listening to the stated and restated cardinal rule: "Don't get out of the car or vehicle." The groups desire to find a tranquil spot to enjoy our packed picnic lunch basket was their only concern. I strongly suggested we wait and use to picnic tables located near the entrance to the park. Once again, the doctor's opted to stop at a somewhat isolated area that featured a phenomenal view of the park and was a photographer's dream come true.

I again reminded them what might appear to be a safe location could actually present secret perils that would not be revealed until a potentially unsafe encounter presented itself. Modeling the value of following the cardinal rule, I remained in the vehicle and stood watch hoping all would go well as they took photos after ignoring all warnings to stay in the vehicle. My mind was racing to the headlines that might appear in the morning paper. The feature article would be filled with this juicy news report. Headline: Visiting medical volunteers after prolonging the lives of many impoverished local Nairobi citizens; lose their own by providing meals for local animals in the Nairobi National Park. Statements would include: numerous reports of park guide's repeated warnings to not leave their vehicles, the medical volunteers were more concerned with snapping pictures, and were themselves snapped up by aggressive and hungry animals.

Safely returning to the car, I felt a sense of relief. Returning to the Methodist Guest House we noticed a pamphlet that had been placed underneath a few magazines. After reading it over, we noticed listed among the many species of wildlife living in Nairobi National park included: buffalo, giraffe, lion, leopard, baboon, zebra, wildebeest, cheetah with over 100 mammal species, 400 migratory and endemic bird species. Who knew? The wide-open grass plains with acacia trees provide areas where any form of life could easy hide and be unseen until it was too late to escape a very bad scenario. Although the panoramic view was lovely and the wind -blown tall grass reminded one of the waves in the sea, this was a potential graveyard without any headstones.

Our efforts in Mathare were successful in many ways. Of the glitches, we encountered running out of medicines limited how many patients we could see and treat. Calculating the amount of medicines brought and then dispensed in relationship to the patients seen our next trip would use this information to help extend out medical services and possibly leave some medication with Florence.

Trip Four – Meet Dr. Sam and Dr. Teresa

Welcoming me back home and work on the KFXX the FAN sports radio station with Mychal, he opened our program with my second trip to Africa. As this working relationship with the local radio station initially sparked my interest in the situation in Rwanda, it also provided an out of the box concept for raising awareness of this situation while at the same time raising funds to be used for a pending fourth return trip to Mathare, Kenya. Mychal asked me to share how things went and if I had any plans to go back. I focused my dialogue on my third trip and how two local doctors and two local nurses and Elsa Marie accompanied me.

Mychal then asked how my return trip to the slums of Mathare was financed. I acknowledged Howard Hedinger's financial support. As it was my intent to make the public aware of my planning a fourth trip to Africa, Mychal's line of questioning helped to keep the public interested in my efforts. I took time to carefully present the facts showing we could provide health care to the residents of Mathare at a different location than trip two. This was the perfect opportunity to help listeners understand some successes and some frustration in conducting a clinic in the slums of Mathare. I reviewed our goals and continued to ask listeners for their assistance in carrying out the foundations action plan.

As my main objective for upcoming trips was to secure funding, I began to look outside the box for ideas that work. What could I possibly do to meet the expenses for a trip? It had to be the direct result of down-sizing. As my personal NBA memorabilia included items that were of great sentimental value, these items would be of interest to many potential buyers. Looking over my prized memorabilia I first selected my treasured John Havlicek belt buckle he gave as gifts to his twelve teammates the night of his retirement. Remembering how Clyde made mention he liked one of my paintings, we spoke about making an exchange with my LeRoy Neiman race car painting, for an authentic Clyde Drexler's signed and worn Olympic jersey.

I then gave thought to a more enterprising idea, worn and signed NBA game shoes. Would collectors, fans or anyone be interested in signed game worn NBA shoes? When speaking with the Trailblazers and visiting teams, the NBA players was very agreeable, as it was a way to provide funds without impacting their personal cash flow. All funds collected and used for expenses we incurred in Africa to include salaries, transportation, housing, and food. We were limited in our medical supplies and making a little go a very long way was the order of every day patient care in the temporary clinic set up.

The need for more medications, medical supplies, and willing volunteers were topics discussed as well as putting questions regarding finding a long-term site for a clinic. Addressed, were details about constructing a building versus finding a building that would meet our current needs with the opportunity to expand if necessary. This campaign proved well received and when one listener asked when and where a meeting would be held I planned for a 1 pm meeting at my restaurant.

Dr. Richard and Dr. Teresa Gipson along with twenty other health care providers were in attendance. Dr. Gipson immediately took charge in recording ideas and was the most vocal about her determination to be an active supporter and participant. Dr. Richard's personality was more subdued but his medical expertise and genuine concern was also unmistakable. Both remained after the twenty interested health care providers left and it was determined a total of thirteen, including Sam, Teresa, Elsa Marie and Jay would be joining me on trip four.

The next step was funding. I contacted the NBPA and requested my retirement severance pay. Using all the $25,000 for the project I purchased airline tickets, rooming accommodations, medical supplies, and brought $5,000.00 in cash to cover all incurred expenses. Local drug chains also donated medicines and supplies as well as selling materials at discounted prices. Jay was able to gather a large quantity of medicines to treat scabies and ringworm, and antibiotics for the well know respiratory conditions such as pneumonia and malaria. I contacted the school principal, to set up a date and times for this visit and they extended an open invitation to return to Mathare and their school. This trip's expenses were over $30,000.00.

We left Portland, Oregon, and landed in Amsterdam staying overnight before arriving in Kenya the following late evening. Airplane food not being either filling or appetizing, once our luggage was picked up, we handed to immigration check-in. We soon were greeted and participated in the well-known and expected five-minute government break. These lapses in service should only be five-minutes long but somehow extended to anywhere from fifteen to twenty-minutes – on a good day. From there we secured ground transportation which made you feel like you were on the auction block as every available taxi and van driver was fighting to be selected to provide you their services. With such a large group, we selected two vans. Once moving along the road to our housing we knew it was late to be served a meal and when we asked one of the van's driver what was nearby he suggested a local chicken restaurant.

The food was said to be good but there was one caveat, it was located in downtown Nairobi near the city Centre. Our driver cautioned the group about getting out of the vans as a group. He strongly advised one person, me, place the order for the group while the rest remained in the van and waited for me to return with the items once the order was place, paid for and ready for pick-up. The group decided to make their own selections and exited their van as if they were still back home.

Before entering the restaurant, a group of ten young boys rushed past the group attempting to grab purses. The driver warned the group to hold on to their possessions and quickly enter the restaurant. He scared them off running after them to give the group the ability to safely enter the restaurant. The incident ended without anything happening. The restaurant menu although it featured chicken was very colorful and we took a few minutes to read over some of the items listed:

Ugali (Cornmeal Staple)–The undeniable most common Kenyan food staple is ugali – usually made from cornmeal that is added to boiling water and heated until it turns into a dense block of cornmeal paste. Ugali has the consistency of a grainy dough and the heaviness of a brick. The waiter explained for many Kenyans, ugali along with a small amount of cooked vegetables or saucy stew is a normal meal.

MENU

Kenyan Pilau (Spiced Rice)–Pilau is a glorified combination of rice cooked with flavor bursting spices like cumin, cardamom, cinnamon, and cloves. The fragrant rice is fantastic to eat with a form of meat stew and a few slices of fresh tomato and onions. Biriyani is another form of spiced rice that is a popular Kenyan food on the coast.

Sukuma Wiki (Collard Greens / Kale)–One of the most popular vegetable Kenyan dishes is sukuma wiki (known as collard greens or a form of kale in English). The nutritious green leafy vegetable is often cooked in oil with a few diced tomatoes, onions, and flavored with a sprinkle of mchuzi mix (Kenyan food secret flavoring salt – MSG) or stock cube flavoring.

Kenyan Stew- Kenyan stew can include several different meats: beef stew, goat stew, chicken stew or any other animal stew. Kenyan stew dishes might also include a few other base vegetable ingredients such as carrots, peppers, peas, or potatoes. The sauce is usually formed from a light tomato base and accented with onion, salt and pepper and that essential mchuzi mix.

Nyama Choma (Roasted Meat) – Pride of Kenyan Food– Any Kenyan food list is not complete without a mention of nyama choma, also known as roasted meat. Goat and beef are the two most common forms of nyama choma, but chicken (kuku choma) and fish (samaki choma) are also valid choices. Fat and the grizzle from the meat is the choice part of the animal, and are often consumed with a quick dip into a pile of salt for extra flavoring! It's also possible at many places to get the "fry," – the fried meat variation.

Matoke (Plantain Banana Stew)–Matoke is originally a dish from Uganda, though it is widely available and popular in Kenya as well. Plantain bananas are cooked up in a pot with some oil, tomatoes, onions, garlic, chilies, meat (optional), and lemon juice. The bananas are cooked until they become soft and begin to form a thick sauce with the other ingredients. The result is a delicious dish that is reminiscent of boiled potatoes in sauce and excellent to eat with rice, ugali, or a chapati.

We felt adventurous as well as hungry and those two combinations almost always result in a pleased palate. You will try anything and it will satisfy your hunger, therefore, it must be good. We ordered the chicken. When our food arrived, we were not disappointed. The waiter told us what to look out for when and if we ventured downtown Nairobi during the day versus downtown Nairobi at night. Days later this advice became the topic of conversation while traveling to the Clinic. "If you value your wallet, don't go downtown at night." We listened to this advice and got back into the awaiting van.

Feeling much better after a pleasing meal, we settled in to get a good night's sleep. The morning came soon enough and we left the Methodist Guest House to meet the principal at the school. The drive to the school was filled mixed conversation about their interest in exploring downtown Nairobi early in the day. Daytime downtown is a hustling bustling kicked up a notch version of any metropolitan city with criminal forces strongly entrenched in the fabric of the life.

Locals know where to go and what to avoid moving along the danger filled streets and side parking lots. Vendors set up tents next to established business establishments and fill the dirt paved parking lot areas eager to sell items and to provide an additional threat from the local lost boys. Their methods vary but the outcome is always the same, we were often told, "If you value your life take care while venturing downtown Nairobi either day or night."

Unlike the original group, the lost boys were another long-term consequence to the Hutu and Tutsi conflicts. Orphans became heads of households due to the increase of HIV infections contracted from rape. Today this term refers to young criminals who prey on anyone they observe with intensity and select and their target. This reminded me of the old-time cartoons where the screen is black and appears that no one is there until or unless two white eyes with black pupils are open. Once a target is selected the eyes open joining in the attack on their victim. Sometimes bumping into you and running fast after snatching your purse, their accomplice races by you on a bike to throw off your concentration and prevent having a one on one encounter with a sidewalk.

Today, the term "Lost Boys" describes those boys directly involved in gang activity and known for criminal and violent behavior. Easily identified by their aggressive actions a local juvenile facility has been established outside the downtown city center. The facility sits alone with warthogs frequently seen living among the vacant property landscape. To visit and enter the facility you must granted permission after writing a formal request. The dark walls and drab interior although stark, provides educational programs to rehabilitate offenders placed by a court appointed judge.

Morning breakfast was bland but necessary to get through the long day ahead. I didn't pack any items from home as I wanted to make sure we could pack as much medical supplies and medications possible. I did decide to do include some food items on my next trip for breakfast has long been acknowledged as the most important meal of the day.

The Methodist guest house was in a neighborhood with other houses, with nice landscaping to give the appearance of an equally pleasant interior. The front of the house had a small community living space, off the one side was a hallway with two to three small bedrooms and off the other side were two to three small bedrooms. In the center of the house directly behind the living space was a small dining area with a small kitchen directly behind it. The kitchen had a pantry, small work table, a stove and oven, and limited countertop space.

Outside the school were children who were denied attendance due to a lack of admission fees. Their desire to enter the barred facility could be seen on their disappointed faces. Although they looked like lost sheep every day as we passed this school they were present as if looking for that one chance to come inside and attend school.

Noticing this group of the kids standing outside the school who wanted to come inside the gate and learn, we opened to gates to let them inside, after treating the enrolled students and staff. They were very well mannered and both curious and interested to find out why we were there and what we were doing at the school. These young African kids understand, very early, the only chance they would ever have a better life was by getting an education. Education was valued they did not need to be told and reminded going to school to obtain an education was important. They knew this to be so by experiencing their living conditions, holding out a hope for a better life and future.

We rode in the ricketiest bus imaginable to and from the guest house every day. We never seemed to have a problem with the bus transporting us from the guest house to the clinic. The bus seemed to have the desire to provide optimal service, but in reality, that was not possible. Its ability to make simple turns around a corner was not consistently performed, and occasionally several of us would get off the bus and walk. At times, when the bus came to a halt, unable to go on, most of us got off, but not except Dr. Teresa. She would sit on the bus hopeful it would resume its mission so she won't have to walk along the dusty road. I'd laughingly say, "Teresa, get your butt off the bus."

The school campus was in the format of an outdoor school using the rectangular format. As you entered the property if you turned immediately to your left the upper grades occupied the first six classrooms. If you walked straight ahead, you were in the primary grades with six classrooms. Continuing down the width of the rectangle and turning left were the administrative rooms and three storage closets. It was on this side to the school campus we asked if we could use to set a clinic to provide health care to patients.

With the doctors setting up in thirteen different stations and with the changes made to the patient numbering in place, we were easily able to treat one hundred sick people per hour, easily. Dr. Sam, Dr. Teresa, the local medical students and nurses treated people by using the time-tested numbering system. We paid the medical students ten dollars per day and the doctors were paid twenty-five dollars per day. Those fees were well above the average salary of three hundred dollars a month that doctors earned. Using the African doctors and nurses the stations at the clinic a bit tight but everyone worked together to pick up the slack. We took breaks during the weekends to explore Nairobi and some went on a safari, whereas I would mostly take the time to catch up on much needed rest and ready myself for the following week of work. This trip turned out to be one of many that Dr. Sam and Dr. Teresa were a part of. Their attendance was a blessing on every trip.

The Kenyan doctors we employed were happy to earn their salary for a day's work. I noticed the Kenyan doctors had a hardened demeanor about them, in terms of bedside manner. I associated the demeanor with the tremendous daily suffering but, I could not ignore the behavior and expressed the importance to stand up and greet each patient. Many of the patients were scared and intimidated as they had not visited or seen a doctor in their lives. The local doctors quickly complied by standing up, extending a handshake and saying a welcome in the patient's language. Offering them a seat, the doctors were then advised to ask questions not only why they were there but personal ones that helped make the make realize there was a personal interest in them. Although this might not have the usual way things were done, for us it was important to stress the need to and make patient feel comfortable such as much a priority as providing a diagnosis of their health.

We were working as a well- tuned engine by providing the most important services to the people one fly remained in the ointment until we met Florence. The language barrier was greatly impacting our effectiveness and efficiency during our trips and with the volume of people treated; we needed the aid of a translator. Florence filled that missing void for us and was more valuable than one could ever describe.

I met Florence in the most technically advanced method known to man. I stepped into a crowed and yelled at the top of my lungs, "Does anyone speak English? We will pay for translators." Florence stepped forward, along with Kimmy a young woman about eighteen years old. They were a tremendous asset to our mission and it was much easier for us to communicate with the patients. Everyone worked well together and supported one another, with even funny moments fit in-between.

We could have used more translators. But with Florence we know had someone from the area who was not only abreast of the local languages but also the customs and being a health care provider was familiar with local diseases and medications. She and the rest of us would laugh at times during the day which made the hours seem to fly by quickly.

The pharmacy was soon identified as the most vital aspect of our efforts. Everything relied on having the pharmacy organized and running smoothly. Once seen by a white doctor patients were convinced whatever medication they received would cure them of all their ailments. As penicillin was not a widely available medication, it was extremely effective. One man approached Dr. Sam and requested a pill that would improve his eyesight. With such confidence being also evident with warm smiles and affectionate hugs, our efforts were rewarding. As 7:00 am to 7:00 pm was the normal work day, Dr. Sam and Dr. Teresa were tireless in their dedication to helping improve the lives of many who would otherwise have suffered and possibly victims of an untimely death.

The powerful antibiotics were responsible for many miracles. Patients we did not think would live to see another day would come back to let us know how much better they were feeling and how appreciative they were. Health care in Africa is a different process altogether. If you enter the hospital for any reason you are not released until you pay the bill in full. In addition, no meals were provided and family members or friends were those you counted on for this assistance. There were many days Florence took me to the Kenyatta Hospital to release patients by covering their medical expenses. It was on one occasion that I noticed a night guard placing a heavy lock and chain on the doors to the nursery. When I asked if there was a problem with babies being stolen, he explained, "Just the opposite, babies were being dropped off if a family could not take care of them."

Of the most unforgettable and incredibly inspiring events of this trip was the knowledge and availability of medical support can influence and change lives in a meaningful way. Three young boys brought their extremely ill mother to the clinic. She was in a very dire state. Following an examination, it was determined she had pneumonia, a respiratory infection. Even if an accurate diagnosis had been made by any medical professional, treatment required an antibiotic, Erythromycin. Since such medications are not readily obtainable due to their expense, the potency for an antibiotic to work is increased. It is also, required that any and all needed medications be provided following a medical diagnosis given by a medical professional.

Both Sam and Teresa did their best to make her comfortable while asking Jay to locate the dosage needed to treat her. Jay, who oversaw the pharmacy, checked to see what antibiotics had been included in the medications we had with us. The most powerful antibiotic we had was Erythromycin, and this was given to the mother by means of an injection. Sam and Teresa informed the family to make sure the mother rested and then the family left the clinic. Three days later, much to everyone's surprise the family returned and the mother walked without assistance and looked like she had been resurrected from the dead. She came back to the clinic facility to personally thank Sam and Teresa for making her get well so she could care for herself and her family.

Treating about two hundred patients a day we safely kept the supplies and medicines in place. This system allowed us more time to treat patients without the procedure of breaking down and setting up over and over. The pharmacy was a very important element of the clinic, and it had glitches because of the penmanship of the doctors when writing out prescriptions. I had to advise the doctors to write more clearly so that the pharmacy could provide the proper medicines.

We adjusted to the local custom of afternoon tea breaks at eleven o'clock each morning and then lunch breaks at one O'clock in the afternoon. I felt uneasy about this custom under the conditions of people sitting and standing, severely exposed to the sun, etc., while our staff drank tea. It was custom, and perhaps they understood. The restrooms; were horrendous as they were just elevated wooden outhouses with holes in the ground. They were hot and full of flies, and the stench was strong enough to make one lose his lunch well before approaching to enter one of them. Many of us attempted to hold our urine and bathroom needs the entire day and until we reached the guest house. That was quite difficult and it meant you'd go all day without drinking anything.

Trip Five:

With our large group of health care providers returning to Portland, Oregon, after a two week stay with me in Africa, the news of our fourth trip was widely spread. Listeners to our KFXX the FAN sports show called in and asked for more details and updates without any probing or prompting from Mychal. He followed their lead by asking for more information and inviting listeners to phone in. I shared my concerns regarding finding a more suitable location to accommodate the many patients who travel many distances to been seen by our health care providers.

Listeners called in to get more updates about the foundations action plan and many wanted to know how and where to make donations. I mentioned, after meeting with KFXX executives, my intention to hold a car raffle using my Porsche 928. Financing for the fifth trip was made possible with the ability to use daily airtime sending out information about the price of tickets, where and how to purchase them. Reminders regarding the date, time and location of the raffle were given daily airtime as well. As this trip, would be taking fifteen medical health care providers funding to cover expenses was a priority. It was shared after holding our most recent meeting with a group of fifteen interested volunteers the cost of our previous trip was $30,000.00, which sponsored thirteen volunteers

The drawing was held at my restaurant and chose someone in attendance to draw the winning ticket as to guarantee the raffle was not fixed or the winner predetermined. My prized Porsche 928 soon had a new owner and the funds were used to set the date of the fifth trip, purchase airline tickets, make rooming reservations, and take care of any other details requiring attention. Any expenses not covered by the proceeds of the raffle were covered by me, including my airfare, accommodations and incidentals.

Our previous trips were in Mathare, a collection of slums in Kibera the largest urban slum in Kenya that is heavily polluted by human refuse, garbage, soot, dust, and other wastes. All slums within Nairobi; Kibera, Mathare, Kawangware, Kiambu, Korogocho, and Mukuru, are contaminated with human and animal feces, due to the open sewage system and the frequent use of "flying toilets". The lack of sanitation combined with poor nutrition among resident's accounts for many illnesses and diseases. We made plans to work in Kibera.

Trip five our first medical clinic set-up in Kibera came about two years later. I contacted a Kenyan doctor, Dr. Stephen Ndombi's. Ndombin's, made arrangements for us to set-up our clinic in a local church. He said it would be the best place because of the spaciousness and opportunities to set-up more stations than we had previously done. A meeting was arranged in the afternoon at my restaurant inviting all interested person to attend. Dr. Sam, Dr. Teresa, Jay and I were present along with ten health care providers and one dentist. I shared a new option for holding the clinic and our progress in meeting our goals listed in our action plan. The space offered was a church with a larger working space with only one downside. There were no indoor bathroom facilities only outhouses.

After each of my previous visits I took the time to review our action plan and determine what improves were being made and which direction to pursue. By this fifth trip I felt comfortable being in charge and delegating assignments to the volunteers matching the needs outlined in our action plan goals as well as meeting the needs of patients seen. Organizing stations, replenishing medical supplies and medicines, employing local doctors and nurse assistance, were addressed by me enabling me to make decisions and effect changes where needed. But on this trip, I did not have to follow the lead of others. If people came in and the doctors felt the treatment required something beyond what we could do, I could decide to have them taken to a hospital.

Our health care services continued until we ran out of medicine, after working ten days, one or two days before our scheduled return home. The lines of patients were still ever present and we would have to pack up and sneak out the back door to avoid having to explain this and feel uncomfortable. The local doctors and nurses continued to see as many patients as possible and could explain the clinic was going to be shut down due to this fact. Building on the success of our first medical clinic set-up in Mathare provided invaluable insight into daily life and Kenyan culture, aspects that govern the structure in this slum. It was perplexing to discover even though we traveled to Africa to provide assistance that would positively impact lives, not everyone was supportive of our success. The high rate of poverty adversely affected some people causing frustration and desperation which manifested itself in their becoming opportunists. There was no "pay it forward," some individuals sought their own interests without consideration of consequences that followed.

This unfortunately was the case with the minister in whose church we planned to use for this trip's clinic. The minister of the church, greeted us and immediately gathered us together to inform us of his agenda for our providing medical services. Respectively listening to his sermon like speech it astonished me his blatant controlling manner. He shared a schedule of our expected daily routine as to where and how we were going to examine, diagnosis, treat and prescribe medication for the people seen. The only point we had in common was seeing as many patients as we could. When the minister finished this communication with us I took charge and immediately set the matter straight. I made it clear, the minister's instructions did not take into any consideration of our plans and itinerary. His plan was for us to work separately and not as a group, walk the slums of Kibera and visit patients in their homes.

Perhaps he wasn't aware we were well -versed in the facts about Kibera the largest slum in Africa housing somewhere between 500,000 and 1,000,000 residents. Many living in this slum are HIV positive or have full-blown AIDS. Clean water is scarce, diseases caused by poor hygiene are prevalent, any of which present many dangers and potential health hazards to our health care providers if they were to follow his agenda. Being in charge I clearly thanked him for the use of his church as the facility to house our clinic and pointed out separating our team and walking the slums of Kibera would not allow us to provide adequate services as intended. In addition, safety was also to be considered and the crime rate in the area was extremely high with reports of assault and rape. If this understanding could not be agreeable we were prepared to use an alternative location.

After stating the only agenda, we were going to follow, it became obvious he considered our presence only as a means to help his own interests of acquiring new parishioners and increase financial support for his congregation. The idea of not having access to providing services to his local parishioners was the key to us remaining at the church.

The Mathare slum in Kibera was extremely dangerous, and we would never have considered as an option going door to door there. Safety notwithstanding, lack of running water would serious endanger both patients and health care providers. I advised him that we were ready and willing to set-up in his church and stay together as a group in exchange for treating the parishioners of his church first. We did just that, and it was beautifully orchestrated.

All the doctors worked to diligently during that on the very hard during the week, especially since two nurses whose airfare and expenses were paid for left working in the clinic after two days. They did not tell anyone they were leaving and returning to the United States. We were getting ready to pack up our supplies for the day when we noticed they had not come down for breakfast. Imagine our surprise when after knocking on their bedroom door and getting no response, we opened the door to discover they had packed up and left without a word.

The local doctors and nurses arrived shortly following this conversation and were pleased to find most were fluent in English which was a great help. We set up twenty-five stations and Jay once again set up and efficient pharmacy. Treating about one hundred people per hour and approximately one thousand per day we safely kept the supplies and medicines in place. Although these numbers were up building in the ability to help patients the lines were extremely long. As agreed we saw the parishioners of the church first and we stayed two weeks.

One of the nurses was unfortunately locked inside an outhouse. She screamed repeatedly, and in her struggling haste to free herself, she fell on the ground; but not in the hole. She was a tough woman and a good sport about it. She carried on but after having to remove her articles of clothing, scrubbing and taking appropriate measures to avoid bacterial infections of sorts.

Outside of the children, many of the patients came to the clinic for treatment of venereal diseases and respiratory problems. Our previous trips were opportunities to evaluate how the operation of a temporary clinic could be improved. It made me more aware of the need to locate and acquire permanent property. With more stable and established accommodation, we could provide health care on a regular basis with local doctors and health care providers. We worked on identifying procedures that worked well and those in need of adjustment to better match efficiency of patient to doctor interactions.

One evening after returning to the Methodist Guest house, Dr. Sam and I stood outside and looked upward at the night sky. As we stood outside gazing upward, Sam continued to share astronomical information I was previously unaware of. The African southern sky is a starry realm richly sown with star clusters, bright and dark gas clouds, and galaxies. From this array five specimens of each class of object have been named the celestial Big Five. The representative of open star clusters is the Southern Pleiades. First amongst the globular star clusters is omega Centauri. Bright nebulae are represented by eta Carinae Nebula. The mysterious dark nebulae are represented by the Coal Sack. And the most splendid galaxy of them all is our own Milky Way Galaxy.

The Big 5 are visible anywhere from within the southern hemisphere. Two of the Big 5 lies in Carina, one lies in Centaurus, and one in Crux. The fifth – the Milky Way – lies in a narrow band dividing the sky in half. The brightest parts of the Milky Way are in Sagittarius, Scutum, Norma and Carina. All five objects will not be visible at the same time. This is mainly because the Milky Way is a large object and it will take more than one session to see it at its full extent. Being in Africa between late June and late August in the early evening we could see the Big Five and the Milky Way.

I asked if stars move in the sky. Sam explained stars do move but very slowly over the course of the night. The entire sky rotates. The motion of stars is quite small at a few or a few tens of km/s. However, they are situated several light years away from us. Let me give you an example. Let a star be situated about 10 light years away from us (note that this is a nearby star) and move at 10 km/s. Then, in 100 years, the movement is approximately 30 billion km. The distance of the star from us in comparison is 90,000 billion kilometers. So, its motion in 100 years is so small compared to its distance that we see the star in the same spot in the sky. However, if one waits for a few hundred thousand years, then one can see the constellations change.

At first I found it difficult to concentrate on Sam's discussion about stars. He then added the constellations we were presently viewing were used by early traveler to navigate the seas and land. Now that was impressive to me. It reminded me of how I needed someone as my compass to guide me through many of the travels I would undertake over the years and those yet to come.

We completed our mission in the projected time of the trip and hired a group of kids to clean up the church. The minister, who had proven to be quite a character from the beginning, was seemingly upset with us. I was initially unsure as to why because his parishioners took full advantage of being the first patients to be treated during our stay. He promoted his church and convinced others to go to his church on Sundays because of the services we were providing. They were all treated first, which the agreement stipulated for us to treat others on his property.

When we had packed up our supplies and proceeded to clean up, at the end, he told us that we did not have to hire the group of kids to clean up and that members of his congregation should have been given such Jobs and paid for their services. The minister showed his anger by presenting us with a bill when our kids finished cleaning up. As this was a matter for discussion, there was no monetary compensation given to his church members and it was now time to think about additional clinic options after the conclusion of the trip.

It was becoming clear that some of the people in Africa had selfish motives of their own and looked for ways to modify our arrangements to fit their secret ulterior motives. Some residents in Mathare had the impression all Americans had money and looked for ways to profit from it. The area was so impoverished people did anything they could to survive. It seemed to be a justification of their actions to foster their survival.

School children going on picnic

While our mission was to be there to help people, I wanted to ensure that it was on terms that were agreeable to me. We had to make sure money was used in the most efficient way possible. I learned unexpected expenses caused the people we came there to assist receive insufficient medical support and food services. Obtaining a suitable location was a concern we needed to find a viable solution to.

Kids getting ready for medical checkup

TRIP 6

Returning home to Portland, Oregon, I arranged a meeting with Dr. Sam and Dr. Teresa When meeting with Dr. Sam and Dr. Teresa we brainstormed some possibilities to find a more permanent location for the clinic. Having met and worked with Florence, I phoned her on a regular basis and asked her to do some fact finding on possible sites to consider for this upcoming sixth trip. With our newly established connection with Florence, I made a sixth trip with my own financial backing, on my own with the sole purpose of finding a location.

In my thirty-plus trips to Africa, each layover held some interesting adventures to recall. One such trip, after meeting my daughter Dana for breakfast in DC, she was working as an intern for Donald Dell, I was headed to Kenya. Checking in at the airport I noticed a large group of armed Special Forces police in several locations. Our original layover as to be London, England but the flight was redirected to Belgium. Of all the layovers during my thirty-three trips to Africa, this was by far the most memorable. Our plane was scheduled to land in London, England, but due the threat of a terrorist attack, we were diverted to Belgium.

Passengers were upset as connecting flights were missed and arrangements made months in advance for a well-deserved vacation were now completely altered. Luggage was somehow misplaced and I feared this problem was somehow going to impact me. A positive was I was traveling alone and did not have to meet anyone until I arrived in Kenya. My connection was changed to Belgium. The city was celebrating the Brussels Flower Show: As was the custom, this was held every October at the capital's Basilica of the Sacred Heart. The beauty of this floral extravaganza, with the local buildings featuring water displays, magnificent floral arrangements, and rare plants was breathtaking.

The fragrances from the variety of beautiful flowers that lined the streets filled the air. My three-day layover was made enjoyed simply due to the festival and all the many activities. These temporarily distracted my attention from my concern that with each passing day my luggage as it had not arrived. During these three days, I made a concerted effort to find a store where I could get some clothes that fit and could replace those still in limbo. To my dismay, there were no shops with extra-large clothing to purchase. My wardrobe would be limited at best. My luggage never did arrive in Kenya or later returned to my when I returned home.

This trip began with lots of rain. Rain in Kibera flooded much of the region and resulted in sticky and thickened mud that caused shoes to be sucked right off one's feet. The roads were a muddy mess and traveling was very difficult as well. Meeting with Florence, we concentrated our efforts on finding a suitable location for our clinic. I brought medicine that Florence could use in her clinic. She took me to visit the clinic she was currently running. Before getting on the road, being concerned about the road conditions I remembered telling her it might not be a good idea to attempt driving on the muddy roads and we should go later or catch a ride. I feared her vehicle would get stuck in the mud. Florence insisted on driving, and just as I anticipated, her vehicle got well stuck in the mud. When we finally made our way to the clinic, I was in utter amazement that the clinic had been set-up and functioning out of such a building.

The size of the clinic was thirty feet by thirty feet, twelve feet by twelve feet, at best; with a tin roof, tin siding, and no running water or apparent electricity. She had only one bed and only one health care worker to assist her. I told Florence that the space was not going to work for us because we needed a larger working area with updated equipment that was more modern. We began to search for a space around the slums and in doing so; we looked at countless places, which resulted in our declining them. After driving around, the streets in Kawangware we drove along a main street with many locals walking by.

On this thoroughfare, we noticed a building under construction with a sign reading: No longer under construction. An older gentleman was walking around the perimeter of the site as if checking on something. I asked Florence to stop the car to determine who this man might be and why there was a sign posted in front. The man on the premises was the owner who was checking to see if any of the materials left on sight were still there as he had just recently run out of money to complete the project. The building located in Kawangware a slum with a prime location. Being on a busy main street it was close to small markets, a medical, the Kawangware Primary School, Kawangware School and Kawangware Academy.

The land owner's finances were strained as building materials could not be left unattended for long at any time as there was a high probability of them being stolen. This required the owner of the property to have to camp out overnight until the building was completed to protect materials from would-be-thieves. Building foundations were also a concern. The ground in Kibera is literally composed of refuse and rubbish. We had to check to ensure this dwelling was not being constructed atop unstable ground so as not to collapse whenever flooding occurred, which is regularly. Sometimes even well-constructed buildings are often damaged by the collapse of nearby collapsed buildings.

The features of the land in Kibera are firm not giving into pressure and cramped. Most roads have limited vehicle access located at the bottoms of steep inclines. Construction efforts became more difficult as all materials had to be carried to the building site by hand.

The builder's unfortunate lack of funding worked to our advantage. We were able work a deal where if we provided him the funds for completion, he would provide us with a lease. The building was approximately three thousand square feet with running water, electricity, solid cinder block construction, and concrete floors, and it was simply a tremendous value from what Florence was ever accustomed to. The building was two stories and had an apartment design for the upstairs. We had at least five beds and a maternity ward. We negotiated with the landowner who was unable to provide funds to complete to work on the potential facility for the clinic and school.

When the building was completed we purchased gas generators to ensure electricity would always be available. It was the general rule at any time during the day electricity would be cut off with no idea when it would be turned back on. While walking at the local mall we found a local artist's mural work on display in the window. After finding out who the artist was and how to contact him we hired him to paint colorful murals on the walls in the clinic and school. The ordinary bland walls needed to help inspire and motivate those who entered the facility to become comfortable and well-cared for. The murals help to foster the meaning of hope with each painting being beautiful and colorful. The staff was both impressed with the results and the residents in the community were anxious to take advantage of all this new facility had to offer at their disposal. The pharmacy itself was larger than the entire clinic Florence was operating in.

Trip Seven

After arranging for the completion and renting of the building for the clinic I returned home to Portland, Oregon, and immediately began to consider how to finance the operation and set-up of the clinic. A local school was sponsoring a walk-a-thon where people were asked to sponsor a student for walking in a school walk-a-thon. Students walked around a high school track and earned money for each lap they completed. You could sign up to sponsor a student for as little as five cents a lap to higher donations per lap or contribute one sum. This gave me the idea of doing a fast.

I shared this idea with Dr. Sam and Dr. Teresa and they both agreed it was doable and offered to join me in this fund-raising event.

For trips eight and nine, funding from fasting proved successful. After presenting the President of American University, Cornelius Kerwin, our proposal to fast on American University's campus he readily agreed. By giving permission to hold these two fasts at American University and help sponsor these events we managed to gather significant proceeds from our efforts for two consecutive years. Our efforts resulted in raising twenty-five thousand dollars each year. The details seemed clear enough but we honestly had no idea what would be involved in NOT eating a single morsel of food for any extended period of time.

The first few hours were easy, and I soon gained a deeper appreciation for why they call the first meal of the day breakfast. By noon reality began to set in as our stomachs began to growl and present the unanswered question, "Where is the beef?" Drinking lots of water was a true blessing. Numerous bottles of water filled us up averting hunger pains until our bodies as it managed to fill us up and avert the pangs of hunger until our bodies no longer questioned if the next meal was coming. By day three we were more comfortable with the lack of solid food, appreciated and enjoyed the refreshing feeling water provided.

We were housed in a camper located on the campus of American University in Washington, DC in the quad. Dr. Sam Richard, Jay, Dr. Teresa Gipson and I were extremely grateful for being allowed to hold this funding event in such a beautiful and congeal setting. We spent most of the seven days thanking our sponsors for their support and giving Project Contact a platform that drew attention to our connection with Africa to sponsors and onlookers. Both fasting sessions were supported by a variety of people who either lived on campus, worked on campus or were curious about the media's coverage media news of our efforts over both each seven-day fasting periods. For every day, we successfully fasted, individuals signed up to donate funding starting at one dollar up to a hundred dollars a day.

Fasting required we expend as little energy as possible. The most difficult part of this challenge experience was moving around the camper to use the facilities and not allowing yourself be drawn by the inviting aroma from the food center which tried to entice our bodies to give into the temptation to eat something. Remaining in the camper for an entire day was very confining and at times it was necessary to step outside and feel connected to the outside world. Mary Graydon center was located directly across from our camper offering free view of students and faculty grabbing a bite here and there. It was apparent that our sense of smell is quite in sensitive when you haven't eaten for any period of time.

We worked at ignoring any visual stimulus, the clear distraction of people eating while sharing a meal and conversation on the lush green grassy area, or walking past the camper to attend a class or appointment. We focused on what needed to be purchased to make the clinic operable both while we were working there and when we returned home and left the management to Florence. But the true highlight of our conversations which It became part of our daily routine was to list the food items we were going to consume when the fast was over. Each morning we compared the list created that day with the days prior. It was like creating a shopping list or identifying the name of the restaurant to make a reservation. We were deciding how to place our order directly after our fast ended. These discussions were always followed by drinking a large bottle of water.

On the final day of the first fasting fund raising event experience, our first agenda was to head directly to a local restaurant. Looking over the menu we didn't allow the waiter to leave but gave him or order as quickly as possible. Our senses were willing and highly stimulated to receive all items ordered, but unfortunately, our bodies were not prepared and comply. We didn't realize time was needed to gradually reintroduce solid food after not having eaten for seven days. Although we felt ready to resume our normal eating routine after this long-awaited activity, our bodies failed to communicate a warning. We didn't realize how going from fasting to eating a regular meal was going to be accepted by our bodies Therefore, after savoring the flavor and texture of all food items our stomachs sent a very clear message, this was not going well. After eating we began to feel strong stomach cramps and immediately rejected our meal.

After our second time, we were more prepared and drank light broth and slowly allowed our bodies to adjust to taking in food.

Denying our bodies of nourishments by choice is not in itself a comparable experience to anyone who has no access to food. However, the feeling of starvation or deprivation of a daily meal, whether large or small, does force one to re-evaluate poverty. You can understand, empathize and become motivated to lessen the suffering of others living anywhere in the world from a lack of food, housing, and the necessities of life.

Fasting will bring that directly to your attention. The question as to what you can or will do about making a difference redefines your priorities and defines who you are as a person. It was an eye-opening experience in many ways. One began to have an understanding for what a human body requires to maintain daily activity and the body's ability to shut down until all efforts for nourishment are addressed in a way that is meaningful and not distressing to one's normal eating habits.

In total over my thirty plus trips to Africa, once we established the Ray of Hope Clinic and School, a variety of structures have been put into place to ensure continuous on-going operation of both. Two years following our fasting funding efforts I met with American University's School of International Service director, Lou Goodman, to suggest a student exchange program to be connected with the Ray of Hope Clinic and School. Google: American University students Nairobi, to see the efforts and achievements made from the university and its students since starting the program in 2005. An apartment was rented to house visiting students who spent one semester in Nairobi. Students worked with Florence in the clinic and help set-up and provide structure for the school and were paid a money stipend to cover expenses and working with Florence in both the clinic and the school. The total stipend allotment for a semester was $10,000.00 for purchasing items if sent from the states would be confiscated before any delivery was possible.

Being introduced into the African cultural norms was an on-going adventure. Students were surprised to find milk and eggs housed outside of local gas stations inside a large white cooler that was not connected to any electricity. Shopping for general food stuffs in the local supermarket could be interrupted at any time if the power went out and the store did not chose to use a generator to restore power. These power outages were generally accepted as the norm and business was conducted as usual. Finding name US brands was another challenge. When looking for potato chips there were no packages labeled Lays. Local potato chips were packaged in clear cellophane packages labeled Potato Chips. These chips were thick and not seasoned and could almost be mistaken for flattened steak fries.

Any and most items were overpriced and many well past the sell by date. Meat shopping was clearly a lesson in getting what you pay for. If vendors had an outdoor stall, many flies visited the area and made the available items less appealing. Indoor stores housed their meats and fish in coolers and without the flies the price of items was doubled. Fresh fruits and veggies were also in outdoor markets and was suggested purchase only if they had skins. Bananas, apples, pears, melons, oranges, etc. were considered safe for consumption.

They developed a new appreciation of beef. While driving out in the rural section of the city one weekend a local farmer was butchering a cow. It was hung on a large stake and cut open to bleed out. From there the farmer with the help of an assistant took down the cow and proceeded to cut it into sections. Driving away from this graphic scene was enough to lessen one's desire to have hamburger or steak for a meal.

Some of my visits were for longer periods of time. A short visit was two weeks and an extended trip would be for a month. Finishing the construction of the clinic presented several challenges. Rooming accommodations were not changed from using the Methodist Guest House to local hotels and sometimes a room extended by local families. Finding workers who were consistent and qualified and trustworthy was the first. Once the building construction was completed we focused on landscaping. We found a rock nursery and purchased a large load of rocks to prevent the dirt from being carried into the building. After a load was delivered, the rocks were stolen and we had to replace this with another load two times. Plants and flowers were taken by local residents for their homes.

Having access to clean drinking water is always a concern especially when needing to sterilize medical equipment and flush toilets being used by staff, patients and later by students. Purchasing large water tanks alerted the community that water was going to, available. After buying water to fill the tanks; this water was stolen by local residents. We paid for multiple deliveries of water until the community was aware that the source of water was not unlimited and if depleted as it currently was the clinic would be able to service the students, staff and patients as originally intended. It makes one wonder how the concept of a garage sale managed to be embraced by the locals without the benefit of financial compensation? Did this appear to individuals as putting out one's trash which means it's available for anyone to take to reinforce the adage: one man's trash is another man's treasure?

David Parris' father approached me while I was working out in Gold's gym. He told me his son a current high school student, wanted to meet with me about obtaining equipment for the Clinic and School. My interest was piqued when the equipment he wanted to share with me was a water filtration system. After meeting with David this equipment as a viable solution for obtaining safe drinking water and was available for purchase. Remembering the problems, we continued to encounter to gain access to clean drinking water this idea was most appealing. It had been the case following several attempts to buy large tanks of drinking water which proved unsuccessful, this equipment just might. In the past when water was purchased from the city and placed near the Clinic and School, locals would come by at night and steal the water. I was willing to give it a try, to eliminate our frustration in meeting the need to provide clean water for both the clinic and school.

David explained if we purchased three containers 500 gallons of filtered clean drinking water would be produced a day. Water was poured into the containers from the local water source and dispenses clean drinking water. Locals would need to bring the water to be filtered and receive clean water when they did so. This was most appealing in resolving two problems: the need for clean drinking water and locals stealing clean drinking water. We took time to calculate the cost and developed an action plan on how funds could be raised to make the purchase. It was arranged for a school raffle to be held featuring warn and signed NBA game shoes to raise money to purchase three filtration containers. Students sold raffle tickets to win worn and signed NBA players Chris Paul and Blake Griffin, on the Los Angeles Clippers, game shoes.

While the clinic was under construction, Sam, Teresa and I met to determine what furnishings, supplies, and medicines we needed to purchase. It was necessary to take into consideration the most common health problems in the area, review patient needs and the services to be provided, the skills and competence of the health care workers, and the resources we would be able to use to purchase supplies and equipment. A budget was used to estimate what quantities of items needing to be purchased as it was important to order the right quantities. It was most important to develop a budget. At this time, there were no donors and all expenses were financed by the three of us.

Florence had employed seven workers at this time, and we voiced our concern as to how salaries, would be included in the budget of on-going expenses. Although, the clinic was to be "free" in theory, if known as such by the community we would see endless lines of patients daily waiting outside the clinic doors. Therefore, we posted information regarding fees for medical services and set up appointments with patients who had some ability to pay. The service fees were determined by which items were used to provide services, what medications were dispensed, and arranging an affordable payment for services.

To support the operation of the clinic and school I send Florence $10,000.00 per year. This covers rent, medical fees for personal illnesses, school administrative costs, replacing clinic medical supplies and equipment. Debra Drayton, a former high school schoolmate, generously provides additional financial assistance to Lydia sending $150 every three months for expenses, after viewing the Project Contact Africa web site. Over the past twenty years, Florence has made it an annual ritual to celebrate the positive contributions of the visiting doctors and medical care providers at her living quarters. Lydia was employed as her house maid. Every year Lydia worked tirelessly to make meals and ensure everyone had a good time. We often spent a few minutes to catch up on how things were going in her personal life. She was very disappointed when her fiancé failed to show up for their scheduled wedding ceremony. Her additional Job responsibilities included working as a maid cleaning the American University student apartment. I send Lydia $400.00 each month for rent, school fees, uniforms and household supply expenses.

With the most recent change in her circumstances she was looking to move into a different living arrangement. Not having the needed funds to do so, we discussed how I could help. It was arranged to move her into new housing and provide furnishings. Her current living space was limited to a shack 12ft x 12ft built with mud walls, a corrugated tin roof with a dirt or concrete floor. Providing funds to continue to support her relocation to another mode of housing continues to this day. Despite improving her former living conditions, she has not invited me to visit as she insists it was too dangerous. Florence later employed Lydia to work in the clinic and school.

Our clinic and school cook is another great hire by Florence. Over 60 years old she adopted a three-year old orphan two years ago. Her child is now five and attends the Ray of Hope School. As the cook, she prepares breakfast seven days a week for all students and staff. Local families are often included whenever possible.

Many of our patients came from a variety of trades. Farming was something that always amazed me as the few products did not appear to be home grown. In a casual conversation one day, I asked if living outside the city limits of Nairobi might be an option for many of the locals living in the slums of Mathare and Kibera. I was told that many of the inhabitants in Mathare and Kibera had been farmers who could not compete with the items sent over from the United States. Local produce could not be sold in local markets to compete with United States subsidized food. The cost for such items was less than local farmers were requesting and there adding the economic impoverished state of the local citizens.

Vanessa came to the Ray of Hope Clinic due to two family medical concerns. Her mother was in the local hospital requiring treatment for pneumonia. For any patient to be released from a hospital procedure or stay a fee is charged and must be paid in full.

Vanessa was unable to pay this bill and came to the clinic requesting assistance. It was on one of our trips that this situation came to our immediate attention. I went to the hospital with Vanessa to pay the charges and once released we made sure her mother was seen on a regular basis to check on her recovery status.

During one of these visits Florence took note of a medical condition Vanessa's son had which required surgery. This procedure was quite expensive and something the clinic was not qualified to take care of. The NBA players were visiting and coming to the clinic one morning were made aware of the seriousness for Vanessa's sons surgery and immediately addressed the issue. World Meta Peace and I arranged for the surgery to be paid for which included the operation and hospital stay fees. When Vanessa's son recovered, he attended the school and funding for school fees, uniforms and supplies have been sponsored by me. I send $3,000.00 a year to fund school fees for her son.

Evelyn is a single mother with six children living in a typical shack, 12ft x 12ft, built with mud walls, a corrugated tin roof with a dirt or concrete floor. Due to being located right next to a sewage system all six children were suffering from chronic respiratory diseases. Her son who was of school age walked to the school every day with his youngest sister. Although she was not school age and eligible to attend, would sit next to him every day in class. She sat quietly, wearing shoes that were worn and several sizes too large for her small feet, an old and dirty dress that was too large, and her hair disheveled. She would not leave her brothers side and having taken notice of this we made the decision to get her shoes, a school uniform and provide daily meals. Every month I send $200 for rent and sponsor four of her six children paying for school fees, uniforms, supplies, transportation to local schools and daily meals.

After this little girl came to my attention I offered to sponsor her. This would not be possible if I excluded her other siblings. Therefore, knowing about the on-going health issues I looked for new housing accommodations for Evelyn and her family. It was arranged after determining the cause of her six children often being sick a change in living quarters was not only needed but would also provide a long-term solution to her children's health issues. Shortly after the family moved the children's health improved. Now they attend school regularly without being sick and we sponsor them financially to continue to live in these upgraded conditions.

The Ray of Hope Clinic was established to: Diagnosis and treatment of common diseases and conditions – including malaria, skin diseases, respiratory infections, anemia and malnutrition. Provide preventive child health – including growth monitoring, immunization and nutrition. Deliver reproductive and sexual health – including antenatal, postnatal and delivery care, family planning and sexually transmitted disease prevention, diagnosis and treatment of STDs. The treatment of injuries – dressing wounds and immobilizing uncomplicated fractures, minor outpatient surgery under local anesthetic and providing basic first aid in emergencies. Arrange for and schedule health education and health promotion – for residents in the community. Space was set-up to make provision for a small delivery room for births and a few short stay beds for very sick patients, and basic laboratory facilities for conducting simple diagnostic tests. I later bought Florence a car which served as an ambulance to convey patients to needed health care facilities.

Nairobi's Kenyatta National Hospital is the main referral for medical treatment. It is also a teaching center and Sam expressed how impressed was with the young doctors who worked with us in the clinic. He mentioned these young doctors were as qualified in not more qualified to work in any health care facility in the world. This helped explain why so many health professionals leave Kenya and find employment abroad.

Medical supplies and equipment to procure included: Supplies – items that need to be replaced on a routine basis, including: disposables, single use items, e.g. disposable syringes and needles; expendables (sometimes also called consumables), items that are used within a short time, e.g. cotton and wool, laboratory stains and tape; reusable items, e.g. catheters and sterilize able syringes; and other items with a short life span, e.g. thermometers.

Equipment – capital equipment and durable items that last for several years, e.g. beds, examination tables, sterilizers, microscopes, weighing scales and bedpans. Refrigerators with two compartments: The main compartment – kept at 0-8°C (or 2-8°C) – for vaccines and some drugs. The freezer compartment – kept below 0°C – for making ice packs. Required the need for non-interrupted electricity. A gas generator was added to this list of necessities.

To provide safe running water: used daily for cleaning, disinfection and sterilization, we purchased clean water (preferably filtered or boiled) for cleaning, disinfecting and sterilizing on a regular scheduled delivery arrangement from the city. This was quite expensive and required an alternative solution that would be more cost effective.

Three months following the opening of the Clinic, we had to reevaluate cost and expense. Despite the $50,000 of donated medicine from the NBA helped tremendously but did not offset the rent, salaries, upkeep and maintenance, and replacement of medical supplies, equipment, and medicines. The financial compensation from paying patients vs. expenditures was in the negative. It then became apparent that any idea of the Clinic being self-sufficient needed to be revised. Reality set in and reminded us of the need to constantly monitor accounts payable against accounts receivable.

Like any new business venture, you obtain the space, the facility, the merchandise, but the upkeep and replacement of items doesn't meet the rent and overall management of the venture. It was then agreed that funding would have to come from us and an all effort to solicit funding was going to have to be explored.

Florence Muyundo took us to see how other facilities in the area operated. We spent quite a lot of time visiting orphanages. We had an additional allotment of food supplies that we could offer to other facilities and Florence knew two that we could support. Shortly, before the end of a long day we stopped at Mother Teresa's Sister of Charity Children's Home. Florence tried to prepare us for the range of physical deformities we would be seeing, but no words could accurately describe what we saw.

The children ranged in age and their twisted bodies prevented them for moving about without assistance. Statistics show a third of the children under the age of five are stunted with more than 15% underweight. The sisters who lived and worked there were very committed to meeting the needs of their charges. Each child did their best to communicate with us their pleasure of our being there.

At facility was neat and clean yet the children need constant attention to changing clothing, toileting and feeding. The cupboards were stocked with limited food staples and our ability to provide rice, beans, and gains for a few months was clearly needed. The attention given to each child was beyond taxing. During our four-hour visit, constant attention was given to keeping floors clean and items available for use. The rooms were small but clean and neat. Special attention was given to the floors as many of the children could not walk and maneuvered around by crawling on the bare floors.

The orphans showed their comfort with their surroundings by reaching out to both give and receive hugs and embraces. They were truly dependent on the sisters for everything. Florence made arrangements with the administrator and we were able to donate a large quantity of food items and cash money to support these efforts. Unlike some of the orphanages we visited, you could tell that the sisters cared about the well-being of the children and were not repulsed by their grotesquely deformed physical conditions.

Each child was spoken to with a calm and quiet tone. All responses were acknowledged to indicate the value and level of understanding being conveyed. When visiting any facility such as this one, you leave with mixed feelings. Do you blame the parents for abandoning their child? Do you appreciate the efforts expended daily by the care-givers? Is it a blessing that parents are not abusing a child who by no fault of their own was born with such a disability? Do you take stock of the situation and provide a long-term support base? We opted to provide on-going support through the food distribution program. When possible financial support was also included in the monthly support of this facility.

We also visited *Mama Ngina Kenyatta Children's Home in Baraka, Africa:* This orphanage housed an average of 75 children and 20 babies. Space in the orphanage was limited and resources scarce. The children depended largely on the generosity of private donors, a small staff, and volunteer care givers to meet their basic needs; such as food, water, clothes, bills, and educational supplies.

Being in the Mathare slum community environment, concern for child development is of no consequential importance, however outreach efforts are resulting in families becoming more empowered to support their own children. The key deterring factor to outreach efforts is that families involved in the outreach program relocate and it is difficult to provide consistent monitoring and care.

Vocational training at Mama Ngina's included: Basic computer skills using donated computers Technical skills including: tailoring, dress-making, carpentry, masonry, mechanics, electronics, computer training, household skills and beauty. Providing Job placement support for high performing students Partnerships with local colleges, universities and vocational facilities enable continued studies past secondary school and financial support to help children aging out of the home to start small businesses.

While visiting Mama Ngina Kenyatta Children's Home we noticed as we walked around the nursery the babies were frequently left unattended and crying for attention. Florence mentioned she knew a young girl of eighteen, Edna, who would be interested in working in the nursery. Having been orphaned herself she had a tender spot in her heart for other orphans who needed as much love and attention as they could be given. I arranged to pay Edna t$200.00 a month to work with the infants in the nursery. When the administrator learned of this financial compensation I was asked to provide the funds directly to the home and they would then disperse it to Edna. When I declined, the home let Edna go and Florence employed her in the clinic.

While at the clinic Edna met Rosemary, who was working there and who had a married daughter living in Italy. An acquaintance of Rosemary's daughter was looking to hire an au pair. Edna was interested and Dr. Teresa and I provide funds to obtain a visa and complete all paperwork to help Edna accept the job. After three payments to a Nigerian agency we realized it was a scam and were contacted a reliable service agency. Airline fare and all required fees were paid by me and Edna was soon off the Italy. She is still working as an au pair, has completed her college education and speaks Italian fluently.

Trip Seven:

Still working at KFXX the Fan sports radio station I began to think outside of the box for alternative ways obtain funding and advertise our efforts in Africa. Working on acquiring medical equipment and on-going needed medicines I broadened my public speaking efforts to increase public awareness. Mychal and I had a conversation one day while on the air about memorable moments while playing in the NBA. I mentioned John Havlicek's final game as a Boston Celtic in the Boston Garden. He mentioned how valuable the belt buckles he gave to his team players must be. I began to think of other items that might be of interest to sports fans. Warn and signed game shoes, portraits signed with letters of authenticity, game jerseys I had hanging in my restaurant, just to name a few ideas for exchanging donations for items of interest.

Relying on my efforts for financial support, Dr. Sam and Dr. Teresa continued to meet and plan our next steps to establish a reasonable budget for expenses and building upkeep and maintenance. Sports fans showed more interest than originally considered and we were ready to finalize plans for trip seven. Despite the many times we had traveled to Africa, that long flight with close seating arrangements always poses stress and strain on my limbs. On this trip the passenger sitting in the middle seat in my row wasn't feeling too well and coughed quite a bit. As there were no alternative seating arrangements on the long flight this made contact with this passenger inevitable.

Landing in Amsterdam and resting the night before flying on to Nairobi my throat started to feel scratchy but I tried not to give it much thought. The first morning of trip seven, immediately after we arrived, I became ill and could not get out of bed. I was disappointed that I would not be able to start working at the clinic as my primary reason for coming was to help the sick. But here I was sick. My room appeared darker and drearier than the night before. My arms and legs ached and my head was spinning. I vaguely remembered having a conversation with both doctors who checked me over and assured me that with some rest I would soon recover.

Drifting off into a fitful sleep I opened my eyes to view seven Lilliputians walking down the hallway into my bedroom. They quickly climbed on top of my bed and after hauling up several bundles of netting proceeded to cover my body with it. "They spoke several languages with smatterings of High and Low Dutch, Latin, French, Spanish, and Italian." Thank goodness English was the language they choose to speak in my presence. I soon realized that this feeling of being securely anchored to a surface was exactly like how Gulliver felt in the account recorded in Gulliver's Travels.

After I was secured with the netting to the satisfaction of the seven Lilliputians they precede to scrupulously inspect each area open between the netting. Using small cone shaped stethoscopes each open area was inspected. After each area was examined they verbally shared their findings. Each one could be clearly heard to say, "You'll be okay, nothing serious. You will be better in two days." Once they had completed their inspection each one worked together to gather the netting. Once it was secured they jumped off the bed and exited the room walking down the hallway. What seemed like a few minutes later both doctors returned from working in the clinic and stopped into check in on me? I asked them if they had spoken with the Lilliputians who came to see me. They looked at each other, and after holding in laughter, smiled and said, "You must really be sick." But in two days I was much better and able to work in the clinic.

The local orphanage facilities came to my attention on trip seven. There were the financial expenses needed for renting the space and salaries for helpers. After realizing the need to provide a stable facility for new mothers and children who were left alone after their families died from AIDS. Over time the children of HIV positive-AIDS parents were living longer and needed adult support and care. Visiting the local facilities showed the desire to meet these needs was evident event but man power 13888 to carry out a successful operation would require on-going funding.

Local funding for the current facility was limited and with the help given by Florence we were able to hire helpers and set up schedules of shifts that met the needs of the current children in the wards. We began to understand the children needed twenty-four-hour care and the increase of consistent funds would have to include salaries, food stuffs, medical supplies, and clothing. Florence organized and coordinated all efforts and was instrumental in supervising effecting positive changes they made for a smoother operation. With the expertise of a local doctor we identified medical care-givers. Nurses, medical students and local doctor's fees for services included daily stipends, meals, transportation and housing when required to meet the needs of the community were identified and paid for. In addition, we could hire care-givers who later became permanent employees for the Ray of Hope Clinic.

Now that we had the space established it was time to put our clinic into operation. We needed medicines and supplies so I began reaching out for help. I contacted, Purvis Short, whom I told of what we were attempting to accomplish. He advised that I contact Billy Hunter, the then executive director of the NBA Players Association, which I did. Billy said it was good to hear from me, which confused me because I did not know him, or did not recall being introduced to him at any time. He said that he knew of me and the struggles I had in the NBA. He also stated that he'd seen a special on ESPN about the clinic and my trips to Africa.

The player's association is an organization that assists the players in many ways and has the best interest of their careers as the cornerstone of what they do. Billy mentioned that even though I had been through difficult periods in the league, I had never asked for anything or sought any help. He looked at the clinic as an opportunity to help people globally and not just me. He organized donations and generated over $50,000 worth of medical supplies for the clinic. Those donations were the building blocks in a new era of our clinic. As a clinic, we had a start.

With a new building and supplies the clinic had become operational. I was proud of our efforts and thought the finished product and success would be ensured by all our solid ground-work and generous donations. As things go in Africa, our mission was far from easy. Instead of the clinic operating with the two people I had envisioned, Florence hired eight employees. There was certainly a necessity for the number of employees but they also required salaries.

The clinic was not advertised as a free clinic, but if people couldn't pay we did not turn anyone away. We had envisioned an offering of treatment at a minimal cost, which could in turn pay; for the required medicines and future operational expenses. Most of the people couldn't pay, or were not able to pay the full amount, however minimal.

This would deter people in the Nairobi hospitals from asking for the treatment they needed because they were not allowed to leave until all expenses incurred during a hospital stay was to be paid in full before being released. There was an incident where a man was not allowed to leave a Nairobi hospital for six months. He had to rely on his family to gather the money to pay the bill and even bring him daily food because it was not provided by the hospital. We understood the value of our services our clinic extended to the community People couldn't pay for quality health care and seemingly serious health issues that were common to treat in America were relieved. Women received in clinic childbirth health care instead of delivering babies in their homes, which saved lives.

Each morning the children would approach me and wait to see what I brought them to eat from the Guest House. I would always take hard boiled eggs, sausages and biscuits. As most families in Kibera don't eat three meals a day this early morning breakfast was truly enjoyed by the children. I watched as they played and waited for them to join me. The first food item to be given was sausage. It was heartwarming to see how each child would share any food item before asking for another helping. This display of comradery explains how these children felt they were part of a whole and not a mere individual. As a unit of one the need to look out for each other was always put first. As for the sausages, I simply could not stomach them. The children loved the sausages the most which made being able to share this treat with them extra special. The hard-boiled eggs were next followed by the biscuits. This was the only guaranteed meal the children would have for the day.

Soon my morning visitors were Joined by friends and within a few days there were several children coming and going to hopefully receive something to eat. I approached Florence with a proposal.

Could it be possible to feed these fifty children consistently and get them into an educational program? We interviewed teachers and hired two Alfred and Evelynn. We changed from sausages, eggs and toast to serve a purple colored porridge. It looked a bit unappetizing to me but the children loved it. Schooling in Africa comes with heavy financial obligations. Students must pay for books, materials and uniforms. Families were unable to provide meals for the day therefore paying such fees was not an option. We then gave some thought to starting a school program to be held on the floor above the clinic. There was adequate space and with two teachers we gave it a go.

The kids, native Swahili speakers, carried limited conversations with us in English. They were always interested in money and this added to their natural inclination for catching on to math patterns. They enjoyed learning tricks to times tables and solving simple teasers with ease. It was exciting to see them learning in a different way and help them to enjoy school more by sharing these little secrets with them. The kids were learning from this small interaction with American educational strategies, but I was beginning to understand that even though the visiting teachers were providing a wonderful learning opportunity with great impact, my efforts would be best served providing medical care.

Interviews were scheduled and preparations arranged for teachers and students to attend classes immediately. Time for students to be measured for uniforms, the daily ordering of food stuffs, and the purchasing of both school and medical supplies quickly fell into place. It also became necessary to provide housing for Florence, Lydia and Vanessa. Relocating to be closer to the Clinic and School was necessary as no one had a car that could provide transportation to and from the clinic both for patients and staff.

I was able to purchase a car for Florence to carry out all administrative duties supporting the activities needing to be addressed use. It was interesting that without the use of credit cards and establishing a line of credit to make monthly payments paying for the car upfront using cash was required. Apartments were one thousand (including utilities) and were rented for Florence, Lydia, Vanessa and visiting

American University students. Later each care-givers family was provided on-going financial assistance.

Trip Eight: School

With the clinic working smoothly as we drove back to the Methodist quest house I began to wonder about opening a school. Although many children attend nursery school, or kindergarten in the private sector until the age of five, for the residents of Kibera that is not always possible. Nursery school lasts one to three years (KG1, KG2, and KG3) and is financed privately as there is no government policy regarding mandatory attendance. Primary school is for students from six to seven years of age, to thirteen to fourteen years of age, and is free in public schools. However, all students are required to wear uniforms, pay fees for lunch and school supplies to attend. Attendance in a preschool is a key requirement for admission into Standard One (First Grade.)

To matriculate to the secondary level there is a national examination at the end of Form Four-The Kenya Certificate of Secondary Education (KCSE), which determines those students who can move forward. A Joint Admissions Board (JAB) is responsible for selecting students who enter public universities. To provide more opportunities for local students to go to school I opened the Ray of Hope Clinic and School in 2008. Working along with Florence we reviewed the space available and included fifth students.

I purchased furniture—student desks, bookcases, student chairs, bulletin boards, chalk boards, teacher desk, and teacher file cabinets. Purchase student supplies: notebooks, pencils, pencil erasers chalk, chalk board erasers, writing paper, staplers, staple remover, three hold punch, student writing tablets, pencil sharpeners, single hold punch, paper clips, file folders, address labels, copy machine, office file cabinet, receipt-voucher forms.

Student school fees, transportation, uniforms and supplies are supported. In addition to feeding students and staff during the week and on the weekend, we have added meat to weekly meals. Meat is and expensive commodity and rarely included in the daily diet. Florence is able to purchase meat for one meal each week for students, staff and local families from a local. The location of the clinic and school in Kawangware is ideal as supermarkets are within a safe walking distance.

We investigated the Educational Services provided in the primary grades, The American University exchange students organized and gathered classroom instruction materials. We then funded all costs related to: direct labor for teachers, curricula and instructional materials, including textbooks, workbooks, and other supplies; furnishings: including desks, chairs, bookcases, and blackboards, bulletin boards, and equipment. Food Services- Meals for staff and students provided breakfast, school lunches, this included weekends. The most unexpected challenge was the maintenance of the floors in the school. Solving this enigma proved to require out of the box thinking. A special paint was needed to prevent erosion due to corrosive agents used on the roads and surfaces in the community. Walking into the building shoes carried this agent and locating a special paint to counter the effects of the corrosive required a lot of research and fact finding.

Having some history with the Portland Public School System it gave me the thought to see whether adopting a sister school in Kenya might be doable. Having to return my concentration on the clinic, this idea was placed on the back burner with a medium level of heat. We organized the medicine into packets and printed cards with numbers to be passed out to the people to see the doctors. The doctors saw the patients in order of those numbered cards and diagnosed illness, identified treatment and wrote an appropriate prescription. The patients would then go to the makeshift pharmacy area to obtain the needed medications.

Although a variety of fund raising events have proved successful. Over the years the expense of educating fifty students has increased with additional impediments to overcome considerations. A one room multi-grade school house model works, but once you have six-year-old with thirteen-year-old students, it becomes increasingly difficult to meet the academic rigors needed to go on to High School. In addition, monthly and yearly school expenses the expenses increase to include transportation to five different schools and these the fees increase to $250 a year per student. High school fees run up to $1,000 a year per student. As children outgrew the educational program at the Clinic and School, fees financed included: uniforms, school supplies, and meals. Fees included uniforms, supplies, meals and a tutoring space for daily educational was started.

On one of my annual trips October of 2013, I met Cheryl Meyers through Dr. Teresa Gipson. Dr. Teresa had invited Cheryl to join her on a visit to a school she was going to be sponsoring, located in a rural area outside Nairobi. Cheryl not comfortable traveling 50 – 60 miles outside of the city Centre in primitive conditions was interested in helping in Africa and Joined Dr. Teresa for a lunch meeting with me. As Dr. Teresa, would no longer be giving financial assistance to the Ray of Hope Clinic and School the opportunity to include her in working with me was fortuitous. We spent the lunch time talking about the clinic and school and arranged for her to come and see how things were going.

Students were now requiring a more structured and formal educational experience from the two-classroom set up currently in place. The students and Cheryl instantly bonded and she replaced Dr. Teresa in both support and financial assistance. Planning and coordinating funds and decisions regarding both the clinic and school are mutually shared. Cheryl has a 501c3 non-profit designation and this has replaced Project Contacts 501c3 status. My monthly contribution of $1,500.00 is sent to Kawangware Kids to share funding for the Ray of Hope Clinic and School.

Fulfilling her desire to reach to more students and families in Africa, and transferred her financial support from Project Contact Africa. Dr. Gipson started her own program and transferred her financial support. Cheryl Meyers stepped in to continuing financial support. Cheryl choose Kawangware Kids as the name of her 501c3. Kawangware is located about 15 miles west of the city Centre, housing approximately 800,000 residents of which 65% are children and youths. Most live on less than one dollar a day. Safe drinking water is scarce and water supplied by city authority is not available every day and is very expensive.

Yearly excursions provide optimal times to hold meetings for on-going operation of clinic and school. During these meetings in

Nairobi with Cheryl and Florence we review the operating budget, reevaluate staff performance, consider which students will be assigned to matriculated schools, calculate transportation fees, uniform and school supplies increases, noon time meal fees at schools, and budget for end of the year celebration and excursion. It's always a pleasure to arrange for outings as the students are well behaved and so appreciative of our efforts. The opportunity to see what adjustments are pending due to the matriculation of students is important to meet the ever-changing needs of both the clinic and school. Status of medical equipment and supplies, including medicines is addressed based on patients treated with the adjustment to provide a supply of medicines most frequently used in the clinic. Florence maintains records on each patient seen and determines what health concerns are most reflected in patient visits.

Our current concerns are providing a program that will prepare students who do not qualify for college admission for employment opportunities. This along with providing Florence with more administrative assistance will be addressed when I can return to Nairobi.

Dr. Sam having heard of the Ngong Hills and as I nicknamed him "Daniel Boone" he wanted to check it out before returning home. We drove 30- minutes from the main city to reach the Ngong Hills, peaks in a ridge along the Great Rift Valley, located southwest near Nairobi, in southern Kenya. The word "Ngong" is an Anglicization of a Maasai phrase "enkong'u emuny" meaning rhinoceros spring, and this name derives from a spring located near Ngong Town.

The Ngong Hills, from the eastside slopes, overlook the Nairobi National Park and, off to the north, the city of Nairobi. The Ngong Hills, from the Westside slopes, overlook the Great Rift Valley dropping over 1000 meters (4,000 feet) below, where Maasai villages have been developed. The peak of the Ngong Hills is at 2460 meters (8070 feet) above sea level.

We left the Methodist Guest House at 9:00 am and arrived at 9:30 am as we were told the best time to go hiking was early in the morning, as later in the day the temperature could get cooler and quite windy. As it was our first time we went with a guard. Our guard took note we were wearing long pants and long sleeved shirts. He mentioned to look out for army ants or "siafu" – safari ants. These were much larger than pinching ants and don't attack in the same way, they will bite, but don't climb all over you. They might ignore you. Pinching ants once they get on you they don't bit at once. They climb inside your clothes and you never feel them. They seem to give a signal and suddenly they all start biting at once. Having very large pinchers, once they grab hold they don't let go.

We were also glad we were dressed appropriately, as it was cool, with our light jackets and comfortable walking shoes. Sam was more interested in the hike but I was keeping a look out for those army ants. Our guard walked with Sam up the seven mills and were warned us of possible attacks on the way. That reinforced my desire to sit on a large rock and wait for their return. The seven-mile trek took Sam to the top of the hills. After resting for a few, what seemed like seconds, I looked down and saw army or pinching ants crawling up my pant legs and felt them biting me. Jumping up I brushed them off and immediately decided to catch up with Sam and the guard.

The relief from the ants could not compare to the view. It was well worth the effort and quite spectacular. We remembered to bring a video camera and tried our best to capture this moment on film. We had to decide whether to walk down the seven miles or hire a taxi to take up back down and then back to the Methodist Guest House. As our guard was in great shape we decided to walk down and then hire a cab. Daniel Boone was not tired at all; he seemed to be rejuvenated by the exercise.

Kibera is the largest slum in the continent of Africa. Limited accommodations such as access to running water, electricity, and toilet facilities continue to be were a daily concern. The streets remain unpaved. Average walking traffic results in red dust permeating the air streets were unpaved and the red dirt filled the air as your feet walked along the roadway. During the rainy season, the steady downpour of water creates large trenches along the side of the well-traveled paths. Some are large enough to more than adequately provide housing for a family of three. During the rainy season, that lined the walkways were so deep they could adequately provide housing for a family of three.

The average Kenyan walks five-miles to work and after putting in a long twelve-hour day, walks five-miles back home earning the average salary of three dollars a day. No one voices voiced any complaints about wages as the unemployment rate is was so high and people lined up outside a business ready and able to replace anyone who might feel bold enough to question how things were being run.

To demonstrate what simple tools are used to complete a task and provide financial support, I once watched as a barber welcomed a client to sit in a shaky looking bar stool, near the road outside in the sun. With nothing wrapped around him to prevent the hair clippings from falling onto his clothing. While engaging in a lively conversation, he proceeded to use a hand-held metal hair cutting tool to cut his clients hair. I was able to recognize this as such after having had one in my home growing up. I watched my father using one such tool to cut my uncle's hair before electric trimmers were available. I hadn't seen one in years but instantly recognized this as such. The client sat patiently in the shaky chair and allowed the barber to practice his skills.

Nights proved to be exceptionally dangerous from criminal entities and flying bathrooms. Sanitation being under par, it was known human waste was placed in plastic bags with the method of disposal being throwing these out in the streets. Poverty was a dilemma to be remedied and lacking public supported provisions for street lighting and ample law enforcement protection, this created the need to be cautious when moving about the city. The lack of street lights necessitated the use of candles to provide light to guide you on the streets.

Another cause for concern was the possibility of fires. Candles were a major supply of great significance every day. People used candles as they dangerous. You might think this was a direct result of poverty and the lack of street lights. Candles were the order of the day. People used candles as they walked the streets and in their homes for lighting. Many cooked meals in the small confines of a structure that one would hardly call a room. The smoke from the cooking process carried permeated the air and leaving the otherwise-white pupils of one's eyes a stark yellow in color.

Walking down the street, the onslaught of flying toilets proved the worse danger to be regularly encountered. Due to poor toilet facilities, plastic bags filled with excrement would be tossed into the air. Some bags landed on roof tops, but the majority lined the streets to be avoided in the darkness. The evening air was filled with the stench of human excrement despite the presence of many varieties of flowers that could have been the source of pleasant floral fragrances.

Being well run by Florence, in 2007 the clinic was in the fifth year of operation, Billy Hunter and the National Basketball Players Association; contacted me about the possibility of having a very large feeding program in Africa. Billy knowing that Feed the Children wanted to use four NBA players Maurice Evans, Theo Ratliff, Ron Artist, and Etan Thomas in a commercial to feature Feed the Children. For filming the commercial, Billy Hunter made the deal that thousands of tons of rice, beans, cornmeal and heating oil would be delivered every month and Project Contact would distribute it to the residents in the slums. Over a three-year period, because of Billy and the players we fed close to two million people.

We did not randomly feed two million people. We established very rigid rules for each family who received food stuff every month. If anyone sold any food item they would no longer qualify for this program. If a failure to adhere to any rules was made known, the person providing evidence of this infraction would receive double the portion of food previously given. It was amazing to watch women, some not weighing one hundred pounds soaking wet, carrying heavy bundles of food stuffs on their heads, backs, and arms with a joyful facial expression knowing that as they knew they would be able to feed their families.

When Feed the Children no longer could provide food stuffs in such large quantities, we were still able to feed eighty thousand to ninety thousand people each year. Since Billy Hunter left the NBPA, we are only able to feed thirty-six thousand people a year. In addition, as the students grow older, the expenses for uniforms, meals and schooling essentials continue to increase. The school accommodations for the younger students have been extended to include transportation to and from schools, with fees for each student's enrollment, supplies, and uniforms.

Florence continues to provide strong leadership in administrative duties and health care. In recent months, her health has been comprised and additional help from Vanessa and Lydia has been necessary with fees that are needed to cover their living expenses. Our original goal is still working with limited funding because those involved in this venture from the beginning continue to work to support the success of providing a hope for the community of Kibera. Yearly, if not bi-yearly, trips are taken by Cheryl Meyers and me to keep abreast of all concerns that may arise.

Taking care of individual families in addition to our fifty students it has become necessary to help move Project Contact Africa forward. Trips to Nairobi now include taking families and school administrators shopping for essentials. These shopping excursions provide on-going support to keep up with student their children's educational opportunities and individual health issues. Most important they sponsor and finance the Ray of Hope's Clinic and School's ability to operate smoothly.

Working out in Gold's Gym one of my workout partners was aspiring to prepare and train for a NBA try-out. His partner, Gezina Lavely, was currently working on starting a taxi cab service for the DC, MD and VA metropolitan area. Purchasing two taxis was the intent and I provided the funds to support her efforts under the stipulation that (1) if successful all information regarding how to and what to do when running a taxi company be given to me for future reference and (2) when the business was on solid ground a contribution would be made to Project Contact Africa for support of the Ray of Hope Clinic and School. Her taxi company is still struggling but the good news is this provides insight on how to move forward in purchasing taxis in Nairobi as potential Job opportunities for graduating seniors.

As we begin to consider the future employment options for the 50 students we have sponsored over the years we began to consider small business ventures. We initially purchased two taxi cabs for use in the states as a measuring guide for how maintenance, fuel expenditures, salaries, with insurance and other amenities influence running a successful taxi company. Then we purchased hair extensions for a cosmetology center, sewing machines for tailoring, dressmaking and alterations. And purchased purses and costume jewelry for a small section within a cosmetology shop of sorts.

When we consider why these ventures were not successful it was mainly due a lack of education. Running any business requires basic math skills which are only the foundation of the concept of marketing. Lack of understanding that maintenance is the key to any successful project is a foreign concept to locals. Looking for a fast buck is more important than any long-term business plan. To reverse this line of thinking, we are contemplating the following: provide schooling for mechanics with the requirement that these skills be used for the upkeep and maintenance of two taxi cabs, schooling on book keeping – ledgers, accounts payable, accounts receivable, purchase order, inventory checks, business letters, ordering, processing, computer skills, scheduling, and more.

Once coursework is passed a contract between graduates and The Ray of Hope Clinic and School must be signed and strictly followed. As taxi's make money all funds must be documented and collected. Any failure to be responsible and reliable would result in consequences. There are many options to pursue, yet the starting up and maintenance of a taxi company is one we are actively pursuing.

Doing a great deal of traveling for the NBPA you could often find me seating in the boarding area in Dulles International Airport. Most people are excited about their plans for a trip whether it is for business or pleasure. Sitting across from me was a family who initiated a conversation. When asked where I was traveling to it was a great opportunity to talk about Project Contact Africa. They soon shared that they were from Somali and currently living in Virginia. Housing and relocating a family to the United States is quite expensive and they were looking to build a home back in Somali. We exchanged contact information and after returning home I did receive a message regarding how their efforts in Somali were going. Sending me a detailed account of where and how much funding was needed to initiate the building of a house, I sent them the three thousand start-up funds. I moved and lost contact with them, I was not able to find out whether their project was ever completed.

Project Contact Africa continues to address local needs here in the United States. During the summer of 2013, after training a local basketball player, driving back home, from Long Beach, California, I was extremely thirsty and made a quick stop at the local Superior Grocer supermarket. While in the check-out line I was behind a customer who did not have enough money to purchase all the items in their shopping cart. It took a few minutes for the customer to decide which items to keep and which to remove.

After the customer checked-out, I asked the manager, Felicia Johnson, if such a situation is an unusual occurrence or does it happen often. She sadly related to me that customers fall sort of funds due to being either unemployed and on assistance or living on limited incomes. I asked if she could take a few minutes to step away from the cash register so we could discuss this further.

Arranging for another checker to take over we walked over to her office. There we discussed what could be done to help someone without making it known so assistance given would not be abused. It was decided each month I would provide funds in the form of gift cards in increments of $50.00. This averages approximately $400.00 a month. The arrangement is, when a customer checking out at the register is short of funds to cover the amount of the sale, funds on a gift card is applied to cover the purchase so all necessary items can be purchased. This system works well, as the customer is unaware of the assistance, and it allows for the purchase of items otherwise unaffordable.

Over the last fifteen years of sending money to Africa, Western Union payments to provide financial support for the maintenance of the Ray of Hope Clinic and School as well as supporting Florence, Vanessa, Lydia, and Evelyn have been a challenge. Restrictions were imposed for sending money on a regular basis. Blocked from using my name to send monthly funds to Africa, I have had to use family member's names as the sender and to date this change is permitted. When contacting, Florence using a phone card, there are occasions when using any phone card is not accepted.

I contacted Western Union asking for the reason my ability to use my personal name when sending monthly funds to was blocked. I was informed over the years too much money has been sent by me personally and it was suspicious. As recipients of these funds in Africa remain the same, if the sender's names are acceptable we can continue with this new procedure. It is important all efforts to ensure financial and administrator matters are covered, funding is received and used to support the efforts of Project Contact Africa. This is quite important as over 100,000 patients have been examined and treated in this clinic, since its inception and we sponsor fifty students and families in the Kawangware community.

Florence continues to provide strong leadership in administrative duties and health care. In recent months, her health has been comprised and additional help from Vanessa and Lydia has been necessary with fees that are needed to cover their living expenses. Our original goal is still working with limited funding because those involved in this venture from the beginning continue to work to support the success of providing a hope for the community of Kibera. Yearly, if not bi-yearly, trips are taken by Cheryl Meyers and myself to keep abreast of all concerns that may arise.

Taking care of individual families in addition to our fifty students it has become necessary to help move Project Contact Africa forward. Trips to Nairobi now include taking families and school administrators shopping for essentials. These shopping excursions provide on-going support to keep up with student their children's educational opportunities and individual health issues. Most important they sponsor and finance the Ray of Hope's Clinic and School's ability to operate smoothly.

Florence, one of the kids Kermit has supported for 9 years

Kermit treaating kid with scabies

The kids Kermit supports

Kids in their sweatsuits

Having fun at picnic #2

Kids going to animal park

Start of our school ten years ago

Kids we've helped for 10 years are getting bigger

Kids can have fun anywhere

CHAPTER 19

By Florence Muyundo

Ray of Hope Community Center

Florence with school children

Florence with kids showing off water filtration system

News in the Mathare community travels fast. While walking in the slums checking on my regular patient's well-being. I noticed the streets were more congested than usual. Several local families were walking in the direction of the local school. I stopped to ask one of the patients who frequents my small clinic to find out what was going on. She told me a group of United States health care providers were granted permission to hold a "free" clinic at the local school. The principal allowed Kermit and his group to use one room in their building if the students attending her school would be seen first. The community was pleased to have this available. Many could not afford to been seen by a doctor to diagnose their current health status and be given medicines need to cure ailments they couldn't afford to buy.

My curiosity was peaked after hearing the local residents talking about a tall Black man from the United States and a team of doctors who were providing medical services and medicine. I walked into the school complex and saw this tall Black man step out of a classroom and yell into the crowd of people, "Does anybody speak English?" I readily replied "I do." He then invited me into the make shift clinic. There were several stations with doctors and nurses trying to gather patient information with the assistance of few qualified translators. Unfortunately, these translators were limited in their knowledge of medical terms which greatly hinder the efficient diagnosis of patient concerns. I immediately engaged my services so that the clinic would be able to complete its mission which was to identify the current status of each patient's health.

It is interesting to note that simply speaking English was indeed beneficial but the ability to understand how to make patient's needs clear to the visiting medical staff needed a lot of work. By showing how to better work with the patients the other translators improved in their communication skills and that helped make the program more along faster and accomplish the goal of meeting the needs of as many people as possible.

I volunteered to return the next day and worked with the team for five consecutive days. There were approximately 25 stations set up to see patients. When the medicines needed by the patients ran out and the medicines left over were not being dispensed it was time to shut down the clinic's operation. Kermit invited me to go with the team to a dinner meal to say thank you and to get better acquainted with the United States health care providers as individuals. We had worked as a team for five days but spending time with them this evening was really a pleasure, making possible the establishment of life-long friendships.

At this time, I had been operating a small clinic in Kibera. Kermit was quite interested in how I ran my clinic and I extended an invitation for him to come and see it when he returned to Kenya. As there were several large duffle bags of unused medicines that needed to be stored until Kermit's return I was asked if my clinic could be used to store the unused medicines. This I did and Kermit was very impressed that all the medicines were there upon his return. His level of trust in my ability to follow through on important matters grew as I was the one person who organized and coordinated Kermit's yearly clinics. Over a five-year period of time I was able to form a system that was efficient and effective in meeting patient needs.

Kermit had a great idea of setting up the pharmacy and how patients were to be seen. He designed a numbering system in which patients were given numbers and then seen using that numbering system. Unfortunately, there was a lack of understanding by the patients. They assumed one number applied to themselves and whomever they brought with them to see a doctor. This meant a mother with six children really needed the numbers 1- 7 but was given the number 1. This was greatly slowly down the progression of patients being seen in addition to an added problem when the mother or patient gave her number to a friend waiting to be seen with a similar large family to be seen by the doctors. I had to explain how the numbering system was to be used and made sure that someone was collecting the numbers after patients were seen.

Dr. Sam, Dr. Teresa and Jay accompanied Kermit on six trips to Africa where we planned how funds were being used and designed a working budget. I would tell my regular patients of their impending arrival which helped the community show up at the clinic in large numbers. Everyone worked long hours to meet the needs of patients.

Sam and Teresa provided all medical assistance at the clinic while Jay dispensed and monitored medication.

I also suggested that instead of bringing a large group of health care providers using local Kenyan doctors, medical students and nurses would prove more effective. First, they would be more aware of current health issues which would facilitate the purchase of medicines most likely to be required to treat problems. In addition, speaking the language would eliminate any language problems and move patients through the clinic faster with a faster diagnosis of current health status. As a result, two United States doctors: Dr. Sam Richard and Dr. Teresa Gipson became the two regular visiting doctors. Kermit agreed and we worked on a salary to be given to the local Kenyan medical professionals. Doctors were paid fifty dollars a day, the medical students were paid twenty dollars a day and nurses were paid ten dollars a day. Each salary was more than the established salary paid in Kenya. Dr. Sam once shared that the quality of the Kenyan medical students was comparable if not in some instances more qualified than United States medical students he had worked with.

When I invited Kermit to visit my clinic on a previous visit we finally made arrangements. The day we selected was quite wet and rainy. I being a local I was familiar with the weather and road conditions and felt confident I could drive the roads and get us there safely. Kermit was quite skeptical and suggested we change to another day. I won on this one and we headed to the clinic. Kermit's apprehension proved true as my car got stuck in the mud. He later commented this visit put more mud on his shoes and pant legs then was left on the road. My clinic space was small and held many challenges. Kermit meet with Dr. Sam and Dr. Teresa and agreed that we could work together and we began to search the Kawangware area for a possible building.

We encountered a partially completed building and met the owner who shared that he was unable to complete the project due to insufficient funds. Kermit arranged with the owner to provide the funds to complete the project if the rent would remain at $1,000.00 a month for 5 years. The Ray of Hope Clinic was now underway. Years later we rented out the upper level to provide a study hall/classroom for the school children. The building is also used as a feeding sight for local students. As we walked around the neighborhood streets throngs of children followed Kermit as if he was the Pied Piper. You read about such characters in books but when you actually see how much of a positive impact one person has on some many those stories come to life.

Whenever we ran out of medicine I made local contact with a pharmacy that sold medicine much cheaper than in the United States and thus eliminated the cost of transportation. With every year as Project Contact Africa continued NBA players came to serve meals, the NBPA union representatives coordinated with Feed the Children and provided over two hundred thousand pounds of rice and beans. When these supplies were depleted I was assigned the task of purchasing large quantities of such staples and rice, beans and other grains. As the main organizer of the meal distribution program we designed a check system in which anyone known to be selling any supplies they received would not only lose the privilege of remaining in the program and the person or persons who reported the incident would receive the offender's food supply. This worked as no one was ever reported nor removed from the program.

At present Project Contact Africa is provides students, staffs and families he sponsors with 1,000 meals every week. This feeding program includes meat on the menu one day a week. In addition, Kermit provides for my rent, bought a car to be used to provide transportation for patients to and from the clinic and in some instances to and from the hospital. He personally sponsors three families paying for their monthly expenses. Funding is also provided to cover school uniforms, school fees and the clinic/school maintenance. Over the past twenty years of working with Kermit and Project Contact Africa the yearly celebrations and holiday parties have been enjoyed by students, staff, and mothers from the community. Students have the opportunity to visit Nairobi and enjoy the many attractions and activities mostly enjoyed by visitors or local residents who can afford such luxuries.

Picnics are the usual agenda as the local parks are well cared for and not frequented by students and their families. In 2015 during his yearly visit unexpected rain necessitated a change in location. Students, staff, and two mothers were given an opportunity to enter the Galleria Mall. The restaurant KFC – Kentucky Fried Chicken was new to all of us. Students enjoyed their meal and to this day still speak about the excursion. We look forward to these yearly visits as Kermit takes Vanessa, Lydia, Evelyn, two mothers and me to the Nakumatt grocery store. It was also on this visit that Kermit took out to eat and American breakfast and it was the first-time Evelyn had been to a restaurant. She was so excited we took photos to show everyone.

The Nakumatt grocery store has items we can only purchase when Kermit takes us. Although he reminds us to stay within his budget there has never been a time when we were able to stick to it. He never objects but simply pays the bill, using cash as checks, debit and/or credit cards are not acceptable. It is dangerous for people to see how many food stuffs we purchase and he and helped us disguise our purchases to get them safely back to our homes. Kermit's sincere concern for the students and families of Kibera is much appreciated and without his continued support the clinic, school, and the lives of each student would be extremely negatively impacted. His funding is consistent and helps make a difference in the lives of many.

Over the years Western Union has not allowed Kermit to send money directly to me. Kermit was able to continue to send needed money using the names of his family members, and we use the names of clinic and school workers to collect these needed funds. Another obstacle is not being able to make phone calls using calling cards. Despite this keeping in regular communication is consistent. When a problem or unexpected expense needs to be addressed, he is always readily available and provides the needed financial assistance requested for the clinic, school, students, families he sponsors and the community. Kermit has been an invaluable help to the students and families of Kibera.

*Florence with Somali refugees the NBA players
helped for 2 years starting businesses*

Taking some of the children's mothers
shopping Florence, Evelyn, Lydia

Some food that they bought

Dr. Stephen Juma Ndombi

Building clinic for Florence

CHAPTER 20

My Experience with Kermit Washington and Project Contact

by Dr. Stephen Juma Ndombi

I wish to start by introducing myself and briefly narrate my experience with the above project which was started many years ago by the 65 year old NBA player and formerly with the Portland Trailblazers basketball team.

My name is Dr. Stephen Juma Ndombi, I am a specialist physican practising in Nariobi, Kenya. I run a private clinic as well as teach as a senior lecturer at the University of Nairobi, Kenya. I first met Kermit in 1996 in Nairobi, when he came to Kenya with a group of NBA basketball players on a mission of assisting disadvantaged children living in slums and shanties in Nairobi and its outskirts. The initial objective appeared to be to assist the children and their poor parents by providing free medical camps and to establish a referral system to and for those who were too sick, to the Kenyatta National Hospital which is the largest and most equipped hospital in Kenya and East and Central Africa.

I gathered that before coming to Kenya, Kermit had been to several other African countries ravaged by civil wars such as Rwanda and Congo. Initially, we ran clinics in primary schools and churches which donated space for our activities offeromg free medicine donated by well wishers in the United States of America following his passionate appeals both on radio and big screen television. The medicines were offered absolutelly free and also minor surgeries were offered for free.

Also accompanying Kermit were some doctors from the United States who could offer free services. One such doctor was Teresa Gipson, a public health expert. On my part, I brought along medical students from the University of Nairobi. Dr. Julius Otido, groups of nurses from the Kenyatta National Referral Hospital who proved-quite valuable. Also assisting us was a retired clinical officer Mrs. Florence Muyundo and the late professor, Job Bwayo, who was the then chairman of the Department of Medical Micro- Biology of the University of Nairobi. On any visit to Kenya by this team, we could serve between 5,000 to 10,000 needy patients within less than a week.

Dr. Gipson with school kids

The initial camp was done in Eastlands slums of Mathare in a primary school before we expandedthe caps to include the largest slum in east Africa known as Kibera and Kawangware slums where the current Project Contact Ray of Hope Clinic and School is located. Also envisioned by Kermit Washington in the intial stages, was to promote education among the kids and youth. A project which culminated into the construction of a clinic and school which sponsors fifty kids education. This is an exceptional gesture not ever done by efforts of a single individual that I am aware of. One require a big heart and exceptional generosity.

At some occasions he would come with a large team of volunteers including his daughter and son on the team to help.

This good work needs to be supported by all well-wishers, on humanitarian ground that includes a feeding program for the very poor and hungry slum dwellers.

CHAPTER 21

Project Contact by Sam Richard MD

Dr. Sam Richard

I first met Kermit after he was asking for volunteers for Project Contact on his radio show, I think it was 1995. I'm not much of a basketball fan, but did know him from this Portland Trailblazer days. In the early 90's Kermit and Michel Thompson had an afternoon radio sports talk show that I loved to listen to on my drive home from work. The show was a real conversation. The two played well off each other, being witty and humorous with interesting things to say. The show was about sports but also so much more. Much like "Car Talk" on NPR, about cars but not really. The manager that broke them up made a terrible decision to separate them. Neither one was the same alone. Even my wife Julia who only considers something a sport only if it takes place on top of a horsed listened to them. I haven't listened to sports talk radio since. Sports talk radio is just a bunch of screaming adolescents these days.

We started having meetings in the back room of Kermit's sport bar and restaurant, Le Slam. Beside myself there were a few others who have been there since the beginning like Jay Donkers. We gathered medicine samples, other necessary medicines and supplies for the trip and talked ourselves into the adventure.

Our first trip was to the slum of Kibera. This slum was the local for the movie "The Constant Gardener" if you want to know what it's like. We used this poor rudimentary school, which consisted of a dirt and weed courtyard, surrounded by corrugated steel roofed lean-tos with packed dirt floors. The school desks and benches were crude; there was no electricity, no running water or plumbing, just a hole the ground out back that really stunk.

The wonderful people of that slum more than made up for it. The kids were bright, respectful, and despite being ragged and worn, their uniforms were neat and clean. So much different than the average entitled American patient (except of course my wonderful patients). The adults came in their best. There were sick people where with just a touch of our- take for granted American medicine really make a difference. No one came in just for pain pills they were looking for treatment. I remember a subsequent trip where a poor widowed woman came in acutely ill and near death. She made her living as a prostitute, there's really not much else to do in the slum for a woman with no skills. Her husband had died, probably of AIDS. She was weak, malnourished dehydrated and febrile and had come in because she could no longer work. She had pneumonia. But with no money, even if we could get her to the hospital she wouldn't be able to afford the antibiotics and IV's. I gave her some IV fluids and a dose of a common antibiotic. I thought I was sending her home to die but planned to see her back the next day for more treatment. There was nothing else we could do.

The next day that woman walked in beaming under her own power. I could hardly recognize her; Kermit had to point her out. Little did everyone know or believe how lucky she was. I think she had pneumococcal pneumonia where just a bit of the right antibiotic at the right time can give a miracle. It made me look like the Great White Doctor. I wasn't a great or even good doctor. I just had the right medicine. It is more important to have the right resources in the right place. A mediocre doctor will do the right thing.

Back then we always stayed at the place called the Methodist Guest House. It is actually more like a minimum-security prison. Gates with guards, walls with sharp broken glass imbedded on the top, ironwork on all the windows. It's a place where missionaries stay on the way to go and do well and give credit to the lord. We always kept a low profile there. Project Contact didn't want your soul and allegiance; we just wanted to be in a place where a little help, either through medicine, education or food might just give you that little boost to a better life. At that time, I was working for the Department of Family Medicine at Oregon Health and Sciences University. They had recruited me to start a community clinic for a place to train their residents. I convinced a couple of my residents to come with us on the next trip. One of them was Theresa Gibson MD who has been instrumental in the growth and vision of Project Contact. Theresa is a gifted and beautiful woman with a personality to match Kermit's (I take great enjoyment in listening to them complain about each other). The medical staff realized early on that just showing up three or four times a year was a good thing but what we needed was an ongoing presence.

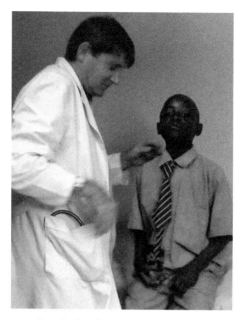

Dr. Richard examining a student

While maintaining the street clinics Kermit was able to get a building built in one of the other slums named Kawangware. Over the years Project Contact's home, The Ray of Hope Clinic has grown to have a pharmacy and laboratory (thank you Ron Artest), a clinic delivering primary care, immunizing children, testing for HIV, and delivering babies. It does a lot of good for the population there. Kermit has also established an elementary school for kids who just can't get into a regular school. Maybe too poor, developmentally delayed, or homeless without a sponsor or guardian. About 50% are HIV positive. Project contact provides the teachers, the books and study plans, the uniforms and hot lunches daily. Certainly, the only good meal of their day.

Kermit loves to feed people. He feeds a group of 85 HIV + people with their families. He figures that must feed at least 850 people a month when you take in all the relatives. This is rice, meat, and vegetables. I remember one dinner in Nairobi and Kermit going over the figures of what it would cost to feed 1,000,000 people for a year. Don't remember the exact number but it wasn't very much.

The medical clinic part I've pretty much worked myself out of a Job. Florence and her staff have done an amazing Job, first rate even by US standards, of providing care in the Ray of Hope Clinic. When I return there I usually go for 1 or 2 weeks of free care and medicine but I now feel they're doing such a good Job that I'm just in the way. The staff there does humor me though.

This last visit I was lucky enough to get to bring my 17-year-old daughter Katie with me. At the time, it was the summer between here junior and senior high school years. I think it is so important for our young people to see the third world up close. Kate was energized by it. I made her do all the scut work- shaving heads and applying gentian violet to the heads for ringworm, applying scabicide from chin to toes for scabies. I'll always remember her face when she got to see a delivery and take care of the newborn. I was so proud of her, she's the only one out of all my five children who wanted to go into medicine and she loved it.

Nairobi is a wonderful vibrant city, perhaps the most forward in Africa as far as human rights, democratic principles and education. I enjoy visiting there, walking downtown, going to the restaurants and haggling with the street market vendors. I once got to go on a long weekend to the Masaai Mara and it was spectacular. The problem is the lack of capital and jobs for most people. If you are the elite, the connected or lucky enough to have a Job it's a very decent place to live. There are roughly 3,000,000 people in Nairobi. 2,000,000 live in the slums. There's no infrastructure, water may be delivered once or twice weekly to a community spigot, and little investment in those places to make them decent to live in. While unskilled workers work for anything, there are also professionals like doctors who make less than 300 us dollars a month.

I remember when I lived in Idaho and all the tillable land in the county would be ready to seed in 48 hours when the time was right. Big tractors, big fields. In Kenya, there are small tractors but mostly 60 workers with hoes doing the tilling. Street repairs are 20 guys with picks working away. Contrast here where capital is cheap and labor is expensive to Kenya where capital is expensive and workers go begging.

On my last couple, recent visits things have gotten better. A new constitution was approved. In my experience (which counts for little), people are healthier. Programs like PETA have provided free HIV testing and more importantly free HIV drugs to treat this disease that has devastated Africa. Before there was no reason to test for HIV, simply because even though there was treatment none but the wealthiest could possibly obtain it. Being an African doctor too often is an exercise in futility the doctor for the poor knows he has this and that treatment for a certain problem but it's pretty much an intellectual discussion because the patient has a tough time just getting the funds to eat. At least here in America we have the option to file bankruptcy if we can't afford an expensive treatment.

Kermit's life from the beginning was an uphill struggle. I would write about rehabilitation and repentance but I think the Kermit NBA incident was just another tough obstacle in a life full of tough obstacles. After reading a lot and thinking about the writings of so called sports experts (doesn't take you too far up the evolutionary ladder, does it?) I think a lot of the continual judgment and criticism after all these years is covert, subtle racism. One sees a lot of this these days with President Obama, another truly American kid whose success was based on merit rather than privilege. We've got a lot of angry white people in this country.

I can't begin to understand why Kermit does what he does. It exhausts me. Why would someone like him work like a dog to support a few poor forsaken people with no resources in a far corner of the world?

The answer is easy. If we're normal good unselfish people we by nature take care of people who are less fortunate than we are. That's what makes us human. Kermit just goes a quantum leap farther. Kermit is a great person and human being. A topic of discussion in sports is should we make heroes out of our athletes just for their athletic greatness. When it comes to Kermit Washington the athletic greatness is just the window dressing, the rest of the man is beautiful.

He possesses all the traits that it takes to be a Great American. A work ethic second to none, unselfishness, putting others ahead of yourself and perseverance in the face of great obstacles.

CHAPTER 22

Eugenia Steininger – "That's it!"

My family first met Kermit when he was working as a co-host with Mychal Thompson for a local sport talk radio station KFXX-The Fan, in Portland, Oregon. As a family, we have always been die-hard Blazer Fans, proud to be season ticket holders for forty-six years. My husband Dale, was a regular on the Persimmon golf course located in Gresham, Oregon. He would frequently see Mychal Thompson carrying a large bucket of golf balls over to the driving range. Not only being an ardent Blazer fan, but an enthusiastic golfer. After hitting balls together one overcast morning, Mychal jokingly called my husband Persimmon Dale. This nickname stuck as Mychal would often mention the improvement of his golf game was directly related to his regular meetings with Persimmon Dale on the driving range. Of course, our beverage of choice will be water. One afternoon, both Kermit and Mychal were holding their sport talk radio broadcast at a local restaurant. Our three sons wanted to go and we decided it would be a great opportunity for the boys and us to listen to a live broadcast. Sometime during the broadcast our youngest son walked over the table where Kermit and Mychal were sitting and promptly sat on Kermit's lap.

Flying by the seat of his pants, he introduced our son as a surprise guest and the show continued as if nothing out of the ordinary had just happened. He was so understanding and kind, from that day forward we became friends. We visited briefly and when I told him I was a nurse, working at Kaiser, we spoke about his relief efforts in Africa. When planning his first trip with a large group of 11 health care workers, which he personally paid all expenses for, he invited me to join him. I was really excited and immediately shared this generous offer with Dale who agreed it would the opportunity of a lifetime. After telling Kermit I would love and be more than willing to go, I made all the necessary arrangements.

As this was going to be my initial introduction to the health care needs of patients in Africa I felt confident that my years as an American nurse had prepared me to be more than qualified for the challenge. I was excited about being regarded as person to include in Kermit's grand plan for Africa and traveling to a country with different cultural traditions. I didn't understand the magnitude of this undertaking but knew it would be successful simply because of Kermit's desire to help others. We had observed his generosity through his Sixth Man Foundation project on numerous occasions and this was one more demonstration of his big heart.

My first trip in 1995, Kermit arranged and paid all expenses for this group of 11. It's been a while and I forgot some of their names, but these are the ones that came to mind: Dr. Gipson, Dr. Sam, a Dr. from Tillamook, three nurses, Elsa Marie, me and a roommate, an ob-gyn nurse practitioner from Kaiser out of Vancouver and her husband an E.R. Dr. at St. Vincent's. A nun sponsored by Clyde Drexler, who was his babysitter also accompanied us. Our daily schedule was to pack up supplies and then set up clinic at a local school. Housing was through the Methodist guest house; the property was set back on a well-manicured and guarded lot. The front and sides of this plain structure was covered with lush flowers and vegetation. You had a choice of a double or single room accommodation.

At times the guest house was used for conventions. It had a swimming pool, but to use it you had to pay an additional fee. There was a laundry facility or you could choose to pay to have your laundry done. There were no dryers and a clothes line was located just outside the kitchen area. There were posted guards with a tall wire fencing surrounding the property. In addition, security gates had been recently installed as the house had been robbed at gun point just a few days before our arrival.

Each room included a simple bed, mattress, and blankets. A small closet was inside the wall, with a small desk in-between the beds with a large pan of boiled water. Because you couldn't drink the water from the faucets dispensing regular water, this was made available and left in every room for use if needed. It was best practice not to drink it, and buy and drink only bottled water.

In the morning, we would get up, have breakfast, usually eggs, either boiled or fried, with African mashed potatoes (ghoughpteighb-teau). Some days we would have porridge similar to our oatmeal, coffee, tea, ham, maybe a banana, an apple or an orange. After the first trip, we were remembered this daily menu and brought peanut butter and jelly to satisfy both our sweet tooth and a provide a meal that would stick to your ribs until lunch. You had to be quick to wash up and use the facilities at any time as the electricity would go out unexpectedly. I personally experienced this when, before meeting with the group for breakfast, I was taking a shower and shampooing my hair, the electricity went out and I had to use the boiled water to rinse out my hair.

Butter was not used for cooking, or serving with bread, but large containers of Mazola corn oil were stocked in a small pantry just off the kitchen. Honestly, most meals were boring and not very tasty. Following this, less than gourmet meal, we packed up the van and drove to the school's make-shift clinic. As most days were long and afforded little time to go out and grab lunch we brought bread and ham, or whatever meat was served along with breakfast, from the guest house for sandwiches.

One day during each of these trips was a mandatory day of work because of a national holiday. We took advantage of this time of the see some of the local sights. One was to the Ngong Hills. The steep trek up the mountain was dangerous in many ways. Armed guards accompanied you all the way up and down. The view was spectacular and would have been even more appreciated if not for the presence of the armed guards. We were told there were poisonous snakes and sometimes questionable person lurking about. This seemed a bit overkill as the mountain was both steep and void of any hiding places for such individual. As we had to pay for this protection it was more likely a scam to collect money from visitors. This trip on our day off we went to see an animal reserve.

The second trip was in 1996. My husband Dale was very uncomfortable about not being to reach me on the phone when he wanted to check on how things were going. Therefore, one this second trip and for the rest of my five trips he came along with me. Elsa Marie helped with coordination but didn't share her arrangements. Each trip daily routine mirrored our first trip with one day off, as we couldn't work due the observance of a national holiday. Dr. Stephen Ndombi, local doctor we worked under, invited us over for the day.

When we were returning from our lunch break, the interpreter did not return. Kermit called out to the waiting patients to see if anyone could speak English. Two young teenagers Kimmy and Joe came forward and offered their assistance. Brother and sister, they brought their mother to the clinic for medical care. That first day we were kindred spirits. On one visit with us to the United States, Kimmy stated she did not know they were poor, and her initial impression of Americans were that everything came easy and the streets were paved with gold. To this day, in 2016, Kimmy and her family stay in touch. They later moved from the "slums" in Kibera to a low socio-economic neighborhood in Mathare.

One afternoon, Kimmy and Joe's mother invited us for lunch. Their apartment was very small I'd guess the dimensions were at best ten feet by ten feet. There was no running water, bathroom amenities were shared by all tenants of this six-floor apartment complex. There was one light bulb for the entire space. The ten foot by ten-foot space was divided into; one bedroom, and a living room where meals were prepared and cooked with only one light bulb. The geographic area was a little bit more comfortable than the housing in the "slums" of Kibera. The family was extremely proud of their home and being able to pay ninety dollars a month in rent.

Kimmy and Joe had a younger brother who was lame. Unable to walk, he would crawl around their apartment. When we walked through the front door, this young man pulled himself up to be supported by the wall so that he could properly greet us. Their mother had prepared a light meal for us and although we had already had eaten the sandwiches we brought for lunch, we didn't want to appear ungrateful and managed to eat her well-cooked meal and enjoy both it and our hosts. We soon understood why there were times when Kimmy would complain her stomach hurt. The cupboards were bare and frequently the family would go several days without having anything to eat.

There were nights were we simply could not face another home cooked meat served at the guest house. We ventured out one evening and found a Chinese restaurant four easy walking blocks away. The entire staff were native Kenyans working in an Asian establishment. Now that is a major paradigm shift. The most difficult aspect of navigating Kenyan streets at night was the lack of lighting. One night while walking home we turned and called out to Kermit only to discover he had fallen into a hole and needed help getting out. He injured his knee and had to some discomfort during the remainder of the trip.

Our third trip was in 1997. One of the patients from our first trip was a small child with a breathing concern. His family lived in the local "slum" and was very grateful for the medical care we could provide. This family later moved to an area outside the city and when they learned the medical team was returning, they made a ten-mile trek to come see us to let us know how much they appreciated how we helped their child get better. We took some time to travel up country and saw a beautiful waterfall, then visited the Baroness Karen Von Blixen-Finede Museum, in Karen, Africa, located southwest of the city center. The town was named after the author of "Out of Africa." There was a small but quaint restaurant located in the front of this coffee farm. Separate and located a few yards from this restaurant was a small bead shop with the bead making facility located directly behind it. A variety of African designed beads were used to create original and unique beads to make jewelry. In comparison to the local markets in downtown Nairobi, this site was an artist's treasure chest filled with interesting local beauty, inviting and safe.

For our first trips, we worked out of a neighborhood school. Jay dispensed the medicines; Dale manned the door, the nurses and doctors examined patients, Kermit applied medication to treat ringworm, and Eugenia treated patient burns, and gave shots and antibiotics. Then on the fifth trip we switched the location of the clinic to a church. The minister limited those who could receive any health care assistance to those who were members of his church. We had to address this issue immediately and open appointments to anyone in need.

Kermit and I flew into Amsterdam and caught the connecting flight into Nairobi. Jay was a Portland, Oregon, pharmaceutical representative who provided antibiotics and other drugs to treat ailments we found to be prevalent on our last trip. Medicines that were labeled out of date but still effective were included among our supplies. One night we decided to eat at the Carnivore restaurant after returning to the guest house looking for a different option for dinner. If we returned to the guest house when the regular dinner meals were served, we could always count on a bland serving of goulash. If we came home after serving hours we would go out to eat dinner at either the Safari Club, The Carnivore or the Sheraton buffet. Evenings gave us the opportunity to unwind and relax before we prepared things for the next day.

One evening returning to the guest house at the end of a long day working in the clinic we went to dinner at the Carnivore. On the menu was a selection of charcoal roasted meats which included: leg of beef, haunch of exotic meat (Ostrich – this was quite dry), leg of pork, leg of lamb, pork spare ribs, rabbit, Crocodile – when available, a variety of deer, water buffalo, snake, chicken tikka, chicken yakitori, chicken wings, chicken livers and gizzards, pork sausages, beef sausages – my favorite was alligator for it reminded me of chicken being moist and quite tasty. Salads and side dishes (mixed salad, rice salad, kidney beans, corn relish, and coleslaw), Sauces: garlic, fruit salsa, sweet and sour, masala, mint, and chili, Choice of desserts: apple pie, cheesecake, strawberries and ice creams, and Kenyan coffee. It was in Africa I first tried Chai tea.

With Jay feeling better Dale and I felt adventurous and convinced him to try out, The Country, a restaurant featuring Ethiopian cuisine. This was something we sampled for the first time. We went out to dinner in a restaurant, The Country, where we tried Ethiopian cuisine for the first time. We were instructed we could only eat with one hand, as one hand was frequently used to address and toileting procedures. We were dropped off by our usual driver and arranged for him to return in two hours to take us back to our accommodations.

For whatever unexpected event prevent his returning to pick us up, we never knew. Seeing our predicament one of the waiters offered to provide us safe transportation home after he had finished his shift. Three hours later at 11:00 pm we walked out of the restaurant to the waiter's car parked in the lot. It was not a luxury item by any stretch of one's imagination. However, three of us squeezed into the back seat and the other two sat in the front seat. As we approached a hill we needed to go up to reach our final destination. It soon became obvious the car lacked the power to do so.

I got out with my two other back seat companions and we pushed and pushed the car up the steep incline. Once the car was relieved of the additional weight of three passengers we braced ourselves and prepared to push it up the hill. We had to remind the waiter, once we got the car moving we would need to stop, get back inside before continuing on own way. Once and again, we arrived safely back to the guest house, but not before the waiter tried to get me to pay more for our recent adventure than the fee for our original driver we had arranged to pick us up or a taxi. This was especially maddening as I had to help push the car up the hill. Outraged by his insolence I had to walk away and simply shake my head. Any desire to return to The Country restaurant anytime soon was quickly squelched, even though their chicken wings were the best I had enjoyed in a long time.

On my last Trip Five 1999 included: Dr. Gipson, Judy Anderson, her husband, her husband's friend, and car dealership person, Pat, a long-time friend of mine, Kermit, Trey, Kermit's 19-year-old son Dale and me. We changed our location to a local church. Trey had no medical training and was assigned to applying medication for ringworm and scabies. It was important he be adequately trained as both ringworm and scabies are highly contagious. The morning before his first day in the clinic, we shared this information with him: Ringworm is easy to visibly detect as it has a red ring of small blisters or is a red ring of scaly skin that grows outward. The infected area may be itchy and red. It is easily spread by direct skin to skin contact from handshakes or hugs. It can also be spread by touching an infected animal or object such as blankets or door knobs. In the clinic, we use an antifungal medication applied to the infected area ONLY using disposable gloves. Ringworm, a common fungal infection of the skin causes a scaly, crusted rash that may appear as round, red patches on the skin.

Living in slum conditions the following ways to avoiding catching ringworm present several challenges. To avoid ringworm, encourage good hand washing and keep feet clean and dry.

It can be successfully treated with antifungal medication used either topically or orally. Ringworm occurs in people of all ages, but it is particularly common in children. It occurs most often in warm, moist climates. It is common to have several areas of ringworm at once in different body areas. The most common occurrences appear on the scalp, between the toes and feet.

Ringworm first appears as a lesion that starts as a flat, scaly patch, but develops a defend border and radiates outwardly. The border becomes red, raised and scaly, while the center clears and reveals fine scaling. The rash can appear anywhere of the body: the arms, legs, face, etc. It may be itchy, but it typically isn't painful. The most frequently used topical anti-fungal treatment in the clinic was Gentian violet an antiseptic purple dye used to treat fungal infections of the skin.

As the ability to clean and sanitize clothing is limited and predominately ineffective due to lack of adequate cleaning supplies, and appliances such as washing machines and dryers, ringworm spreads rapidly to all members of the household. Once receiving treatment, it is expected this condition will reoccur.

Scabies and ringworm occurs more commonly in developing world countries and tropical climates. These two skin diseases were frequently treated in the clinic. One of the three most common skin disorders in children, along with the ringworm and bacterial skin infections, we were mindful to bring a large quantity of Kwell lotion and Gentian violet. Kermit's son Trey accompanied us on this trip. His first experience working in the slums of Kibera, he was unfamiliar with both skin diseases. Dr. Sam and Dr. Teresa took time to bring him up-to-date on what signs and symptoms to look for, which medicines were used to treat each disease, and how to apply the medications. The need to wear, change, and dispose of gloves after dispensing each treatment, and most important to wash his hands after removing tainted gloves was emphasized.

Trey learned, scabies is an itchy highly contagious skin disease caused by an infestation by the itch mite. Direct skin-to-skin contact is the most common means of transmission. The mites that cause the condition burrow into the skin to infect humans. They are so tiny it's not possible to see them with the naked eye. Signs and symptoms of scabies include a skin rash composed of small red bumps and blisters that affects specific areas of the body. He was advised to look for pimple like rashes on the wrist, elbows, armpits, nipple, waist belt line, buttocks, in between the fingers, above the neck, on palms of hands and the soles of feet. Other symptoms can include tiny red burrows on the skin and relentless itching. The itching skin leads to frequent scratching while may lead to other infections.

Crowded living conditions in the slums of Kibera increased the risk of transmission. Areas with a lack of access to water also have higher rates of disease. Bedding and clothing used three days before receiving treatment should be washed in hot water and dried in a hot dryer.

Of the several creams and lotions available with a doctor's prescription, we used Kwell. This cream is a topical cream which contains chemicals that kill scabies mites and their eggs. It is generally considered safe for adults, pregnant women, and children ages 2 months and older. This medicine is not recommended for nursing mothers. The cream kills the mites promptly but the itching doesn't stop entirely for several weeks. It was applied over all the body from the neck down, and left on for at least eight hours. A second treatment is needed if new burrows or a rash appear. As scabies spreads, so easily, the clinic recommended treatment for all household members and other close contacts, even if they showed no signs of scabies infestation.

Unlike the schools, this church had outhouses. During our lunchtime break, Pat and I walked over to find an outhouse that was available. I opened the door and was immediately greeted with the noxious fumes that come with discarded human waste. We always stuffed alcohol wipes up our nostrils to help reduce the smell. When ready to leave, the outhouse opening the door became a real challenge. I continually pulled at the door handle but it appeared to be stuck. The door opened easily enough when I entered, but now it was very difficult to open from the inside. I kept pulling and, pulling and, calling out for help. Finally, the door opened and the force with which I exerted to get it open threw me back inside and I fell into the open hole. I was soon sucked into the hole covering my body up to my elbows in its contents.

Try as I might, no amount of cleaning supplies helped get any relief from the stains and stench from the hole's contents. I couldn't get clean. I kept putting alcohol wipes up my nostrils, but they failed to provide any relief. Everyone was laughing so hard they couldn't stop for at least five minutes to help me get out of the hole. I was the first to leave the van and jumped into a soap filled tub to rid myself of the awful smell and the accompanying waste that had attached to my clothing and skin.

Upon returning home the red dirt came along with us. In Africa, this red dirt was everywhere. Our daily inhaling of the dust was left in our noses and lungs. When we would blow our noses, there would be remnants of this dust and dirt in our Kleenex for several days.

As the professional NFL season was starting, Dale remembered Joe, Kimmy's brother, had never played with an NFL football, a major-league baseball or game regulation NBA basketball. Using this as an excuse to visit our local sports store, Dale decided to send one of each of these items to Joe shortly after we settled back into our normal daily routines. Once the package Dale sent Joe arrived in Africa, the customs agent would not release this package to Joe. The agent insisted a price, bribe, for receipt of packages from the States, was set in stone and must be paid. Joe shared this information with Dr. Stephen Ndombi who had established a close working relationship with this customs agent.

Dr. Ndombi had an exclusive bargaining agreement with this custom agent to receive medications sent from the States to Nairobi only released in a previously identified location. Once contact was made with the custom agent Dr. Ndombi could collect Joe's package. It was difficult to tell which made Joe happier, the package and its contents or what Dr. Ndombi had arranged to collect the package.

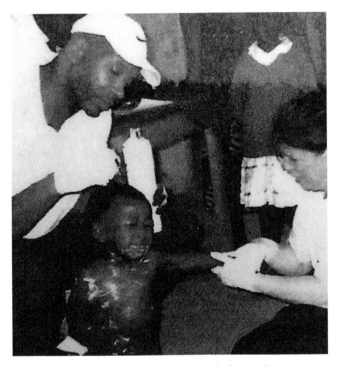

Eugenia and Kermit treating kids in Africa

CHAPTER 23

Juanita and Howard Hedinger

It doesn't matter where I live or where I vacation, working out in the gym is the one activity I will always make time for. The people who join you in an exercise routine soon become added to your circle of friends. While living in Portland, Oregon, in 1994 this proved to be the case when meeting a local model for Nike, named Juanita. While working out at Gold's gym my conversation about my newest Africa project were shared with her. She was dating Howard Hedinger, president of American Steel. She shared she had been sponsoring a young African girl for fifteen-plus years and took an active interest in my plans for my next trip to Africa. Mr. Hedinger was interested in helping Juanita contact her sponsored child and was also supportive of Project Contact Africa's efforts. This trip became a fact-finding excursion.

Howard and Juanita traveled with me to Nairobi. Juanita discovered her sponsored child was living in a small town near Nairobi. Once we arrived and checked into our hotel she made numerous phone calls and could contact an agency that was willing to come to the hotel and drive Juanita to where the child was living. While Juanita left on her mission, Howard accompanied me to visit the slums of Kibera and walked around. Noticing the lack of water, he donated funds to build a well for the local residents. Later, he paid the air fare for two doctors to travel with me and work in our make shift clinic.

Juanita arranged for me to meet Howard and the next trip to Africa was on the way. We flew out of Portland, in Howard's private jet landing in Los Angeles, California to make our connecting flight to London, England. We missed our connecting flight and Howard made the necessary arrangements for us to continue our trip. The small private jet was phenomenal. Luxury at a level one could truly appreciate when you otherwise travel by commercial jets and suffer the long-leg short-leg room constant scenario.

We landed in LAX international airport with time to spare and leisurely waited to make our connecting flight. While waiting for the scheduled flight to Heathrow, England, Juanita was eager to begin her quest and soon to be adventure into the uncharted regions in Africa. And her plan to contact people who said they would be able to locate and take her to meet her sponsored girl. Her success in carrying out her plan depended on if the contact numbers she was given were accurate and working. The most current numbers she was given were provided with basic suggestions from a recognized assistance organization who knew how to make a meeting a success.

Upon arriving in London, Howard hired a chauffeured Rolls Royce to pick us up and take us the hotel. The hotel fee was over my budget, but well worth it. The room was plush and decorated a small like small cottage with all the amenities and more. Meals were five-star quality, and the mints under the pillow literally melted in your mouth. The weather was sunny and mild when we landed but needed to take a short nap before falling on our faces. Waking up to the sound of rain hitting the windows, was a surprise but not being sure if I'd ever make it England again decided to venture out to look around the city even if it was dark and wet outside.

After living in Portland, Oregon, where it rains on a regular basis, taking a walk on the rainy streets of London, England did not present an issue. The concierge at the hotel told me the weather on the day we arrived was the first dry, sunny day in forty-five days. This reminded me of my first forty-five days of constant rain in Oregon, first traded from the San Clippers. Therefore, walking a few blocks to see Buckingham Palace was definitely a must do. The directions given were easy to follow. But somehow I managed to walk right past the gates. I'm not sure which was more of a surprise, that Buckingham Palace was located on a major busy street or there were no guards in full dress stationed outside. Without the legendary palace guards stationed out front, and few street lights, to help you read signs, it was easy to miss one of the best-known points of interest.

Being late in the evening, rainy and dark I can't verify if the guards remain in place without a blink, as there weren't any. There were none stationed outside the palace gates. Having heard a lot about fish and chips. I stopped at a local stand to order some. The fish was just okay but the fries were really soggy. I missed the crispy American French fries and McDonald's fillet of fish sandwich. Having satisfied my basic questions about London, England, it was time to return to the hotel and go back to sleep. In the morning breakfast was a feast. The small private eating area provided lots of counter space for several silver trays filled with a welcomed variety of options. There were scrambled, hard-boiled eggs, eggs benedict, oatmeal, and steak. Bread items included scones, biscuits, bagels, and toast. Fresh fruit strawberries, bananas, oranges, apples, and an assortment of raisins made choosing what to eat a tasty enigma.

After eating breakfast, we left the hotel and were again driven to the airport in a chauffeured Rolls Royce. The ride was short and soon we were checked in and boarding the plane to Nairobi, Kenya. The contrast between the affluence we experienced in London, England, with the airport in Nairobi, Kenya was just the beginning of many. Both Howard and Juanita were ready to hit the ground running. After checking into the second high-level hotel accommodations; Juanita proceeded to make phone calls and I took Howard for a tour of Kibera. The "slums" were hot and dusty. He watched as locals carrying large empty water containers on their heads passed by to make the long climb up hill to re-fill their tanks with water.

Visiting several homes which were virtually sheds covered with thin tin roofs was quite an eye-opening experience. Stepping inside the floors were simply dirt, there were no windows or furniture. In the center of this one room was a small cooking grill very similar to a Japanese hibachi. The doorway provided the only ventilation and was always accessible. Howard was so touched by these deplorable conditions that he agreed to provide some funding for my Project Contact Africa.

Juanita was successful in connecting with people who knew where her sponsored girl was living. A woman drove to the hotel and told her the drive would take took over an hour. Without any hesitation Juanita got into the awaiting car to meet her ward. Nothing anyone could have said was going to persuade her to wait and have someone accompany her or at best travel in a more reliable running vehicle. She had come this far and was willing to do whatever it took her efforts to be successful.

She left mid-day from the hotel and returned well after dinner. She was more satisfied than tired. She had accomplished her goal. In most cases the funding given organizations to sponsor children never reach the pictured recipient. Thankfully this was not the case in this instance. The visit went well, but I'm not sure if there was any further communication after the two met. Returning home Howard did follow through with his support in Africa.

CHAPTER 24

Teacher Trip

Young reader taking a break from class

Upon my return home from my first trip to Goma, Zaire, Africa, the Oregonian, the Portland area local newspaper printed an informative article about my recent connection with the North West Medical Team and the American Red Cross Africa relief efforts. Donations poured in and many positive actions were the direct result of this media coverage.

With regularly scheduled assemblies to reward academic performance and improvement several teachers approached me about the possibility of going on a future trip to Africa. With the amount of interest to help Africa growing, I scheduled an "are you interested" meeting at my restaurant.

The meeting went well and resulted in three teachers committing to accompany me on my fourth trip make a trip to Nairobi, Kenya. As we had established a relationship with local schools in Africa after they hosted our clinics, it was brought to our attention, the children's educational needs were not being addressed. Without having a true understanding of how the educational system works in Africa, teachers drew from their teaching related their educational experiences and collected supplies, pencils, crayons, composition paper, and easy to read primer books to bring to Africa for students to use in their classrooms. Realizing how much all children love recess, they decided to include in their boxes of supplies basketballs, regular gym balls and jump ropes.

Leaving Portland, Oregon, despite being excited about working with the children in Africa, the plane ride was exceedingly long for them. When we landed in Amsterdam it was time to walk around and loosen up their legs. We then landed in Nairobi, Kenya. The teacher's first impression of the city was shown on their faces. Walking through the Nairobi airport the visible neglect of the building impacted me as if it was my first time visiting the country. It soon became necessary to adjust expectations and questions were raised as to whether the supplies brought were a match with what was needed.

Settling into The Methodist guest house was their first introduction to daily life in Africa. The property being surround by tall wire fencing, an armed guard, and lush flowers and vegetation indicated a stark contrast existed between what was American normal and African normal. One clearly saw a serene setting separated and guarded to keep out the dangers anyone might experience when outside this protected area.

Entering the house, the plain and simple décor helped the teachers understand what down-sizing would look like for any American. Necessities were available although not up to date. If an item was functioning at a basic level, it was kept and maintained. As for food stuffs, if you were able to feel satisfied, then it was time to move on and try not to crave something that would not be available. Knowing how bland the morning breakfast had been reported to the teachers, a large box in front of Costco items selected were specifically packed and brought with us. Pancake mix, maple syrup, Ritz crackers, Graham cracker cookies, cold cereals, powdered milk, tea, hot chocolate mix, coffee creamer, hot cereals, M & M's plain and peanut, cans of soup, chili with and without meat, Kraft macaroni and cheese, mashed potato buds, corn bread mix, stuffing, and canned vegetables were among the care packages welcomed extras.

It was only going to be a week-long trip but with the locals wanting to taste these delectable items it was known they Would not go very far. Sweets were not part of a meal or included on the day's menu. Snacks did not exist and oddly enough milk and eggs were kept out of the refrigerator and sold at gas stations. This made one wonder if these items were safe to eat.

Settling in didn't take very long but being extremely tired from traveling, early to bed and early to rise was the order of the day. The morning arrived with the teachers ready to visit the school, observe the status of things and determine what could be accomplished during their visit. Driving down the heavily trafficked roads, the locals were walking, driving, riding bikes, or pushing wooden carts in round-abouts to continue with their daily routine.

Before dropping us off at the clinic, the first morning feeling like myself, our driver noticed he was running low on gas. He tried to stop before picking us up but the traffic was a bit heavy he said. He did mention having to do this before taking us back to the Methodist Guest House after we finished our day in the clinic. A local gas station was located along the outskirts of Kibera, the slum where we were holding the clinic. Located near the Carnivore restaurant and the airport.

The gas station had a small local market within five to ten yards from the gas pumps. Outside the little market was a medium sized white freezer with the lid open resting against the outside wall, with milk and eggs inside but not connected to any electrical socket. As the driver got out of the mini-van I stepped outside to check the final cost so I could give the driver the money to take inside and pay.

Tried and eager to stretch their legs the group opened the mini-van sliding door and looking to see what the local store might carry that might be a good potential snack for later stated their intent to go inside. Sitting on a hill directly in front of us were three very sinister looking men. They looked like they were not doing well, as their clothing was tattered and their faces rough from the weather and elements. As they take a quite appraisal of me, the mini-van, and the white people trying to exit from the van, it was soon apparent they meant no good. I then told the group to get back inside the van and no matter what might transpire do not open windows and lock the doors.

No sooner had these words of caution left my lips, one of the men approached me for money. The other two walked to each side of the van and asked for money from the outside. I again, stated we were not giving any money to anyone but the store to pay for gas. Not pleased, the one man speaking with me tried his best to intimidate me by having his two companions join him next to me. I focused my attention on the main leader of this threatening crew and moved past him to give the driver the money he needed to pay for the gas. I watched to make sure he entered and exited the store without having an altercation with these thugs. I waited until he opened his door, then opened mine and we drove off.

My concern will always be to keep my companions safe. Thank goodness this time I could deflect a potentially dangerous situation. Just another opportunity to demonstrate "If you value your wallet." Don't do it.

Driving up to the school, it was nothing as expected. The property perimeter was enclosed by a tall wire fence, with a lock and a manned employee who would unlock the gate and let people inside. Outside were several children who could not enter the property as they did not have school uniforms. The students inside the fenced in property wore green and white pin-stripe uniforms. Most wore welcoming smiles to their visitors, but their uniforms were very unkempt. Buttons were missing, either too small or too big, needing cleaning and repair. Shoes fell in the same category, either too small or too big. But it was clear each child was ecstatic about being inside the fenced in property.

Designed in the American outside school format, the typical rectangular framework the inner courtyard, reserved for recess was void of any physical education structures or supplies for student use. Upper grades were on the left side with primary on the right. The main offices were in-between lower grades and upper grades. There was a closet where supplies and all recreational materials were stored. Every closet that housed supplies was locked. Classrooms had one blackboard that was rough due to being covered with tiny pebbles. This made writing with chalk that also had tiny pebbles mixed in it very difficult.

The students sat in rows on wooden benches with attached desktops. Desks had no name tags and walls were stark without colorful decorations around the room. Students kept miniature black and white notebooks in their pockets, pencils we brought were the size of golf pencils, and there no pencil sharpeners anywhere. Razor blades were put inside student mouths so no one would steal them. There were no textbooks or reading materials. Crayons were not going to be useful and the mere basics were much to be desired. The pencils would be helpful and the composition paper, but it was clearly not enough for every student. The closet with its lock was an indication that the administration would decide who would be benefit from the supplies we donated to the school.

Daily, the local teachers would ask if the American teachers would sponsor their families. They were relentless in their requests and made the teachers feel uncomfortable. It was clear another group of American teachers were not going to return. The current educational system in place did not allow nor encourage individuality. Students were more concerned with matriculating through the system to acquire knowledge and master a skill required to earn a living. With each year, the fees for schooling increased and thus requesting help from "rich Americans" was the considered acceptable. Thus, the relentless requests for American's supporting the pursuit of higher education.

Students took numerous tests and if their scores met admission requirements the first available slot would be offered and filled. Students didn't apply for positions they were interested in they merely took tests and were satisfied having the opportunity to continue learning. The American teachers tried to introduce new ideas but local teachers were not open to suggestions. Their form of lesson plans was repeated activities that fostered memorization of information, lacking any sign of creativity. There were no workshops for educators to be trained on new programs and the be provided support to introduce programs and strategies to students. What worked in the past was the way to continue to work forever, not in the present or distant future.

This was noted when students were asked by one visiting teacher to solve a math problem using a visual math strategy. The principal interrupted the lesson and told the guest teacher that was not something students needed to understand. Both embarrassed and upset, the visiting teacher soon realized the mind set for the students was to be a cookie cutter design each willing to accept the system in place. The Consensus was if it's not broke don't fix it.

My most vivid memory was watching the kids outside the school wanting to come inside the gate and learn, but were prevented due to finances. School fees, uniforms and supplies were mandatory to meet the basic admissions and entrance requirements. These children had absolutely nothing but were very well mannered and wanted to be in school. The young African children had an understanding, very early, that the only chance they would ever have a meaningful life was to get an education. Education was highly valued and children and families took this opportunity very seriously. Children did not have to be told that going to school to get an education was important. They knew it simply by living a life that would continue to be passed down to them as it was passed down from their grandparents to their parents. Simply waking up to another day presented the stark and harsh realities of what life was but with some intervention might not always be.

The kids although native Swahili speakers managed to carry on limited conversations with us. They were always interested in money and this added to their natural inclination for catching on to math patterns. They enjoyed learning tricks to multiplication tables and solving simple teasers with ease. It was exciting to see them learning in a different way and help them enjoy school more by sharing these little secrets with them. The kids were learning from this small inter-action with American educational strategies, but I was beginning to understand that even though the visiting teachers were providing a wonderful learning opportunity with great impact, my efforts would be best served providing medical care. We introduced the students to the few American food items we brought with us. Candy of any kind was a favorite.

Surprisingly enough, Kool-Aide topped the children's palates for stimulating their taste buds. The visiting dentists noted what good condition most patient's teeth were in despite the lack of an estab-lished oral hygiene regime of brushing three times a day and flossing. Most patient's dental health was very good. This was attributed to the lack of consuming sweets and sugary beverages. Drinking any fla-vored beverage that was cold was something very odd. Most students had never tasted anything cold or refrigerated. The idea of a cold drink was entirely new. Drinking most if not all beverages at room or outside temperatures, as having a refrigerator was out of the ques-tion. Even though it was eighty degrees outside, the children would sit and shiver as they drank this new tasting and cold beverage. It was a very rare treat for them.

We spent time investigating the conditions in the slums. The roads were not paved and after a rain we drove through muddy ter-rain. If we walked the roads like the locals, we could see the inside of these huts and see what different areas our patients came from. Living in such conditions made it was virtually impossible to stay clean. Throughout these walks we noticed there were no street lights and no wires to gain access to electricity. The idea of running water was out of the question as we constantly watched women and chil-dren hauling water from a water source in the far distance.

The need for a well-organized clinic that our visiting healthcare professionals could provide necessities for the present and formu-late all changes for future trips. The ultimate goal was for a clinic develop into a system that was on-going with a continuous beneficial impact. I soon realized for about one dollar per day, a local African health care provider could be working with us and continue after we left. This arrangement being more effective due to understanding the languages spoken and the general medical concerns of the patients. Translation was the biggest obstacle that needed to be addressed.

After finding someone was well-versed in speaking English, I asked about Kip Keino, the Olympic long distance runner who throughout his career, Kip earned almost a dozen medals, half of which were gold, for being an amazing middle to long distance runner. Kip was almost late for his own race and had to (literally) run to get there, then won a gold medal anyway, despite another major adversity in that race, an injury. I was intrigued to speak with him about his commendable work ethic. His training style was more vigorous than standards set in America. I was interested in what his workout routine entailed and how making it through his strenuous training sessions resulted in athletic success.

I was told he still lives in the Nandi Hills, Rift Valley, Kenya. The 164-mile drive from the Nairobi to Eldoret took about two hours and 46 minutes. Our vehicle traveled over very dangerous and poorly constructed roadways. The driver clocked in at 70 mph which made the drive more treacherous as the recommended 60 mph would have only made the trip travel time three hours and 12 minutes. The road was dusty and bumpy, there were no lane barriers, combined with altitude, driving techniques, condition of vehicles, and weather ranked this road among the world's most unsafe. There were lots of heavy trucks and the driver told us recently a fatal accident between a heavy truck and Matatu claimed several lives. It became apparent that it was not so much the road conditions but the drivers who were the main road hazard. I asked about available transportation and managed to hire a driver.

This ride holds first place for the most dangerously travel route. The two-lane paved highway was filled with potholes. Eager and unskilled drivers passed one another with little regard for safety. The landscape looked void of any life form. I asked the driver f it would be safe to walk across the lush green terrain. He informed me that during the day I might be safe in attempting the excursion, however, at night my chances were greatly reduced to slim if not none. The terrain might appear to be calm and serene, but housed all sorts of wild animals. Every animal residing in this jungle wooded area: elephants, lions, snakes and hyenas would attack you and fight for choice limbs to eat.

The small town of Eldoret, was thriving with residents. The town was surrounded by prime agricultural lands. Looking around the view reminded one of a western movie with the town center separated from the homesteads and farm land. This said the frequent customers moving around the strip of merchants confirmed that this city was growing and known at the fifth largest city outside of Nairobi. A local restaurant featured the best tea and coffee in the world. The sidewalks were constructed with planks of wood. There was little shade from any awnings or roof type structures. After a brief restroom break we continued.

Upon our arrival, our car was eagerly greeted by several multiple aged children. At first I considered this might be an orphanage of some sort, but was immediately informed I was the guest of The Kip Keino Primary School. Since January 1999, the school has provided a quality primary school education to hundreds of students from the Eldoret highlands in western Kenya. In December 2005, the school ranked #1 in the District out of 400 primary schools for the Kenya Certificate of Education Exam for Grade 8 students. All Kip Keino School students who sat for the exam passed and were called to placements in secondary school.

The Kip Keino School is providing a quality education and first class-facilities to the orphans from the Lewa Children's Home and many other deserving children. More than just a top-notch education, the school provides employment to 20 teachers and 31 non-teaching staff from the local region, contributing to the local economy. Bread and Water for Africa has provided critical funds for school construction and for supplemental equipment, supplies and materials such as computers, library books and musical instruments.

Today, the Kip Keino School is one of the best primary schools in the country and more than half of their students join prestigious national schools while the rest that can go on to secondary school join country schools and well performing private schools.

The students informed me Kip was somewhere on the property attending to school business. Students took me on a tour of the twenty-acreage property. When we approached a short fence, I attempted to climb over it to shorten the distance between myself and the buildings in the foreground. Limited in their able to speak English, they did their best to stop me from going over the fence. Before I could place my leg over the short wooden fence my student guide stopped me. I tried to insist I was more than capable of making it over safely when I was told to wait for a moment. They worked at controlling laughing at what might happen. The student guide reached for a long stick and proceeded to place it in the grassy yard I was attempting to enter. The stick sunk down for several feet almost covering it. That meant the grass I thought was rooted on solid ground merely on the top of some really mushy stuff. I was then told cow manure was placed on the other side of this fenced in area and had I not stopped I would be standing up to my waist covered in cow manure.

I began to pay closer attention to the words from the students taking me around the property. Just before reaching the building that stood closer in the foreground, I spotted a rather slim but athletic looking man walking towards us. I then met the legendary Kip Keino. Soft-spoken, Kip greeted me and recognized who I was. Both realizations made quite an impression on me. He walked me to his humble living space and showed me numerous newspaper clippings, awards, and his prized Olympic medal display. We exchanged experiences in our sports careers that were too memorable to be forgotten by ourselves and the world at large. He was most interested in my all too well-known altercation while playing in the NBA.

I shared with him my reasons for coming to Africa being to establish a health clinic in the slums of Kibera. He expressed his support and then told me how he came to get involved with his school. We ended our conversations on such an upbeat note I was even more motivated than before to move forward. Although we haven't been in contact since that day in Eldoret, Africa, the continued success of his efforts is well documented.

CHAPTER 25

Billy Hunter

Billy Hunter, Executive Director of the NBPA

When I accepted the position as director of the National Basketball Player Association Union, I occasionally spent time reflecting on the careers of various former NBA players. One such player that I became interested in was Kermit Washington. In Kermit's case, I began to inquire about his whereabouts, wondering how the Rudy Tomjanovich incident affected him. I was curious to know how the incident impacted his post-NBA life. I suspected that his professional life had been severely limited by the incident, since he had been so negatively represented in the press. And this was that persona non-grata at the NBA. What little I knew of him convinced me that he was a decent person and the incident with Rudy T. was a mistake.

In retrospect, I believe our meeting was providential since unbeknownst to me, Robert Gaston, director of Security at the NBPA office, had received a letter from Kermit requesting financial assistance from the union to acquire prescription medicines for his Project Contact Africa efforts in Nairobi, Kenya. I learned that Kermit had visited Rwanda during the Hutu/Tutsi uprising and slaughtering of eight hundred thousand civilians. After experiencing firsthand, the horrors of such devastation, Kermit was forced to find some way to aid the cause of the survivors who had fled into neighboring Kenya. Though the task was monumental, he began by exhausting his personal resources to purchase medicines, bandages, crutches, etc., for delivery to Kenya. Realizing such efforts would be ongoing with constantly increasing expenses, he began searching for alternative ways to fund the venture. Kermit contacted the NBA but did not receive any acknowledgment of assistance from his inquiries. He then sought the help of the NBPA by writing to Robert Gaston.

Kermit had focused his attention on the camps of Kibera and Kawangware. Both camps were located outside the city limits of Nairobi where most of the refugees from Rwanda had fled. Others in the camps included the poorest Kenyans, as well as refugees from the six countries that bordered Kenya. Many of the inhabitants of the two camps were HIV positive or undergoing the full-blown effects of AIDS. Because he was trying to make a connection with the union, I extended an invitation for him to come in and meet with me.

The outreach for assistance was clearly expressed in the interview we had. He also expressed confidence that the NBPA could leverage medicines and medical supplies from American pharmaceutical companies, medical supply companies, and drugstore chains such as CVS, Rite Aid, and Walgreens. Drugstores around the country had available great sources of unused/expired drugs which had a longer shelf life than I had previously been aware of and could be used to combat illnesses. I assigned Megan Inaba to head up the project, and she urged friends to give us all their unused/expired medicines.

I recall a conversation with Dave Bing in which he stated that he sat on the board of an American pharmaceutical company and could convince the company to aid our project. He was instrumental in gathering a large supply of needed medicines identified by the health-care providers in Kenya. As word began to spread in the outlining areas around Kibera and Kawangware, the number of potential patients began to increase. Free medical assistance for HIV and AIDS, along with respiratory diagnosis, was passed throughout the slums and out into the bush.

Larry Jones, the founder of Feed the Children, was a key contact for getting medicines and facilitating shipment from the United States to Africa. Larry had a contact in Germany who made us aware of a company in Germany that would be able to provide medicines and transport supplies from the United States and Germany into Kenya. Larry was already regularly shipping clothing and food through the Abandoned Baby Clinic in Dogaretti.

As things evolved, Kermit talked about other things we could help with. He had just set up the purchase of a building outside the slums of Kibera to be managed by a native Kenyan, Florence Muyundo. Florence was the neighborhood health-care provider who was looking for a space to operate a clinic connected with Kermit's Project Contact Africa. Larry and I arranged to purchase and send medicines to open this clinic, later named Ray of Hope. We learned how inflated the prices were for medicines. Prices varied in the United States, Europe, and India. Actually, India had the best prices for purchasing medicines with the average cost of $0.05 per pill as compared to $5.00 to $10.00 per pill when purchased in the United States.

Knowing the situation in India, the United States government made it difficult to purchase and transport large supplies of medicines from India to Africa. We were immediately faced with bureaucratic tape. Kermit was expending a great amount of effort in his determination to acquire needed medicines, and that really impressed me. It built up my trust in him as a person. I was impressed years earlier upon learning that Kermit had been selected academic first-team all-American while attending the American University in Washington, DC.

He always demonstrated sensitivity and compassion for his fellow men. Being a black athlete, this was rarely seen except in the cases of Jim Brown, Cookie Gilchrist, Kareem Abdul Jabbar, Bill Russell, Mohamad Al, John Carlos, and Tommie Williams, to name a few one can identify, for displaying similar compassion for others. Far too often black athletes are afraid to exercise the power and influence they possess to make a difference in the world. Kermit's tenacity in this regard greatly impressed me.

Contributions made to help the children in Kenya facing HIV and AIDS was an ongoing battle as the many patients were dying and being buried as fast as their medical needs could be addressed. With the permission of the executive committee of the NBPA, I issued checks from the union to Project Contact Africa to help stop the onslaught of death. I made the NBA players aware of Kermit's efforts and decided to take a group of five players over to Kenya to see how dire the situation was and to gain an understanding of why funding was being provided. The trip was essential to spread among players what efforts were being expended and garner their continued support of these efforts.

We arrived in Nairobi and went to the slums of Kibera. This was about nine years ago, in 2007. Players in the group were familiar with Soweto, South Africa, the apartheid struggle, Steven Biko, and Joseph Mandela, but one could not begin to imagine what true reality was. It is safe to say that Soweto is like Rodeo Drive in Beverly Hills when compared to Kibera. Kibera is the largest slum on the African continent, with approximately one million inhabitants. The US slums do not begin to compare with it. The trip was eye-opening and enlightening and awakened one's soul. Seeing how people struggled, the poor quality of life, despair, and the daily level of abject poverty brought all the players to tears at some time during the trip.

Metta World Peace (Ron Artest) bought a video camera and spent time filming the Kibera community. He felt his colleagues in the NBA needed to see and understand how black refugees in Kibera struggled daily to survive life without any meaning and happiness. He personally donated funds to Project Contact Africa to alleviate this struggle for the Kibera community. He walked the slums and admitted the word "slum" did not accurately describe what he was documenting.

Larry Jones informed me of the World Food Project sponsored by the United Nations and the countries that contributed to the program. We learned that Taiwan was a major contributor of rice and that the ambassador to the United Nations was an avid National Basketball Association fan. Larry arranged a meeting with the ambassador, who expressed a willingness to partner with Feed the Children Inc. and the NBPA. The Taiwanese government donated ten thousand tons of rice, equal to twenty million pounds of rice. The cost of shipping was split between Feed the Children and the NBPA.

The Kenyan government barred the importation of the rice into the country. Larry Jones spent an inordinate amount of time and energy lobbying the Kenyan government for its permission. When his efforts proved worthless, he was forced to seek the assistance of the Anglican Church of Kenya. We were informed by several sources that it would be impossible to import ten thousand tons of rice into the country. The government of the People's Republic of China did not want the Taiwanese government to get any positive publicity, so we had to limit the importation of the rice to 5,000 tons and give half (2,500 tons) to the archbishop of the Anglican Church.

To facilitate this transaction, we had to cut a deal with the archbishop of the Anglican Church and agree to split the rice (five thousand tons) with the archbishop. We were able to import ten million tons of rice to Africa. Kermit's Project Contact Africa was included in this arrangement.

Once the rice arrived in Africa, it was stored in a large warehouse in Mombasa. From Mombasa rice was transported to the warehouse in Nairobi. Some of the rice was exchanged for beans, corn, and grains such as millet and barley. Over a three-year period eight million meals were delivered to the people of Kibera, Kawangware, and Dogaretti. Because of Kermit's Project Contact Africa, Feed the Children, and the NBPA Union, 125,000 meals were provided each week to the residents of the slums. The NBA players got to see all of these efforts and how people's lives were being positively changed for the better. Project Contact Africa made direct distributions of foodstuffs for three years and had continued over the past ten years to provide over two million meals served in the Kawangware area. Kermit and Project Contact Africa and Florence Muyundo provided monthly reports to keep the NBPA abreast of how this feeding program was moving forward over the years.

I distinctly remember at one distribution site young children were lined up with their metal dishes to receive a meal. It was explained that for many, if not all, of the children in line, this would be the only meal they would have for the day and, in some cases, the week. It was a Friday, and many children saved a portion of their meal to be eaten over the weekend, as they would have to wait until Monday before eating again. There was one young five-year-old boy who came to my attention. He wore a stained pair of pants, and I asked the school principal why his pants were stained. The principal explained that this child, like most of the younger students, would put a portion of their food in their pockets to take home and share with their families. Although the students in line ranged from five years of age to twelve years of age, it was noted that the younger children were more likely to take food home and share with siblings and families.

It was as a direct result of working with Kermit on his Project Contact Africa that we became friends. Later I offered him a Job working for the National Basketball Players Association Union and must admit he was the hardest worker, most diligent, and sincere in his interest that every player's needs be met. When asked by me to pursue contacting former players to provide financial compensation for licensing, dues, and workmen's compensation, he contacted the most eligible players. He worked tirelessly to comply with my directive to contact every player, if at all possible.

I continue to make contributions to support Kermit's Project Contact Africa efforts even though we are both no longer affiliated with the National Basketball Players Association. Working with him on his project and as his boss was a pleasure and privilege I appreciate even to this day.

Robyn Hunter and Ron Artest giving out treats to kids

Billy and NBA players feeding millions of African kids

NBA players with CEO of Feed the Children at Ray of Hope School serving meals to students

Theo Ratliff playing with the orphans

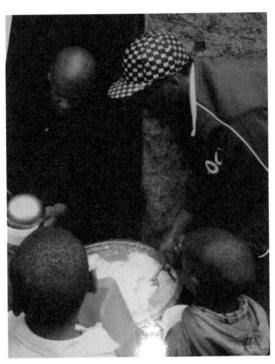

Maurice Evan and Meta World feeding the hungry in Kenya

CHAPTER 26

National Basketball Players Association

While working in Nairobi, Kenya, to distribute the medicines donated to the Ray of Hope Clinic and School from the National Basketball Association (NBPA Union) with Billy Hunter, the executive director, I expressed my interest in working for Billy and the NBPA when a position became available. One year later Billy phoned me after Darnell Valentine left his position, opening a position I felt qualified to apply for. Billy asked me to meet with him in New York to talk about the possibility of my securing this vacancy, before offering me the Job.

I drove up to New York and stayed in a hotel located on Washington Avenue, and my room number was 24, my favorite number. As things go, I do believe in signs, I felt confident—no, I knew I would get the Job. This position was truly a perfect match for me. I would be working with players, this has always been my strength, to establish and nurture personal relationship with athletes.

In my meeting with Billy we talked about the job description and mission of the union to be there for the players, to include education on finance, health, adherence to league rules and regulations regarding drugs, alcohol, and demonstration of acceptable behavior. The main objective was to provide an awareness of league expectations and consequences to eliminate fines, suspensions, or all adverse actions.

I was excited about the position as it would give me the opportunity to share my personal mistakes and successes to help players make better, informed choices and decisions that would positively impact their present and future lives. After joining the NBPA working my first Rookie Transition Program (a program for potential NBA draft choices) held in Orlando, Florida, the need to be able to provide assist in making these transitions from college into professional basketball as smooth as possible was my number one concern to be addressed for every player. With the enormous changes in salaries, the face of the NBA was very different. Now "hanger-oners" were more blatant in their motives to secure as much monetary gains from players without any regard for the interest of the players they sought to exploit. Such individuals were so consumed with their own interests, the same slogan "Don't you trust me?" was the usual opening and closing phrase to most conversation.

With players entering the league at much younger ages than when I played, they are more vulnerable to the unknown selfish interests of their "friends." Back then very few players left school early to sign NBA contracts. Today it is more the norm than not. The money being offered is such a big draw that the willingness to jump into the big leagues is too good to refuse.

The Rookie Transition Program was very well organized. We held break-out sessions led by professionals sporting PhDs who kept discussions focused on the subject matter being presented. By keeping these sessions small and focusing on one main topic per session, questions could be formed and relevant answers if they were easily understood and more likely to be later applied and valued by the participants.

Despite the structure of the sessions, potential draftees were filled with anxiety as they had not yet been drafted by any NBA team. It was stressed throughout the sessions and repeatedly emphasized *not* to sign over a power of attorney, explained what percentage was reasonable for attorneys and agents to request and receive, and how not to be fooled by inflated fees. Each player was urged to *not* sign anything without sending copies of all paperwork to the union for their review. If they felt pressured or uncomfortable, this was a true sign to seek the guidance and support being offered by the NBPA. The league's drug testing policy was thoroughly discussed with consequences resulting from the failure to pass these stressed. The topic most widely explored was the PAY, the difference between actual paycheck vs. contract monies. Revealing to the rookies' deductions such as: federal tax withholdings, FICA, and additional expenses taken from every paycheck became a game stopper for many. It took a while for the reality that signing a million-dollar contract did not mean you were actually paid a million dollars to set in. Awareness of this *need to know* information would encourage living within a budget, putting money aside in savings or well-researched investments, and reducing retail therapy opportunities came as a big surprise to many ifs not all.

Purvis Short was my direct supervisor. He kept me abreast of policy NBA and procedures as well as his expectations concerning fulfilling my Job requirements. He was diligent in meeting deadlines and including all details concerning my Job responsibilities to demonstrate my ability to support the NBPA's mission. He was always available for a quick conversation and strengthened our professional relationship and personal friendship. You couldn't ask for a better boss.

The Top 100 camp was another NBPA program held at the University of Virginia, in Charlottesville, Virginia directly following the end of the high school academic year. My first camp was a true revelation. The talent displayed by these one hundred high school seniors was phenomenal attending the camp coming from schools across the country. We held instructive sessions for both players and their parents about topics such as: what to expect from college recruiters, what courses to take to qualify for enrollment requirements from Division I schools, what to expect from college recruiters who will come and visit you in your homes. The top qualified coaches in the country provided instruction with opportunities to participate in one on one demonstrations. Most players were recognized as the top players in their city or state, but they were now in the company of similar recognized athletes. It was a great opportunity to learn about one's strengths and one's weaknesses and truly assess what level of excellence they had achieved and what level they needed to reach to develop their talent.

The NBPA had a talented group of working professionals: Purvis Short (Roy Hinson, George Johnson, Tim McCormick, and Frank Berkowski— each assigned a group of five NBA teams to work with during the season) and assistant Lupercia Ten. Teams were assigned based on your home location or your primary residence. The expectation was to attend all home games played by your assigned team(s). Prior to each game I visited touch base and discuss needs or concerns they may be having or answer any questions asked whether about personal issues, professional advice, or ideas on how to improve their performance. It was a good way to have a friendly conversation without imposing on the need to focus on the game at hand. Any updated NBA information was shared, but primarily it was a time to continue developing meaningful relationships between players the union and, most important, with me.

All concerns were immediately addressed and dealt with by myself or the union if necessary. Nothing went unresolved, and an area of concern was addressed to provide a solution with support with a positive outcome. Players became more like friends than mere names on any NBA team roster.

In late September seminars were held for players drafted by NBA teams and were identified as NBA rookies. Sessions were led by referees, coaches, former players, and professionals on how to talk and interact in a positive way with the media.

When living in Los Angeles, California, I was assigned the Los Angeles Lakers and the Los Angeles Clipper teams and games to attend. When a player asked to work out with me in weight lifting of learning basketball skills, it allowed me the opportunity to share what I had learned from world-champion bodybuilders from Gold's Gym and basketball skills from Pete Newell's Big Man's Camps.

It is to be noted that the biggest obstacle facing the NBPA and players is *apathy*. Being paid such large salaries, players get comfortable and complacent forgetting how the love for the game brought them to this point. It didn't seem relevant for them to plan for the future and attend meetings or seminars that provided basic information that will help them to make better choices and decisions right now that can impact their financial and personal well-being.

Getting players to think as a *unit* and not as individuals is something I continued to stress when working for the NBPA.

Working for the NBPA challenged me to take a risk and venture into the modern technology oriented world. At first completing expense reports, sending memos, and forwarding meeting agendas were considered tasks I needed to address. Later these became avenues to better organize my thoughts and communicate in written formats to document my improvement in mastering the use of technology.

CHAPTER 27

Theo Ratliff

Theo Ratliff comforts an orphan in Kenya

Making that trip to Nairobi, Kenya, with fellow players to work with Kermit Washington's Project Contact Africa was an opportunity of a lifetime. The office staff of the NBPA made arrangements for five NBA players to participate in this humanitarian work to provide medical supplies and meals in conjunction with the Feed the Children organization.

NBA players were first made aware of the opportunity to make this trip based on the respect we felt for Kermit's efforts through his Project Contact Africa. We were aware that Kermit had founded a clinic and school and was providing medical supplies and a feeding program in Kibera. When the opportunity was discussed and presented to make a trip to join with Feed the Children and Kermit's Project Contact Africa, five NBA players volunteered to participate.

In the year 2007 we visited the slums of Kibera and served meals of rice and beans to the children who were attending the Ray of Hope School founded and supported since 1994 by Kermit's Project Contact Africa. With this firsthand look at a third world country, it made an impression on every one on how to accurately define and document what poverty and impoverishment is. In most instances, it reminded me of what life was like in the United States in the 1930s when electricity, water, and basic necessities were scarce. I can still see Florence Owens Thompson's black-and-white photo of Dorothea Lange (1936) entitled *The Migrant Mother*, who was destitute during the Great Depression in the Dust Bowl of America, and even those conditions could not mirror what we were eyewitnesses of.

It was heartwarming to see that children are children wherever you go. Despite being hungry the children were filled with energy. They were just like my own children who are always eager to play and interact with others. There was an innocence about them that made you want to know more about them. And to understand how they managed to remain optimistic about life while struggling to survive from one day to the next. Being able to provide a meal to each one of these children who had not eaten for three to four days gave me a feeling that words can never describe. We were touched by their desire to share their meals with their families. As of the younger children would eat a small portion of their meal and put the rest aside to take home to their siblings and family members.

Kermit had been working for over twenty years in Nairobi, Kenya, which touched each one of us, especially Metta World. Meta was so impressed by athletic prowess displayed by Kenyan runners he gave serious thought to training in Nairobi. Runners were mandated to run three times every day. Their second run was the nine-mile run up the Ngnog Hills, peaks in a ridge along the Great Rift Valley, located southwest near Nairobi, in southern Kenya. He documented the conditions and personally donated funding to Project Contact Africa and wanted to return and in the city to help provide more support and public awareness of what conditions were like and the efforts being made to improve conditions.

I brought my wife with me on this trip, and she was also deeply moved by the reality of life in the slums of Kibera. We felt blessed and honored that our family and lifestyle was one of comfort and privilege. We were fortunate enough to provide some financial assistance to five Somali refugee families living in the slums. Kermit keeps in touch with them, and three of the five families were able to start small businesses that have helped them to be self-sufficient and provide financial assistance to others. Kermit often referred to the original Sixth Man Foundation concept to provide a helping hand and not a handout.

Seeing how poverty can overwhelm the lives of many, it made all of us realize what a tremendous problem exists in third world countries. Through the efforts of Feed the Children, we were able to serve over two million meals and distribute sixty pounds of rice, beans, and grain. To this day Kermit's Project Contact Africa is providing one thousand meals every week to Kibera residents at various feeding centers, including the Ray of Hope Clinic and School.

As the time, we spent among that Kibera community our group of NBA delegates wanted to show our respect and thanks for the efforts being done for the people who were no longer statistics but individuals with warm personalities and the ability to be happy if given the support needed to overcome their current circumstances in life.

When you are experiencing dire situations that face people daily, you come to have a deeper understanding of the anxieties and stresses that confront people who want to enjoy their lives and not simply endure daily life simply to add one more day to their existence. Playing with the children, sharing their history as they could best relate it to us helped to deepen our commitment to continue whatever efforts the NBPA could provide.

We soon became aware of how, actions maintained or neglected, create a domino effect. We realized we could make a difference by reversing a negative set of circumstances by turn it around to become a very positive forward moving venture to support Billy's efforts, Feed the Children's commitment, and Kermit's Project Contact Africa. We could work together as players providing on-going life sustaining aid if we remained cognizant of the real situation. Seeing what the actual state of the community, the measures in place, and measures needed to be added, we collaborated to formulate a plan of action. This plan would be designed and financially supported to make life less stressful and present positive changes for the residents of Kibera.

This trip was one that will always give me a feeling of purpose in my life and to make sure that I help myself and my family appreciate the benefits we have and the need to share these with others. But the need to be aware of and provide assistance whenever it is within your ability to do so is a lesson I will always strive to keep close to my mind and heart and, therefore, readily apply.

CHAPTER 28

Etan Thomas

In 2007 when Billy Hunter was the director of the National Basketball Player Association Union, I served on a committee with several other NBA players. Billy spoke to us about Kermit Washington's Project Contact Africa in Nairobi, Kenya. He extended an invitation for five players to take a fact-finding/humanitarian trip to support Kermit's efforts in the slums of Kibera. The opportunity sounded interesting, and I agreed to go along. Knowing Kermit—who he was, what he was doing, and what kind of help he was requesting—made deciding to participate in such a trip easy.

Visiting the areas in Nairobi, it was overwhelming to be an eye-witness to the level of poverty which impacted so many people daily. It was equally confounding to see a dichotomy of lifestyles within a few miles of each other. There were areas in Nairobi where homes and garages were similar to those found in most middle- to upper-class families, and there were such devastated areas like the slums in Kibera and Kawangware. As we walked within the slums and among its residents, we were extremely moved with the sincere outward display of appreciation for our presence. Seeing how a simple metal serving bowl filled with rice and beans was so instrumental in the physical and emotional well-being of so many people, often moved us to tears. We also visited an orphanage that cared for infants that were HIV positive or abandoned by families that simply could not care for their needs. We tried to hold as many as we could to silence their cries for the need to be held and cared for.

Larry Jones, who worked along with Billy Hunter of the NBPA, and the five of us who served meals to as many people we could reach showed me that there were programs and individuals who were sincere in their concern and efforts to help people. It was truly good to see people helping others, and it was particularly rewarding to have the opportunity to be actively involved in sincere efforts to make the lives of those in such dire situations better. The feeding program continued for three years serving meals to over two hundred million people. Kermit's Project Contact Africa feeds one thousand meals a week from his Ray of Hope health clinic and school as he continues to support his relief efforts in Kibera.

This trip heightened my social consciousness for the need to help without the underlying objective of gaining something in return. Kermit's program reinforced my view that when you donate to any cause that says their mission is focused on making a difference, it is all too rare to actually see that this is the true reality. By taking this trip I could see along with the other players that every penny donated or supplied by Kermit's personal funds was used to support Kermit's feeding program, the clinic, and the school.

What Kermit Washington did for me was to show firsthand how funding was being used and what was actually being accomplished on an ongoing basis. It made me look at people to gain a better understanding of why their lives were as they were and that when anyone or any organization uses all its financial support to consistently provide assistance, there can be an alleviation to the state of poverty if only for a limited amount of time and in a limited way. There is hope that as long as there are people like Kermit Washington and organizations like Project Contact Africa, helping others will have long-term beneficial results for both recipients and donors of such genuine assistance.

CHAPTER 29

When one door closes – another door opens

Training Robert Sacre of the Lakers

Teaching basketball is an art. Pete Newell was a master whose expertise has changed and continues to influence player performance. The game is a marriage between the mental and physical components when working in harmony with one another produces a well-rounded and gifted player on the court. The ability to read the moves of an opponent and place oneself in the optimal position to respond to those moves makes or breaks a great player's performance on the court. Learning any skill requires patience to practice that skill with repetition for both emphasis and mastery. The ability to understand how and when to apply those skills is the key to Pete Newell's Big Man moves. In every scenario, the moves make the man. Working with Pete helped me learn the moves, successfully apply them and know how to use them to identify the strengths and weaknesses of players who aspire to join the ranks of professional NBA greats.

Once a relationship has been established between myself and the players I work with my biggest challenge is to develop within each player the confidence they will achieve their goal to become an NBA player. It is essential each player believe in themselves and demonstrate their talent to distinguish them as the key component to compliment a team. With so many gifted athletes on the court today, recognizing how your talents can be observed and considered as valuable to a team separates the want the be player from the player chosen. Displaying this on the court, a player will be better equipped to stand out and be noticed. Confidence must be evident in both body language and on the court performance.

The ability to play with maximum endurance is acquired through intense training. Lifting weights provides strength, cardio workouts builds stamina, and practicing Pete's moves develops knowledge. If all three are working together, the well-rounded athlete is prepared to meet any challenge set before them on the basketball court. One must not forget the importance of the heart being the seat of motivation. This influences how a player's performance is demonstrated by applying all three components consistently. Experiencing successful performances helps the heart to motivate the athlete to continue striving for working with diligence and not to become complacent. Working out becomes the natural part of their daily life-style. Every session is fulfilling and informative. Identifying through analysis of their performance focusing on what went well and what did not, allows time for self-reflection. Mentally, players need to envision success by considering working out as on-going, equivalent to breathing.

When working with players who aspire to become NBA players, I share with them the value of setting goals. To help them understand the importance of doing so told them how doing these on two separate occasions greatly influenced my career in the NBA. As a college junior before the basketball season began I recorded on a sheet of paper the name of schools we would play and set a goal as to which games we would win and which we would lose. I placed this information in a sealed envelope to look at after the season ended. When I opened this envelope each one of my goals was achieved.

Later, while sitting on the Los Angeles Laker bench I again thought about NBA career goals and wrote each one down on a sheet of paper. I included no longer being a bench warmer or in the F-troop as the Lakers used to identify ones who rarely got a chance to play. Added the amount of playing time in minutes I wanted to play, becoming a starter, being a team captain, making the All-Star game, etc. I placed this sheet of paper in a sealed envelope and after ten years found it. Upon opening it each one of my goals were met.

The power of setting goals helped me in my career and would be equally beneficial to anyone who did the same and accessed the power of positive thinking and visualization.

Adopting this philosophy, is what influenced my continuing to enjoy working out and the ability to work out with the players I train. Being recognized for this has a had a dual impact on my post NBA career. If viewed as an asset I am contacted and asked to work with players or my skills are considered a threat and dismissed, limiting my delegating assignments to menial tasks. Fortunately, long term relationships with David Falk and Billy Hunter have been both a source of financial and professional support.

While working for the NBPA I was contacted by Los Angeles Laker Robert Sacre. The Lakers were one of the teams the NBPA assigned me to along with Los Angeles Clippers, Denver Nuggets, Utah Jazz, and the Dallas Mavericks. Robert and I met during the NBPA rookie transition seminars held in New York. The sessions focused on helping rookies gain a clear basic understanding of NBA life and pitfalls to avoid. When drafted by the Lakers, Robert and I focused our work-outs on weight training, and conditioning. We would meet at Gold's Gym in Santa Monica five days a week. As our work-out sessions progressed having worked for years until the tutelage of Pete Newell, I put into practice his keen observation skills of how a player performed on the court. I noticed if he practiced with consistency to learn and apply positioning strategies in playing his position in a professional the game of basketball, his game would improve. I was unable to share include this component in the workout sessions with Robert as the Laker team had already made arrangements for someone to work with him on basketball strategies.

Following the regular 2015 season, I was contacted by David Falk offering me the opportunity to work with another Los Angeles Laker player, Roy Hibbert. We made arrangements and focused on mastering basketball skills. Living in Los Angeles presents many challenges for professional athletes. Earning a substantial salary can either motivate one to work harder to maintain the lifestyle they have become used to or make one complacent and comfortable. Hibbert made the commitment to work with me and was always on time and focused. We worked together at a local gym in the Jewish Community Center.

Months my employer informed me my services were no longer needed by the NBPA. Not quite ready to slip into the retirement mode, I decided to continue working out using this time to adjust to my new situation. I was then contacted by Alex Stephenson's parents, who were aware of my working with players on weight training, conditioning, and basketball strategies, and we scheduled a meeting. Alex had attended the NBPA's Top 100 camp as he was recognized as a graduating senior who demonstrated an interest in pursuing the career of an NBA player. Parents were also invited to attend the camp, and while there Alex's parents met and developed a friendship with George Johnson.

George and I held the same Job assignments while employed by the NBPA. Alex's parents asked George who would the best person to work with Alex for him to achieve his goal of playing in the NBA. George recommended me. After receiving a phone call from his parents, we arranged a meeting. We discussed their son Alex's desire to earn a spot on an NBA team they had heard I was the go-to man. We arranged for Alex to work with me three days a week. Being a strong and capable player, his needed a combination of basketball skills and getting into game playing shape to achieve his goal. Mid-way into our training, his agent arranged for him to try-out with a team and he soon came to understand the meaning of being in basketball game shape.

I continued to focus Alex's attention on his acquisition of this game breaking changer. Alex played well in the first half of a game, but tired out as the game progressed to record the final score. I explained: if a jockey is given entry to the Kentucky Derby riding a mule, with the other entrants riding Secretariats, the odds of the jockey on the mule being able to run in and finish the race is slim if not none, as slim left town yesterday. As being in game shape with the physical stamina able to display full effort until the game ending buzzer sounds, was the key to his making an impression on coaches and or representative of NBA teams. We then focused on increasing his stamina.

After speaking with the coordinator of the NBA summer league held in Las Vegas, Nevada, about Alex he as giving the opportunity to participate. Making an impression on a few coaches he later Joined the D league and later moved into the NBA for a few weeks.

Billy Hunter then called and asked if I would be interested in working with Sooren Derboghosian. A recent UCLA graduate who saw limited playing time while there. We met and set up a schedule to work-out together. His major skill lies in his consistent ability to make baskets. He lost weight, enduring the rigorous weight-lifting under myself and Danny Padilla: the well-known body builder working on weight training, strengthening skills, nutrition, learning, practicing and implementing Pete Newell's Big Man's Camp moves, and building court stamina running daily.

Brian Taylor a former, San Diego Clipper teammate, joined me in working with both Alex and Sooren in March of 2016.

The NBPA was very helpful and supportive of sponsoring Project Contact Africa funding for the Ray of Hope Clinic and School. When that door closed another opened to take time to work on this book and to pursue another career path. Ever since meeting with Pete Newell and learning how to work with players an understanding the game in the pro ranks, I have been asked to train and focus on one on one basic basketball moves with Alex Stephenson and Sooren Derboghosian.

Alex was picked up from the D-league by the Los Angeles Clippers and moved up play in a few NBA games before being cut. Hopefully, Sooren will be ready to try out for an NBA team by participating in the 2016 Summer League in Las Vegas, Nevada. Both players display a keen desire to learn the game and work with weight training to improve strength and endurance. There is a great need to understand the difference between being in shape and being in shape to play basketball. The knowledge and experience gained from Pete Newell and weight training from the best body builders in the world at Gold's Gym has provided me with the ability to share this with others. This new focus continues to be one of the most enjoyed Jobs I have had in recent years.

In working with locals, it soon becomes apparent most business ventures include an agenda that is disclosed over time. Poverty shapes individual's basic needs, wants, and these are met and or acquired. Coming from the United States many Africans assume you have an unlimited source of funds and seek assistance. Having close connections with Florence has made efforts to meet financial obligations in Kibera, Mathare, and Kwangware a process that has and continues to work out for the benefit of the continuation of operating the clinic, school, sponsored families and feeding the community. When I am asked, "How can I help?" or "How much can I donate?" I always respond, "You need to make a trip with me." As every penny of funds received are directly used to sponsor a family, support the clinic and school, purchase medical supplies and equipment, and continue our daily feeding program. By actually seeing what contributing funds can accomplish, then deciding how you want these funds to be distributed should be an individual choice. Everything will continue to be done to continue meeting current and future needs with the concerted intent to making a meaningful difference.

CHAPTER 30

You Have to Do Something

It always amazes me the sensations of waking up in one geographic location and then over a period of hours going to sleep in another. The travel to Africa is always a challenge with airline seats featuring limited leg room and hours of being suspended in space with the hope of safely arriving on land. After landing and taking off numerous times in extended hours in the air, it is not a serious concern as to exactly where you land, just as long as you land safely. You need to remember not to drink the water or use it to brush your teeth. The simple actions you take for granted present potential dangers when not in your natural surroundings.

All in all, when in Africa, I continually consider the many things I normally take for granted. Daily visits to the Ray of Hope Clinic and School in Africa present numerous opportunities to do that during my day. Looking out the hotel window, watching people moving about, it was time to visit the clinic and check on things. Florence was already there getting the day's routine under way. The students were eagerly waiting for their morning meal and greeting me with warm smiles and hugs. The reality was that with Project Contact Africa's consistent support, these small children are continuing to grow up with a focus on securing their desire to improve their futures through the ability to have access to educational opportunities for increased learning.

Over the years it can be noted how all the students regularly attend schools to succeed in fulfilling goals and dreams. From the first time, we saw the building, one can't help but observe how major improvements both in the physical structure, the administration, and the programs have resulted in positive changes for the community of Kawangware. Families continue to require financial assistance, and on every visit the excursion to the local grocery store is the one venture most anticipated and appreciated. Entering the grocery store, the thrill of meeting the challenge to shop for items much needed but too expensive to purchase on a regular basis, with spontaneity and success, fills the air. Eyes widen at the choices available, and the only detriment is the knowledge of a set budget for the excursion, which streamlines choices from the wants to the needs element for the day. Being aware of which supplies are the best choices to select, it is noted that in addition there is always one item or two included to make the excursion special and memorable.

Packing up purchases is the biggest demonstration of skill and genius exhibited by the shoppers. It is important that it not be observed by anyone what items are being purchased and placed in a vehicle. Great care is taken to pack items in brown paper boxes to appear as if supplies do not include foodstuffs. I rarely enter the grocery store with the intent of accompanying the shoppers. I stroll up and down the aisles with the sole purpose of reminding everyone of the budget and the need to buy items that are normally not within their budget restrictions. Meat is a valuable and expensive commodity, but without refrigeration it is not something you would buy a large quantity of, but you can purchase a limited amount to be used immediately.

Beans, rice, grains, and cooking oil are the staples. Butter is not a staple, but large containers of oil is a necessity used daily in all meal preparations. Items I would have placed in a shopping cart are not available, and the substitutions considered staples are quite interesting. One can never be more impressed by the ingenuity displayed by the shoppers when choosing what products to put in their shopping carts.

Since meeting Florence in 1997, she has worked exclusively with Project Contact Africa to establish and maintain the Ray of Hope Clinic and School. She continues to spearhead the daily feeding program by purchasing foodstuffs, organize transportation to and from the clinic for patients, locate and purchase medical supplies, purchase food, contact local resources to acquire supplies and medical professionals, provide additional tutoring for all students, maintain all financial records, and communicate on a regular basis to help supporters remain in touch with the daily operation of the Ray of Hope Clinic and School.

In 2008 Lydia was hired to maintain and manage apartments for American University students who attended the School of International Service foreign exchange students. Knowing the dean, Lou Goodman, I inquired about the programs that were currently available for students participating in oversees programs. We discussed the Ray of Hope Clinic and School and developed a program that sent over fifteen to twenty students every semester. This program was in place for over five years. Students worked in the clinic and in the school with students while attending regular courses delivered by Kenyan professors. The curriculum was approved by American University and was later moved to South Africa. When the five-year program was moved, Lydia remained with the Ray of Hope Clinic and School and was given monthly funds to support herself and her two children. The apartments are no longer used by Project Contact Africa, and Lydia works when needed at the facility.

Sam continues to support our efforts with the Ray of Hope Clinic and School. Teresa opened her own school in a more rural area of Africa as of October 2013 and Cheryl Meyers stepped in to support our efforts.

At the end of each school year, a special excursion is planned for the students and staff. Arriving at the clinic and school, the excitement and anticipation can be felt in the air. The positive energy is both stimulating and rewarding. The students and staff who all have worked hard share the opportunity to be commended and supported for the sincere efforts that continue to positively impact all. It would be an oversight not to mention this activity with the students and staff as sharing in such a joyous occasion helps everyone to be more determined to maintain their goals with the knowledge that all efforts will be recognized and appreciated.

It clearly is one activity the students enjoy, and it provides them with an opportunity to be introduced to foods and establishments they would not likely have access to. Kentucky Fried Chicken was our most recent excursion. Of the many excursions taken to the Nairobi National Park, The Giraffe Center on the edge of the Nairobi National Park, picnics at Jeevanjee Gardens, grocery shopping at Nakumatt and lunch at KFC in the Galleria Shopping Mall, Java (Valley Arcade), Uhuru Park is considered to be the most beautiful and popular inner city park in Nairobi. The recreation park features a variety of natural play areas for children, an artificial lake and several national monuments, and the Jolly Roger Theme Park.

Taking Florence, Vanessa, Lydia, Evelyn and two mothers from the community shopping at Nakumatt is always an adventure. The grocery store is located inside the guarded Galleria shopping mall. To gain access to the many retail shops and entertainment experiences, a guard must admit you. If you don't look a certain way or have some history with the guards, you are not likely to be granted entry to the premises. Back packs and large purses must be checked in with the guards before entering the Nakumatt grocery store.

As you walk inside you see seven workers walking up and down each aisle. They are there to help in locating items and to guarantee that nothing is stolen. This means that while shopping you constantly interact with a store employee. This might sound expensive but the daily salary for these employees is less than $2.00 a day.

On my last visit in 2015 we had planned to picnic at Jeevanjee Gardens but it was raining. We considered other options and decided to go to the Galleria Shopping Mall after learning the students, two mothers and most of the administrative staff had never been there. KFC's was located there and fried chicken with all the trimmings was a new and quite enjoyed experience. The conversations held throughout the restaurant varied from the menu items, the mall itself and appreciating how the rain made this year's celebration different from others. This willingness to show concern and actively support others to make each day of their lives meaningful and rewarding I will continue to provide financial and any other assistance, along with many others who are caring and passionate to enhance and show appreciation for the value of life.

CHAPTER 31

Inception and On-going
Sixth-Man Foundation and Project
Contact Africa Non-Profit efforts:

If it weren't for the Blazers and their fans, this would have never come about. When I started the Sixth Man Foundation, I was doing well financially, and I wanted to thank the people of Portland. They're the greatest fans in the world. We were treated like family. I wanted to give back their kindness. In the early years, the sole supporter was Nike founder, Phil Knight–who donated thousands of shoes to inner-city kids who made academic improvement.

I made a commitment with owner Larry Weinberg to come-back and play as a Portland Trail Blazer and donate my full salary to helping the people of Portland through the Sixth Man Foundation.

1. When come-back attempt did not happen, organized an All-Star Game held at the Memorial Coliseum in Portland, Oregon. Raised $56,000.00 as start-up money.

2. I purchased and sold a Leroy Neiman limited painting (low number) in (1973). A donor requested a Clyde Drexler signed game worn Olympic Jersey. This jersey was sold and donated funds for upcoming trips to Africa for healthcare workers to the 6th Man Foundation.

3. Donated my 928 Porsche in Portland for charity start-up funds. Automobile purchased for $50,000.00. Held a radio auction. Sold raffle tickets for $20.00 each.

4. I purchased and had signed NBA jerseys: Shawn Kemp; Scottie Pippin, Michael Jordan, Clyde Drexler, all Trail Blazers.

5. I paid for four healthcare workers airfares, hotel and housing with stop in Amsterdam.

6. I paid round trip airfare, accommodations and additional expenses to Nairobi, Kenya ($2,500.00) after received communication requesting assistance in locating family members separated during genocide in Rwanda, for translator in Goma, Zaire (Vienne.)

7. I paid airfare and all expenses for doctors and nurses to travel to Nairobi to provide free medical assistance at a self-made clinic.

8. Medicine was donated from medical companies in Portland, Oregon, Jay Donkers.

9. I paid $25,000.00 for airfare and hotel expenses for 15 healthcare workers for travel to and from Nairobi and work in a ten-day sponsored free clinic for Kibera slum residents.

10. My severance and retirement money from the NBA was the source of this funding. During my first days in Nairobi I was robbed of $5,000.00 to be used to pay for teaching staff and administration. I had to use my personal funds to recover this amount to pay fees.

11. While conducting a free clinic with Dr. Gipson and Richard we needed the assistance of someone who spoke English and had medical experience. It was there we met Florence Muyundo, and established administrative staffing and building arrangements for current the school and clinic. After visiting Florence's clinic, the facility was so poorly outfitted to provide adequate services we discussed the need to find a better location and use this for the cur-

rent school and clinic. We were able to find a building facility in the local village of Kawangware. This location was selected because the current owner had stopped construction due to a lack of funds and I was able to negotiate monthly rent fees provided we financed the completion of the building property.

12. I paid to complete the project and signed a contract for a set monthly fee of $1,000.00. Once construction was completed we paid for furnishing the clinic – with medical and office materials, built a water tower, correct wiring of electrical outlets.

13. Monthly fees to run the clinic, including administrative fees to Florence of $800.00, I hired and paid with personal funds one artist (he had a showing at a local gallery and the manager found the artist and arranged for us to meet) to paint (mural fee was $3,500.00 in addition to walls and other areas requiring painting), landscape – including purchasing greenery and rocks), and other matters that required attention to provide quality medical care, etc.

14. The NBPA brought over $50,000.00 work of medicine and supplies to support the opening of the clinic.

15. I purchased an automobile for Florence to use as transportation and as an ambulance when needed.

16. Two apartments were paid for one to be used by Florence and the second to house students (American University foreign exchange program with School of International Service) and volunteer doctors and nurses working in the clinic to provide extra help for Florence and the community. Both apartment monthly rental fees were $800.00/ apartment not including utilities.

17. When working in the free clinic it was noticed that there were numerous children hanging around the clinic. These children included some who were homeless and HIV positive but all were hungry and eager to receive a meal. We

then started feeding children breakfast which led to establishing a daycare center which later became the school and clinic in Nairobi. The initial number of students grew to 55. Some of these students are HIV positive and were abandoned by family either through death of situational poverty.

18. As the children grew in age and required additional educational opportunities we hired teachers a salary of $400.00/month for 2 teachers. As these children continued to grow and met school age requirements it became evident that we would need to place them in schools and provide financial assistance for uniforms, school fees and supplies.

19. As the children were placed in neighborhood schools and additional expense of transportation and increased schooling fees each year was provided by the project. School fees vary depending on the age and grade level requirements but all 55 students (up to current – we provide breakfast before going to school, pay for round trip transportation to seven different schools to and from the clinic – uniforms, school supplies, during the weekend we fund a tutoring program which includes meals.) This arrangement for weekend support was the direct result of learning students did not eat on the weekends but waited to be fed on returning to school. Children prior to this arrangement did not have meat unless provided by the project.

20. Purses, jewelry, sewing machines I purchased to start small business opportunities for local families of students who attend school and clinic.

21. I purchased hair extensions to start up small business in Nairobi, Kenya for $20,000.00 to provide on-going financial assistance to school and clinic. We are still waiting to see if that venture is going to be successful.

22. I provide extra funding to Florence when expenses exceed monthly allowance.

23. Fasted – went without food had only water for 7 days for two consecutive years on American University campus. (Fast for Funding) – With Dr. Teresa Gipson and Richard.

24. Over the years, used my NBA connections, to gather autographed shoes from Kobe Bryant, Dwight Howard, Steve Nash and Carmelo Anthony, among others as auction items.

25. Ron Artest's donation to create a medical lab at the clinic and pay for operation for Kenyan student and discharge fees from hospital.

26. The medical clinic features four patient rooms, a pharmacy and a lab and brings more than 40 healthy Kenyan babies into the world every month. Between 20 and 30 people visit the clinic every day for medical care.

27. Roughly 50 kids, between the ages of 3 and 10, attend classes five days a week. Some are HIV positive. They live in poverty and receive little educational guidance at home so they fall behind educated peers in every measurable barometer. The goal is to catch them up and send them back into the Kenyan school system with the tools to graduate and go on to college.

28. The kids are fed two meals a day during the school week –usually grains and beans but sometimes meat – and the school gives grains and beans to their families, providing food for up to eight people in each family every day.

29. The school features two classrooms and a library and Gipson and Washington acquired laptop computers through grants. When the kids learn enough to catch up to their grade, Dr. Gipson and I paid for uniforms, books and supplies to support the children so they can return to public school and continue with their education.

30. I used funds from all Academic All American speaking engagements to sponsor doctor trips to Africa.

31. I return to Nairobi every year, sometimes paying for doctors and nurses to join me and provide medical help.

32. I initiated with Lewis Goodman (Dean of the School of International Service) a study abroad program in the slums of Nairobi. 20 students worked in the school and clinic. 202-885-2000 per semester.

33. I paid for apartments (Students, guest health care professionals – 2 years-2008-2011) and Florence (3 years-2008-2011) ($800.00 plus utilities and housekeeper = $1,000.00/apartment/month)

34. I paid for furnishings for both apartments–$9,000.00 Nakumatt-store

35. Organized water purifying program for filtration tanks which last for years to help purify drinking liquids – particularly contaminated water to purified drinking water. Students given memorabilia to purchase containers.

36. I pay Superior Grocery Store Manager Felecia:–Between $300.00–$500.00/month $10,000.00 donated to Gezina Lavely to start up **first** cab company from my personal funds.

37. $10,000.00 was donated to Gezina Lavely to start up **second** cab company from my personal funds.

38. I provide Florence funds to cover monthly fees vary depending on school needs – recent (5/2015) visit was $1,400.00

39. I paid $2,000.00 for Doctors and Nurses paid for flights and hotel accommodations for two doctors, Elsa Marie and a nurse. After working in the clinic, I paid for hotel and meals for 2 days in Amsterdam for the doctors and nurses.

40. I worked with Feed the Children to provide meals for millions of kids in Nairobi, Kenya.

41. I personally sponsor 22 students with financial support for school feed, uniforms, meals, transportation to and from school.

42. I pay for counselor fees to keep track of student's progress to address any concerns.

43. I paid $2,000.00 hospital fees for 10 Kenyan family members.

44. Edna worker at school/clinic in Nairobi –I paid $2,000.00, for airfare and expenses to go to Italy for school. Contact Florence Muyundo

45. We paid $100.00/month financial assistance each to each 5 Somali families for 4 years. (2011-2013)

46. I provided $3,500.00 my bonus NBA check donated to LAPD detective Eddie Jordan to sponsor 30 inner city teenagers and 5 chaperones Disneyland field trip.

47. $21,500.00 personal funds were donated from my personal memorabilia items: John Havlicek retirement belt buckle–$5,000.00, signed Michael Jordan game shoes–$1,000.00, signed Kobe Bryant game shoes–$1,000.00, Laker team shoes signed–$8,000.00 , signed portrait of Michael Jordan–$1,000.00, signed Klay Thompson game shoes–$500.00, organized – planned All-Star game in Portland, Oregon – John Stockton, Purvis Short, Dominique Wilkins; Red Auerbach Boston Celtic memorabilia – signed game jerseys–$5,000.00.

48. I paid for Edna to supervise orphans ($200/month from 2009-2011) then worked in Clinic ($200/month) and relocation trip to Italy ($1,500).

49. I pay for Evelyn and her seven children. Rent and school fees. (2013-present) $200.00/month plus school fees and food stuffs.

50. I pay Vanessa Lubanga pay for her rent and school fees. ($5,000/year – 2006-present)

51. I pay Lydia Wepukhunu pay ($300/month plus rent (2005 – present) plus $300.00 three times a year for school and material fees in Nairobi (Secondary school fees are higher than elementary school fees.) Additional: $2,000 gifts for holidays and food stuffs.

52. Florence Muyundo I pay for all expenses when her health is compromised. (2004-2006 $500/month) (2006-2012 $2,000/month apartment/administrative salary) (2012 -present $10,000/year)

53. Teresa Gipson was paid ($1,000/month – 2008-10/012013 for Ray of Hope Clinic and School support)

54. Cheryl Meyers is paid ($1,500/month – Kawangware Kids 10/01/2013-present)

Yearly visit ($10,000.00) for 50 student/8 administrators/2 community mother's celebration. Group excursions to: Nairobi National Park, The Giraffe Center on the edge of the Nairobi National Park, picnics at Jeevanjee Gardens, grocery shopping at Nakumatt and lunch at KFC in the Galleria Shopping Mall, Java (Valley Arcade), Uhuru Park. is the most beautiful and popular inner city park in Nairobi and it offers a wide range of fun and exciting activities such as boat riding on the lake, camel riding, picnic with friends and family. The recreation park features a variety of natural play areas for children, an artificial lake and several national monuments, and the Jolly Roger Theme Park. Include air fare, hotel, meals – with staff and administrators, gifts, replacing clinic and school supplies.

From the authors:

Thank you for reading our publication. We hope you enjoyed reading it as much as we did in writing it. Please note all the information included is accurate and was verified by the following document.

DESERT POLYGRAPH

LAS VEGAS, NEVADA
TELEPHONE: (760) 427-8975
DHARAM.SAMRA@YAHOO.COM
NEVADA LICENSE: 2269E

4/12/2017

Kermit Washington Polygraph Examination

Examiner's Conclusion: **No Deception Indicated**

EXAMINATION:

On 4/12/2017, Kermit Washington appeared for a polygraph examination at his request. Washington signed a consent form stating he was voluntarily submitting to the examination. A copy of the form is on file. During the pre-test interview the polygraph instrument and examination procedures were explained.

Washington presented himself in a neat well dressed manner. He was polite, alert, and responsive during the pre-test interview. His demeanor was friendly and cooperative. I determined Washington was a suitable candidate for a polygraph examination.

PRE-TEST INTERVIEW:

At the beginning of the pre-test interview Washington explained he had written a book and wanted to use polygraph test results to prove the contents of the book were true.

TEST PROCEDURE:

Following the pre-test interview, a series of two Utah Zone Comparison Tests (Utah ZCT) utilizing relevant, neutral, and comparison questions were designed and administered utilizing a Lafayette LX-5000 computerized instrument. Each question on the examination was reviewed and discussed with Washington prior to the instrument phase of the examination.

The following questions were among those that appeared in the polygraph examination.

UTAH, ZCT:

R1: Is everything about Africa in your book true?
Answer: "Yes."

R2: Is everything you wrote in your book about Africa true?
Answer: "Yes."

R3: Is everything in your book about Africa true?
Answer: "Yes."

1

DESERT POLYGRAPH

LAS VEGAS, NEVADA
TELEPHONE: (760) 427-8975
DHARAM.SAMRA@YAHOO.COM
NEVADA LICENSE: 2269E

NOTE:

The Utah ZCT is a validated testing format approved and listed by the American Polygraph Association. The Utah ZCT was scored as instructed using the Empirical Scoring System (ESS).

TEST DATA ANALYSIS & RESULTS:

The examination chart data was analyzed and numerically scored. Washington did not produce any significant physiological reactions to the relevant questions. This procedure resulted in a finding of: **No Deception Indicated.**

EXAMINER'S PROFESSIONAL OPINION:

Washington's answers to the relevant test questions are considered to be: **Truthful.**

POST-TEST INTERVIEW:

No post-test interview was conducted.

Dharam K. Samra
Polygraph Examiner
Las Vegas, Nevada

2

CHAPTER 32

Glossary of Persons of Interest/Players

Glossary 1: Abdul Jeelani: Abdul Qadir Jeelani (born Gary Cole) is a retired American professional basketball player. He was a 6'8" and 210 lb. small forward and played collegiately at the University of Wisconsin–Parkside. He had a brief career in the National Basketball Association (NBA).

Jeelani was drafted on June 8, 1976 by the NBA's Cleveland Cavaliers in the third round of the 1976 draft, but he was later waived in October of that year. He was later signed by the Detroit Pistons on September 2, 1977 but was again waived a month later, prior to the start of the 1977-78 season. He played one season with the Portland Trail Blazers in 1979–80 and was made available in the expansion draft on May 28, 1980, where he was taken by the Dallas Mavericks prior to their inaugural season in 1980–81. He was part of the starting lineup for the Mavericks' first NBA game in 1980 and scored the first points in franchise history. In his first season with the Mavs, he seemed to have a knack for scoring in the final quarter of games. As of January 20, 1981, when he had played 43 games, 142 of his 350 points had come in the last period.

Glossary 2: Adrian Dantley played 15 seasons in the National Basketball Association (NBA). A forward/guard and six-time NBA

All-Star, he was inducted into the Basketball Hall of Fame in 2008. In the 1976 NBA draft Dantley was drafted sixth overall by the Buffalo Braves. He became the third Buffalo player in five years to receive the NBA Rookie of the Year Award when he won it after the 1977 season.

In his seven years with the Jazz, Dantley picked up all six of his All-Star appearances and two All-NBA second-team honors.

Dantley finished his career with an average of 24.3 points per game. He scored his points with a mix of flat-footed mid-range jump shots, high-percentage opportunities close to the basket, and frequent trips to the free throw line. For his career, he shot .540 from the floor-16th in NBA history-and .818 from the free throw line. He led the league in free throws six times and ranks sixth all-time in that category. He shares the record with Wilt Chamberlain for the most, free throws made in a regular-season NBA game with 28.

Glossary 3: Artis Gilmore: Artis Gilmore an American retired basketball player who played in the American Basketball Association (ABA) and National Basketball Association (NBA). Gilmore was inducted into the Naismith Memorial Basketball Hall of Fame on August 12, 2011. A star center during his two collegiate years at Jacksonville University, in Jacksonville, Florida, Gilmore led the Dolphins to the NCAA Division I championship game in 1970, where his team was beaten 80-69 by the UCLA Bruins. Gilmore remains the top player in rebounds per game in the history of NCAA Division I basketball.

Gilmore followed five All-Star seasons with the Kentucky Colonels of the ABA by becoming the first overall pick of the 1976 NBA dispersal draft, which was held after the ABA was disbanded, as four teams transferred to the NBA. In Gilmore's complete pro basketball career, he was an eleven-time All-Star, the ABA Rookie of the Year, and an ABA MVP, and he remains the NBA career leader for field goal percentage. Nicknamed "The A-Train", the 7'2" (2.18 m) Gilmore once played in 670 consecutive games.

Glossary 4: Austin Carr, Austin Carr, (a 6-foot 4-inch (1.93 m), 200 lb. (91 kg) shooting guard first came to prominence as a highly recruited player for the University of Notre Dame, arriving after having scored more than 2,000 points during his high school career. Carr lived up to his lofty billing by ending his three-year career at Notre Dame with 2,560 points (an average of 34.5 points per game), ranking him fifth all-time in college basketball history at the time of his departure. During his final two seasons, Carr became only the second college player ever to tally more than 1,000 points in a season, joining Pete Maravich in that select group. Carr holds NCAA tournament records for most points in one game (61 vs. Ohio in 1970), most field goals in one game (25), and most field goals attempted in one game (44). His record scoring average of 50 points per game in seven NCAA playoff games may never be broken.

Recently, ESPN named Carr the 22nd greatest college basketball player of all time. Carr moved onto the professional ranks as the first overall selection of the Cleveland Cavaliers in the 1971 NBA Draft. Carr was also selected in the 1971 ABA Draft by the Virginia Squires, but signed with the Cavaliers on April 5, 1971. Carr's first season in the NBA was marred by a series of injuries that limited his output. During the 1971 preseason, he broke his foot and missed the first month of the season. Less than one month after returning to the court, he was sidelined again by another foot injury, missing another seven weeks. Upon his return, he began to display the skills which made him the top selection in the NBA draft and was named to the 1972 NBA All-Rookie Team. Following the conclusion of his first season, Carr had surgery to clear up any lingering foot problems.

Two months into the 1974–75 season, he suffered a knee injury that put him out of the lineup indefinitely. His absence in the lineup likely prevented the Cavaliers' from capturing their first-ever playoff berth, with the team's bid falling one game short

However, during the next three seasons, Carr played a role in three straight playoff appearances for the team.

Glossary 5: Bernard King: Bernard King is an American retired professional basketball player at the small forward position in the National Basketball Association (NBA). He played 14 seasons with the New Jersey Nets, Utah Jazz, Golden State Warriors, New York Knicks and the Washington Bullets. He was inducted into the Naismith Memorial Basketball Hall of Fame on September 8, 2013.

At 6'7" and 205 pounds, Bernard King epitomized the explosive, high-scoring NBA small forward of the 1980s. With his long arms and quick release, King was a tremendous scorer. Speed permeated his game, whether cutting to the hoop or finishing on the fastbreak. King led the NBA in scoring in the 1984–85 season with 32.9 points per game and was selected twice to the All-NBA First Team and four times to the NBA All-Star Game.

In 1977–78, his rookie season, he set a New Jersey Nets franchise record for most points scored in a season with 1,909, at 24.2 points per game. He would later surpass this record with his 2,027-point season in 1983–84, earning the first of his back-to-back All-NBA First Team selections.

January 31 and February 1, 1984, King made history by becoming the first player since 1964 to score at least 50 points in consecutive games. He scored 50 points on 20 for 30 shooting with 10 free throws. King followed this with another 50-point performance at Dallas, setting a Reunion Arena single-game scoring record in the process. He scored 11 points in both the first and second quarters and 14 points in both the third and fourth quarters. King drew 13 fouls on Mavericks defenders, including Mark Aguirre, who fouled out. King shot 20 for 28 from the field with 10 free throws in the 105–98 win over the Dallas Mavericks.

The next season, King lit up the New Jersey Nets for 60 points in a losing effort, becoming just the tenth player in NBA history to score 60 or more points in a single game. King had scored 40 points by halftime, and finished the game with 19 of 30 shooting from the field and 22 of 26 from the free throw line.

At the peak of his career, however, King suffered a devastating injury to his right leg while planting it under the hoop attempting to block a dunk by Kansas City King Reggie Theus. The March 23, 1985 injury, which included a torn anterior cruciate ligament, torn knee cartilage, and broken leg bone, required major reconstruction, causing King to miss all of the 1985-86 season. To that point no NBA player had returned to form after such a potentially career-ending injury, surgery, and loss of time.

Rehabilitating completely out of the media spotlight, King drove himself back into competitive shape. Despite averaging 22.7 points per game during his first six games back, he had not recovered his pre-injury explosiveness and was released by the Knicks at the end of the 1987 season. He used the 1987-88 to solidify his come-back with the Washington Bullets, then launched into three straight plus 20 point seasons, peaking at a remarkable 28.4 as a 34-year-old in 1990-91. Having played 81games in 1988-89 and all 82 in 1989-90 he had proved the naysayers wrong both on his skills and durability, then walked away on-top as the 1990-91 NBA's #3 scorer and an All-Star for a final time. After a year-and-a-half hiatus, King returned for an ill-fated 32-game stint with the New Jersey Nets at the end of the '93 season, when knee problems forced him permanently to the sidelines.

Glossary 6: Bertil Fox: Bertil Fox won the 1969 Junior Mr. Britain at 18. He went on to win nearly every major bodybuilding contest outside of the IFBB, including the 1976 AAU Mr. World, the amateur 1977 NABBA Mr. Universe and the professional NABBA Mr. Universe in 1978 and 1979.

Glossary 7: Bill Cartwright: Bill Cartwright A 7'1" (2.16 m) center, he played 16 seasons for the New York Knicks, Chicago Bulls and Seattle Super Sonics, helping the Bulls capture consecutive championships in 1991, 1992 and 1993. Cartwright was the third overall pick in the 1979 NBA draft selected by the New York Knicks. As a member of the Knicks, he made his only All-Star Game appearance in his rookie year of 1979-80. Cartwright averaged more than 20 points per game in his first two seasons for the Knicks. His playing time decreased during his time in New York, initially due to injury (he suffered four separate fractures to his left foot) and then due to the arrival of number-one pick Patrick Ewing which changed Cartwright's role to that of a backup center.

Glossary 8: Bill Russell: Bill Russell: William Felton "Bill" Russell is an American retired professional basketball player. Russell played center for the Boston Celtics of the National Basketball Association

(NBA) from 1956 to 1969. A five-time NBA Most Valuable Player and a twelve-time All-Star, he was the centerpiece of the Celtics dynasty, winning eleven NBA championships during his thirteen-year career. Along with Henri Richard of the National Hockey League's Montreal Canadians, Russell holds the record for the most championships won by an athlete in a North American sports league

Russell is widely considered one of the best players in NBA history. He was listed as between 6 ft. 9 in (2.06 m) and 6 ft. 10 in (2.08 m), and his shot-blocking and man-to-man defense were major reasons for the Celtics' success. He also inspired his teammates to elevate their own defensive play. Russell was equally notable for his rebounding abilities. He led the NBA in rebounds four times, had a dozen consecutive seasons of 1,000 or more rebounds, and remains second all-time in both total rebounds and rebounds per game. He is one of just two NBA players (the other being prominent rival Wilt Chamberlain) to have grabbed more than 50 rebounds in a game. Though never the focal point of the Celtics' offense, Russell also scored 14,522 career points and provided effective passing.

Russell is one of only seven players in history to win an NCAA Championship, an NBA Championship, and an Olympic Gold Medal. He was inducted into the Naismith Memorial Basketball Hall of Fame and the National Collegiate Basketball Hall of Fame. He was selected into the NBA 25th Anniversary Team in 1971 and the NBA 35th Anniversary Team in 1980, and named as one of the 50 Greatest Players in NBA History in 1996, one of only four players to receive all three honors. In 2007, he was enshrined in the FIBA Hall of Fame. In 2009, the NBA announced that the NBA Finals Most Valuable Player trophy would be named the Bill Russell NBA Finals Most Valuable Player Award in honor of Russell.

Russell was an elite help defender who allowed the Celtics to play the so-called "Hey, Bill" defense: whenever a Celtic requested additional defensive help, he would shout "Hey, Bill!" Russell was so quick that he could run over for a quick double team and make it back in time if the opponents tried to find the open man. He also became famous for his shot-blocking skills: pundits called his blocks "Wilsonburgers", referring to the Wilson NBA basketballs he "shoved back into the faces of opposing shooters". This skill also allowed the other Celtics to play their men aggressively: if they were beaten, they knew that Russell was guarding the basket. This approach allowed the Celtics to finish with a 44–28 regular season record, the team's second-best record since beginning play in the <u>1946–47 season</u>, and guaranteed a post-season appearance.

Russell became the first African American head coach in NBA history, and commented to journalists: "I wasn't offered the Job because I am a Negro, I was offered it because Red figured I could do it." The Celtics' championship streak ended that season at eight, however, as Wilt Chamberlain's Philadelphia 76ers won a record-breaking 68 regular season games and overcame the Celtics 4–1 in the Eastern Finals. The Sixers simply outpaced the Celtics, shredding the famous Boston defense by scoring 140 points in the clinching Game 5 win. Russell acknowledged his first real loss in his career (he had been injured in 1958 when the Celtics lost the NBA Finals) by visiting Chamberlain in the locker room, shaking his hand and saying, "Great". However, the game still ended on a high note for Russell. After the loss, he led his grandfather through the Celtics locker rooms, and the two saw white Celtics player <u>John Havlicek</u> taking a shower next to his black teammate <u>Sam Jones</u> and discussing the game. Suddenly, Russell Sr. broke down crying. Asked by his grandson what was wrong, his grandfather replied how proud he was of him, being coach of an organization in which blacks and whites coexisted in harmony.

Glossary 9: Bill Walton: Bill Walton: William Theodore "Bill" Walton III is an American retired <u>basketball</u> player and <u>television</u> <u>sportscaster</u>. Walton achieved superstardom playing for <u>John Wooden</u>'s powerhouse <u>UCLA Bruins</u> in the early 1970s, winning three successive College Player of the Year Awards, while leading the Bruins to two <u>Division I national titles</u>. He then went on to have a prominent career in the <u>National Basketball Association</u> (NBA) where he was a <u>league Most Valuable Player</u> (MVP) and won two <u>NBA championships</u>. His professional career was significantly hampered by multiple foot injuries. Walton was inducted into the <u>Naismith Memorial Basketball Hall of Fame</u> on May 10, 1993 and the Oregon Sports Hall of Fame that same year. He spent the 1987-88 season on the injured list. He attempted a comeback in February 1990, but injury intervened and he retired from the game.

Glossary 10: Billy Gaskins: Billy Gaskins – 1970 NBA Draft, round 9, Pick 8, Portland Trailblazers.

Glossary 11: Billy Hunter: George William "Billy" Hunter is a former executive director of the National Basketball Players Association (NBPA), the players' union of the National Basketball Association (NBA). He is also a former American football wide receiver in the National Football League (NFL) for the Washington Redskins and Miami Dolphins.

Glossary 12: Billy Ray Bates: Billy Ray Bates is a retired American professional basketball player. Bates played shooting guard at McAdams High in Mississippi and attended Kentucky State University. Bates played four seasons in the National Basketball Association for the Portland Trail Blazers, Washington Bullets and Los Angeles Lakers. He has the highest playoffs points per game for a non-starter in NBA history.

Glossary 13: Bob Gross: Bob Gross: Robert Edwin Gross is a retired American basketball player formerly in the NBA. A 6'6" (1.98 m) 200 lb. (91 kg) forward, he attended Seattle University and California State University, Long Beach, and was selected in the 1975 NBA Draft by the Portland Trail Blazers. He was also selected in the 1975 ABA Draft by the San Diego Sails. Gross was the starting small forward for the Blazers during their only championship season (1976-77). He left the NBA in 1983 with career averages of 8.9 points, 4.4 rebounds, 1.3 assists and 1.12 steals a game.

Gross' number 30 jersey was retired on December 18, 2008 during the Trail Blazers' home game against the Phoenix Suns

Glossary 14: Bob Lanier: Bob Lanier: Robert Jerry Lanier, Jr. is a retired American professional basketball player who played for the Detroit Pistons and Milwaukee Bucks of the National Basketball Association (NBA).

Lanier was inducted into the Naismith Memorial Basketball Hall of Fame in 1992. Lanier was drafted number one overall by the National Basketball Association's Detroit Pistons and was named to the All-Rookie Team following the 1970-71 season. He starred for Detroit until being traded to the Milwaukee Bucks in 1980. In his five seasons with the Bucks, they won the division championship each year. The same year he retired, in 1984, he was awarded the Oscar Robertson Leadership Award.

According to Kareem Abdul-Jabbar, Lanier would smoke cigarettes during halftime breaks. Abdul-Jabbar would try to take advantage of this by forcing Lanier to run more during the second half.

At the Naismith Memorial Basketball Hall of Fame in Springfield, Massachusetts, visitors are able to compare the size of their foot to that of Lanier's. The largest shoe ever created by shoe company Allen Edmonds was a size 22 for Lanier.

The basketball court at Lanier's *alma mater*, St. Bonaventure, is named after him.

Glossary 15: Bob McAdoo: Bob McAdoo: Robert Allen McAdoo is an American former professional basketball player and coach. He played 14 seasons in the National Basketball Association (NBA), where he was a five-time NBA All-Star and named the NBA Most Valuable Player in 1975. He won two NBA championships with the Los Angeles Lakers in the 1980s.

McAdoo played at the center and power forward positions. In his 21-year playing career, he spent 14 years in the NBA and his final seven in the Lega Basket Serie A in Italy. He was inducted into the Naismith Memorial Basketball Hall of Fame in 2000. McAdoo is one of the few players who have won both NBA and FIBA European Champions Cup titles as a player. He later won three more NBA titles in 2006, 2012 and 2013 as an assistant coach with the Miami Heat

McAdoo enjoyed memorable end to his NBA career, winning two NBA titles with the Los Angeles Lakers in 1982 and 1985 as the team's sixth man. His teammates on those Showtime Lakers included Magic Johnson, Kareem Abdul-Jabbar, James Worthy, Michael

Cooper, Byron Scott, Kurt Rambis, and Jamaal Wilkes. He finished his NBA career with the Philadelphia 76ers in the 1985–86 season.

Glossary 16: Bob Whitmore: Bob Whitmore: attended University of Notre Dame, was drafted by the Boston Celtics April 6, 1969 in round 8 with pick 9 in the 1969 NBA draft.

Glossary 17: Bobby Jones: Robert Clyde "Bobby" Jones is a retired American professional basketball player in the American Basketball Association (ABA) and National Basketball Association (NBA). Bobby Jones was one of the most admired defenders ever to wear an NBA uniform; he was also considered one of the most virtuous. While most other players depended on the occasional thrown elbow, hip-check, or grab of the uniform to gain an advantage, Jones relied on hustle and determination. It was Jones' stellar defense along with his other specialties such as leadership that made him a standout sixth man. Opposing teams could ill afford to relax on defense when Jones came off the bench, and they also had to work a lot harder on offense to get the ball in or even near the basket.

A 12-year pro career that featured eight selections to the NBA All-Defensive First Team; the first-ever NBA Sixth Man Award; membership on the ABA All-Rookie Team; four appearances in the NBA All-Star Game and one in the ABA All-Star Game; and perhaps most prized, an NBA Championship with the Philadelphia 76ers in 1983. Above all, Jones's value as a player was evidenced by the fact that his teams never missed the playoffs.

Glossary 18: Brad Davis: Brad Davis: Davis was selected by the Los Angeles Lakers in the first round (15th pick overall) of the 1977 NBA Draft. Davis played for the Lakers for parts of two seasons and then for the Indiana Pacers for parts of two seasons. In between, he played with the Great Falls Sky of the Western Basketball Association. He played only part of the 1979-1980 NBA season for the Utah Jazz. In between his time with the Pacers and Jazz, he played with the Anchorage Northern Knights of the CBA during the 1979-80 basketball season.

In April 1992, Davis retired after 15 NBA seasons, and he was the final Maverick remaining from the team's first season in 1980-81. On November 14, 1992, Davis was the first Maverick to have his number retired when his #15 jersey was raised to the rafters of Reunion Arena.

Glossary 19: Brian Taylor: Brian Taylor: Brian Dwight Taylor is a retired American professional basketball player. A 6'2" guard from Princeton University, he was selected by the Seattle SuperSonics in the second round of the 1972 NBA Draft. However, he began his professional career with the New York Nets of the American Basketball Association, for whom he played four seasons, appearing in two ABA All-Star Games. He Joined the NBA as a member of the Kansas City Kings in 1976, and he averaged a career-high 17 points per game in 1976-77. He also played for the Denver Nuggets and San Diego Clippers, before retiring in 1982 with 7,868 career points.

Glossary 20: Brian Winters: Brian Winters: Brian Joseph Winters is an American former basketball player and coach. He attended academic and athletic powerhouse Archbishop Molloy High School in Queens, New York, graduating in 1970. He then played collegiately with the University of South Carolina and was the 12th pick in the 1974 NBA Draft, taken by the Los Angeles Lakers. He made the NBA All-Rookie Team with the Lakers, and was then traded to the Milwaukee Bucks as part of the trade that brought Kareem Abdul-Jabbar to the Lakers. He had a productive, if unspectacular, nine-year career that included two appearances in the NBA All-Star Game and playing on six playoffs teams. Winters averaged 16.2 points and 4.1 assists over his career, with his best years coming from 1975 to 1979 when he averaged over 19 points and slightly less than 5 assists per game. His number 32 was retired by the Bucks.

Glossary 21: Bruce Pearl: Bruce Allan Pearl is an American college basketball coach, and the head coach of the Auburn Tigers men's basketball program. He previously served as the head coach of the University of Tennessee Volunteers men's team, among others. He is a graduate of Boston College, where he obtained his first position as an assistant basketball coach. He was the first coach to lead the Volunteers to a national #1 ranking.

During his playing career, Scott suited up for the Lakers, Indiana Pacers and Vancouver Grizzlies. Scott was a key player for the Lakers during the Showtime era, being a starter alongside Magic Johnson, James Worthy, Kareem Abdul-Jabbar and A. C. Green. He played for the Lakers for 10 consecutive seasons (1983–1993). During that time, he was on three NBA championship teams (1985, 1987, and 1988). As a rookie, Scott was a member of the 1984 all-rookie team, averaging 10.6 PPG in 22 MPG. He led the NBA in three-point field goal percentage (.433) in 1984-85. In 1987-88, Scott enjoyed his best season, leading the NBA champion Lakers in scoring, averaging a career-best 21.7 ppg, and in steals (1.91 spg). He was the Lakers' starting shooting guard from 1984 until 1993. In 1996-97, the last year of Scott's playing career in the NBA, he went back to the Lakers and proved to be a valuable mentor for a team featuring Shaquille O'Neal, Eddie Jones, Nick Van Exel and 18-year-old rookie Kobe Bryant.

Glossary 22: Bud Stallworth: Bud Stallworth–Isaac (Bud) Stallworth: Stallworth was selected 7th overall by the Seattle SuperSonics in the 1972 NBA Draft, and by the Denver Rockets in the 1972 ABA Draft After two seasons with the Sonics, he was made available in the 1974 expansion draft to be selected by the New Orleans Jazz for whom he played for three seasons. His playing career was cut short due to a back injury sustained in an automobile accident in 1977.

Glossary 23: Byron Scott: Byron Scott: Byron Antom Scott is an American professional basketball former head coach and player. He last coached the Los Angeles Lakers of the National Basketball Association (NBA). As a player, he won three NBA championships with the Lakers during their Showtime era in the 1980s. Selected by the San Diego Clippers in the first round, with the fourth pick of the 1983 NBA draft, Scott was traded to the Los Angeles Lakers in 1983 in exchange for Norm Nixon.

Glossary 24: Caldwell Jones: Caldwell Jones: Caldwell "Pops" Jones (August 4, 1950 – September 21, 2014) was an American professional basketball player. Jones was drafted from Albany State College (Georgia) by the Philadelphia 76ers with the 14th pick in the 1973 NBA Draft. He played three seasons in the American Basketball Association and 14 seasons in the NBA, most extensively with the Philadelphia 76ers. Jones led the ABA in blocked shots in the 1973-74 season, and played in the 1975 ABA All-Star Game. He shares (with Julius Keye) the ABA's all-time record for blocked shots in a game with 12.

Glossary 25: Calvin Mack – Mack Calvin: Calvin Mack – Mack Calvin: He played seven seasons (1969–1976) in the now-defunct American Basketball Association (ABA) and four seasons in the National Basketball Association (NBA).

Calvin began his professional career with the ABA's Los Angeles Stars, averaging 16.8 points per game in his first season to make the ABA All-Rookie Team. The following season, he averaged a career-high 27.2 points for The Floridians, in the process setting the ABA records for most free throws made (696) and most free throws attempted (805) in one season. Calvin also played for the ABA's Carolina Cougars, Denver Nuggets, and Virginia Squires before the ABA-NBA merger in 1976. He also briefly coached the Squires during the 1975–1976 season. During his ABA career, he tallied 10,620 points and 3,067 assists (second in ABA history behind only Louie Dampier's 4,044) and appeared in 5 All-Star games.

Calvin Joined the Lakers for the 1976–77 NBA season but he was never able to match the same level of production he reached while in the ABA. He spent his four seasons in the NBA with five teams—the Lakers, the San Antonio Spurs, the Denver Nuggets (which had Joined the NBA in 1976), the Utah Jazz, and the Cleveland Cavaliers—before retiring in 1981 with an NBA career scoring-average of 7.0 points per game.

Glossary 26: Calvin Murphy: Calvin Murphy: Calvin Jerome Murphy is a retired American professional basketball player who played as a guard for the NBA's San Diego/Houston Rockets from

1970-1983. Standing at a height of 5 feet 9 inches (1.75 m), Murphy has the distinction of being the shortest NBA player inducted into the Basketball Hall of Fame, and to play in an NBA All-Star Game (the latter since tied by Isaiah Thomas in 2016). In his first season, Murphy was nominated to the NBA All-Rookie team. A diminutive guard at 5 feet 9 inches (175 cm), Murphy was known for his quickness and defensive ability.

Murphy was one of the best free-throw shooters ever, setting NBA records for most consecutive free throws made and for the highest free throw percentage in a single season (1980-1981). Both records have since been broken. He set many other records within the Rockets organization, including that of all-time leading scorer until that record was broken in 1994 by Hakeem Olajuwon. The Rockets made it to the NBA Finals in 1981, losing to the Boston Celtics in six games. After retiring from the NBA in 1983, Calvin Murphy was inducted into the Basketball Hall of Fame in 1993.

Glossary 27: Calvin Natt: Calvin Natt: Calvin Leon Natt is a retired American professional basketball player. A 6'6" (1.98 m) forward, Natt played at Northeast Louisiana University under coach Lenny Fant. After college, he played 11 NBA seasons (1979-1990), spending time with the New Jersey Nets, Portland Trail Blazers, Denver Nuggets, San Antonio Spurs, and Indiana Pacers. He represented the Nuggets in the 1985 NBA All-Star Game, and retired with 10,291 career points. Natt's nickname was "Pit Bull."

Glossary 28: Casey Viator: Casey Viator: Casey Viator was the youngest ever AAU Mr. America–gaining the title at the age of 19 in 1971. The following year, he came in sixth in the 1969 Teen Mr. America, but won in the categories Best arms, Best Abs, Best Chest, Best Legs and Most Muscular. In 1970, Casey Viator's upper arm measured at 19 5/16 inches, and his forearm at 15 7/16 inches. All in the same year, Viator won three separate bodybuilding championships; Teen Age Mr. America, Jr. Mister America, and lastly, the title of Mr. America. In 1982 he capped off his bodybuilding career by placing third in the Mr. Olympia competition.

Glossary 29: Cazzie Russell: Cazzie Lee Russell is an American former professional <u>basketball</u> player and coach.

In 1966, Russell averaged 30.8 points per game and was named the College Basketball Player of the Year. <u>Crisler Arena</u>, which opened in 1967, has been dubbed *The House that Cazzie Built*.

Russell spent twelve seasons in the <u>NBA</u> (<u>1966</u>–<u>1978</u>), and is best remembered for his five seasons with the <u>New York Knicks</u> (<u>1966</u>–<u>71</u>). Russell was the NBA's first draft pick in 1966, and was named to the 1967 <u>All-Rookie Team</u>. He was later part of the famous <u>1970</u> Knicks team that won the NBA championship over the <u>Los Angeles Lakers</u>. Russell played in the <u>1972 NBA All-Star Game</u> while with the <u>Golden State Warriors</u>. When he played for the Lakers, he was the last player to wear #32 prior to <u>Magic Johnson</u>.

In 2006, Russell was voted as one of the <u>100 Legends of the IHSA Boys Basketball Tournament</u>, a group of former players and coaches in honor of the 100 anniversary of the <u>IHSA boys basketball tournament</u>. Russell received the Bobby Jones Award in 2015 at the Athletes in Action All Star Breakfast, which is held each year at the NBA All Star Weekend. In 2016 Russell was the recipient of the Coach Wooden "Keys to Life" Award at the Athletes in Action Legends of the Hardwood Breakfast, which is held each year at the Final Four.

Glossary 30: Cedric Maxwell: Cedric Maxwell: Cedric Bryan Maxwell is a retired American professional <u>basketball</u> player now in <u>radio broadcasting</u>. Nicknamed *"Cornbread"*, he played 11 seasons in the <u>National Basketball Association</u> (NBA), and played a key role in two championships with the <u>Boston Celtics</u>.

Maxwell was best known for his moves near or beneath the basket. He was very effective in the low post, faking defenders into the air, drawing contact, then making high percentage shots (and sometimes drawing a foul) using either his jump-hook close to the basket or going up against the glass. It was rare that Maxwell took an outside jump shot, especially when Celtic teammates like Bird or Tiny Archibald were on the floor. This helped the Celtics run a balanced offense with a formidable inside game that was hard for most teams to defend.

Maxwell, in addition to being a dangerous scorer and a colorful character, was a clutch performer in the playoffs. Maxwell was named MVP of the 1981 NBA Finals. Three years later, Maxwell scored 24 points against the Los Angeles Lakers in the decisive game-seven victory during the 1984 NBA Finals. Before the game, he told his teammates to "climb on my back, boys." Maxwell's colorful side was also on display in the series as he mocked second-year Laker forward James Worthy's inability to make free throws during overtime of game 4 by walking across the lane between free throws with his hands around his own neck, suggesting Worthy's choking under pressure. Maxwell also made fun of Kurt Rambis prior to Game 4 of the 1984 Finals, wearing Rambis's trademark glasses and inadvertently missing a long range shot in front of loyal Rambis fans known as the "Rambis Youth". The following season, after an injury, Maxwell lost his starting role to Kevin McHale, who had spent two seasons coming off the bench and was the two-time reigning Sixth Man of the Year.

Maxwell was the 22nd former Celtic to have his jersey (number 31) retired by the Celtics (December 15, 2003).

Glossary 31: Charlie Scott: Charlie Scott:: Charles Thomas Scott is an American former professional basketball player. He played two seasons in the now-defunct American Basketball Association (ABA) and eight seasons in the National Basketball Association (NBA). Scott was drafted by the Boston Celtics in 1970 but he had already signed a contract with the Virginia Squires of the ABA. Scott was named ABA Rookie of the Year after averaging 27.1 points per game. During his second season with the Squires, he set the ABA record for highest scoring average in one season (34.6 points per game). However, he became dissatisfied with life in the ABA and Joined the NBA's Phoenix Suns in 1972. At that point, he briefly went by the name Shaheed Abdul-Aleem.

Scott continued his stellar play in the NBA, representing the Suns in three straight NBA All-Star Games (1973, 1974, and 1975), then went to the Celtics for the 1975-76 NBA season where he won a championship ring against the Suns. Scott later played for the Los Angeles Lakers and Denver Nuggets. He retired in 1980 with 14,837 combined ABA/NBA career points.

Glossary 32: Chris Dickerson: Chris Dickerson One of the world's most titled bodybuilders, Dickerson's competitive career spanned thirty years; he was known for both his heavily muscled, symmetrical physique and for his skills on the posing dais. Dickerson first entered bodybuilding competition in 1965 by taking third- place at that year's Mr. Long Beach competition.

He was the first African-American AAU Mr. America, the oldest and first openly gay winner of the IFBB Mr. Olympia contest at age 43, and one of only two bodybuilders (along with Dexter Jackson) to win titles in both the Mr. Olympia and Masters Olympia competitions. Dickerson won the Mr. Olympia once (1982), a distinction he shares with Samir Bannout (1983) and Dexter Jackson (2008).

Glossary 33: Chris Mullin: Chris Mullin: Christopher Paul Mullin (born July 30, 1963) is an American retired basketball player and current head coach of the St. John 's Red Storm. He previously served as special advisor for the Sacramento Kings and general manager of the Golden State Warriors. He is a two-time Olympic Gold medalist and a two-time Naismith Memorial Basketball Hall of Fame inductee (in 2010 as a member of the 1992 United States men's Olympic basketball team ("The Dream Team"), and in 2011 for his individual career).

Mullin played shooting guard and small forward in the NBA from 1985 to 2001. Mullin was chosen as the seventh pick by the Golden State Warriors in the first round of the 1985 NBA draft. He returned to the Olympics in 1992 as a member of the "Dream Team", which was the first American Olympic basketball team to include professional players.

He played with the Warriors from the 1985–86 until the 1996–97 season. Thereafter, Mullin played with the Indiana Pacers from 1997 until the 1999–2000 season. He retired after the 2000–01 season, playing for his original team, the Warriors.

Glossary 34: Chris Washburn: Chris Washburn: Washburn left N.C. State after the 1985-86 season and was selected by the Golden State Warriors with the third overall pick of the 1986 NBA Draft. He was the third consecutive Atlantic Coast Conference player taken in that draft, following North Carolina center Brad Daugherty (Cleveland Cavaliers) and Maryland forward Len Bias (Boston Celtics).

The Warriors brought in center Joe Barry Carroll to help Washburn's development but to no avail. The highlight of Washburn's career might have come in an October exhibition game in his rookie season against the Knicks. In a 23-point loss, he scored 16 points. Tendinitis in his knee led Washburn to taking anti-inflammatory medicine, which led to a kidney infection in January 1987. After returning to the Warriors in late March, the player remained ineffective.

Washburn played 72 games over two seasons (1.5 seasons with the Warriors and part of another with the Atlanta Hawks), averaging 3.1 points and 2.4 rebounds per game.

Glossary 35: Clyde Drexler: Clyde Drexler: Clyde Austin "The Glide" Drexler is an American retired professional basketball swingman. During his career, he was a ten-time All-Star, and named one of the 50 Greatest Players in NBA History. Drexler won an Olympic gold medal in 1992 as part of the 1992 United States men's Olympic basketball team ("The Dream Team") and an NBA Championship in 1995 with the Houston Rockets. He is a two-time Naismith Memorial Basketball Hall of Fame inductee (being inducted 2004 for his individual career, and in 2010 as a member of the "Dream Team").

Glossary 36: Collis Jones: Collis Jones: Collis Jones is a former college and professional basketball player. Born in Washington, D.C., he attended the University of Notre Dame. He currently ranks 17th on the Notre Dame all-time scoring list with 1,367 points. Throughout his career, he has averaged 16.1 points per game, which ranks 19th in school history. He also stands at eighth place in Fighting Irish history in rebounds (884), ninth in rebounding average (10.4 rpg), 13th in field goals attempted (1,242), 15th in field goals made (567), and 22nd in free throws attempted (360). He led the 1969-70 and 1970-71 squads in rebounding with averages of 12.4 and 13.1 rpg, respectively. He was selected in the first round of the 1971 NBA Draft by the Milwaukee Bucks and also in the 1971 American

Basketball Association player draft by the Dallas Chaparrals.[1] He played exclusively in the American Basketball Association, including for the Kentucky Colonels, Memphis Sounds and Baltimore Claws.

Glossary 37: Connie Hawkins: Connie Hawkins: Cornelius L. "Connie" Hawkins is an American former American Basketball League, National Basketball Association and American Basketball Association player, Harlem Globetrotter, Harlem Wizard and New York City playground legend. It was on the New York City courts that he earned his nickname *The Hawk.*

In 1969, Hawkins hit the ground running in his first season with the Suns, when he played 81 games and averaged 24.6 points, 10.4 rebounds and 4.8 assists per game. In the final game of his rookie season, Connie had 44 points, 20 rebounds, 8 assists, 5 blocks and 5 steals. The Suns finished third in the Western Conference, but were knocked out by the Los Angeles Lakers in a great seven-game series in which Hawkins carried the Suns against a team that had future Hall of Famers Wilt Chamberlain, Elgin Baylor and Jerry West. For the series, Hawkins averaged 25 points, 14 rebounds and 7 assists per game.

Hawkins missed 11 games due to injury during the 1970–71 season, averaging 21 points per game. He matched those stats the next year, and was the top scorer on a per-game basis for the Suns in 1971–72. However, he averaged only 16 points per game for the Suns in 1972–73, and was traded to the Lakers for the next season.

Injuries limited his production in 1974–75, and Hawkins finished his career after the 1975–76 season, playing for the Atlanta Hawks.

Glossary 38: Curtis Perry: Curtis Perry: Curtis R. Perry is a retired American basketball player. Born in Washington, D.C., he attended Southwest Missouri State University and played at forward. Perry was selected by the San Diego Rockets in the third round of the 1970 NBA Draft and by the Virginia Squires in the 1970 ABA Draft. Perry played for the NBA's San Diego Rockets/Houston Rockets (1970–71), Milwaukee Bucks (1971–74) and Phoenix Suns (1974–78). He helped the Bucks win the 1971-72 and 1972-73 NBA Midwest

Division titles, and the 1973-74 NBA Western Conference championship, as well as helping the Phoenix Suns win the 1975-76 NBA Western Conference championship. In the <u>1976 Finals, Perry was a key player in "the greatest game ever played"</u>[2][3][4][5] in NBA history.

In 8 seasons, he played in 480 games and had 13,656 minutes played, a .455 field goal percentage (1,904 for 4,188), .699 free throw percentage (770 for 1,101), 4,239 rebounds, 906 assists, 1,670 personal fouls and 4,578 points. He averaged 9.5 points, 8.8 rebounds and 1.9 assists per game.

Glossary 39: Dan Issel: Dan Issel: Daniel Paul Issel is a retired American <u>Hall of Fame</u> professional basketball player and coach. An outstanding collegian at the <u>University of Kentucky</u>, he was twice named an <u>All American</u> en route to a still school record 25.7 points per game. The <u>ABA</u> <u>Rookie of the Year</u> in 1971, he was a six-time <u>ABA All-Star</u> and one-time <u>NBA All-Star</u>.

Upon Issel's graduation in 1970 he was drafted by the <u>Detroit Pistons</u> of the <u>NBA</u> and the <u>Kentucky Colonels</u> of the <u>ABA</u>. Issel signed to play basketball for the Colonels and the ABA. In his rookie season, Dan Issel led the ABA in scoring with 29.9 points per game, and averaged 13.2 rebounds per game.

Wearing number 44, Issel is the Nuggets' second all-time leading scorer. He accumulated over 27,000 points in his combined ABA and NBA career, trailing only <u>Kareem Abdul-Jabbar</u>, <u>Wilt Chamberlain</u> and <u>Julius Erving</u> upon his retirement. Issel currently ranks #9 on the all-time combined ABA/NBA scoring list. He missed only 24 games in 15 seasons, earning him the moniker, "the Horse". He was part of the <u>Naismith Memorial Basketball Hall of Fame</u> Class of 1993.

Glossary 40: Dan Roundfield: Dan Roundfield 6'8" <u>forward</u>/<u>center</u> He spent 12 seasons in the <u>American Basketball Association</u> and <u>National Basketball Association</u>, playing for the <u>Indiana Pacers</u> (1975–1978), <u>Atlanta Hawks</u> (1978–1984), <u>Detroit Pistons</u> (1984–1985), and <u>Washington Bullets</u> (1985–1987).

Roundfield earned a reputation as a strong rebounder and tenacious defender, and during his career he was named to five NBA All-Defensive teams and three <u>All-Star</u> teams. His <u>nickname</u> was Dr.

Rounds. He was selected to the NBA Eastern Conference All-Star team in three consecutive seasons from 1980-1982.

Glossary 41: Darryl Dawkins: Darryl Dawkins: was an American professional basketball player, most noted for his days with the NBA's Philadelphia 76ers and New Jersey Nets, although he also played briefly for the Detroit Pistons and Utah Jazz late in his career. His nickname, *"Chocolate Thunder"*, was bestowed upon him by Stevie Wonder. He was known for his powerful dunks, which led to the NBA adopting breakaway rims due to his shattering the backboard on two occasions in 1979.

Dawkins averaged double figures in scoring nine times in his 14 years in the NBA, often ranking among the league leaders in field-goal percentage. He also played in the NBA Finals three times as a member of the Philadelphia 76ers in the late 1970s and early 1980s. On the flip side, Dawkins set an NBA record for fouls in a season (386 in 1983–84).

In a game against the Kansas City Kings at Municipal Auditorium on November 13, 1979, Dawkins threw down such a massive dunk that the backboard shattered, sending the Kings' Bill Robinzine ducking. Three weeks later he did it again, this time at home against the San Antonio Spurs at the Spectrum. A few days after that the NBA ruled that breaking a backboard was an offense that would result in a fine and suspension.

Dawkins named the first backboard-breaking dunk "The Chocolate-Thunder-Flying, Robinzine-Crying, Teeth-Shaking, Glass-Breaking, Rump-Roasting, Bun-Toasting, Wham-Bam, and Glass-Breaker-I-Am-Jam."

He named other dunks as well: the Rim Wrecker, the Go-Rilla, the Look Out Below, the In-Your-Face Disgrace, the Cover Your Head, the Yo-Mama, the Spine-Chiller Supreme, and the Greyhound Special (for the rare occasions when he went coast to coast). The 76ers also kept a separate column on the stat sheet for Dawkins's self-created nicknames: "Sir Slam", "Dr. Dunkenstein", and "Chocolate Thunder."

At one point, Dawkins claimed to be an alien from the planet Lovetron, where he spent the off-season practicing "interplanetary funkmanship" and where his girlfriend Juicy Lucy lived.

The 1983–84 campaign was Dawkins' last full season. Injuries limited him to 39 games in 1984–85. Midway through the 1985–86 season, he slipped in his bathtub and injured his back. At the time, Dawkins was averaging 15.3 points and shooting .644 from the floor, but the injury sidelined him for 31 of the Nets' final 32 games. Dawkins tried to come back over the next three seasons with the Nets, the Utah Jazz and Detroit Pistons, but back problems limited him to 26 games during those seasons. He attempted a comeback in 1994, attending Denver Nuggets training camp, and again in 1995 with the Boston Celtics.

Glossary 42: Dave Bing: Dave Bing: an American businessman, retired Hall of Fame basketball player, and former mayor of Detroit, Michigan. After starring at Syracuse University, Bing played 12 seasons in the National Basketball Association (NBA) as a guard for the Detroit Pistons (1966 to 1975), Washington Bullets (1975 to 1977), and Boston Celtics (1977–78). During his career, he averaged over 20 points and six assists per game and made seven NBA All-Star appearances, winning the game's Most Valuable Player award in 1976. After retiring, the Pistons celebrated his career accomplishments with the retirement of his #21 jersey. In addition, he was elected to the Naismith Memorial Basketball Hall of Fame and named one of the NBA's 50 Greatest Players of all-time.

Glossary 43: Dave Cowens: Dave Cowens: NBA Career: Despite some critics who felt Cowens was too small to play center, Cowens was selected as the fourth overall pick by the Boston Celtics during the 1970 NBA draft, largely at the recommendation of former Celtics center Bill Russell. During his rookie year, Cowens averaged 17.0 points per game and 15.0 rebounds per game. He was named to the NBA All-Rookie First Team and shared the NBA's Rookie of the Year honors with Portland's Geoff Petrie. He also led the league in personal fouls that same year.

In 1973, Cowens averaged 20.5 ppg and 16.2 rpg while help-ing the Celtics to a league best 68-14 record. He was chosen the NBA MVP as well as MVP of the All-Star Game that same season. Cowens and fellow Celtic Bill Russell both have the distinction of being named MVP of the league but not being included on the All-NBA First Team that year.

Cowens retired in 1980. Cowens played for the Bucks during the 1982-83 season before retiring for good. During his NBA career, Cowens averaged 17.6 points and 13.6 rebounds per game, was selected to seven All-Star Games, was named to the All-NBA Second Team three times, and was named to the All-NBA Defensive First Team in 1976 and All-NBA Defensive Second Team in 1973 and 1980. He was a member of the Celtics' 1974 and 1976 NBA Championship teams.

Cowens' playing credo was all-out intensity at both ends of the court, a style that never wavered during his 11-year NBA career. As a testament to his all-around ability, Cowens is one of only four players (Scottie Pippen, Kevin Garnett and LeBron James are the others) to lead his team in all five major statistical categories for a season: points, rebounds, assists, blocks, and steals. He accomplished the feat in the 1977–78 season.

Glossary 44: Dave Twardzik: Dave Twardzik: David John Twardzik (born September 20, 1950) is an American former professional bas-ketball player. He was a point guard in both the American Basketball Association (ABA) and the National Basketball Association (NBA). He is best known for being a starter on the Portland Trail Blazers team that won the 1977 NBA Finals.

Twardzik grew up in Middletown, Pennsylvania, and played collegiately at Old Dominion University, where he was a two-time All-American and led the Monarchs to the 1971 NCAA Division II title game. He was drafted by the Trail Blazers in 1972, but elected to play for the Virginia Squires of the ABA. Twardzik played for the Squires for four seasons until the team (and the ABA) came to an end, folding just prior to the ABA-NBA merger in June 1976. After the ABA-NBA merger Twardzik signed with the Blazers (who held his NBA rights). He would be the starting point guard of the Blazers team which won the NBA title in 1977. He played for four seasons total in Portland, and retired at the end of the 1979–80 season because of injury. His jersey number (13) was retired by the team.

After his retirement from playing, he began an NBA coaching and front-office career. He served in Portland's front office through 1985, and worked as an assistant coach for the Indiana Pacers from 1986 through 1989. He has also worked for the Detroit Pistons, Charlotte Hornets, Los Angeles Clippers, Golden State Warriors, and the Denver Nuggets. In 2003, he became Director of Player Personnel for the Orlando Magic, and was promoted to assistant general manager in 2005. He held that position until 2012.

In 1995, Twardzik was inducted into the Virginia Sports Hall of Fame.

Glossary 45: Dave Wyman: David Matthew Wyman is a former professional football player, a linebacker in the National Football League for nine seasons with the Seattle Seahawks and Denver Broncos. He was selected by the Seahawks in the second round of the 1987 NFL Draft with the 45th overall selection. Wyman played six seasons for the Seahawks, but left as a free agent before the 1993 season[3] and played his final three years with the Broncos.

Glossary 46: David Falk: David Falk is a sports agent who primarily works with basketball players in the National Basketball Association. Falk began his career representing professional tennis players for Donald Dell's ProServ and is best known for representing sports icon Michael Jordan for the entirety of Jordan's career. Besides Jordan, Falk has represented more than 100 other NBA players, and is generally considered to be the most influential player agent the NBA has seen. During the peak years of Falk's career in the 1990s, he was often considered the second-most powerful person in the NBA behind Commissioner David Stern, and in 2000 he had at least one client on all but two NBA teams. He was listed among the "100 Most Powerful People in Sports" for 12 straight years from 1990 to 2001 by *The Sporting News*, and was also named one of the Top 50 Marketers in the United States by Advertising Age in 1995.

Falk negotiated the then-highest contracts in NBA history for Patrick Ewing and Danny Ferry. He also negotiated professional sports' first $100 million contract for Alonzo Mourning as part of an unprecedented free agency period, during which his company, FAME, changed the entire salary structure of the NBA, negotiating more than $400 million in contracts for its free agent clients in a six-day period.

In January 2007, Falk re-launched FAME, and today serves as its founder and CEO. He represented nine players in 2012; in the prime of his sports agent career in the 1990s he represented as many as 40 players at a time.

Glossary 47: David Halberstam David Halberstam was an American Journalist and historian, known for his work on the Vietnam War, politics, history, the Civil Rights Movement, business, media, American culture, and later, sports Journalism. He won a Pulitzer Prize for International Reporting in 1964. Later in his career, Halberstam turned to sports, publishing *The Breaks of the Game*, an inside look at Bill Walton and the 1979-80 Portland Trail Blazers basketball team. In 2007, while doing research for a book, Halberstam was killed in a car crash.

Glossary 48: David Thompson: David Thompson was the No. 1 draft pick of both the American Basketball Association (Virginia Squires) and the National Basketball Association (Atlanta Hawks) in the 1975 drafts of both leagues. He eventually signed with the ABA's Denver Nuggets. Explaining his choice between the establishment NBA and the ABA—which offered less real money (but more "deferred" over the life of the contract)—Thompson said when he met with the Hawks, the organization had seemed almost uninterested, to the point of treating him to a meal at McDonald's. Thompson also told the Denver Nuggets he wanted his friend and point guard at N.C. State Monte Towe to have a chance to play in the NBA, and Denver signed Towe to a 2-year contract.

Thompson and Julius Erving were the finalists in the first ever Slam-Dunk Competition, held at the 1976 ABA All-Star Game at McNichol's Sports Arena in Denver. The competition organizers had arranged the seedings to assure a final round pairing these two dynamic players. Erving won with the first ever foul-line dunk, to this day the standard for leaping and dunking prowess. Thompson, inexplicably, performed even more difficult dunks in warmups, but not in the competition itself—including a dunk called the "cradle the baby" whereby he cradled the ball in the crook of his arm, raised it above the rim, and punched it through. (See *Loose Balls* by Terry Pluto) Thompson won the MVP of the 1976 ABA All-Star Game, and as a prize, he received a credenza television set.

After the ABA-NBA merger in 1976, Thompson continued with the Nuggets through the 1981–82 season, after which he was traded on June 17, 1982 to the Seattle SuperSonics.

Thompson made the NBA All-Star Game four seasons, and reached his peak in 1978 season. On April 9, 1978, the last day of the regular NBA season, Thompson scored 73 points against the Detroit Pistons in an effort to win the NBA scoring title (he barely lost the scoring title to San Antonio's George Gervin, who scored 63 points in a game played later that same day). He also led the Denver Nuggets to the NBA playoffs, but they lost to the eventual Western Conference champion Seattle SuperSonics.

After the 1978 season, Thompson signed a record-breaking contract for $4 million over five-years. That amount was more than any basketball player ever had previously been paid. However, from that point, injuries and persistent problems with substance abuse would trouble Thompson and to the significant detriment of the remainder of his NBA career, which came to an end after the 1983–84 season. He severely injured his knee at the notorious Studio 54, epicenter of the New York party scene and antithesis of his humble beginnings. He attempted a comeback with the Indiana Pacers in 1985 but was unsuccessful.

Glossary 49: Dean Meminger: Dean Peter Meminger was an American basketball player. Meminger was drafted in the first round (16th overall) of the 1971 NBA Draft by the New York Knicks, with whom he played from 1971 to 1974 and 1976-1977 As a rookie reserve guard in 1971-72, Meminger averaged 4.6 points in 15 minutes per game, followed by 5.7 points in 18 minutes per game in

1972-73. In that season, Meminger helped the Knicks win their second-ever NBA championship. Playing on a team which featured star guards Walt Frazier, Earl Monroe and Dick Barnett, in Game 7 of the 1973 Eastern Conference finals he replaced Monroe in the second quarter, frustrated the hot-shooting Boston Celtics guard Jo White and scored 13 points. After knocking the Celtics out of the playoffs, the Knicks beat the Los Angeles Lakers for the title. In the postseason, Meminger played in all 17 games for the Knicks, making 31 of 56 field goal attempts for a team-leading .554 percentage.

In Meminger's third season of 1973-74, his playing time increased to 26.7 minutes per game as he averaged 8.3 points and 3.6 rebounds per game (both career highs) and 2.1 assists. In 1974-75, Meminger played for the Atlanta Hawks, averaging career highs of 27.2 minutes, 5.0 rebounds and 1.5 steals per game in addition to 7.9 points per game. In 1975-76 with the Hawks, his fifth NBA season, he averaged over 20 minutes per game. The 1976-77 season was his sixth and final NBA season as he returned to the Knicks and averaged 7.9 minutes per game.

Glossary 50: Dennis Johnson: Dennis Johnson: Dennis Wayne Johnson nicknamed "DJ", was an American professional basketball player for the National Basketball Association's (NBA) Seattle SuperSonics, Phoenix Suns and Boston Celtics and coach of the Los Angeles Clippers.

A prototypical late bloomer, Johnson overcame early struggles and had a successful NBA playing career. Drafted 29th overall in 1976 by the Seattle SuperSonics, Johnson began his professional career as a shooting guard. He eventually led the Sonics to their only NBA championship in 1979, winning the Finals MVP Award. After a short stint with the Phoenix Suns, he became the starting point guard for the Boston Celtics, with whom he won two more championships. Johnson was voted into five All-Star Teams, one All-NBA First and one Second Team, and nine consecutive All-Defensive First and Second Teams. Apart from his reputation as a defensive stopper, Johnson was known as a clutch player who made several decisive plays in NBA playoffs history.

The Celtics franchise has retired Johnson's #3 jersey, which hangs from the rafters of the TD Garden, the home arena of the team. On April 5, 2010, the Naismith Memorial Basketball Hall of Fame officially announced that Johnson had been posthumously elected to the Hall. He was formally inducted on August 13. He is considered by several sports journalists to be one of the most under-rated players of all time.

Glossary 51: Don Adams: Don Adams INSERT: Don Lamar Adams was an American professional basketball small forward. He was 6 ft. 6 in 210 lb. and was selected in the 8th round of the 1970 NBA Draft by the San Diego Rockets. In his NBA career, Adams averaged 8.7 points per game, 5.6 rebounds per game and 1.8 assists per game. In the ABA, Adams averaged 10.1 points per game, 5.1 rebounds per game and 3.9 assists per game.

Glossary 52: Don Chaney: Don Chaney: most notable for his long stints as a player on the Boston Celtics. Chaney played basketball in college for the University of Houston, where he was a teammate of future Basketball Hall-of-Famer Elvin Hayes. Chaney played all 40 minutes of the famed "Game of the Century" at the Astrodome. That year Chaney became the first-round pick (12th overall) of the Boston Celtics in the 1968 NBA Draft; he was also drafted by the Houston Mavericks of the American Basketball Association.

Don became a 1969 NBA Finals champion with the Boston Celtics during his rookie year. He would also help the Celtics toward winning the 1974 NBA Finals. He had two stints with the Boston Celtics (1968–1975, and 1977–1980), for which he is most notable. He also had a short two season stint with the Los Angeles Lakers from 1976–1978, and also played in the ABA for one year with the Spirits of St. Louis from 1975-1976. Chaney was mostly known for his defensive skills, providing adequate numbers in minutes off the bench.

Chaney is the only Boston Celtic who played with both Bill Russell (1956–1969) and Larry Bird (1979–1992). Awards: 1969 NBA Finals and 1974 NBA Finals champion, NBA All-Defensive second team (1972, 1973, 1974, 1975 and 1977)NBA Coach of the

Year Award with the Houston Rockets for the 1990-91 season, after leading the Houston Rockets to a 50-32 record. Louisiana Sports Hall of Fame (1991), Gold medal-winning US national team at the 1994 FIBA World Championship in Toronto, assistant coach.

Glossary 53: Don Ford: Don Ford–Donald J. "Don" Ford is a retired American professional basketball player who played in the NBA. He was a 6'9" (2.06 m), 215 lb. (97.5 kg) forward. Ford was selected with the second pick of the sixth round of the 1975 NBA Draft by the L.A. Lakers. He spent four-and-a-half seasons with the Lakers before he was traded along with a 1980 first round draft pick to the Cleveland Cavaliers in exchange for Butch Lee and a 1982 first round draft pick, which ultimately became first overall pick James Worthy.

After he was released by the Cavaliers in 1982, Ford spent two years playing professionally in Italy. Over 474 NBA games, he averaged 6.4 points, 3.6 rebounds and 1.4 assists.

Glossary 54: Don Nelson: Donald Arvid "Don" Nelson (born May 15, 1940) is an American former NBA player and head coach. He coached the Milwaukee Bucks, the New York Knicks, the Dallas Mavericks, and the Golden State Warriors.

An innovator, Nelson is credited with, among other things, pioneering the concept of the point forward, a tactic which is frequently employed by teams at every level today. His unique brand of basketball is often referred to as Nellie Ball. He was named one of the Top 10 coaches in NBA history. On April 7, 2010, he passed Lenny Wilkens for first place on the all-time NBA wins list with 1,333 wins.[1] His all-time record is 1,335–1,063.

He was drafted 19th overall by the Chicago Zephyrs of the NBA. He played for the Zephyrs one season, and was acquired by the Los Angeles Lakers in 1963. After two years with the Lakers, he was signed by the Boston Celtics.

Nelson would average more than 10 points per game every season between 1968–69 and 1974–75 (before the introduction of the three-point shot). He led the NBA in field-goal percentage in 1974–75. Nelson was coined as one of the best "sixth men" ever to play in the NBA. He was also known for his distinctive one-handed style for shooting free throws. He would place the ball in his shooting hand, lean in almost off-balance and toe the free-throw line with his right foot and his left leg trailing. He would then push the ball toward the basket completely with his right hand while springing with his right knee and lifting the trailing foot in a sort of "hop". This technique helped him to a career 76.5% free-throw shooting percentage.

Nelson retired as a player following the 1975–76 season. His number 19 jersey was retired to the Boston Garden rafters in 1978.

Glossary 55: Donald Dell: Donald Dell is an attorney and was a professional tennis player, U.S. Davis Cup captain, and administrator. Dell was one of the first professional sports agents, having represented professional tennis players Arthur Ashe, Stan Smith, Jimmy Connors, and Ivan Lendl during pro tennis' golden age (1975 to 1985). He was also the founder of Professional Services (ProServ), one of the nation's first sports marketing firms established in 1970 with co-founder, Frank Craighill, a fellow law partner. He was Big Ten #1 Singles Champion in 1969.

Clients of ProServ dominated the leadership roles of the ATP in its formative years. ProServ and one of its young agents, David Falk, would go onto to represent professional basketball players such as: Patrick Ewing, John Lucas, and Michael Jordan selected Dell's ProServ and Falk as his first sports agent after leaving the University of North Carolina.

Glossary 56: Doug Collins: Doug Collins: Paul Douglas "Doug" Collins is an American retired basketball player. He was the first overall pick of the 1973 NBA draft and a three-time NBA All-Star. Collins was drafted first overall by the Philadelphia 76ers. He played eight seasons for Philadelphia, and was an All-Star three times. In 1976-77, he Joined Julius Erving leading the Sixers to the NBA Finals, where they lost to the Portland Trail Blazers.

A rash of injuries to his feet and left knee beginning in 1979, would end Collins' career in 1981. In all, he played 415 NBA games, scoring 7427 points (17.9 per game).

Glossary 57: Duck Williams: Duck Williams: Donald Edgar "Duck" Williams is an American former professional basketball player. He played in the National Basketball Association for the New Orleans Jazz during the 1979–80 season. Playing for Notre Dame's Fighting Irish he was the 96th player picked in the fifth round of the 1978 NBA draft as a point guard.

Glossary 58: Earl Tatum: Earl Tatum: William Earl Tatum is a retired American professional basketball player born in Mount Vernon, New York. He was a 6'4½" (194 cm) 185 lb. (84 kg) guard who played high school basketball at Mount Vernon, where he was selected large-school player of the year by the New York State Sportswriters Association in 1972, and collegiately at Marquette University.

Tatum was selected with the 4th pick of the second round in the 1976 NBA Draft by the Los Angeles Lakers. He played for five teams in 4 years, his final season spent with the Cleveland Cavaliers in 1979–80.

Glossary 59: Eddie Johnson: Eddie Johnson spent 17 seasons in the NBA and a year in the Euroleague midway through his career. With nearly 1,200 games in the NBA, he is notable for having scored the most career points of a player to never play in an NBA All-Star game. Johnson played for the Kings, the Phoenix Suns, the Seattle SuperSonics, the Charlotte Hornets, the Indiana Pacers, the Houston Rockets, and Greek team Olympiacos (1994–1995) before retiring from basketball in 1999. Although his 19,202 points over 1,199 NBA games was the 22nd highest total in NBA history at the time of his retirement, Johnson was never selected to play in the All-Star game nor ever chosen for an All-NBA team. In fact, the "awards highlight" of his career occurred in 1989, when he received the NBA Sixth Man of the Year Award as a member of the Suns. Johnson's career point total of 19,202 is also higher than all but 30 inductees into the Naismith Memorial Basketball Hall of Fame.

Glossary 60: Elgin Baylor: Elgin Baylor: is an American retired basketball player, coach, and executive. He played 13 seasons as a small forward in the National Basketball Association (NBA) for the

Minneapolis/Los Angeles Lakers, appearing in eight NBA Finals. Baylor was a gifted shooter, strong rebounder, and an accomplished passer. Renowned for his acrobatic maneuvers on the court, Baylor regularly dazzled Lakers fans with his trademark hanging jump shots. The No. 1 draft pick in 1958, NBA Rookie of the Year in 1959, and an 11-time NBA All-Star, he is regarded as one of the game's all-time greatest players. In 1977, Baylor was inducted into the Naismith Memorial Basketball Hall of Fame.

Glossary 61: Elmore Smith: Elmore Smith: Elmore Smith is a retired American professional basketball player born in Macon, Georgia. A 7'0" center from Kentucky State University, he played in the National Basketball Association from 1971 to 1979. He was a member of the Buffalo Braves, Los Angeles Lakers, Milwaukee Bucks, and Cleveland Cavaliers.

Smith is best remembered for his shot-blocking, earning him the nickname "Elmore the Rejector". He led the league in total blocked shots twice (in 1974 and 1975), and holds the NBA record for most blocked shots in a game since 1973, with 17. He achieved this mark against the Portland Trail Blazers on October 28, 1973, while playing for the Lakers. Smith's average of 4.85 blocks per game from the 1973–74 season (the first season blocked shots were officially recorded in the NBA) is the third highest ever. He was also a skilled rebounder, and he averaged a double-double (13.4 points, 10.6 rebounds) over the course of his career.

Glossary 62: Elvin Hayes: Elvin Hayes Joined the San Diego/Houston Rockets in 1968, the Washington Bullets in 1972 and the Houston Rockets in 181. He is a member of the NBA's 50th Anniversary All-Time Team, and an inductee in the Naismith Memorial Basketball Hall of Fame. San Diego/Houston Rockets.

Hayes Joined the NBA with the San Diego Rockets in 1968 and in his rookie year, he scored a career-high 54 points against the Detroit Pistons on November 11 of that year. As a rookie, Hayes led the NBA in scoring with 28.4 points per game, averaged 17.1 rebounds per game, and was named to the NBA All-Rookie Team.

Hayes' scoring average is the fifth best all-time for a rookie, and he remains the last rookie to lead the NBA in scoring average.

Desiring to finish his playing career in Texas and preferably Houston, Hayes was sent back to the Rockets for second-round draft picks in 1981 (Charles Davis) and 1983 (Sidney Lowe) on June 8, 1981. The "Big E" closed out his career with the Rockets in 1984. Hayes had a career scoring average of 21.0 points and 12.5 rebounds per game. He played at least 80 games in every season. He ranks fourth in NBA history in total rebounds, behind Chamberlain, Russell and Kareem Abdul-Jabbar.

Glossary 63: Ernie DiGregorio: Ernest "Ernie" DiGregorio, known as "Ernie D," is an American former National Basketball Association player. He was the 1973-74 NBA Rookie of the Year and holds the NBA rookie record for assists in a single game with 25. Due to a severe knee injury suffered early in DiGregorio's professional career, he played only five NBA seasons.

He was selected third overall by the Buffalo Braves in the 1973 NBA Draft out of Providence College, and won the NBA Rookie of the Year Award in 1973-74 after averaging 15.2 points and leading the league in both free throw percentage and assists per game.[1] DiGregorio still holds the NBA rookie record for assists in a single game with 25 (a record now shared with Nate McMillan). He would never again come close to that level of production, but managed to have a decent NBA career, most of which he spent with the Braves.

During the 1976-77 season, Di Gregorio led the league in free throw percentage a second time, with a then-NBA record 94.5%. Ernie after playing 27 games with the Braves in the 1977-78 season, DiGregorio was traded to the Los Angeles Lakers, but he played in a Lakers uniform in only 25 games before being waived. The Boston Celtics signed him as a free agent but he played only sparingly for the rest of the season. He would not play in the NBA again, although he did not formally retire until 1981. In 1999, he was elected to the National Italian American Sports Hall of Fame.

Glossary 64: Etan Thomas: Dedrick Etan Thomas (/ɛtɑːˈn/; born April 1, 1978) is an American retired professional basketball player who played 9 seasons in the <u>NBA</u>. He is also a published poet, free-lance writer, and motivational speaker. Without ever playing a game for the Mavericks, he was traded to the <u>Washington Wizards</u> in 2001. He averaged 4.3 points and 3.9 rebounds throughout the 2001–02 season.

On June 23, 2009, he was traded along with <u>Oleksiy Pecherov</u>, <u>Darius Songaila</u>, and a first-round draft pick to the <u>Minnesota Timberwolves</u> for <u>Randy Foye</u> and <u>Mike Miller</u>. On July 27, 2009, he was traded to the <u>Oklahoma City Thunder</u> along with a 2010 second-round draft pick and a conditional 2010 second-round draft pick in exchange for guards <u>Chucky Atkins</u> and <u>Damien Wilkins</u>. On September 2, 2010, it was announced that the <u>Atlanta Hawks</u> had signed Thomas.

Glossary 65: Fat Lever: Fat Lever: Lever was selected by the <u>Portland Trail Blazers</u> as the 11th pick in the <u>1982 NBA draft</u> out of <u>Arizona State</u>. While at ASU, his guard-tandem teammate was <u>Byron Scott</u> who left school early (1983) to sign with the <u>San Diego Clippers</u>. He was considered one of the NBA's best <u>point guards</u> in the late 1980s while playing for the <u>Denver Nuggets</u>. Despite his size (6 feet 3 inches) he regularly led the Nuggets in <u>rebounding</u>.

Lever was traded by the Nuggets to the <u>Dallas Mavericks</u> in 1990 for the Mavs' #9 pick in the <u>1990 NBA draft</u> plus Dallas' first-round pick in the <u>following one</u>. The Nuggets subsequently traded the #9 pick and their own #15 pick to the <u>Miami Heat</u> for the Heat's #3 pick in the 1990 draft, with Denver sending the Mavs' 1991 first rounder (which was originally the <u>Detroit Pistons</u>' pick they acquired in the <u>Mark Aguirre/Adrian Dantley</u> trade) to the <u>Washington Bullets</u> along with <u>Michael Adams</u>, for the Bullets' first round pick in the 1991 Draft.

Lever sat out the entire <u>1992-93 season</u> due to knee injury. He finished his career with the Mavericks in 1994 with career averages of 13.9 points, six rebounds, 6.2 assists and 2.22 steals per game. He is the Nuggets' all-time franchise leader in steals and was 2nd in career assists. He is one of only three players in NBA history to record 15 plus points, rebounds and assists in a single <u>playoff</u> game (the others being <u>Jason Kidd</u> and <u>Wilt Chamberlain</u>). Among Lever's career achievements were making two <u>NBA All-Star</u> teams, an All-NBA Second Team in 1987, an All-Defensive Second Team in 1988, and, as of 2014, ranking 6th on the all-time list of Most Triple-Doubles in the Regular Season with 43 over 11 seasons, ahead of players like <u>Michael Jordan</u> (28) and <u>Clyde Drexler</u> (25).

Glossary 66: Floyd Lewis: Floyd Lewis: 1973 NBA draft: Round 11, Pick 4, Cleveland Cavaliers.

Glossary 67: Franco Columbu: Franco Columbu won the title of <u>Mr. Olympia</u> in 1976 and 1981. At 5 feet 5 in. in height, Columbu was shorter than most of his bodybuilding competitors. In 1977, Columbu competed in the first *World's Strongest Man* competition and was in fifth place in total points during the competition; a remarkable outing, considering that Franco weighed much less than all his competitors. Then came the refrigerator race, which called for a downhill race in which a heavy, bulky, unwieldy refrigerator is strapped to the racer's back While ahead, Franco stumbled, and was shown on national television collapsing with a grotesquely dislocated leg. This ended his participation in the World's Strongest Man contest, in the end, he finished in fifth place. After <u>Arnold Schwarzenegger</u>'s comeback victory in the 1980 Mr. Olympia, Franco followed suit and won the 1981 Mr. Olympia.

Glossary 68: Frank Zane: Frank Zane is a three-time <u>Mr. Olympia</u> (1977 to 1979). His reign represented a shift in emphasis from <u>mass</u> to <u>aesthetics</u>. Zane's proportionate physique featured the second thinnest waistline of all the Mr. Olympias (after <u>Sergio Oliva</u>), with his wide shoulders making for a distinctive V-taper. His abdominals were considered by some bodybuilders to be the best in bodybuilding history. He stood at 5'9" and had a self-declared competition weight of 198 pounds when he won Mr. Olympia (He weighed over 200 lbs. when he competed in the 1960s). Zane is one of only three people who have beaten <u>Arnold Schwarzenegger</u> in a bodybuilding contest (1968 <u>Mr. Universe</u> in Miami, FL) and one of the very few Mr. Olympia winners under 200 pounds. Overall, he competed for over 20 years (retiring after the 1983 Mr. Olympia contest) and won

Mr. America, Mr. Universe, Mr. World and Mr. Olympia during his illustrious career.

Glossary 69: Fred Carter: Fredrick James Carter is an American former professional basketball player and coach. A 6' 3" guard from Mount St. Mary's University, Carter was selected by the Baltimore Bullets in the third round of the 1969 NBA Draft. He played eight seasons (1969–1977) in the NBA as a member of the Bullets, Philadelphia 76ers, and Milwaukee Bucks, scoring 9,271 career points. Carter was the leading scorer on the 1973 Sixers team that lost an NBA record 73 of 82 regular-season games.

On December 1, 2007, Carter had his jersey, number "33", retired at halftime of the Mount St. Mary's v. Loyola men's basketball game at Coach Jim Phelan Court in Knott Arena in Emmitsburg, MD. A crowd of over 2,000, mixed with Mount and Loyola students, Mount and Loyola alumni, and Emmitsburg residents cheered the "Mad Dog" for his importance to not only the men's basketball program, but the integration of the school back in the 1960s, as Carter became the first African-American student on the campus when he began attending school there. He is also known for popularizing the "fist bump."

Glossary 70: Fred J. Foster was an American professional basketball player. He was drafted in the third round of the 1968 NBA Draft by the Cincinnati Royals and was also selected in the 1968 American Basketball Association draft by the Kentucky Colonels. In his rookie season with the Royals, Foster made his debut on October 19, 1968 as the Royals' last man in in a win over the Detroit Pistons. For the season, he averaged 3.4 points per game.

Foster came on strong in his second season, 1969–70, when he averaged 14.8 points and 4.8 rebounds per game, both career highs. He also had career highs in minutes per game (28.1) and field goal percentage (.449). He twice had a single-game career best of 32 points—on January 7, 1970 against the Milwaukee Bucks when he made 13 field goals and was 6-for-6 at the free throw line, and again on February 15 against the San Diego Rockets.

In 1970-71, after playing one game with the Royals, he was traded along with Connie Dierking to the Philadelphia 76ers for Darrall Imhoff and a future draft pick. For the season, Foster averaged 5.5 points and 2.3 rebounds per game. In 1971-72, he was a steady contributor, averaging 23 minutes per game and 11.9 points and 3.7 rebounds per game. He had a season-high 30 points on February 10, 1972 against the Golden State Warriors.

Prior to the 1972-73 season, on July 31, 1972, Foster was traded to the Portland Trail Blazers for a future draft pick, then on the same day Portland traded him to the Detroit Pistons for Terry Dischinger. In 23.2 minutes per game, he averaged 8.7 points per game. On October 8, 1973, he was waived by the Pistons and three weeks later signed as a free agent with the Cleveland Cavaliers for the 1973-74 season, averaging 4.8 points per game. In 1974-75, he upped his average to 6.9 points per game.

He did not play in the 1975-76 season, and in 1976-77 he returned to the NBA, signing as a free agent with the Buffalo Braves, for whom he averaged 3.9 points per game in his eighth and final NBA season.

Glossary 71: Fred Slaughter: Fred Slaughter is an American former college basketball player for the UCLA Bruins. He won a national championship with the Bruins in 1964, and was later one of the early African Americans to become a sports agent.

Growing up in Kansas, Slaughter was a dual-sport athlete in basketball and track before leaving home to attend University of California, Los Angeles (UCLA). He continued in both sports in college, and he helped UCLA basketball coach John Wooden win the first of his 10 national championships in 12 seasons. In addition to his undergraduate degree, Slaughter also earned an Master of Business Administration (MBA) and a law degree before becoming a sports agent in 1969. He spent almost a decade as an administrator at the UCLA School of Law before leaving in 1980 to become a full-time agent. Slaughter has represented professional basketball and American football players. He was also the labor union leader for referees in the National Basketball Association (NBA).

Glossary 72: Freeman Williams: Freeman Williams is a retired American professional basketball player. He was the 1978 NCAA men's basketball Division I scoring champion, and the Portland State University all-time scoring leader. Williams was the NCAA Division I national men's basketball individual scoring leader in 1977 and 1978. Williams was a consensus second team All-American in 1978. He is second in Division I history in scoring, trailing only Pete Maravich. He was born in Los Angeles, California.

He was a 1978 first round draft pick (8th overall) by the Boston Celtics. His pro playing career started in 1978 with the San Diego Clippers. He finished in the top 10 for three-point field goals in three consecutive seasons, 1980 through 1982. In December 1980, Freeman became the first Clippers player to win a Player of the Month award, and the only one in franchise history until Elton Brand did so 25 years later.

In September 1982, Freeman Williams was traded by the Atlanta Hawks along with John Drew, and cash to the Utah Jazz in exchange for Dominique Wilkins who was drafted by the Jazz and refused to sign.[4] After that season (1982–83), Williams only played in 27 more games: 18 with Utah in 1983 and nine with the Washington Bullets in 1986.

Glossary 73: Gary Close: Gary E. Close is a basketball coach. Close was an assistant coach with the Stanford Cardinal and the Iowa Hawkeyes before taking a head coaching position at Regina High School in Iowa City, Iowa. He Joined the Badgers in 2003. He resigned his position on March 30, 2016 after 13 years with the team.

Glossary 74: George Gervin: George Gervin, nicknamed "The Iceman," is an American retired professional basketball player who played in both the American Basketball Association (ABA) and National Basketball Association (NBA) for the Virginia Squires, San Antonio Spurs, and Chicago Bulls. Gervin averaged at least 14 points per game in all 14 of his ABA and NBA seasons, and finished with an NBA career average of 26.2 points per game. Gervin is widely regarded to be one of the greatest shooting guards in NBA history.

Gervin's first NBA scoring crown came in 1978, when he narrowly edged <u>David Thompson</u> for the scoring title by seven hundredths of a point (27.22 to 27.15). Although Thompson came up with a memorable performance for the last game of the regular season, scoring 73 points, Gervin maintained his slight lead by scoring 63 points (including a then NBA record 33 points in the second quarter) in a loss in his last game of the season. With the scoring crown in hand, he sat out some of the third, and all of the fourth quarter.

Gervin went on to lead the NBA in scoring average three years in a row from 1978 to 1980 (with a high of <u>33.1 points per game</u> in 1979-80), and again in 1982. Prior to <u>Michael Jordan</u>, Gervin had the most scoring titles of any guard in league history. In 1981, while sitting out three games due to injury, Gervin's replacement, <u>Ron Brewer</u>, averaged over 30 ppg. When Gervin returned, he scored 40+ points. When asked if he was sending a message, Gervin said, "Just the way the Lord planned it" and added, "Ice be cool" (with Ron Brewer).

The last NBA game of Gervin's career was April 20, 1986, Jordan's remarkable 63-point game against the <u>Boston Celtics</u> in the playoffs. Gervin recorded an assist and a personal foul in five minutes of play for the Bulls.

Glossary 75: George Johnson: George Johnson: George Thomas Johnson (born December 18, 1948) is a retired American professional <u>basketball</u> player. A 6'11" <u>forward</u>/<u>center</u> born in <u>Tylertown, Mississippi</u> and from <u>Dillard University</u>, he played in 13 <u>NBA</u> seasons (1972–1983; 1984–1986) as a member of the <u>Golden State Warriors</u>, the <u>Buffalo Braves</u>, the <u>New Jersey Nets</u>, the <u>San Antonio Spurs</u>, the <u>Atlanta Hawks</u>, and the <u>Seattle SuperSonics</u>.

Johnson was a key reserve on the Warriors team that won the <u>NBA Championship</u> in 1975, and he grabbed 5,887 <u>rebounds</u> in his career. Johnson led the NBA in <u>blocked shots</u> per game three times, led the NBA in disqualifications in <u>1977–78</u> with 20, and was named to the NBA All-Defensive Second Team in <u>1980-81</u>. He <u>blocked at least 10 shots in a game six times during his NBA career</u>.

Inspired by his teammate Rick Barry, Johnson shot his free throws underhanded.

Glossary 76: George Leftwich: George Leftwich: While engaged in a playground battle during his high school days, Leftwich had the chance to go against Elgin Baylor. Though he suffered a knee injury that would end his chances at a NBA career, Leftwich dodged two bullets during his 1962 car accident. Leftwich was a great rebounder as a guard and ranked second on the team in rebounds during the 1959-60 season. In 2006, Leftwich was inducted into the D.C. Metropolitan Basketball Hall of Fame. Coach Leftwich is acknowledged as being a great teacher, great student of the game that was apparent in his on the court performance and as a coach.

Glossary 77: George McGinnis: George McGinnis: George F. McGinnis is an American retired professional basketball player who played 11 seasons in the American Basketball Association (ABA) and National Basketball Association (NBA). He was drafted into the ABA from Indiana University in 1971. In the 1970–71 season at Indiana, McGinnis became the first sophomore to lead the Big Ten in scoring and rebounding. He averaged 29.9 points per game in his lone season in Bloomington earning All-American and All-Big Ten Honors in 1971.

George McGinnis was one of the marquee players of the ABA, and later teamed up with fellow ABA alumni Julius Erving and Caldwell Jones on the Philadelphia 76ers that made the NBA Finals in 1977.

McGinnis is one of four players (the others are Roger Brown, Reggie Miller, and Mel Daniels) to have his jersey (#30) retired by the Pacers.

Of all former ABA and NBA regular season MVPs, George McGinnis (ABA 1974–75) is the only player meeting the five-year retirement eligibility criterion not inducted into the Naismith Memorial Basketball Hall of Fame.

ABA and NBA accomplishments: Member of the 1972 and 1973 Indiana Pacers ABA championship teams, Second Team All-ABA selection in 1973, Two All-ABA First Team selections (1974–

1975), Three ABA All-Star selections (1973–1975), Selected as ABA Co-MVP, with Julius Erving, in 1975, Won the ABA scoring title in 1975, First Team All-NBA selection in 1976, Second Team All-NBA selection in 1977, Three NBA All-Star selections (1976, 1977 and 1979), Member of the ABA's All-Time Team., Number retired by Indiana Pacers.

Glossary 78: Greg Butler: Gregory Edward "Greg" Butler, is an American former professional basketball player who was selected by the New York Knicks in the 2nd round (37th overall) of the 1988 NBA Draft. A 6'11" center from Stanford University, Butler played in 3 NBA seasons from 1988-1991. He played for the Knicks and Los Angeles Clippers. In his NBA career, Butler played in 55 games and scored a total of 76 points.

Glossary 79: Greg DeFerro: Greg DeFerro, in 1979, IFBB Mr. International, five top 4 placing in IFBB shows from 1981-1984. He participated in the following shows: 1984 IFBB World Pro 2nd, 1983 IFBB Grand Prix Las Vegas (Caesars) 4th, 1983 IFBB Night Of The Champions 2nd, 1983 IFBB World Pro 2nd, 1982 IFBB Night Of The Champions 9th, IFBB 1981 IFBB Grand Prix California 6th, 1981 IFBB Grand Prix New England 4th, 1981 IFBB Pro World NP, 1980 IFBB World Pro 6th, 1979 IFBB Mr. International 1st, and 1977 IFBB Mr. USA 3rd.

Glossary 80: Gus Johnson: Gus Johnson: Gus Johnson was an American professional basketball player in the National Basketball Association (NBA). A 6 ft. 6 in (1.98 m), 235-pound (107 kg) forward-center he spent nine seasons with the Baltimore Bullets, and his final season was split between the Phoenix Suns and the Indiana Pacers of the ABA.

One of the first forwards to frequently play above the rim, Johnson combined an unusual blend of strength, jumping ability, and speed; he was one of the first dunk shot artists in the NBA. His nickname "Honeycomb" was given to him by his college coach. He had a gold star drilled into one of his front teeth and shattered three backboards during his career.

As a member of the Baltimore Bullets, Johnson was voted to the All-Rookie Team for 1963–64. He played in five NBA All-Star Games, was named to four All-NBA Second Teams, and was twice named to the All-NBA Defense First Team. His No. 25 jersey was retired by the Bullets franchise. With the Pacers, he was a member of the 1973 ABA championship team.

Johnson was inducted into the Naismith Memorial Basketball Hall of Fame in 2010. Injuries limited Johnson's pro basketball career to 10 seasons, and this no doubt prevented post-career honors such as inclusion on the NBA 50 Greatest Players Ever list, and a delayed induction into the Hall of Fame. His induction in 2010 came 37 years after his final game and 23 years following his death.

Glossary 81: Eric "Hank" Gathers was an American college basketball star at Loyola Marymount University who collapsed and died during a game. He was the second player in NCAA Division I history to lead the nation in scoring and rebounding in the same season. He originally played at the University of Southern California, but transferred with teammate Bo Kimble to LMU after his freshman year. Gathers was listed as 6'7" in height.

Due to NCAA regulations, Gathers and Kimble could not play in the season following their transfer. They helped lead the Lions to a 28–4 record in 1987–88. Gathers led the team that year in both scoring and rebounding, averaging 22.5 points and 8.7 rebounds per game, and he was named to the All-West Coast Conference (WCC) first team and was awarded the WCC Tournament Most Valuable Player (MVP). In the 1988–89 season, Gathers became the second player in NCAA Division I history to lead the nation in scoring and rebounding in the same season, averaging 32.7 points and 13.7 rebounds per game. He was named WCC Player of the Year and again won the WCC Tournament MVP. On December 30, 1988, he scored a career-high 49 points along with 26 rebounds in a 130–125 win over Nevada.

As a senior in 1989–90, he was a candidate for player of the year and had been projected as an NBA lottery pick. Gathers' teams led Division I in scoring in 1988 (110.3 points per game), 1989 (112.5), and 1990 (122.4). LMU's 122.4 point per game in 1990 is still a record as of April 2012. As of April 2012, Loyola Marymount held the five highest combined score games in Division I history. Four of the five occurred during Gathers' career, including a record 331 in the 181–150 win over United States International University on January 31, 1989.

At 6'7" and 210 pounds, Gathers was Loyola Marymount's strongest inside player. He had a high field goal percentage because he seldom shot from beyond 10 feet. He used his power and quickness for follow-up baskets and scoring on fast breaks. "I don't care much about the points," said Gathers. "In fact, I should lead the nation in scoring because of my rebounding. Anybody can score 30 points a night if that's what he's concentrating on. But rebounding is special because it comes from the heart.

Glossary 82: Howard Hedinger: Mr. Howard H. Hedinger has been a director of Sirena Apparel Group, Inc. since May 1997. Since 1959, Mr. Hedinger has been an executive officer and director of American Steel, a West Coast steel service center chain based in Portland, Oregon. American Steel is a subsidiary of American Industries, which has interests in real estate and other investments. Since the 1970s, Mr. Hedinger has been the President and Chairman of American Industries. Mr. Hedinger is a board member of American Steel LLC.

Glossary 83: Howard Wright: Howard Gregory Wright is an American professional basketball player. Born in San Diego, California, he is a 6'8" (203 cm) 220 lb. (100 kg) forward and played collegiately at Stanford University from 1987–1989.

Wright played for the NBA's Dallas Mavericks, Atlanta Hawks, and Orlando Magic. He also played in the Continental Basketball Association for the Tri-City Chinook.

Glossary 84: Jack Sikma: Jack Sikma a seven-time NBA All-Star with the Seattle SuperSonics, who drafted him in the first round with the eighth overall pick of the 1977 NBA draft. He was a seven-time NBA All-Star with the Seattle SuperSonics, who drafted him in the first round with the eighth overall pick of the 1977 NBA draft. In 1979, he won an NBA championship with Seattle. Sikma finished his playing career with the <u>Milwaukee Bucks</u>. He was known for his distinctive curly, blonde hair along with his patented step back behind the head jumper during his playing days.

Sikma was one of the most accurate shooting centers in NBA history. He holds the rare distinction of leading the league in free-throw percentage (92.2%) while playing the center position during the 1987–88 season; he averaged 84.9% in free-throw shooting for his career. Sikma also made over 200 three-pointers during his career with a 32.8% three-point accuracy.

Glossary 85: Jamaal Wilkes: Jamaal Wilkes: Jamaal Abdul-Lateef (born Jackson Keith Wilkes), better known as Jamaal Wilkes, nicknamed "Silk", is a retired American <u>basketball</u> player who played the <u>small forward</u> position and won four <u>NBA</u> championships with the <u>Golden State Warriors</u> and <u>Los Angeles Lakers</u>. He was a three-time <u>NBA All-Star</u> and the 1975 <u>NBA Rookie of the Year</u>. He was inducted into the <u>Naismith Memorial Basketball Hall of Fame</u>, and his jersey No. 52 was <u>retired</u> by both the Lakers and the Bruins.

Wilkes converted to <u>Islam</u> and legally changed his name to Jamaal Abdul-Lateef in 1975, but he continued to use his birth surname only for purposes of public recognition.

One of the smoothest, steadiest and most productive forwards to ever play in the NBA (he possessed a deadly accurate jump shot from the corner that <u>Hall of Fame</u> Laker announcer <u>Chick Hearn</u> dubbed the "20 foot layup") Jamaal "Smooth as Silk" Wilkes won championships at the scholastic, collegiate and professional levels.

In March 2007, he was inducted into the <u>Pac-10 Men's Basketball Hall of Honor</u>. One of the most memorable games of his career was the series clinching Game 6 of the <u>1980 NBA Finals</u> against the <u>Philadelphia 76ers</u>; Wilkes had 37 points and 10 rebounds, but was overshadowed by rookie teammate <u>Magic Johnson</u>, who started at center in place of an injured <u>Kareem Abdul-Jabbar</u> and finished with 42 points, 15 rebounds, and 7 assists. "Jamaal Wilkes had an unbelievable game," said Johnson in 2011. "Everybody talked about my 42 [points], but it was also his [37-point effort]." Wilkes missed the first seven games of the 1984 Playoffs due to a <u>gastrointestinal</u>

virus. When he returned to action on May 8, he received a standing ovation from the Forum crowd.

For his career, Wilkes registered 14,664 points (17.7 ppg) and 5,117 rebounds (6.2 rpg), averaging 16.1 ppg in 113 postseason games. He played in the 1976, 1981, and 1983 All-Star Games and was named to the NBA All-Defensive Team twice. The Sporting News named Wilkes to its NBA All-Pro Second Team three years. On April 2, 2012, Wilkes was announced as a member of the Naismith Memorial Basketball Hall of Fame induction class of 2012. He formally entered the Hall on September 7. On December 28, 2012, the Lakers retired Wilkes' jersey, number 52, and on January 17, 2013, UCLA retired his collegiate jersey, also number 52.

Glossary 86: James Brown: James Brown: After failing to make a roster spot when he tried out for the NBA's Atlanta Hawks in the mid-1970s, Brown entered the corporate world, working for such companies as Xerox and Eastman Kodak. Brown went into sports broadcasting in 1984 when he was offered a Job doing Washington Bullets television broadcasts. He later moved on to an anchor position at WDVM-TV (later WUSA) in Washington and to some work at CBS Sports.

Glossary 87: James Edwards: James Franklin Edwards is a retired American professional basketball player. Nicknamed "Buddha" for his appearance (he often sported a Fu Manchu mustache) and stoic demeanor, the 7'0" Though he never appeared in an All-Star Game, Edwards was a reliable low-post scorer, averaging 12.7 points per game over his career.

He retired with 14,862 career points and 6,004 career rebounds. Edwards played 19 years (1977–1996) in the National Basketball Association, playing both the center and power forward positions. Edwards was drafted by the Los Angeles Lakers on June 10, 1977 and made his NBA debut on October 18. Edwards was then traded to the Indiana Pacers. This is where Edwards played a majority of his career and averaged his best scoring numbers, averaging 15.9 points during his four years with the franchise. Edwards spent a short period of time with the Cleveland Cavaliers. Edwards was then traded to the

Phoenix Suns. Edward's most remembered years in the NBA was his three seasons with the Detroit Pistons. He was a key member of the 1989 and 1990 NBA champion Detroit Pistons, starting most of the team's games in 1990. Edwards was known for his turn-around fade away jump shot that was difficult to block. He was then traded to the Los Angeles Clippers. He spent his 18th season with the Portland Trail Blazers. Edwards spent his final season with the Chicago Bulls. He won a third championship in the final season of his career, with the 1996 Chicago Bulls, where he saw limited playing time.

Glossary 88: James Lofton: James David Lofton is a former American football player and coach. He is a former coach for the San Diego Chargers but is best known for his years in the National Football League as a wide receiver for the Green Bay Packers (1978–1986), Los Angeles Raiders (1987–1988), the Buffalo Bills (1989–1992), Los Angeles Rams (1993) and Philadelphia Eagles (1993). He was also the NCAA champion in the long jump in 1978 while attending Stanford University. He is a member of the Pro Football Hall of Fame.

Lofton was drafted in the first round (sixth overall) of the 1978 NFL Draft by the Green Bay Packers. He was named to the NFL Pro Bowl eight times (seven with the Packers, one with the Bills). He was also named to four All-Pro teams. He also played in three Super Bowls during his career with the Bills.[4] Lofton was inducted into the Pro Football Hall of Fame in 2003.

In his 16 NFL seasons, Lofton caught 764 passes for 14,004 yards and 75 touchdowns. He averaged 20 yards per catch or more in five seasons, leading the league in 1983 and 1984 with an average of 22.4 and 22 yards respectively. He also rushed 32 times for 246 yards and one touchdown.

Lofton is the first NFL player to record 14,000 yards receiving and was the second, one game after Drew Hill to score a touchdown in the 1970s, 1980s, and 1990s. During his nine seasons in Green Bay, Lofton played in seven Pro Bowls and left as the team's all- time leading receiver with 9,656 yards (since broken by Donald Driver). In 1991, Lofton became the oldest player to record 1,000 receiving yards in a season (since broken by Jerry Rice). On October 21, of that same year, Lofton became the oldest player to record 200 yards receiving as well as 200 yards from scrimmage in a game (35 years, 108 days). He is also the 2nd oldest player to have 200+ all-purpose yards in a game behind Mel Gray, (35 years, 204 days)

Glossary 89: James Worthy: James Worthy: James Ager Worthy is an American retired Hall of Fame professional basketball player.

Named one of the 50 Greatest Players in NBA History, **"Big Game James"** was a seven-time NBA All-Star, three-time NBA champion and the 1988 NBA Finals MVP. A standout at the University of North Carolina, the 6 ft. 9 in (2.06 m) small forward shared College Player of the Year honors en route to leading the Tar Heels to the 1982 NCAA Championship. Named the tournament's Most Outstanding Player, he was #1 pick of the 1982 NBA draft of the reigning NBA Champion Los Angeles Lakers.

Glossary 90: Jerome Kersey: Jerome Kersey: was an American professional basketball player in the National Basketball Association (NBA). He played for the Portland Trail Blazers (1984–1995), Golden State Warriors (1995–96), Los Angeles Lakers (1996–97), Seattle SuperSonics (1997–98), San Antonio Spurs (1998–2000), and Milwaukee Bucks (2000–01).

The Trail Blazers selected Kersey in the second round of the 1984 NBA draft from Longwood University (then Longwood College) in Farmville, Virginia. He was a member of the Spurs during their 1999 NBA Finals victory over the New York Knicks. Following his playing career, Kersey worked with his former Portland teammate and then-head coach of the Milwaukee Bucks Terry Porter as an assistant in 2005.

Glossary 91: Jerome Whitehead: Jerome Whitehead: Jerome Whitehead was an American professional basketball player. He was selected by the San Diego Clippers in the 2nd round (41st overall) of the 1978 NBA Draft. A 6'10" center-forward from Marquette University, Whitehead played in 11 NBA seasons from 1978 to 1989. He played for the Clippers, Utah Jazz, Dallas Mavericks, Cleveland Cavaliers, Golden State Warriors and San Antonio Spurs. In his NBA career, Whitehead played in 679 games and scored a total of 4,423 points.

Glossary 92: Jerry Chambers: Jerry Chambers: a retired American professional basketball player. At 6'5" and 185 pounds, he played as a forward. Chambers attended the University of Utah during the mid-1960s, winning the NCAA Basketball Tournament Most Outstanding Player award in 1966, despite his Runnin' Utes finishing fourth at the Final Four. He was the only player to ever earn MOP for a fourth-place team, and unless the third-place game is reinstated—it was abolished after the 1981 Final Four—he will remain the only player ever to attain this feat. His 143 points in four games remains an NCAA Tournament record, with 70 of them coming in the Final Four—38 against eventual national champion Texas-Western, and 32 more in the third-place game against Duke.

He played four professional seasons in the National Basketball Association as a member of the Los Angeles Lakers, Phoenix Suns, Atlanta Hawks, and Buffalo Braves. In 1968, he was involved in one of the most significant transactions in NBA history when the Lakers traded him, Archie Clark and Darrall Imhoff to the Philadelphia 76ers for Hall-of-Famer Wilt Chamberlain. Chambers never played for the 76ers, as they traded him to Phoenix in 1969.

From 1972 to 1974, Chambers played in the rival American Basketball Association as a member of the San Diego Conquistadors and the San Antonio Spurs. He retired with 2,667 combined NBA/ABA career points.

Glossary 93: Jerry West: Jerry Alan West is an American retired basketball player who played his entire professional career for the Los Angeles Lakers of the National Basketball Association (NBA). His nicknames include "Mr. Clutch", for his ability to make a big play in a clutch situation, such as his famous buzzer-beating 60-foot shot that tied Game 3 of the 1970 NBA Finals against the New York Knicks; "The Logo", in reference to his silhouette being incorporated into the NBA logo; "Mr. Outside", in reference to his perimeter play with the Los Angeles Lakers; and "Zeke from Cabin Creek", for the creek near his birthplace of Chelyan, West Virginia. Playing the small forward position early in his career, West was a standout at East Bank High School and at West Virginia University, leading the Mountaineers to the 1959 NCAA championship game, earning the NCAA Final Four Most Outstanding Player honor despite the loss. He then embarked on a 14-year career with the Los Angeles Lakers, and was the co-captain of the 1960 U.S. Olympic gold medal team in Rome, a squad that would be inducted as a unit into the Naismith Memorial Basketball Hall of Fame in 2010.

West's NBA career was highly successful. Playing the guard position as a professional, he was voted 12 times into the All-NBA First and Second Teams, was elected into the NBA All-Star Team 14 times, and was chosen as the All-Star MVP in 1972, the same year that he won the only title of his career. West holds the NBA record for the highest points per game average in a playoff series with 46.3. He was also a member of the first five NBA All-Defensive Teams (one second, followed by four firsts), which were introduced when he was 32 years old. Having played in nine NBA Finals, he is also the only player in NBA history to be named Finals MVP despite being on the losing team (1969). West was inducted into the Naismith Basketball Hall of Fame in 1980 and voted as one of the 50 Greatest Players in NBA history in 1996.

He was a loner. His high-pitched voice earned him the nickname "Tweety Bird", and he spoke with such a thick Appalachian accent that his teammates also referred to him as "Zeke from Cabin Creek" (his nickname acknowledged his country roots, and his accent was so thick that he squeaked his nickname sheepishly–"Zeek fr'm Cab'n Creek"). However, West soon impressed his colleagues with his defensive hustle, with his vertical jump—he could reach up 16 inches above the rim when he went up—and with his work ethic, spending countless extra hours working on his game.[15] On the floor, West scored 17.6 points, grabbed 7.7 rebounds and gave 4.2 assists per game.

Glossary 94: Jim Brewer: James Turner Brewer is a retired American National Basketball Association player. Brewer was the first notable player to come out of Proviso East High School, which has one of the most successful high school basketball programs in Illinois. In

1969, Brewer, playing center, led his team to the first of four state championships. Brewer was followed at Proviso East by other future NBA players, notably Doc Rivers, Michael Finley, Dee Brown, and Shannon Brown. The 6'9" 210 pound forward then attended the University of Minnesota, where he was a teammate of future Baseball Hall-of-Famer Dave Winfield. Brewer played in the 1972 Summer Olympics, including the United States' controversial loss to the Soviet Union, before being drafted by the Cleveland Cavaliers in the first round (2nd pick) of the 1973 NBA Draft. When Brewer scored a basket at a Cavaliers home game, the public address announcer would declare, "Two for the Brew!" Brewer played nine seasons in the NBA from 1973 to 1982.

Glossary 95: Jimmy Paxson – James Joseph "Jim" Paxson is an American retired professional basketball player. A first round selection (12th overall) of the Portland Trail Blazers in the 1979 NBA Draft, Paxson played for Portland and the Boston Celtics of the NBA from 1979-1990 and was twice an All-Star. The 6-foot-6 Paxson was an NBA All-Star in 1983 and 1984. He also earned All-NBA Second Team honors in 1984 after averaging 21 points per game. He spent nine seasons with Portland (1979-1988) and, after being traded to Boston in February 1988, spent two full seasons with Boston (1988-1990). When he was traded from Portland, he left as the team's all-time leading scorer.

Glossary 96: Jim Price: James E. "Jim" Price is a retired American professional basketball player. After starring at the University of Louisville, the 6' 3" Price was drafted by the Los Angeles Lakers in the second round of the 1972 NBA Draft. Price would go on to play seven NBA seasons (1972–1979), spending time with the Lakers, Milwaukee Bucks, Buffalo Braves, Denver Nuggets and Detroit Pistons. He was an All-Star in 1975, and he retired with 5,088 career points.

Glossary 97: Joe White: Henry "Jo" White is an American former professional basketball player. As an amateur, he played basketball at the University of Kansas and represented the U.S. Men's Basketball team during the 1968 Summer Olympics. As a professional, he is best known for his ten-year stint with the Boston Celtics of the NBA, where he led the team towards two NBA championships, played nine seasons, and set a franchise record of 488 consecutive games played. White was inducted into the Naismith Memorial Basketball Hall of Fame in 2015.

White was drafted in 1969 in the first round (9th pick overall) by the NBA's Boston Celtics. White was also drafted by the Dallas Cowboys and the Cincinnati Reds.

In 1974, White and the Celtics reached the 1974 NBA Finals. They would face the Milwaukee Bucks who were returning with their championship-winning core from the 1971 NBA Finals, including future Hall of Fame members Kareem Abdul-Jabbar and Oscar Robertson. With the Bucks starting point guard, Lucius Allen, injured at the onset of the playoffs, White would lead a small, quick line-up (featuring undersized, All-Star Cowens at Center) towards the first Celtics championship in the Post-Russell era. The following season, White led the Celtics in minutes in a season where they would finish 1st in NBA Atlantic Division with a 60-22 record but lost the Eastern Conference Finals.

In 1976, White was part of a dominance Celtics squad which featured 5 veterans averaging double-digit scoring. During the playoffs, White led the Celtics to the NBA championship and was a starring player in what is often referred to as "the greatest game ever played" in NBA history. In the triple overtime win against the Phoenix Suns in game 5 of those finals, White was the game's high scorer with 33 points, had a game high 9 assists, leading the Celtics to a 128-126 win. Logging 60 minutes of play time, only the Suns' Garfield Heard (61) played more minutes. White was named the most valuable player of the 1976 NBA Finals.

White went on to become one of professional basketball's first "iron men", playing in all 82 games for five consecutive seasons during the 1970s and setting a franchise record of 488 consecutive games played. White suffered an injury during the 1977-78 season. With the end of the streak, White and the aging Celtics became a less effective squad and followed their championship with an exit from playoff semifinals in 1977 and then two losing seasons.

White would retire in 1981 with the Kansas City Kings.

Glossary 98: Joe Barry Carrol: Joe Barry Carroll is a retired American professional basketball player who spent ten seasons in the NBA.

Carroll was selected by the Golden State Warriors with the first overall pick of the 1980 NBA Draft. Many have labeled Carroll as one of the biggest busts in NBA Draft history, giving him the nicknames "Joe Barely Cares" and "Just Barely Carroll" for his perceived indifference to the game. A great deal of Carroll's negative press, however, can reasonably be attributed by the fact that he often declined interviews and the fact that the Warriors traded Robert Parish and the draft choice used to select Kevin McHale to the Boston Celtics for the first overall pick used to select Carroll. During his first few seasons, however, Carroll was actually a very productive player. He averaged 18.9 points and 9.3 rebounds as a rookie. He scored a game high of 46 points and led the Warriors with 121 blocks during his first season, while being named an NBA All-Rookie First Team selection.

Throughout his career as a Warrior, he is a top ten career franchise leader in defensive rebounds (3rd), offensive rebounds (4th), and points per game (8th), total points (9th) and steals (9th). He scored at least 1,000 points in each of his seasons as a Warrior. He left Golden State as the franchise leader in blocks with 837, which is currently the second most behind Adonal Foyle's 1,090 from 1997 to

Joe Barry retired from the NBA in 1991. He ended his career with totals of 12,455 points and 5,404 rebounds, 4 times topping 20+ point a game in scoring. He appeared in 19 playoff games, where he averaged 27 minutes, 5 rebounds and 13.7 points per game.

Over his career, he averaged 17.7 points, 7.7 rebounds, 1.8 assists, 1 steal, 1.6 blocks per game, with a .474 field goal and .747 free throw percentage in 705 games. He averaged 32 minutes of playing time per game.

Glossary 99: John Arrillaga: John Arrillaga is an American real estate mogul and philanthropist. He is one of the largest landowners in Silicon Valley He is well known for his generous support of Stanford

University.[6] The alumni center, the Frances C. Arrillaga Building, is named in memory of his first wife, and various other athletic facilities carry his surname. In May 2006, Arrillaga gave $100 million to Stanford.[7]

In June 2013, he again donated to Stanford, writing a check for $151 million, making it the largest individual donation in the school's history.

Glossary 100: John Barnhill: John Anthony "Rabbit" Barnhill was an American former professional basketball player. From 1962 to 1969, Barnhill played in the National Basketball Association as a member of the St. Louis Hawks, Detroit Pistons, Baltimore Bullets, and San Diego Rockets. He averaged 8.6 points per game in his NBA career. Barnhill later spent time in the rival American Basketball Association, mainly as a member of the Indiana Pacers. Additionally, Barnhill was selected in three separate NBA expansion drafts in three consecutive years, 1966 (Chicago Bulls), 1967 (San Diego Rockets), and 1968 (Phoenix Suns).

Glossary 101: John Drew: John Drew a 6'6" guard, he played 11 seasons in the NBA. Drew was a two-time NBA All-Star. Selected by the Atlanta Hawks with the 7th pick (in the 2nd round) of the 1974 NBA Draft, Drew quickly made an impact with the club, averaging 18.5 points per game, 10.7 rebounds per game, and leading the NBA in offensive rebounding during his rookie season (Drew was named to the NBA All-Rookie Team for his efforts). From 1974 to 1982, the immensely talented Drew starred for the Hawks, with whom he was a two-time All-Star, averaging more than 20 points per game on five occasions. After being traded by Atlanta for Dominique Wilkins, Drew played three seasons (1982-1985) with the Utah Jazz, retiring with 15,291 career points.

Glossary 102: John Havlicek: John Havlicek: John Joseph "Hondo" Havlicek (/ˈhævlɪtʃɛk/ *HAV-lə-chek*; born April 8, 1940) is a retired American professional basketball player who competed for 16 seasons with the Boston Celtics, winning eight NBA championships, four of them coming in his first four seasons.

In the <u>National Basketball Association</u>, only teammates <u>Bill Russell</u> and <u>Sam Jones</u> won more championships during their playing careers. Havlicek is widely considered to be one of the greatest players in the history of the game and was inducted as a member of the <u>Naismith Memorial Basketball Hall of Fame</u> in 1984.

Havlicek was drafted by both the Celtics and the <u>NFL's</u> <u>Cleveland Browns</u> in 1962. After competing briefly as a wide receiver in the Browns' training camp that year, he focused his energies on playing for the Celtics, with head coach <u>Red Auerbach</u> later describing him as the "guts of the team." He was also known for his stamina, with competitors saying that it was a challenge just to keep up with him.

Nicknamed '*Hondo*', (a name inspired by the <u>John Wayne movie of the same name</u>), Havlicek revolutionized the "<u>sixth man</u>" role, and has been immortalized for his clutch steal in the closing seconds of the 1965 Eastern Conference championship.

Havlicek is the Celtics' all-time leader in points and games played, scoring 26,395 points (20.8 points per game, 13th all-time in points scored in the NBA), and playing in 1,270 games (17th all-time). He became the first player to score 1,000 points in 16 consecutive seasons, with his best season coming during the <u>1970-71 NBA season</u> when he averaged 28.9 points per game.

Havlicek shares the <u>NBA Finals</u> single-game record for most points in an overtime period (9 in a May 10, 1974 game vs. the <u>Milwaukee Bucks</u>), and was named that year's NBA Finals MVP.

Aside from being a great sixth man at the start of his career, Havlicek became known for his ability to play both forward and guard, his relentlessness and tenacity on both offense and defense, his outstanding skills in all facets of the game, his constant movement, and his tireless ability to run up and down the court. As a result of his endurance, he was a devastating fast break finisher, one who could suddenly score in bunches when his Celtics team would shut out the other team and grab defensive rebounds. Although he did not have a high field goal percentage, he was a clutch outside shooter with great range. He was also the type of player who would do what it took to help his team score a victory, such as grab a crucial rebound, draw a charge, come up with a steal in a key defensive moment, or settle the team with a clutch basket or assist.

Glossary 103: John Shumate: John Shumate: John Henry Shumate is a retired American professional basketball player and coach. A 6'9" forward/center from the University of Notre Dame, Shumate played five seasons (1975–1978; 1979–1981) in the NBA as a member of the Phoenix Suns, Buffalo Braves, Detroit Pistons, Houston Rockets, San Antonio Spurs and Seattle SuperSonics. He earned NBA All-Rookie Team honors in his first season after averaging 11.3 points per game and 5.6 rebounds per game. Over the course of his career, Shumate averaged 12.3 points and 7.5 rebounds.

Glossary 104: John Thompson: John Thompson attended Archbishop Carroll High School, Thompson emerged as a standout center, playing in three consecutive City Championship games (1958–60). In 1959, Carroll All-Mets Thompson, Monk Malloy, George Leftwich and Tom Hoover won over Cardozo 79–52. The next year, Thompson and Leftwich led the Lions over the Ollie Johnson/Dave Bing led Spingarn, 69–54. During his senior year, Thompson led Carroll to a 24–0 record, preserving their 48-game winning streak along the way. Carroll capped off the undefeated 1960 season with a 57–55 win over St Catherine's Angels of Racine, WI in the Knights of Columbus National Championship Tournament with Thompson pacing the Lions with 15 points. Thompson finished the season as the top scorer in the Washington Catholic Athletic Conference, averaging 21 points per game. A former college basketball coach for the Georgetown Hoyas. He is now a professional radio and TV sports commentator. In 1984, he became the first African-American head coach to win a major collegiate championship, capturing the NCAA Men's Division I Basketball Championship when Georgetown, led by Patrick Ewing, defeated the University of Houston 84–75.

Glossary 105: John Tresvant: John Tresvant: a retired American basketball player. A native of Washington, D.C., he played high school football and baseball, but not basketball as he was cut from the team. After graduating, he Joined the U.S. Air Force. He was stationed at

Paine Field in Everett, Washington and repaired aircraft radar units. He grew several inches and was playing AAU basketball when Seattle University spotted him and gave him a scholarship after his military stint was up.

A 6'7" forward/center, Tresvant played three seasons at Seattle. He averaged 17.9 points and 14 rebounds per game as a senior, and 12.6 and 11.1, respectively, in his three-year career at Seattle. In 1963, he snared 40 rebounds in a game against the University of Montana at the Seattle Center Arena, the fourth-highest total in NCAA history.

He was selected in the fifth round (40th overall) of the 1964 NBA Draft by the St. Louis Hawks. He played nine seasons in the league with St. Louis, the Detroit Pistons, the Cincinnati Royals, the Seattle SuperSonics, the Los Angeles Lakers, and the Baltimore Bullets, posting NBA career averages of 9.2 points and 6.3 rebounds.

Glossary 106: Jr. Bridgeman: Jr. Bridgeman: Ulysses Lee "Junior" Bridgeman is a retired American basketball player. A 6'5" guard/forward from the University of Louisville, Bridgeman was drafted by the Los Angeles Lakers in 1975 and immediately traded with Brian Winters, David Meyers and Elmore Smith to the Milwaukee Bucks for Kareem Abdul-Jabbar. Bridgeman went on to have a solid 12-year NBA career, spent mostly with the Bucks, and he scored 11,517 total points. Although he was a sixth man for most of his career, he averaged double figures in scoring for nine consecutive seasons. He played in 711 games for the Bucks, still the most in franchise history, although he started only 105 times. His #2 jersey was retired by the Bucks franchise in 1988.

Glossary 107: Julius Erving: Julius Erving commonly known by the nickname Dr. J, Erving helped legitimize the American Basketball Association (ABA) and was the best-known player in that league when it merged with the National Basketball Association (NBA) after the 1975–76 season.

Erving won three championships, four Most Valuable Player Awards, and three scoring titles with the ABA's Virginia Squires and New York Nets (now the NBA's Brooklyn Nets) and the NBA's

Philadelphia 76ers. He is the sixth-highest scorer in ABA/NBA history with 30,026 points (NBA and ABA combined). He was well known for slam dunking from the free throw line in slam dunk contests and was the only player voted Most Valuable Player in both the American Basketball Association and the National Basketball Association.

Erving was inducted in 1993 into the Basketball Hall of Fame and was also named to the NBA's 50th Anniversary All-Time team. In 1994, Erving was named by *Sports Illustrated* as one of the 40 most important athletes of all time. In 2004, he was inducted into the Nassau County Sports Hall of Fame.

Many consider him one of the most talented players in the history of the NBA; he is widely acknowledged as one of the game's best dunkers. Dr. J" brought the practice into the mainstream. His signature dunk was the "slam" dunk, since incorporated into the vernacular and basic skill set of the game in the same manner as the "crossover" dribble and the "no look" pass.

Glossary 108: K.C. Jones: K. C. Jones is a retired American professional basketball player and coach (K. C. Jones is his full name). He is best known for his association with the Boston Celtics of the National Basketball Association (NBA), with which he won 11 of his 12 NBA Championships (eight as a player, one as an assistant coach, and two as a head coach.)

In NBA history, only teammates Bill Russell (11 championships) and Sam Jones (10 championships) have won more championship rings during their playing careers. After Boston lost to the Philadelphia 76ers in the 1967 playoffs, Jones ended his playing career.

Glossary 109: Kareem Abdul-Jabbar: Kareem Abdul-Jabbar born Ferdinand Lewis Alcindor, Jr. is an American retired professional basketball player who played 20 seasons in the National Basketball Association (NBA) for the Milwaukee Bucks and Los Angeles Lakers. During his career as a center, Abdul-Jabbar was a record six-time NBA Most Valuable Player (MVP), a record 19-time NBA All-Star, a 15-time All-NBA selection, and an 11-time NBA All-Defensive

Team member. A member of six NBA championship teams as a player and two as an assistant coach, Abdul-Jabbar twice was voted NBA Finals MVP. In 1996, he was honored as one of the 50 Greatest Players in NBA History. NBA coach Pat Riley and players Isiah Thomas and Julius Erving have called him the greatest basketball player of all time.

At the time of his retirement in 1989, Abdul-Jabbar was the NBA's all-time leader in points scored (38,387), games played (1,560), minutes played (57,446), field goals made (15,837), field goal attempts (28,307), blocked shots (3,189), defensive rebounds (9,394), and personal fouls (4,657). He remains the all-time leading scorer in the NBA, and is ranked 3rd all-time in both rebounds and blocks. In 2007 ESPN voted him the greatest center of all time, in 2008 they named him the "greatest player in college basketball history," and in 2016 they named him the second-best player in NBA history.

He played 20 seasons in the National Basketball Association (NBA) for the Milwaukee Bucks and Los Angeles Lakers. During his career as a center, Abdul-Jabbar was a record six-time NBA Most Valuable Player (MVP), a record 19-time NBA All-Star, a 15-time All-NBA selection, and an 11-time NBA All-Defensive Team member. A member of six NBA championship teams as a player and two as an assistant coach, Abdul-Jabbar twice was voted NBA Finals MVP. In 1996, he was honored as one of the 50 Greatest Players in NBA History.

Glossary 110: Karl Malone: Karl Anthony Malone is an American retired professional basketball player. Nicknamed "The Mail Man", Malone played the power forward position and spent his first 18 seasons (1985–2003) in the National Basketball Association (NBA) with the Utah Jazz and formed a formidable duo with his teammate John Stockton. Malone also played for the Los Angeles Lakers. Malone was a two-time NBA Most Valuable Player, a 14-time NBA All-Star, and an 11-time member of the All-NBA first team. He scored the second most career points in NBA history (36,928) (second behind Kareem Abdul-Jabbar), and holds the records for most free throws attempted and made, in addition to co-holding the record for the most first team All-NBA elections in history (tied with Kobe Bryant). He is considered among the greatest power forwards in NBA history.

Glossary 111: Kelvin Ransey: Kelvin Ransey–Point Guard, Draft: Chicago Bulls, 1st round (4th pick, 4th overall), 1980 NBA Draft, Seasons as a Blazer: 2 (1980-1982) Career statistics in Portland: 15.6 points, 7.0 assists. The worst thing that happened for Kelvin Ransey was being traded by the Trail Blazers to Dallas after the 1982 season. Then again, it could also be considered the best thing.

Favorite Blazer memory In December of 1980, we won 13 games, but there were two in particular that I remember: One at the Lakers, when they had Magic and Kareem, and another at home against Philadelphia, on a lob pass with one second left. Those memories were great.

The bad part about the trade for Ransey was that he liked it in Portland. As a slashing, high scoring point guard, he had found a cohesion with backcourt mate Jim Paxson, as well as big men Mychal Thompson and Calvin Natt. "I really thought we had a good team, with good chemistry," Ransey said. "If they would have built around us, I felt they could have had a championship-caliber team in a couple of years. But for some reason, they felt the need to trade me. I never did understand it, to this day."

Glossary 112: Kenneth Howard Norton, Sr. best known as Ken Norton, was an American professional boxer. He was the WBC world heavyweight champion from 1977 to 1978 and is best known for his trilogy with Muhammad Ali, in which he defeated Ali in their first bout by split decision over twelve rounds in March 1973. Their rematch also ended in a split decision, this time in favor of Ali. The third fight was won by Ali, but many observers thought Norton had won. He also is known for his classic title fight with Larry Holmes in June 1978. In 1992, Norton was inducted into the International Boxing Hall of Fame.

Glossary 113: Kenny Carr: Kenny Carr: a 6'7" forward from North Carolina State University, Carr won a gold medal with the United States national basketball team at the 1976 Summer Olympics. He was selected by the <u>Los Angeles Lakers</u> with the sixth overall pick of the <u>1977 NBA Draft</u>, and he played 10 seasons (1977–1987) in the NBA with the Lakers, <u>Cleveland Cavaliers</u>, <u>Detroit Pistons</u>, and <u>Portland Trail Blazers</u>. Carr scored 7,813 points in his NBA career and grabbed 4,999 <u>rebounds</u>.

Glossary 114: Kenny Boyd: **Ken Boyd** is an American retired <u>basketball</u> player born in <u>Frederick, Maryland</u>. A 6'5" forward from <u>Boston University</u>, Boyd was selected by the <u>New Orleans Jazz</u> in the 9th round of the <u>1974 NBA Draft</u>. He played six games for the Jazz during the <u>1974-75 NBA season</u>, averaging 3.2 points, 0.8 rebounds, and 0.3 assists per game.

Glossary 115: Kent Benson: Kent Benson: Michael Kent Benson is a retired American collegiate and professional <u>basketball</u> player. Having had a prolific career during the 1970s and 1980s, he scored a career high of 38 points, playing college basketball and later spending 11 seasons in the NBA for four different teams. After graduating from <u>Indiana University</u> in 1977, he was the number one draft pick of the <u>1977 NBA Draft</u> by the <u>Milwaukee Bucks</u>. Two minutes into his very first game as a professional, however, <u>Los Angeles Lakers</u> center <u>Kareem Abdul-Jabbar</u> punched Benson in retaliation for an overly aggressive elbow, causing his jaw to be broken. Abdul-Jabbar broke his hand in the incident and was out for two months; otherwise, he could have potentially been suspended by the NBA.

Benson never quite lived up to the potential of a number one NBA draft pick. Twice in his career, he was traded for a player that helped his former team get "over the hump" and contend for an NBA title. In 1980, the Bucks traded him to the <u>Detroit Pistons</u> for <u>Bob Lanier</u>, who would help the Bucks to consecutive conference finals appearances in 1983 and 1984. In 1986, the Pistons traded him along with <u>Kelly Tripucka</u> to the <u>Utah Jazz</u> for <u>Adrian Dantley</u>, who would help lead the Pistons to the Eastern Conference finals in 1987 and the NBA Finals in 1988.

Benson spent 11 seasons in the <u>NBA</u> with Milwaukee, Detroit, Utah and Cleveland. He averaged 9.1 points per game in 680 regular season games. He wore jersey #54 for his entire career.

Glossary 116: Kevin Duckworth: Kevin Jerome Duckworth was an American professional basketball player at center in the National Basketball Association, drafted in 1986 in the second round by the San Antonio Spurs. Before completing his rookie season with the Spurs, he was traded to the Portland Trail Blazers where he spent most of six seasons and was named the NBA's Most Improved Player and a two-time All-Star. After playing with three more teams he retired in 1997 and returned to Oregon where he would later work for the Trail Blazers' organization.

Duckworth was the ninth pick in the 2nd round of the 1986 NBA draft, chosen by the San Antonio Spurs. Later that season, he was traded to the Portland Trail Blazers for rookie Walter Berry.

In 1991 Duckworth was selected as an NBA All-Star for a second time. At the end of 1992–93, Duckworth was traded to the Washington Bullets for forward Harvey Grant. Duckworth played two seasons with the Bullets. During the 1994-95 season, traded to the Milwaukee Bucks for the 1995-96 season, missing most of the season due to injuries. He then played for the Los Angeles Clippers in 1996–97, after which he retired from professional basketball.

Glossary 117: Kevin Kunnert: Kevin Robert Kunnert is a retired American basketball player in the NBA. A 7'0" and 230 lb. center-forward, was drafted out of the University of Iowa by the Chicago Bulls in the first round (12th overall) of the 1973 NBA Draft. He also helped the Houston Rockets to a Central Division title during the 1976-77 season. Career History: 1973 – 1974 Buffalo Braves, 1974 -1978 Houston Rockets, 1978-1979 San Diego Clippers, 1979-1982 Portland Trailblazers. Career History: Points: 4,602 (8.3) ppg; Rebounds: 4.031 (7.3 rpg); Assists: 784 (1.4) apg.

Glossary 118: Kiki Vandeweghe: Ernest Maurice "Kiki" Vandeweghe III is a German-born professional basketball player. Vandeweghe was drafted 11th overall in the 1980 NBA Draft by the Dallas Mavericks, but refused to play for Dallas and demanded a trade (for virtually the remainder of his career, he was subjected to boos whenever he played in Dallas). He got his wish, and was traded to the Nuggets on December 3 of that same year. As a member of the Nuggets,

Vandeweghe was twice selected to the NBA Western Conference All-Star team, in 1983 and 1984. He was second in scoring in 1983, averaging 26.7 points, and 3rd in 1984 with a career-high 29.4 points.

During the 1983-84 Nuggets season, Vandeweghe scored 50 or more points in two NBA record-setting games. The former game, on December 13, 1983, in which he had a career-high 51 points, is also the highest combined scoring game in NBA history, a 186-184 triple-overtime loss to the Detroit Pistons.[2] Vandeweghe subsequently had 50 points in another high-scoring game, this one a 163-155 win over the San Antonio Spurs on January 11, 1984 (at the time, the highest combined scoring NBA *regulation* game of all time).

In the summer of 1984, Vandeweghe was traded to the Portland Trail Blazers in exchange for Calvin Natt, Wayne Cooper, Fat Lever, and two draft picks. Vandeweghe had several productive seasons in Portland, where he averaged nearly 25 points a game. He paired with Clyde Drexler to form a dynamic scoring duo. However, during the 1987–88 season, Vandeweghe suffered a back injury and lost his starting Job to Jerome Kersey. He was traded the next year to the New York Knicks (where his father played his entire career), with whom he played for several years apart from half a season with the Los Angeles Clippers before retiring from the league after the 1992–93 season.

As a player, Vandeweghe was regarded as an excellent scorer and outside shooter, averaging 20 points for seven consecutive seasons. His offensive repertoire was essentially limited to a single move, the stepback, but he was so proficient at this lone move that it was often referred to as the "Kiki Move" toward the end of his career. Vandeweghe's teams qualified for the NBA playoffs in 12 of his 13 seasons in the league, although none of his teams ever won the NBA championship.

Glossary 119: Kip Keino: Kipchoge Hezekiah "Kip" Keino is a retired Kenyan track and field athlete and two-time Olympic gold medalist. Kip Keino was among the first in a long line of successful middle and long distance runners to come from Nandi, Kenya, and has helped and inspired many of his fellow countrymen and women to become the athletics force that they are today. In 2012, he was of one of 24 athletes inducted as inaugural members of the International Association of Athletics Federations Hall of Fame.

Glossary 120: Larry Bird: Larry Bird played for the Boston Celtics of the National Basketball Association (NBA). in 1978, Bird started at small forward and power forward for thirteen seasons, spearheading one of the NBA's most formidable frontcourts that included center Robert Parish and forward Kevin McHale. Bird was a 12-time NBA All-Star and was named the league's Most Valuable Player (MVP) three consecutive times (1984–1986). He played his entire professional career for Boston, winning three NBA championships and two NBA Finals MVP awards.

He was a member of the 1992 United States men's Olympic basketball team ("The Dream Team") that won the gold medal at the 1992 Summer Olympics. Bird was voted to the NBA's 50th Anniversary All-Time Team in 1996 and inducted into the Naismith Memorial Basketball Hall of Fame] in 1998 (and was inducted again 2010 as a member of the "Dream Team").

Glossary 121: Larry Smith: Larry Smith is a former American professional basketball player. A 6'8" forward/center from Alcorn State University, Smith spent 13 seasons (1980–1993) in the National Basketball Association (NBA), playing for the Golden State Warriors, Houston Rockets, and San Antonio Spurs. Smith received NBA All-Rookie Team Honors in 1981, and would become one of the best rebounders of the 1980s. He had career averages of 9.2 rebounds and 25.9 minutes per game.

Glossary 122: Larry Steele: Larry Nelson Steele is a former professional basketball player, best known for being on the Portland Trail Blazers team that won the 1977 NBA Finals.

Born in Greencastle, Indiana, Steele grew up in Bainbridge, Indiana, and played collegiately at the University of Kentucky under coach Adolph Rupp. As a junior at Bainbridge High School, he had a high game of 46 points and 38 points as a high game during senior year. He scored a total of 1,646 high school points. His senior year he was selected All-County, All-Sectional, All-Regional, All-

He was drafted by the Trail Blazers in 1971, with the 2nd pick in the 3rd round (37th overall) and by the Kentucky Colonels in the 1971 American Basketball Association draft. In 1974 he was drafted again by the Kentucky Colonels in the 5th round of the ABA draft of NBA players. He Joined the Trail Blazers at the start of the Blazers' second season and became a roster mainstay for nine years before injuries forced him into retirement at the end of the 1979-80 season. His 610 games in a Portland uniform ranks sixth on the club's all-time list.

Steele played his entire NBA career for the team (retiring from basketball at the end of the 1979-80 season). Steele led the NBA in steals in the 1973-74 NBA season— the first year steals were recorded by the league with 2.68 swipes per game. He played 20.7 MPG on the 1977 championship team (starting in only nine games) averaging 10.3 points per game. During his nine-year NBA career, all with the Trail Blazers, he averaged 8.2 points, 2.9 assists, 1.39 steals and 24.2 minutes while starting 337 games.

His Trailblazers jersey number (15) was retired by the team on October 11, 1981 and he was selected as a member of the Indiana Basketball Hall of Fame's 1992 Silver Anniversary Team. In 2003, he was inducted into the Indiana Basketball Hall of Fame.

Glossary 123: Lee Haney: Lee Haney is the joint record holder along with Ronnie Coleman for winning the most Mr. Olympia titles, with eight wins. His bodybuilding titles include: 1979 Teen Mr. America Tall, 1st, 1982 Junior Nationals Heavyweight & Overall, 1st, 1982 Nationals Heavyweight & Overall, 1st, 1982 World Amateur Championships Heavyweight, 1st, 1983 Grand Prix England, 2nd, 1983 Grand Prix Las Vegas, 1st, 1983 Grand Prix Sweden, 2nd, 1983 Grand Prix Switzerland, 3rd, 1983 Night of Champions, 1st, 1983 Mr. Olympia, 3rd, 1983 World Pro Championships, 3rd, 1984 Mr. Olympia, 1st, 1985 Mr. Olympia, 1st, 1986 Mr. Olympia, 1st, 1987 Mr. Olympia, 1st, 1987 Grand Prix Germany (II), 1st, 1989 Mr. Olympia, 1st, 1990 Mr. Olympia, 1st and 1991 Mr. Olympia, 1st.

Glossary 124: Lenny Wilkens: Leonard Randolph "Lenny" Wilkens is an American retired basketball player and coach in the National

Basketball Association (NBA). He has been inducted three times into the Naismith Memorial Basketball Hall of Fame, first in 1989 as a player, as a coach in 1998, and in 2010 as part of the 1992 United States Olympic "Dream Team", for which he was an assistant coach. He is also a 2006 inductee into the College Basketball Hall of Fame.

Wilkens was a combined 13-time NBA All-Star as a player (nine times) and as a head coach (four times), was the 1993 NBA Coach of the Year, won the 1979 NBA Championship as the head coach of the Seattle SuperSonics, and an Olympic gold medal as the head coach of the 1996 U.S. men's basketball team.

Glossary 125: Lionel Hollins: Lionel Eugene Hollins is a former professional basketball player. During his ten-year NBA career playing as a point guard he played for five teams, averaging 11.6 points and 4.5 assists per game.

Drafted by the Portland Trail Blazers with the sixth pick of the 1975 NBA Draft out of Arizona State University, Hollins was bestowed All-Rookie first team honors that season, averaging 10.8 points in 78 games for the Blazers. Prior to his two seasons at Arizona State, he played two years[1] at Dixie College in St. George, Utah.

He was a member of Portland's 1976–77 National Basketball Association championship team, and made his only All-Star Game appearance one year later. He was a member of the NBA All-Defensive team twice, in 1978 and 1979. On April 18, 2007, the Portland Trail Blazers retired his #14 jersey.

Glossary 126: Lonnie Shelton: Lonnie Jewel Shelton is a retired American National Basketball Association player who played in 1976–1985. He played college basketball for Oregon State University. Shelton was drafted by the Memphis Sounds (soon to become the Baltimore Claws) of the American Basketball Association in 1975 but elected to stay in college. He was then selected by the New York Knicks in the second round of the 1976 NBA Draft. Shelton stayed with the Knicks for 2 seasons, later playing 5 seasons with the Seattle SuperSonics and finishing his career playing for the Cleveland Cavaliers for 3 seasons. Shelton led the NBA in personal fouls in his first two seasons with New York. In 1979, his first season with the SuperSonics, Shelton was the team's starting power forward and helped the SuperSonics win the NBA Finals. Shelton was one of three SuperSonics represented in the 1982 NBA All-Star Game (along with Jack Sikma and Gus Williams) and was named to the NBA's 1982 2nd All-Defense Team.

Glossary 127: Lou Ferrigno: Lou Ferrigno, in 1969, won his first major titles, IFBB Mr. America and IFBB Mr. Universe, four years later. Early in his career he lived in Columbus and trained with Arnold Schwarzenegger. In 1974, he came in second on his first attempt at the Mr. Olympia competition. He then came third the following year, and his attempt to beat Arnold Schwarzenegger was the subject of the 1975 documentary *Pumping Iron*. The documentary made Ferrigno famous.

Glossary 128: Lucius Allen: Lucius Oliver Allen, Jr. is an American former professional basketball player. Allen played 10 years in the NBA for four different teams. His highest scoring average was 19.1 points per game, during the 1974–75 season. Part of the way through that season he was traded to the Los Angeles Lakers after playing with the Milwaukee Bucks since the 1970–71 season. He was inducted into the Pac-12 Conference men's basketball Hall of Honor on March 16, 2013.

Glossary 129: Magic Johnson: Earvin "Magic" Johnson Jr. is an American retired professional basketball player who played point guard for the Los Angeles Lakers of the National Basketball Association (NBA) for 13 seasons. Johnson was selected first overall in the 1979 NBA draft by the Lakers. He won a championship and an NBA Finals Most Valuable Player Award in his rookie season, and won four more championships with the Lakers during the 1980s. Johnson retired abruptly in 1991 after announcing that he had contracted HIV, but returned to play in the 1992 All-Star Game, winning the All-Star MVP Award. After protests from his fellow players, he retired again for four years, but returned in 1996, at age 36, to play 32 games for the Lakers before retiring for the third and final time.

Johnson's career achievements include three <u>NBA MVP</u> <u>Awards</u>, nine <u>NBA Finals</u> appearances, twelve <u>All-Star</u> games, and ten <u>All-NBA</u> First and Second Team nominations. He led the league in regular-season <u>assists</u> four times, and is the NBA's all-time leader in average assists per game, at 11.2.[2] Johnson was a member of the <u>1992 United States men's Olympic basketball team</u> ("The Dream Team"), which won the <u>Olympic</u> gold medal in 1992. After leaving the NBA in 1992, Johnson formed the Magic Johnson All-Stars, a <u>barnstorming</u> team that travelled around the world playing <u>exhibition games</u>. Johnson was honored as one of the <u>50 Greatest Players in NBA History</u> in 1996.

Johnson is one of only seven players in history to win an NCAA Championship, an NBA Championship, and an Olympic Gold Medal.[4] He became a two-time inductee into the <u>Basketball Hall of Fame</u>—being enshrined in 2002 for his individual career, and again in 2010 as a member of the "Dream Team".

Glossary 130: Marc Mills: Marc Mills: co-founded PRC – Pacific Rim Capital, Mr. Mills is the Vice President, Headquarters Marketing, for Capital Associates Portfolio Company. He has held marketing and management positions with Capital Associates International and Beverly Hills Savings. Graduated from Harvard University and later secured a degree in Finance from the London School of Economics.

Glossary 131: Marc Splaver: Mr. Splaver was a 1970 journalism graduate of American University and had worked as an assistant in the sports information office. He also worked as a part-time news aide at The Washington Post. He became Sports Information Director at AU after graduation, remaining there until he Joined the Bullets in 1974. Marc Splaver was the director of public relations of the Bullets since the team was moved from Baltimore in 1973. Splaver won the first NBA Public Relations Director award, presented by the Professional Basketball Writers' Association.

Glossary 132: Marques Johnson: Marques Johnson: small forward played in the National Basketball Association from 1977–1989, where was a five-time All-Star. He spent a majority of his career with the Milwaukee Bucks. A forward/guard and six-time NBA All-Star, he was inducted into the Basketball Hall of Fame in 2008. A small forward he played in the National Basketball Association (NBA) from 1977–1989, where was a five-time All-Star. He spent a majority of his career with the Milwaukee Bucks. Johnson was the third overall pick in the 1977 NBA Draft by the Milwaukee Bucks. He played seven seasons with Milwaukee before finishing his NBA career with the Los Angeles Clippers and the Golden State Warriors. Johnson helped lead Milwaukee to several division titles (1980, 1981, 1982, 1983, and 1984). In his second season in 1978–79, he was the NBA's third leading scorer (25.6 PPG), behind George Gervin (29.6) and Lloyd Free (28.8). Johnson claims to have coined the term *point forward*, a position he played out of necessity in 1984.

Glossary 133: Marvin Barnes: Marvin Jerome Barnes was an American professional basketball player. As a 6'8" forward, he was drafted by the Philadelphia 76ers with the second overall pick in the first round of the 1974 NBA Draft and by the Spirits of St. Louis in the 1974 ABA Draft. Barnes opted for the ABA and played for the Spirits in the American Basketball Association from 1974 to 1976 before playing in the National Basketball Association from 1976 to 1980. He had his greatest success in the ABA, where he starred for the Spirits and was named Rookie of the Year for the 1974–75 season. He also shares the ABA record for most two-point field goals in a game, with 27. In 2005, the ABA 2000, the second incarnation of the ABA, named one of their divisions after him.

In March 2008, Providence College retired his jersey, honoring him along with Ernie DiGregorio and Jimmy Walker. He still co-holds (since tied by MarShon Brooks) the school single-game scoring record of 52 points.

Glossary 134: Maurice Lucas: Maurice Lucas was an American professional basketball player. The first two years of his post collegiate career were spent in the American Basketball Association (ABA) with the Spirits of St. Louis and Kentucky Colonels. He then played twelve seasons in the National Basketball Association (NBA) with the Portland Trail Blazers, New Jersey Nets, New York Knickerbockers,

Phoenix Suns, Los Angeles Lakers and Seattle SuperSonics. The starting power forward on the Trail Blazers' 1976–77 NBA Championship team, he was nicknamed *The Enforcer* because of his primary role on the court which was best exemplified in Game 2 of the NBA Finals that season.

In his fourteen-year professional basketball career–two in the ABA and 12 in the NBA–Lucas scored 14,857 points and gathered 9,306 rebounds. He was a five-time All-Star–one in the ABA and four in the NBA. He was named to the 1978 All-NBA-Defense First team, the 1978 All-NBA Second team and the 1979 All-NBA-Defense Second team.

Glossary 135: Mel DeLaura: Mel DeLaura an assistant strength conditioning coach at Southern Methodist University (SMU). Received free agent contract with NFL Atlanta Falcons and Washington Redskins as a wide receiver. In Atlanta during training camp suffered a torn quad muscle injury that prevented him from pursuing an NFL career. Employs plyometrics: aerobic exercise to improve jumping and quickness. He attended Hawaii Pacific University and received his bachelor's degree in sports and recreational administration.

Glossary 136: Ron Artest: Metta World Peace born Ronald William Artest, Jr., is an American professional basketball player for the Los Angeles Lakers of the National Basketball Association (NBA). He was known as Ron Artest before legally changing his name in September 2011.

World Peace gained a reputation as one of the league's premier defenders as he won the NBA Defensive Player of the Year Award in 2004, when he was also named an NBA All-Star and earned All-NBA honors. He won an NBA championship in 2010 as a member of the Los Angeles Lakers.

NBA Teams: Chicago Bulls (1999–2002)_Indiana Pacers (2002–2006Sacramento Kings (2006–2008)_Los Angeles Lakers (2009–2013)_New York Knicks (2013–2014)_China and Italy (2014–2015) Return to the Lakers (2015–present) On September 24, 2015, World Peace signed with the Los Angeles Lakers, returning to the franchise for a second stint.

Glossary 137: Michael Jordan: Michael Jeffrey Jordan. Jordan Joined the NBA's Chicago Bulls in 1984 as the third overall draft pick. He quickly emerged as a league star, entertaining crowds with his prolific scoring. His leaping ability, illustrated by performing slam dunks from the free throw line in slam dunk contests, earned him the nicknames "Air Jordan" and "His Airness". He also gained a reputation for being one of the best defensive players in basketball.In 1991, he won his first NBA championship with the Bulls, and followed that achievement with titles in 1992 and 1993, securing a "three-peat". Although Jordan abruptly retired from basketball before the beginning of the 1993–94 NBA season to pursue a career in baseball, he returned to the Bulls in March 1995 and led them to three additional championships in 1996, 1997, and 1998, as well as a then-record 72 regular-season wins in the 1995–96 NBA season. Jordan retired for a second time in January 1999, but returned for two more NBA seasons from 2001 to 2003 as a member of the Wizards.

Jordan's individual accolades and accomplishments include five Most Valuable Player (MVP) Awards, ten All-NBA First Team designations, nine All-Defensive First Team honors, fourteen NBA All-Star Game appearances, three All-Star Game MVP Awards, ten scoring titles, three steals titles, six NBA Finals MVP Awards, and the 1988 NBA Defensive Player of the Year Award. Among his numerous accomplishments, Jordan holds the NBA records for highest career regular season scoring average (30.12 points per game) and highest career playoff scoring average (33.45 points per game). In 1999, he was named the greatest North American athlete of the 20th century by ESPN, and was second to Babe Ruth on the Associated Press's list of athletes of the century. Jordan is a two-time inductee into the Basketball Hall of Fame, having been enshrined in 2009 for his individual career, and again in 2010 as part of the group induction of the 1992 United States men's Olympic basketball team ("The Dream Team").

Glossary 138: Micheal Ray Richardson: Micheal Ray Richardson The New York Knicks drafted him with the fourth overall pick in the 1978 NBA Draft, and he was billed as "the next Walt Frazier." Two picks later, the Boston Celtics drafted Larry Bird. In his second year,

Richardson became the third player in NBA history (1. <u>Slick Watts</u>–1976, 2. <u>Don Buse</u>–1977 to lead the league in both assists (10.1) and steals (3.2), setting Knicks franchise records in both categories.

What is most appreciated about having this opportunity to play with such NBA All-Stars was being selected to replace an injured Scott Wedman by the NBA coaches. I was at home thinking about having a few days off and watching the All-Star Game as usual on TV. The phone rang and the secretary in the front office told me I was selected to replace Wedman in the upcoming All-Star Game. I had to ask if this was a joke, as the reality of such a possibility seemed unimaginable. Not only was the opportunity of a lifetime, with playing in front of my Washington, DC family and friends an added bonus. Although I was in a state of shock I packed my bags and was ready to board the plane leaving Portland.

The pre-game activities were filled with players making a few classic remarks about one another, showing how each appreciated being there and the level of competitive spirit was still alive and well. The gifts and memorabilia given still holds sentimental value.

Being held at the Capital Center in Landover, Maryland with an attendance of 19,035 on February 3, 1980. I played fourteen minutes, had 1- FGM – field goal made, 6 FGA – field goal attempts, 1 PFS- personal foul shot, and 2 PTS – points. It was exciting and nerve wracking at the same time to be playing with such greats. Although it was cold outside I was warmed by the exhilaration of simply being a part of the game. Not expecting to be a starter and content to be included in the game, the final score of East – 144 and West – 136. We went into overtime and Larry Bird, with 1:40 left in the game, made the first 3-pointer in All-Star Game history. The crowd went crazy.

Glossary 139: Moses Malone: Moses Malone played in both the American Basketball Association and the National Basketball Association from 1974 through 1995. A <u>center</u> was named the <u>NBA Most Valuable Player</u> (MVP.)

Malone led the NBA in rebounding six times, including a record five-straight seasons (1981–1985). He finished his career as the all-time leader in offensive rebounds after leading both the

ABA and NBA in the category a combined nine times. Malone was nicknamed "Chairman of the Boards" for his rebounding prowess. [1] Combining his ABA and NBA statistics, he ranks seventh all-time in career points (29,580) and third in total rebounds (17,834). He was named to both the ABA All-Time Team and the NBA's 50th Anniversary All-Time Team. Malone won his only NBA championship in 1983, when he was both the league and Finals MVP with the Philadelphia 76ers. He was inducted into the Naismith Memorial Basketball Hall of Fame in his first year of eligibility in 2001.

He was selected in the third round of the 1974 ABA Draft by the Utah Stars. He was named an ABA All-Star as a rookie and played two seasons in the league until it merged with the NBA in 1976. He landed in the NBA with the Buffalo Braves, who traded him after two games to the Houston Rockets. Malone became a five-time All-Star in six seasons with the Rockets. After leading the NBA in rebounding in 1979, he was named league MVP for the first time. He led the Rockets to the NBA Finals in 1981, and won his second MVP award in 1982. Malone was traded to Philadelphia the following season, when he repeated as MVP and led the 76ers to a championship in his first year. In his first of two stints with Philadelphia, he was an All-Star in each of his four seasons. Following another trade, Malone was an All-Star in his only two seasons with the Washington Bullets (known later as the Wizards). He signed as a free agent with the Atlanta Hawks, earning his 12th straight and final All-Star selection in his first season. In his later years, he played with the Milwaukee Bucks before returning to the 76ers and completing his career with the San Antonio Spurs.

Glossary 140: Muhammad Ali, born Cassius Marcellus Clay, Jr., was an American Olympic and professional boxer and activist. He is widely regarded as one of the most significant and celebrated sports figures of the 20th century. From early in his career, Ali was known as an inspiring, controversial and polarizing figure both inside and outside the ring.

Glossary 141: Mychal Thompson: Mychal George Thompson is a retired Bahamian basketball player. He played the power forward and center positions for the University of Minnesota and the NBA's Portland Trail Blazers, San Antonio Spurs and Los Angeles Lakers. The Portland Trail Blazers made Thompson the number one pick in the 1978 NBA draft, the first foreign-born player to be selected first.

Thompson was a fixture in the Portland lineup for eight years (though one season was missed due to injury), where he started at both power forward and center positions. He was named to the 1979 All-Rookie team, and had his statistically best season in 1981–82, where he averaged over 20 points and 11 rebounds per game. In the 1986 off-season, Thompson was traded to the Spurs in exchange for center/forward Steve Johnson.

Thompson played only half a season with the Spurs, before he was traded again, this time to Los Angeles for center/forward Frank Brickowski, center Pétur Guðmundsson and a 1990 first-round draft choice. He was brought to the Lakers in February 1987 to back up Kareem Abdul-Jabbar and defend Boston Celtics forward Kevin McHale. This gave the Lakers a team that had four players who were overall #1 selections in the NBA draft, the others being Abdul-Jabbar, Magic Johnson, and James Worthy. Of those four, Thompson is the only one not enshrined in the Naismith Memorial Basketball Hall of Fame. Thompson helped the Showtime Lakers win consecutive titles in 1987 and 1988, and he retired in 1991.

Glossary 142: Nate Archibald: Nate "Tiny"Archibald spent 14 years playing in the NBA, most notably with the Cincinnati Royals, Kansas City–Omaha Kings and Boston Celtics. In 1991 he was enshrined in the Naismith Memorial Basketball Hall of Fame. Archibald was a willing passer and an adequate shooter from midrange. However, it was his quickness and speed and shiftiness that made him difficult to guard in the open court, as he would regularly drive past defenders on his way to the basket. He is the only player in NBA history to lead the league in scoring and assists in the same season.

His scoring average of 34.0 points per game broke the NBA record for a guard. His 910 assists that season (11.4 assists per game) was also an NBA record at the time, breaking Guy Rodgers' mark of 908. He was named the Sporting News NBA MVP that season.

Archibald was an All-NBA First Team selection three times (1973, 1975, 1976) and an All-NBA Second Team selection two times (1972, 1981). A six-time NBA All-Star Game selection (1973, 1975, 1976, 1980, 1981, and 1982), he was named the 1981 NBA All-Star Game MVP. Archibald led the NBA in free throws made three times and free throw attempts twice. He competed in 876 professional games, scored 16,841 points (18.8 points per game), and dished out 6,476 assists. He was named to the NBA's 50th Anniversary All-Time team. Nate Archibald was inducted to the Naismith Basketball Hall of Fame in 1991.

Glossary 143: Nick Weatherspoon: Nick Levoter Weatherspoon was an American professional basketball player. He was a 6' 7" small forward. Weatherspoon scored 1,431 points at Canton McKinley High School, holding the Bulldog scoring record for 37 years until Raymar Morgan broke it during the 2005–06 season. He was an All-American at the University of Illinois before being selected by the Capital Bullets with the 13th pick of the 1973 NBA Draft. Named to the 1974 NBA All-Rookie Team, Weatherspoon spent a total of seven seasons in the NBA with the Bullets, the Seattle SuperSonics, the Chicago Bulls, and the San Diego Clippers.

Glossary 144: Norm Nixon: Norman Ellard Nixon is an American retired professional basketball player for the NBA, who spent twelve seasons with the Los Angeles Lakers and the San Diego/Los Angeles Clippers.

Nixon was the 22nd overall pick in the 1977 NBA Draft by the Los Angeles Lakers. He played for the Lakers for six successful seasons and helped the Showtime Lakers win NBA championships in 1980 (4–2) and 1982 (4–2), both against the Philadelphia 76ers. The same two teams would meet in the 1983 NBA Finals, but Philadelphia won this series four games to none. In the 1978 (Seattle SuperSonics), 1979 (Seattle), and 1981 (Houston Rockets) playoffs, the Lakers were eliminated by the eventual Western Conference champion. He led the team in scoring in the 1982 playoffs.

During his NBA career, Nixon scored 12,065 points (15.7 points per game) and had 6,386 assists (8.3) in 768 games played.

Although he had impressive statistics, he may be remembered most for faking a <u>free throw</u> at the end of a Lakers-<u>San Antonio Spurs</u> game on November 30, 1982, which caused a double lane violation. The referees erroneously ordered a jump ball, instead of requiring Nixon to re-shoot the free throw. The Lakers got the ball and Nixon made a field goal to tie the game, where they prevailed in overtime. The last three seconds of the game were later replayed in April 1983.

Glossary 145: Ollie Johnson: Oliver "Ollie" Johnson is a retired American <u>basketball</u> player. He was an <u>All-American</u> forward at the <u>University of San Francisco</u> and a first round draft pick in the <u>National Basketball Association</u> (NBA) in 1965.

(Early Years in DC) Johnson, a 6'7 power forward, was a 3 time All Interhigh and 2 time All MET playing for William Roundtree at Spingarn HS. Johnson teamed with Dave Bing to win the DC Interhigh Titles in 60 and 61....and City Championship vs DeMatha in 1961, in front of a sold-out crowd (10,500) at the U of Maryland's Cole Field House. Johnson averaged 19.9 pts and 17.5 rebounds for his senior season.

Johnson played college basketball at the University of San Francisco from 1962 to 1965. At USF, Johnson was a first team All-<u>West Coast Conference</u> pick each of his three years there (freshmen were ineligible) and was named <u>WCC player of the year</u> as a junior and senior. Johnson led the Dons to WCC championships and <u>NCAA tournament</u> appearances in all three of his seasons. The Dons lost in the West regional final in consecutive years to eventual champion <u>UCLA</u>. In the <u>1965 NCAA tournament</u>, Johnson led all players in scoring in rebounding average as he tallied 36 points and 18.5 rebounds per game.

For his career, Ollie Johnson scored 1,668 points (19.9 per game) and grabbed 1,323 rebounds (15.8 per game), ranking him in the school's top ten all-time in both categories. In addition to his conference accolades, Johnson was named an All-American in 1964 and 1965.

Johnson was drafted in the first round of the <u>1965 NBA Draft</u> by the <u>Boston Celtics</u> (8th pick overall), but he never played in the NBA. After being cut by the Celtics, he played for the San Francisco

Athletic Club in the <u>Amateur Athletic Union</u>, where he was named an <u>AAU All-American</u> in 1965. He then played overseas in the <u>Basketball League Belgium</u> for three seasons.

Glossary 146: Oscar Robertson: Oscar Palmer Robertson, nicknamed "The Big O", is an American retired <u>National Basketball Association</u> player who played for the <u>Cincinnati Royals</u> and <u>Milwaukee Bucks</u>. The 6 ft. 5 in (1.96 m), 220 lb. (100 kg Robertson played at <u>point guard</u> and was a 12-time <u>All-Star</u>, 11-time member of the <u>All-NBA Team</u>, and one-time winner of the <u>MVP</u> award in 14 professional seasons. He is the only player in NBA history to average a <u>triple-double</u> for a season. He was a key player on the team which brought the Bucks their only NBA title in the <u>1970–71 NBA season</u>. His playing career, especially during high school and college, was plagued by <u>racism</u>.

From a historical perspective, however, Robertson's most important contribution was made not on the court, but rather *in* <u>court</u>. It was the year of the landmark *Robertson v. National Basketball Ass'n*, an <u>antitrust</u> suit filed by the NBA's Players Association against the league. As Robertson was the president of the Players Association, the case bore his name. In this suit, the proposed <u>merger</u> between the NBA and <u>American Basketball Association</u> was delayed until 1976, and the college draft as well as the free agency clauses were reformed. Robertson himself stated that the main reason was that clubs basically owned their players: players were forbidden to talk to other clubs once their contract was up, because free agency did not exist back then. Six years after the suit was filed, the NBA finally reached a settlement, the <u>ABA-NBA merger</u> took place, and the Oscar Robertson suit encouraged signing of more free agents and eventually led to higher salaries for all players.

Robertson was elected to the <u>Wisconsin Athletic Hall of Fame</u> in 1995.

Glossary 147: Otis Birdsong: Otis Birdsong spent twelve seasons in the NBA and appeared in four NBA All-Star Games. He spent twelve seasons (1977–1989) in the <u>NBA</u> and appeared in four <u>NBA All-Star Games</u>. Birdsong was the second player chosen in the 1977 NBA draft when he was taken by the Kansas City Kings. He scored over 12,000 career points, averaging 18 points per game, in 12 seasons with the Kings, the New Jersey Nets and the Boston Celtics. He was a member of the <u>All-NBA Second Team</u> in 1981.

Glossary 148: Pam Dukes: Pamela Camille "Pam" Dukes (-Boyer, -Brown) 1987 NCAA Champion in the indoor shot put with a toss of 57-1...1992 Olympian in the shot put in Barcelona, Spain... No. 6 on the All-time Stanford shot put list with a toss of 51-7 Â½ (15.74m) 2-time All-American at Stanford in the shot put (1985-86). Pam Dukes finished fifth in the shot put at the 1987 Pan American Games and fourth in discus throw at the 1991 Pan American Games.
Personal Best: SP – 18.11 (1987).

Glossary 149: Patrick James "Pat" Riley is an American professional basketball executive, and a former coach and player in the <u>National Basketball Association</u> (NBA). He has been the team president of the <u>Miami Heat</u> since 1995, a position that enabled him to serve as their *de facto* general manager and as their head coach in two separate tenures (1995 through 2003, and 2005 through 2008).
Widely regarded as one of the greatest NBA coaches of all time, Riley has served as the <u>head coach of five championship teams</u> and an assistant coach <u>to another</u>. He was named <u>NBA Coach of the Year</u> three times (<u>1989–90</u>, <u>1992–93</u> and <u>1996–97</u>, as head coach of the <u>Los Angeles Lakers</u>, <u>New York Knicks</u> and <u>Miami Heat</u>, respectively). He was <u>head coach of an NBA All-Star Game team</u> nine times: eight times with the <u>Western Conference</u> team (<u>1982</u>, <u>1983</u>, <u>1985–1990</u>, all as head coach of the <u>Lakers</u>) and once with the Eastern team (<u>1993</u>, as head coach of the <u>Knicks</u>). In 1996 he was named one of the 10 Greatest Coaches in the NBA history. As a player, he played for the <u>Los Angeles Lakers</u>' championship team in 1972. Riley most recently won the <u>2012</u> and <u>2013 NBA championships</u> with the <u>Miami Heat</u> as their team president. He is the first North American sports figure to win a championship as a player, coach (both assistant and head), and executive. He received the <u>Chuck Daly Lifetime Achievement Award</u> from the NBA Coaches Association on June 20, 2012. Riley

finished his NBA playing career with a 7.4 points per game scoring average and a field-goal percentage of 41.4%.

Glossary 150: Patrick McEnroe: Patrick John McEnroe is a former professional tennis player and the former captain of the United States Davis Cup team, is the younger brother of John McEnroe. He won one singles title and 16 doubles titles, including the 1989 French Open Men's Doubles. His career-high rankings were World No. 28 in singles and World No. 3 in doubles.

Glossary 151: Paul Westphal: Paul Westphal, as a player, he won an NBA championship with the Boston Celtics in the 1974 NBA Finals. In addition to being a five-time All-Star selection, from 1977 to 1981, Westphal earned three All-NBA First Team selections and one Second Team honor.

After three seasons in Boston, including a championship ring in 1974, he was traded to the Phoenix Suns. In 1976, Westphal helped the Suns reach their first-ever Finals appearance, where they played the Celtics. Game 5 of that series is often called "the greatest game ever played" in NBA history.

With time winding down in regulation and the Suns trailing 94–91, Westphal poked the ball away from JoJo White, took a long pass from Dennis Awtrey, and hit a breakaway layup. He was fouled on the play and hit the free throw to tie it at 94–94.

In the second overtime, with 15 seconds left and the Suns trailing 109–108 after just making a basket, Westphal stole the ball from John Havlicek after Havlicek received the inbounds pass. This began a chain of events that culminated with Curtis Perry hitting a jumper to give the Suns a 110–109 lead.

After the Perry basket and a Celtics timeout, Havlicek got the ball with five seconds left and hit a bank shot to put the Celtics up 111–110. The buzzer sounded and Celtic fans poured on the floor, thinking the Celtics had won. However, referee Richie Powers correctly ruled that Havlicek's shot went through the basket with two seconds left on the clock. After one second was placed back on, Westphal, sensing that the Suns could get a better shot off if the ball was inbounded at half court, called a timeout that the Suns didn't have while preparing to inbound the ball from under the Celtics' basket. A <u>technical foul</u> was assessed; the Celtics made the subsequent free throw and increased their lead to 112–110. The resulting timeout call allowed Phoenix to inbound the ball at midcourt, rather than go the full length of the court. (As a result of this play, the NBA changed the rules prior to the following season.) <u>Garfield Heard</u> then made a shot for the Suns that sent the game into triple-overtime.

With 20 seconds left in the third overtime and the Celtics seemingly in control at 128–122, Westphal scored two quick baskets to cut it to 128–126 and nearly made a steal at midcourt after the second, but failed and the Celtics ran out the clock to the victory.

Glossary 152: Pete Maravich: Peter Press "Pistol Pete" Maravich was an American professional <u>basketball</u> player. He played for three <u>NBA</u> teams. He is still the <u>all-time leading</u> <u>NCAA</u> <u>Division I</u> scorer with 3,667 points scored and an average of 44.2 points per game. All of his accomplishments were achieved before the <u>three-point</u> line and shot clock were introduced to NCAA basketball and despite being unable to play varsity as a freshman under then-NCAA rules. One of the youngest players ever inducted into the <u>Naismith Memorial Basketball Hall of Fame</u>, Maravich was cited by the Hall as "perhaps the greatest creative offensive talent in history". In an April 2010 interview, Hall of Fame player <u>John Havlicek</u> said that "the best ball-handler of all time was Pete Maravich.

Realizing that his knee problems would never go away, Maravich retired at the end of that season. It is noteworthy that the NBA instituted the 3-point shot just in time for Pistol Pete's last season in the league. He had always been famous for his long-range shooting, and his final year provided an official statistical gauge of his abilities. Between his limited playing time in Utah and Boston, he made 10 of 15 3-point shots, giving him a career 67% completion rate behind the arc.

During his ten-year career in the NBA, Maravich played in 658 games, averaging 24.2 points and 5.4 assists per contest. In 1987, he was inducted into the <u>Naismith Memorial Basketball Hall of Fame</u>, and his #7 jersey has been retired by both the Jazz and the <u>New Orleans Pelicans</u>.

Glossary 153: Pete Newell: Peter Francis Newell was an American college men's basketball coach and basketball instructional coach. He coached for 15 years at the University of San Francisco, Michigan State University and the University of California, Berkeley, compiling an overall record of 234 wins and 123 losses. He led the University of California to the 1959 NCAA men's basketball championship, and a year later coached the gold medal-winning U.S. team at the 1960 Summer Olympics, a team that would be inducted as a unit to the Naismith Memorial Basketball Hall of Fame in 2010. After his coaching career ended he ran a world-famous instructional basketball camp and served as a consultant and scout for several National Basketball Association (NBA) teams. He is often considered to be one of the most influential figures in the history of basketball.

Considered "America's Basketball Guru", Newell conducted an annual training camp for centers and forwards known simply as "Big Man Camp", which has since been informally dubbed "Pete Newell's Big Man Camp". The camp originated when word spread that Newell was working with Kermit Washington. After Washington's game rapidly improved, more and more big men started to work with Newell, and he later opened the camp. The camp's impressive participants list features over 200 current and former NBA players. Newell attracted this list of players due to his reputation of teaching footwork, being what one publication described as "The Footwork Master". Former attendees include Shaquille O'Neal, Hakeem Olajuwon, Bill Walton, and many others. The camp was almost seen as standard for players coming out of college into the NBA; according to ESPN's Ric Bucher, "[f]or the past 24 years, every big man of any significance has spent at least one summer week trying to get close enough to Pete." From the time Newell opened the camp in 1976 until his death, he never accepted any money for his services, stating that "I owe it to the game. I can never repay what the game has given me." The camp has taken place in Honolulu, Hawaii and most recently Las Vegas, Nevada.

Glossary 154: Phil Ford: Phil Jackson Ford Jr. is a retired American professional basketball player in the National Basketball Association. The second pick in the first round of the draft, Ford was NBA Rookie of the Year with the Kansas City Kings in 1979. In 482 NBA games, Ford scored 5,594 points, an 11.6 average, and had 3,083 assists, an average of 6.4 per game. He retired from the NBA in 1985.

Glossary 155: Phil Knight: Philip Hampson "Phil" Knight (born February 24, 1938) is an American business magnate and philanthropist. A native of Oregon, he is the co-founder and chairman of Nike, Inc., and previously served as CEO of the company. A graduate of the University of Oregon and Stanford Graduate School of Business (Stanford GSB), he has donated hundreds of millions of dollars to both schools. Jeff Johnson, a friend of Knight, suggested calling the firm "Nike," named after the Greek winged goddess of victory. Nike's "swoosh" logo, is now considered one of the most powerful logos in the world.

Glossary 156: Purvis Short: Purvis Short is a retired American professional basketball player who played with the Golden State Warriors, Houston Rockets and New Jersey Nets of the National Basketball Association (NBA) from 1978 to 1990. A 6'7" small forward, Short averaged 17.3 points per game over his twelve-season career in the NBA. He is currently the Warriors seventh all-time leading scorer.

Short was selected fifth overall in the 1978 NBA Draft. Short was affectionately nicknamed "Rainbowman" because of the distinctive rainbow-like high arc of his jump shots, something he stated he obtained in high school. He was a role player and sixth man his first few years in the league. Short was a starter by the 1984-85 season, and scored a career high 59 points in a game against the New Jersey Nets in 1984.

Short started working out with Pete Newell during the off-seasons, which Short later claimed help improve his shooting skills significantly. During a November 17, 1984 game against the New Jersey Nets, Short scored a career high 59 points during a 131-114 loss. He hit 20 of 28 field goal attempts and 15 free throws. At the time, only nine other players had scored more points in one game, and it was the most points scored in the NBA since David Thompson and George Gervin respectfully scored 73 and 63 points in a game on April 9, 1978. Excluding Wilt Chamberlain's many games of 60 or over points as a Warrior, it was also the third highest total in franchise history, behind Joe Fulks' 63 points in 1949 and Rick Barry's 64 points in 1974. He also scored 57 points against the San Antonio Spurs and 46 against the Washington Bullets that season. Short finished the 1984-85 season with an average of 28.0 points per game, and was the NBA's fourth leading scorer. During the off-season, Short got involved in a contract dispute and held out for four weeks, but the Warriors managed to come to a contract agreement with him.[11] He ended up with a 25.5 points per game average in 64 games in 1985-86, finishing fifth in the league in scoring. Short missed two months early in the 1986-87 season due to knee surgery.[12] He missed further time with a pulled thigh muscle in March. Golden State reached the playoffs, an achievement Short later recalled as "the best time" in his Warriors career. He ended up appearing in 34 games that year, with an 18.3 points per game average.

Glossary 157: Randy Smith: Randolph "Randy" Smith was an American professional basketball player who set the NBA record for consecutive games played. From 1972–1982, Smith played in every regular season game, en-route to a then-record of 906 straight games (since broken by A. C. Green.)

The highlight of Smith's career was the 1978 NBA All-Star Game, where he came off the bench to lead all scorers with 27 points, and was named the game's Most Valuable Player.

Iron Man Streak: On November 3, 1982, Smith played in his 845th consecutive NBA game, breaking Johnny Kerr's iron man record. The game was a 130–111 loss to the Philadelphia 76ers in which Smith started and scored 14 points. Smith's iron man streak ended at 906 games when he played his last game with the Clippers on March 13, 1983. The record was later surpassed by A. C. Green in 1997.

Atlanta Hawks: Smith was traded to the Atlanta Hawks, where he played fifteen games before retiring.

Glossary 158: Red Auerbach: Red Auerbach: Arnold Jacob "Red" Auerbach was an American basketball coach of the Washington Capitals, the Tri-Cities Blackhawks and the Boston Celtics. After he retired from coaching, he served as president and front office executive of the Celtics until his death. As a coach, he won 938 games (a record at his retirement) and nine <u>National Basketball Association</u> (NBA) <u>championships</u> in ten years (a number surpassed only by <u>Phil Jackson</u>, who won 11 in twenty years). As general manager and team president of the Celtics, he won an additional seven NBA titles, for a grand total of 16 in a span of 29 years, making him one of the most successful team officials in the history of North American professional sports.

Auerbach is remembered as a pioneer of modern basketball, redefining basketball as a game dominated by team play and defense and for introducing the <u>fast break</u> as a potent offensive weapon. He groomed many players who went on to be inducted into the <u>Basketball Hall of Fame</u>. Additionally, Auerbach was vital in breaking down color barriers in the NBA. He made history by drafting the first <u>African-American</u> NBA player, <u>Chuck Cooper</u> in 1950, and introduced the first <u>African-American</u> starting five in 1964. Famous for his polarizing nature, he was well known for smoking a cigar when he thought a victory was assured, a habit that became, for many, "the ultimate symbol of victory" during his <u>Boston</u> tenure.

In 1967, the <u>NBA Coach of the Year</u> award, which he had won in 1965, was named the "Red Auerbach Trophy," and Auerbach was inducted into the Basketball Hall of Fame in 1969. In 1980, he was named the greatest coach in the history of the NBA by the Professional Basketball Writers Association of America, and was <u>NBA Executive of the Year</u> in 1980. In addition, Auerbach was voted one of the <u>NBA 10 Greatest Coaches in history</u>, was inducted into the <u>National Jewish Sports Hall of Fame</u>, and is honored with a retired number 2 jersey in the <u>TD Garden</u>, the home of the Boston Celtics.

Glossary 159: by the <u>Chicago Bulls</u> with the 9th pick of the <u>1978 NBA Draft</u>. A 6'7" guard, Theus averaged 16.3 points per game during his first season and was the runner-up for the <u>1979 NBA Rookie of the Year Award</u>. He garnered the nickname "Rush Street Reggie" while playing in Chicago for owning an apartment on that street and having an active social life around that area, being frequently spotted at the city night spots. He followed his stellar rookie campaign with a strong sophomore season, in which he averaged 20.2 points and 6.3 assists for the Bulls. In 1981, Theus appeared in his first All-Star Game; he appeared again in 1983, during a season in which he averaged a career high 23.8 points per game.

Glossary 160: Rick Barry–Richard Francis Dennis "Rick" Barry III is an American retired professional basketball player who played in both the American Basketball Association (ABA) and National Basketball Association (NBA). Named one of the 50 Greatest Players in history by the NBA in 1996, Barry was known for his unorthodox but effective underhand free throw shooting technique, and at the time of his retirement in 1980, his .900 free throw percentage ranked first in NBA history.[1] In 1987, Barry was inducted into the Naismith Memorial Basketball Hall of Fame, Wilt Chamberlain, and Pete Maravich, in endorsing Spalding's line of rubber basketballs, with a signature "Ernie D." ball making up part of the collection.

Nicknamed the "Miami Greyhound" by longtime San Francisco-area broadcaster Bill King because of his slender physical build and remarkable quickness and instincts, the 6'7" Barry won the NBA Rookie of the Year Award after averaging 25.7 points and 10.6 rebounds per game in the 1965-66 season. The following year, he won the 1967 NBA All-Star Game MVP award with a 38-point outburst and led the NBA in scoring with a 35.6 point per game average — which still ranks as the eighth- highest output in league annals. Teamed with star center Nate Thurmond in San Francisco, Barry helped take the Warriors to the 1967 NBA Finals, which they lost to the Philadelphia 76ers in six games. Including a 55-point outburst in Game 3, Barry averaged 40.8 points per game in the series, an NBA Finals record that stood for three decades.

Glossary 161: Robbie Robinson: Robby Robinson is an American former professional bodybuilder. Known early in his career as Robin Robinson, he is also known as The Black Prince and Mr. Lifestyle. He won various competitions including Mr. America, Mr. World, Mr. Universe, Masters Olympia, and other titles of the International Federation of Body Building & Fitness (IFBB), and appeared in several films (including the landmark semi-documentary *Pumping Iron*) over a 27-year career as a professional bodybuilder, retiring from competition in 2001 at the age of 56.

Glossary 162: Robert Sacre: Robert Sacre is a professional <u>basketball</u> player for the <u>Los Angeles Lakers</u> of the <u>National Basketball Association</u> (NBA). A <u>dual citizen</u> of both the United States and Canada, he has played for the <u>Canadian national basketball team</u>. Los Angeles Lakers (2012–present.)

On June 28, 2012, the <u>Los Angeles Lakers</u> selected Sacre with the last pick (60th) in the <u>2012 NBA draft</u>. He Joined the Lakers for the 2012 NBA Summer League. On September 7, 2012, he signed his first professional contract with the Lakers. On October 31, 2012, he made his NBA debut against the <u>Portland Trail Blazers</u>, playing 49 seconds in a 116-106 loss. He scored his first points on November 4, 2012, in a victory against the <u>Detroit Pistons</u>. During his rookie season, he had multiple assignments with the <u>Los Angeles D-Fenders</u> of the <u>NBA D-League</u>.

On January 8, 2013, he made his first career start against the <u>Houston Rockets</u>, finishing with 10 points, four blocked shots and three rebounds in a 125–112 loss.[1] Even before the start, he was already a Lakers' fan favorite for his celebratory moves supporting his teammates while on the bench. The moves are in part inspired by the <u>Yosemite Sam</u> cartoon character in *Looney Tunes*.

On July 10, 2013, Sacre re-signed with the Lakers on a reported three-year deal.

Glossary 163: Ron Brewer: Ronald Charles "Ron" Brewer is a retired American professional <u>basketball</u> player. A 6'4" (1.93 m) <u>guard</u> from the <u>University of Arkansas</u>, he was selected by the <u>Portland Trail Blazers</u> in the first round of the Draft. Ron Brewer was selected by the Trail Blazers with 7th pick in the <u>1978 NBA Draft</u>, and was named to the 1978-79 <u>NBA All-Rookie Team</u>, Brewer was drafted directly after <u>Larry Bird</u> and ahead of notable NBA players such as <u>Reggie Theus</u> and <u>Maurice Cheeks</u>.

Brewer went on to spend eight seasons in the league with six teams—the Trail Blazers, <u>San Antonio Spurs</u>, <u>Cleveland Cavaliers</u>,

Golden State Warriors, New Jersey Nets, and Chicago Bulls—and finished his career in 1986 with 5,971 total points (11.9 ppg).

Glossary 164: Ronald "Ron" Townson was an American vocalist. He was an original member of The 5th Dimension, a popular vocal group of the late 1960s and early 1970s. Born in St. Louis in 1933, Townson started singing at age six and was a featured soloist on various choirs throughout his school years. His grandmother inspired him to sing and his parents arranged for him to have private singing and acting lessons. During high school, he appeared for three seasons in productions of Bloomer Girl, Annie Get Your Gun and Show Boat; he also won third place in the Missouri State trials for the Metropolitan Opera.

Glossary 165: Roy Hibbert: Roy Denzil Hibbert is a Jamaican-American professional basketball player for the Los Angeles Lakers of the National Basketball Association (NBA). He is a two-time NBA All-Star, and earned NBA All-Defensive second team honors 2014.

Hibbert was drafted 17th overall by the Toronto Raptors in the 2008 NBA draft. On July 9, 2008, his rights were traded to the Indiana Pacers. On July 15, he signed his first professional contract with the Pacers.

In 2012, he was selected to the 2012 NBA All-Star Game as a reserve for the East. Playing just 10 minutes, Hibbert only recorded 3 points, on 1-3 shooting. Hibbert was selected as an All-Star reserve for the East in 2014. Playing only 12 minutes, he tallied 8 points on 4-5 shooting. At the end of the season, Hibbert finished second in the Defensive Player of the Year voting with 166 out of the 1125, losing to Joakim Noah, who had 555 of the points. Hibbert averaged 2.2 blocks per game. On July 9, 2015, Hibbert was traded to the Los Angeles Lakers in exchange for a future second-round pick. He made his debut for the Lakers in the team's season opener against the Minnesota Timberwolves on October 28, recording 12 points and 10 rebounds in a 112–111 loss.

Glossary 166: Rudy Tomjanovich: Rudolph "Rudy" Tomjanovich, Jr. is an American retired basketball player and coach who coached the Houston Rockets to two consecutive NBA championships. He was an All-Star forward for the Rockets during his playing career. *The Kermit Washington incident*–Despite Tomjanovich's noteworthy career as a player, he is perhaps best remembered for an infamous occurrence at the height of his playing career. In a December 9, 1977 game, the Los Angeles Lakers' Kermit Washington punched Tomjanovich. The blow shattered Tomjanovich's jaw and face and inflicted life-threatening head injuries, leaving him sidelined for five months. He eventually made a full recovery, but his playing career slowly came to a halt and he was forced to retire in his mid-30s.

Glossary 167: Sam Lacey: Samuel "Sam" Lacey was an American basketball player. Lacey was drafted in the first round (fifth overall) of the 1970 NBA Draft by the Cincinnati Royals. He played 13 seasons (1970–1983) in the National Basketball Association as a member of the Royals, Kansas City Kings, New Jersey Nets and Cleveland Cavaliers. He averaged over 10 rebounds per game in his first six seasons, and was the NBA's third leading rebounder in the 1974–75 season. Lacey's most productive NBA season came in 1973–74 when he averaged 14.2 points and 13.4 rebounds per game. He was named an All-Star in 1975, and finished the season averaging 11.5 points, 14.2 rebounds, and 5.3 assists per game.

Lacey is one of only five NBA players (along with Hakeem Olajuwon, Julius Erving, David Robinson and Ben Wallace) to have registered 100 blocks and 100 steals in six consecutive seasons His #44 jersey was retired by the Sacramento Kings. He is also one of three NBA players (along with Wes Unseld and Reggie Evans) to total at least 30 rebounds and fewer than 10 points in the first two games of the season.

When Lacey retired in 1983, he had accumulated 9,687 rebounds and a total of 10,303 points. As of 2014, Lacey ranks 40th overall for total rebounds in NBA history.

Glossary 168: Samir Bannout: Samir Known as "the Lion of Lebanon", Samir Bannout won the Mr. Olympia title in 1983. At that time, only six men had held this most prestigious title since the contest began in 1965. The extreme muscular definition that

Bannout achieved in his lower back region helped to shape "Lebanon Cedar" when referring the shape made visible during a back pose on the competition stage. Bannout took 4th place at the 1982 Mr. Olympia contest and returned the following year to take home the title in 1983.

After placing 6th at the 1984 Olympia, the IFBB suspended him for three years as punishment for his participation at the World Championship competition of a rival federation, the WABBA. (The real reason was because Samir had an argument with one of the officials over mistreatment.) Bannout did not again get a top six placing again at a Mr. Olympia contest despite competing at the event many more times. In 1990 he won his second IFBB pro show, the IFBB Pittsburgh Pro Invitational. His professional career lasted 17 years.

Glossary 169: Dr. Samuel Richard: Graduated in 1979 from the Oregon Health Science University of Medicine with Healthgrades honor roll recognition. Residency Hospital Contra Costa Medical Services, 1982. Specialty Family Medicine.

Glossary 170: Scott Wedman: Scott Dean Wedman is an American former professional basketball player who played several seasons in the National Basketball Association (NBA). He was drafted by Kansas City-Omaha Kings in the first round in the 1974 NBA draft. Wedman was a proficient shooter. He represented the Kansas City Kings twice in the NBA All-Star Game. During his time in Kansas City, Wedman gained the nickname "The Incredible Hulk" because of his extensive sessions in the weight room. On March 4, 1979, Wedman was involved in a 1-car accident in which his Porsche overturned on a rainy highway in Kansas City. At the time, doctors credited his conditioning with keeping him out of action for only a few games. October 16, 1987, he was traded by the Celtics with Sam Vincent to the Seattle SuperSonics for a 1989 second-round draft choice. However, he retired and did not play a game for the SuperSonics.

Glossary 171: Sergio Oliva: Sergio Oliva, in 1966, won the AAU Jr. Mr. America and again he claimed the trophy for "Most Muscular".

He then Joined the International Federation of Body Builders <u>IFBB</u> in which he won both the professional Mr. World and Mr. Universe Contests. In 1967, he won the prestigious Mr. Olympia contest, making him the undisputed world champion of bodybuilding. Oliva then went on to win the <u>Mr. Olympia</u> title three years in a row, at 5 feet 11 inches and at a contest weight that went from 225 lbs. up to his most massive at 255 lbs.

Glossary 172: Shaquille O'Neal: Shaquille Rashaun O'Neal (/ʃə'kiːl/ *shə-KEEL*; nicknamed Shaq (/'ʃæk/ *SHAK*), is a retired American professional <u>basketball</u> player who is currently an analyst on the television program *Inside the NBA*. Listed at 7 ft. 1 in (2.16 m) tall[1] and weighing 325 pounds (147 kg), he was one of the heaviest players ever to play in the NBA. O'Neal played for six teams throughout his 19-year NBA career.

O'Neal's individual accolades include the 1999–2000 <u>MVP award</u>, the 1992–93 <u>NBA Rookie of the Year award</u>, 15 <u>All-Star game</u> selections, three All-Star Game MVP awards, three <u>Finals MVP</u> awards, two <u>scoring titles</u>, 14 <u>All-NBA team</u> selections, and three <u>NBA All-Defensive Team</u> selections. He is one of only three players to win <u>NBA MVP</u>, <u>All-Star game MVP</u> and <u>Finals MVP</u> awards in the same year (2000); the other players are <u>Willis Reed</u> in <u>1970</u> and <u>Michael Jordan</u> in <u>1996</u> and <u>1998</u>. He ranks <u>7th all-time in points scored</u>, 5th in <u>field goals</u>, <u>13th in rebounds</u>, and <u>7th in blocks</u>. Largely due to his ability to <u>dunk</u> the basketball, O'Neal also ranks 3rd all-time in field goal percentage (58.2%). O'Neal was elected into the <u>Naismith Memorial Basketball Hall of Fame</u> in 2016.

Glossary 173: Shawn Kemp: Shawn Travis Kemp is an American retired professional <u>basketball</u> player, who played in the <u>National Basketball Association</u> (NBA) for 14 seasons. He was a six-time <u>NBA All-Star</u> and a three-time <u>All-NBA Second Team</u> member.

Glossary 174: Sid Catlett: Sid Catlett, (born in <u>Washington, D.C.</u>, he attended the <u>University of Notre Dame</u>.) He currently ranks 17th on the Notre Dame all-time scoring list with 1,367 points. Throughout his career, he has averaged 16.1 points per game, which ranks 19th in school history. He also stands at eighth place in Fighting Irish history in rebounds (884), ninth in rebounding average (10.4 rpg), 13th in field goals attempted (1,242), 15th in field goals made (567), and 22nd in free throws attempted (360). He led the 1969-70 and 1970-71 squads in rebounding with averages of 12.4 and 13.1 rpg, respectively. Sydney Leon "Sid" Catlett, a small forward was selected by the Cincinnati Royals in the 4th round (55th pick overall) of the 1971 NBA Draft. He played for the Royals (1971–72) in the NBA for 9 games.

Glossary 175: Sidney Wicks: Sidney Wicks is a retired American basketball player. A native of California, he played college basketball for the UCLA Bruins and played professionally in the National Basketball Association (NBA) from 1971 to 1981. In the NBA he played for the Portland Trail Blazers, Boston Celtics, and San Diego Clippers, earning NBA Rookie of the Year in 1972 as well as four all-star selections.

The Portland Trail Blazers selected Wicks with the second pick of the 1971 NBA draft., Wicks was named NBA Rookie of the Year, and played in the NBA All-Star Game that season. Wicks played for the Trail Blazers from 1971 to 1976, earning a total of four selections as an All-Star (1972–1975) and averaging over 20 points per game each of his first four seasons. He holds the Blazers' franchise record for rebounds in a game with 27, and averaged 22.3 points per game and 10.3 rebounds a game in his five years with the team.

Glossary 176: Spencer Haywood: Spencer Haywood decided to turn pro after his sophomore year, but National Basketball Association (NBA) rules, which then required a player to wait until his class graduated, prohibited him from entering the league. As a result, he Joined the Denver Rockets of the American Basketball Association (ABA).

In his rookie season, Haywood led the ABA in scoring at 30.0 points per game and rebounding at 19.5 rebounds per game while leading the Rockets to the ABA's Western Division Title. He was named both the ABA Rookie of the Year and ABA MVP during the 1969–70 season, and became the youngest ever recipient of the MVP at the age of 21. His 986 field goals made, 1,637 rebounds, and 19.5

rebound per game average are the all-time ABA records for a season. Haywood also won the ABA's <u>1970 All-Star Game</u> MVP that year after recording 23 points, 19 rebounds, and 7 blocked shots for the West team.

Haywood was named to the All-NBA First Team in 1972 and 1973 and the All-NBA Second Team in 1974 and 1975. Haywood's 29.2 points per game in the 1972–73 season and 13.4 rebounds per game in 1973–74 are still the single-season record averages for the SuperSonics for these categories. Haywood played in four <u>NBA All-Star Games</u> while with Seattle, including a strong 23 point 11 rebound performance in 1974. In the 1974–75 season, he helped lead the SuperSonics to their first playoff berth. Overall, during his five seasons with Seattle, Haywood averaged 24.9 points per game and 12.1 rebounds per game. Haywood's no. 24 jersey was retired by the SuperSonics during a halftime ceremony on February 26, 2007.

Glossary 177: Steve Johnson: Clarence Stephen "Steve" Johnson is a retired American professional <u>basketball</u> player, who played for numerous NBA teams. He played the <u>power forward</u> and <u>center</u> positions. He was generally regarded as a good low-post offensive player, but as a poor defender and rebounder (and as a foul-prone player as well).

He was drafted the following summer, with the 7th pick overall, by the <u>Kansas City Kings</u>, and played with the Kings for 2½ seasons before being traded to the <u>Chicago Bulls</u>. After a season and a half with the Bulls, Johnson played a season with the <u>San Antonio Spurs</u>. While with the Spurs, Johnson led the <u>league in field goal percentage</u> at 0.632 — one of the highest in NBA history.

During the 1986 off-season, Johnson was traded to the <u>Portland Trail Blazers</u> for longtime Blazers' fixture <u>Mychal Thompson</u>; the team intended to start Johnson at power forward alongside defensive-minded center <u>Sam Bowie</u>. Five games into the season, however, Bowie suffered a broken leg (one of many such injuries he would endure in his ill-fated career), and Johnson was moved to the starting center role, with aging veteran <u>Caldwell Jones</u> replacing him at power forward. That year, Johnson enjoyed his best season as a pro, averaging nearly 17 points a game, and shooting a respectable 0.555 from the field.

The next season, Bowie again broke his leg, and Johnson assumed the starting center position. Unfortunately for him, he would himself be injured, and was replaced in the lineup by Kevin Duckworth, whose stellar play earned him the Job permanently. Nevertheless, Johnson earned a selection on the West All-Star team, but was unable to play due to injury. An attempt to start both players in a dual-post configuration, and the Johnson/Duckworth controversy was one of several which distracted the team in the 1988-89 season (which led to a losing record and a first-round playoff sweep). After that season, the rather unhappy Johnson was left unprotected in the 1989 NBA expansion draft, and was selected by the Minnesota Timberwolves. Johnson, unhappy with being drafted by an expansion team, played only 4 games for the Timberwolves before being traded to the Seattle SuperSonics; he played only 21 games for the Sonics that season. He played 24 games for the Golden State Warriors the following year; and retired at the conclusion of the 1990-1991 season.

Johnson holds the NCAA single season and career records for field goal percentage. He led the NBA in personal fouls during the 1981-82 and 1986-87 seasons, and led the NBA in disqualifications during the 1981-82, 1985-86, and 1986-87 seasons.

Glossary 178: Stu Lantz: Stuart Burrell "Stu" Lantz is a retired American basketball player and the current television commentator for the Los Angeles Lakers of the National Basketball Association (NBA) on Time Warner Cable SportsNet. He has been the Lakers' color commentator since 1987, sharing the microphone with Chick Hearn, Paul Sunderland, Joel Meyers and now Bill Macdonald. Lantz has winning numerous awards for his work along the way. The Southern California Sports Broadcasters Association has named Lantz best radio commentator in six of the last seven years.

Lantz played in the National Basketball Association from 1968 until 1976. He was drafted by the San Diego Rockets in the third round (1st Pick, 23rd Overall) of the 1968 NBA Draft and by the Oakland Oaks in the 1968 ABA Draft after attending the University of Nebraska.

Glossary 179: Swen Nater: Swen Erick Nater is a retired Dutch professional basketball player, primarily in the American Basketball Association (ABA) and National Basketball Association (NBA). He is the only player to have led both the NBA and ABA in rebounding. Nater was a two-time ABA All-Star and was the 1974 ABA Rookie of the Year.

Nater was drafted by The Floridians in the 1972 ABA Draft, and then by the Virginia Squires in the June 1972 ABA dispersal draft after the Floridians' demise. Nater was also drafted in the first round of the 1973 NBA Draft with the 16th overall pick by the Milwaukee Bucks; he is the only NBA first round pick who played in the NCAA without ever starting a college game. In August 1973, he opted to sign with the Squires. On November 21, 1973 the Squires traded Nater to the San Antonio Spurs for a draft pick and $300,000.

With the Spurs, Nater was the American Basketball Association Rookie of the Year and led the ABA in field goal percentage in 1974. He led the ABA in rebounding in 1975. He was named to the All-ABA Second Team in 1974 and 1975, and participated in the ABA All-Star Game both seasons. During his three seasons in the ABA, Nater played for the Spurs, Squires, and the New York Nets.

Nater's NBA career began with the Milwaukee Bucks, and he was traded after one season to the Buffalo Braves. When the Braves played in San Diego, Nater became a local favorite. Nater led the NBA in rebounding average during the 1979-80 season, making him the only player ever to lead both the NBA and ABA in rebounding.

Before the 1983-84 season, Nater was traded by the Clippers along with a just-drafted Byron Scott to the Los Angeles Lakers for Norm Nixon, Eddie Jordan, and a 1986 second-round draft pick (which would eventually be dealt to the Phoenix Suns and become Jeff Hornacek). Nater and Scott helped lead the Lakers to the NBA Finals that year, but the next season the team did not offer him a guaranteed contract.

Glossary 180: T.R. Dunn: Theodore Roosevelt "T. R." Dunn is an American former professional basketball player who used to be an assistant coach for the Houston Rockets of the National Basketball Association (NBA).

A star at the <u>University of Alabama</u>, the 6'4" Dunn was selected by the <u>Portland Trail Blazers</u> in the second round of the <u>1977 National Basketball Association Draft</u>. He went on to have a productive 14-year career with three teams: the Portland Trail Blazers (1977–1980), the <u>Denver Nuggets</u> (1980–1988;1989–1991), and the <u>Phoenix Suns</u> (1988–1989). Dunn was named to the NBA's All-Defensive Second Team three times during his career, and he was widely regarded as one of the best <u>rebounding guards</u> of the 1980s.

Dunn retired in 1991 with 5,033 career points and 4,371 career rebounds.

Glossary 181: Teresa Gipson: Graduated from Georgetown University School of Medicine in 1994. Specialty Family Medicine. Recognized on Healthgrades honor roll.

Glossary 182: Terry Porter: Terry Porter is an American college <u>basketball</u> coach and former player in the <u>National Basketball Association</u> (NBA). Drafted 24th by the <u>Portland Trail Blazers</u> in the <u>1985 NBA draft</u>. In Portland, he played ten seasons with two <u>All-Star Game</u> appearances. Porter spent 17 years in the NBA as a player.

Going into the <u>1985 NBA Draft</u>, on June 18, 1985 the <u>Portland Trail Blazers</u> selected Porter with the 24th overall pick in the NBA Draft.

During his decade-long tenure in Portland, Porter went to the <u>NBA Finals</u> twice and continues to hold the NBA Finals single-game record for the most, free throws made, none missed—15 (June 7, 1990 at <u>Detroit</u>). He was the recipient of the <u>J. Walter Kennedy Citizenship Award</u> in 1993, and remains as the Trail Blazers' all-time assists leader with 5,319. Porter signed as a free agent with the <u>Minnesota Timberwolves</u> prior to the 1995-96 season and helped the Wolves clinch their first-ever playoff berth in 1996-97 and their first winning season the following year.

He signed with the <u>Miami Heat</u> before the 1998–99 campaign, and signed with the <u>San Antonio Spurs</u> prior to the 1999-2000 season. He retired after the 2001-02 season, having never been traded during his NBA career. Porter's teams compiled a record of 815-547 (.598) during his career, and only once failed to make the <u>postseason</u>.

In 1,274 career games, Porter averaged 12.2 points, 5.6 assists and 1.24 steals during a career that included two All-Star berths (1991, 1993), two trips to the NBA Finals (1990, 1992) and 15,586 career points. He is 12th on the NBA's all-time assist list (7,160). Porter has played for five of the top 36 coaches (games won) in NBA history: Pat Riley (1,210), Rick Adelman (945), Jack Ramsay (864), Gregg Popovich (797) and Flip Saunders (636).

On December 16, 2008, the Trail Blazers retired Porter's #30 jersey.

Glossary 183: Theo Ratliff: Theophalus Curtis "Theo" Ratliff is an American retired professional basketball player who last played with the NBA's Los Angeles Lakers. Primarily a center, he was an excellent shot-blocker who has led the league three times in blocks per game. As of 2011, he is ranked 18th all-time in career blocks, and 13th all-time in career blocks per game.

Ratliff was selected with the 18th pick of the 1995 NBA draft by the Detroit Pistons, for whom he played 2½ seasons. During the 1997–98 season he was traded to the Philadelphia 76ers. He played in Philadelphia for three seasons, and was voted Eastern Conference starting center of the 2001 All-Star Game, but was unable to play due to injury. He was a key fixture on the 2000-01 Sixers team that made it to the NBA finals.

Ratliff was signed by the Los Angeles Lakers on July 22, 2010 to a 1-year deal. In December 2011, Ratliff retired from basketball.

Glossary 184: Tim Bassett: Eugene Timothy "Tim" Bassett is a retired American basketball player. He was selected by the Buffalo Braves in the 7th round (106th pick overall) of the 1973 NBA Draft and by the San Diego Conquistadors in the second round of the 1973 ABA Supplemental Draft. He played for the San Diego Conquistadors (1973–75) and New York Nets (1975–76) in the American Basketball Association (ABA) and, after the 1976 ABA-NBA merger, he played for the Nets (1976–79) and the San Antonio Spurs (1979–80) in the NBA for 473 games.

Glossary 185: Todd Litchi: Todd Samuel Lichti is a retired American professional basketball player. At 6'4" (1.93 m) and 205 lb. (93 kg) he played at guard. He was selected with 15th pick in the 1989 NBA draft by the Denver Nuggets where he stayed for 4 years. He also had short spells with Orlando Magic, Golden State Warriors and Boston Celtics before moving to Australia to play for the Perth Wildcats.

Lichti started his professional career when he was drafted via the 15th overall pick by the Denver Nuggets in the 1989 NBA Draft. With the Nuggets, he performed well in his first season (8 points per game), and continued to improve in his second season (14 points per game), before knee injuries limited him to 29 of 82 contests. Various injuries (including being involved in a serious car accident, which killed his fiancée, Kirstin Gravrock of Bellevue, Washington) further kept him from playing at a competitive level. Lichti stayed on in Denver for two more seasons until August 19, 1993, when he was traded to the Orlando Magic for Brian Williams. He played a combined 13 games with three different teams before being waived by the Golden State Warriors in 1993-94, his final NBA season.

Glossary 186: Tom Abernathy: Thomas Craig "Tom" Abernethy is a retired American professional basketball player. Born and raised in South Bend, Indiana, Abernathy starred at St. Joseph's High School and Indiana University, the 6'7" Abernethy was drafted by the Los Angeles Lakers in the third round of the 1976 NBA Draft. He spent five years in the league as a member of the Lakers, Golden State Warriors and Indiana Pacers. He amassed 1,779 career NBA points.

Glossary: 187: Tom Burleson: Tommy Loren Burleson is an American former professional basketball player. A 7'2" center. Burleson was also a member of the 1972 U.S. Olympic Basketball Team that lost an epic and controversial gold medal game to the Soviet Union. The entire 1972 Olympic Basketball team believed they had been cheated and voted unanimously to not accept the silver.

Drafted by the Seattle SuperSonics as the third overall player in the 1974 NBA Draft, Burleson was named to the 1974–75 NBA All-Rookie Team. Playing under coach Bill Russell, Burleson recorded strong playoff performances in both 1975 and 1976 for Seattle. For his playoff career, Burleson averaged over 20 points, 10 rebounds, and two blocks per game. His second season as a professional proved to be his best, as he averaged 15.6 points, 9.0 rebounds, and 1.8 blocks per game. Just as he began to dominate the NBA game, he was injured breaking up a fight between his teammate and an opposing team member. The injury was instrumental in his steady decline over the next several years.

Burleson was known throughout his amateur and pro career as a good shot blocker. He played eight seasons in the NBA with three different teams (Seattle, the Kansas City Kings and the Atlanta Hawks. In 2002, Burleson was named to the ACC 50th Anniversary men's basketball team honoring the fifty greatest players in Atlantic Coast Conference history.

Glossary 188: Tom Davis: Thomas "Dr. Tom" Davis is an American former college men's basketball coach. He served as the head coach at Lafayette College, Boston College, Stanford University, the University of Iowa, and Drake University from 1971 to 2007.

Stanford and Iowa: He would accept a position at Stanford University before taking over as the head coach at the University of Iowa in 1986. While at Iowa, he led the Hawkeyes to nine NCAA Tournaments, including a pair of Sweet Sixteen appearances as well as an Elite Eight. The Hawkeyes also made two NIT appearances. He is the winningest coach in the University of Iowa history. His team was ranked number one during the 1986-87 season.

March 21, 2007 Davis announced his retirement from college coaching.

Glossary 189: Tom Owens: Thomas William Owens is a retired American professional basketball player. A 6'10" center born in the Bronx, New York and from the University of South Carolina, Owens played five seasons (1971–1976) in the American Basketball Association and seven seasons (1976–1983) in the National Basketball Association as a member of the Carolina Cougars, Memphis Pros, Memphis Sounds, Spirits of St. Louis, Indiana Pacers, Kentucky Colonels, San Antonio Spurs, Houston Rockets, Portland Trail Blazers, and Detroit Pistons. He scored 9,898 points and grabbed

5,985 rebounds in his ABA/NBA career. He has one son, Thomas William Owens Jr., born October 21, 1972.

Late in his career, Owens was involved in one of the most one-sided trades in NBA history. After the 1980-81 season, the Blazers traded him to the Pacers and got the Pacers' 1984 draft pick in return. Owens was traded to the Pistons after the season and retired a year later. Four years later, the Pacers finished with the worst record in the Eastern Conference. However, because of the trade, the Pacers were left as bystanders in one of the deepest drafts ever, featuring such future stars as Michael Jordan, Sam Bowie, Hakeem Olajuwon, Sam Perkins, Charles Barkley and John Stockton. The pick acquired from Indiana turned out to be the one the Blazers famously used to select Bowie while Jordan was still available.

Glossary 190: Tom Platz: Tom Platz became famous for his remarkable leg development. He developed a high intensity, high volume method of leg training, which led to his unparalleled size and definition for his time. Platz began his competitive bodybuilding career in the 1973 Mr. Adonis competition. He competed as an amateur until he won the 1978 World Amateur Championships middleweight division. In 1978 and after completing his degree at Wayne State University, he moved to California. He arrived there with $50 and a dream to win Mr. Olympia. For the following nine years Platz competed as a professional, aiming for Mr. Olympia. Though Platz never took first at the Olympia competition, he had a string of top ten finishes, with a third position in 1981 being his best.

Platz became famous for his remarkable leg development. He developed a high intensity, high volume method of leg training, which led to his unparalleled size and definition for his time. Regardless of what was found lacking elsewhere, it is still widely claimed in bodybuilding circles that Platz holds the mark for the best legs in bodybuilding of his time and some of the best legs in bodybuilding ever. Flex readers agree: In a "best body parts of the 20th century" poll, Platz was deemed to have the best quads and hamstrings of all time.

Tom Platz retired from professional bodybuilding competition in 1987 and did a 'Comeback' in 1995 when he was awarded Honorary Mr. America. He still promotes the sport wholeheartedly.

Tom says, "I just want to give back to the sport I love which has been really great to me."–Wikipedia. He played the part of "Body Builder" in the 1990 film <u>Book of Love</u>. His character portrayed the <u>Charles Atlas</u>-like character from those "tired of bullies kicking sand in your face and stealing your girlfriend"-type of advertisements that were in a lot of comic books for decades.

Platz was and is one of the most sought-after guest speakers in the world of bodybuilding, nutrition and general fitness. He was a Professor and the Director of Bodybuilding Sciences at ISSA for 14 years. Tom has a Masters in Fitness Science, Bachelors in Science Physiology and Nutrition from <u>Wayne State University</u> and <u>Michigan State University</u>, and a Master's in Business Administration from the <u>University of California</u>.

Glossary 191: Truck Robinson: Leonard Eugene Robinson is a retired American <u>power forward</u>. He played in the NBA for the <u>Washington Bullets</u> (1974–77), <u>Atlanta Hawks</u> (1977), <u>New Orleans Jazz</u> (1977–79), <u>Phoenix Suns</u> (1979–82), and <u>New York Knicks</u> (1982–85).

He helped the Bullets win the 1975 NBA Eastern Conference and the Suns win the 1981 NBA Pacific Division. Robinson was named to the 1978 East All-Star Team and the 1981 West All-Star Team. He was named to the 1978 All-NBA First Team. Robinson led the NBA in minutes played (3,638), defensive rebounds (990), total rebounds (1,288) and rebounds per game (15.7) during the 1977-78 season.

He ranks 86th on the NBA/ABA career offensive rebounds list (1,985), 43rd on the career defensive rebounds list (5,282), 81st on the total rebounds list (7,267) and 73rd on the career rebounds per game list (9.4). In 11 seasons Robinson played in 772 games, stayed 25,141 minutes on the court and had a .483 field goal percentage (4,816 for 9,971), .662 free throw percentage (2,355 for 3,556), 7,267 total rebounds (1,985 offensive and 5,282 defensive), 1,348 assists, 533 steals, 510 blocks, 2,253 personal fouls and 11,988 points.

January 12 the Jazz traded Robinson to the <u>Phoenix Suns</u> for two players and two first-round draft picks. Over his next three seasons with the Suns, Robinson averaged at least 17 points and 9 rebounds each year. Following the 1981–82 campaign he was traded to the <u>New York Knicks</u> for <u>Maurice Lucas</u>. In 1982–83 Robinson suffered through the worst slump of his career, averaging just 9.5 points and 8.1 rebounds. Fans began complaining about their "truck with four flat tires." He played another full season for New York—with similar results—before retiring in 1984–85.

In 11 NBA seasons Robinson amassed 11,988 points and 7,267 rebounds.

Glossary 192: Wally Walker: Walter Frederick "Wally" Walker is an American former professional <u>basketball</u> player. His playing career averages were 7.0 points and 3.1 rebounds during eight years with Portland, Seattle and Houston. He won two championship rings (with Portland and Seattle) in his first and third seasons. He was a starter for the Sonics in 1981-82 and the next season for the Houston Rockets. He ended his NBA career in 1984.

Glossary 193: Walter Davis: Walter Davis a 6'6" forward/guard, Davis spent 15 years in the National Basketball Association, spending the bulk of those years with the Phoenix Suns. The Suns selected Davis with the fifth pick of the <u>1977 NBA Draft</u>. He made an immediate impact, playing in 81 games and averaging <u>24.2 points per game</u> in his first season, which would also be his career-high. He won the 1978 <u>Rookie of the Year Award</u>, and earned second team <u>All-NBA</u> honors. Over his first ten seasons, Davis averaged over 20 <u>points</u> per game six times, and earned trips to six <u>All-Star Games</u>.

Over his career, Davis averaged 18.9 points, 3.8 <u>assists</u> and 3.0 <u>rebounds</u> per game. Davis was affectionately known as "The Greyhound" for his speedy style and sleek physical appearance. Suns broadcaster <u>Al McCoy</u> created many alternate nicknames for him, including "The Candyman," and "The Man with the Velvet Touch." Davis is the Suns' all-time leading scorer with 15,666 points.

Glossary 194: Wes Unseld: Westley Sissel "Wes" Unseld is an American former <u>basketball</u> player. He spent his entire <u>NBA</u> career with the <u>Baltimore/Capital/Washington Bullets</u>, and was inducted into the <u>Naismith Memorial Basketball Hall of Fame</u> in 1988.

Unseld was drafted by the <u>Kentucky Colonels</u> in the 1968 <u>American Basketball Association</u> draft, and was drafted second overall in the first round by the <u>Baltimore Bullets</u> in the <u>1968 NBA Draft</u>, helping lead the Bullets (who had finished in last place in the Eastern division the previous year) to a 57–25 record and a division title.

Unseld averaged <u>18.2 rebounds per game</u> that year, and became only the second player ever to win both <u>Rookie of the Year</u> and <u>Most Valuable Player</u> in the same season (<u>Wilt Chamberlain</u> being the first). Unseld was also named to the <u>NBA All-Rookie First Team</u>, and also claimed the <u>Sporting News</u> MVP that year. He was one of the best defensive players of his era, and in 1975, he led the NBA in rebounding. The following season, he led the NBA in field goal percentage with a .561 percentage. Unseld was inducted into the <u>Naismith Memorial Basketball Hall of Fame</u> in 1988, and in 1996, he was named as one of the NBA's <u>50 Greatest Players</u> of all time.

Glossary 195: Wilt Chamberlin: Wilton Norman "Wilt" Chamberlain was an American <u>basketball</u> player. He played for the <u>Philadelphia/San Francisco Warriors</u>, the <u>Philadelphia 76ers</u>, and the <u>Los Angeles Lakers</u> of the <u>National Basketball Association</u> (NBA); he played for the <u>University of Kansas</u> and also for the <u>Harlem Globetrotters</u> before playing in the NBA. The 7 foot 1-inch Chamberlain weighed 250 pounds as a rookie before bulking up to 275 and eventually to over 300 pounds with the Lakers. He played the <u>center</u> position and is widely considered one of the greatest and most dominant players in NBA history.

Chamberlain holds numerous <u>NBA records</u> in scoring, <u>rebounding</u> and durability categories. He is the only player to <u>score 100 points in a single NBA game</u> or average more than 40 and 50 points in a season. He also won seven scoring, nine <u>field goal percentage</u>, and eleven rebounding titles, and led the league in <u>assists</u> once. Chamberlain is the only player in NBA history to average at least 30 points and 20 rebounds per game in a season, a feat he accomplished seven times. He is also the only player to average at least 30 points and 20 rebounds per game over the entire course of his NBA career.

Chamberlain was subsequently enshrined in the <u>Naismith Memorial Basketball Hall of Fame</u> in 1978, elected into the NBA's

35th Anniversary Team of 1980, and chosen as one of the <u>50 Greatest Players in NBA History</u> of 1996. Chamberlain was known by various <u>nicknames</u> during his basketball playing career. He hated the ones that called attention to his <u>height</u> such as "<u>Goliath</u>" and "Wilt the <u>Stilt</u>", which was coined during his <u>high school</u> days by a <u>Philadelphia</u> <u>sportswriter</u>. He preferred "The Big Dipper", which was inspired by his friends who saw him dip his head as he walked through <u>doorways.</u>

Glossary 196: World be Free: World B. Free (born Lloyd Bernard Free) is an American former professional <u>basketball</u> player who played in the <u>National Basketball Association</u> (NBA) from 1975–1988. Free was known as the "Prince of Midair" as well as "All-World".

Free played for the <u>San Diego Clippers</u>, <u>Philadelphia 76ers</u>, <u>Golden State Warriors</u>, <u>Cleveland Cavaliers</u> and <u>Houston Rockets</u> in the <u>National Basketball Association</u>. He got his name from his days in <u>Brooklyn</u>, where a friend nicknamed him "World" because of his 44-inch vertical leap and 360 degree dunks. He was known for taking high risk shots and playing flamboyantly.

His best season was <u>1979–80</u> with the Clippers, averaging 30.2 points per game, as well as 4.2 assists per game and 3.5 rebounds per game in 68 games. He was an <u>All-Star</u> that season as well, although the Clippers failed to make the playoffs. During the <u>1984–85</u> season, Free became the 39th player in league history to surpass 15,000 career points.

Free loved to go one-on-one against a defender and either whirl around him or take a jump shot. His shot was possibly his greatest strength: a soft, high-arching lob that stayed in the air longer than the average jump shot and was very straight when he was "on" that it barely jostled the net. When he was younger, on the playgrounds of New York City, his jump shot was a flat line drive, but he was tired of having the ball blocked, so he developed a new style of shooting. Free admired Muhammad Ali. On December 8, 1981, he legally changed his first name to World· According to Free, "the fellas back in <u>Brownsville</u> gave me the nickname "World" when I was in junior high... they just started calling me 'all-world', because all-city and all-county and things like that weren't good enough. Finally, they just started calling me World... I'm still the same guy I was when I was Lloyd, though. I'll say what I'm going to do, and then I'll go out and do it."

Trying to stop Wicks from driving

NBPA Players Billy Hunter, Maurice Evans. Theo Ratliff,
Etan Thomas, Meta World, Kermit, all in Africa

Freshman Year at American U

My last college game,
American vs. Louisville

Coach Tom Young and me

9. *Pete Newell*

Driving on George Washington's Burrell

*Steve Garrett and Wilbur Thomas – winning
our 20th game against LaSalle*

Pete and I demonstrating a technique at a Big Man's Camp

677

Third year with the Lakers

At Blazer game with son Trey

Team Reunion at AU 2015

Trying to check Wes Unseld

*Going for a block
against the Lakers*

Making a pass with the Blazers

First year with the Lakers

Breakaway Dunk

Getting ready to join Celtics

JOHNNY LLOYD
MAC's leading free-throw shooter;
averaging 15 points per game

Johnny Lloyd

Only game I fouled out of, against LaSalle

Danny Padilla our trainer and workout partners Roy
Hibbert and Sorren Derboghosian Pakajaki

Working with NBA union

Kermit and brother Chris

Coach Young   *Teammates*

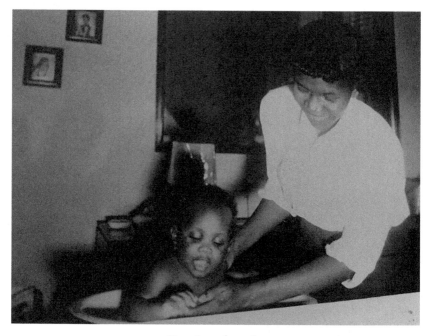

Kermit and mother

Kermit's mother

Pat, Kermit's college girlfriend

Kermit, his daughter and father

Car Kermit raffled off to pay for doctor's expenses to Africa

At AU with Pete Delaven and Steinnie

Clinic in Kenya with Florence, Richard, and his daughter

School kids in Kenya

School kids in Kenya getting ready for picnic

Kenya school kids with giraffe

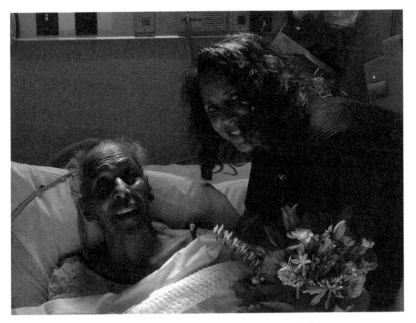

Kermit's father towards the end of his life

Maurice Evans just having fun with kids

ALL ABOUT THE
AUTHOR PATRICIA

After reading a quote "While lying on their death beds people are surrounded by regrets." Patricia removed one regret and met her goal to write a book. Traveling to Camas, Washington to visit with grandchildren provided the time and opportunity to share the challenges overcome by Kermit over his lifetime. Conversations led to writing down notes, holding interviews and finally a manuscript to publish. Her goal was to accurately record and portray the many experiences Kermit's life has experienced with honesty and clarity.

ALL ABOUT THE
AUTHOR KERMIT

· ·

Born in the nation's capital, Washington, DC Kermit is best known for "*the incident*" from 1977 while playing in the NBA for the Los Angeles Lakers. To this day when people mention his name this if the first impression that comes to mind. However, what is not known is the man behind the stigma who has had many positive impacts on the lives of many. His journey to clarify the man behind "*the incident*" and share his many adventures complete with challenges and obstacles will provide the reader with an accurate portrayal of the man, Kermit Washington.

CPSIA information can be obtained
at www.ICGtesting.com
Printed in the USA
BVOW05s2021100717

488740BV00007BA/10/P